# THE CHILDREN'S WONDERLAND OF STORIES

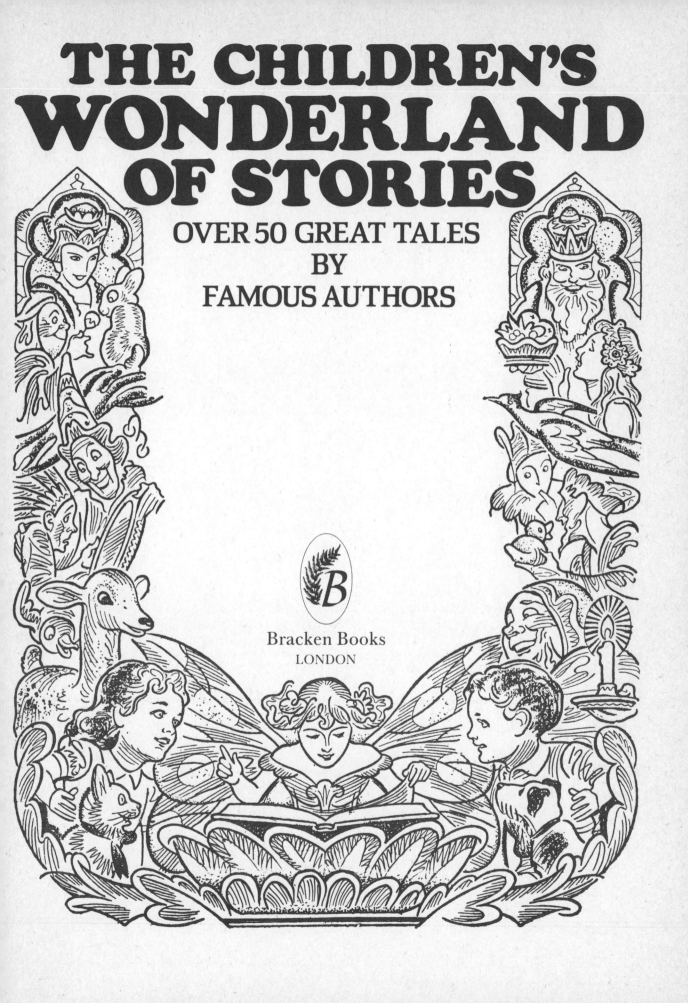

# THE CHILDREN'S
# WONDERLAND
## OF STORIES

### OVER 50 GREAT TALES
### BY
### FAMOUS AUTHORS

Bracken Books
LONDON

*First published 1939.*

*This edition published by Bracken Books, a
division of Bestseller Publications Ltd,
Brent House, 24–28 Friern Park, North
Finchley, London N12 9DA in 1986.*

*ISBN 1 85170 037 4*

*'Sea Fever' is reprinted with permission of
Macmillan Publishing Company from
Peoms by John Masefield. (New York:
Macmillan, 1953), and the Society of
Authors, London.*

*The publishers have made every effort to trace
all holders of copyright material. They
acknowledge with thanks permission to reprint
all such material and if any such
acknowledgement has been inadvertently
omitted they hope that the copyright holders
will accept their apology.*

*Printed and bound by Kultura, Hungary.*

# CONTENTS

# COLOUR ILLUSTRATIONS

# INTRODUCTION

What a wonderful collection of stories there is in this book to carry you off to Wonderland. In this great selection you can find many favourites to while away a winter evening or to read before you go to bed. The first story is the *Tales of Robin Hood* that great favourite for generations of girls and boys: read of the adventures of Robin Hood and Maid Marian, Friar Tuck, Little John and the wicked Sheriff of Nottingham: read *The Water Babies* by Charles Kingsley which tells you the adventures of Poor Tom and introduces you to those two tremendous ladies Mrs Doasyouwouldbedoneby and Bedonebyasyoudid: read *Robinson Crusoe*, that classic story of a desert island, that was based on the real life story of Alexander Selkirk who was marooned for six years: read some of the lovely fairy tales written by the Brothers Grimm or the Dane, Hans Christian Andersen. All these are well known and delightful stories which have charmed children for many years.

But there are other stories in this book which are, perhaps, not quite so well known. Read some of the American writers Mark Twain, whose hero Tom Sawyer is a particular favourite; read Nathaniel Hawthorne and Henry Longfellow two more great American authors: read some of the poems that we have included. It may not be very fashionable to read poetry nowadays but try some of the nonsense verses of Edward Lear to start with. Lear was really a painter and illustrated lovely books on animals and parrots but he wrote these very funny poems to amuse the children of his patrons. Also read the first poem in the book *Sea Fever* by John Masefield, if you have ever been to the seaside on a cold wet grey day you can read the poem and imagine the grey waves and breaking seas. We do hope that you enjoy the selection that we have included and if you do, let us know and we will let you know of another book which you might enjoy as well.

The Editors.

# Tales of Robin Hood

*Adapted from W. J. Thoms*

## ROBIN HOOD'S DELIGHTS

N a midsummer's day in the morning, Robin Hood, with Little John and Will Scarlock, did walk forth betimes, and wished that on the way they might meet with some adventure that might be worthy of their valour. They had not walked long by the forest side, but, behold, three of the keepers of the king's game appeared, with their forest-bills in their hands and well appointed with falchions and bucklers to defend themselves.

"Lo, here," saith Robin Hood, "according to our wish, we have met with our mates, and before we part from them we will try what metal they are made of."

"What! Robin Hood!" cried one of the keepers.

"I, the same," replied Robin.

"Then have at you," said the keeper. "Here are three of us and three of you; we will single out ourselves one to one; and, bold Robin, I for my part am resolved to have a bout with thee."

"Content with all my heart," said Robin Hood, "and fortune shall determine who shall have the best, the outlaws or the keepers."

With that they did lay down their coats, which were all of Lincoln green, and fell to it for the space of two hours with their brown bills, in which hot exercise Robin Hood, Little John, and Scarlock had the better, and, giving the rangers leave to breathe, demanded of them how they liked them.

"Why, good stout blades, i' faith," said the keeper that fought with Robin; "we commend you, but let us make trial whether you are as good at your sword and buckler as you have been at your quarter-staff."

"Why, do you doubt it?" said Robin Hood; "we shall satisfy you in that immediately."

With that, having laid down their staves and thrown off their doublets, they fell to it pell-mell; and dealt their blows unmercifully sore, which were carefully always defended with their bucklers. At the last, Robin Hood, observing Little John and Will Scarlock begin to give ground, which they never did in all their lives before, called out for a little space to breathe.

"Good boys, i' faith," said he to the keepers, "and the best that ever I dealt withal. Let me know your names, and for the time to come I will give that respect unto you that belongs unto your valour."

"Tush," replied one of the keepers, "ye lose time in asking after our names; if thou wilt have any more to do with our hands or our swords, we are for thee."

"Lo, here, according to our wish, we have met with our mates," said Robin Hood.

"I see that you are stout men," said Robin Hood; "we will fight no more in this place; but come with me to Nottingham (I have silver and gold enough about me), and there we will go to the King's Head tavern; and after we are weary we will lay down our arms, and become sworn brothers to one another. I love those men that will stand to it, and scorn to turn their backs on a foe."

"With all our hearts, jolly Robin," said the keepers to him; so, putting up their swords, and on their doublets, they went to Nottingham, where for three days' space they were very merry, and in the end parted good friends.

## ROBIN HOOD'S PROGRESS

THE name of Robin Hood did now begin to grow famous up and down the country; those who had occasion to go from one market to another were either afraid of him, and did forbear to go those ways where his haunts were, or else they were in fee with him, and every quarter did give him money, that with their goods and cattle they might pass by unmolested.

This he considered to be a secure and thriving way to fill his pockets, wherefore he contracted with all the graziers and rich farmers thereabouts, who had rather to give him every quarter a certain sum of money, than to be liable to those dangers, both by day and by night, which before did too much afflict them.

Robin Hood, in the meantime living high, and being out of any fear of hues and cries, or constables' warrants, would repair oftentimes to the town of Nottingham, where he would constantly make merry at the King's Head, and no guest was more respected than himself.

It so fell out that the king, lying at that time at a great earl's house not far from Nottingham, the townsmen and some others of the countryside did intend to delight his majesty with the honest exercise and game of archery. Thither were going many of the rangers of Sherwood Forest, and thither was going Robin Hood himself, but so disguised that it was not easy for any one to know him.

The foresters meeting him, demanded of him whither he was going, and he answered, to the shooting-match, to which purpose he had taken his bow of yew along with him.

" Thou shoot," said one of the foresters, " alas, you boy, thou art not able to bend a bow of yew, much less to draw it being bent—thou shoot before the king ! "

" I will hold you twenty mark," said Robin Hood, " that I will shoot a good buck one hundred rod off and kill him dead in the place."

" A hundred mark on that," said the foresters.

" Down with your dust," said Robin, and having told down the money,

*He let fly at a fat buck.*

with which he did go always provided, he bended his bow, and, having drawn a broad arrow up to the head of it, he did let it fly at a fat buck, one hundred rod or more. The arrow, entering in between the ribs of the buck, made him give a jump from the ground and fall down dead on the place, which Robin espying, " The wager," said he, " is mine, if it were for a thousand pounds."

" It is none of thine," said the foresters, and began to threaten him with violence, if he did not let the money alone, and get him suddenly gone.

" I will go," returned Robin Hood, smiling though angry, " but the money shall go with me."

With that he blew his horn, and on three or four of his men running up, the foresters made away with all the speed they could, though several were left dead on the plain.

" Now to your costs," said Robin Hood, " you have found me to be an archer," and taking up the money with him, withdrew into the forest to avoid all further danger that might ensue, and the spilling of more blood.

In the meantime, the townsmen of Nottingham, hearing that Robin Hood was abroad, and that some of the foresters were slain, did go forth in great numbers, hoping that Robin Hood was either slain or so hurt that they might now take him before the king. Robin, however, having sent some stinging arrows amongst them, they found to their costs that he was safe enough from being hurt or endangered.

## ROBIN HOOD AND THE BUTCHER

Not long afterwards Robin Hood, walking in the forest as was his daily custom, observed a butcher riding along the way, having on his mare's back good store of meat, which he was to sell in the market.

" Good morrow, good fellow," said Robin to the butcher.

" Good fellow," replied the butcher, " heaven help me from Robin Good fellow, for if I meet with him I may chance to fall short of my journey, and my meat of the market."

" I like thy company well," said Robin Hood. " What hast thou to sell ? "

" Flesh, master," said the butcher, " with which I am going to Nottingham market."

" What is the price of thy flesh and of the mare that bears it ? " asked Robin ; " tell me, for if thou wilt use me well I will buy both."

" Four marks," said the butcher, " I cannot bate anything of it."

" Sit down, then, and tell thy money," said Robin Hood ; " I will try for once if I can thrive by being a butcher."

The money being told, Robin Hood got up on the mare, and rode away with the meat to Nottingham market, where he made such good pennyworths that he had sold all his meat by ten o'clock in the morn ; he gave more meat for one penny than others could do for five.

The butchers in the market that had their stands by him said one to another, " Certainly this man's meat is bad and tainted, or else he has stolen it."

*Robin Hood had sold all his meat by ten o'clock.*

"Whence cometh he?" asked another; "I have never seen him before."

"That will I tell you by-and-by," said a third butcher, who stepping to Robin Hood said unto him, "Brother, thou art the freest butcher that ever came to this market. We be all of a trade; come, let us dine together."

"No man can deny a butcher so fair an invitation," said Robin, and, going with him to the inn, the table was suddenly covered and furnished, and the best man in the company being to say grace, Robin Hood at the upper end of the table did put off his bonnet.

"God bless us all," he said, "and our meat upon this place; a cup of sack is good to nourish the blood, and so I end my grace."

Robin Hood was no sooner sat, but he called for a cup of sack, and drank to them all, desiring them to be merry, for if there were five pounds to pay, he would pay it, every farthing.

"Thou art the bravest blade," said the butchers, "that ever came to Nottingham market."

The sheriff, who was newly alighted, and had taken his chamber at the inn, hearing of what was going on, said the stranger must be some prodigal that had sold his land, and would now spend it all at once. This, coming to Robin Hood's ear, he, after dinner, took the opportunity to speak unto him.

"Well, my good fellow," said the sheriff, "thou hast made a good bargain to-day; hast thou any more horned beasts to sell?"

"Yes, that I have," said Robin Hood to master sheriff, "I have two or three hundred, and a hundred acres of good land to keep them on as ever the crow flew over, which, if you will buy of me, I will make you as good assurance of it as ever my father made me."

The sheriff being a greedy man, and thinking to get the better of the deal, commanded his horse to be brought forth, and, taking some money with him for the purchase, he rode with Robin Hood, who led him into the forest for a mile or two outright. The sheriff, being laden with good store of gold, grew more and more uneasy at the place, and did wish himself at Nottingham again.

"And why so?" asked Robin Hood.

"I tell thee plainly," said the sheriff, "I do not like thy company."

"No," said Robin, "then I will provide you better."

"God keep me from Robin Hood," cried the sheriff, "for this is the haunt he useth."

Robin, smiling, observed a herd of three hundred gallant deer, feeding in the forest by him, and demanded of the sheriff how he liked these horned beasts, assuring him that they were the best that he could show him. With that he blew his horn, whereupon Little John, with fifty more of his men, came presently in, to whom Robin Hood imparted that he had brought the sheriff of Nottingham to dine with him.

"He is welcome," said Little John; "I know he hath store of gold and will honestly pay for his dinner."

"I," said Robin Hood, "never doubt it." Taking off the sheriff's case, he took to himself the three hundred pounds that were in it; then, leading him back through the forest, he desired him to remember him kindly to his wife, and so went laughing away.

## ROBIN HOOD AND THE BEGGAR

ROBIN HOOD took not any long delight in the mare which he bought of the butcher, but having now supplied himself with good store of money, which he got by the sheriff of Nottingham, he bought him a stout horse, and, riding one day on him towards Nottingham, it was his fortune to meet with a poor beggar.

Robin, who was of a jovial spirit, observing the beggar to have several sorts of bags, which were fastened to his patched coat, did ride up to him, and, giving him the time of day, demanded of him what countryman he was.

"A Yorkshireman," said the beggar, "and I would desire of you to give me something."

"Give thee," said Robin Hood, "why, I have nothing to give thee. I am a poor ranger in the forest, and thou seemest to be a lusty knave. Shall I give thee a good beating over the shoulder?"

"Content, content," said the beggar, "durst lay my coat and all my bags to a threaden point, thou will repent it."

At that Robin alighted, and the beggar and he fell to it, he with his sword and buckler, and the beggar with his long quarter-staff, who so well defended himself that, let Robin Hood do what he could, he could not come within the beggar, and nothing vexed him more than to find that the beggar's staff was as hard as iron itself. So, however, was not Robin Hood's head, for the beggar with all his force did let his staff descend with such a side blow that Robin, for all his skill, could not defend it.

The blood came trickling down his face, which, turning his courage into fury, he let fly at him with his trusty sword, and doubled blow on blow, but, perceiving that the beggar did not hold him so hard to it, he cried out to him to hold his hand.

"That will I not do," said the beggar, "unless thou wilt resign unto me thy horse and thy sword, and thy clothes, with all the money thou hast in thy pockets."

"The change is uneven," said Robin Hood, "but for once I am content."

So, putting on the beggar's clothes, the beggar was the gentleman, and Robin Hood the beggar, who entering into Nottingham town with his patched coat and several wallets, heard that three brethren were that day to suffer at the gallows, being condemned for killing the king's deer. He made no more ado but went directly to the sheriff's house, where a young gentleman, seeing him stand by the door, demanded of him what he would have. Robin returned answer that he came to crave neither meat nor drink, but the lives of those three brothers who were condemned to die.

"That cannot be," said the young gentleman, "for they are all this day to suffer according to law, for stealing of the king's deer, and they are already conveyed out of town to the place of execution."

"I will be there presently," said Robin Hood, who, coming presently to the gallows, found many making great lamentations for them.

Robin Hood did comfort them, and assured them they should not die. Blowing his horn, behold on a sudden a hundred brave archers came unto him, by whose help, having released the prisoners, and killed the hangman, and hurt many of the sheriff's officers, he took those who were condemned to die for killing the king's deer along with him. The three brothers, being very thankful for the safety of their lives, became afterwards of the band of Robin Hood.

*The beggar and Robin Hood fell to.*

## A COMBAT WITH A VALIANT YOUNG GENTLEMAN

ROBIN HOOD now did wish he had continued his butcher's trade a little longer, for provisions grew scarce, and he had not therewith to maintain his band and himself. Riding, therefore, forth to see what good fortune he could be master of, he met with a young gentleman that had shot a buck.

Robin was not far off when it was done, and praised him for his archery, and offered him a place in his service, to be one of his yeomen. The young gentleman, disdaining his offer, told him if he would not begone he would kick him out of that place, whereupon Robin assured him that he had men enough to take his part if he would but blow his horn.

"Sound it, and thou darest," said the gentleman, "I can draw out a good sword that shall cut thy throat and thy horn too."

These rough words made Robin Hood so impatient that he did bend his bow, which, the gentleman observing, said unto him, "I am as ready for that as you, but then one, if not both of us, shall be surely slain; it were far better to try it out with our swords and bucklers."

"Content," said Robin Hood, "we can nowhere find a more fitting place than under the shadow of this oak."

They drew out their swords, and to it they went. Robin Hood gave the young gentleman a cut on the right elbow, and a little prick on his left shoulder, which the gentleman returned with advantage, insomuch that both of them taking space to breathe a little, Robin Hood demanded of him if he had never seen nor heard of him before.

"I know not who you are," said the gentleman, "but my name is Gamwel. I was born in Maxfield, and for killing my father's steward I am forced hither to seek my uncle, known to most folk by the name of Robin Hood."

"Why, I am the man," said Robin, and throwing down his sword and buckler he made haste to embrace him whom before he had so rashly wounded. Then Robin communicated what had passed to Little John, and gave his kinsman a place next to Little John, Little John being always next to himself.

Not long afterwards he travelled into the north, where a bonny Scot offered him his service, but Robin refused to entertain him. At that time the battle grew hot betwixt the Scots and the English. "Fight on, my merry men all," cried Robin, turning to the English, "our cause is just, we shall not be beaten, and though I am compassed about, with my sword I will cut my way through the midst of my enemies."

## ROBIN HOOD AND THE BISHOP

ROBIN HOOD, being returned with renown into Nottinghamshire, did walk forth one morning on foot, to see how affairs stood in the world. He had not gone far when he beheld a bishop riding towards London, and attended by one hundred followers. He perceived that the bishop had notice of him, and did steal into an old woman's house. She asked him who he was, to whom he revealed that he was the famous outlaw, commonly called by the name of Robin Hood.

TALES OF ROBIN HOOD

Robin Hood took the friar on his back, and, not speaking the
least word to him, carried him over the water. (Page 21)

THE FROG PRINCE

The frog seemed to relish his dinner, but every bit that
the King's daughter ate nearly choked her. (Page 27)

*Robin Hood, in danger of being captured, escapes by the help of an old woman.*

" If thy name be so," said the old woman, " I will do the best I can to provide for thee, for I do well remember it is not long since I received some kindness from thee. The best way that I can advise thee to conceal thyself is to put on my clothes, and I will put on thine."

"With all my heart," said Robin ; so, putting on her gray coat, he gave her his green one, with his doublet and breeches, and his bow, and those few arrows he had.

This was no sooner done but the bishop's men, with their swords drawn, entered into the house, did take the old woman, believing she had been Robin Hood, and did set her on a milk white steed, the bishop following himself on a dapple gray, being overjoyed at the great purchase he had made.

In the meantime, Robin Hood, being dressed in an old woman's clothes, with a rock and a spindle in his hand, did address himself straight to his company, and Little John, beholding him coming over the green, cried out, " Oh ! who is she that yonder is coming towards us, and looketh so like a witch ? I will shoot her dead, and being dead will nail her to the earth with one of my broad arrows."

" Hold thy hand," cried Robin, " I am thy master," and coming nearer he told them what had befallen at the old woman's house, and, to confirm what he said, they beheld the bishop with a gallant train riding up that way. The bishop, espying a hundred bold bowmen standing near a tree, in the way where he was to pass, demanded of his prisoner who they were.

" Marry," replied the old woman, " I think it is Robin Hood and his company."

" Who art thou, then ? " said the bishop.

" Why, I am just a simple old woman," replied his prisoner.

" Then woe is me ! " said the bishop.

He had scarce finished when Robin Hood called out to him and bade him stay, and taking hold of his horse tied the bishop fast to a tree. Next he took from the cases on the sumpter-horse five hundred pounds, which being done, Robin Hood smiling on Little John, and all his band laughing at one another, Robin Hood bade Little John give the bishop his horse and let him go.

First, however, they made him sing a mass; then they set him on his horse again, with his face towards the tail, and, bidding him to pray for Robin Hood, they suffered him to go forward on his journey.

## FAMOUS ARCHERY BEFORE THE QUEEN

ROBIN HOOD, having on all hands supplied himself with good store of gold, sent thereof a considerable present to the queen, begging her to ask his majesty for a pardon for himself and his band. The queen accepted the gift, and sent one of her pages, Richard Patrington, by name, to advise Robin to come to London.

Great was the haste that Patrington made, and, being well mounted, he covered within the space of two days and less, so long a journey. Being come to Nottingham, he found so much friendship that, on the next morning, he was brought to Robin's place, where he delivered his message from the queen, and Robin assured him that he would not fail to wait upon her majesty.

Immediately he clothed the chiefest of his men in Lincoln green, with black hats and white feathers, all alike, and himself in scarlet, and thus attended, he came to London to the queen.

"Welcome Locksly," said she, "the king is now gone into Finsbury Field to be present at a great game of shooting with the long-bow, and you come very seasonable unto it. Do you go before; I will presently be there myself."

When Robin Hood was come into Finsbury Field, the king spake unto his bow-bearer, and bade him to measure out the line, to know how long the mark should be; and the queen, not long afterwards, being sat next unto him, the king asked of her for what wager they should shoot.

The queen made answer, " The wager is three hundred tuns of Rhenish wine, and three hundred tuns of beer, and three hundred of the fattest bucks that run on Dallum plains."

" Beshrew me," said the king, " it is a princely wager indeed; well, mark out the ground."

This immediately was done, and though it was in length full fifteen score, Clifton, a famous archer about the town, boasted that he would hit the clout every time.

And now the king's archers had shot three goals and were three for none; but the queen, nothing discouraged, desired to know if any would be on her side. Sir Richard Lee, who was descended from the noble family of the Gowers, and was standing close unto her, was unwilling to lay one wager, while the Bishop of Hereford told her bluntly that he would not bet one penny on her side.

" For," said he, " those that shoot on the king's side are excellent archers, and those that you have made choice of, we know not who they are or whence they come. I durst wager all that I have about me against them."

" What is that ? " asked Robin Hood.

" Fifteen score nobles," said the bishop, " and that is almost one hundred pounds."

" It is right," said Robin Hood, " I will lay with you," and, taking his bag of money from his side, he threw it down upon the green.

William Scarlock being present, said, " I will venture my life that I know beforehand who will win this wager."

Now the archers did begin to shoot again, and now those whom the queen made choice of were equal to those of the king's side, they were both three and three. Whereupon the king spake aloud to the queen and said the next three must pay for all.

Robin Hood in the first place shot, and with such skill that his arrow entered into the clout ; and almost touched the black ; he on the king's side that did second him did also shoot well, and came very near unto the clout.

Then shot Little John and hit the black, at which the ladies laughed aloud, being now almost sure that the game would go on their side, which Midge, the miller's son, confirmed. I know not at that time whether I may most commend his art or his fortune ; but so it was that he cleft the very pin in the middle of the black, and that with such a twang of his bow that it seemed to proclaim the victory before the arrow came unto the mark.

The queen, having thus won the wager, fell down on her knees before the king, and besought his majesty that he would not be angry with any there present who were on her side. This, the king (the day being meant for mirth), promised, although he did not well understand what she did mean by that petition.

This being granted, the queen said aloud, " Then welcome Robin Hood, and welcome Little John, welcome Midge, the miller's son, and welcome every one of Robin Hood's company that is now in the field."

" Is this Robin Hood ? " asked the king ; " I thought he had been slain at the palace gate in the north."

The Bishop of Hereford, turning to the king, said unto him, " May it please your Majesty, this bold outlaw, Robin Hood, three weeks ago last Saturday, took from me five hundred pounds in gold, and bound me fast to a tree, and afterwards made me sing a mass, to him and to those of his most unruly company that were with him."

Robin Hood laughed heartily.

" What if I did ! " he cried, " I was full glad of it, for I have not heard mass before in many a year ; and for recompense of it, behold, sir bishop, here is half your gold."

" No, no," cried Little John, " that must not be, for, master, before we go we are to give gifts to the king and queen's officers, and the bishop's gold will serve for all."

So the king and queen took pleasure in their visit to the greenwood, and their hearts warmed towards Robin Hood and his merry men.

## ROBIN HOOD AND THE CURTAL FRIAR

ROBIN HOOD, being now grown most famous for his skill in archery, and being high in the favour of Queen Katherine, did return with much honour into Nottinghamshire. Forthwith he set aside a day of mirth for all his companions, and wagers were laid amongst them, who should succeed at this exercise, and who at that.

Some did contend who should jump farthest, some who should throw the bar, some who should be swiftest afoot in a race five miles in length ; others there were with whom Little John was most delighted, who did strive which of them should draw the strongest bow, and be the best marksman.

" Let me see," said Little John, " which of you can kill a buck, and who can kill a doe, and who is he can kill a hart, being distance from it by the space of five hundred foot."

With that, Robin Hood going before them, they went directly to the forest, where they found good store of game feeding before them. William Scarlock, that drew the strongest bow of them all, did kill a buck ; and Little John made choice of a fat doe, and the well-directed arrow did enter into the very heart of it ; and Midge, the miller's son, did kill a hart above five hundred foot distant from him.

The hart falling, Robin Hood stroked him gently on his shoulder, and said unto him, " God's blessing on thy heart, I will ride five hundred miles to find a match for thee."

William Scarlock hearing him speak these words, smiled, and said unto him, " Master, what needs that ? Here is a curtal friar * not far off, that for a hundred pound will shoot at what distance you choose to fix, either with Midge or with yourself. An excellent archer is he, and will draw a bow with great strength ; he will shoot with yourself, and with all the men you have, one after another."

" Sayest thou so ? " replied Robin Hood, " by the grace of God, I will neither eat nor drink, till I see this friar thou dost speak of."

Having prepared himself for his journey, he took Little John and fifty of his best archers with him, whom he placed at a convenient spot, as he himself thought fitting. This being done, he ran down into the dale, where he found the curtal friar walking by the water side. He no sooner espied him, but he took unto him his broad sword and buckler, and put on his head a steel bonnet. The friar not knowing who he was, nor for what reason he came, did arm himself to encounter him.

Robin Hood coming near unto him, alighted from his horse, which he tied to a thorn that grew hard by, and looking on the friar said unto him, " Carry me over the water, thou curtal friar, or else thy life lies at stake."

The friar made no more ado, but took up Robin Hood and carried him on his back through the deep water. He spake not so much as one word to him, but, having carried him over, he gently laid him down on the side of the bank. This being done, the friar said to Robin Hood, " It is now my turn ; therefore, carry me over the water, thou bold fellow, or be sure I shall make thee repent it."

* Curtal Friar, a friar wearing a short frock.

Robin Hood took the friar on his back, and, not speaking the least word to him, carried him over the water and laid him gently down on the side of the bank. Then turning to him, he spake thus unto him as at first, and bade him carry him over the water once more, or he should answer it with his life.

The friar, in a smiling manner, took him up, and spake not a word till he came in the midst of the stream, where, being up the middle and higher, he did shake him from off his shoulders, and said unto him, " Now choose thee, bold fellow, whether thou wilt sink or swim."

Robin Hood, being soundly washed, did swim to a bush of broom on the other side of the bank ; the friar swam to a willow tree which was not far from it. Robin Hood, taking his bow in his hand, and one of his arrows, did shoot at the friar, which the friar caught on his buckler of steel. " Shoot

*The friar smilingly took Robin Hood on his back.*

on, shoot on, thou bold fellow," he said ; " if thou shootest at me a whole summer's day, I will stand thy mark still."

" That will I try," said Robin, and shot arrow after arrow at him, until he had not one left in his quiver. He then laid down his bow, and drew out his sword, which but two days before had been the death of three men.

Now hand to hand they meet with sword and buckler ; the steel buckler defends whatsoever blow is given : sometimes they make at the head, sometimes at the foot, sometimes at the side ; sometimes they strike directly down, sometimes they come in foot and arm with a full thrust at the body ; and being ashamed that so long they cannot hurt one another, they multiply their blows ; they hack, they hew, they slash, they foam. At last Robin Hood desired the friar to hold his hand, and to give him leave to blow his horn.

" Thou wantest breath to sound it," said the friar ; " take thee a little rest, for we have been five hours at it by Fountain Abbey clock."

Robin Hood took his horn from his side, and, having sounded it three times, behold where fifty lusty men, with their bended bows, came to his assistance.

The friar, wondering at it, said, " Whose men be these ? "

" They are mine," said Robin, " what is that to thee ? "

" False loon," said the friar, and making a little pause, " thou soundest thy horn three times, let me now but whistle three times."

" With all my heart," said Robin, " I were to blame if I should deny thee that boon."

With that the friar set his fist to his mouth, and whistled three times so shrilly that the place echoed again with it, and, behold, three-and-fifty fair ban-dogs (their hairs rising on their backs showing their rage) were almost on the backs of Robin Hood and his companions.

" Here is for every one of thy men a dog," said the friar, " and two for thee."

" That is foul play," said Robin Hood.

He had scarce spoken that word, but two dogs came upon him at once, one before, another behind him, who, although they could not touch his flesh (his sword had made so swift a despatch of them), yet they tore his coat in two pieces.  By this time his men had so lain about them that the dogs began to fly back, and their fury to be confined to barking.  Little John did so bestir himself that the curtal friar, admiring his courage and nimbleness, did ask him who he was.

He made him answer.  " I will tell the truth and not lie.  I am he who is called Little John, and do belong to Robin Hood, who hath fought with thee this day, five hours together, and if thou wilt not submit unto him this arrow shall make thee."

The friar, perceiving how much he was overpowered, and that it was impossible for him to deal with so many at once, did make a compact with Robin Hood.  The articles of agreement were these :—

That the friar should abandon Fountain Dale and Fountain Abbey, and live with Robin Hood at his place not far from Nottingham, where, for saying of mass, he should receive a noble for every Sunday throughout the year, and for saying of mass on every Holyday, a new change of garments.

Thus, by the courage of Robin Hood and his yeomen, the friar was forced at the last to submit, having for seven long years kept Fountain Dale, not all the powers thereabouts being able to bring him on his knees.

## THE NOBLE FISHERMAN

THE countryside and the cities being full of the doings of Robin Hood and his companions, he resolved with himself to make some adventure at sea, and to try if he could be as famous at sea.  Having therefore called all his yeomen together, he did communicate unto them his plan, but none of them would consent unto it, nor any of them would so much as go along with him on such an expedition.  Little John, in whom he much trusted, and who was partaker with him in all his schemes, and in all his dangers, was absolutely against it, and told him it was a madness in him to harbour any thought of such an adventure.

Wherefore Robin Hood did go by himself to Scarborough, where, being clad in a seaman's habit, he came to a woman's house by the waterside, and desired employment. The good woman, seeing him a tall, likely fellow, did ask him what his name was, and he made answer that it was Simon over the Lee.

" It is a good name," said she, " and I hope thou wilt make a good servant. If thou wilt be my servant, I will give thee any wages that in reason thou wilt demand. I have a ship of my own, as good as any that sails upon the sea, and neither thou nor it shall want for any accommodation."

Robin Hood being content to serve, took token money from her, and on the next morning, the wind being fair, the ship put forth to sea, where Robin Hood had not been long, before he fell very sick, the sea and he not being able to agree. Besides, he was so utterly useless that the master of the ship repented a thousand times that he ever took him along with him, and every one would call him the tall, unwieldy lubber.

When others, as they were a-fishing, would cast into the sea their baited hooks, he would throw in nothing but his bare line, without any hook or bait at all. This mistake, amongst many others, made him so ridiculous, that a thousand times he wished himself again either in Sherwood Forest or in Plumpton Park.

At last the master of the ship espied a Spanish man-of-war to make up to him, wherefore he made away from her with all the speed he could ; but, it being impossible to outsail her, they yielded themselves lost, and all the goods in the ship. Robin Hood, who called himself Simon over the Lee,

*Taking his bow and arrows up on deck, he killed Spaniard after Spaniard.*

seeing all men in despair, took courage to himself, and bade his master but give him his bow and his arrows, and he would deal well enough with them all.

"Thou deal with them!" said the master; "I think we all fare the worse in the ship, for such a lubber as thou art."

Robin grew angry at these words; nevertheless, taking his bow and arrows in his hand, he went up to the deck, and, drawing his arrow up to the very head, killed one Spaniard, and by and by another and another.

The master of the ship, seeing the Spaniards to drop so fast, encouraged his men and boarded the ship, where Robin Hood, alias Simon, behaved himself so manfully that, by his particular valour, they possessed themselves of the ship, in which they found twelve thousand pounds. Half of this money Robin Hood set aside for his dame and her children, and the other half he offered to his companions in the ship.

"No," said the master, "it must not be so, Simon, for you have won it with your own hands, and you shall be master of it."

"Why then," cried Robin Hood, "it shall be as I have said. Half of it shall go to the dame and her children, and (since you refuse my bounty) the other half shall be for the building of an alms-house for the comfort of the poor!"

# Sea Fever

## by JOHN MASEFIELD

I MUST down to the seas again, to the lonely seas and the sky,
  And all I ask is a tall ship and a star to steer her by,
And the wheel's kick and the wind's song and the white sail's shaking,
And a grey mist on the sea's face and a grey dawn breaking.

I must down to the seas again, for the call of the running tide
Is a wild call and a clear call that may not be denied;
And all I ask is a windy day with the white clouds flying,
And the flung spray and the blown spume, and the sea-gulls crying.

I must down to the seas again to the vagrant gypsy life,
To the gull's way and the whale's way where the wind's like a whetted knife;
And all I ask is a merry yarn from a laughing fellow-rover,
And quiet sleep and a sweet dream when the long trick's over.

# THE·FROG PRINCE

*from " Grimms' Fairy Tales "*

IN olden times, when to wish was to have, there lived a King whose daughters were all beautiful. But the youngest was so fair that the Sun himself, although he saw her often, was enchanted every time she came out into the sunshine.

Near the castle of this King was a large and gloomy forest, and in the midst grew an old linden-tree, beneath whose branches splashed a little fountain. So when the days were very warm, the King's youngest daughter ran off to the wood, and sat down by the side of the fountain. When she felt dull, she would often amuse herself by throwing a golden ball up in the air and catching it. This was her favourite form of play.

Now, one day it happened that this golden ball did not fall down into her hand, but on the grass; and then it rolled past her into the fountain. The child followed the ball with her eyes, but it disappeared beneath the water which was so deep that no one could see to the bottom. Then she began to lament, and to cry louder and louder; and as she wailed, a voice called out, "Why do you weep, O Princess? Your tears would move even a stone to pity." She looked around to the spot from which the voice came, and saw a Frog stretching his fat ugly head out of the water.

"Ah! you old water-paddler," said she, "was it you that spoke? I am crying for my golden ball, which has slipped away into the water."

"Well, now, do not cry," answered the Frog; "I can tell you what to do. But what will you give me if I fetch your plaything up again?"

25

" What will you have, dear Frog ? " said she. " My dresses, my pearls and jewels, or the golden crown that I wear ? "

The Frog answered :

" Dresses, jewels, or golden crowns are not for me ; but if you will love me, and let me be your companion and playmate, and sit at your table, and eat from your little gold plate, and drink out of your cup, and sleep in your little bed—if you will promise me all these, then will I dive down and fetch up your golden ball."

" Oh, I will promise you all," said she, " if you will only get my ball."

But she thought to herself, " What is the silly Frog croaking about ? Let him stay in the water with his frogs ; he cannot be company for any human being." The Frog, as soon as he had received her promise, drew his head under the water, and dived down. Presently he swam up again with the ball in his mouth, and threw it on the grass. The Princess was full of joy when she again saw her beautiful plaything ; and, taking it up, she ran off immediately.

" Stop ! stop ! " cried the Frog ; " take me with you. I cannot run as you can."

But all his croaking was useless ; although it was loud enough, she did not hear it, but, hastening home, soon forgot the poor Frog, who was obliged to leap back into the fountain.

The next day, when the Princess was sitting at table with her father and all his courtiers, and was eating from her little gold plate, something was heard coming up the marble stairs, *splish-splash*, *splish-splash* ; and, when it arrived at the top, it knocked at the door, and a voice said, " Open the door, youngest daughter of the King, and let me in ! "

So she rose and went to see who it was that called her ; but, when she opened the door and caught sight of the Frog, she shut it again with great vehemence, and sat down at the table, looking very pale. The King saw that her heart was beating violently, and asked her if it was a giant come to fetch her away who stood at the door.

" Oh, no ! " answered she ; " it is no giant, but an ugly Frog."

" What does the Frog want with you ? " said the King.

" Oh, dear father, when I was sitting yesterday playing by the fountain, my golden ball fell into the water, and this Frog fetched it up again because I cried so much ; but first, I must tell you, he pressed me so much that I promised him that he should be my companion. I never thought that he could come out of the water ; but somehow he has jumped out, and now he wants to come in here."

At that moment there was another knock, and a voice said :

" Youngest Princess,
          Open the door.
     Have you forgotten
     Your promises made,
     At the fountain so clear
     'Neath the lime-tree's shade ?
     Youngest Princess,
          Open the door."

Then the King said, "What you have promised, that you must do; go and let him in."

So she went and opened the door, and the Frog hopped in after her right up to her chair: and, as soon as she was seated, the Frog said, "Take me up." She hesitated so long that at last the King ordered her to obey. And as soon as the Frog sat on the chair, he jumped on to the table and said, "Now push your plate near me, that we may eat together." She did so, but, as every one saw, very unwillingly.

The Frog seemed to relish his dinner, but every bit that the King's daughter ate nearly choked her. At last the Frog said, "I am satisfied, but

*"Do take me up, or I will tell your father," said the Frog.*

feel very tired; will you carry me upstairs now to our room, and make our bed ready that we may sleep?"

At this speech the Princess began to cry, for she was afraid of the cold Frog, and dared not touch him; and besides, he actually wanted to sleep in her beautiful, clean bed!

Her tears only made the King very angry, and he said, "He who helped you in the time of your trouble, must not now be despised." So she took the Frog up with two fingers, and put him in a corner of her room. But, as she lay in her bed, he crept up to it, and said, "I am so very tired that I shall sleep well; do take me up, or I will tell your father." This speech put her in a passion, and catching up the Frog, she threw him with all her strength against the wall, saying, "Now, will you be quiet, you ugly Frog?"

But, as he fell, he was changed from a frog into a handsome Prince with beautiful eyes, and after a little while he became, with her father's consent, her dear companion and playmate. Then he told her how he had been changed by a wicked witch, and that no one but herself could have had the power to take him out of the fountain; and that on the morrow they would go together to his own kingdom.

The next morning, as soon as the sun rose, a carriage, drawn by eight white horses, with white ostrich feathers on their heads, and golden bridles, drove up to the door of the palace, and behind the carriage stood the trusty Henry, the servant of the young Prince. When his master was changed into a frog, trusty Henry had grieved so much that he had bound three iron bands round his heart, for fear it should break with sorrow.

Now that the carriage was ready to carry the young Prince to his own country, the faithful Henry helped in the bride and bridegroom, and placed himself in the seat behind, full of joy at his master's release. They had not gone far when the Prince heard a crack, as if something had broken behind the carriage; so he put his head out of the window and asked Henry what was broken, and Henry answered, " It was not the carriage, my master, but a band which I bound round my heart when it was in grief because you were changed into a frog."

Twice afterwards on the journey there was the same noise, and each time the Prince thought that it was some part of the carriage that had given way. But it was only the breaking of the bands which bound the heart of the trusty Henry, who was thenceforward free and happy.

---

# The Shepherd Boy's Song

*by* JOHN BUNYAN

He that is down need fear no fall,
    He that is low no pride;
He that is humble ever shall
    Have God to be his guide.

I am content with what I have,
    Little be it or much:
And, Lord, contentment still I crave,
    Because thou savest such.

Fulness to such a burden is
    That go on pilgrimage:
Here little, and hereafter bliss,
    Is best from age to age.

# THE VALIANT LITTLE TAILOR

*from " Grimms' Fairy Tales "*

ONE summer's morning a Tailor was sitting on his bench by the window in very good spirits, sewing away with all his might, and presently up the street came a peasant woman, crying, " Good preserves for sale ! Good preserves for sale ! "

This cry sounded nice in the Tailor's ears, and, sticking his diminutive head out of the window, he called out, " Here, my good woman, just bring your wares here ! " The woman mounted the three steps up to the Tailor's house with her heavy basket, and began to unpack all the pots together before him. He looked at them all, held them up to the light, put his nose to them, and at last said, " These preserves appear to me to be very nice, so you may weigh me out four half-ounces, my good woman ; I don't mind even if you make it a quarter of a pound." The woman, who expected to have met with a good customer, gave him what he wished, and went away grumbling, very much dissatisfied.

" Now ! " exclaimed the Tailor, " Heaven will send me a blessing on this preserve, and give me fresh strength and vigour ; " and, taking the bread out of the cupboard, he cut himself a slice the size of the whole loaf, and spread the preserve upon it. " That will taste by no means badly," said he ; " but, before I have a bite, I will just get this waistcoat finished." So he laid the bread down near him and stitched away, making larger and larger stitches every time for joy.

Meanwhile, the smell of the preserve mounted to the ceiling, where flies were sitting in great numbers, and enticed them down, so that soon a regular swarm of them had settled on the bread. " Hallo ! Who invited you ? " exclaimed the Tailor, hunting away the unbidden guests ; but the

29

flies, not understanding his language, would not be driven off, and came again in greater numbers than before.

This put the little man in a boiling passion, and, snatching up in his rage a piece of cloth, he brought it down with an unmerciful swoop upon them. When he raised it again, he counted no fewer than seven lying dead before him with outstretched legs. " What a fellow you are ! " said he to himself, wondering at his own bravery. " The whole town shall know of this."

In great haste he cut himself out a band, hemmed it, and then put on it in large characters, " SEVEN AT ONE BLOW ! " " Ah," said he, " not one city alone ; the whole world shall know it ! " and his heart fluttered with joy, like a lambkin's tail.

The little Tailor bound the belt round his body, and prepared to travel forth into the wide world, thinking the workshop too small for his valiant deeds. Before he set out, however, he looked round his house to see if there was anything he could take with him ; but he found only an old cheese, which he pocketed ; and, seeing a bird before the door, which was entangled in the bushes, he caught it and put that in his pocket also. Directly after, he set out bravely on his travels ; and, as he was light and active, he felt no weariness. His road led him up a hill, and when he reached the highest point of it he found a great Giant sitting there, who was looking about him very composedly.

The little Tailor, however, went boldly up, and said, " Good-day, comrade ; in faith, you sit there and see the whole world stretched below you. I am also on my road thither to try my luck. Have you a mind to go with me ? "

The Giant looked contemptuously at the little Tailor, and said, " You vagabond ! you miserable fellow ! "

" That may be," replied the Tailor ; " but here you may read what sort of a man I am ; " and, unbuttoning his coat, he showed the Giant his belt. The Giant read, " Seven at one blow ! " and, thinking they were men whom the Tailor had slain, he had a little respect for him. Still, he wished to prove him first ; so, taking up a stone, he squeezed it in his hand, so that water dropped out of it.

" Do that after me," said he to the other, " if you have any strength."

" If it be nothing worse than that," said the Tailor, " that's play to me." And, diving into his pocket, he brought out the cheese and squeezed it till the whey ran out of it, and said, " Now, I think that's a little better."

The Giant did not know what to say, and could not believe it of the little man ; so, taking up another stone, he threw it so high that one could scarcely see it with the eye, saying, " There, you mannikin, do that after me."

" Well done ! " said the Tailor ; " but your stone must fall down again to the ground. I will throw one up which shall not come back," and, dipping into his pocket, he took out the bird and threw it into the air. The bird, rejoicing in its freedom, flew straight up, and then far away, and did not return. " How does that little affair please you, comrade ? " asked the Tailor.

" You can throw well, certainly," replied the Giant ; " now let us see if you are in trim to carry something out of the common." So saying, he led him to a huge oak-tree, which lay upon the ground, and said, " If you are strong enough, just help me to carry this tree out of the forest."

" With all my heart," replied the Tailor. " Do you take the trunk upon your shoulder, and I will raise the boughs and branches, which are the heaviest, and carry them."

The Giant took the trunk upon his shoulder; but the Tailor seated himself on a branch, so that the Giant, who was not able to look round, was forced to carry the whole tree and the Tailor besides. He, being behind, was very merry, and chuckled at the trick, and presently began to whistle the song, " There rode three tailors out at the gate," as if the carrying of trees were child's play. The Giant, after he had staggered along a short distance with his heavy burden, could go no farther, and shouted out, " Do you hear? I must let the tree fall." The Tailor, springing down, quickly embraced the tree with both arms, as if he had been carrying it, and said to the Giant, " Are you such a big fellow, and yet cannot you carry this tree by yourself? "

Then they journeyed on farther, and as they came to a cherry-tree, the Giant seized the top of the tree where the ripest fruits hung, and, bending it down, gave it to the Tailor to hold, bidding him eat. But the Tailor was much too weak to hold the tree down; and when the Giant let go, the tree flew up in the air, and the Tailor was carried with it. He came down on the other side, however, without any injury, and the Giant said, " What does that mean? Have you not strength enough to hold that twig? " " My strength did not fail me," replied the Tailor. " Do you suppose that that was any hard thing for one who has killed seven at one blow? I have sprung over the tree because the hunters were shooting below there in the thicket. Spring after me if you can." The Giant made the attempt, but could not clear the tree, and stuck fast in the branches; so that in this affair, too, the Tailor was the better man.

After this the Giant said, " Since you are such a valiant fellow, come with me to our house and stop a night with us." The Tailor consented, and followed him; and when they entered the cave, there sat by the fire two other Giants, each having a roast sheep in his hand, of which he was eating. The Tailor sat down, thinking, " Ah, this is much more like the world than is my workshop." And soon the Giant showed him a bed where he might lie down and go to sleep. The bed, however, was too big for him, so he slipped out of it and crept into a corner.

When midnight came, and the Giant thought the Tailor would be in a deep sleep, he got up, and, taking a great iron bar, beat the bed right through at one stroke, and supposed he had given the Tailor his death-blow. At the earliest dawn of morning the Giants went forth into the forest, quite forgetting the Tailor, when presently up he came, quite merry, and showed himself before them. The Giants were terrified, and, fearing he would kill them all, they ran away in great haste.

The Tailor journeyed on, always following his nose, and after he had wandered some long distance, he came into the courtyard of a royal palace; and as he felt rather tired he laid himself down on the grass and went to sleep. Whilst he lay there the people came and viewed him, and read upon his belt, " Seven at one blow." " Ah! " said they, " what does this great warrior here in time of peace? This must be some mighty hero."

So they went and told the King, thinking that, should war break out, here was an important and useful man, whom one ought not to part with at any price. The King took counsel, and sent one of his courtiers to the Tailor to ask for his fighting services, if he should be awake. The messenger stopped at the sleeper's side, and waited till he stretched out his limbs and opened his eyes, and then he laid before him his message. " Solely on that account did I come here," was the reply ; " I am quite ready to enter into the King's service." Then he was conducted away with great honour, and a fine house was appointed him to dwell in.

The courtiers, however, became jealous of the Tailor, and wished he were a thousand miles away. " What will happen ? " said they to one another. " If we go to battle with him, when he strikes out seven will fall at every blow, and nothing will be left for us to do."

In their rage they came to a resolution to resign, and they all went together to the King, and asked his permission, saying, " We are not prepared to keep company with a man who kills seven at one blow." The King was grieved to lose all his faithful servants for the sake of one, and wished that he had never seen the Tailor, and would willingly have now been rid of him. He dared not, however, dismiss him, because he feared that the Tailor would kill him and all his subjects, and place himself upon the throne.

For a long time he deliberated, till at last he came to a decision ; and, sent for the Tailor. " In a certain forest in my kingdom," said the King, " there live two Giants, who, by murder, rapine, fire, and robbery, have committed great havoc, and no one dares to approach them without perilling his own life. If you overcome and kill both these Giants, I will give you my only daughter in marriage, and the half of my kingdom for a dowry : a hundred knights shall accompany you too, to assist you."

" Ah, that is something for such a man as I," thought the Tailor to himself ; " a beautiful Princess and half a kingdom are not offered to one every day." So he replied, " Oh, yes, I will soon manage these two Giants, and a hundred horsemen are not necessary for that purpose ; he who kills seven at one blow need not fear two."

Thus talking, the little Tailor set out, followed by the hundred knights, to whom he said, as soon as they came to the borders of the forest, " Stay you here ; I would rather meet these Giants alone." Then he sprang off into the forest, peering about him right and left ; and after a while he saw the two Giants lying asleep under a tree, snoring so loudly that the branches above them shook violently. The Tailor, full of courage, filled both his pockets with stones and clambered up the tree. When he got to the middle of it he crept along a bough, so that he sat just above the sleepers, and then he let fall one stone after another upon the breast of one of them. For some time the Giant did not stir, until, at last awakening, he pushed his companion, and said, " Why are you beating me ? "

" You are dreaming," he replied ; " I never hit you." They laid themselves down again to sleep, and presently the Tailor threw a stone down upon the other. " What is that ? " he exclaimed. " What are you knocking me for ? "

" I did not touch you ; you must dream," replied the first. So they wrangled for a few minutes ; but, being both very tired with their day's

THE VALIANT LITTLE TAILOR

His road led him up a hill, and when he reached the highest point
of it he found a great Giant sitting there. (Page 30)

**RAPUNZEL**

Then Rapunzel let down her tresses,
and the witch mounted up. (Page 36)

*The unicorn fixed its horn fast in the trunk.*

work, they soon fell asleep again. Then the Tailor began his sport again, and, picking out the biggest stone, threw it with all his force upon the breast of the first Giant. "That is too bad!" he exclaimed; and, springing up like a madman, he fell upon his companion, who felt equally aggrieved. They set to in such good earnest, that they rooted up trees and beat one another about until they both fell dead upon the ground.

Now the Tailor jumped down, drew his sword, and, cutting a deep wound in the breast of each, he went to the horsemen, and said, "The deed is done? I have given each his death-stroke; but it was a hard job, for they uprooted trees to defend themselves with; still, all that is of no use when such a one as I come, who killed seven at one stroke."

"Are you not wounded, then?" asked they.

"That is not to be expected: they have not touched a hair of my head," replied the little man. The knights could scarcely believe him, till, riding away into the forest, they found the Giants lying in their blood and the uprooted trees around them.

The Tailor now demanded of the King his promised reward; but the King repented his promise, and began to think of some new scheme to get rid of the hero. "Before you receive my daughter and the half of my kingdom," said he, "you must perform one other heroic deed. In the forest there runs wild a unicorn, which commits great havoc, and which you must first of all catch."

"I fear still less for a unicorn than I do for two Giants! 'Seven at one blow!' that is my motto," said the Tailor. Then he took with him a rope and an axe, and went away to the forest. He had not to search long, for presently the unicorn came near and prepared to rush at him as if it would pierce him on the spot. "Softly, softly!" he exclaimed; "that is not done so easily." And, waiting till the animal was close upon him, he sprang nimbly behind a tree.

The unicorn, rushing with all its force against the tree, fixed its horn so fast in the trunk that it could not draw it out again, and so it was made prisoner. " Now I have got mý bird," said the Tailor ; and, coming from behind the tree, he first bound the rope around its neck, and then, cutting the horn out of the tree with his axe, he led the animal before the King.

The king, however, would not yet deliver up the promised reward, and made a third request, that, before the wedding, the Tailor should catch a wild boar which did much injury, and he should have the huntsmen to help him. " With pleasure," was the reply ; " it is mere child's play." The hunstmen, however, he left behind, to their entire content, for this wild boar had already so often hunted them, that they had no pleasure in hunting it. As soon as the boar perceived the Tailor, it ran at him with gaping mouth and gnashing teeth, and tried to throw him on the ground ; but our flying hero sprang into a little chapel which was near, and out again at a window on the other side in a trice. The boar ran after him, but he, skipping round, shut the door behind it, and there the raging beast was caught, for it was much too unwieldy and heavy to jump out of the window. The Tailor now called the huntsmen up, that they might see his prisoner with their own eyes ; but our hero presented himself before the King, who was compelled now, whether he would or no, to keep his promise, and surrender his daughter and the half of his kingdom.

So the wedding was celebrated with great splendour, though with little rejoicing, and out of a Tailor was made a King.

Some little while afterwards the young Queen heard her husband talking in his sleep, and saying, " Boy, make me a waistcoat, and stitch up these trousers, or I will lay the yard-measure over your ears ! " Then she found of what condition her lord was, and complained in the morning to her father, and begged he would deliver her from her husband, who was nothing else than a tailor. The King comforted her by saying, " This night leave your chamber door open ; my servants shall stand without, and when he is asleep they shall enter, bind him, and bear him away to a ship, which shall carry him forth into the wide world." The wife was contented with his proposal ; but the King's armour-bearer, who had overheard all, went to the young King and disclosed the whole plot.

" I will shoot a bolt upon this affair," said the brave Tailor. In the evening, at their usual time, they went to bed, and when his wife believed he slept she got up, opened the door, and laid herself down again. The Tailor, however, only feigned to be asleep, and began to exclaim in a loud voice, " Boy, make me this waistcoat, and stitch up these trousers, or I will beat the yard-measure about your ears ! Seven have I killed with one blow ; two Giants have I slain ; a unicorn have I led captive ; and a wild boar have I caught ; and shall I be afraid of those who stand without my chamber ? "

When the servants heard these words spoken by the Tailor, a great fear overcame them, and they ran away as if the wild huntsmen were behind them ; neither afterwards durst any man venture to oppose him. Thus became the Tailor a King, and so he remained the rest of his days.

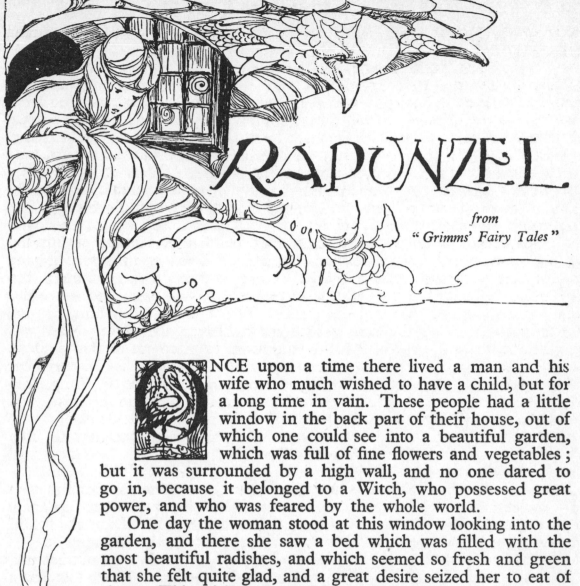

# RAPUNZEL

*from*
*"Grimms' Fairy Tales"*

ONCE upon a time there lived a man and his wife who much wished to have a child, but for a long time in vain. These people had a little window in the back part of their house, out of which one could see into a beautiful garden, which was full of fine flowers and vegetables; but it was surrounded by a high wall, and no one dared to go in, because it belonged to a Witch, who possessed great power, and who was feared by the whole world.

One day the woman stood at this window looking into the garden, and there she saw a bed which was filled with the most beautiful radishes, and which seemed so fresh and green that she felt quite glad, and a great desire seized her to eat of them. This wish tormented her daily, and as she knew that she could not have them, she fell ill, and looked very pale and miserable. This frightened her husband, who asked her, "What ails you, my dear wife?"

"Ah!" she replied, "if I cannot get any of those radishes to eat out of the garden behind the house, I shall die!"

The husband, loving her very much, thought, "Rather than let my wife die, I must fetch her some radishes, cost what they may."

So, in the gloom of the evening, he climbed the wall of the Witch's garden, and, snatching a handful of radishes in great haste, brought them to his wife, who made herself a salad with them, which she relished extremely. However, they were so nice and so well flavoured, that the next day after she felt the same desire for the third time, and could not get any rest, so that her husband was obliged to promise her some more.

So, in the evening, he made himself ready, and began clambering up the wall; but, oh! how terribly frightened he was, for there he saw the old Witch standing before him. "How dare you," she began, looking at

35

him with a frightful scowl—" how dare you climb over into my garden to take away my radishes like a thief? Evil shall happen to you for this."

" Ah ! " replied he, " let pardon be granted before justice. I have only done this from a great necessity : my wife saw your radishes from her window, and took such a fancy to them that she would have died if she had not eaten of them." Then the Witch ran after him in a passion, saying, " If she behave as you say, I will let you take away all the radishes you please ; but I make one condition—you must give me your child. All shall go well with it, and I will care for it like a mother."

In his anxiety the man consented, and when the child was born the Witch appeared at the same time, gave the child the name " Rapunzel," and took it away with her.

Rapunzel grew to be the most beautiful child under the sun, and when she was twelve years old the Witch shut her up in a tower, which stood in a forest, and had neither stairs nor door, and only one little window just at the top. When the Witch wished to enter, she stood beneath, and called out :

> " Rapunzel ! Rapunzel !
> Let down your hair."

For Rapunzel had long and beautiful hair, as fine as spun gold ; and, as soon as she heard the Witch's voice, she unbound her tresses, opened the window, and then the hair fell down twenty ells, and the Witch mounted up by it.

After a couple of years had passed away, it happened that the King's son was riding through the wood, and came by the tower. There he heard a song so beautiful that he stood still and listened. It was Rapunzel, who, to pass the time of her loneliness away, was exercising her sweet voice. The King's son wished to ascend to her, and looked for a door in the tower, but he could not find one.

So he rode home, but the song had touched his heart so much that he went every day to the forest and listened to it ; and as he thus stood one day behind a tree, he saw the Witch come up, and heard her call out :

> " Rapunzel ! Rapunzel !
> Let down your hair."

Then Rapunzel let down her tresses, and the Witch mounted up. " Is that the ladder on which one must climb ? Then I will try my luck too," said the Prince ; and the following day, as he felt quite lonely, he went to the tower, and said :

> " Rapunzel ! Rapunzel !
> Let down your hair."

Then the tresses fell down, and he climbed up.

Rapunzel was much frightened at first when a man came in, for she had never seen one before ; but the King's son talked in a loving way to her, and told how his heart had been so moved by her singing that he had no peace until he had seen her himself.

*" You will never see her again."*

So Rapunzel lost her terror, and when he asked her if she would have him for a husband, and she saw that he was young and handsome, she thought, " Any one may have me rather than the old woman : " so, saying " Yes," she put her hand within his. " I will willingly go with you, but I know not how I am to descend. When you come, bring with you a skein of silk each time, out of which I will weave a ladder, and when it is ready I will come down by it, and you must take me upon your horse."

Then they agreed that they should never meet till the evening, as the Witch came in the daytime. The old woman found out nothing, until one day Rapunzel innocently said, " Tell me, mother, how it happens you find it more difficult to come up to me than the young King's son, who is with me in a moment ! "

" Oh, you wicked child ! " exclaimed the Witch ; " what do I hear ? I thought I had separated you from all the world, and yet you have deceived me." And, seizing Rapunzel's beautiful hair in a fury, she gave her a couple of blows with her left hand, and, taking a pair of scissors in her right, *snip, snap,* she cut off all her beautiful tresses, and they fell upon the ground. Then she was so hard-hearted that she took the poor maiden into a great desert, and left her to die in great misery and grief.

But in the evening of the same day on which she had carried off Rapunzel, the old Witch bound the shorn tresses fast above to the window-latch, and when the King's son came, and called out :

" Rapunzel ! Rapunzel !
Let down your hair."

she let them down. The Prince mounted ; but when he got to the top he found, not his dear Rapunzel, but the Witch, who looked at him with furious and wicked eyes.

" Aha ! " she exclaimed scornfully, " you would fetch your dear wife ; but the beautiful bird sits no longer in her nest, singing ; the cat has taken her away, and will now scratch out your eyes. To you Rapunzel is lost ; you will never see her again."

The Prince lost his senses with grief at these words, and sprang out of the window of the tower in his bewilderment. His life he escaped with, but the thorns into which he fell put out his eyes. So he wandered, blind, in the forest, eating nothing but berries and roots, and doing nothing but weep and lament for the loss of his dear wife.

He wandered about thus, in great misery, for some few years, and at last arrived at the desert where Rapunzel, with her twins—a boy and girl—which had been born, lived in great sorrow. Hearing a voice which he thought he knew, he followed in its direction; and, as he approached, Rapunzel recognised him, and fell upon his neck and wept. Two of her tears moistened his eyes, and they became clear again, so that he could see as well as ever.

Then he led her away to his kingdom, where he was received with great demonstrations of joy, and where they lived long, contented and happy.

What became of the old Witch no one ever knew.

# Washing

### by JOHN DRINKWATER

What is all this washing about,
Every day, week in, week out?
From getting up till going to bed,
I'm tired of hearing the same thing said.
Whether I'm dirty or whether I'm not,
Whether the water is cold or hot,
Whether I like or whether I don't,
Whether I will or whether I won't.—
" Have you washed your hands, and washed your face? "
I seem to *live* in the washing-place.

Whenever I go for a walk or ride,
As soon as I put my nose inside
The door again, there's some one there
With a sponge and soap, and a lot they care
If I have something better to do,
" Now wash your face and your fingers too."

Before a meal is ever begun,
And after ever a meal is done,
It's time to turn on the waterspout.
Please, what *is* all this washing about?

# THE TINDER-BOX

*from " Andersen's Fairy Tales "*

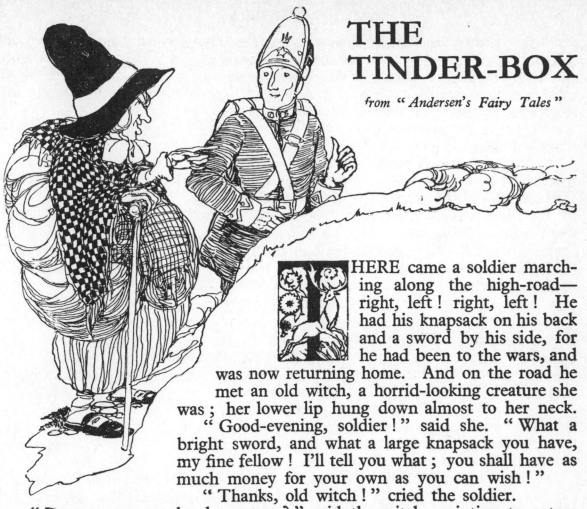

HERE came a soldier marching along the high-road— right, left ! right, left ! He had his knapsack on his back and a sword by his side, for he had been to the wars, and was now returning home. And on the road he met an old witch, a horrid-looking creature she was ; her lower lip hung down almost to her neck.

" Good-evening, soldier ! " said she. " What a bright sword, and what a large knapsack you have, my fine fellow ! I'll tell you what ; you shall have as much money for your own as you can wish ! "

" Thanks, old witch ! " cried the soldier.

" Do you see yonder large tree ? " said the witch, pointing to a tree that stood close by the wayside. " It is quite hollow within. Climb up to the top, and you will find a hole large enough for you to creep through, and thus you will get down into the tree. I will tie a rope round your waist, so that I can pull you up again when you call me."

" But what am I to do down in the tree ? " asked the soldier.

" What are you to do ? " repeated the witch. " Why, fetch money, to be sure ! As soon as you get to the bottom, you will find yourself in a wide passage ; it is quite light, more than a hundred lamps are burning there. Then you will see three doors ; you can open them, the keys are in the locks.

" On opening the first door you will enter a room. In the midst of it, on the floor, lies a large chest ; a dog is seated on it, his eyes are as large as teacups ; but never you mind, don't trouble yourself about him ! I will lend you my blue apron ; you must spread it out on the floor, then go briskly up to the dog, seize him, and set him down on it ; and after that is done, you can open the chest, and take as much money out of it as you please.

" That chest contains none but copper coins ; but if you like silver better, you have only to go into the next room ; there you will find a dog with eyes as large as mill-wheels, but don't be afraid of him ; you have only to set him down on my apron, and then rifle the chest at your leisure.

"But if you would rather have gold than either silver or copper, that is to be had, too, and as much of it as you can carry, if you pass on into the third chamber. The dog that sits on this third money-chest has two eyes, each as large as the round tower. A famous creature he is, as you may fancy; but don't be alarmed, just set him down on my apron, and then he will do you no harm, and you can take as much golden treasure from the chest as you like."

"Not a bad plan that, upon my word!" said the soldier. "But how much of the money am I to give you, old woman? For you'll want your full share of the plunder I've a notion!"

"Not a penny will I have," returned the witch. "The only thing I want you to bring me is an old tinder-box which my grandmother left there by mistake last time she was down in the tree."

"Well then, give me the rope to tie round my waist, and I'll be gone," said the soldier.

"Here it is," said the witch; "and here is my blue apron."

So the soldier climbed the tree, let himself down through the hole in the trunk, and suddenly found himself in the wide passage, lighted up by many hundred lamps, as the witch had described.

He opened the first door. Bravo! There sat the dog with eyes as large as teacups, staring at him in utter amazement.

"There's a good creature!" quoth the soldier, as he spread the witch's apron on the floor, and lifted the dog upon it. He then filled his pockets with the copper coins in the chest, shut the lid, put the dog back into his place, and passed on into the second apartment.

Huzza! There sat the dog with eyes as large as mill-wheels.

"You had really better not stare at me so," remarked the soldier, "it will make your eyes weak!" and he set the dog down on the witch's apron. But when, on raising the lid of the chest, he beheld the vast quantity of silver money it contained, he threw all his pence away in disgust, and hastened to fill his pockets and his knapsack with the pure silver.

And he passed on into the third chamber. Now, indeed, that was terrifying! The dog in this chamber actually had a pair of eyes each as large as the round tower, and they kept rolling round and round in his head like wheels.

"Good-evening!" said the soldier, and he lifted his cap respectfully, for such a monster of a dog as this he had never in his life before seen or heard of. He stood still for a minute or two, looking at him; then thinking, the sooner it was done the better, he took hold of the immense creature, removed him from the chest to the floor, and raised the lid of the chest.

Oh, what a sight of gold was there! Enough to buy not only all Copenhagen, but all the cakes and sugar-plums, all the tin soldiers, whips, and rocking-horses in the world! Yes, he must be satisfied now.

Hastily the soldier threw out all the silver money he had stuffed into his pockets and knapsack, and took gold instead; not only his pockets and knapsack, but his soldier's cap and boots he crammed full of gold—bright gold! heavy gold! He could hardly walk for the weight he carried. He lifted the dog on the chest again, banged the door of the room behind him, and called out through the tree:

*She saw the dog
vanish into a large house.*

"Hallo, you old witch! pull me up again!"

"Have you got the tinder-box?" asked the witch.

"Upon my honour, I'd quite forgotten it!" shouted the soldier, and back he went to fetch it. The witch then drew him up through the tree, and now he again stood in the high-road, his pockets, boots, knapsack, and cap stuffed with gold pieces.

"Just tell me now, what are you going to do with the tinder-box?" inquired the soldier.

"That's no concern of yours," returned the witch. "You've got your money; give me my tinder-box this instant!"

"Well, take your choice," said the soldier. "Either tell me at once what you want with the tinder-box, or I draw my sword, and cut off your head."

"I won't tell you!" screamed the witch.

So the soldier drew his sword and cut off her head. There she lay, but he did not waste time in looking at what he had done. He made haste to knot all his money securely in the witch's blue apron, made a bundle of it, and slung it across his back, put the tinder-box into his pocket, and went straight to the nearest town.

It was a large, handsome town—a city, in fact. He walked into the first hotel in the place, called for the best rooms, and ordered the choicest and most expensive dishes for his supper, for he was now a rich man, with plenty of gold to spend.

The servant who cleaned his boots could not help thinking they were disgracefully shabby and worn to belong to such a grand gentleman; however, next day he provided himself with new boots and very gay clothes besides.

Our soldier was now a great man, and the people of the hotel were called in to give him information about all the places of amusement in the city, and about their King, and the beautiful Princess, his daughter.

" I should rather like to see her ! " observed the soldier ; " just tell me when I can."

" No one can see her at all," was the reply ; " she dwells in a great copper palace, with ever so many walls and towers round it. No one but the King may go and visit her there, because it has been foretold that she will marry a common soldier, and our King would not like that at all."

" Shouldn't I like to see her though, just for once," thought the soldier ; but it was of no use for him to wish it.

And now he lived such a merry life ! He went continually to the theatre, drove out in the Royal Gardens, and gave much money in alms to the poor —to all, in fact, who asked him.

And this was well done in him ; to be sure, he knew by past experience how miserable it was not to have a shilling in one's pocket.

He was always gaily dressed, and had such a crowd of friends, who, one and all, declared he was a most capital fellow, a real gentleman ; and that pleased our soldier uncommonly.

But, as he was now giving and spending every day, and never received anything in return, his money began to fail him, and at last he had only twopence left, and was forced to remove from the splendid apartments where he had lodged hitherto, and take refuge in a little bit of an attic-chamber, where he had to brush his boots and darn his clothes himself, and where none of his friends ever came to see him, because there were so many stairs to go up, it was quite fatiguing.

It was a very dark evening and he could not afford to buy himself so much as a rushlight. However, he remembered, all at once, that there were a few matches lying in the tinder-box that the old witch had made him fetch out of the hollow tree.

So he brought out this tinder-box and began to strike a light ; but no sooner had he rubbed the flint-stone and made the sparks fly out than the door burst suddenly open, and the dog with eyes as large as teacups, and which he had seen in the cavern beneath the tree, stood before him, and said, " What commands has my master for his slave ? "

" Upon my honour, this is a pretty joke ! " cried the soldier. " A fine sort of tinder-box this is, if it will really provide me with whatever I want. Fetch me some money this instant ! " said he to the dog ; upon which the creature vanished, and lo ! in half a minute he was back again, holding in his mouth a large bag full of pence.

So now the soldier understood the rare virtue of this charming tinder-box. If he struck the flint only once, the dog that sat on the chest full of copper came to him ; if he struck it twice, the dog that watched over the silver answered his summons ; and if he struck it three times, he was forthwith attended by the monstrous guardian of the golden treasure.

The soldier could now remove back to his princely apartments ; he bought himself an entirely new suit of clothes, and all his friends remembered him again, and loved him as much as ever.

But one evening the thought occurred to him, " How truly ridiculous it is that no one should be allowed to see this Princess ! They all say she is so very beautiful; what a shame it is that she should be mewed up in that great copper palace with the towers guarding it round! And I do want so to see her! Where's my tinder-box, by the by?" He struck the flint, and lo! before him stood the dog with eyes as large as teacups.

"It is rather late, I must own," began the soldier; "but I do want to see the Princess so much, only for one minute, you know!"

And the dog was out of the door, and, before the soldier had time to think of what he should say or do, he was back again with the Princess sitting asleep on his back. A real Princess was this, so beautiful, so enchantingly beautiful! The soldier could not help himself; he knelt down and kissed her hand.

The dog ran back to the palace with the Princess that very minute. However, next morning, while she was at breakfast with the King and Queen, the Princess said that she had had such a strange dream during the past night. She had dreamt that she was riding on a dog, an enormously large dog, and that a soldier had knelt down to her, and kissed her hand.

"A pretty sort of dream, indeed!" exclaimed the Queen.

And she insisted that one of the old ladies of the court should watch by the Princess's bedside on the following night, in case she would again be disturbed by dreams.

The soldier longed so exceedingly to see the fair Princess of the copper palace again; accordingly, next evening the dog was summoned to fetch her. So he did, and ran as fast as he could; however, not so fast but that the ancient dame watching at the Princess's couch found time to put on a pair of waterproof boots before running after them.

*"Stop, stop, little 'prentice!" cried the soldier.*

She saw the dog vanish into a large house; then, thinking to herself, "Now I know what to do," she took out a piece of chalk and made a great white cross on the door. She then went home and betook herself to rest, and the Princess was home almost as soon.

But on his way the dog chanced to observe the white cross on the door of the hotel where the soldier lived; so he immediately took another piece of chalk and set crosses on every door throughout the town. And this was wisely done on his part.

Early in the morning came out the King, the Queen, the old court dame, and all the officers of the royal household, every one of them curious to see where the Princess had been.

" Here it is ! " exclaimed the King, as soon as he saw the first street-door with a cross chalked on it.

" My dear, where are your eyes ? This is the house," cried the Queen, seeing the second door bear the cross.

" No, this is it surely—why, here's a cross, too ! " cried all of them together, on discovering that there were crosses on all the doors. It was evident that their search would be in vain, and they were obliged to give it up.

But the Queen was an exceedingly wise and prudent woman ; she was good for something besides sitting in a state carriage, and looking very grand and condescending. She now took her gold scissors, cut a large piece of silk stuff into strips, and sewed these strips together, to make a pretty, neat little bag. This bag she filled with the finest, whitest flour, and with her own hands tied it to the Princess's waist ; and when this was done, again took up her golden scissors and cut a little hole in the bag, just large enough to let the flour drop out gradually all the time the Princess was moving.

That evening the dog came again, took the Princess on his back, and ran away with her to the soldier. Oh, how the soldier loved her, and how he wished he were a prince, that he might have this beautiful Princess for his wife !

The dog never perceived how the flour went drip, drip, dripping all the way from the palace to the soldier's room, and from the soldier's room back to the palace. So next morning the King and Queen could easily discover where their daughter had been carried ; and they took the soldier and cast him into prison.

And now he sat in the prison. Oh ! how dark it was, and how wearisome, and the turnkey kept coming in to remind him that to-morrow he was to be hanged.

This piece of news was by no means agreeable ; and the tinder-box had been left in his lodgings at the hotel. When morning came, he could, through his narrow iron grating, watch the people all hurrying out of the town to see him hanged ; he could hear the drums beating, and presently, too, he saw the soldiers marching to the place of execution. What a crowd there was rushing by ! Among the rest was a shoemaker's apprentice in his leathern apron and slippers ; he bustled on with such speed that one of his slippers flew off and bounded against the iron staves of the soldier's prison window.

" Stop, stop, little 'prentice ! " cried the soldier ; " it's of no use for you to be in such a hurry, for none of the fun will begin till I come, but if you'll oblige me by running to my lodgings and fetching me my tinder-box, I'll give you twopence. But you must run for your life ! "

The shoemaker's boy liked the idea of earning twopence ; so away he raced after the tinder-box, returned, and gave it to the soldier, and then —ah, yes, now we shall hear what happened then.

Outside the city a gibbet had been erected ; round it were marshalled the soldiers with many hundred thousand people—men, women, and children ; the King and Queen were seated on magnificent thrones, exactly opposite the judges and the whole assembled council.

Already had the soldier mounted the topmost step of the ladder, already was the executioner on the point of fitting the rope round his neck when, turning to their Majesties, he began to entreat most earnestly that they would suffer a poor criminal's innocent fancy to be gratified before he underwent his punishment. He wished so much, he said, to smoke a pipe of tobacco, and as it was the last pleasure he could enjoy in this world, he hoped it would not be denied him.

The King could not refuse this harmless request, accordingly the soldier took out his tinder-box and struck the flint. Once he struck it, twice he struck it, three times he struck it, and lo ! all the three wizard dogs stood before him—the dog with eyes as large as teacups, the dog with eyes as large as mill-wheels, and the dog with eyes each as large as the round tower !

" Now help me, don't let me be hanged ! " cried the soldier. And forthwith the three terrible dogs fell upon the judges and councillors, tossing them high into the air, so high that on falling down to the ground again they were broken in pieces.

" We will not——" began the King, but the monster dog with eyes as large as the round tower did not wait to hear what his Majesty would not ; he seized both him and the Queen, and flung them up into the air after the councillors. And the soldiers were all desperately frightened, and the people shouted out with one voice, " Good soldier, you shall be our King, and the beautiful Princess shall be your wife, and our Queen ! "

So the soldier was conducted into the royal carriage, and all the three dogs bounded to and fro in front, little boys whistled upon their fingers, and the guards presented arms.

The Princess was forthwith sent for and made Queen, which she liked much better than living a prisoner in the copper palace. The bridal festivities lasted for eight whole days, and the three wizard dogs sat at the banquet-table, staring about them with their great eyes.

# THE CONSTANT TIN SOLDIER

*from " Andersen's Fairy Tales "*

HERE were once five-and-twenty tin soldiers, all brothers, for they had all been made out of one old tin spoon. They carried muskets in their arms, and held themselves very upright, and their uniforms were red and blue—very gay indeed.

The first word they heard in this world, when the lid was taken off the box in which they lay, was " Tin soldiers ! " It was a little boy who made this exclamation, clapping his hands at the same time. They had been given to him because it was his birthday, and he now set them out on the table.

The soldiers resembled each other to a hair—one only was rather different from the rest ; he had but one leg, for he had been made last, when there was not quite tin enough left. However, he stood as firmly upon his one leg as the others did upon their two ; and this identical tin soldier it is whose fortunes seem to us worthy of record.

On the table where the tin soldiers were set out were several other playthings, but the most charming of them all was a pretty pasteboard castle. Through its little windows one could look into the rooms. In front of the castle stood some tiny trees, clustering round a little mirror intended to represent a lake, and waxen swans swam in the lake and were reflected on its surface.

All this was very pretty, but prettiest of all was a little damsel standing in the open doorway of the castle ; she, too, was cut out of pasteboard, but she had on a frock of the clearest muslin, a little sky-blue ribbon was flung across her shoulders like a scarf, and in the midst of this scarf was set a bright gold wing. The little lady stretched out both her arms, for she was a dancer, and raised one of her legs so high in the air that the tin soldier could not find it, and fancied that she had, like him, only one leg.

" That would be just the wife for me," thought he, " but then, she is of rather too high rank ; she lives in a castle. I have only a box ; and besides, there are all our five-and-twenty men in it; it is no place for her.

"However, there will be no harm in my making acquaintance with her," and so he stationed himself behind a snuff-box that stood on the table; from this place he had a full view of the delicate little lady, who still remained standing on one leg, yet without losing her balance.

When evening came, all the other tin soldiers were put away into the box, and the people of the house went to bed. The playthings now began to play in their turn; they pretended to visit, to fight battles, and give balls. The tin soldiers rattled in the box, for they wanted to play too, but the lid would not come off. The nut-crackers cut capers, and the slate-pencil played at commerce on the slate; there was such a racket that the canary bird woke up, and began to talk too, but he always talked in verse.

The only two who did not move from their places were the tin soldier and the little dancer; she constantly remained in her graceful position, standing on the point of her foot, with outstretched arms; and, as for him, he stood just as firmly on his one leg, never for one moment turning his eyes away from her.

Twelve o'clock struck. Crash! Open sprang the lid of the snuff-box, but there was no snuff inside it; no, out jumped a little black conjurer, in fact it was a Jack-in-the-box. "Tin soldier!" said the conjurer, "wilt thou keep thine eyes to thyself?"

But the tin soldier pretended not to hear.

"Well, only wait till to-morrow!" quoth the conjurer.

When the morrow had come, and the children were out of bed, the tin soldier was placed on the window-ledge, and, whether the conjurer or the wind occasioned it, all at once the window flew open, and out fell the tin soldier, head foremost from the third story to the ground.

A dreadful fall was that! His one leg turned over and over in the air, and at last he rested, poised on his soldier's cap, with his bayonet between the paving stones.

The maid-servant and the little boy immediately came down to look for him; but, although they very nearly trod on him, they could not see him. If the tin soldier had but called out, "Here I am!" they might easily have found him; but he thought it would not be becoming for him to cry out, as he was in uniform.

It now began to rain; every drop fell heavier than the last; there was a regular shower. When it was over two boys came by. "Look!" said one, "here is a tin soldier; he shall have a sail for once in his life."

So they made a boat out of an old newspaper, put the tin soldier into it, and away he sailed down the gutter, both the boys running along by the side and clapping their hands. The paper boat rocked to and fro, and every now and then veered round so quickly that the tin soldier became quite giddy; still he moved not a muscle, looked straight before him, and held his bayonet tightly clasped.

All at once the boat sailed under a long gutter-board; he found it as dark here as at home in his own box.

"Where shall I get to next?" thought he. "Yes, to be sure, it is all that conjurer's doing! Ah, if the little maiden were but sailing with me in the boat I would not care for its being twice as dark!"

Just then a great water-rat that lived under the gutter board darted out. " Have you a passport ? " asked the rat. " Where is your passport ? "

But the tin soldier was silent, and held his weapon with a still firmer grasp. The boat sailed on, and the rat followed. Oh! how furiously he showed his teeth, and cried out to sticks and straws, " Stop him, stop him ! he has not paid the toll ; he has not shown his passport ! "

But the stream grew stronger and stronger. The tin soldier could already catch a glimpse of the bright daylight before the boat came from under the tunnel, but at the same time he heard a roaring noise, at which the boldest heart might well have trembled. Only fancy ! where the tunnel ended the water of the gutter fell perpendicularly into a great canal ; this was as dangerous for the tin soldier as sailing down a mighty waterfall would be for us.

He was now so close that he could no longer stand upright ; the boat darted forwards ; the poor tin soldier held himself as stiff and immovable as possible ; no one could accuse him of having even blinked. The boat spun round and round three, nay, four times, and was filled with water to the brim ; it must sink. The tin soldier stood up to his neck in water ; deeper and deeper sank the boat, softer and softer grew the paper. The water went over the soldier's head, and he thought of the pretty little dancer whom he should never see again, and these words rang in his ears :

" Wild adventure, mortal danger
Be thy portion, valiant stranger ! "

The paper now tore asunder, the tin soldier fell through the rent ; but, in the same moment, he was swallowed up by a large fish. Oh, how dark it was, worse even than under the gutter-board, and so narrow too ! But the tin soldier's resolution was as constant as ever ; there he lay, at full length, shouldering his arms.

The fish turned and twisted about, and made the strangest movements. At last he became quite still ; a flash of lightning, as it were, darted through him. The daylight shone brightly and some one exclaimed, " Tin soldier ! "

The fish had been caught, taken to the market, sold, and brought home into the kitchen, where the servant girl was cutting him up with a large knife.

She seized the tin soldier by the middle with two of her fingers, and took him into the parlour, where every one was eager to see the wonderful man who had travelled in the maw of a fish ; however, our little warrior was by no means proud. They set him on the table, and there—no, how could anything so extraordinary happen in this world ?—the tin soldier was in the very same room in which he had been before.

He saw the same children, the same playthings stood on the table, among them the beautiful castle with the pretty little dancing maiden, who was still standing upon one leg, while she held the other high in the air ; she, too, was constant. It quite affected the tin soldier ; he could have found it in his heart to weep tin tears, but such weakness would have been unbecoming in a soldier. He looked at her and she looked at him, but neither spoke a word.

And now one of the little boys took the soldier and threw him without ceremony into the stove. He did not give any reason for so doing, but no doubt the conjurer in the snuff-box must have had a hand in it.

The tin soldier now stood in a blaze of red light; he felt extremely hot. Whether this heat was the result of the actual fire or of the flames of love within him, he knew not. He had entirely lost his colour. Whether this change had happened during his travels, or were the effect of strong emotion, I know not. He looked upon the little damsel, she looked upon him, and he felt that he was melting; but, constant as ever, he still stood shouldering his arms.

A door opened, the wind seized the dancer, and, like a sylph, she flew straightway into the stove to the tin soldier; they both flamed up into a blaze, and were gone. The soldier was melted to a hard lump, and when the maid took out the ashes the next day she found his remains in the shape of a little tin heart; of the dancer there remained only the gold wing, and that was burned black as coal.

# The Littlest One

*by* MARION ST. JOHN WEBB

I'm sittin' on the doorstep,
    And I'm eating bread an' jam,
And I aren't a-cryin' really,
    Though I speks you think I am.

I'm feelin' rather lonely,
    And I don't know what to do,
'Cos there's no one here to play with,
    And I've broke my hoop in two.

I can hear the children playing,
    But they sez they don't want me
'Cos my legs are rather little,
    An' I run so slow, you see.

So I'm sittin' on the doorstep,
    And I'm eating bread an' jam,
And I aren't a-cryin' really,
    Though it feels as if I am.

# THE BRONZE PIG

*from " Andersen's Fairy Tales "*

IN the city of Florence is a little by-lane called Porta Rosa. There, in front of a vegetable market, stands a bronze pig, from whose mouth pure fresh water ever flows.

Old age has turned the colour of the pig to a greenish-black, but its snout shines as if it were polished daily—as, indeed, it is by the children and the beggars, who seize it with their hands and hold their mouths close to it, that they may drink its cool waters. It is a pretty picture to see the animal with a handsome, half-naked lad astride on its back, or with his ripe red lips close to the bronze snout.

The place is easily found. The first beggar a visitor meets on the streets of Florence will show him the way to the metal pig.

It was winter, and the mountains around were covered with snow. In the gardens of the Grand Duke's castle, under a roof of arching pines, where thousands of roses blossom all through the year, a little ragged boy had been sitting the whole day long. He was like Italy herself—fair, smiling, and yet suffering.

The boy was hungry and thirsty, but no one offered him either food or drink, and when night came and the gardens were closed, the gate-keeper drove him out. For a long while he stood idly dreaming on the bridge that crosses the Arno, and watching the stars that twinkled in the waters beneath as they flowed on towards the marble bridge.

He wandered on to the bronze pig, knelt down and wound his arms round its rough neck, put his lips to the polished snout, and took a long draught of the cool water. Beside it lay one or two chestnuts and a few lettuce leaves, and these were the child's supper.

The street for the time was his own—no one else was near—and he climbed up on the back of the pig, leaned his curly head on its neck, and before he felt his utter weariness, he was sound asleep.

At midnight the bronze pig moved, and spoke. "Hold fast, little boy," it said; "I am going to have a run."

Off went the pig at a goodly pace, and carried him first to a street where all seemed astir with life. The bronze horse, which carries the statue of the duke, neighed aloud as they passed; and the painted coat-of-arms on the court-house shone like living pictures; a strange life stirred on every side. The groups of marble figures started to sudden life, and a cry of pain burst from the lips of the women, and was borne far and wide across the square.

In the court before the palace, where the nobles keep high festival, the bronze pig stood still for a moment.

"Hold fast," it said, "hold fast. I am going upstairs now."

The boy, trembling, half in fear and half in joy, was borne through a long gallery. The walls were covered with costly paintings, statues stood all around, and the light was as clear as at noonday. A side-door opened, and there, in the wondrous light, stood a lovely marble woman; her fair limbs moved, dolphins gathered at her feet, and a bright light shone from her clear eyes. It was one of the most famous statues in the world.

Beside her stood groups of marble figures that seemed alive—handsome men, one of them sharpening his sword, and wrestlers in deadly strife. The sword was sharpened, and the battle fought for the goddess of beauty.

But none of the pictures dared to come out of their frames. The goddess of beauty, the swordsman, and the others remained in their places. All were spell-bound by the radiant glory that streamed down from the pictures of the Virgin and the saints.

In every room the child beheld beauty and splendour. The bronze pig carried him slowly through it all, and, in the ever-changing loveliness, one scene made the boy forget what went before.

But at last they came to a picture, which went straight to the boy's heart. It is the descent of Christ into Hades. Round the crucified Saviour throng groups of heathen, and the loveliest thing in all the picture is the happy look on the faces of the children. In full confidence of heaven, two of them clasp each other in love, and one little lad beckons to another, and points to himself as if to say, "We are going to heaven!" The older people stand in doubtful hope, or bow humbly before the Saviour.

The child gazed longest of all on this picture, and the bronze pig stood still before it. A low soft sigh was heard, and the boy, who did not know if it came from the animal or the canvas, stretched out his arms to the smiling children. But the pig ran hastily away with him through the open doorway

"Thanks to you, dear, kind pig!" said the boy, as they went down th staircase.

"Thanks to you also," answered the bronze pig. "We have been helpful to each other. It is only when I have an innocent child on my back that I have the power of running at all. Now, see! I may pass under the light of the lamp that hangs below the picture of the Virgin, but I may not enter the church. So long, however, as I carry you, I may look in from without. But do not get off, or at once I shall lie dead as you see me in the Porta Rosa."

"I will stay with you," said the boy, as they hurried on through the streets till they reached the square before a great church.

The doors opened wide, lights shone from the altar and streamed across the lonely square. From a tomb in the left aisle a wondrous light gleamed, and round it thousands of glancing stars glittered. It is the grave of Galileo— a simple monument, with a ladder of stone on a blue ground—a glowing ladder by which prophets are caught up, like Elijah, to the heavens.

In the right aisle, the statues and tombs seem full of life. Here stand the great painter, and the famous poet wearing his laurel crown, and all the great and good men who are the pride and the glory of Italy.

The folds of the marble drapery seemed to move, the figures raised their heads and gazed towards the altar, where, amid outbursts of music, white-robed boys swung their golden censers, from which a heavy fragrance was wafted out into the square.

The boy held out his hand towards the bright scene, and in a moment the pig hurried him away. The wind whistled past him, the church doors creaked as they swung close, and the boy felt chill as ice. For a little he seemed to know nothing, and then he opened his eyes.

It was broad daylight. He was still sitting on the back of the bronze pig, which stood where it always did, in the street of Porta Rosa.

Fear filled the heart of the child when he thought of her whom he called mother. Yesterday, she had sent him out to beg, and he had been given nothing. Again he threw his arms around the neck of the bronze pig, kissed it, and nodded good-bye to it.

Sick at heart, hungry, and thirsty, he wended his way along a lane, hardly broad enough to let a donkey with a pack-saddle pass along. An iron-bound door admitted him to a number of dirty staircases leading to the houses ranged round the courtyard. In the middle of the yard was a well, from which water was carried up to the houses in buckets hung on creaking chains.

As the poor boy went slowly upward, two Russian sailors, coming down in headlong haste, nearly overturned him.

"What have you brought?" demanded a black-haired handsome woman who followed them.

"Don't be angry," pleaded the boy; "they gave me nothing—nothing at all"; and he clutched his mother's dress as if to kiss it.

They entered the wretched room, and the woman took up the chafing-dish at whose charcoal embers Italians are used to warm themselves, and, pushing the boy aside with her elbow, said, "Come, you have brought some money."

The poor lad began to sob and cry, and the woman kicked him roughly.

"Be still!" she cried, swinging the dish, "or I will break your head."

"What are you doing to the boy?" said a neighbour, who had heard his cry of fear, and who came in with chafing-dish also in her hands.

"The child is mine," answered the woman; "I can murder him if I like, and you also."

She raised her chafing-dish, and at the same time her neighbour lifted hers in self-defence. The two clay dishes clashed together so violently that they were shivered to pieces, while the room was filled with a blinding shower of embers and dust.

The child ran out in the bustle that followed. He ran through the courtyard and out into the street until he could breathe freely. Before him stood the church whose doors had opened to him the night before; he entered, and kneeling at the first tomb he came to—it was that of the famous painter—he sobbed aloud.

Mass was being sung, and the people came and went. But no one seemed to notice the child; only one elderly man paused for a moment to look at him, and then passed on.

Sad and weary, and faint from hunger, the boy crept into a corner amongst the marble statues and fell asleep. It was growing dark when some one pulled his coat, and he started up to find the same old man standing before him.

"Are you ill?" asked the man. "Where do you live? Have you been here all day?"

When the boy answered his questions, the old man took him to his house, which was in a side-street nearby. They entered the workshop of a glove-maker, where a woman was busy sewing. A little poodle, whose hair was cut so close that you could see the pink skin beneath, was jumping about on the table, and sat up to greet the child.

"Innocent things soon find each other out," said the woman, fondling both child and dog.

The good people gave the boy food and drink, and told him he might stay overnight with them, and that next day the old glove-maker would see his mother. They gave him a little bed—poor, indeed, but rich and kingly to the child who had so often slept on cold, hard steps. He slept sweetly, and dreamed of the lovely pictures he had seen, and of the bronze pig.

Next morning the glove-maker went out; but the boy was not hopeful, for he feared he would just have to go back to his mother.

When the old man came back, he spoke for a long while with his wife, who nodded and smiled to the child, and stroked his head.

"He is a beautiful boy," she said; "he will make as famous an apprentice as you did. Look how delicate his fingers are! Madonna has surely meant him to be a glove-maker."

The boy stayed in the house, and the woman taught him to sew. He ate well, slept well, learned to play, and began to tease Bellissima, the little dog. Then the woman would scold him, and then he would take it to heart, and sit in sorrow in his lonely chamber.

This room looked out on the street, where skins were hung to dry, and the windows were iron-barred on the outside. The boy could not sleep at such times, and the bronze pig was always in his thoughts. Suddenly he heard the sound of "Pit-pat! pit-pat!" and he sprang to the window. It was certainly the bronze pig, but it had gone past.

"Help the gentleman to carry his colour-box," said Madame to the boy one morning.

The painter was their neighbour, who just then was passing with a huge roll of canvas under his arm. The boy took the colour-box and followed the painter. When they reached the gallery, they went up the stairs on which the bronze pig had carried him, and again he saw the groups of statues and the pictures that hung all round the walls.

They paused in front of the picture of Christ. The beautiful children smiled, as they had done before, in confident hope of heaven, and the boy now smiled back to them, for this was *his* heaven.

"You may go home now," said the painter, when the boy stood still, after the easel was set up.

"May I see you paint?" asked the boy. "May I look on while you put the picture on your white canvas?"

*" Oh, you wicked boy, why did you take her out?"*

"I am not going to paint yet," said the painter, taking up his crayon.

His hand moved quickly, his eye measured the picture before him and with a few bold strokes he made the figure of Christ stand out on the canvas.

"Now, go home with you!" cried the painter, and slowly and silently the boy went home, sat down at the table, and began to sew gloves.

All day long, however, his thoughts were of the picture gallery. He worked badly and pricked his fingers with the needle, but he did not tease Bellissima. As evening fell, he stole out.

The night was cold, but starlit and bright, and he wandered on through the deserted streets till he stood before the bronze pig. He kissed it, and mounted on its back.

"Oh, you dear pig," he said, "how I have longed for you! We must have a run together to-night."

The pig stood motionless, with the clear spring water flowing from its snout. Something pulled gently at the boy's dress, and, on looking down, he saw the little half-shorn Bellissima, barking as if to say, " Here am I too ! What are you sitting there for ? "

A fiery dragon would not have frightened the boy more than did Bellissima in that place and at that hour of the night.

Bellissima without her wraps ! What would become of him ? Her mistress never allowed her out in winter without being *dressed*, as she called it. She had to wear a little jacket of lambskin, cut out and made specially for her. It was trimmed with bows and hung with little bells, and was tied on with scarlet ribbon.

But here was Bellissima out of doors, at night, and not dressed. What would happen ? The thought put an end to all the boy's dreams and fancies. He kissed the bronze pig, took Bellissima, shivering with cold, under his arm, and ran towards the house as fast as he could.

" What are you running off with ? " cried two policemen, at whom Bellissima barked. " Where have you stolen that dog ? "

" Oh, give it back to me ! " cried the child, as they took the little dog from him.

" If you have not stolen it," they said, " you can tell them at home to send for it to the police-station."

As the policemen marched off with Bellissima, the poor lad did not know what to do—whether to jump into the Arno, or to go home and confess everything.

" They will certainly kill me," he thought ; " but I will gladly die, and then I shall go to the Madonna." So he went home chiefly that he might be killed.

The door was closed, and he could not reach up to the knocker ; but a stone lay near, and with that he rattled against the wood.

" Who is there ? " said a voice from within.

" It is I," said the boy. " Bellissima is gone—gone to the police-station ; let me in, and then kill me."

Madame, in terror, glanced at the wall, where the little lambskin jacket hung, as usual, in its place.

" Bellissima at the police-station ! " she cried. " Oh, you wicked boy, why did you take her out ? She will be frozen ! Think of the poor little thing among all those rough men ! "

The old man went out in search ; the woman mourned her loss ; and the boy sat down and cried. All the neighbours came in, and among them was the painter, who took the boy between his knees and drew from him the whole story of the bronze pig and the picture gallery. It was at the best a puzzling story, but the painter comforted the boy and tried to soothe the woman. But she would not be comforted till her husband came back with Bellissima from the police-station.

Then there was an outburst of joy all round. The painter petted the boy, and gave him a handful of sketches.

Such funny heads were there, and splendid drawings ! And among them was a sketch of the bronze pig. How delightful ! only a few strokes, and there was the pig—and the house behind it was there too !

Next day, at early dawn, the boy took up a lead-pencil and tried to make a copy of the bronze pig on the back of one of the drawings. When finished, it leaned perhaps too much to one side, looked rather too much up and down, and had one leg thin and one thick; but every one could see it was the bronze pig. The boy himself was overjoyed.

The next day another bronze pig was sketched on the back of another drawing, and it was a hundred times better. The third was so good that every one owned how well it was done.

Meanwhile the making of gloves fared badly, and the lad's messages in the city fared even worse. The bronze pig had taught the lad that all pictures can be set down on paper; and all Florence is a picture-book to any one who can only turn the leaves.

In one street there is a column on which stands Justice, with eyes bandaged and with a balance in her hand. She, too, was set down on paper by the little apprentice of the glove-maker. For long, his little collection contained only studies of still life; but one day Bellissima came playing round the boy.

"Stand still," he cried, "and then you shall come into my gallery."

Bellissima refused to stand still, and the boy was forced to tie her by the head and the tail. Then she struggled and pulled till the string was pulled quite tight.

"Oh, you wicked, wicked boy!" cried Madame, who was attracted by the barking; "my poor dog!"

She was unable to utter another word, but she drove him from the house as an unthankful rascal, and then went back to grieve over the half-strangled Bellissima.

At that very moment the painter was coming up the staircase, and—this is the turning-point of the whole story.

In 1834, there was an exhibition of paintings in the Academy of Art, where two pictures, hung side by side, made all visitors stop to look.

In the smaller picture a merry little lad was shown as drawing a closely-clipped white poodle, which evidently would not be still and was therefore tied up by its head and its tail. There was truth in the painting that spoke straight to every heart.

The painter, the people said, was a poor Florentine, who had been taken out of the streets when quite young by an old glove-maker. A well-known young painter had discovered the boy's talent, and took charge of him when he was driven out of the house because he had tied up his mistress's poodle by the head and the tail to make a drawing of her.

The picture showed—and the larger one beside it showed more clearly—that the apprentice glove-maker had become a great painter.

In the second picture, a beautiful, ragged boy sat sleeping in the empty street, his head resting on the bronze pig that stands near the Porta Rosa. All knew the spot. The boy's arms were thrown round the pig's neck, the boy was sound asleep, and the lamp in front of the Madonna cast a bright light upon his pale and lovely face.

It was a wonderful painting in a rich frame of gold. From each corner hung a laurel wreath; a black ribbon was twined among the green leaves, and the whole was draped with long heavy folds of crape.

The young artist was dead.

# THE WILD SWANS

from " Andersen's Fairy Tales "

FAR hence, in a country whither the swallows fly in our winter-time, there dwelt a King who had eleven sons, and one daughter, the beautiful Elise. The eleven brothers went to school with stars on their breasts, and swords by their sides ; they wrote on golden tablets with diamond pens, and could read either with a book, or without one ; in short, it was easy to perceive that they were princes. Their sister Elise used to sit upon a little glass stool, and had a picture-book which had cost the half of a kingdom. Oh, the children were so happy ! But happy they were not to remain always.

Their father, the King, married a very wicked Queen, who was not at all kind to the poor children ; they found this out on the first day after the marriage, when there was a grand gala at the palace ; for when the children played at receiving company, instead of giving them as many cakes and sweetmeats as they liked, the Queen gave them only some sand in a little dish, and told them to imagine that was something nice.

The week after, she sent the little Elise to be brought up by some peasants in the country, and it was not long before she told the King so many falsehoods about the poor Princes, that he would have nothing more to do with them.

" Away out into the world, and take care of yourselves," said the wicked Queen ; " fly away in the form of great speechless birds." But she could not make their transformation so disagreeable as she wished—the Princes were changed into eleven white swans. Sending forth a strange cry, they flew out of the palace windows, over the park and over the wood.

It was still early in the morning when they passed by the place where Elise lay sleeping in the peasant's cottage ; they flew several times round the roof, stretched their long necks, and flapped their wings, but no one either heard or saw them ; they were forced to fly away, up to the clouds, and into the wide world ; so on they went to the forest, which extended as far as the seashore.

The poor little Elise stood in the peasant's cottage amusing herself with a green leaf, for she had no other plaything. She pricked a hole in the leaf and peeped through it at the sun, and then she fancied she saw her brothers' bright eyes, and whenever the warm sunbeams shone full upon her cheeks, she thought of her brothers' kisses.

One day passed exactly like the other. When the wind blew through the thick hedge of rose-trees, in front of the house, she would whisper to the roses, " Who is more beautiful than you ? " but the roses would shake their heads and say, " Elise." And when the peasant's wife sat on Sundays at the door of her cottage reading her hymn-book, the wind would rustle in the leaves and say to the book, " Who is more pious than thou ? "—" Elise," replied the hymn-book. And what the roses and the hymn-book said, was no more than the truth.

Elise, who was now fifteen years old, was sent for to return home ; but when the Queen saw how beautiful she was, she hated her the more, and would willingly have transformed her like her brothers into a wild swan ; but she dared not do so, because the King wished to see his daughter.

So the next morning the Queen went into a bath which was made of marble, and fitted up with soft pillows and the gayest carpets ; she took three toads, kissed them, and said to one, " Settle thou upon Elise's head, that she may become dull and sleepy like thee." " Settle thou upon her forehead," said she to another, " and let her become ugly like thee, so that her father may not know her again."—And " Do thou place thyself upon her bosom," whispered she to the third, " that her heart may become corrupt and evil, a torment to herself."

She then put the toads into the clear water, which was immediately tinted with a green colour, and having called Elise, took off her clothes and made her get into the bath—one toad settled among her hair, another on her forehead, and the third upon her bosom ; but Elise seemed not at all aware of it. She rose up, and three poppies were seen swimming on the water.

Had not the animals been poisonous and kissed by a witch, they would have been changed into roses whilst they remained on Elise's head and heart —she was too good for magic to have any power over her. When the Queen perceived this, she rubbed walnut juice all over the maiden's skin, so that it became quite swarthy, smeared a nasty salve over her lovely face, and entangled her long thick hair. It was impossible to recognise the beautiful Elise after this.

When her father saw her, he was shocked, and said she could not be his daughter ; no one would have anything to do with her but the mastiff and the swallows ; but they, poor things, could not say anything in her favour.

Poor Elise wept, and thought of her eleven brothers, not one of whom she saw at the palace. In great distress she stole away and wandered the whole day over fields and moors, till she reached the forest. She knew not where to go, but she was so sad, and longed so much to see her brothers, who had been driven out into the world, that she determined to seek and find them.

She had not been long in the forest when night came on, and she lost her way amid the darkness. So she lay down on the soft moss, said her evening prayer, and leaned her head against the trunk of a tree. It was still in the forest, the air was mild, and from the grass and mould around gleamed the green light of many hundred glowworms; and when Elise lightly touched one of the branches hanging over her, bright insects fell down upon her like falling stars.

All the night long she dreamed of her brothers. They were all children again, played together, wrote with diamond pens upon golden tablets, and looked at the pictures in the beautiful book which had cost half of a kingdom.

But they did not, as formerly, make straight strokes and pot-hooks upon the tablets; no, they wrote of the bold actions they had performed, and the strange adventures they had encountered, and in the picture-book everything seemed alive. The birds sang, men and women stepped from the book and talked to Elise and her brothers. However, when she turned over the leaves, they jumped back into their places, so that the pictures did not get confused together.

When Elise awoke the sun was already high in the heavens. She could not see it certainly, for the tall trees of the forest entwined their thick-leaved branches closely together, and, as the sunbeams

*Three poppies were seen swimming on the water.*

played upon them, they looked like a golden veil waving to and fro. The air was fragrant, and the birds perched upon Elise's shoulders. She heard the noise of water; there were several springs forming a pool, with the prettiest pebbles at the bottom; bushes were growing thickly round. But the deer had trodden a broad path through them, and by this path Elise went down to the water's edge. The water was so clear that, had not the boughs and bushes around been moved by the wind, you might have fancied they were painted upon the smooth surface, so distinctly was each little leaf mirrored upon it.

As soon as Elise saw her face reflected in the water, she was quite startled, so brown and ugly did it look; however, when she wetted her little hand, and rubbed her brow and eyes, the white skin again appeared. So Elise took off her clothes, stepped into the fresh water, and in the whole world there was not a king's daughter more beautiful than she then appeared.

After she dressed herself, and braided her long hair, she went to the bubbling spring, drank out of the hollow of her hand, and then wandered farther into the forest. She did not know where she was going, but she thought of her brothers, and of the good God who, she felt, would never forsake her. He it was who made the wild crab-trees grow in order to feed the hungry, and who showed her a tree whose boughs bent under the weight of their fruit. She made her noonday meal under its shade, propped up the boughs, and then walked on amid the dark twilight of the forest.

It was so still that she could hear her own footsteps, and the rustling of each little withered leaf that was crushed beneath her feet. Not a bird was to be seen; not a single sunbeam penetrated through the thick foliage; and the tall stems of the trees stood so close together, that when she looked straight before her, she seemed encircled by trellis-work. Oh! there was a loneliness in this forest such as Elise had never known before.

And the night was so dark! Not a single glow-worm sent forth its light. Sad at heart she lay down to sleep, and then it seemed to her as if the boughs above her opened, and she saw an Angel looking down with gentle aspect, and a thousand little cherubs all around him. When she awoke in the morning she could not tell whether this was a dream, or whether she had really been so watched.

She walked on and met an old woman with a basket full of berries; the old woman gave her some of them, and Elise asked if she had seen eleven princes ride through the wood.

"No," said the old woman, "but I saw yesterday eleven swans with golden crowns on their heads swim down the brook near this place."

And she led Elise to a precipice, the base of which was washed by a brook; the trees on each side stretched their long leafy branches  vards each other, and where they could not unite, the roots had dise gaged themselves from the earth and hung over the water.

Elise bade the old woman farewell, and wandered by the side of the stream till she came to the place where it reached the open sea.

The beautiful sea lay stretched out before the maiden's eyes, but not a ship, not a boat was to be seen; how was she to go on? She observed the little stones on the shore, all of which the waves had washed into a round form; glass, iron, stone, everything that lay scattered there, had been moulded into shape, and yet the water which had done this was much softer than Elise's delicate little hand. "It rolls on unweariedly," said she, "and subdues what is so hard; I will be no less unwearied! Thank you for the lesson you have given me, ye bright rolling waves; some day, my heart tells me, you shall carry me to my dear brothers!"

There lay upon the wet sea-grass eleven white swan-feathers; Elise collected them together; drops of water hung about them, whether dew or tears she could not tell. She was quite alone on the seashore, but she did not care for that; the sea presented an eternal variety to her, more indeed in a few hours than the gentle inland waters would have offered in a whole year.

When a black cloud passed over the sky, it seemed as if the sea were saying, "I too can look dark;" and then the wind would blow and the waves fling out their white foam. But when the clouds shone with a bright red tint, and the winds were asleep, the sea also became like a rose-leaf in hue. It was now green, now white; but as it reposed peacefully, a slight breeze on the shore caused the water to heave gently like the bosom of a sleeping child.

At sunset Elise saw eleven wild swans with golden crowns on their heads flying towards the land; they flew one behind another, looking like a streaming white ribbon. Elise climbed the precipice, and concealed herself behind a bush; the swans settled close to her, and flapped their long white wings.

As the sun sank beneath the water, the swans also vanished, and in their place stood eleven handsome princes, the brothers of Elise. She uttered a loud cry, for although they were very much altered, Elise knew them to be her brothers. She ran into their arms, called them by their names—and how happy were *they* to see and recognise their sister, who was now grown so tall and so beautiful! They laughed and wept, and soon told each other how wickedly their step-mother had treated them.

"We," said the eldest of the brothers, "fly or swim as long as the sun is above the horizon, but, when it sinks below, we appear again in our human form. We are therefore obliged to look out for a safe resting-place, for, if at sunset we were flying among the clouds, we should fall down as soon as we resumed our own form. We do not dwell here. A land quite as beautiful as this lies on the opposite side of the sea, but it is far off. To reach it, we have to cross the deep waters, and there is no island midway on which we may rest at night; one little solitary rock rises from the waves, and upon it we find only just room enough to stand side by side.

"There we spend the night in our human form, and when the sea is rough, we are sprinkled by its foam; but we are thankful for this resting-place, for without it we should never be able to visit our dear native country. Only once in the year is this visit to the home of our fathers permitted. We require two of the longest days for our flight, and can remain here only eleven days, during which time we fly over the large forest whence we can see the palace in which we were born, where our father dwells, and the tower of the church in which our mother was buried.

"Here even the trees and bushes seem of kin to us; here the wild horses still race over the plains, as in the days of our childhood; here the charcoal burner still sings the same old tunes to which we used to dance in our youth; here we are still drawn, and here we have found thee, thou dear little sister! We have yet two days longer to stay here; then we must fly over the sea to a land beautiful indeed, but not our fatherland. How shall we take thee with us? We have neither ship nor boat!"

"How shall I be able to release you?" said the sister. And so they went on talking almost the whole of the night. They slumbered only a few hours.

Elise was awakened by the rustling of swans' wings which were fluttering above her. Her brothers were again transformed, and for some time flew around in large circles. At last they flew far, far away; one of them remained behind; it was the youngest, and he laid his head in her lap and she stroked his white wings. They remained the whole day together. Towards evening the others came back, and when the sun set, they stood again on the firm ground in their natural form.

"To-morrow we shall fly away, and may not return for a year, but we cannot leave thee; hast thou courage to accompany us? My arm is strong enough to bear thee through the forest; shall we not have strength enough in our wings to carry thee over the sea?"

"Yes, take me with you," said Elise. They spent the whole night in weaving a mat of the pliant willow bark and the tough rushes, and their mat was thick and strong. Elise lay down upon it, and when the sun rose, and the brothers were again transformed into wild swans, they seized the mat with their beaks and flew up high among the clouds with their dear sister, who was still sleeping. The sunbeams shone full upon her face; so one of the swans flew over her head, and shaded her with his broad wings.

They were already far from land when Elise woke; she thought she was still dreaming, so strange did it appear to her to be travelling through the air, and over the sea. By her side lay a cluster of pretty berries, and a handful of delicious roots. Her youngest brother had laid them there; and she thanked him with a smile, for she knew him as the swan who flew over her head and shaded her with his wings.

They flew so high that the first ship they saw beneath them seemed like a white seagull hovering over the water. Elise saw behind her a large cloud, which looked like a mountain, and on it she saw the shadows of herself and the eleven swans. It formed a picture more splendid than any she had ever yet seen. Soon, however, the sun rose higher, the cloud remained far behind, and then the floating shadowy picture disappeared.

*She stroked his white wings.*

The whole day they continued to fly with a whizzing noise, somewhat like an arrow; but yet they went slower than usual—they had their sister to carry. A heavy tempest gathered as the evening approached; Elise anxiously watched the sun. It was setting; still the solitary rock could not be seen; it appeared to her that the swans plied their wings with increasing vigour.

Alas! it would be her fault if her brothers did not arrive at the place in time! they would become human beings when the sun set, and if this happened before they reached the rocks, they must fall into the sea and be drowned. She prayed to God most fervently; still no rock was to be seen; the black clouds drew nearer, violent gusts of wind announced the approach of a tempest, the clouds rested upon a huge wave which rolled quickly forwards, and one flash of lightning rapidly succeeded another.

The sun was now on the rim of the sea. Elise's heart beat violently; the swans shot downwards so swiftly that she thought she must fall. But again they began to hover; the sun was half sunk beneath the water, and at that moment she saw the little rock below her; it looked like a seal's head when he raises it just above the water. And the sun was sinking fast—it seemed scarcely larger than a star—her foot touched the hard ground, and the sun vanished like the last spark on a burnt piece of paper.

Arm in arm stood her brothers around her; there was only just room for her and them—the sea beat tempestuously against the rock, flinging over them a shower of foam. The sky seemed in a blaze, with the fast succeeding flashes of fire that lightened it, and peal after peal rolled on the thunder, but sister and brothers kept firm hold of each other's hands. They sang a psalm, and their psalm gave them comfort and courage.

By daybreak the air was pure and still, and, as soon as the sun rose, the swans flew away with Elise from the rock. The waves rose higher and higher, and when they looked from the clouds down upon the blackish-green sea, covered with white foam, they might have fancied that millions of swans were swimming on its surface.

As day advanced, Elise saw floating in the air before her a land of mountains with glaciers, and in the centre, a palace a mile in length, with splendid colonnades, surrounded by palm-trees and gorgeous-looking flowers as large as mill-wheels. She asked if this was the country to which they were flying, but the swans shook their heads, for what she saw was the beautiful airy castle of the fairy Morgana, where no human being was admitted. Whilst Elise still bent her eyes upon it, mountains, trees, and castle all disappeared, and in their place stood twelve churches with high towers and pointed windows —she fancied she heard the organ play, but it was only the murmur of the sea. She was now close to these churches, but behold! they changed into a large fleet sailing under them; she looked down and saw it was only a sea-mist passing rapidly over the water. An endless variety floated before her eyes, till at last the land to which she was going appeared in sight. Beautiful blue mountains, cedar woods, towns, and castles rose to view. Long before sunset Elise sat down among the mountains, in front of a large cavern; delicate young creepers grew thickly around, so that it appeared covered with gay embroidered carpets.

"Now we shall see what thou wilt dream of to-night!" said her youngest brother, as he showed her the sleeping chamber destined for her.

"Oh, that I could dream how you might be freed from the spell!" said she; and this thought filled her mind. She prayed for God's help, nay, even in her dreams she continued praying, and it appeared to her that she was flying up high in the air towards the castle of the fairy Morgana. The fairy came forward to meet her, radiant and beautiful, and yet she fancied she resembled the old woman who had given her berries in the forest, and told her of the swans with golden crowns.

"Thou *canst* free thy brothers," said she; "but hast thou courage and patience enough? The water is indeed softer than thy delicate hands, and yet can mould the hard stones to its will, but then it cannot feel the pain which thy tender fingers will feel ; it has no heart and cannot suffer the anxiety and grief which thou must suffer. Dost thou see these stinging-nettles which I have in my hand ? There are many of the same kind growing round the cave where thou art sleeping ; only those that grow there or on the graves in the churchyard are of use, remember that !

" Thou must pluck them although they will sting thy hand, thou must trample on the nettles with thy feet, and get yarn from them, and with this yarn thou must weave eleven shirts with long sleeves ; throw them over the eleven wild swans and the spell is broken. But mark this : from the moment that thou beginnest thy work till it is completed, even should it take thee years, thou must not speak a word ; the first syllable that escapes thy lips will fall like a dagger into the hearts of thy brothers ; on thy tongue depends their life. Mark well all this ! "

And at the same moment the fairy touched Elise's hands with a nettle, which made them burn like fire, and Elise awoke. It was broad daylight, and close to her lay a nettle like the one she had seen in her dream. She fell upon her knees, thanked God, and then went out of the cave in order to begin her work. She plucked with her own delicate hands the stinging-nettles ; they burned large blisters on her hands and arms, but she bore the pain willingly in the hope of releasing her dear brothers. She trampled on the nettles with her naked feet, and spun the green yarn.

At sunset came her brothers. Elise's silence quite frightened them ; they thought it must be the effect of some fresh spell of their wicked step-mother. But when they saw her blistered hands, they found out what their sister was doing for their sakes. The youngest brother wept, and, when his tears fell upon her hands, Elise felt no more pain, and the blisters disappeared.

The whole night she spent in her work, for she could not rest till she had released her brothers. All the following day she sat in her solitude, for the swans had flown away ; but never had time passed so quickly. One shirt was ready ; she now began the second.

Suddenly a hunting horn resounded among the mountains. Elise was frightened. The noise came nearer, she heard the hounds barking ; in great terror she fled into the cave, bound up the nettles which she had gathered and combed into a bundle, and sat down upon it.

In the same moment a large dog sprang out from the bushes. Two others immediately followed, they barked loudly, ran away, and then returned. It was not long before the hunters stood in front of the cave ; the handsomest among them was the King of that country ; he stepped up to Elise. Never had he seen a lovelier maiden.

" How camest thou here, thou beautiful child ? " said he.

Elise shook her head ; she dared not speak, for a word might have cost her the life of her brothers, and she hid her hands under her apron lest the King should see how she was suffering.

" Come with me," said he, " thou must not stay here ! If thou art good as thou art beautiful, I will dress thee in velvet and silk, I will put a gold crown upon thy head, and thou shalt dwell in my palace ! " So he lifted her upon his horse, while she wept and wrung her hands ; but the King said, " I only desire thy happiness ! thou shalt thank me for this some day ! " and away he

THE TINDER BOX

He opened the first door. Bravo! There sat the dog with eyes as
large as tea-cups, staring at him in utter amazement. (Page 40)

THE WILD SWANS

They all crowded about her, and were on the point of
snatching away the shirts, when eleven white swans came flying
towards the cart. (Page 68)

rode over mountains and valleys, holding her on his horse in front, whilst the other hunters followed.

When the sun set, the King's magnificent capital with its churches and domes lay before them, and the King led Elise into the palace, where, in a marble hall, fountains were playing, and the walls and ceilings displayed the most beautiful paintings. But Elise cared not for all this splendour; she wept and mourned in silence, even whilst some female attendants dressed her in royal robes, wove costly pearls in her hair, and drew soft gloves over her blistered hands.

And now she was full dressed, and, as she stood in her splendid attire, her beauty was so dazzling that the courtiers all bowed low before her; and the King chose her for his bride, although the Archbishop shook his head, and whispered that the "beautiful lady of the wood must certainly be a witch, who had blinded their eyes, and infatuated the King's heart."

But the King did not listen; he ordered that music should be played. A sumptuous banquet was served up, and the loveliest maidens danced round the bride; she was led through fragrant gardens into magnificent halls, but not a smile was seen to play upon her lips, or beam from her eyes. The King then opened a small room next her sleeping apartment; it was adorned with costly green tapestry, and exactly resembled the cave in which she had been found; upon the ground lay the bundle of yarn which she had spun from the nettles, and by the wall hung the shirt she had completed. One of the hunters had brought all this, thinking there must be something wonderful in it.

"Here thou mayst dream of thy former home," said the King; "here is the work which employed thee; amidst all thy present splendour it may sometimes give thee pleasure to fancy thyself there again."

When Elise saw what was so dear to her heart, she smiled, and the blood returned to her cheeks; she thought her brothers might still be freed, and she kissed the King's hand. He pressed her to his heart, and ordered the bells of all the churches in the city to be rung, to announce the celebration of their wedding. The beautiful dumb maiden of the wood was to become Queen of the land.

The Archbishop whispered evil words in the King's ear, but they made no impression upon him; the marriage was solemnised, and the Archbishop himself was obliged to put the crown upon her head. In his rage he pressed the narrow rim so firmly on her forehead that it hurt her; but a heavier weight—sorrow for her brothers—lay upon her heart, and she did not feel bodily pain. She was still silent, a single word would have killed her brothers; her eyes, however, beamed with heartfelt love to the King, so good and handsome, who had done so much to make her happy.

She became more warmly attached to him every day. Oh! how much she wished she might confide to him all her sorrows. But she was forced to remain silent; she could not speak until her work was completed. To this end she stole away every night, and went into the little room that was fitted up in imitation of the cave; there she worked at her shirts, but by the time she had begun the seventh, all her yarn was spent.

She knew that the nettles she needed grew in the churchyard, but she must gather them herself; how was she to get them?

" Oh, what is the pain in my fingers compared to the anguish my heart suffers ! " thought she. " I must venture to the churchyard ; the good God will protect me ! "

Fearful, as though she were about to do something wrong, one moonlight night she crept down to the garden, and through the long avenues into the lonely road leading to the churchyard. She saw sitting on one of the broadest tombstones a number of ugly old witches. They took off their ragged clothes as if they were going to bathe, and digging with their long lean fingers into the fresh grass, drew up the dead bodies and devoured the flesh.

Elise was obliged to pass close by them, and the witches fixed their wicked eyes upon her ; but she repeated her prayer, gathered the stinging-nettles, and took them back with her into the palace. One person only had seen her ; it was the Archbishop, who was awake when others slept. Now he was convinced that all was not right about the Queen : she must be a witch, who had, through her enchantments, infatuated the King and all the people.

In the Confessional he told the King what he had seen, and what he feared ; and, when the words came from his lips, the images of the saints shook their heads as though they would say, " It is untrue ; Elise is innocent ! " But the Archbishop explained the omen otherwise ; he thought it was a testimony against her that the holy images shook their heads at hearing of her sin.

Two large tears rolled down the King's cheeks ; he returned home in doubt ; he pretended to sleep at night, though sleep never visited him ; and he noticed that Elise rose from her bed every night, and every time he followed her secretly and saw her enter her little room.

His countenance became darker every day ; Elise perceived it, though she knew not the cause. She was much pained, and besides, what did she not suffer in her heart for her brothers ! Her bitter tears ran down on the royal velvet and purple ; they looked like bright diamonds, and all who saw the magnificence that surrounded her, wished themselves in her place.

She had now nearly finished her work, only one shirt was wanting ; unfortunately, yarn was wanting also ; she had not a single nettle left. Once more, only this one time, she must go to the churchyard and gather a few handfuls. She shuddered when she thought of the solitary walk and of the horrid witches, but her resolution was as firm as her trust in God.

Elise went, the King and Archbishop followed her ; they saw her disappear at the churchyard door, and, when they came nearer, they saw the witches sitting on the tombstones as Elise had seen them, and the King turned away, for he believed her whose head had rested on his bosom that very evening to be amongst them. " Let the people judge her ! " said he. And the people condemned her to be burned.

She was now dragged from the King's apartments into a dark damp prison, where the wind whistled through the grated window. Instead of velvet and silk, they gave her the bundle of nettles she had gathered ; on that she must lay her head, and the shirts she had woven must serve her as mattress and counterpane. But they could not have given her anything she valued so much ; and she continued her work, at the same time praying

*This night she must finish her work.*

earnestly to her God.  The boys sang scandalous songs .about her in front of her prison ; not a soul comforted her with one word of love.

Towards evening she heard the rustling of swans' wings at the grating. It was the youngest of her brothers who had at last found his sister, and she sobbed aloud for joy, although she knew that the coming night would probably be the last of her life ; but then her work was almost finished, and her brother was near.

The Archbishop came in order to spend the last hour with her ; he had promised the King he would ; but she shook her head, and entreated him with her eyes and gestures to go.  This night she must finish her work, or all she had suffered—her pain, her anxiety, her sleepless nights—would be in vain.  The Archbishop went away with many angry words, but the unfortunate Elise knew herself to be innocent, and went on with her work.

Little mice ran busily about and dragged the nettles to her feet wishing to help her ; and the thrush perched on the iron bars of the window, and sang all night as merrily as he could, that Elise might not lose courage.

It was still twilight, just one hour before sunrise, when the eleven brothers stood before the palace gates, requesting an audience with the King.  But it could not be, they were told ; it was still night, the King was asleep, and they dared not wake him.  They entreated, they threatened ; the guard came up, and the King himself at last stepped out to ask what was the matter.  At that moment the sun rose, the brothers could be seen no longer, and eleven white swans flew away over the palace.

The people poured forth from the gates of the city ; they wished to see the witch burned.  One wretched horse drew the cart in which Elise was placed, a coarse frock of sackcloth had been put on her, her beautiful long hair hung loosely over her shoulders, her cheeks were of a deadly paleness, her lips moved gently, and her fingers wove the green yarn. Even on her way to her cruel death she did not give up her work; the ten shirts lay at her feet, and she was now labouring to complete the eleventh. The rabble insulted her.

"Look at the witch, how she mutters! She has not a hymn-book in her hand; no, there she sits with her accursed hocus-pocus. Tear it from her; tear it into a thousand pieces!"

And they all crowded about her, and were on the point of snatching away the shirts, when eleven white swans came flying towards the cart; they settled all round her, and flapped their wings. The crowd gave way in terror.

"It is a sign from Heaven! She is certainly innocent!" whispered some; they dared not say so aloud.

The Sheriff now seized her by the hand; in a moment she threw the eleven shirts over the swans, and eleven handsome princes appeared in their place. The youngest had, however, only one arm, and a wing instead of the other, for one sleeve was deficient in his shirt—it had not been quite finished.

"Now I may speak," said she: "I am innocent!"

And the people who had seen what had happened bowed before her as before a saint. She, however, sank lifeless in her brothers' arms; suspense, fear, and grief had quite exhausted her.

"Yes, she is innocent," said her eldest brother, and he now related their wonderful history. Whilst he spoke a fragrance as delicious as though it came from millions of roses diffused itself around, for every piece of wood in the funeral pile had taken root and sent forth branches. A hedge of blooming red roses surrounded Elise, and above all the others blossomed a flower of dazzling white colour, bright as a star. The King plucked it and laid it on Elise's bosom, whereupon she awoke from her trance with peace and joy in her heart.

And all the church-bells began to ring of their own accord; and birds flew to the spot in swarms; and there was a festive procession back to the palace, such as no king has ever seen equalled.

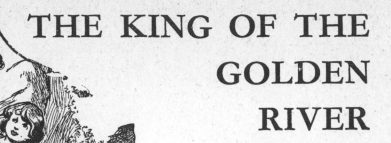

# THE KING OF THE GOLDEN RIVER

*by*

JOHN RUSKIN

### CHAPTER I

HOW THE AGRICULTURAL SYSTEM OF THE
BLACK BROTHERS WAS INTERFERED WITH BY
SOUTH-WEST WIND, ESQUIRE

IN a secluded and mountainous part of Stiria there was, in old time, a valley of the most surprising and luxuriant fertility. It was surrounded on all sides by steep and rocky mountains, rising into peaks, which were always covered with snow, and from which a number of torrents descended in constant cataracts. One of these fell westward, over the face of a crag so high that, when the sun had set to everything else, and all below was darkness, his beams still shone full upon this waterfall, so that it looked like a shower of gold. It was, therefore, called by the people of the neighbourhood, the Golden River.

It was strange that none of these streams fell into the valley itself. They all descended on the other side of the mountains, and wound away through broad plains and by populous cities. But the clouds were drawn so constantly to the snowy hills, and rested so softly in the circular hollow, that in time of drought and heat, when all the country round was burned up, there was still rain in the little valley ; and its crops were so heavy, and its hay so high, and its apples so red, and its grapes so blue, and its wine so rich, and its honey so sweet, that it was a marvel to every one who beheld it, and was commonly called the Treasure Valley.

The whole of this little valley belonged to three brothers, called Schwartz, Hans, and Gluck. Schwartz and Hans, the two elder brothers, were very ugly men, with overhanging eye-brows and small dull eyes, which were always half shut, so that you couldn't see into *them*, and always fancied they saw very far into *you*.

They lived by farming the Treasure Valley, and very good farmers they were. They killed everything that did not pay for its eating. They shot the blackbirds, because they pecked the fruit ; and killed the hedgehogs, lest they should suck the cows. They poisoned the crickets for eating the crumbs in the kitchen ; and smothered the cicadas, which used to sing all summer in the lime trees. They worked their servants without any wages,

till they would not work any more, and then quar-
relled with them, and turned them out of doors
without paying them.

It would have been very odd if, with such a farm
and such a system of farming, they hadn't got very
rich; and very rich they *did* get. They generally
contrived to keep their corn by them till it was very
dear, and then sell it for twice its value. They had
heaps of gold lying about on their floors, yet it was
never known that they had given so much as
a penny or a crust in charity. They never
went to mass; they grumbled perpetually at
paying tithes; and were, in a
word, of so cruel and grinding
a temper, as to receive from
all those with whom they had
any dealings, the nick-name of
the " Black Brothers."

The youngest brother,
Gluck, was as completely
opposed, in both appearance
and character, to his seniors
as could possibly be imagined
or desired. He was not above
twelve years old, fair, blue-
eyed, and kind in temper to
every living thing. He did
not, of course, agree particularly well with his brothers,

*He used sometimes to clean plates.*

or rather, they did not agree with *him*. He was usually appointed to the
honourable office of turnspit, when there was anything to roast, which was
not often; for, to do the brothers justice, they were hardly less sparing
upon themselves than upon other people. At other times he used to
clean the shoes, floors, and sometimes the plates, occasionally getting what
was left on them, by way of encouragement, and a wholesome quantity of
dry blows, by way of education.

Things went on in this manner for a long time. At last came a very
wet summer, and everything went wrong in the country around. The hay
had hardly been got in, when the haystacks were floated bodily down to
the sea by an inundation; the vines were cut to pieces with the hail; the
corn was all killed by a black blight.

Only in the Treasure Valley, as usual, was all safe. As it had rain when
there was rain nowhere else, so it had sun when there was sun nowhere else.
Everybody came to buy corn at the farm, and went away pouring male-
dictions on the Black Brothers. They asked what they liked, and got it,
except from the poor people, who could only beg, and several of whom were
starved at their very door, without the slightest regard or notice.

It was drawing towards winter, and very cold weather, when one day the
two elder brothers had gone out, with their usual warning to little Gluck,

who was left to mind the roast, that he was to let nobody in, and give nothing out. Gluck sat down quite close to the fire, for it was raining very hard, and the kitchen walls were by no means dry or comfortable looking. He turned and turned, and the roast got nice and brown.

"What a pity," thought Gluck, "my brothers never ask anybody to dinner. I'm sure, when they've got such a nice piece of mutton as this, and nobody else has got so much as a piece of dry bread, it would do their hearts good to have somebody to eat it with them."

Just as he spoke, there came a double knock at the house door, yet heavy and dull, as though the knocker had been tied up—more like a puff than a knock.

"It must be the wind," said Gluck; "nobody else would venture to knock double knocks at our door."

No; it wasn't the wind: there it came again very hard, and what was particularly astounding, the knocker seemed to be in a hurry, and not to be in the least afraid of the consequences. Gluck went to the window, opened it, and put his head out to see who it was.

It was the most extraordinary looking little gentleman he had ever seen in his life. He had a very long nose, slightly brass-coloured, and expanding towards its termination into a development not unlike the lower extremity of a key-bugle; his cheeks were very round, and very red, and might have warranted a supposition that he had been blowing a refractory fire for the last eight-and-forty hours; his eyes twinkled merrily through long silky eyelashes; his moustaches curled twice round like a corkscrew on each side of his mouth; and his hair, of a curious mixed pepper-and-salt colour, descended far over his shoulders. He was about four feet six in height, and wore a conical pointed cap of nearly the same altitude, decorated with a black feather some three feet long. His doublet was prolonged behind into something resembling a violent exaggeration of what is now termed a "swallow tail," but was much obscured by the swelling folds of an enormous black, glossy looking cloak, which must have been very much too long in calm weather, as the wind, whistling round the old house, carried it clear out from the wearer's shoulders to about four times

*"Hollo!" said the little gentleman.*

his own length. Gluck was so perfectly paralysed by the singular appearance of his visitor, that he remained fixed without uttering a word, until the old gentleman, having performed another, and a more energetic concerto on the knocker, turned round to look after his fly-away cloak.   In so doing he caught sight of Gluck's little yellow head jammed in the window, with its mouth and eyes very wide open indeed.

" Hollo ! " said the little gentleman, " that's not the way to answer the door :  I'm wet, let me in."

To do the little gentleman justice, he *was* wet.  His feather hung down between his legs like a beaten puppy's tail, dripping like an umbrella ; and from the ends of his moustaches the water was running into his waistcoat pockets, and out again like a mill stream.

" I beg pardon, sir," said Gluck,  " I'm very sorry, but I really can't."

" Can't what ! " said the old gentleman.

" I can't let you in, sir—I can't, indeed ;  my brothers would beat me to death, sir, if I thought of such a thing.  What do you want, sir ? "

" Want ? " said the old gentleman petulantly.  " I want fire and shelter ; and there's your great fire there blazing, crackling, and dancing on the walls, with nobody to feel it.  Let me in, I say ;  I only want to warm myself."

Gluck had had his head, by this time, so long out of the window, that he began to feel it was really unpleasantly cold, and when he turned, and saw the beautiful fire rustling and roaring, and throwing long bright tongues up the chimney, as if it were licking its chops at the savoury smell of the leg of mutton, his heart melted within him that it should be burning away for nothing.

" He does look *very* wet," said little Gluck ;  " I'll just let him in for a quarter of an hour."

Round he went to the door, and opened it ;  and as the little gentleman walked in, there came a gust of wind through the house, that made the old chimneys totter.

" That's a good boy," said the little gentleman.  " Never mind your brothers.  I'll talk to them."

" Pray, sir, don't do any such thing," said Gluck.  " I can't let you stay till they come ;  they'd be the death of me."

" Dear me," said the old gentleman, " I'm very sorry to hear that.  How long may I stay ? "

" Only till the mutton's done, sir," replied Gluck, " and it's very brown."

Then the old gentleman walked into the kitchen, and sat himself down on the hob, with the top of his cap accommodated up the chimney, for it was a great deal too high for the roof.

" You'll soon dry there, sir," said Gluck, and sat down again to turn the mutton.  But the old gentleman did *not* dry there, but went on drip, drip, dripping, among the cinders, and the fire fizzed, and sputtered, and began to look very black and uncomfortable :  never was such a cloak ;  every fold in it ran like a gutter.

" I beg pardon, sir," said Gluck at length, after watching the water spreading in long, quicksilver-like streams over the floor for a quarter of an hour ;  " mayn't I take your cloak ? "

" No, thank you," said the old gentleman.

"Your cap, sir?"

"I am all right, thank you," said the old gentleman rather gruffly.

"But—sir—I'm very sorry," said Gluck, hesitatingly; "but—really, sir—you're—putting the fire out."

"It'll take longer to do the mutton, then," replied his visitor drily.

Gluck was very much puzzled by the behaviour of his guest; it was such a strange mixture of coolness and humility. He turned away at the string meditatively for another five minutes.

"That mutton looks very nice," said the old gentleman at length. "Can't you give me a little bit?"

"Impossible, sir," said Gluck.

"I'm very hungry," continued the old gentleman: "I've had nothing to eat yesterday, nor to-day. They surely couldn't miss a bit from the knuckle!"

He spoke in so very melancholy a tone, that it quite melted Gluck's heart.

"They promised me one slice to-day, sir," said he; "I can give you that, but not a bit more."

"That's a good boy," said the old gentleman again.

Then Gluck warmed a plate, and sharpened a knife.

"I don't care if I do get beaten for it," thought he.

Just as he had cut a large slice out of the mutton, there came a tremendous rap at the door. The old gentleman jumped off the hob, as if it had suddenly become inconveniently warm. Gluck fitted the slice into the mutton again, with desperate efforts at exactitude, and ran to open the door.

"What did you keep us waiting in the rain for?" said Schwartz, as he walked in, throwing his umbrella in Gluck's face.

"Ay! what for, indeed, you little vagabond?" said Hans, administering an educational box on the ear, as he followed his brother into the kitchen.

"Bless my soul!" said Schwartz when he opened the door.

"Amen," said the little gentleman, who had taken his cap off, and was standing in the middle of the kitchen, bowing with the utmost possible velocity.

"Who's that!" said Schwartz, catching up a rolling-pin, and turning to Gluck with a fierce frown.

"I don't know, indeed, brother," said Gluck in great terror.

"How did he get in?" roared Schwartz.

"My dear brother," said Gluck, deprecatingly, "he was so *very* wet!"

The rolling-pin was descending on Gluck's head; but, at the instant, the old gentleman interposed his conical cap, on which it crashed with a shock that shook the water out of it all over the room. What was very odd, the rolling-pin no sooner touched the cap, than it flew out of Schwartz's hand, spinning like a straw in a high wind, and fell into the corner at the farther end of the room.

"Who are you, sir?" demanded Schwartz, turning upon him.

"What's your business?" snarled Hans.

"I'm a poor old man, sir," the little gentleman began very modestly, "and I saw your fire through the window, and begged shelter for a quarter of an hour."

" Have the goodness to walk out again, then," said Schwartz. " We've quite enough water in our kitchen, without making it a drying house."

" It is a cold day to turn an old man out in, sir ; look at my gray hairs."

They hung down to his shoulders, as I told you before.

" Ay ! " said Hans, " there are enough of them to keep you warm. Walk ! "

" I'm very, very hungry, sir ; couldn't you spare me a bit of bread before I go ? "

" Bread indeed ! " said Schwartz ; " do you suppose we've nothing to do with our bread, but to give it to such red-nosed fellows as you ? "

" Why don't you sell your feather ? " said Hans, sneeringly. " Out with you."

" A little bit," said the old gentleman.

" Be off ! " said Schwartz.

" Pray, gentlemen."

" Off, and be hanged ! " cried Hans, seizing him by the collar. But he had no sooner touched the old gentleman's collar, than away he went after

*Away he went after Hans and the rolling-pin.*

the rolling-pin, spinning round and round, till he fell into the corner on the top of it.

Then Schwartz was very angry, and ran at the old gentleman to turn him out ; but he also had hardly touched him, when away he went after Hans and the rolling-pin, and hit his head against the wall as he tumbled into the corner. And so there they lay, all three.

Then the old gentleman spun himself round with velocity in the opposite direction ; continued to spin until his long cloak was all wound neatly about him ; clapped his cap on his head, very much on one side (for it could not stand upright without going through the ceiling), gave an additional twist to his corkscrew moustaches, and replied with perfect coolness.

" Gentlemen, I wish

you a very good morning. At twelve o'clock to-night I'll call again; after such a refusal of hospitality as I have just experienced, you will not be surprised if that visit is the last I ever pay you."

"If ever I catch you here again," muttered Schwartz, coming, half frightened, out of the corner —but, before he could finish his sentence, the old gentleman had shut the house door behind him with a great bang: and there drove past the window, at the same instant, a wreath of ragged cloud, that whirled and rolled away down the valley in all manner of shapes; turning over and over in the air; and melting away at last in a gush of rain.

"A very pretty business, indeed, Mr. Gluck!" said Schwartz. "Dish the mutton, sir. If ever I catch you at such a trick again— bless me, why, the mutton's been cut!"

*"What's that?" cried Schwartz.*

"You promised me one slice, brother, you know," said Gluck.

"Oh! and you were cutting it hot, I suppose, and going to catch all the gravy. It'll be long before I promise you such a thing again. Leave the room, sir; and have the kindness to wait in the coal-cellar till I call you."

Gluck left the room melancholy enough. The brothers ate as much mutton as they could, locked the rest in the cupboard, and proceeded to get very drunk after dinner.

Such a night as it was! Howling wind, and rushing rain, without intermission. The brothers had just sense enough left to put up all the shutters, and double bar the door, before they went to bed. They usually slept in the same room.

As the clock struck twelve, they were both awakened by a tremendous crash. Their door burst open with a violence that shook the house from top to bottom.

"What's that?" cried Schwartz, starting up in his bed.

"Only I," said the little gentleman.

The two brothers sat up on their bolster, and stared into the darkness. The room was full of water, and by a misty moonbeam, which found its way through a hole in the shutter, they could see, in the midst of it, an enormous foam globe, spinning round, and bobbing up and down like a cork, on which, as on a most luxurious cushion, reclined the little old gentleman, cap and all. There was plenty of room for it now, for the roof was off.

"Sorry to incommode you," said their visitor, ironically. "I'm afraid your beds are dampish; perhaps you had better go to your brother's room: I've left the ceiling on there."

They required no second admonition, but rushed into Gluck's room, wet through, and in an agony of terror.

"You'll find my card on the kitchen table," the old gentleman called after them. "Remember, the *last* visit."

"Pray Heaven it may!" said Schwartz, shuddering. And the foam globe disappeared.

Dawn came at last, and the two brothers looked out of Gluck's little window in the morning. The Treasure Valley was one mass of ruin and desolation. The inundation had swept away trees, crops, and cattle, and left, in their stead, a waste of red sand and gray mud.

The two brothers crept shivering and horror-struck into the kitchen. The water had gutted the whole first floor; corn, money, almost every movable thing had been swept away; and there was left only a small white card on the kitchen table. On it, in large, breezy, long-legged letters, were engraved the words:

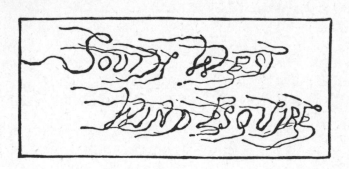

## CHAPTER II

### OF THE PROCEEDINGS OF THE THREE BROTHERS AFTER THE VISIT OF SOUTH-WEST WIND, ESQUIRE; AND HOW LITTLE GLUCK HAD AN INTERVIEW WITH THE KING OF THE GOLDEN RIVER.

SOUTH-WEST WIND, ESQUIRE, was as good as his word. After the momentous visit above related, he entered the Treasure Valley no more; and, what was worse, he had so much influence with his relations, the West Winds in general, and used it so effectually, that they all adopted a similar line of conduct.

So no rain fell in the valley from one year's end to another. Though everything remained green and flourishing in the plains below, the inheritance of the Three Brothers was a desert. What had once been the richest soil in the kingdom, became a shifting heap of red sand ; and the brothers, unable longer to contend with the adverse skies, abandoned their valueless patrimony in despair, to seek some means of gaining a livelihood among the cities and people of the plains. All their money was gone, and they had nothing left but some curious old-fashioned pieces of gold plate, the last remnants of their ill-gotten wealth.

"Suppose we turn goldsmiths ? " said Schwartz to Hans, as they entered the large city. " It is a good knave's trade ; we can put a great deal of copper into the gold without any one's finding it out."

The thought was agreed to be a very good one ; they hired a furnace, and turned goldsmiths. But two slight circumstances affected their trade : the first, that people did not approve of the coppered gold ; the second, that the two elder brothers, whenever they had sold anything, used to leave little Gluck to mind the furnace, and go and drink out the money in the ale-house next door.

So they melted all their gold without making money enough to buy more, and were at last reduced to one large drinking mug, which an uncle of his had given to little Gluck, and which he was very fond of, and would not have parted with for the world ; though he never drank anything out of it but milk and water.

The mug was a very odd mug to look at. The handle was formed of two wreaths of flowing golden hair, so finely spun that it looked more like silk than metal ; and these wreaths descended into, and mixed with, a beard and whiskers of the same exquisite workmanship, which surrounded and decorated a very fierce little face, of the reddest gold imaginable, right in the front of the mug, with a pair of eyes in it which seemed to command its whole circumference. It was impossible to drink out of the mug without being subjected to an intense gaze out of the side of these eyes ; and Schwartz positively averred, that once, after emptying it, full of Rhenish, seventeen times, he had seen them wink !

When it came to the mug's turn to be made into spoons, it half broke poor little Gluck's heart ; but the brothers only laughed at him, tossed the mug into the melting-pot, and staggered out to the ale-house : leaving him as usual, to pour the gold into bars, when it was all ready.

When they were gone, Gluck took a farewell look at his old friend in the melting-pot. The flowing hair was all gone ; nothing remained but the red nose, and the sparkling eyes, which looked more malicious than ever.

" And no wonder," thought Gluck, " after being treated in that way."

He sauntered disconsolately to the window, and sat himself down to catch the fresh evening air, and escape the hot breath of the furnace. Now this window commanded a direct view of the range of mountains which, as I told you before, overhung the Treasure Valley, and more especially of the peak from which fell the Golden River.

It was just at the close of the day ; and, when Gluck sat down at the window, he saw the rocks of the mountain tops, all crimson and purple with the sunset; and there were bright tongues of fiery cloud burning and quivering about them; and the river, brighter than all, fell, in a waving column of pure gold, from precipice to precipice, with the double arch of a broad purple rainbow stretched across it, flushing and fading alternately in the wreaths of spray.

" Ah ! " said Gluck aloud, after he had looked at it for a little while, " if that river were really all gold, what a nice thing it would be."

" No, it wouldn't, Gluck," said a clear metallic voice, close at his ear.

" Bless me, what's that ? " exclaimed Gluck, jumping up. There was nobody there. He looked round the room, and under the table, and a great many times behind him, but there was certainly nobody there; and he sat down again at the window.

This time he didn't speak, but he couldn't help thinking again that it would be very convenient if the river were really all gold.

" Not at all, my boy," said the same voice, louder than before.

" Bless me ! " said Gluck again, " what *is* that ? "

He looked again into all the corners, and cupboards, and then began turning round, and round, as fast as he could in the middle of the room, thinking there was somebody behind him, when the same voice struck again on his ear. It was singing now very merrily, " Lala-lira-la "; no words, only a soft running effervescent melody, something like that of a kettle on the boil. Gluck looked out of the window. No, it was certainly in the house. Upstairs, and downstairs. No, it was certainly in that very room, coming in quicker time, and clearer notes, every moment. " Lala-lira-la."

All at once it struck Gluck that it sounded louder near the furnace. He ran to the opening, and looked in : yes, he was right, it seemed to be coming, not only out of the furnace, but out of the pot. He uncovered it, and ran back in a great fright, for the pot was certainly singing ! He stood in the farthest corner of the room, with his hands up, and his mouth open, for a minute or two, when the singing stopped, and the voice became clear and pronunciative.

" Hollo ! " said the voice.

Gluck made no answer.

" Hollo ! Gluck, my boy," said the pot again.

Gluck summoned all his energies, walked straight up to the crucible, drew it out of the furnace, and looked in. The gold was all melted, and its surface as smooth and polished as a river; but instead of reflecting little Gluck's head, as he looked in, he saw meeting his glance from beneath the gold, the red nose and sharp eyes of his old friend of the mug, a thousand times redder and sharper than ever he had seen them in his life.

" Come, Gluck, my boy," said the voice out of the pot again, " I'm all right; pour me out."

But Gluck was too much astonished to do anything of the kind.

" Pour me out, I say," said the voice rather gruffly.

Still Gluck couldn't move.

" *Will* you pour me out ? " said the voice passionately, " I'm too hot."

By a violent effort, Gluck recovered the use of his limbs, took hold of the crucible, and sloped it, so as to pour out the gold. But instead of a liquid stream, there came out, first, a pair of pretty little yellow legs, then some coat tails, then a pair of arms stuck akimbo, and, finally, the well-known head of his friend the mug; all which articles, uniting as they rolled out, stood up energetically on the floor, in the shape of a little golden dwarf about a foot and a half high.

"That's right!" said the dwarf, stretching out first his legs, and then his arms, and then shaking his head up and down, and as far round as it would go, for five minutes, without stopping; apparently with the view of ascertaining if he were quite correctly put together, while Gluck stood contemplating him in speechless amazement.

He was dressed in a slashed doublet of spun gold, so fine in its texture, that the prismatic colours gleamed over it, as if on a surface of mother-of-pearl;

*Gluck sloped it, so as to pour out the gold."*

and, over this brilliant doublet, his hair and beard fell full half-way to the ground, in waving curls, so exquisitely delicate, that Gluck could hardly tell where they ended; they seemed to melt into air. The features of the face, however, were by no means finished with the same delicacy; they were rather coarse, slightly inclining to coppery in complexion, and indicative, in expression, of a very pertinacious and intractable disposition in their small proprietor.

When the dwarf had finished his self-examination, he turned his small sharp eyes full on Gluck, and stared at him deliberately for a minute or two. "No, it wouldn't, Gluck, my boy," said the little man.

This was certainly rather an abrupt and unconnected mode of commencing conversation. It might, indeed, be supposed to refer to the course of Gluck's thoughts, which had first produced the dwarf's observations out of the pot; but whatever it referred to, Gluck had no inclination to dispute the dictum.

"Wouldn't it, sir?" said Gluck, very mildly and submissively indeed.

"No," said the dwarf, conclusively, "No, it wouldn't." And with that, the dwarf pulled his cap hard over his brows, and took two turns, of three feet long, up and down the room, lifting his legs up very high, and setting them down very hard.

This pause gave time for Gluck to collect his thoughts a little, and, seeing no great reason to view his diminutive visitor with dread, and feeling his curiosity overcome his amazement, he ventured on a question of peculiar delicacy.

"Pray, sir," said Gluck, rather hesitatingly, "were you my mug?"

On which the little man turned sharp round, walked straight up to Gluck, and drew himself to his full height.

"I," said the little man, "am the King of the Golden River."

Whereupon he turned about again, and took two more turns, some six feet long, in order to allow time for the consternation which this announcement produced in his auditor to evaporate. After which, he again walked up to Gluck and stood still, as if expecting some comment on his communication.

Gluck determined to say something at all events.

"I hope your Majesty is very well," said Gluck.

"Listen!" said the little man, deigning no reply to this polite inquiry. "I am the King of what you mortals call the Golden River. The shape you saw me in, was owing to the malice of a stronger king, from whose enchantments you have this instant freed me. What I have seen of you, and your conduct to your wicked brothers, renders me willing to serve you; therefore, attend to what I tell you. Whoever shall climb to the top of that mountain from which you see the Golden River issue, and shall cast into the stream at its source, three drops of holy water, for him, and for him only, the river shall turn to gold. But no one failing in his first, can succeed in a second attempt; and if any one shall cast unholy water into the river, it will overwhelm him, and he will become a black stone."

So saying, the King of the Golden River turned away, and deliberately walked into the centre of the hottest flame of the furnace. His figure became red, white, transparent, dazzling—a blaze of intense light—rose, trembled, and disappeared. The King of the Golden River had evaporated.

"Oh!" cried poor Gluck, running to look up the chimney after him; "oh, dear, dear, dear me! My mug! my mug! my mug!"

# CHAPTER III

### HOW MR. HANS SET OFF ON AN EXPEDITION TO THE GOLDEN RIVER, AND HOW HE PROSPERED THEREIN.

THE King of the Golden River had hardly made the extraordinary exit related in the last chapter, before Hans and Schwartz came roaring into the house very savagely drunk.

The discovery of the total loss of their last piece of plate had the effect of sobering them just enough to enable them to stand over Gluck, beating him very steadily for a quarter of an hour; at the expiration of which period they

**THE KING OF THE GOLDEN RIVER**

The old gentleman walked into the kitchen,
and sat himself down on the hob. (Page 72)

THE WATER BABIES

And inside it, looking very much ashamed of himself, sat his
friend the lobster twiddling his horns. (Page 110)

dropped into a couple of chairs, and requested to know what he had got to say for himself.

Gluck told them his story, of which, of course, they did not believe a word. They beat him again, till their arms were tired, and staggered to bed.

In the morning, however, the steadiness with which he adhered to his story obtained him some degree of credence ; the immediate consequence of which was, that the two brothers, after wrangling a long time on the knotty question, which of them should try his fortune first, drew their swords and began fighting. The noise of the fray alarmed the neighbours, who, finding they could not pacify the combatants, sent for the constable.

Hans, on hearing this, contrived to escape, and hid himself ; but Schwartz was taken before the magistrate, fined for breaking the peace, and, having drunk out his last penny the evening before, was thrown into prison till he should pay.

When Hans heard this, he was much delighted, and determined to set out immediately for the Golden River. How to get the holy water, was the question. He went to the priest, but the priest could not give any holy water to so abandoned a character. So Hans went to vespers in the evening for the first time in his life, and, under pretence of crossing himself, stole a cupful, and returned home in triumph.

Next morning he got up before the sun rose, put the holy water into a strong flask, and two bottles of wine and some meat in a basket, slung them over his back, took his alpine staff in his hand, and set off for the mountains.

On his way out of the town he had to pass the prison ; and as he looked in at the windows, whom should he see but Schwartz himself peeping out of the bars, and looking very disconsolate.

" Good-morning, brother," said Hans ; " have you any message for the King of the Golden River ? "

Schwartz gnashed his teeth with rage, and shook the bars with all his strength ; but Hans only laughed at him ; and, advising him to make himself comfortable till he came back again, shouldered his basket, shook the bottle of holy water in Schwartz's face till it frothed again, and marched off in the highest spirits in the world.

It was, indeed, a morning that might have made any one happy, even with no Golden River to seek for. Level lines

*Hans shook the bottle of holy water in Schwartz's face.*

of dewy mist lay stretched along the valley, out of which rose the massy mountains—their lower cliffs in pale gray shadow, hardly distinguishable from the floating vapour, but gradually ascending till they caught the sunlight, which ran, in sharp touches of ruddy colour, along the angular crags, and pierced, in long level rays, through their fringes of spear-like pine. Far above, shot up red splintered masses of castellated rock, jagged and shivered into myriads of fantastic forms, with here and there a streak of sunlit snow, traced down their chasms like a line of forked lightning ; and, far beyond, and far above all these, fainter than the morning cloud, but purer and changeless, slept in the blue sky, the utmost peaks of the eternal snow.

The Golden River, which sprang from one of the lower and snowless elevations, was now nearly in shadow ; all but the uppermost jets of spray, which rose like slow smoke above the undulating line of the cataract, and floated away in feeble wreaths upon the morning wind.

On this object, and on this alone, Hans' eyes and thoughts were fixed ; forgetting the distance he had to traverse, he set off at an imprudent rate of walking, which greatly exhausted him before he had scaled the first range of the green and low hills.

He was, moreover, surprised, on surmounting them, to find that a large glacier, of whose existence, notwithstanding his previous knowledge of the mountains, he had been absolutely ignorant, lay between him and the source of the Golden River. He entered on it with the boldness of a practised mountaineer ; yet he thought he had never traversed so strange or so dangerous a glacier in his life. The ice was excessively slippery, and out of all its chasms came wild sounds of gushing water ; not monotonous or low, but changeful and loud, rising occasionally into drifting passages of wild melody, then breaking off into short melancholy tones, or sudden shrieks resembling those of human voices in distress or pain. The ice was broken into thousands of confused shapes, but none, Hans thought, like the ordinary forms of splintered ice. There seemed a curious *expression* about all their outlines—a perpetual resemblance to living features, distorted and scornful. Myriads of deceitful shadows, and lurid lights, played and floated about and through the pale blue pinnacles, dazzling and confusing the sight of the traveller ; while his ears grew dull and his head giddy with the constant gush and roar of the concealed waters.

These painful circumstances increased upon him as he advanced ; the ice crashed and yawned into fresh chasms at his feet, tottering spires nodded around him, and fell thundering across his path ; and though he had re-peatedly faced these dangers on the most terrific glaciers, and in the wildest weather, it was with a new and oppressive feeling of panic terror that he leaped the last chasm, and flung himself, exhausted and shuddering, on the firm turf of the mountain.

He had been compelled to abandon his basket of food, which became a perilous encumbrance on the glacier, and had now no means of refreshing himself but by breaking off and eating some of the pieces of ice. This, however, relieved his thirst ; an hour's repose recruited his hardy frame, and with the indomitable spirit of avarice, he resumed his laborious journey.

His way now lay straight up a ridge of bare red rocks, without a blade of grass to ease the foot, or a projecting angle to afford an inch of shade from the south sun. It was past noon, and the rays beat intensely upon the steep path, while the whole atmosphere was motionless, and penetrated with heat. Intense thirst was soon added to the bodily fatigue with which Hans was now afflicted; glance after glance he cast on the flask of water which hung at his belt.

"Three drops are enough," at last thought he; "I may, at least, cool my lips with it."

He opened the flask, and was raising it to his lips, when his eye fell on an object lying on the rock beside him; he thought it moved. It was a small dog, apparently in the last agony of death from thirst. Its tongue was out, its jaws dry, its limbs extended lifelessly, and a swarm of black ants were crawling about its lips and throat. Its eye moved

*He hurled it into the centre of the torrent.*

to the bottle which Hans held in his hand. He raised it, drank, spurned the animal with his foot, and passed on. And he did not know how it was, but he thought that a strange shadow had suddenly come across the blue sky.

The path became steeper and more rugged every moment; and the high hill air, instead of refreshing him, seemed to throw his blood into a fever. The noise of the hill cataracts sounded like mockery in his ears; they were all distant, and his thirst increased every moment.

Another hour passed, and he again looked down to the flask at his side; it was half empty; but there was much more than three drops in it. He stopped to open it, and again, as he did so, something moved in the path above him. It was a fair child, stretched nearly lifeless on the rock, its breast heaving with thirst, its eyes closed, and its lips parched and burning. Hans eyed it deliberately, drank, and passed on. And a dark gray cloud came over the sun, and long, snake-like shadows crept up along the mountain sides.

Hans struggled on. The sun was sinking, but its descent seemed to bring no coolness ; the leaden weight of the dead air pressed upon his brow and heart, but the goal was near. He saw the cataract of the Golden River springing from the hill-side, scarcely five hundred feet above him. He paused for a moment to breathe, and sprang on to complete his task.

At this instant a faint cry fell on his ear. He turned, and saw a gray-haired old man extended on the rocks. His eyes were sunk, his features deadly pale, and gathered into an expression of despair.

" Water ! " he stretched his arms to Hans, and cried feebly, " Water ! I am dying."

" I have none," replied Hans ; " thou hast had thy share of life."

He strode over the prostrate body, and darted on. And a flash of blue lightning rose out of the East, shaped like a sword ; it shook thrice over the whole heaven, and left it dark with one heavy, impenetrable shade.

The sun was setting ; it plunged towards the horizon like a red-hot ball.

The roar of the Golden River rose on Hans' ear. He stood on the brink of the chasm through which it ran. Its waves were filled with the red glory of the sunset : they shook their crests like tongues of fire, and flashes of bloody light gleamed along their foam. Their sound came mightier and mightier on his senses ; his brain grew giddy with the prolonged thunder.

Shuddering, he drew the flask from his girdle, and hurled it into the centre of the torrent. As he did so, an icy chill shot through his limbs ; he staggered, shrieked and fell. The waters closed over his cry. And the moaning of the river rose wildly into the night as it gushed over

*The Black Stone.*

## CHAPTER IV

HOW MR. SCHWARTZ SET OFF ON AN EXPEDITION TO THE GOLDEN RIVER, AND
HOW HE PROSPERED THEREIN.

POOR little Gluck waited very anxiously alone in the house for Hans' return.
Finding he did not come back, he was terribly frightened, and went and told
Schwartz in the prison all that had happened. Then Schwartz was very
much pleased, and said that Hans must certainly have been turned into a
black stone, and he should have all the gold to himself. But Gluck was very
sorry, and cried all night.

When he got up in the morning, there was no bread in the house, nor
any money; so Gluck went and hired himself to another goldsmith, and he
worked so hard, and so neatly, and so long every day, that he soon got
money enough together to pay his brother's fine; and he went and gave
it all to Schwartz, and Schwartz got out of prison. Then Schwartz was
quite pleased, and said he should have some of the gold of the river. But
Gluck only begged he would go and see what had become of Hans.

Now when Schwartz had heard that Hans had stolen the holy water,
he thought to himself that such a proceeding might not be considered altogether correct by the King of the Golden River, and determined to manage
matters better. So he took some more of Gluck's money, and went to a
bad priest, who gave him some holy water very readily for it. Then Schwartz
was sure it was all quite right.

So Schwartz got up early in the morning before the sun rose, and took
some bread and wine in a basket, and put his holy water in a flask, and set
off for the mountains. Like his brother he was much surprised at the sight
of the glacier, and had great difficulty in crossing it, even after leaving his
basket behind him.

The day was cloudless, but not bright: there was a heavy purple haze
hanging over the sky, and the hills looked lowering and gloomy. And as
Schwartz climbed the steep rock path, the thirst came upon him, as it had
upon his brother, until he lifted his flask to his lips to drink. Then he saw
the fair child lying near him on the rocks, and it cried to him, and moaned
for water.

"Water, indeed," said Schwartz; "I haven't half enough for myself,"
and passed on.

And as he went he thought the sunbeams grew more dim, and he saw a
low bank of black cloud rising out of the West; and, when he had climbed for
another hour, the thirst overcame him again, and he would have drunk.
There he saw the old man lying before him on the path, and heard him cry
out for water.

"Water, indeed," said Schwartz, "I haven't half enough for myself,"
and on he went.

Then again the light seemed to fade from before his eyes, and he looked
up, and behold, a mist, of the colour of blood, had come over the sun;
and the bank of black cloud had risen very high, and its edges were tossing

*He gave all his money to Schwartz.*

and tumbling like the waves of the angry sea. And they cast long shadows, which flickered over Schwartz's path.

Then Schwartz climbed for another hour, and again his thirst returned; and as he lifted his flask to his lips, he thought he saw his brother Hans lying exhausted on the path before him, and, as he gazed, the figure stretched its arms to him, and cried for water.

"Ha, ha," laughed Schwartz, " are you there? remember the prison bars, my boy. Water, indeed! do you suppose I carried it all the way up here for *you*?"

And he strode over the figure. Yet, as he passed, he thought he saw a strange expression of mockery about its lips. And, when he had gone a few yards farther, he looked back; but the figure was not there.

And a sudden horror came over Schwartz, he knew not why; but the thirst for gold prevailed over his fear, and he rushed on. And the bank of black cloud rose to the zenith, and out of it came bursts of spiry lightning, and waves of darkness seemed to heave and float between their flashes, over the whole heavens. And the sky where the sun was setting was all level, and like a lake of blood; and a strong wind came out of that sky, tearing its crimson clouds into fragments, and scattering them far into the darkness.

And when Schwartz stood by the brink of the Golden River, its waves were black, like thunder clouds, but their foam was like fire; and the roar of the waters below and the thunder above met as he cast the flask into the stream. And, as he did so, the lightning glared in his eyes; and the earth gave way beneath him, and the waters closed over his cry. And the moaning of the river rose wildly into the night, as it gushed over the

TWO BLACK STONES.

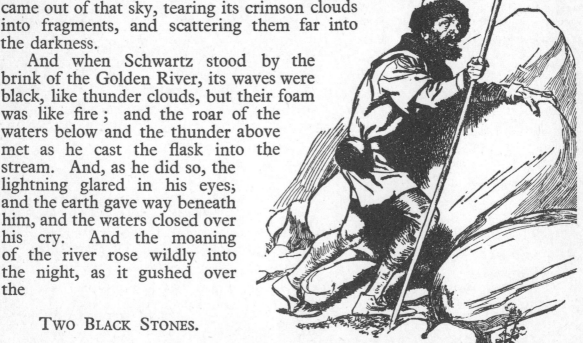

*A sudden horror came over Schwartz.*

## CHAPTER V

HOW LITTLE GLUCK SET OFF ON AN EXPEDITION TO THE GOLDEN RIVER, AND HOW HE PROSPERED THEREIN ; WITH OTHER MATTERS OF INTEREST.

WHEN Gluck found that Schwartz did not come back, he was very sorry, and did not know what to do. He had no money, and was obliged to go and hire himself again to the goldsmith, who worked him very hard, and gave him very little money.

So, after a month or two, Gluck grew tired, and made up his mind to go and try his fortune with the Golden River.

" The little king looked very kind," thought he. " I don't think he will turn me into a black stone."

So he went to the priest, and the priest gave him some holy water as soon as he asked for it. Then Gluck took some bread in his basket, and the bottle of water, and set off very early for the mountains.

If the glacier had occasioned a great deal of fatigue to his brothers, it was twenty times worse for him, who was neither so strong nor so practised on the mountains. He had several very bad falls, lost his basket and bread, and was very much frightened at the strange noises under the ice.

He lay a long time to rest on the grass, after he had got over, and began to climb the hill just in the hottest part of the day. When he had climbed for an hour, he got dreadfully thirsty, and was going to drink like his brothers, when he saw an old man coming down the path above him, looking very feeble, and leaning on a staff.

" My son," said the old man, " I am faint with thirst, give me some of that water."

Then Gluck looked at him, and when he saw that he was pale and weary, he gave him the water ; " Only pray don't drink it all," said Gluck.

But the old man drank a great deal, and gave him back the bottle two-thirds empty.

Then he bade him good speed, and Gluck went on again merrily. And the path became easier to his feet, and two or three blades of grass appeared upon it, and some grasshoppers began singing on the bank beside it ; and Gluck thought he had never heard such merry singing.

Then he went on for another hour, and the thirst increased on him so that he thought he should be forced to drink. But, as he raised the flask, he saw a little child lying panting by the roadside, and it cried out piteously for water.

Then Gluck struggled with himself, and determined to bear the thirst a little longer ; and he put the bottle to the child's lips, and it drank it all but a few drops. Then it smiled on him, and got up, and ran down the hill ; and Gluck looked after it, till it became as small as a little star, and then turned and began climbing again. And then there were all kinds of sweet flowers growing on the rocks, bright green moss, with pale pink starry flowers, and soft belled gentians, more blue than the sky at its deepest, and pure white transparent lilies. And crimson and purple butterflies

*" Don't be frightened, it's all right."*

darted hither and thither, and the sky sent down such pure light, that Gluck had never felt so happy in his life.

Yet, when he had climbed for another hour, his thirst became intolerable again; and, when he looked at his bottle, he saw that there were only five or six drops left in it, and he could not venture to drink. And, as he was hanging the flask to his belt again, he saw a little dog lying on the rocks, gasping for breath—just as Hans had seen it on the day of his ascent. And Gluck stopped and looked at it, and then at the Golden River, not five hundred yards above him; and he thought of the dwarf's words, " that no one could succeed, except in his first attempt; " and he tried to pass the dog, but it whined piteously, and Gluck stopped again. " Poor beastie," said Gluck, " it'll be dead when I come down again, if I don't help it." Then he looked closer and closer at it, and its eye turned on him so mournfully, that he could not stand it.

" Confound the King and his gold too," said Gluck; and he opened the flask, and poured all the water into the dog's mouth.

The dog sprang up and stood on its hind legs. Its tail disappeared, its ears became long, longer, silky, golden; its nose became very red, its eyes became very twinkling; in three seconds the dog was gone, and before Gluck stood his old acquaintance, the King of the Golden River.

" Thank you," said the monarch; " but don't be frightened, it's all right; " for Gluck showed manifest symptoms of consternation at this unlooked-for reply to his last observation.

" Why didn't you come before," continued the dwarf, " instead of sending me those rascally brothers of yours, for me to have the trouble of turning into stones? Very hard stones they make too."

" Oh, dear me!" said Gluck, " have you really been so cruel?"

" Cruel!" said the dwarf, " they poured unholy water into my stream: do you suppose I'm going to allow that?"

" Why," said Gluck, " I am sure, sir—your Majesty, I mean—they got the water out of the church font."

"Very probably," replied the dwarf; "but," and his countenance grew stern as he spoke, "the water which has been refused to the cry of the weary and dying, is unholy, though it had been blessed by every saint in heaven; and the water which is found in the vessel of mercy is holy, though it had been defiled with corpses."

So saying, the dwarf stooped and plucked a lily that grew at his feet. On its white leaves there hung three drops of clear dew. And the dwarf shook them into the flask which Gluck held in his hand.

"Cast these into the river," he said, "and descend on the other side of the mountains into the Treasure Valley. And so good speed."

As he spoke, the figure of the dwarf became very indistinct. The playing colours of his robe formed themselves into a prismatic mist of dewy light: he stood for an instant veiled with them as with the belt of a broad rainbow. Then the colours grew faint, the mist rose into the air; the monarch had evaporated.

And Gluck climbed to the brink of the Golden River, and its waves were as clear as crystal, and as brilliant as the sun. And, when he cast the three drops of dew into the stream, there opened, where they fell, a small circular whirlpool, into which the waters descended with a musical noise.

Gluck stood watching it for some time, very much disappointed, because not only the river was not turned into gold, but its waters seemed much diminished in quantity.

Yet he obeyed his friend the dwarf, and descended the other side of the mountains, towards the Treasure Valley; and, as he went, he thought he heard the noise of water working its way under the ground. And, when he came in sight of the Treasure Valley, behold, a river, like the Golden River, was springing from a new cleft of the rocks above it, and was flowing in innumerable streams among the dry heaps of red sand.

*The Black Brothers*

And as Gluck gazed, fresh grass sprang beside the new streams, and creeping plants grew, and climbed among the moistening soil. Young flowers opened suddenly along the river sides, as stars leap out when twilight is deepening, and thickets of myrtle, and tendrils of vine, cast lengthening shadows over the valley as they grew. And thus the

B.F.            H

Treasure Valley became a garden again, and the inheritance, which had been lost by cruelty, was regained by love.

And Gluck went, and dwelt in the valley, and the poor were never driven from his door : so that his barns became full of corn, and his house of treasure. And for him the river had, according to the dwarf's promise, become a River of Gold.

And to this day the inhabitants of the valley point out the place where the three drops of holy dew were cast into the stream, and trace the course of the Golden River under the ground, until it emerges in the Treasure Valley. And at the top of the cataract of the Golden River are still to be seen two BLACK STONES, round which the waters howl mournfully every day at sunset ; and these stones are still called by the people of the valley

## THE BLACK BROTHERS

# The Banks o' Doon

### *by* ROBERT BURNS

Ye banks and braes o' bonnie Doon,
How can ye bloom sae fresh and fair?
How can ye chant, ye little birds,
And I sae weary fu' o' care?
Thou'lt break my heart, thou warbling bird,
That wantons thro' the flowering thorn :
Thou minds me o' departed joys,
Departed never to return.

Aft hae I roved by bonnie Doon,
To see the rose and woodbine twine ;
And ilka bird sang o' its love,
And fondly sae did I o' mine.
Wi' lightsome heart I pu'd a rose,
Fu' sweet upon its thorny tree ;
And my fause lover stole my rose,
But ah ! he left the thorn wi' me.

# THE WATER BABIES

## by CHARLES KINGSLEY

*(Abridged and Adapted)*

## CHAPTER I

ONCE upon a time there was a little chimney-sweep, and his name was Tom.

One day a smart little groom rode into the court where Tom lived. Tom was just hiding behind a wall, to heave half a brick at his horse's legs; but the groom halloed to him to know where Mr. Grimes, the chimney-sweep, lived. Now, Mr. Grimes was Tom's own master, and Tom was a good man of business, and always civil to customers, so he put the half-brick down quietly behind the wall, and proceeded to take orders.

Mr. Grimes was to come up next morning to Sir John Harthover's, at the Place, for his old chimney-sweep was gone to prison, and the chimneys wanted sweeping. Then the groom rode away, not giving Tom time to ask what the sweep had gone to prison for.

His master was so delighted at his new customer that he knocked Tom down out of hand. When he got up at four the next morning, he knocked Tom down again, in order to teach him that he must be an extra good boy that day. So he and his master set out; Grimes rode the donkey in front, and Tom, with the brushes, walked behind; out of the court, and up the street, past the closed window-shutters, and the winking, weary policemen, and the roofs all shining gray in the gray dawn.

Soon the road grew white, and the walls likewise; and at the wall's foot grew long grass, and gay flowers, all drenched with dew; and they heard the skylark saying his matins high up in the air, and the pit bird warbling in the sedges, as he warbled all night long. On they went; and Tom looked, and looked, for he never had been so far into the country before; and longed to get over a gate, and pick buttercups, and look for birds' nests in the hedge ; but Mr. Grimes was a man of business, and would not hear of that.

Soon they came up with a poor Irishwoman, trudging along with a bundle at her back. She had neither shoes nor stockings, and limped as if she were tired and footsore ; but she was a very tall and handsome woman, with bright gray eyes, and heavy, black hair hanging about her cheeks. And she took Mr. Grimes's fancy so much, that, when he came alongside, he called out to her :

" This is a hard road for a gradely foot like that. Will ye up, lass, and ride behind me ? "

But, perhaps, she did not admire Mr. Grimes's look and voice ; for she answered quietly :

" No, thank you ; I'd sooner walk with your little lad here."

" You may please yourself," growled Grimes, and went on smoking. So she walked beside Tom, and talked to him, and asked him where he lived, and all about himself, till Tom thought he had never met such a pleasant-spoken woman.

At last, at the bottom of a hill, they came to a spring ; and there Grimes stopped. Without a word, he got off his donkey, and clambered over the low road wall, and knelt down, and began dipping his ugly head into the spring—and very dirty he made it.

Tom was picking the flowers as fast as he could. The Irishwoman helped him, and showed him how to tie them up ; and a very pretty nosegay they made between them. But when he saw Grimes actually wash, he stopped, quite astonished ; and when Grimes had finished, and began shaking his ears to dry them, he said :

" Why, master, I never saw you do that before."

" Nor will again, most likely. 'Twasn't for cleanliness I did it, but for coolness. I'd be ashamed to want washing every week or so, like any smutty collier lad."

" I wish I might go and dip my head in," said poor little Tom. " It must be as good as putting it under the town pump ; and there is no beadle here to drive a chap away."

" Thou come along," said Grimes ; " what dost want with washing thyself ? "

" I don't care for you," said naughty Tom, and ran down to the stream, and began washing his face. Grimes dashed at him and tore him up from his knees, and began beating him.

" Are you not ashamed of yourself, Thomas Grimes ? " cried the Irishwoman, over the wall.

Grimes looked up, startled at her knowing his name ; but all he answered was, " No, nor never was yet ; " and went on beating Tom.

" True for you. If you ever had been ashamed of yourself, you would have gone over into Vendale long ago."

" What do you know about Vendale ? " shouted Grimes ; but he left off beating Tom.

" I know about Vendale, and about you, too. I know, for instance, what happened in Aldermire Copse, by night, two years ago come Martinmas."

" You do ? " shouted Grimes ; and leaving Tom, he climbed up over the wall, and faced the woman. Tom thought he was going to strike her; but she looked him too full and fierce in the face for that.

"Yes; I was there," said the Irishwoman quietly; "and if you strike that boy again, I can tell what I know."

Grimes seemed quite cowed, and got on his donkey without another word.

"Stop!" said the Irishwoman. "I have one more word for you both; for you will both see me again before all is over. Those that wish to be clean, clean they will be; and those that wish to be foul, foul they will be. Remember!"

She turned away, and went through a gate into the meadow. Grimes stood still a moment. Then he rushed after her, shouting, "You come back!" But when he got into the meadow, the woman was not there. Had she hidden away? There was no place to hide in. But Grimes looked about, and Tom also; but look where they would, she was not there.

Grimes came back again, as silent as a post, for he was a little frightened; and getting on his donkey, filled a fresh pipe, and smoked away, leaving Tom in peace. And now they had gone three miles and more, and come to Sir John's lodge gates. Grimes rang at the gate, and out came a keeper on the spot, and opened.

"I was told to expect thee," he said. "I may as well walk up with thee to the hall."

They walked up a great lime avenue, a full mile long. Tom had never seen such enormous trees, and, as he looked up, he fancied that the blue sky rested on their heads. Tom and his master did not go in through the great iron gate, but round the back way, and a very long way round it was; and into a little back door, where the ash-boy let them in, yawning horribly; and then in a passage the housekeeper met them, and she gave Grimes solemn orders about "You will take care of this, and take care of that," as if he was going up the chimneys, and not Tom.

Grimes listened, and said, every now and then, under his voice, "You'll mind that, you little beggar?" and Tom did mind, all at least that he could. Then the housekeeper turned them into a grand room, all covered up with sheets of brown paper, and bade them begin; and so after a whimper or two, and a kick from his master, into the grate Tom went, and up the chimney.

How many chimneys Tom swept I cannot say; but he swept so many that he got quite tired, and puzzled too, and at last he came down the wrong one, and found himself standing on the hearthrug in a room the like of which he had never seen before.

The room was all dressed in white—white window curtains, white bed curtains, white furniture, and white walls, with just a few lines of pink here and there. The carpet was gay all over with little flowers; and the walls were hung with pictures in gilt frames, which amused Tom very much. But the two pictures which took his fancy most were, one a man in long garments, with little children and their mothers round him, who was laying his hand upon the children's heads. That was a very pretty picture, Tom thought, to hang in a lady's room. For he could see that it was a lady's room by the dresses which lay about.

The next thing he saw, and that too puzzled him, was a washing-stand, with ewers and basins, and soap and brushes and towels, and a large bath full of clean water—what a heap of things all for washing! " She must be a very dirty lady," thought Tom, " by my master's rule, to want as much scrubbing as all that. But I don't see a speck about the room, nor even on the very towels."

And then, looking toward the bed, he saw the dirty lady, and held his breath with astonishment.

Under the snow-white coverlet, upon the snow-white pillow, lay the most beautiful little girl Tom had ever seen. Her cheeks were almost as white as the pillow, and her hair was like threads of gold spread all about over the bed. She might have been as old as Tom, or maybe a year or two older ; but Tom did not think of that. He thought only of her delicate skin and golden hair, and wondered whether she was a real live person, or one of the wax dolls he had seen in the shops. But when he saw her breathe, he made up his mind that she was alive, and stood staring at her, as if she had been an angel out of heaven.

No. She cannot be dirty. She never could have been dirty, thought Tom to himself. Then he thought, " And are all people like that when they are washed ? "

Turning round, he suddenly saw, standing close to him, a little ugly, black, ragged figure, with bleared eyes and grinning white teeth. He turned on it angrily. What did such a little black ape want in that sweet young lady's room ? And behold ! it was himself, reflected in a great mirror the like of which Tom had never seen before.

Tom, for the first time in his life, found out that he was dirty ; and burst into tears with shame and anger ; and turned to sneak up the chimney again to hide ; and upset the fender, and threw the fire-irons down, with a noise as of ten thousand tin kettles tied to ten thousand mad dogs' tails.

Up jumped the little white lady in her bed, and, seeing Tom, screamed as shrill as any peacock. In rushed a stout old nurse from the next room, and seeing Tom likewise, made up her mind that he had come to rob, plunder, destroy, and burn ; and dashed at him, as he lay over the fender, so fast that she caught him by the jacket.

But she did not hold him. Tom doubled under the good lady's arm across the room, and out of the window in a moment. Down he went, like a cat, and across the garden lawn, and over the iron railings, and up the park toward the wood, leaving the old nurse to scream murder and fire at the window.

The under-gardener saw Tom, and, with all the other servants and Sir John himself, gave chase. Up the park and over the wall Tom went, until he got on to a wide moor, and no one saw him except the Irishwoman who had been kind to him on the road. At last he began to get a little hungry, and very thirsty ; for he had run a long way, and the sun had risen high in the heavens, and the rock was as hot as an oven. But he could see nothing to eat anywhere, and still less to drink.

So he went on and on, till his head spun round with the heat, and he thought he heard church-bells ringing, a long way off. And in a minute more, when he looked round, he stopped again, and said, "Why, what a big place the world is!"

Down below he saw a deep, deep green and rocky valley, very narrow, and filled with woods; but through the woods, hundreds of feet below him, he could see a clear stream! Then, by the stream, he saw the roof of a little cottage, and a little garden set out in squares and beds. And there was a tiny little red thing moving in the garden, no bigger than a fly. As Tom looked down he saw that it was a woman in a red petticoat. Ah! perhaps she would give him something to eat. And there were the church bells ringing again. Surely there must be a village down there, and he could get down in five minutes.

Tom was wrong about getting there in five minutes, for the cottage was more than a mile off, and a good thousand feet below.

*There lay the most beautiful little girl
that Tom had ever seen.*

However, down he went, like a brave little man as he was, though he was very footsore, and tired, and hungry, and thirsty; while the church-bells rang so loud, he began to think that they must be inside his own head, and the river chimed and tinkled far below; and this was the song which it sang:

> "Clear and cool, clear and cool,
> By laughing shallow, and dreaming pool:
> Cool and clear, cool and clear,
> By shining shingle, and foaming wear;
> Under the crag where the ouzel sings,
> And the ivied wall where the church-bell rings,
> Undefiled, for the undefiled;
> Play by me, bathe in me, mother and child."

So Tom went down; and all the while he never saw the Irishwoman going down behind him.

# CHAPTER II

A MILE off, and a thousand feet down.

At last Tom got to the bottom. He lay down on the grass and fell asleep till the beetles ran over him, and the flies settled on his nose. Then he woke up, and stumbled away, down over a low wall, and into a narrow road, and up to the cottage door.

He peeped in, half-afraid. And there sat by the empty fireplace, which was filled with a pot of sweet herbs, the nicest old woman that ever was seen, in her red petticoat and clean white cap. At her feet sat the grandfather of all the cats; and opposite her sat, on two benches, twelve or fourteen neat, rosy, chubby children learning their Chris-cross-row; and gabble enough they made about it.

Such a pleasant cottage it was, with a shiny, clean stone floor, and a cuckoo clock in the corner, which began shouting as soon as Tom appeared; not that it was frightened at Tom, but that it was just eleven o'clock.

" What art thou, and what dost thou want ? " cried the old dame. " A chimney-sweep ! Away with thee ! I'll have no sweeps here."

" Water," said poor little Tom, quite faint; and sank down upon the doorstep, and laid his head against the post.

The old dame looked at him through her spectacles one minute, and two, and three; and then she said, " He's sick; and a bairn's a bairn, sweep or none."

" Water," said Tom.

" Water's bad for thee; I'll give thee milk." And she toddled off into the next room, and brought a cup of milk and a bit of bread. Tom drank the milk off at one draught, and then looked up, revived.

" Where didst come from ? " said the dame.

" I came from the Place ; " and Tom told all the truth in a few words.

" Bless thy little heart ! Why, God's guided the bairn, because he was innocent. Why dost not eat thy bread ? It's good enough, for I made it myself."

" I can't," said Tom, and he laid his head on his knees, and then asked, " Is it Sunday ? "

" No, then; why should it be ? "

" Because I hear the church-bells ringing so."

" Bless thy pretty heart ! The bairn's sick. Come wi' me, and I'll hap thee up somewhere. If thou wert a bit cleaner, I'd put thee in my own bed, for the Lord's sake. But come along here."

But when Tom tried to get up, he was so tired and giddy, that she had to help him. She put him in an outhouse upon soft sweet hay and an old rug, and bade him sleep off his walk, and she would come to him when school was over, in an hour's time.

But Tom did not fall asleep. Instead of it he turned and tossed and kicked about in the strangest way, and felt so hot all over that he longed to get into the river and cool himself. Then he heard the church-bells ring so loud, close to him too, that he was sure it must be Sunday, in spite of what the old dame had said.

All of a sudden he found himself, not in the outhouse on the hay, but in the middle of a meadow, over the road, with the stream just before him, saying continually, " I must be clean, I must be clean." He had got there on his own legs, between asleep and awake. But he was not a bit surprised, and lay down on the grass, and looked into the clear limestone water, with every pebble at the bottom bright and clean, while the little silver trout dashed about in fright at the sight of his black face ; and he dipped his hand in and found it so cool, cool, cool ; and he said, " I will be a fish ; I will swim in the water ; I must be clean, I must be clean."

He pulled of all his clothes in such haste that he tore some of them, which was easy enough with such ragged old things. He put his poor hot sore feet into the water, and then his legs ; and the farther he went in, the more the church-bells rang in his head. And all the while he saw the Irishwoman, not behind him this time, but in front.

Just before he came to the riverside, she had stepped down into the cool, clear water, and her shawl and her petticoat floated off her, and green water-weeds floated round her sides, and the white water-lilies floated round her head, and the fairies of the stream came up from the bottom and bore her away ; for she was the queen of them all.

" I have brought you a new little brother," she said, " and watched him safe all the way here. But mind, maidens, he must not see you, or know that you are here. You must not play with him, or speak to him, or let him see you ; but only keep him from being harmed."

Then the fairies were sad, because they could not play with their new brother, but they always did what they were told. All this Tom, of course, never saw or heard : for he was so hot and thirsty, and longed so to be clean for once, that he tumbled himself as quick as he could into the clear cool stream.

He had not been in it two minutes before he fell fast asleep, into the quietest, sunniest, cosiest sleep that ever he had in his life ; and he dreamed about the green meadows and the tall elm trees, and the sleeping cows, and after that he dreamed of nothing at all. The reason of his falling into such a delightful sleep is very simple ; and yet hardly any one has found it out. It was merely that the fairies took him.

The kind old dame came back at twelve, when school was over, to look at Tom ; but there was no Tom there. So she went in again quite sulky, thinking that little Tom had tricked her. But she altered her mind the next day.

When Sir John and the rest of them had run themselves out of breath, and lost Tom, they went back again, looking very foolish. They looked more foolish still when they heard the whole story from Miss Ellie, the little lady in white. All she had seen was a poor little black chimney-sweep, crying and sobbing, and going to get up the chimney again. Of course, she was very much frightened ; and no wonder. But that was all. The boy had taken nothing in the room ; by the mark of his little sooty feet, they could see that he had never been off the hearthrug till the nurse caught hold of him. It was all a mistake.

The next day Sir John and the rest went out again, and when they came to the old dame's school, all the children came out to see. The old dame came out too ; and when she saw Sir John she curtsied very low, for she was a tenant of his.

" Well, dame, how are you ? " said Sir John.

" Blessings on you as broad as your back, Harthover," says she—she didn't call him Sir John, but only Harthover, for that is the fashion in the North country—" and welcome into Vendale ; but you're no hunting the fox this time of the year ? "

" I'm looking for a lost child, a chimney-sweep, that has run away."

" Oh, Harthover, Harthover," says she, " ye were always a just man and a merciful ; and ye'll no harm the poor little lad if I give you tidings of him ? "

" Not I, not I, dame. I'm afraid we hunted him out of the house all on a miserable mistake, and——"

Whereat the old dame broke out crying, without letting him finish his story.

" So he told me the truth after all, poor little dear ! Ah, a body's heart'll guide them right, if they will but hearken to it." And then she told Sir John all.

And Tom ?

Ah, now comes the most wonderful part of this wonderful story. Tom, when he woke, found himself swimming about in the stream, being about four inches long, with something which he mistook for a lace frill round his neck, till he pulled at it, found he hurt himself, and made up his mind that it was part of himself, and best left alone.

In fact, the fairies had turned him into a water-baby.

A water-baby ? You never heard of a water-baby. Perhaps not. That is the very reason why this story was written.

Good Sir John did not understand all this, and he took it into his head that Tom was drowned. Then Sir John did something as like crying as ever he did in his life, and the groom-boy cried, and the huntsman cried, and the dame cried, and the dairymaid cried, and the old nurse cried (for it was somewhat her fault), and My Lady cried. And the little girl would not play with her dolls for a whole week, and never forgot poor little Tom.

And always after this, the old dame sang an old, old song, as she sat spinning. The children could not understand it, but they liked it none the less for that ; for it was very sweet, and very sad. And these are the words of it :

> " When all the world is young, lad,
>     And all the trees are green ;
> And every goose a swan, lad,
>     And every lass a queen ;
> Then hey for boot and horse, lad,
>     And round the world away ;
> Young blood must have its course, lad,
>     And every dog his day.

" When all the world is old, lad,
And all the trees are brown ;
And all the sport is stale, lad,
And all the wheels run down ;
Creep home, and take your place there,
The spent and maimed among ;
God grant you find one face there,
You loved when all was young."

And all the while Tom was swimming about in the river, with a pretty little lace collar of gills about his neck, as lively as a grig, and as clean as a fresh-run salmon.

## CHAPTER III

TOM felt himself quite at home in the water, and what is better still, he was clean. He was very happy in the water. He had nothing to do now but enjoy himself, and look at all the pretty things which are to be seen in the cool clear water-world, where the sun is never too hot, and the frost is never too cold.

Sometimes he went along the smooth gravel waterways, looking at the crickets which run in and out among the stones, as rabbits do on land ; or he went into a still corner, and watched the caddises eating dead sticks as greedily as you would eat plum pudding, and building their houses with silk and glue. Very fanciful ladies they were ; none of them would keep to the same materials for a day. One would begin with some pebbles ; then she would stick on a piece of green wood ; then she found a shell, and stuck it on too ; then she stuck on a piece of rotten wood, then a very smart pink stone, and so on, till she was patched all over like an Irishman's coat.

Then she found a long straw, five times as long as herself, and said, " Hurrah !

*The fairies had turned him into a water-baby.*

my sister has a tail, and I'll have one too;" and she stuck it on her back, and marched about with it quite proud, though it was very inconvenient indeed. And, at that, tails became all the fashion among the caddis-baits in that pool, and they all toddled about with long straws sticking out behind, tumbling over one another, and looking so ridiculous, that Tom laughed at them till he cried.

Now you must know that all the things under the water talk; only not such a language as ours; but such as horses, and dogs, and cows, and birds talk to each other; and Tom soon learned to understand them; so that he might have had very pleasant company if he had been a good boy. But I am sorry to say, he was too like some other little boys, very fond of hunting and tormenting creatures for mere sport. Some people say that boys cannot help it; boys can help it, and must help it.

Tom, however, pecked and howked the poor water-things about sadly, till they were all afraid of him, and got out of his way, or crept into their shells; so he had no one to speak to or play with. The water-fairies, of course, were very sorry to see him so unhappy, and longed to take him and tell him how naughty he was, and teach him to be good, and to play and romp with him, too; but they had been forbidden to do that. Tom had to learn his lesson for himself as many another foolish person has to do.

At last one day he found a caddis, and wanted it to peep out of its house; but its house door was shut. He had never seen a caddis with a house door before; so what must he do, the meddlesome little fellow, but pull it open, to see what the poor lady was doing inside. So Tom broke to pieces the door, which was the prettiest little grating of silk, stuck all over with shining bits of crystal; and when he looked in, the caddis poked out her head, and it had turned into just the shape of a bird's. But when Tom spoke to her she could not answer; for her mouth and face were tied up in a new nightcap of neat pink skin. However, if she didn't answer, all the other little caddises did; for they held up their hands and shrieked, "Oh, you nasty, horrid boy; there you are at it again! And she had just laid herself up for a fortnight's sleep, and then she would have come out with such beautiful wings, and flown about, and laid such a lot of eggs: and now you have broken her door, and she can't mend it, because her mouth is tied up for a fortnight, and she will die. Who sent you here to worry us out of our lives?"

Tom swam away. He was very much ashamed of himself. Then he came to a pool full of little trout, and began tormenting them, and trying to catch them. But as Tom chased them, a huge old brown trout, ten times as big as he was, ran right against him, and knocked all the breath out of his body; and I don't know which was the more frightened of the two.

Then he went on sulky and lonely, as he deserved to be; and under a bank he saw a very ugly, dirty creature sitting, about half as big as himself; which had six legs, and a big stomach, and a funny head with two great eyes, and a face just like a donkey's.

"Oh," said Tom, "you are an ugly fellow to be sure!" and he began making faces at him; and put his nose close to him, and halloed at him, like a very rude boy.

When, hey presto! all the thing's donkey-face came off in a moment, and out popped a long arm with a pair of pincers at the end of it, and caught Tom by the nose.

"Yah! ah! Oh, let me go!" cried Tom.

"Then let me go," said the creature. "I want to be quiet. I want to split."

Tom promised to let him alone, and he let go. "Why do you want to split?" said Tom.

"Because my brothers and sisters have all split, and turned into beautiful creatures with wings; and I want to split too. I will split!"

He swelled himself, and puffed, and stretched himself out stiff, and at last—crack, puff, bang—he opened all down his back, and then up to the top of his head. Out of his inside came the most slender, elegant, soft creature, as soft and smooth as Tom; but very pale and weak. It

*I don't know which was the more frightened of the two.*

looked about a bit and then walked up a grass stem to the top of the water. Tom went to the top of the water, too, and peeped out to see what would happen.

As the creature sat in the warm, bright sun, a wonderful change came over it. It grew strong and firm; the most lovely colours began to show on its body, blue and yellow and black, spots and bars and rings; out of its back rose four great wings of bright brown gauze; and its eyes grew so large that they filled all its head, and shone like ten thousand diamonds.

"Oh, you beautiful creature!" said Tom; and he put out his hand to catch it. But the thing whirred up into the air, and hung poised on its wings a moment, and then settled down again by Tom quite fearless.

"No!" it said, "you cannot catch me. I am a dragon-fly now, the king of all the flies; and I shall dance in the sunshine, and hawk over the river, and catch gnats, and have a beautiful wife like myself." And he flew away into the air, and began catching gnats.

"Oh, come back, come back," cried Tom. "I have no one to play with, and I am so lonely here. If you will but come back I will never try to catch you."

"I don't care whether you do or not," said the dragon-fly; "for you can't. But when I have had my dinner, and looked a little about this pretty place, I will come back, and have a little chat about all I have seen in my travels. Why, what a huge tree this is! and what huge leaves on it!"

It was only a big dock; but you know the dragon-fly had never seen any but little water-trees; so it did look very big to him. The dragon-fly did come back, and chatted away to Tom. He was very fond of talking about all the wonderful things he saw in the trees and meadows; and Tom liked to listen to him, for he had forgotten all about them. So, in a little while, they became great friends. I am very glad to say that Tom learned such a lesson that day, that he did not torment creatures for a long time after.

He was basking at the top of the water one hot day in July, when he saw a dark gray little fellow with a brown head. He was a very little fellow indeed; but he made the most of himself, as people ought to do. Instead of getting away, he hopped upon Tom's finger, and cried out in the tiniest, shrillest, squeakiest little voice you ever heard:

"Much obliged to you, indeed; but I don't want it yet."

"Want what?" said Tom, quite taken aback by his impudence.

"Your leg, which you are kind enough to hold out for me to sit on. I must go and see after my wife for a few minutes. Dear me! what a troublesome business a family is! When I come back, I shall be glad of it, if you'll be so good as to keep it sticking out just so;" and off he flew.

Tom thought him a very cool sort of personage; and still more so, when, in five minutes, he came back, and said, "Ah, you were tired waiting! Well, your other leg will do as well."

And he popped himself down on Tom's knee, and began chatting away in his squeaking voice.

"So you live under water? It's a low place. I lived there for some time, and was very shabby and dirty. But I didn't choose that that should last. So I turned respectable, and came up to the top, and put on this gray suit. It's a very business-like suit, I think, don't you?"

"Very neat and quiet indeed," said Tom.

"Yes, one must be quiet and neat and respectable, and all that sort of thing, when one becomes a family man. But I'm tired of it, that's the truth. I've done quite enough business in the last week, to last me my life. So I shall put on a ball dress, and go out and be a smart man, and see the gay world, and have a dance or two. Why shouldn't one be jolly if one can?"

And, as he spoke, he turned quite pale, and then quite white.

"Why, you're ill!" said Tom. But he did not answer.

"You're dead," said Tom, looking at him as he stood on his knee as white as a ghost.

"No, I ain't!" answered a little squeaking voice over his head. "This is me up here, in my ball dress; and that's my skin. Ha! ha! Ain't I a pretty fellow now?"

And so he was; for his body was white, and his tail orange, and his eyes all the colours of a peacock's tail. And the whisks at the end of his tail had grown five times as long as they were before.

"Ah!" said he, "now I shall see the gay world." He began flirting and flipping up and down, and singing:

"My wife shall dance, and I shall sing,
　　So merrily pass the day;
For I hold it for quite the wisest thing,
　　To drive dull care away."

He danced up and down for three days and three nights, till he grew so tired that he tumbled into the water, and floated down. But what became of him Tom never knew, and he himself never minded; for Tom heard him singing to the last, as he floated down:

"To drive dull care away-ay-ay!"

One day Tom had a new adventure. He was sitting on a water-lily leaf, he and his friend the dragonfly, watching the gnats dance. The dragonfly had eaten as many as he wanted, and was sitting quite still and sleepy, for it was very hot and bright.

Suddenly, Tom heard the strangest noise up the stream; cooing and grunting, and whining and squeaking, as if you had put into a bag two stock-doves, nine mice, three guinea-pigs, and a blind puppy, and left them there to settle themselves and make music.

He looked up the water, and there he saw a sight as strange as the noise; a great ball rolling over and over down the stream, seeming one moment of soft brown fur, and the next of shining glass: and yet it was not a ball; for sometimes it broke up and streamed away in pieces, and then it joined again.

Tom asked the dragonfly what it could be; but, of course, with his short sight, he could not even see it, though it was not ten yards away. So he took the neatest little header into the water, and started off to see for himself; and, when he came near, the ball turned out to be four or five beautiful creatures, many times larger than Tom, who were swimming about, and rolling, and diving, and twisting, and wrestling, and cuddling, and kissing, and biting, and scratching, in the most charming fashion that ever was seen.

But, when the biggest of them saw Tom, she darted out from the rest, and cried in the water-language, sharply enough, "Quick, children, here is something to eat, indeed!" and came at poor Tom, showing such a wicked pair of eyes, and such a set of sharp teeth in a grinning mouth, that Tom slipped in between the water-lily roots as fast as he could, and then turned round and made faces at her.

"Come out," said the wicked old otter, "or it will be worse for you."

But Tom looked at her from between two thick roots, and shook them with all his might, making horrible faces all the while.

"Come away, children," said the otter in disgust, "it is not worth eating, after all. It is only a nasty eft, which nothing eats, not even those vulgar pike in the pond."

"I am not an eft!" said Tom; "efts have tails."

"You are an eft," said the otter, very positively; "I see your two hands quite plain, and I know you have a tail."

"I tell you I have not," said Tom.

"I say you are an eft, and therefore you are, and not fit for gentlefolk like me and my children. You may stay here till the salmon eat you "(she knew the salmon would not, but she wanted to frighten poor Tom). "Ha! ha! they will eat you, and we will eat them;" and the otter laughed a wicked, cruel laugh.

"What are salmon?" asked Tom.

"Fish, you eft, great fish, nice fish to eat. They are lords of the fish, and we are lords of the salmon;" and she laughed again. "We hunt them up and down the pools, and drive them up into a corner, the silly things; and we catch them, and then throw them away, and go and catch another. They are coming soon, children, coming soon; I can smell the rain coming up off the sea, and then hurrah for the salmon, and plenty of eating all day long."

"Where do they come from?" asked Tom, who kept himself very close, for he was considerably frightened.

"Out of the sea, eft, the great wide sea, where they might stay and be safe if they liked. But out of the sea the silly things come, into the great river down below, and we come up to watch them; and when they go down again, we go down and follow them. And there we fish for the bass and the pollock, and have jolly days along the shore, and toss and roll in the breakers, and sleep snug in warm, dry crags. Ah, that is a merry life, too, children, if it were not for those horrid men."

"What are men?" asked Tom; but somehow he seemed to know before he asked.

"Two-legged things, eft; and, now I come to look at you, they are actually something like you, if you had not a tail " (she was determined that Tom should have a tail), "only a great deal bigger, worse luck for us."

Tom could not help thinking of what the otter had said about the great river and the broad sea. He could not tell why; but the more he thought, the more he grew discontented with the narrow little stream in which he lived, and all his companions there; and wanted to get out into the wide, wide world, and enjoy all the wonderful sights of which he was sure it was full.

Once he had set off to go down the stream, but the stream was very low; and when he came to the shallows he could not keep under water, for there was no water left to keep under. So the sun burned his back and made him sick; and he went back again, and lay quiet in the pool for a whole week more.

Then, on the evening of a very hot day, he saw a sight. He had been very stupid all day, and so had the trout; for they would not move an inch to take a fly, though there were thousands on the water, but lay dozing at the bottom under the shade of the stones; and Tom lay dozing too, and was glad to cuddle their smooth, cool sides, for the water was quite warm and unpleasant. But, toward evening, it grew suddenly dark, and Tom looked up and saw a blanket of black clouds lying right across the valley above his head. There was not a whisper of wind, nor a chirp of a bird to be heard; and next a few great drops of rain fell plop into the water, and one hit Tom on the nose, and made him pop his head down quickly enough.

Then the thunder roared, and the lightning flashed, and leaped from cliff to cliff, till the very rocks in the stream seemed to shake; and Tom looked up at it through the water, and thought it the finest thing he ever saw in his life. Then rain came down by bucketfuls, and the hail hammered like shot on the stream, and churned it into foam; and soon the stream rose, and rushed down, higher and higher.

And now, by the flashes of the lightning, Tom saw a new sight—all the bottom of the stream alive with great eels, turning and twisting along, all down the stream and away. And he could hear them say to each other, "We must run, we must run. What a jolly thunderstorm! Down to the sea, down to the sea!"

Then the otter came by with all her brood, twining and sweeping along as fast as the eels themselves; and she spied Tom as she came by, and said: "Now is your time, eft, if you want to see the world. Come along, children, never mind those nasty eels; we shall breakfast on salmon to-morrow. Down to the sea, down to the sea!"

Them came a flash brighter than all the rest, and by the light of it—in the thousandth part of a second they were gone again—three beautiful little white girls, with their arms twined round each other's necks, floating down the torrent, as they sang, "Down to the sea, down to the sea!"

"Down to the sea?" said Tom; "everything is going to the sea, and I will go too. Good-bye, trout." But the trout were so busy gobbling worms that they never turned to answer him.

When the daylight came, Tom found himself out in the salmon river. And there he stopped. He got a little frightened. "This must be the sea," he thought. "What a wide place it is! If I go on into it I shall surely lose my way, or some strange thing will bite me. I will stop here and look out for the otter, or the eels, or some one to tell me where I shall go."

Then he waited, and slept, too, for he was quite tired with his night's journey; and, when he woke, he saw a sight which made him jump up. Such a fish! ten times as big as the

*Three beautiful little white girls floated down the torrent.*

biggest trout, and a hundred times as big as Tom, sculling up the stream past him, as easily as Tom had sculled down.

Such a fish ! shining silver from head to tail, and here and there a crimson dot ; with a grand hooked nose and grand curling lip, and a grand bright eye, surveying the water, right and left, as if all belonged to him. Surely he must be the salmon, the king of all the fish. The salmon looked at him full in the face, and then went on without minding him, with a swish of two of his tail, which made the stream boil again. And, in a few minutes, came another, and then four or five, and so on ; and all passed Tom, rushing and plunging up the cataract with strong strokes of their silver tails, now and then leaping clean out of the water and up over a rock, shining gloriously, for a moment, in the bright sun ; while Tom was so delighted that he could have watched them all day long.

At last came up one bigger than all the rest ; but he came slowly, and stopped, and looked back, and seemed very anxious and busy. Tom saw that he was helping another salmon, an especially handsome one, who had not a single spot upon it, but was clothed in pure silver from nose to tail.

" My dear," said the great fish to his companion, " you really look dreadfully tired, and you must not over-exert yourself at first. Do rest yourself behind this rock ; " and he shoved her gently with his nose to the rock where Tom sat. Then he saw Tom, and looked at him very fiercely, one moment, as if he were going to bite him.

" What do you want here ? " he said fiercely.

" Oh, don't hurt me ! " cried Tom. " I only want to look at you ; you are so handsome."

" Ah ! " said the salmon, very stately but very civilly. " I really beg your pardon ; I see what you are, my little dear. I have met one or two creatures like you before, and found them very agreeable and well-behaved. Indeed, one of them showed me a great kindness lately, which I hope to be able to repay. I hope we shall not be in your way here. As soon as this lady is rested, we shall proceed on our journey."

What a well-bred old salmon he was !

" So you have seen things like me before ? " asked Tom.

" Several times, my dear. Indeed, it was only last night that one at the river's mouth came and warned me and my wife of some new stake-nets which had got into the stream, and showed us the way round them, in the most charmingly obliging way."

" So there are babies in the sea ? " cried Tom, and clapped his little hands.

" Were there no babies up this stream ? " asked the lady salmon.

" No ! and I grew so lonely, for I had nothing to play with but caddises and dragon-flies and trout."

" Ugh ! " cried the lady, " what low company ! "

" My dear, if he has been in low company, he has certainly not learned their low manners," said the salmon.

" No, indeed, poor little dear ; but how sad for him to live among such people as caddises ! "

## CHAPTER IV

So the salmon went up, after Tom had warned them of the wicked old otter ; and Tom went down, but slowly and cautiously, coasting along the shore. He was many days about it, for it was many miles down to the sea ; and perhaps he would never have found his way, if the fairies had not guided him, without his seeing their fair faces, or feeling their gentle hands.

And, as he went, he had a very strange adventure. It was a clear, still September night, and the moon shone so brightly down through the water that he could not sleep. At last he came up to the top, and sat upon a little point of rock. And suddenly he saw a beautiful sight. A bright, red light moved along the riverside, and threw down into the water a long tap-root of flame. Tom must needs go and see what it was ; so he swam to the shore, and met the light as it stopped over a shallow run at the edge of a low rock.

There, underneath the light, lay five or six large salmon, looking up at the flame with their great goggle eyes, and wagging their tails, as if they were very much pleased with it. Tom came to the top, to look at this wonderful light nearer, and he saw on the bank three great two-legged creatures, one of whom held the light, flaring and spluttering, and another a long pole. He knew that they were men, and was frightened, and crept into a hole in the rock, from which he could see what went on.

The man with the torch bent down over the water, and, looking earnestly in, said :

" Tak' that muckle fellow, lad ; he's ower fiteen punds ; and haud your hand steady."

Tom felt that there was some danger coming, and longed to warn the foolish salmon, who kept staring up at the light as if he was bewitched. But, before he could make up his mind, down came the pole through the water ; there was a fearful splash and struggle, and Tom saw that the poor salmon was speared right through, and was lifted out of the water.

Then, from behind, there sprang on these three men three other men ; and there were shouts, and blows, and words that Tom recollected to have heard before ; and he shuddered and turned sick at them now, for he felt somehow that they were strange, and ugly, and wrong, and horrible. And it all began to come back to him. They were men, and they were fighting ; savage, desperate, up-and-down fighting, such as Tom had seen too many times before.

All of a sudden there was a tremendous splash, and a frightful flash, and a hissing, and all was still. For into the water, close to Tom, fell one of the men ; he who held the light in his hand. Tom heard the men above run along, seemingly looking for him ; but he drifted down into the deep hole below, and there lay quite still, and they could not find him.

Tom waited a long time, till all was quiet, and then he peeped out, and saw the man lying. " Perhaps," he thought, " the water has made him fall asleep, as it did me." He grew more and more curious, he could not tell why. He must go and look at him. He would go very quietly, of course ;

so he swam round and round him, closer and closer; and, as he did not stir, at last he came quite close and looked him in the face. The moon shone so bright that Tom could see every feature; and, as he saw, he recollected, bit by bit, that it was his old master, Grimes. Tom turned tail, and swam away as fast as he could.

"Oh, dear me!" he thought, "now he will turn into a water-baby. What a nasty, troublesome one he will be! And, perhaps, he will find me out and beat me again."

And, for a long time, he was fearful lest he should meet Mr. Grimes, suddenly, in some deep pool. He could not know that the fairies had carried him away, and put him, where they put everything which falls into the water, exactly where it ought to be. Then Tom went on down the stream, till he saw, a long way off, a red buoy through the fog. And then he found, to his surprise, the stream turned round, and running up inland.

It was the tide, of course; but Tom knew nothing of the tide. He only knew that in a minute more the water, which had been fresh, turned salt all round him. And then there came a change over him. He felt strong, and light, and fresh, and gave, he did not know why, three skips out of the water, a yard high, and head over heels, just as the salmon do when they first touch the noble, rich salt water.

He did not care now for the tide being against him. The red buoy was in sight, dancing in the open sea; and to the buoy he would go, and to it he went. He passed great shoals of bass and mullet, leaping and rushing in after the shrimps; and once he passed a great black shining seal, who was coming in after the mullet. The seal put his head and shoulders out of the water, and stared at him, and Tom, instead of being frightened, said, "How d'ye do, sir; what a beautiful place the sea is!" And the old seal, instead of trying to bite him, looked at him with his soft, sleepy, winking eyes, and said, "Good tide to you, my little man; are you looking for your brothers and sisters? I passed them all outside."

"Oh, then," said Tom, "I shall have playfellows at last," and he swam on to the buoy, and got upon it (for he was quite out of breath) and sat there, and looked round for water-babies; but there were none to be seen. Then he began to ask all the strange things which came in and out of the sea if they had seen any water-babies; and some said "Yes," and some said nothing at all.

But, one day, among the rocks, he found a playfellow. It was not a water-baby, alas! but it was a lobster; and a very distinguished lobster he was. Tom had never seen a lobster before; and was mightily taken with this one; for he thought this the most curious, odd, ridiculous creature he had ever seen. He had one claw knobbed and the other jagged; and Tom was delighted in watching him hold on to the seaweed with his knobbed claw, while he cut up salads with his jagged one, and then put them into his mouth, after smelling at them, like a monkey.

But Tom was most astonished to see how he fired himself off—snap! like the leap-frogs which you make out of a goose's breast-bone. Certainly he took the most wonderful shots, and backward, too. For if he wanted to go into a narrow crack, ten yards off, what do you think he did? If he had gone in head foremost, of course he could not have turned round. So

*"But it was a water-baby and I heard it speak,"* cried Ellie.

he used to turn his tail to it, and lay his long horns straight down his back to guide him, and twist his eyes back till they almost came out of their sockets, and then made ready, present! fire! snap! and away he went, pop into the hole; and peeped out, and twiddled his whiskers, as much as to say, "You couldn't do that!"

Tom asked him about water-babies. "Yes," he said. He had seen them often. But he did not think much of them. They were meddlesome little creatures, that went along helping fish and shells which got into scrapes. For his part, he should be ashamed to be helped by little soft creatures that had not even a shell on their backs.

He was a conceited fellow, the old lobster, and not very civil to Tom; and you will hear how he had to alter his mind before he was done, as conceited people generally have. But he was so funny, and Tom so lonely, that he could not quarrel with him; and they used to sit in holes in the rocks, and chat for hours.

And, about this time, there happened to Tom a very strange and important adventure—so important, indeed, that he was very near never finding the water-babies at all.

I hope that you have not forgotten the little white lady all this while. At least, here she comes, looking like a clean, white, good little darling, as she always was, and always will be. For it befell in the pleasant short December days, when the wind always blows from the south-west, that Sir John was so busy hunting, that nobody at home could get a word out of him, so My Lady determined to leave him, and started for the seaside with all her children.

Now, it befell that, on the very shore, and over the very rocks where Tom was sitting with his friend the lobster, there walked one day the little white lady, Ellie herself, and with her a very wise man indeed—Professor Ptthmllnsprts. Ellie and he were walking on the rocks, and he was showing her about one in ten thousand of all the beautiful and curious things which are to be seen there. But little Ellie was not satisfied with them at all; and at last she said honestly, "I don't care about all these things, because they can't play with me, or talk to me. If there were little children now in the water, as there used to be, and I could see them, I should like that. I know there used to be children in the water, and mermaids too, and mermen. I saw them all in a picture at home, of a beautiful lady sailing in a car drawn by dolphins, and babies flying round her, and one sitting on her lap ; and the mermaids swimming and playing, and the mermen trumpeting on conch shells."

But the professor had not the least notion of allowing that things were true, merely because people thought them beautiful.

Just then, groping with his net under the weeds, he caught poor little Tom. He felt the net very heavy ; and lifted it out quickly, with Tom all entangled in the meshes.

" It is a water-baby ! " cried Ellie ; and, of course, it was.

" Water-fiddlesticks, my dear ! " said the professor ; and he turned away and poked Tom with his finger, for want of anything better to do. " You must have dreamed of water-babies last night, your head is so full of them."

Now Tom had been in the most horrible and unspeakable fright all the while, and had kept as quiet as he could. But, when the professor poked him, it was more than he could bear ; and, between fright and rage, he bit the professor's finger till it bled.

" Oh ! ah ! yah ! " he cried ; and dropped him on to the seaweed, and thence he dived into the water, and was gone in a moment.

" But it was a water-baby, and I heard it speak ! " cried Ellie. " Ah, it is gone ! " And she jumped down off the rock, to try and catch Tom before he slipped into the sea.

Too late, and, what was worse, as she sprang down, she slipped, and fell some six feet, with her head on a sharp stone. The professor picked her up, and tried to waken her, and called to her, and cried over her, for he loved her very much : but she would not waken at all. So he took her up in his arms and carried her to her governess, and they all went home ; and little Ellie was put to bed, and lay there quite still ; only now and then she woke up and called out about the water-baby.

And, after a week, one moonlight night, the fairies came flying in at the window and brought her such a pretty pair of wings that she could not help putting them on ; and she flew with them out of the window, and over the land and over the sea, and up through the clouds, and nobody heard or saw anything of her for a very long while.


CHAPTER V

BUT what became of little Tom ?

He slipped away off the rocks into the water, as I said before. But he could not help thinking of little Ellie. He thought about her all that day, and longed to have had her to play with ; but he had very soon to think of something else. He was going along the rocks in three-fathom water, when he saw a round cage of green withes ; and inside it, looking very much ashamed of himself, sat his friend the lobster, twiddling his horns.

"What! have you been naughty, and have they put you in the lock-up?" asked Tom.

The lobster felt a little indignant at such a notion, but he was too much depressed in spirits to argue; so he only said, "I can't get out."

"Why did you get in?"

"After that nasty piece of dead fish." He had thought it looked and smelled very nice when he was outside, and so it did, for a lobster; but now he turned round and abused it because he was angry with himself.

"Where did you get in?"

"Through that round hole at the top."

"Then why don't you get through it?"

"Because I can't! I have jumped upward, downward, backward, and sideways, at least four thousand times; and I can't get out: I always get up there, and can't find the hole."

Tom looked at the trap, and having more wit than the lobster, he saw plainly enough what was the matter; as you may if you will look at a lobster-pot.

"Stop a bit," said Tom. "Turn your tail up to me, and I'll pull you through hindforemost, and then you won't stick in the spikes." Tom reached and clawed down the hole after him, till he caught hold of him; and then, as was to be expected, the clumsy lobster pulled him in head foremost.

"Hallo! here is a pretty business," said Tom. "Now take your great claws, and break the points off those spikes, and then we shall both get out easily."

"Dear me, I never thought of that," said the lobster; "and after all the experience of life that I have had!"

But they had not got half the spikes away when they saw a great dark cloud over them; and, lo and behold, it was the otter! How she did grin and grin when she saw Tom. "Yar!" said she, "you little meddlesome wretch, I have you now! I will serve you out for telling the salmon where I was!" And she crawled all over the pot to get in. Tom was horribly frightened, and still more frightened when she found the hole in the top, and squeezed herself right down through it, all eyes and teeth. But no sooner was her head inside than valiant Mr. Lobster caught her by the nose and held on.

And there they were all three in the pot, rolling over and over, and very tight packing it was. And the lobster tore at the otter, and the otter at the lobster, and both squeezed and thumped poor Tom till he had no breath left in his body; and I don't know what would have happened to him if he had not at last got on the otter's back, and safe out of the hole.

He was right glad when he got out; but he would not desert his friend who had saved him; and the first time he saw his tail uppermost he caught hold of it, and pulled with all his might. But the lobster would not let go.

"Come along," said Tom; "don't you see she is dead?" And so she was, quite drowned and dead.

"Come along, you stupid old stick-in-the-mud," cried Tom, "or the fisherman will catch you!"

But the lobster would not let go.

*The clumsy lobster pulled him in head foremost.*

Tom saw the fisherman haul him up the boat-side, and thought it was all up with him. But when Mr. Lobster saw the fisherman, he gave such a furious and tremendous snap, that he snapped out of his hand, and out of the pot, and safe into the sea. But he left his knobbed claw behind him; for it never came into his stupid head to let go after all, so he just shook his claw off as the easier method.

And now happened to Tom a most wonderful thing, for he had not left the lobster five minutes before he came upon a water-baby. A real live water-baby, sitting on the white sand, very busy about a little point of rock. And when it saw Tom it looked up for a moment, and then cried, "Why, you are not one of us. You are a new baby! Oh, how delightful!"

And it ran to Tom, and Tom ran to it, and they hugged and kissed each other for ever so long. At last Tom said, "Oh, where have you been all this while? I have been looking for you so long, and I have been so lonely."

"We have been here for days and days. There are hundreds of us about the rocks. How was it you did not see us, or hear us, when we sing and romp every evening, before we go home?"

Tom looked at the baby again, and then he said:

"Well, this is wonderful! I have seen things just like you again and again, but I thought you were shells, or sea-creatures. I never took you for water-babies like myself."

"Now," said the baby, "come and help me at this poor, dear little rock; a great clumsy boulder came rolling by in the last storm, and knocked all its head off, and rubbed off all its flowers. And now I must plant it again with seaweeds, and coralline, and anemones."

So they worked away at the rock, and planted it, and smoothed the sand down round it, and capital fun they had till the tide began to turn. And then Tom heard all the other babies coming laughing and singing and shouting and romping; and the noise they made was just like the noise of the ripple.

In they came, dozens and dozens of them, some bigger than Tom, and some smaller, all in the neatest little white bathing dresses; and when they found that he was a new baby, they hugged him and kissed him and danced round him, and there was no one ever so happy as poor little Tom.

"Now then," they cried all at once, "we must come away home, or the tide will leave us dry. We have mended all the broken seaweed, and put all the rock-pools in order, and planted all the shells again in the sand, and nobody will see where the ugly storm swept in last week."

And this is the reason why the rock-pools are always so neat and clean; because the water-babies come inshore after every storm to sweep them out, and put them all to rights again. And where is the home of the water-babies? In St. Brandan's fairy isle.

Now when Tom got there, he found that the isle stood all on pillars, and that its roots were full of caves; all curtained and draped with seaweeds, purple and crimson, green and brown; and strewn with soft white sand, on which the water-babies sleep every night. There were water-babies in thousands, more than Tom, or you either, could count.

But I wish Tom had given up all his naughty tricks, and left off tormenting dumb animals now that he had plenty of playfellows to amuse him. Instead of that, I am sorry to say, he tickled the madrepores, to make them shut up; and frightened the crabs, to make them hide in the sand and peep out at him with the tips of their eyes; and put stones into the anemones' mouths, to make them fancy that their dinner was coming. The other children warned him, and said, "Take care what you are at. Mrs. Bedonebyasyoudid is coming." But Tom never heeded them, being quite riotous with high spirits and good luck, till, one Friday morning early, Mrs. Bedonebyasyoudid came.

A very tremendous lady she was; and when the children saw her they all stood in a row, very upright indeed, and smoothed down their bathing dresses, and put their hands behind them, just as if they were going to be examined by the inspector. She had on a

*They put him in the middle and danced round him.*

black bonnet, and a black shawl, and a pair of large spectacles, and a great hooked nose, hooked so much that the bridge of it stood quite up above her eyebrows; and under her arm she carried a great birch-rod. Indeed, she was so ugly that Tom was tempted to make faces at her; but he did not; for he did not admire the look of the birch-rod under her arm.

She looked at the children one by one, and seemed very much pleased with them, though she never asked them one question about how they were behaving; and then began giving them all sorts of nice sea-things; sea-cakes, sea-apples, sea-bullseyes, sea-toffee; and to the very best of all she gave sea-ices, made out of sea-cows' cream, which never melt under water.

Now little Tom watched all these sweet things given away, till his mouth watered, and his eyes grew as round as an owl's. For he hoped that his turn would come at last; and so it did. For the lady called him up, and held out her fingers with something in them, and popped it into his mouth; and, lo and behold, it was a nasty, cold, hard pebble.

" You are a very cruel woman," said he, and began to whimper.

" And you are a very cruel boy; who puts pebbles into the sea-anemones' mouths, to take them in, and make them fancy that they had caught a good dinner! As you did to them, so I must do to you."

" Who told you that? " said Tom.

" You did yourself, this very minute."

Tom had never opened his lips; so he was very much taken aback indeed.

" Now go, and be a good boy, and I will put no more pebbles in your mouth, if you put none in other creatures'."

" I did not know there was any harm in it," said Tom.

" If you do not know that things are wrong, that is no reason why you should not be punished for them; though not as much, not as much, my little man " (and the lady looked very kindly, after all), " as if you did know."

Then the strange fairy smiled, and said:

" Yes. You thought me very ugly just now, did you not? "

Tom hung down his head, and got very red about the ears.

" And I am very ugly. I am the ugliest fairy in the world; and I shall be, till people behave themselves as they ought to do. And then I shall grow as handsome as my sister, who is the loveliest fairy in the world; and her name is Mrs. Doasyouwouldbedoneby. And now do you be a good boy, and do as you would be done by; and then, when my sister comes on Sunday, perhaps she will take notice of you, and teach you how to behave."

Tom determined to be a very good boy all Saturday; and he was; and when Sunday morning came, sure enough, Mrs. Doasyouwouldbedoneby came too. I cannot tell you what the colour of her hair was, or of her eyes; no more could Tom; for, when any one looks at her, all they can think of is, that she has the sweetest, kindest, tenderest, merriest face they ever saw, or want to see. When the children saw her, they climbed into her lap, and clung round her neck, and caught hold of her hands; and those who could get nowhere else sat down on the sand, and cuddled her feet, and Tom stood staring at them.

" And who are you, you little darling? " she said.

" Oh, that is the new baby! " they all cried, pulling their thumbs out of their mouths; "and he never had any mother," and they all put their thumbs back again.

"Then I will be his mother, and he shall have the very best place; so get out, all of you, this moment."

She took Tom in her arms, and laid him in the softest place of all, and kissed him, and patted him, and talked to him tenderly and low; and Tom looked up into her eyes, and loved her, and loved, till he fell fast asleep. When he woke, the lady was nursing him still.

"Don't go away," he said. "This is so nice. I never had any one to cuddle me before."

"You have not sung us one song," said the children.

"Well, I have time for only one. So what shall it be?"

"The doll you lost!" cried all the babies at once.

So the strange fairy sang:

*Lo and behold, it was a nasty, cold, hard pebble.*

"I once had a sweet little doll, dears,
　　The prettiest doll in the world;
Her cheeks were so red and so white, dears,
　　And her hair was so charmingly curled.
But I lost my poor little doll, dears,
　　As I played in the heath one day;
And I cried for her more than a week, dears,
　　But I never could find where she lay.

"I found my poor little doll, dears,
　　As I played in the heath one day;
Folks say she is terribly changed, dears,
　　For her paint is all washed away.
And her arm trodden off by the cows, dears,
　　And her hair not the least bit curled;
Yet, for old sakes' sake she is still, dears,
　　The prettiest doll in the world."

"Now," said the fairy to Tom, "will you be a good boy and torment no more sea-beasts till I come back?"

"And you will cuddle me again?" said poor little Tom.

"Of course I will, you little duck."

So Tom really tried to be a good boy, and tormented no sea-beasts after that as long as he lived; and he is quite alive, I assure you, still.

## CHAPTER VI

Now you may fancy that Tom was good, when he had everything that he could want or wish, but you would be very much mistaken. For he grew so fond of the sea-bullseyes and sea-lollipops, that his foolish head could think of nothing else; and he was always longing for more, and wondering when the strange lady would come again and give him some.

Then he began to watch the lady to see where she kept the sweet things; and began hiding, and sneaking, and following her about, and pretending to be looking the other way, till he found out that she kept them in a beautiful mother-of-pearl cabinet, away in a deep crack of the rocks.

He longed to go to the cabinet, and yet he was afraid; and then he longed again and was less afraid; and at last, by continual thinking about it, he longed so violently that he was not afraid at all. One night, when all the other children were asleep, and he could not sleep for thinking of lollipops, he crept away among the rocks, and got to the cabinet, and behold! it was open.

But, when he saw all the nice things inside, instead of being delighted, he was quite frightened, and wished he had never come there. And then he would only touch them, and he did; and then he would only taste one, and he did; and then he would only eat two, and then three, and so on, and then he was terrified lest she would come and catch him, and began gobbling them down so fast that he did not taste them, or have any pleasure in them; and then he felt sick, and would have only one more; and then only one more again; and so on till he had eaten them all up.

And all the while, close behind him, stood Mrs. Bedonebyasyoudid. She took off her spectacles, because she did not like to see too much; and in her pity she arched up her eyebrows into her very hair, and her eyes grew so wide that they would have taken in all the sorrows of the world, and filled with great big tears, as they too often do.

She said nothing at all about the matter, not even when Tom came next day with the rest for sweet things. He was horribly afraid of coming; but he was still more afraid of staying away, lest any one should suspect him. He was dreadfully afraid, too, lest there should be no sweets, and lest then the fairy should inquire who had taken them. But, behold! she pulled out just as many as ever, which astonished Tom, and frightened him still more.

And, when the fairy looked him full in the face, he shook from head to foot; however, she gave him his share like the rest, and he thought, within himself, that she could not have found him out. But when he put the sweets into his mouth, they made him so sick that he had to get away as fast as he could. Then, when next week came, he had his share again; and again the fairy looked him full in the face; but more sadly than she had ever looked. And when Mrs. Doasyouwouldbedoneby came, he wanted to be cuddled like the rest; but she said very seriously:

"I should like to cuddle you; but I cannot, you are so horny and prickly."

Tom looked at himself, and he was all over prickles, just like a sea-egg.

What could Tom do now but go away and hide in a corner and cry? For nobody would play with him, and he knew full well why. And he was so miserable all that week that when the ugly fairy came and looked at him once more full in the face, he could stand it no longer, and thrust the sweetmeats away, saying, "No, I don't want any; I can't bear them now," and then burst out crying, poor little man, and told Mrs. Bedonebyasyoudid every word as it happened.

He was horribly frightened when he had done so; for he expected her to punish him very severely. But instead, she only took him up and kissed him, which was not quite pleasant, for her chin was very bristly indeed; but he was so lonely-hearted, he thought that rough kissing was better than none.

"I will forgive you, little man," she said. "I always forgive every one the moment they tell me the truth of their own accord."

"Then you will take away all these nasty prickles?"

"That is a different matter. You put them there yourself, and only you can take them away; so I shall fetch you a schoolmistress, who will teach you how to get rid of your prickles." And so she went away.

Tom was frightened at the notion of a schoolmistress; but he comforted himself at last that she might be something like the old woman in Vendale—which she was not in the least; for, when the fairy brought her, she was the most beautiful little girl that ever was seen, with long curls floating behind her like a golden cloud, and robes floating all round her like a silver one.

*Poor Tom burst out crying.*

"There he is," said the fairy; "and you must teach him to be good, whether you like or not."

"I know," said the little girl; but she did not seem quite to like, for she put her finger in her mouth, and looked at Tom under her brows; and Tom put his finger in his mouth, and looked at her under his brows, for he was horribly ashamed of himself.

The little girl seemed hardly to know how to begin; and perhaps she would never have begun at all if poor Tom had not burst out crying, and begged her to teach him to be good, and help him to cure his prickles; and at that she grew so tender-hearted that she began teaching him as prettily as ever child was taught in the world.

She taught Tom every day in the week; only on Sundays she always went away home, and the kind fairy took her place. And before she had taught Tom many Sundays, his prickles had vanished quite away, and his skin was smooth and clean again.

"Dear me!" said the little girl: "why, I know you now. You are the very same little chimney-sweep who came into my bedroom."

"Dear me!" cried Tom. "And I know you, too, now. You are the very little white lady whom I saw in bed." And he jumped round and round her till he was quite tired.

Then they began telling each other all their story—how he had got into the water, and she had fallen over the rock; and how he had swum down to the sea, and how she had flown out of the window; and how this, that, and the other, till it was talked out; and then they both began over again, and I can't say which of the two talked fastest. Then they set to work at their lessons again, and both liked them so well that they went on till seven full years were past.

You may fancy that Tom was quite content and happy all these seven years; but the truth is, he was not. He had always one thing on his mind, and that was—where little Ellie went, when she went home on Sundays. To a very beautiful place, she said. But what was the beautiful place like, and where was it? All that good little Ellie could say was, that it was worth all the rest of the world put together. And of course that only made Tom all the more anxious to go likewise.

"Miss Ellie," he said at last, "I will know why I cannot go with you when you go home on Sundays, or I shall not have peace, and give you none either."

"You must ask the fairies that."

So when the fairy, Mrs. Bedonebyasyoudid, came next, Tom asked her.

"Little boys who are only fit to play with sea-beasts cannot go there," she said. "Those who go there must go first where they do not like, and do what they do not like, and help somebody they do not like."

"Why, did Ellie do that?"

"Ask her."

And Ellie blushed, and said, "Yes, Tom, I did not like coming here at first; I was so much happier at home, where it is always Sunday. And I was afraid of you, Tom, at first, because—because——"

"Because I was all over prickles? But I am not prickly now, am I, Miss Ellie?"

"No," said Ellie. "I like you very much now; and I like coming here, too."

"And perhaps," said the fairy, "you will learn to like going where you don't like, as Ellie has."

But Tom put his finger in his mouth, and hung his head down; for he did not see that at all. And, when Ellie went home on Sunday, he fretted and cried all day, and did not care to listen to the fairy's stories about good children, though they were prettier than ever. All the while he was eaten up with curiosity to know where Ellie went; so that he began not to care for his playmates, or for the sea-places, or anything else.

"Well," he said, at last, "I am so miserable here, I'll go; if only you will go with me?"

"Ah!" said Ellie, "I wish I might; but the worst of it is, that the fairy says that you must go alone if you go at all. Now, don't poke that poor crab about, Tom" (for he was feeling very naughty and mischievous), "or the fairy will have to punish you."

"I know what she wants me to do," he said, whining most dolefully. "She wants me to go after that horrid old Grimes. And if I find him, he will turn me into a chimney-sweep again, I know. That's what I have been afraid of all along."

"No, he won't—I know as much as that. Nobody can turn water-babies into sweeps, or hurt them at all, as long as they are good."

"Ah," said naughty Tom, "I see what you want; you are persuading me all along to go, because you are tired of me."

Little Ellie opened her eyes very wide at that, and then she cried, "Oh, Tom, where are you?"

And Tom cried, "Oh, Ellie, where are you?"

For neither of them could see each other—not the least. Little Ellie vanished quite away. Who was frightened then but Tom? He swam up and down among the rocks, into all the halls and chambers, faster than ever he swam before, but could not find her. At last he went up to the top of the water and began crying and screaming for Mrs. Bedonebyasyoudid—which perhaps was the best thing to do—for she came in a moment.

"Oh!" said Tom. "Oh dear, oh dear! I have been naughty to Ellie, and I have killed her—I know I have killed her."

"Not quite that," said the fairy; "but I have sent her away home, and she will not come back again for I do not know how long."

"How cruel of you to send Ellie away!" sobbed Tom. "However, I will find her again, if I go to the world's end to look for her."

The fairy did not slap Tom, and tell him to hold his tongue; but she took him on her lap very kindly; just as her sister would have done. Then she told him how he had been in the nursery long enough, and must go out now and see the world, if he intended ever to be a man; and how he must go all alone by himself. At last she comforted poor little Tom so much that he was quite eager to go, and wanted to set out that minute. "Only," he said, "if I might see Ellie once before I went!"

"Why do you want that?"

"Because—because I should be so much happier if I thought she had forgiven me."

And in the twinkling of an eye there stood Ellie, smiling, and looking so happy that Tom longed to kiss her ; but was still afraid it would not be respectful.

" I am going, Ellie ! " said Tom.  " I am going, if it is to the world's end.  But I don't like going at all, and that's the truth."

" Pooh ! pooh ! pooh ! " said the fairy.  " You will like it very well indeed, you little rogue, and you know that at the bottom of your heart."

## CHAPTER VII

" Now," said Tom, " I am ready to be off, if it's to the world's end."

" Ah ! " said the fairy, " that is a brave, good boy.  But you must go farther than the world's end, if you want to find Mr. Grimes ; for he is at the Other-end-of-Nowhere.  You must go to Shiny Wall, and through the white gate that never was opened."

" Oh, dear ! " said Tom.  " But I do not know my way to Shiny Wall."

" Little boys must take the trouble to find out things for themselves, or they will never grow to be men ; so that you must ask all the beasts in the sea and the birds in the air."

" Well," said Tom, " it will be a long journey, so I had better start at once.  Good-bye, Miss Ellie ; you know I am getting a big boy, and I must go out and see the world."

" I know you must," said Ellie ; " but you will not forget me, Tom. I shall wait here till you come."  And she shook hands with him, and bade him good-bye.  Then Tom set out, and swam a long, long way without getting tired.  One day he met a ship, far larger than he had ever seen— a gallant steamer, with a long cloud of smoke trailing behind ; and he wondered how she went on without sails, and swam up to her to see.  A lady came out, with a baby in her arms.  She leaned over the quarter gallery, looking down at the water ; and as she looked she sang :

" Soft, soft wind, from out the sweet south sliding,
　　Waft thy silver cloud-webs athwart the summer seas ;
Thin, thin thread of mist on dewy fingers twining
　　Weave a veil of dappled gauze to shade my babe and me.

" Deep, deep Love, within thine own abyss abiding,
　　Pour Thyself abroad, O Lord, on earth and air and sea ;
Worn weary hearts within Thy holy temple hiding,
　　Shield from sorrow, sin, and shame, my helpless babe and me."

Her voice was so soft and low, and the music of the air so sweet, that Tom could have listened to it all day.  But, as she held the baby over the gallery rail, to show it the dolphins leaping and the water gurgling in the ship's wake, lo ! and behold, the baby saw Tom.  He was quite sure of that ; for when their eyes met, the baby smiled and held out his hands ;

and Tom smiled and held out his hands too; and the baby kicked and leaped, as if it wanted to jump overboard to him.

Then Tom swam northward again, day after day, till at last he met the King of the Herrings, and he asked him the way to Shiny Wall.

"If I were you, young gentleman, I should go to the Allalonestone, and ask the last of the Gairfowl."

Tom thanked him, and went onward for seven days and seven nights, until he saw the last of the Gairfowl, standing up on the Allalonestone. A very grand old lady she was, standing bolt upright, like some old Highland chieftainess. On her nose was a large pair of spectacles, and instead of wings she had two little feathery arms, with which she fanned herself.

Tom came up to her, and made his bow, and the first thing she said was, "Have you wings? Can you fly?"

"Oh, dear, no, ma'am; I should not think of such a thing," said cunning little Tom, who had seen that the old lady had no wings herself.

"Then I shall have great pleasure in talking to you, my dear. It is quite refreshing nowadays to see anything without wings." And she talked for a long while, until at last she got out of breath. Then Tom asked if she knew the way to Shiny Wall.

"Oh, you must go, my little dear—you must go. Let me see—I am sure—that is—really, my poor old brains are getting quite puzzled. Do you know, my little dear, I am afraid, if you want to know, you must ask some of these vulgar birds about, for I have quite forgotten."

But a flock of Mother Carey's Chickens came along. They were so pretty that Tom fell in love with them at once; and he asked them the way to Shiny Wall.

"Shiny Wall?" they whistled. "Do you want Shiny Wall? Then come with us, and we will show you."

A long, long way they went, skimming along over the crests of the foam, and they saw thousands of birds and many wonderful things. At last they found a ship that had been wrecked, and there, in a little cot, lay a baby fast asleep; the very same baby, Tom saw at once, which he had seen in the singing lady's arms. He went up to it, and wanted to wake it; but behold, from under the cot jumped a little black and tan terrier dog, and began barking and snapping at Tom, and would not let him touch the cot; and he and the dog fought and struggled, for he wanted to help the baby, and did not want to throw the dog overboard; but, as they were struggling, there came a tall green sea, and swept them all into the waves.

"Oh! the baby, the baby!" screamed Tom; but the next moment he saw the cot settling down through the green water with the baby, smiling on it, fast asleep; and he saw the fairies come up from below, and carry baby and cradle gently down in their soft arms; and then he knew it was all right, and that there would be a new water-baby in St. Brandan's Isle.

And the poor little dog? Why, after he had kicked and coughed a little, he sneezed so hard, that he sneezed himself clean out of his skin, and turned into a water dog, and jumped and danced round Tom, and ran over the crests of the waves, and snapped at the jelly-fish and mackerel, and followed Tom all the way.

At last they came to Shiny Wall, which was all made of ice. There was no gate, so Tom dived right under the wall, down to the bottom of the sea, where it was pitch dark. And yet he was not a bit frightened. Why should he be ?

At last he came up on the other side, and there he saw a white marble lady, sitting on a white marble throne. This was Mother Carey, and she told Tom the way to the Other-end-of-Nowhere. He and the dog went under the sea, a long, long way, and saw wonderful things, more wonderful than anything you can think of.

At last they came to the Other-end-of-Nowhere. Tom saw a great building before him, and he walked towards it, wondering what it was, and having a strange fancy that he might find Mr. Grimes inside it, till he saw, running toward him, and shouting " Stop ! " three or four people, who, when they came nearer, were nothing else than policemen's truncheons, running along without legs or arms. Tom was not astonished. Neither was he frightened, for he had been doing no harm.

So he stopped ; and, when the foremost truncheon came up and asked his business, he showed a letter from Mother Carey ; and the truncheon looked at it in the oddest fashion ; for he had one eye in the middle of his upper end, so that when he looked at anything, being quite stiff, he had to slope himself, and poke himself, till it was a wonder why he did not tumble over.

" All right—pass on," said he at last. And then he added : " I had better go with you, young man ; " so the truncheon coiled its thong neatly round its handle, to prevent tripping itself up—for the thong had got loose in running—and marched on by Tom's side.

" Why have you no policeman to carry you ? " asked Tom, after a while.

" Because we are not like those clumsy-made truncheons in the land-world, which cannot go without having a whole man to carry them about. We do our own work for ourselves."

" Then why have you got a thong to your handle ? " asked Tom.

" To hang ourselves up by, of course, when we are off duty."

Tom had got his answer, and had no more to say, till they came up to the great iron door of the prison. And there the truncheon knocked twice, with its own head. A wicket in the door opened, and out looked a tremendous old brass blunderbuss, charged up to the muzzle with slugs, who was the porter ; and Tom started back a little at the sight of him.

" What is this ? " he asked in a deep voice, out of his broad bell mouth.

" If you please, sir, it is only a young gentleman from Her Ladyship, who wants to see Grimes, the master sweep."

" Grimes ? " said the blunderbuss. And he pulled in his muzzle, perhaps to look over his prison list.

" Grimes is up chimney No. 345," he said, from inside. " So the young gentleman had better go on to the roof."

Tom looked up at the enormous wall, and wondered how he should ever get up ; but the truncheon whisked round, and gave him such a shove behind as sent him up the roof in no time, with his little dog under his arm. And there he walked along the leads, till he met another truncheon, and told him his errand.

" Very good," it said. " Come along ; but it will be of no use. He thinks about nothing but beer and pipes, which are not allowed here, of course."

At last they came to chimney No. 345. Out of the top of it, his head and shoulders just showing, stuck poor Mr. Grimes. In his mouth was a pipe; but it was not alight, although he was pulling at it with all his might.

"Attention, Mr. Grimes," said the truncheon; "here is a gentleman come to see you." But Mr. Grimes only kept grumbling, "My pipe won't draw. Did I ask to stay and never get my pipe, nor my beer, nor nothing fit for a beast, let alone a man?"

"No," answered a solemn voice behind. "No more did Tom, when you behaved to him in the very same way."

It was Mrs. Bedonebyasyoudid. And, when the truncheon saw her, it started bolt upright.—Attention!— and made a low bow. And Tom made his bow, too.

*He sneezed himself clean out of his skin, and turned into a water-dog.*

"Oh, ma'am," he said, "don't think about me; that's all past and gone. But may not I help poor Mr. Grimes? Mayn't I try and get some of these bricks away, that he may move his arms?"

"You may try, of course," she said.

So Tom pulled and tugged at the bricks; but he could not move one.

"Oh, dear," he said. "I have come all this way, through all these terrible places, to help you, and now I am of no use at all."

"You are a good-natured, forgiving little chap," said Grimes; "but you'd best be off. The hail's coming on soon, and it will beat the eyes out of your little head."

"That hail will never come any more," said the strange lady. "I have told you before what it was. It was your mother's tears. But she is gone to heaven now, and will weep no more for her graceless son."

Then Grimes was silent a while; and then he looked very sad.

"So my old mother's gone, and I never there to speak to her! Ah! a good woman she was, and might have been a happy one, in her little school there in Vendale, if it hadn't been for me and my bad ways."

Then Mr. Grimes cried very much, and was so sorry for his wickedness that the good fairy let him come out of the chimney. He was sent to sweep out the crater of Mount Etna, and if he did that well he would get another chance.

"And now," said the fairy to Tom, "your work here is at an end. You may as well go back again. Shut your eyes."

Tom did so, and when he opened them he saw St. Brandan's Isle reflected double in the still broad silver sea. And, as Tom neared the island, there sat upon a rock the most graceful creature that ever was seen, looking down, with her chin upon her hand, and paddling with her feet in the water. And when they came to her she looked up, and behold it was Ellie.

"Oh, Miss Ellie," said he, "how you are grown!"

"Oh, Tom," said she, "how you are grown, too!"

So he stood and looked at Ellie, and Ellie looked at him; and they stood and looked for seven years more, and neither spoke nor stirred. At last they heard the fairy say: "Attention, children! Are you never going to look at me again?"

They looked—and both of them cried out at once, "Oh, who are you, after all?"

"You are our dear Mrs. Doasyouwouldbedoneby."

"No, you are good Mrs. Bedonebyasyoudid; but you are grown quite beautiful now!"

The fairy smiled; then she turned to Ellie.

"You may take him home with you now on Sundays, Ellie. He has won his spurs in the great battle, and become fit to go with you and be a man; because he has done the thing he did not like."

So Tom went home with Ellie on Sundays, and sometimes on week days, too; and he has become a great and clever man, and does many things for children and grown-up people too. And all from what he learned when he was a water-baby under the sea.

---

# The Sad Story of a Little Boy that Cried

ANON

ONCE a little boy, Jack, was, oh! ever so good,
  Till he took a strange notion to cry all he could.

So he cried all the day, and he cried all the night,
He cried in the morning and in the twilight;

He cried till his voice was as hoarse as a crow,
And his mouth grew so large it looked like a great O.

It grew at the bottom and grew at the top;
It grew till they thought that it never would stop.

Each day his great mouth grew taller and taller,
And his dear little self grew smaller and smaller.

At last, that same mouth grew so big that—alack!—
It was only a mouth with a border of Jack.

# ROBINSON CRUSOE

*Adapted from the story by*
**DANIEL DEFOE**

## CRUSOE'S EARLY ADVENTURES

ROBINSON CRUSOE, the hero of this story, was born in the city of York in the year 1632. He was the third son of the family, and his father wished to make him a lawyer; but young Crusoe longed to go to sea.

His father, a wise and grave man, earnestly advised him not to become a sailor. Calling Crusoe one morning into his room, where he was confined with illness, he spoke to his son very warmly upon the subject. While his father was speaking Crusoe observed that he wept bitterly, and when he told the lad that in time to come he might have leisure to repent and none to assist him, the old gentleman was so moved that he could not go on.

Crusoe was much affected by his father's words, and resolved to think no more of going abroad. But a few weeks wore off this strong impression, and he determined to run away.

Being at Hull one day with a companion who was going to sea, Crusoe was persuaded to set off with him. He left on board the vessel, which was bound for London, and did not even send word of his departure to his father or mother.

The ship had no sooner reached the open sea than the wind began to blow fiercely, and the sea to rage mightily. Sick in body and mind, our young scapegrace began to reflect on his wickedness in leaving home without the consent of his parents.

Meanwhile, the storm raged, and the sea ran high; but, at last, the weather changed; and, on the sixth day of the voyage, the ship came to anchor in Yarmouth Roads. Here another storm, more fierce than the former one, burst over them; and so severe was it, that the sailors were forced to cut away the masts.

In the middle of the night the ship sprang a leak, when all hands, our hero included, were ordered to take turns at the pumps. A gun, fired as a signal of distress, so frightened young Crusoe that he fell down in a swoon.

At last the shipwrecked crew were taken off in a boat, leaving the water-logged vessel to her fate. After much labour, they were safely landed near Yarmouth, to which place they wended their way on foot.

After being shipwrecked on his first voyage, you might think that our runaway hero would have returned home to his parents ; but no. Having some money, he travelled to London by land, and there began to look out for the chance of another voyage.

In London, he fell in with a captain who traded on the coast of Guinea, and he, taking a fancy to our young unfortunate, offered him a free passage and a chance of trading with the natives.

Entering into an engagement with the captain, who was an honest, plain-dealing man, Crusoe went the voyage with him, taking as his share in the venture about forty pounds' worth of toys, and such trifles as his friend directed him to buy.

The voyage proved successful in all respects. The captain showed himself a true friend, taught Crusoe how to keep an account of the ship's course, take observations, and, in short, to understand many things necessary in the sailing of a ship. The instruction was a delight both to Crusoe and the captain, the result being that the young man became both sailor and merchant.

His share of the profits at the end of the voyage amounted to nearly three hundred pounds, and the possession of this sum led Crusoe to embark on further ventures. He determined to become a Guinea trader, and though his friend, the captain, died soon after the voyage, the young man resolved to go on the same journey again on his own account. The party sailed in the same vessel as before, the captain now being the man who had served as mate with Crusoe's friend, the old captain. It was, he tells us, the most unhappy voyage he ever made.

While the ship was making her way between the Canary Islands and the coast of Africa, she was surprised in the early morning by a Moorish pirate from Salee, a port of Morocco. Crusoe's people crowded on as much sail as they dared, and fled from the pirate vessel ; but as the Moor gained on the English ship, they determined to flee no more, but to make a fight for life and liberty. They had twelve guns to the pirate's eighteen.

About three in the afternoon the Moor came abreast of the English vessel, which poured in a broadside of eight guns, causing the pirate to sheer off a little. Before withdrawing the Moors returned the fire, sending in small shot from nearly two hundred men on board their ship. However, not a man was lost, as the sailors kept under cover.

But the Moors were not going to give up so easily. The second attack was successful. Nearly sixty Moors boarded the English ship, and at once began hacking and cutting at the rigging. A desperate fight was waged : twice the Englishmen cleared the decks of their enemies, but the ship being disabled, three men killed, and eight wounded, they were forced to surrender.

They were carried as prisoners into Salee, where Crusoe was lucky enough to be kept at the coast and not carried up country to the Emperor's court as the others were. The pirate captain retained him as a slave because he was young and active, and fit to give help both on shore and afloat.

## CRUSOE'S ESCAPE

FOR some time Crusoe endured the misery of being a slave, but all the time it was in his mind to escape at the first opportunity. The adventurous man's story is told here in his own words.

" As my master had taken me home, I was in hopes that he would take me with him when he went to sea again, believing that it would be some time or other his fate to be captured by a Spanish or Portuguese man-of-war, and that then I should be set at liberty.

" But this hope of mine was taken away. When he went to sea, he left me on shore to look after his little garden and do the common drudgery of slaves about his house, and when he came home again from his cruise, he ordered me to lie in the cabin, to look after the ship.

" Here I thought of nothing but my escape, and what method I might take to effect it. I had no fellow-slave. No Englishman, Irishman, or Scotsman was then there, but myself. So that for a long time, though I often pleased myself with the imagination, yet I never had the least encouraging prospect of putting it in practice.

" After two years, an odd circumstance presented itself, which put the whole thought of making some attempt for my liberty again in my head. My master, lying at home longer than usual, without fitting out his ship, used constantly, once or twice a week, sometimes oftener, if the weather was fair, to take the ship's pinnace, and go out into the road a-fishing. As he always took me and a youth named Xury with him to row the boat, we made him very merry and I proved very skilful in catching fish. At other times he would send me with a Moor, one of his kinsmen, and Xury, to catch a dish of fish for him.

" It happened one time that going a-fishing in a calm morning, a fog rose so thick, that though we were not half a league from the shore, we lost sight of it. Rowing we knew not whither, or which way, we laboured all day, and all the next night.

" When the morning came, we found we had pulled off to sea, instead of pulling in for the shore, and that we were at least two leagues from the land. However, we got well in again, though with a great deal of labour. and some danger, for the wind began to blow pretty fresh in the morning ; but, particularly, we were all very hungry.

" My master, warned by this disaster, resolved to take more care for the future ; and, having lying by him the long-boat of our English ship which he had taken, he resolved he would not go a-fishing any more without a compass and some provision. He therefore ordered the carpenter of his ship to build a little state-room or cabin in the middle of the long-boat, like that of a barge, with a place to stand behind it to steer, and haul home the main-sheet. He also had room made before for a hand or two to stand and work the sails.

" She had what we call a shoulder-of-mutton sail. The boom jibbed over the top of the cabin, which lay very snug and low, and had in it room for him to lie. There was also space for a slave or two, and a table to eat on, with some small lockers to hold his bread, rice, and coffee.

" We were frequently out with this boat a-fishing ; and as I was most dexterous to catch fish for him, he never went without me. It happened one day that he had appointed to go out in this boat, either for pleasure or for fish, with two or three Moors of some distinction, for whom he had made extra provision.

" He had therefore sent on board the boat overnight a larger store of provisions than usual, and had ordered me to get ready three guns, with powder and shot, which were on board his ship ; for that they designed some sport of fowling as well as fishing.

" I got all things ready as he had directed, and waited the next morning with the boat washed clean, and everything to accommodate his guests. By-and-by my master came on board alone, and told me his guests had put off going, and ordered me, with the man and boy, as usual, to go out with the boat, and catch them some fish, for that his friends were to sup at his house. He commanded that as soon as I had caught some fish, I should bring it to his house ; all of which I prepared to do.

" This moment my former ideas of deliverance darted into my thoughts, for now I found I was like to have a little ship at my command. My master being gone, I prepared to furnish myself, not for fishing business, but for a voyage, though I knew not, neither did I so much as consider, whither I would steer ; for anywhere to get out of that place was my way.

" My first contrivance was to make a pretence to speak to this Moor, to get something for our subsistence on board ; for I told him we must not presume to eat of our master's bread. He said that was true ; so he brought a large basket of rusk, or biscuit of their kind, and three jars with fresh water, into the boat.

" I conveyed a great lump of beeswax into the boat which weighed above half a hundredweight, with a parcel of twine or thread, a hatchet, a saw, and a hammer, all of which were of great use to us afterwards, especially the wax to make candles.

" Another trick I tried upon him, ' Moley,' said I, ' the guns are on board the boat ; can you not get a little powder and shot ? It may be we may kill some birds for ourselves, for I know he keeps the gunner's stores in the ship.'

" ' Yes,' said he, ' I'll bring some ; ' and accordingly he brought a great pouch, which held about a pound and a half of powder, or rather more, and another with shot, that had five or six pounds, with some bullets, and put all into the boat. At the same time I had found some powder of my master's in the great cabin. Thus furnished with everything needful, we sailed out of the port to fish.

" The guard in charge of the castle, which is at the entrance of the port, knew who we were and took no notice of us. We were not above a mile out of the port before we hauled in our sail, and set us down to fish.

" The wind blew from the north-north-east, which was contrary to my desire, for had it blown southerly, I had been sure to have made the coast of Spain, and at least reached the Bay of Cadiz. But my resolutions were, that no matter how the wind blew, I would be gone from that horrid place where I was, and leave the rest to fate.

"After we had fished for some time, and caught nothing—for when I had fish on my hook I would not pull them up, that he might not see them—I said to the Moor, ' This will not do—our master will not be thus served—we must stand farther off.' He, thinking no harm, agreed, and being in the head of the boat, set the sails.

"As I had the helm, I ran the boat out nearly a league farther, and then brought her to, as if I would fish. When, giving the boy the helm, I stepped forward to where the Moor was, and, making as if I stooped for something behind him, I took him by surprise and tossed him clear overboard into the sea.

"He rose immediately, for he swam like a cork, and begged to be taken in. He told me he would go all over the world with me. He swam so swiftly after the boat, that he would have reached me very quickly, there being but little wind, had I not stepped into the cabin, and fetching one of the fowling-pieces, aimed at him.

"Then I told him I had done him no hurt, and if he would be quiet I would do him none—' But,' said I, ' you swim well enough to reach the shore, and the sea is calm ; make the best of your way to shore, and I will do you no harm ; but if you come near the boat, I'll shoot you through the head, for I am resolved to have my liberty.'

"So he turned himself about and swam for the shore, and I make no doubt but he reached it with ease, for he was an excellent swimmer.

"I then asked Xury if he would be true to me. The boy smiled in my face, and spoke so innocently that I could not mistrust him. He swore to be faithful to me and go all over the world with me.

"While I was in view of the Moor that was swimming, I stood out directly to sea with the boat, rather stretching to windward that they might think me gone towards the mouth of the strait. But as soon as it grew dusk in the evening, I changed my course, and steered directly south and by east, bending my course a little towards the east, that I might keep in with the shore. Having a fair fresh gale of wind, and a smooth quiet sea, I made such sail that, I believe, by the next day at three o'clock in the afternoon, when I first made the land, I could not be less than one hundred and fifty miles south of Morocco."

Crusoe, however, was so afraid of falling again into the hands of the Moors that he would not stop or go on shore. For five days he sailed on ; then he made for the coast, believing that if any vessels had been in pursuit of him they would have given up the chase by that time.

He had no idea where he had anchored ; he saw no people, nor did he desire to see any. All he wanted was fresh water, and if possible some food. Into the creek they sailed in the evening, having determined to go on shore at night and examine the country. But when darkness came on they heard so many noises, barking, roaring, and howling, that Xury begged him not to go ashore till daylight.

They lay at anchor all night, but could not sleep because of the horrible noises made by wild beasts. In the morning, however, they were compelled to go ashore to search for water, as they had not a pint left in the boat.

Xury offered to go, and on Crusoe asking him why he volunteered, the lad answered, " If wild mans come, they eat me, you go away."

" Well, Xury," replied Crusoe, touched by the boy's affection, " we will both go, and if the wild mans come, we will kill them. They shall eat neither of us."

Then they hauled the boat as near the land as they thought right and waded ashore, carrying nothing but their arms and two jars for water. Crusoe did not like to go far from the boat, fearing that savages might appear and cut off their way of escape. The boy, however, spying a low-lying part of the land, about a mile away, went off to it, and, before long, Crusoe saw him running towards him.

At first he thought the lad was chased by savages but as Xury came nearer, Crusoe found that he was carrying an animal something like a hare only larger. This made a splendid meal for them, and with the water which Xury had found in the valley they refilled their vessels. Having done so they prepared to continue their journey, having seen no traces of human beings in that part of the country.

And now our hero found himself in an awkward position. He had been one voyage to the Canaries and knew in a general way where they lay, but he had no means of discovering where he himself was at the moment. It was useless, therefore, for him to try to reach these islands ; his only hope was to keep along the coast till he came to that part where English vessels traded. So far as he could make out, the coast he was passing must lie between the country of the Negroes and the Emperor of Morocco's dominions. It was waste and uninhabited, the Negroes having deserted it because of the Moors, who by reason of its barrenness did not think it worth keeping.

Once or twice in the daytime Crusoe imagined he saw the peak of Teneriffe in the Canaries and twice he tried to make his way in that direction. But the winds were contrary and the sea ran too high to sail his little vessel with safety. Therefore he resolved to keep to his first plan and sail down the coast.

Several times they had to land for fresh water and on one of these occasions a little adventure happened to them. They had come to anchor, when Xury called quietly to Crusoe, saying they had better lie farther off the shore. " For," he continued, " look—yonder lies a dreadful monster, on the side of that hillock, fast asleep."

Looking where the lad pointed, Crusoe saw a huge lion and said to the boy, " Xury, you shall go ashore and kill him."

Xury was frightened, declaring that the monster would swallow him at one bite. Bidding the boy keep still, Crusoe loaded three guns and prepared to shoot the lion. The first shot broke the beast's leg above the knee.

Up he started, growling with rage and pain, but his leg gave way and down he fell. Once more he jumped up, on three legs this time, but Crusoe shot him in the head, and Xury, finding courage, ran up to the struggling animal, and, putting a pistol to its ear, shot it dead.

After this adventure, the two wanderers continued their journey down the coast, living very sparingly because their provisions were running short. They did not go ashore any oftener than they were obliged to do for fresh

water. Crusoe's aim was
to reach the river Gam-
bia, where he hoped to
meet some European
vessel.

Soon he perceived
that the land was in-
habited in two or three
places. As they sailed
by, the people stood on
the shore looking at
them, and Crusoe saw
that they were quite
black and carried lances.
From some of these
people he obtained pro-

*The first shot broke the beast's leg.*

visions, and set off once more on his journey. About a fortnight later
when he had almost given way to despair, a Portuguese vessel hove in
sight and the wanderers were taken on board, the captain and crew
treating them very kindly.

The captain took charge of Xury, promising to look after him and treat
him well. The goods Crusoe had on board his little craft he sold for two
hundred and twenty pieces of eight, and with this sum he landed in the
Brazils.


## CRUSOE GOES AGAIN TO SEA

CRUSOE next turned planter, buying a piece of uncleared land with his
money, and growing various kinds of food stuffs.

He had a neighbour named Wells, and, because their plantations were
close together, the two men became friends. They both planted for food
rather than for profit; but by degrees they began to prosper and in the
third year tried growing tobacco. For this they required more help than they
could find close at hand.

At the end of four years Crusoe had not only learned the language of the
country but had become friendly with his fellow-planters as well as with
the merchants of their port, San Salvador. Often and often he had given
them an account of his two voyages to the coast of Guinea, the manner of
trading with the natives there, and how easy it was to purchase on the coast
not only ivory and gold dust but negro slaves. All one had to pay for
these things were beads, toys, knives, scissors, hatchets, bits of glass and
such like.

One morning, after he had been talking over the matter with some
planters and merchants whom he knew, he had visitors. They were three of
his friends who told him that, having thought very seriously upon what
Crusoe had said, they had a proposal to make. They all owned plantations
and needed help to cultivate them, and therefore they were going to fit out
a ship to sail for Guinea in search of slaves.

They offered Crusoe the command of the expedition, promising him an equal share with themselves in the profits, without his having to provide any of the stock. The perils of the sea must have had a charm for young Crusoe, for he dared them again this time, and that, too, on an evil errand.

Crusoe's story of his voyage and shipwreck is so graphic that it had best be given in his own words.

" Our ship," he says, " was about one hundred and twenty tons burden. It carried six guns, and fourteen men, besides the master, his boy, and myself. We had on board no large cargo of goods, except of such toys as were fit for our trade with the negroes, such as beads, bits of glass, shells, and odd trifles, especially little looking-glasses, knives, scissors, hatchets, and the like.

" The same day I went on board we set sail, standing away to the northward on our own coast.

" We passed the Line in about twelve days' time, and were, by our last observation, in seven degrees, twenty-two minutes, northern latitude, when a violent tornado, or hurricane, took us quite out of our knowledge.

" In this distress, besides the terror of the storm, one of our men died of the fever, and one man and the boy were washed overboard. About the twelfth day, the weather abating a little, the master made an observation as well as he could, and found that he was in about twenty-two degrees of longitude. He therefore began to consult with me what course he should take, for the ship was leaky and very much disabled, and he was going directly back to the coast of Brazil.

" With the design of standing away for Barbadoes we changed our course, and steered away north-west by west, in order to reach some of our English islands, where I hoped for relief; but our voyage was otherwise determined.

" A second storm came on us, which carried us away westward, and drove us out of the very way of all human commerce. Therefore, had all our lives been saved as to the sea, we were rather in danger of being devoured by savages than ever returning to our own country.

" In this difficulty, the wind still blowing very hard, one of our men, early in the morning, cried out, ' Land ! ' We had no sooner run out of the cabin to look out, in hopes of seeing whereabouts in the world we were, when the ship struck on a sandbank, and in a moment, her motion being so stopped, the sea broke over her in such a manner that we expected we should all have perished immediately.

" Now, though we thought that the wind did a little abate, yet the ship having thus struck on the bank, we were in a dreadful condition indeed, and had nothing to do but to think of saving our lives as well as we could.

" We had a boat at our stern, just before the storm, but she was first staved by dashing against the ship's rudder, and, in the next place, she broke away, and either sunk or was driven off to sea, so there was no hope from her. We had another boat on board, but how to get her off into the sea was a doubtful thing. However, there was no room to debate, for we fancied the ship would break in pieces every minute.

" In this distress the mate of our vessel laid hold of the boat, and, with the help of the rest of the men, got her slung over the ship's side, and getting all into her, let go, and committed ourselves, being eleven in number, to God's mercy and the wild sea.

" And now our case was very dismal indeed. We all saw plainly that the sea went so high that the boat could not live, and that we should be certainly drowned. As to making sail, we had none, nor, if we had, could we have done anything with it. So we worked at the oar towards the land, though with heavy hearts, for we all knew that when the boat came nearer the shore she would be dashed in a thousand pieces by the breach of the sea.

" After we had rowed, or rather driven, about a league and a half, as we reckoned it, a raging wave, mountain-like, came rolling astern of us, and plainly bade us expect a watery grave. In a word, it took us with such a fury that it overset the boat at once, and we were all swallowed up in a moment.

" Nothing can describe the confusion of thought which I felt when I sank into the water. Though I swam very well, yet I could not deliver myself from the waves so as to draw breath, till that wave having driven me, or rather carried me, a vast way on towards the shore, and having spent itself, went back, and left me on the land almost dry, but half-dead with the water I took in. I had so much presence of mind, as well as breath left, that, seeing myself nearer

*They offered Crusoe command of the expedition.*

the mainland than I expected, I got on my feet and endeavoured to make towards the land as fast as I could, before another wave should return and take me up again.

" The wave that came on me again buried me at once twenty or thirty feet deep in its own body. I could feel myself carried with a mighty force and swiftness towards the shore a very great way, but I held my breath, and assisted myself to swim still forward with all my might.

" I was ready to burst with holding my breath, when, as I felt myself rising up so, to my immediate relief, I found my head and hands shoot out above the surface of the water. And though it was not two seconds of time that I could keep myself so, yet it relieved me greatly—gave me breath and new courage. I was covered again with water a good while, but not so long, but I held it out.

" Finding the water had spent itself and began to return, I struck forward against the return of the waves, and felt ground again with my feet. I stood still a few moments to recover breath and till the water went from me, and then took to my heels and ran, with what strength I had, farther towards the shore. Twice more I was lifted up by the waves and carried forwards as before, the shore being very flat.

" The last time of those two had well near been fatal to me. The sea, having hurried me along as before, landed me, or rather dashed me, against a piece of rock, and that with such force as it left me senseless, and indeed helpless, as to my own deliverance ; for the blow, taking my side and breast, beat the breath, as it were, quite out of my body, and had it returned again immediately I must surely have been strangled in the water.

" I recovered a little before the return of the waves, and, seeing I should be covered again with the water, I resolved to cling fast by a piece of the rock, and so to hold my breath, if possible, till the wave went back.

" Now, as the waves were not so high as at first, being near land, I held on till the wave abated, and then fetched another run, which brought me so near the shore, that the next wave, though it went over me, did not so swallow me up as to carry me away.

" The next run I took I got to the mainland, where, to my great comfort, I clambered up the cliffs of the shore, and sat me down on the grass, free from danger, and quite out of the reach of the water.

" I was now landed and safe on shore, and began to look up and thank God that my life was saved, in a case wherein there was, some minutes before, scarce any room to hope. I believe it is impossible to express to the life what the delights and transports of the soul are when it is so saved, as I may say, out of the very grave."

## CRUSOE LANDS ON THE ISLAND

As soon as he recovered himself somewhat, Crusoe walked about on the shore making a thousand gestures impossible to describe, so joyful was he at his deliverance from the sea. He never saw his companions afterwards, or any sign of them, except three of their hats, one cap, and two odd shoes which were cast ashore.

After comforting himself for some time with the thought of his escape, he began to look around to see into what kind of place he had been cast. Then his feelings changed, and he began to think that even death would have been better than being placed in the position in which he found himself. He was wet, he had no clothes except those he had on, nor had he anything to eat or drink.

He could see no other prospect than to perish of hunger or be killed by wild beasts. To make the matter worse, he possessed no weapon either to hunt and kill animals for food, or to defend himself against attack from wild creatures.

Poor Crusoe ! all he possessed was a knife, a pipe, and a little tobacco. Having found a stream of fresh water, he drank of it ; put a little tobacco in his mouth, to deaden the feeling of hunger ; cut a short, stout stick, with which to defend himself, climbed a tree, in which to rest ; and, being very tired, slept soundly among the branches until broad daylight.

On waking, he found, to his surprise, that the waves had lifted the ship and driven her close to a rock, where she lay nearly upright within a mile of the shore. Shortly after noon, when the tide had ebbed so as to leave the ship but a quarter of a mile from the shore, Crusoe swam out to her, clambered on board, and filled his pockets with biscuits, which he ate as he searched the ship from end to end.

Next he made a raft of some spare spars ; then, having broken open and emptied three of the sailors' sea-chests, he lowered them on to his raft. Having done this, he filled one with provisions, another with weapons, powder, and shot, and also secured the carpenter's tools. With these prizes he reached the shore in safety.

His next work was to explore the country on which he had been cast ; so, having armed himself he climbed a hill, and found that he was on an island, which appeared to support neither wild animals nor human beings.

Returning to his raft, he managed to get his cargo ashore ; and, having built a rude hut with the chests and boards he brought from the ship, he fell asleep.

Next day he swam out to the ship again ; built a second raft ; and, having loaded it with weapons, powder, bullets, shot, clothes, and bedding, he regained the shore in safety. His next labour was to make a tent with a sail and some poles, and in it to place any articles that the sun or rain could spoil. Then, blocking up the entrance to his tent, Crusoe went to bed for the first time on the island.

After this he made voyages every day to the vessel, and brought away, as he says in his narrative, " all that one pair of hands could bring." But one night it blew very hard ; and, in the morning, when he looked out, no ship was to be seen.

Selecting a little plain on the side of a hill, the seaward face of which was very steep, Crusoe built a fort, consisting of two rows of sharp-pointed stakes, which formed a fence so strong that neither man nor beast could pass either through it or over it. The entrance to this fort was not by means of a door, but by a short ladder, which he drew up after him ; and in this enclosure, he stowed away all his stores.

In the midst of his work Crusoe found time to go out once at least every day with his gun. This served the double purpose of providing him with amusement and acquainting him with the products of the island.

The first time he went out he discovered there were goats on the island. One of these he killed and carried home for food. A kid, which was with the old goat, followed Crusoe

*Crusoe walked about on the shore making a thousand gestures.*

to his fort, but his hopes of rearing it as a domestic animal came to nothing; the creature would not be tamed, and finally our hero killed and ate it. These two animals served him as food for a long time.

He also made a large double tent of sail-cloth, one within the other; and he dug a cave behind the tent, to serve as a cellar and storehouse.

Crusoe had been cast upon his island on the last day of September, and, after he had been there for ten or twelve days, it came into his head that he would lose all account of time unless he had some kind of calendar. That he might reckon correctly he made a great wooden cross, cutting into it the words:

I CAME ON SHORE HERE ON THE
30TH OF SEPTEMBER, 1659.

Then he set up the cross on the shore where he had first landed.

On the sides of the cross he cut a notch every day with his knife, every seventh notch being as long again as the rest, and every first day of the month as long again as that long one. Thus he was enabled to keep his reckoning of days, weeks, months, and years.

We must not omit to mention that Crusoe carried off from the wreck two cats; and that the dog which was on board the wreck followed his first cargo to shore, and became his trusty companion for many years.

Having put all his stores in order, he went to work to make some necessary articles, and managed to construct a table and a chair of the short pieces of board which he brought from the ship. He also put up shelves and pegs in his cave, upon which to place or hang his guns, tools, and weapons.

As he had brought pens, ink, and paper from the wreck, Crusoe kept a journal, in which he wrote a strict account of all his doings as long as his ink lasted.

One of the entries in his journal runs as follows:

" *Nov.* and *Dec.*—In searching the woods, I found a tree of that wood, or like it, which in the Brazils they call the iron tree, for its exceeding hardness. With great labour and almost spoiling my axe, I cut a piece, and brought it home too, with difficulty enough, for it was exceeding heavy. I worked this by little and little into the form of a shovel or spade, the handle exactly shaped like ours in England, only that, the broad part having no iron shod upon it at bottom, it would not last me so long. However, it served well enough for the uses which I had occasion to put it to; but never was a shovel, I believe, made after that fashion.

" I still wanted a basket or a wheelbarrow. I fancied I could make all but the wheel, but that I had no notion of, neither did I know how to go about it. Besides, I had no possible way to make the iron gudgeons for the spindle, or axis of the wheel to run in, so I gave it over. As for carrying away the earth which I dug out of the cave, I made me a thing like a hod, which the labourers carry mortar in when they serve the bricklayers."

In the midst of his labours Crusoe, in rummaging about, found a little bag in which corn for the fowls had been kept in the ship on a previous voyage. He saw nothing in the bag but husks and dust, and, as he wanted to use it for some purpose, he shook out the husks.

This was before the rainy season, and, not expecting that anything would happen, our hero forgot all about the matter. About a month afterwards, however, he was surprised to see green shoots appearing, and, in a day or two he discovered that he had some ten or twelve ears of barley growing at his door.

*He set up the cross on the shore.*

These grains he saved, sowing them next season, and by continuing the process for four years, was able to supply himself with barley for food.

A violent storm and an earthquake gave Crusoe a great fright ; but the latter heaved the wreck up, and laid it so that Crusoe could cut up the beams and take out the ironwork.

The fear of being swallowed up by an earthquake troubled him so much that he could not sleep peacefully at night. Yet he felt afraid to lie without a fence round him, lest he might be attacked by savage animals or men. He resolved, therefore, to build a wall with piles and cables in a circle as he had already done, and set up his tent in it when the work was finished.

At once he began operations, but the bad condition of his tools caused him great anxiety. He had three large axes and any number of small hatchets, but they had been so much used for cutting hard and knotty wood that their edges were knotched and dull. Though he possessed a grindstone he could not turn it and grind the tools at the same time. By hard thought, however, he contrived a wheel with a string, by means of which he could turn the grindstone with his foot ; and thus have both hands free to work with the tools.

For two days he sharpened his tools and then he was able to cut out the beams from the ship. This consumed some time, but it provided him with employment and supplied him with many useful articles.

*I worked it into the form of a shovel or spade.*

## CRUSOE'S JOURNAL

CRUSOE was cast ashore on the " Isle of Despair," as he called it, on the thirtieth of September, 1659, and had spent nearly nine months there, when one morning, in June, 1660, he found a large turtle. In his journal he wrote as follows :

" *June* 17*th* I spent in cooking the turtle. I found in her three score eggs, and her flesh was to me, at that time, the most savoury and pleasant that I ever tasted in my life, having had no flesh but of goats and fowls since I landed in this horrid place."

Soon after this Crusoe was seized with so violent an ague that he was unable to leave his bed or take any food. So weak was he that, though almost perishing of thirst, he could not even get himself a drink of water. In his journal he wrote an account of this illness.

" *June* 28.—Having been somewhat refreshed with sleep, and feeling a little better, I decided to get something to refresh and support myself in the event of being again unable to attend my wants. The first thing I did, I filled a large bottle with water and set it on my table in reach of my bed. Then I got me a piece of goat's flesh, and broiled it on the coals, but could eat very little.

" After I had eaten, I tried to walk, but found myself so weak that I could hardly carry my gun. However, I went a little way, sat down on the ground, and looked on the sea which was just before me, and very calm and smooth. I then returned to my retreat, and soon afterwards fell into a sound sleep, and waked no more till, by the sun, it must be near three o'clock in the afternoon of the next day. Nay, to this hour, I am partly of the opinion that I slept all the next day and night, and till almost three the day after. If such was not the case I know not how I should lose a day of my reckoning of the days of the week, as it appeared some years afterwards, I had done. If I had lost it by crossing and recrossing the equator I should have lost more than one day, but in my account it was lost, and I never knew which way.

" Be that, however, one way or other, when I awoke, I found myself exceedingly refreshed, and my spirits lively and cheerful. Having got up, I felt stronger than I had been the day before, and, what was still better, I was very hungry.

" My heart was so touched with my deliverance," the journal continues, " that I kneeled down and gave God thanks aloud for my recovery from sickness. I then took the Bible and began seriously to read it."

Having been ten months on the island, Crusoe began to survey it. He discovered a fertile valley, in which he found tobacco, growing wild ; sugarcanes, also wild and imperfect for lack of culture ; melons on the ground ; and grapes on vines which climbed up the trees. The latter he dried in the sun, and so made raisins of them. Cocoa, orange, lemon, and citron trees were also abundant.

In this fruitful part of the island our castaway built a kind of bower, surrounded with a strong fence. " I fancied now," he wrote in his journal,

" that I had my country house and my sea-coast house, and this work employed me till the beginning of August."

About the end of August one of Crusoe's cats, which had disappeared, came home with three kittens. Nothing further of moment happened to our hero, until he had been on the island a year. " I kept this day as a solemn fast," he wrote in his journal, " setting it apart for a religious exercise. I did not taste the least refreshment for twelve hours, even till the going down of the sun. I then ate a biscuit-cake and a bunch of grapes, and went to bed, finishing the day as I began it.

" I found now that the seasons of the year might generally be divided, not into summer and winter, as in Europe, but into the rainy seasons and the dry seasons, two of each. . . . After I had found, by experience, the ill consequences of being abroad in the rain, I took care to provide myself with a supply of provisions beforehand, that I might not be obliged to go out during the rainy season. . . . In this time I found much employment . . . in making a great many baskets."

Having thus passed the rainy season in comparative comfort, Crusoe resolved to survey the island again. So, taking his gun, his hatchet, and a good supply of food, he set out, accompanied by his dog. It was in the course of this journey that he caught the young parrot, which he taught in after years to call him by name.

On the other side of the island our explorer found an abundance of turtles, a large number of fowls, and many goats. In this journey his dog seized a young kid. The following account of this adventure is in Crusoe's own words :

" I, running in to take hold of it, caught it and saved it alive from the dog. I had a great mind to bring it home if I could. I had often been musing whether it might not be possible to get a kid or two, and so raise a breed of tame goats, which might supply me when my powder and shot should be spent.

" I made a collar for this little creature, and, with a string which I made of some rope-yarn, which I always carried about me, I led him along, though with some difficulty, till I came to my bower, and there I enclosed him and left him, for I was very impatient to be at home."

And now began the third year of Crusoe's exile on the island, his daily life, as described by himself, being as follows :

" I was very seldom idle, having regularly divided my time according to the several daily employments that were before me. I set apart some time for reading the Scriptures. I went abroad with my gun three hours every morning, and spent some time arranging, curing, preserving, and cooking what I had killed.

" In the middle of the day, when the sun was in the zenith, the violence of the heat was too great to stir out, so that for about four hours in the evening was all the time I could be supposed to work."

While Crusoe's corn was growing, he found that he was in danger of losing it all, by enemies of several sorts. A fence with which he surrounded his corn-plot kept out the goats, which would have devoured the corn in the blade ; but the birds seemed likely to eat the whole crop when it was in the ear.

*I made a great many baskets.*

Going along by the place to see how it throve, he saw his little crop surrounded by birds of various sorts. Angry at this, Crusoe fired at them, killing three. Immediately a flock rose from the corn itself where they had been feeding.

Taking up the three birds he had killed, our hero hung them in chains on a tree as a warning to their fellows. The effect was startling.

Not only did the birds leave the corn alone, but they actually forsook that part of the island as long as the scarecrows were hanging there.

In December, Crusoe reaped his corn, cutting off the ears, and threshing it by rubbing it out with his hand.

The next work of the lone castaway was an endeavour to make pots and pans of clay, in which, after many struggles, he succeeded. He also made a pestle and mortar of hard wood, with which to grind his corn ; and he baked his bread on tiles of his own making.

And, now, Crusoe attempted a much greater undertaking, none other than that of building a boat. Here is his account of the matter :

" To work I went, and felled a cedar tree. It was five feet ten inches diameter at the lower part next the stump, and four feet eleven inches diameter at the end of twenty-two feet, after which it lessened for a while, and then parted into branches.

" It was not without infinite labour that I felled this tree. I was twenty days hacking and hewing at it at the bottom. I was fourteen more getting the branches and limbs and the vast spreading head cut off with my axe and hatchet.

" After this it cost me a month to shape it, and dub it to a proportion, and to something like the bottom of a boat, that it might float upright as it ought to do. It cost me nearly three months more to clear the inside and work it out, so as to make an exact boat of it.

" This I did indeed without fire, by mere mallet and chisel, and by the dint of hard labour, till I had brought it to be a very handsome canoe, and big enough to have carried six-and-twenty men, and consequently big enough to have carried me and all my cargo.

" When I had gone through this work, I was extremely delighted with it. The boat was really much bigger than I ever saw a canoe, that was made of one tree, in my life. Many a weary stroke it had cost, you may be sure.

" There remained nothing but to get it into the water. Had I been able to do this, I make no question but I should have begun the maddest voyage, and the most unlikely to be performed, that ever was undertaken."

But, when his canoe was finished, he could not launch it, because it was too large and heavy.

" In the midst of this undertaking," he wrote in his journal, " I finished my fourth year in this place, and kept my anniversary with the same devotion, and with as much comfort, as ever before."

By this time, Crusoe had worn out most of the clothes which he removed from the wreck ; but, as he had preserved the skins of all the animals he killed, he set to work to clothe himself in these. First, he made a cap, with the hair on the outside to shoot off the rain. This being a success, he made a suit of clothes, consisting of a loose waistcoat and breeches. Then he spent much time and trouble in making an umbrella.

" I cannot say," he wrote, " that after this, for five years, any special thing happened to me. I lived on in the same course, in the same posture and place, just as before. The chief thing I was employed in, besides my yearly labour of planting my barley and rice, and curing my raisins, of both which I always kept up just enough to have a sufficient stock for the year's provisions beforehand, was my daily exercise of going out with my gun. I made a canoe, which, at last, I finished ; so that by digging a canal to it, six feet wide and four feet deep, I brought it into the creek, which was almost half a mile distant. . . . As I had a boat, my next design was to sail it round the island."

## CRUSOE'S SAILING ADVENTURE

FITTING up his little boat with a mast and sail, and getting stores and provisions aboard, occupied some time ; but, on the sixth of November, in the sixth year of his captivity, he set out. After being nearly carried out to sea by a powerful current, and partly driven back again by one in a contrary direction, he fell in with a fair wind, which served him to return to the island.

On landing, Crusoe fell on his knees and gave God thanks for his deliverance from danger. He also put aside all further thoughts of making his escape by the boat, which he had previously entertained. He laid the vessel up in a little harbour, and returned to his fortress, content to dispense with the result of the labour of so many months.

*Crusoe makes a boat.*

Finding that his powder began to run short, Crusoe trapped some goats and tamed them, so as to have a supply of food always at hand ; and these he shut in an enclosure, which occupied him fully three months to fence in. In about a year and a half, he was the proud possessor of a flock of twelve goats, which increased to forty-three in two more years ; so that he now had milk, and made butter and cheese.

These additional comforts rendered Crusoe more cheerful, as the following extract from his journal bears witness :

" It would have made you smile to have seen me and my little family sit down to dinner. There was my majesty, the prince and lord of the whole island. I had the lives of all my subjects at absolute command. . . .

" Then to see how like a king I dined, too, all alone, attended by my servants. Poll, as if he had been my favourite, was the only person permitted to talk to me. My dog, which was now grown very old and feeble, sat always at my right hand ; my two cats sat, one on one side of the table and one on the other, expecting now and then a bit from my hand, as a mark of special favour. . . .

" Be pleased to take a sketch of my figure as follows :

" I had a great high shapeless cap, made of goat's skin, with a flap hanging down behind, as well to keep the sun from me as to shoot the rain off from running into my neck, nothing being so hurtful in these climates as the rain on the flesh under the clothes.

" I had a short jacket of goat's skin, the skirts coming down to about the middle of my thighs ; and a pair of open-kneed breeches of the same. The breeches were made of the skin of an old he-goat, whose hair hung down such a length on either side, that, like pantaloons, it reached to the middle of my legs. Stockings and shoes I had none. I had made me a pair of something, I scarce knew what to call them, like buskins, to flap over my legs, and lace on either side, but of a most barbarous shape, as indeed were all the rest of my clothes.

" I had on a broad skin belt, which I drew together with two thongs instead of buckles. In a kind of frog on either side of this, instead of a sword and dagger hung a little saw and a hatchet—one on one side and one on the other. I had another belt, not broad, but fastened in the same manner, which hung over my shoulder. At the end of it, under my left arm, hung two pouches, both made of goat's skin too, in one of which hung my powder, and in the other my shot. At my back, I carried my basket ; on my shoulder, my gun ; and, over my head, a clumsy, ugly, goat's skin umbrella."

But Crusoe was destined to suffer a rude awakening from his peaceful slumberous existence. The incident which caused it shall be told in his own words.

" It happened one day about noon, going towards my boat, I was exceedingly surprised with the print of a man's naked foot on the shore, which was very plain to be seen in the sand. I stood like one thunderstruck. I listened, I looked round me—I could hear nothing, nor see anything. . . . I could see no other impression but that one. . . .

" Lost in thought, I returned to my fort . . . terrified to the last degree. . . . When I came to my castle, for so I think I called it ever after this, I fled into it like one pursued. . . . Never alarmed hare fled to cover, or fox to earth, with more terror of mind than I to this retreat.

" I had no sleep that night. . . .

" It came into my thoughts one day that all my fears might be a mere imagination of my own, that this foot might be the print of my own foot, when I came on shore from my boat. . . . Now I began to take courage, and to peep abroad again ; for I had not stirred out of my castle for three days and nights, so that I began to starve for provisions. . . .

" When I came to measure the mark with my own foot, I found my foot not so large by a great deal. . . . This filled my head with new imaginations, so that I shook with cold like one who is ill, and I went home again, filled with the belief that some man or men had been on shore there."

## CRUSOE DISCOVERS A CAVE

SOME time after the adventure of the footprint, Crusoe wandered to a part of the island he had never visited before ; and, looking out to sea, saw a boat at a great distance. He found, too, that visits of savages to this side of the island were by no means of rare occurrence ; for on the shore, he came upon charred human bones, the place where a fire had been made, and a circle dug in the earth, where these savages had sat to enjoy their horrid feast.

Naturally this event made him fear lest the savages should discover him ; but after a time, his uneasiness began to wear off. Still he was much more cautious than he had hitherto been, in moving about the island.

In his journal we find the following entry of his doings in connection with this unwelcome visit of the cannibals :

"After thinking over the matter carefully for a time, I determined to look for a place where I could hide myself, and from which I could watch any savages who might land on the island. At length I found a place on the side of the hill, where I was satisfied I might securely wait till I saw any of the boats coming, and might then, even before they would be ready to come on shore, convey myself unseen into the thickets

*I loaded the fowling-piece with near a handful of swan-shot of the largest size.*

of trees, in one of which there was a hollow large enough to conceal me entirely. Here I might sit, and observe all their doings, and take my full aim at their heads, when they were so close together as that it would be next to impossible that I should miss my shot, or that I could fail wounding three or four of them at once.

" In this place, then, I resolved to fix my design; and accordingly I prepared two muskets and my ordinary fowling-piece. Two muskets I loaded with a brace of slugs each, and four or five smaller bullets, about the size of pistol bullets, and the fowling-piece I loaded with near a handful of swan-shot of the largest size. I also loaded my pistols with about four bullets each. In this posture, well provided with ammunition for a second and third charge, I prepared myself for my expedition.

" After I had thus laid the scheme of my design, I made my tour every morning up to the top of the hill, which was from my castle about three miles or more, to see if any boats were coming near the island or standing towards it. I began to tire of this hard duty, after I had for two or three months constantly kept my watch.

" For more than a year after this I kept myself as much retired as possible. I seldom went from my cell, other than on my constant employment, namely, to milk my goats and manage my little flock in the wood, which, as it was quite on the other part of the island, was entirely out of danger. For certain it is that these savage people, who sometimes haunted this island, never came with any thoughts of finding anything here, and consequently never wandered off from the coast. I doubt not but they might have been several times on shore after my fears of them had made me cautious, as well as before. Indeed, I looked back with some horror on the thoughts of what my condition would have been if I had suddenly met them and been discovered before that, when unarmed, except with one gun, and that loaded often only with small shot.

" I walked everywhere, peeping and peering about the island, to see what I could get. What a surprise I should have been in if, when I discovered the print of a man's foot, I had, instead of that, seen fifteen or twenty savages, and found them pursuing me, and, by the swiftness of their running, no possibility of my escaping them."

While searching for a hiding-place from which he could watch the doings of these savages, should they come to the island again, Crusoe discovered a small cave or grotto, which he fitted up as a kind of fort, storing there his powder and all his spare arms. The discovery of this cave had not been made without a surprise; for, when he first entered it, he saw two shining eyes, and heard the sigh of some creature in pain. This turned out to be an old he-goat, which died, and was buried by Crusoe beneath the floor of the cave.

## CRUSOE SAVES FRIDAY

IT was not until the month of December, during Crusoe's twenty-third year of residence upon the island, that he was surprised at seeing a fire upon the shore, and nine naked savages dancing round it. They had reached the island, as was plain to see, in two canoes; another party, in three canoes, visited the other side of Crusoe's kingdom, indulging in a cannibal feast, and leaving behind a number of human bones, the remains of their horrible banquet.

As soon as he saw they had gone, Crusoe put two guns on his shoulder, two pistols in his belt, and hung a sword by his side. Then with all speed he ran to the hill where he had first seen the canoes of the savages. He perceived that there must have been three other canoes at the place, and, looking out farther, saw them all at sea together.

Once more he felt uneasy, and lived in constant fear of their taking him by surprise. However, it was more than fifteen months before any of the savages came to the island again.

In the middle of the following May, there was a great storm, in the midst of which Crusoe heard the sound of guns from a ship in distress.

He wrote in his journal:
' I brought together all the dry wood I could get at hand, and, making a good handsome pile, I set it on fire on the hill. The wood was dry, and blazed freely, and, though the wind blew very hard, yet it burnt fairly out. As soon as ever my fire blazed up, I heard another gun, and after that several others, all from the same quarter. I plied my fire all night long till day broke ; and when it was broad day, and the air cleared up, I saw some-

*Crusoe rushed on the foremost of the cannibals, and felled him with the stock of the gun.*

thing at a great distance at sea, full east of the island.

" I looked frequently at it all that day, and soon perceived that it did not move, so I presently concluded that it was a ship at anchor. I took my gun in my hand, and ran towards the south-east side of the island, to the rocks, and getting up there, the weather by this time being perfectly clear, I could plainly see, to my great sorrow, the wreck of a ship cast away in the night on those concealed rocks.

" I never knew whether any were saved out of that ship or not ; and had only the affliction, some days after, to see the body of a drowned boy come ashore at the end of the island which was next the wreck."

When the waves subsided, and the sea was calm, Crusoe set out in his boat and reached the wreck, which was jammed between two rocks. A hungry, half-starved dog jumped out of the ship into our hero's boat ; but that seemed to be the only living being left on board the broken vessel. Laden with the dog and a couple of chests from the wreck, with a powder-horn, some fire-irons, kettles, and a gridiron, Crusoe reached his island at the close of day, tired out with his exertions.

B.F.

In the chests he found shirts, handkerchiefs, and neckties. The tills in the great chests contained bags of money and ingots of gold. With regard to the latter, Crusoe wrote in his journal as follows :

" I had more wealth, indeed, than I had before, but was not at all the richer. I had no more use for it than the Indians of Peru had before the Spaniards came thither."

About a year and a half elapsed, when, one morning, Crusoe was surprised at seeing five canoes come ashore together. The savages landed, to the number of about thirty, and began to dance round a fire which they kindled. Then, two miserable wretches were dragged from the boats, one of whom was immediately knocked down and killed with a club.

The second ran, as fast as his legs could carry him, towards Crusoe's castle, followed by three of the savages. He swam across the creek ; but only two of his pursuers did so ; for it seemed that the third could not swim.

Crusoe now appeared upon the scene. Beckoning to the fugitive, he slowly advanced towards the pursuers.

Crusoe did not wish to fire lest the noise should bring all the other savages about him ; but rushing on the foremost of the cannibals, he felled him with the stock of the gun. The other savage did not understand what had happened ; but, seeing an enemy, he fitted an arrow to his bow and was just about to fire when Crusoe shot him. The poor fugitive savage slowly approached his rescuer, knelt down, kissed the ground at Crusoe's feet, then laid his head on the ground, at the same time placing his deliverer's foot upon it.

When the savage who had been knocked down began to recover, the fugitive signed to Crusoe to lend him his sword, which he no sooner received than he ran to his enemy and cut off his head. Having buried the two dead savages in the sand, Crusoe conducted his new companion to the cave, where he gave him food, and bade him sleep.

" After my savage had slumbered, rather than slept, above half an hour," wrote Crusoe, " he waked, and came out of the cave to me, for I had been milking my goats in the enclosure just by.

" When he espied me, he came running to me, laying himself down again on the ground, with all the possible signs of a humble, thankful disposition, making many antic gestures to show it.

" At last, he laid his head flat on the ground, close to my foot, and placed my other foot upon his head, as he had done before. After this, he made all the signs to me of subjection, servitude, and submission imaginable, to let me know how much he would serve me as long as he lived.

" In a little time, I began to speak to him, and teach him to speak to me. First, I made him know his name should be Friday, which was the day I saved his life, and I called him so for the memory of the time."

Upon visiting the spot where the savages had landed, Crusoe found the place covered with human bones, and saw all the tokens of the terrible triumphant feast they had held there after a victory over their enemies. Having buried the bones and other remains of the cannibals' feast, our hero returned to his castle, accompanied by Friday.

# CRUSOE RETURNS HOME

IT was well for Crusoe that he had a companion, or the constant dread of the savages might have unsettled his mind ; but his self-appointed task of teaching Friday employed him, and gave him an interest in life.

Let us now turn again to Crusoe's journal.

" Some time after this," he wrote, " we were on the top of the hill, from which I had on a clear day seen the mainland. Suddenly Friday began jumping and dancing, and when I asked him what was the matter, he exclaimed, ' O joy ! O glad ! There see my country.'

" I said to him, ' Friday, do not you wish yourself in your country ? '

" ' Yes,' he said, ' I would be much O glad to be at my own people.'

" ' What would you do there ? ' said I ; ' would you turn wild again, and eat men's flesh again, and be a savage as you were before ? '

" He looked full of concern, and, shaking his head, said, ' No, no ! Friday tell them to live good, tell them to pray God, tell them to eat corn bread, cattle flesh, milk, no eat man again.'

" ' Why, then,' said I to him, ' they will kill you !' He looked grave at that, and then said, ' No, they no kill me ; they willingly love learn '— he meant by this, they would be willing to learn. He added, they learned much of the white mans that came in the boat.

" Then I asked if he would go back to them. He told me he would go, if I would go with him. ' I go !' said I, ' why, they will eat me if I come there !' ' No, no,' says he, ' me make them no eat you, me make them much love you.' Then he told me how kind they were to seventeen white men who came on shore in distress."

Soon they set to work to make a large canoe, in which to escape to the mainland ; and, for this purpose, Friday selected the tree, for he knew the right kind. A month's hard labour was expended on the boat, and a fortnight in launching her on great rollers ; but, when she was in the water, she would have carried twenty men, although she was very easily managed. Two months were occupied in rigging and fitting out this new vessel with a mast, sails, and a rudder.

Before the boat was completed, another party of savages, in three canoes, numbering one-and-twenty, and bearing a white man as a prisoner, landed on the island. Crusoe and Friday, arming themselves, fired at the savages, killing and wounding several of them. They then rushed down to the shore, where Crusoe cut the bonds which bound the white prisoner, who turned out to be a Spaniard, put arms into his hands, and bade him fight for his life.

The white man, nothing loath, attacked two of his would-be murderers like a fury ; but was likely to have come off badly in his encounter with a third, had not Crusoe shot the savage. Such of the invaders as were unhurt escaped in one of the canoes. Crusoe, jumping into one which they had left, found another poor creature therein, bound hand and foot, and almost dead with fright.

As this prisoner appeared to be Friday's fellow-countryman, he was instructed to inform him of his deliverance; and, strange to say, in the prisoner, he discovered his own father. This strange discovery put a stop to the pursuit of the other savages, who were now almost out of sight.

As soon as Crusoe had secured the rescued prisoners and given them shelter and a place to rest in, he began to think of making some further provision for them.

Having killed a goat he took one of the hindquarters, and, chopping it into small pieces, made a very good dish of broth and flesh with barley and rice added thereto. This he cooked outside and, having set a table for his guests, joined them and ate his dinner with them.

Having now a larger family to feed, Crusoe and his three companions dug up more ground, sowing it with barley and rice. As the season was a favourable one, they reaped a plentiful harvest.

Sending the Spaniard with Friday's father, in one of the canoes which the savages had left behind, to the mainland, in order to bring away some of his friends there, Friday and his master were again left alone.

They had been gone only eight days, when Friday espied a boat's crew of white men, rough seamen, who landed with three prisoners, whom they treated with much unkindness.

When they had landed Crusoe saw that they were Englishmen. In all there were eleven, of whom the three were unarmed. One of them seemed to be entreating for life with all the energy of despair. Here we shall let Crusoe tell his own story.

" I was perfectly confounded at the sight, and knew not what the meaning of it could be. Friday called out to me, in English, as well as he could, ' O master ! you see English mans eat prisoners as well as savage mans.'

" ' Why, Friday,' said I, ' do you think they are going to eat them, then ? '

" ' Yes ' says Friday, ' they will eat them.' "

" ' No, no, Friday,' said I ; ' I am afraid they will murder them, indeed, but you may be sure they will not eat them.'

" All this while I had no thought of what the matter really was, but stood trembling with the horror of the sight, expecting every moment that the three prisoners would be killed. Once I saw one of the villains lift up his arm with a great cutlass, to strike one of the poor men.

" I wished heartily now for our Spaniard, and the savage that was gone with him, or that I had any way to have come undiscovered within shot of them, that I might have rescued the three men, for I saw no firearms they had among them.

" After I had observed the rough usage of the three men by the insolent seamen, I observed the fellows run scattering about the land, as if they wanted to see the country. I observed, also, that the three other men had liberty to go where they pleased ; but they sat down all three on the ground, and looked like men in despair.

" On this I resolved to make myself known to them, and learn something of their condition. I came as near them undiscovered as I could, and then, before any of them saw me, I called aloud to them, in Spanish, ' What are ye, gentlemen ? '

"They started up at the noise, and were ten times more confounded when they saw me, and the uncouth figure that I made. They gave no answer at all, but I thought I perceived them just going to fly from me, when I spoke to them in English. 'Gentlemen,' said I, 'do not be surprised at me ; perhaps you may have a friend near you, when you did not expect it.'

"'Aid must be sent directly from Heaven,

*Suddenly Friday began jumping and dancing.*

then,' said one of them, very gravely to me, pulling off his hat at the same time, 'for our condition is past the help of man.'

"'Pray, lay aside your fears,' I said. 'I am a man—an Englishman, and disposed to assist you ; you see I have one servant only—we have arms and ammunition. Tell us freely, can we serve you ? What is your case ? '"

Then, while the rough seamen were wandering about on the island, Crusoe learned that they had mutinied against the three prisoners, who turned out to be the captain, the mate, and a passenger of their ship.

Arming his new acquaintances, they set upon the ringleaders of the mutineers, one of whom was killed on the spot, and the others severely wounded, upon which the rest submitted. The ship fired several signals and waved flags for the boat to return; but, when these proved fruitless, they sent out another boat, having a crew of ten men provided with firearms.

Eight of them landed in search of their comrades, leaving two only to mind the boat. Having knocked down one of these, the captain summoned the other to surrender, which he did. The plan of the defenders was to watch for the

*He joined his guests and ate dinner with them.*

other mutineers in the dark, and to fall upon them suddenly, so as to make sure work with them.

It was several hours before they came back to their boat, which they were surprised to see fast aground in the creek, and their two men gone. Suddenly, they were fired upon ; when the boatswain, the ringleader of the mutiny, was killed on the spot, and another man was mortally wounded. In great fear, they all laid down their arms, and begged for their lives. The prisoners were divided, and safely secured where they could do no harm ; and then arrangements were made to seize the ship. In this enterprise, also, the captain was successful.

Crusoe now decided to try to return to his native country ; and, having left some of the mutineers upon the island, he went on board the ship, taking his goatskin cap, his umbrella, and one of his parrots, as relics.

As he left the island on the nineteenth of December, 1686, he had lived there rather more than twenty-eight years ; and, when he reached England, in June, 1687, he had been absent thirty-five years. He now resolved to seek some information with regard to his plantation in Brazil, and of the fate of his partner. With this end in view, he went to Lisbon, where he found his old friend, the captain who first rescued him off the coast of Africa. Having laid claim to his estates in Brazil, our hero found himself the owner of fifty thousand pounds, and a rich plantation in Brazil.

---

# The Shortest Tale in the World

### by STEPHEN SOUTHWOLD

" WHICH do you like better, short tales or long ones ? " asked the broken-clawed Lobster, smiling amiably at the young Jack Crab.

" Short ones."

" Then I'll tell you the shortest tale in the world."

" Hurry up, then. Granny's waiting."

" Once upon a time there was a bloater."

" Yes, Go on."

" That's all."

" All ! it can't be all. What did he say ? "

" Nothing.  Bloaters don't."

" What did he do ? "

" Nothing. Bloaters can't."

" But, but——"

" No ' buts ' ; you cut along home and tell it to your Granny. Next time I'll tell you the longest story in the world."

" What's it about ? "

" An eel that swallowed its tail."

" Yes. What else ? "

" Made itself into a ring, you know. No beginning and no end. Ha ! ha ! ha ! " And the Lobster went off into fits of laughter.

# LEGENDS OF OUR ISLANDS

## ULPH'S HORN

*A Yorkshire Legend by John R. Crossland*

HERE is preserved in York Minster a long drinking-horn which is very probably part of the tusk of an elephant. It is some three feet in length, and when it came at first into the possession of the Minster, it was most beautifully decorated with gold, modelled in ancient designs. During the time of Cromwell, however, after the Civil War, the destructive agents of the Lord Protector, in ransacking the stately Minster and destroying its decorations, tore off the gold and left the bare horn. Later, after the Restoration of the Monarchy, the horn was re-decorated with silver gilt. There is a legend concerning the horn, and here it is.

When the Danes were in England, and were the ruling power in the north, there was a certain sub-king of the kingdom of Deira named Ulph, or Olphus. He had four sons, who had all been trained in the art of war, and the eldest would naturally follow his father as sub-king of the province.

It happened, however, that in one of the many skirmishes that continually occurred in this troublous region, the eldest son Adelbert was killed. Ulph mourned for his son, but took consolation in the fact that three more lusty fellows yet remained to him, and the eldest of these would be able to rule in his stead when his term of life was over.

Now Ulph was a man of great strength and bravery. He was, moreover, an upright man, who loved honesty of purpose and devotion to duty. His son Adelbert had left an orphan child, a sweet little girl by name Adelwynne, and Ulph had taken his grandchild into his home to bring her up in comfort and happiness as befitted a princess. He would walk round the castle grounds with the girl, and loved to have her company and hear her prattle more than anything life held for him.

One day they were strolling round the grounds, happy in each other's company—for Ulph was indeed a father to the child—when, in the course of their conversation the king said :

" Thou art very sweet, Adelwynne. Thine eyes are blue like unto those of my dead wife, thy grandmother the queen Helena. I do wish, however, that thou wert a boy ! "

" Why should you wish that, dear grandfather ? " replied the girl. " If I had been a boy perhaps I should have caused you more trouble than ever can be caused by a mere girl. Look, I might have been timid in war, and dubbed a coward by my followers. Again, I might have been a tyrant, hated by all the countryside. No, dear grandfather, it is best I am a girl."

" Perchance thou art right. Thou art young but thy tongue speaks great wisdom," murmured Ulph, as he placed his arm tenderly round her shoulders. " Let us walk on."

They strolled along awhile, until they came to an arbour under the palace wall, where Adelwynne often sat during the sunny summer days. She ran on before the king, to take her seat in the shade and prepare a place for her grandfather.

Ulph watched her lovingly as her light feet sped across the grass. Then, as she came abreast of the arbour, he saw her stop, place her hand before her eyes, and stand still, as though she had seen something which had given her a shock. He hurried to the arbour, and the sight that met his gaze was one which filled him with great anger. There lay his second son, Kerdic, who was his heir. He was in a drunken sleep, and an overturned goblet by his side told its silent tale.

In a great passion, Ulph strode up to the sleeping prince and stirred him roughly with his foot.

" Is this beast a son of mine ? " he cried, but the prince made no sign that he had heard, for he was deep in wine.

" Get up, thou drunken sluggard," cried the king, but Kerdic never heard the command.

" And thinkest thou that thou shalt lead the royal line in the kingdom of Deira ? " scoffed Ulph. " Never shalt thou reign in my kingdom. Thou art no longer my son. Come, Adelwynne, let us go into the purer air and leave this sot to sleep off his wine.

" The crown shall be thine, my daughter," he continued, as they walked away.

" Not so, lord," returned the maiden, " for thou hast yet two sons who will, ere long, return to the palace. One of these will assuredly prove himself fitted to wear the crown. Torfrid is due to-day, back from his hunting, and Edmund, who has been warring in the north, has sent messages ahead to say he draws near home. Let us wait for their return."

" I have little faith in my sons," retorted Ulph, " but I will bear me in patience till they return, and then choose my heir."

The sound of a horn was heard, and ere long two companies, with men and banners, approached the castle walls. Ulph hurried his little charge to a sheltered corner where they might observe what took place, and to witness the entry of the brothers to the castle.

It was soon seen that a quarrel was in progress, and as the companies neared the gate the brothers called a halt.

Above the gate, hidden from view, the king and Adelwynne heard what ensued. Truly, there was a bitter quarrel raging, and harsh words were passed in ever rising tones between the brothers.

Torfrid was raging and shouting, while Edmund was speaking more quietly though with a deeper cunning and bitterness. They were quarrelling about a lady they had both seen, and with whom they had both fallen in love. Torfrid claimed that he had become betrothed to her ere he left the northern land where was her home. Edmund laughed and said that he had left men in her home to guard her and to watch the family treasures too.

" I care not for the treasure, but give me my bride," shouted Torfrid.

Edmund laughed in his face, and told him to go hunting and forget about one who could never be his.

" Wait until father dies," retorted his brother. " Then I will descend with my army on thee and thy princess. I will slay thee with mine own hands. harry thy kingdom, and drive the lady to her knees to beg for mercy. Then shall she be mine at last."

Above the gate, Ulph turned sadly to Adelwynne and shook his head.

*Lifting the horn, he drained it at a draught.*

" I once had a son, dear girl," he moaned, " but he, brave Adelbert, lies dead, and in an honoured grave. I have no other child but thee, for these two are no longer of my flesh and blood. Kerdic is but a wine-wit, Torfrid a would-be murderer of his own brother, while Edmund, cunning and sly, is but an arrant coward. Dear child, to thee shall go my title and my lands. Thou shalt be queen of Deira when I am called to rest. Thou shalt wed thy cousin Edwy, who is brave and manly. Together shall ye rule, but thou shalt be the chief, the Queen of my province."

" Not so, dear lord," begged the girl, with tears of gratitude in her eyes.

" Thou shalt be Queen of Deira," cried Ulph, raising his right hand above his head. " By Woden do I swear it ! "

" What have we to do with Woden ? " pleaded Adelwynne, taking the king's other hand in hers. " Thine eldest son is dead, and thy living sons are unworthy. Yet there is a worthy heir."

" And who may it be, if not thy dear, sweet self ? " asked the king.

" The Lord Christ," exclaimed Adelwynne, her face suffused with a radiant smile. " Give thy lands to Christ, and let His Holy Church guard thy province and thy people. Naught shall harm thy subjects then, and thy soul shall rest in peace."

" Adelwynne, my child," replied the king brokenly, " thou art better than a son to me. It shall be as thou sayest. The kingdom shall belong to God."

Taking his largest drinking-horn, the king ordered that it be filled to the brim with wine and carried into the Church of York. Then he followed quickly, and, marching boldly to the steps of the altar, took the horn in both hands as he knelt in reverence. Lifting the horn he drained it at a draught and laid it empty on the altar.

"Be this the token that I give my lands to Christ and my people to the care of His Holy Church," he cried.

A ballad which has been written of this event closes the story thus : Said Ulph to the priest—

"Keep my horn, O holy father ; so, from age to age be known,
Power is a trust from heaven ; kings have nothing of their own ;
Never shall a son unworthy sit upon my father's throne ! "

So the horn passed into the keeping of the Minster, and the lands of Ulph passed at his death into the ownership of the Church. Thus were foolish men and unworthy sons fitly punished for their sins, and the king was at last at peace with the world.

# THE BOGGART

### A Lancashire Legend by W. Langley Roberts

OUR story is laid in one of Lancashire's most secluded villages, surrounded by tall trees and woodlands. All the beauty of the bluebell is here when spring blows her trumpets through the woodland. This is "Boggart-Hole," for here dwells the mysterious boggart.

And what pranks did he play in the green-wood ! Many had heard his shrill high-pitched laugh in the woods, and some had even had their flowers jerked from their hands, or their hair pulled, or their noses tweaked by his mischievous little fingers.

The boggart enjoyed his merry jests in the dell until the winter approached, and he began to look out for a warm house in which he could live in comfort through the cold weather.

He chose an old-fashioned house not far from the boggart-hole, where lived a worthy farmer named George Cheetham, and soon the whole household began to be plagued and tormented by his tricks.

Now, although no one had actually seen him, the traces of his handiwork were everywhere. The men had their spades and tools hidden, and were often to be seen wandering about the farmyard and out-buildings in bewilderment on mornings after the goblin had been at work ; for he could often be heard at his tricks as soon as ever the clock in the kitchen had struck the hour of midnight.

The maids, too, would find their pots and pans in all manner of strange places, although sometimes his tricks took a more pleasant form, and at times they would arise in the morning to find everything in its place. What is more, on these occasions, pots and pans would have been scrupulously cleaned and scoured, the cream churned for them, and the pewter and brass in the kitchen polished till they gleamed like silver and gold in the early morning sunshine.

But the children of the farmer would sometimes have their very food snatched away from them by his quick fingers, and often their basins of bread and milk would be flung to the ground by an unseen hand, even before their contents had been tasted.

Now one day it happened that one of the children was playing near the foot of the stairs, and seeing a small hole in the woodwork, he put in it a shoehorn with which he was playing. Out flew the shoehorn again and hit the child on the head, and so it was that whoever put anything into the hole was sure to be rewarded with a sharp blow from it as it flew back again. So it was thought that this was the boggart's lair, and this his peep-hole from which he espied all that took place in the house.

It was a time of cold and bitter weather, and Christmas was drawing near. The " waits " had been to the farm with their fiddles, music and Christmas wishes.

After their departure the farmer and his family sat round the fire. A

*Many had heard his shrill, high-pitched laugh in the woods.*

merry yarn had just been told by one of the company. Clearly above the general merriment was heard the fluty laugh of the boggart.

" Well laughed, Boggart ! " cried Robert, the farmer's second son. " Thou'rt a fine tyke, I'se warrant, if one could just catch a glent of thee."

So the story-telling continued, but all noticed that however jolly the story, or however loud the laughter, not another sound was heard from the goblin that night.

Now Robert, who was rather short in stature, slept with the eldest son John, who was just as tall as Robert was small. No sooner were they asleep that night than they were awakened by the thin voice of the boggart crying out :

" Little tyke, indeed ! Little tyke thyself ! Ho, ho, ho ! I'll show thee. I'll have my laugh now. Ho, ho, ho ! "

In the darkness the voice sounded so shrill and clear that it scared them both terribly, and no sooner was the strange laughter ended than Robert felt his feet seized and he was dragged to the foot of the bed. Then, immediately afterwards he was pulled in the opposite direction to the pillow again. Again and again this was repeated. One moment he would be at the foot of the bed, and the next his head would be level again with that of his tall brother John.

" Short and long won't match ! Short and long won't match ! Ho, ho, ho ! " laughed the boggart, who repeated this cry every time he tried to make the brothers equal in stature. He played this trick on the weary and sleepless brothers hundreds of times during the night. The brothers dared not move, so great was their fright, till at last the early morning light shone through the bedroom window.

" Now we'se ha' some rest, happen," said John, as he tried to rearrange the bedclothes.

" Boggart knows no rest ! Boggart knows no rest ! Ho, ho, ho ! " came the dreadful voice of the goblin, and the sufferers had to give up all hope of sleep in that room.

When the farmer heard the story from his sons, he decided that they should sleep in another room, and leave the boggart free to enjoy himself in the room in which they had passed such an unpleasant night.

But from that day the boggart's tricks became more and more unbearable. Each night brought fresh torments and frights. The stillness of the night was disturbed by heavy footsteps which seemed to range over the whole house. Pots and pans clattered, dishes crashed, and each morning they arose expecting to find a scene of havoc and ruin. Yet, strange to say, nothing was broken, and all things remained in their places.

Night became for them a time of dread and sleeplessness, until the farmer and his wife could bear it no longer and decided to move.

So the furniture was loaded on the carts, and with the last load went the farmer and his wife. On their way to the new home they were met by a neighbouring farmer.

" Hey, John," says he, " thou're surely never leaving th'owd whoam ? " (the old home).

" Aye," replied the farmer. " I'm like tha secs, for yon boggart torments us soa we ne'er get a wink o' sleep at neet ; and as for't wife and childer, they're fair skeered to deeath, so we'm fain to flit like."

He had just got so far with his explanation, when, out of a churn on the cart, a shrill voice cried out :

" Aye, aye, neighbour, we're flitting a' reet, as tha sees."

" Rot thee, boggart ! " cried the farmer angrily. " If I'd known tha'd be flitting too I'd ne'er ha' stirred a peg."

Then turning to his wife, he said :

" It's no manner o' use, my dear, we may as well turn back to th'owd house as be plagued again in another."

Return they did, and the legend is that the boggart behaved himself much better after this occurrence.

# THE LAIDLEY WORM OF SPINDLESTON

*A Northumbrian Legend by Margaret Tynedale*

"NEWS, Your Highness ! A royal messenger ! "

"A messenger ? From my father ? " asked the Princess Margaret eagerly.

It was a very lonely life that the little princess led in the royal castle of Bamburgh. Her mother was dead ; her only brother, the Childe (or knight) of the Wynd, had sailed away to seek fame and fortune in other lands, and had not been heard of for so many years that she feared he was dead too. And lately the king, her father, after years of mourning, had gone forth once more among his people, and she missed him sorely.

News at last ! Yes, news indeed ! The king was to be wed once more, and would shortly return to Bamburgh with his bride. At once the royal city was plunged into all the bustle of preparations. Nobles and chieftains of Bernicia (as that part of Northumbria was then called) came flocking in to do homage to their sovereign. But the fair Margaret's heart misgave her, as she gazed from her bower window, watching and waiting for the royal procession. She longed for her father's return ; but what would this new stepmother be like ? Could she love her too ?

At length she heard the well-known horn, and from her lofty window she could see the cavalcade approaching. Calling her maidens, she descended to the great hall to welcome her sire, and to be presented to his new queen. It was with very mixed feelings that the shy little maiden stepped forward to greet the newcomer. Her beauty was marvellous to behold, and her manner outwardly kindly ; but in reality her heart was as hard as stone. She had been bewitched in childhood ; and with the gift of magic beauty she had received the fatal power of casting spells.

Fancy her envy on seeing that the sweet and gentle princess was attracting far more attention than she with all her arts could command. And when one young knight so completely lost his heart to the lovely Margaret that he praised her aloud in glowing terms, calling her peerless among women, the jealous queen's anger burst all bounds. This was too much ! Such a rival must be swept from her path.

So, like the witch she really was, she uttered a dreadful curse. The Princess Margaret, she said, should turn into a laidley worm (which means a loathsome serpent or dragon) and should spread terror through the land. But there was a limit to her power for evil over one who was good and pure ; some loophole of escape she was bound to leave, but she made it as small as she could. On one condition could the victim be released, and that was the return of the absent brother—the Childe of the Wynd—he alone could break the spell.

Cruelly she smiled as she made this last condition—small chance was there of his ever coming back, she thought—for like many others she believed him dead.

Margaret laughed aloud at her cruel stepmother's threat. Really it was too absurd to frighten her—how could she turn into a laidley worm? She had done nothing to merit such a fate. There was no question now of loving her father's new wife, but at least she knew of one who would be ready to champion her should trouble threaten—and the thought was comforting.

And so presently she retired to her dainty bower, and fell peacefully asleep. Did she dream of threats and curses, of the brother she longed for, or of the brave young knight who had looked on her with such admiration? Perhaps. But in the morning when her maidens came to wait upon her, they fled in terror from the venomous beast which they found coiled upon the fair princess's bed. Their shrieks echoed through the castle, and even the warders shrank from the dreadful creature as she crawled down the stairs and out through the gate into the open country.

Two or three miles away, among the crags of Spindleston, she found a cave, and here she took up her abode. But at night she came out to feed upon the neighbouring fields and gardens, and her poisonous breath scorched even what she did not eat.

> " For seven miles east, and seven miles west,
>     And seven miles north and south,
>     No blade of grass or corn could grow,
>     So venomous was her mouth."

So runs the old ballad. In sheer despair, the king's retainers set apart seven cows for the dragon's special use, and every night took the milk to a large stone trough near the mouth of the cave, that the Worm might quench her raging thirst.

Terror reigned; famine threatened. The tale of woe spread far and wide, till at last it reached the ears of the Childe of the Wynd, as he sat at a feast of victory. Wild with wrath, he told the dread tidings to his faithful followers. With drawn swords they one and all vowed never to rest or feast again until their beloved princess should be restored and avenged. But how to get there?

They built a stout ship with masts of rowan-wood, for of such wood was made the cross on which our Redeemer suffered, and therefore no enchantment could touch it. Bravely they sailed homeward, and in seven days the look-out sighted a massive castle poised upon a mighty rock.

" That indeed is my father's keep, the castle by the sea," exclaimed the eager Childe, and would have made straight for the shore.

But the wicked queen had seen the gallant craft, and guessed its errand. Promptly she sent her imps to intercept it, but they were powerless against the rowan-tree mast, and returned baffled. Then she sent warriors to the attack, but they were mere mortals, and the Childe and his band were more than a match for them.

Then came trouble from an unexpected quarter. The Laidley Worm herself failed to recognise her deliverer, and in her fear she lashed the water with her tail until the waves grew so rough that landing was impossible. But Childe Wynd was not dismayed; quickly he changed his course, and made for Budle Bay, where he landed safely. Mounting his trusty steed, he rode to Spindleston, where the dragon had retreated. Throwing his bridle over a stone pillar (whence the place takes its name) he drew his " berry- brown " sword and went on foot to find her.

Face to face at last, she recognised her long-lost brother. In his presence her speech returned to her, and she begged him to " quit his sword, and give her kisses three "—truly a strange request ! Nothing daunted, the Childe bent low his stalwart frame, and caressed the fearsome beast, which then turned tail and retreated into her cave. A moment later, who should emerge but the Princess Margaret, a beautiful maiden once more.

Quick as thought her brother pulled off his crimson cloak to wrap around that delicate form ; and gathering her into his strong arms, lifted her upon his horse. And so they returned in triumph to Bamburgh Castle, to a father's love and his subjects' joy.

*The beauty of Princess Margaret was marvellous to behold.*

But the Childe's mission was not yet completed ; he had broken the wicked spell which had enslaved his beloved sister—he had still to avenge her wrongs. Where was the enemy ?

" Fetch forth the miscreant witch ! " he thundered. And high and low they sought her, till at last she was discovered cowering in terror in her bower, for well she knew her hour had come. Vainly she tried to pray, but the power to do so had long since deserted her, for she had sold her soul to evil.

And now she was to pay the price.

Brave and true himself, the Childe of the Wynd hated anything mean and cruel. And in no measured terms he told his unkind stepmother just what he thought of her. Before his righteous indignation she paled and trembled. The avenging prince knew something about magic arts, and when he sentenced her to the doom she had prepared for his sister, and bade her " squat, crawl, hiss, spit, in likeness of an ugly toad," she knew there was no help for her. Hardly had he ceased speaking when the change took place—and as a toad she hissed her helpless rage, for she could do no more harm.    The warders chased her from the castle gates, but no one killed her.

> " And on the lands near Ida's towers
>     A loathsome toad she crawls,
>     And venom spits on everything
>     That cometh nigh the walls."

At length, however, she took refuge at the bottom of the castle well ; and it is popularly believed that she is there yet !

And so was the wicked queen paid out for her jealousy, and the long-lost heir and his fair sister restored to their home.

Until comparatively recent times the cave and trough could still be seen at Spindleston, but have since been destroyed by a quarry, the Spindle Stone alone remaining.

# Two Scottish Legends

### By M. V. Jack

## I

## THE SEAL WOMAN

### I

SOMEWHERE on the rocky West Coast lived a lonely young fisherman to whom these happenings befell.

In the curve of a bay his hut stood, between the woods and the shingle, and often he would go to the water's edge to look out over the dreaming expanse, and listen to the weird cadences of the seal-music, thinking (as who would not in the circumstances?) of the mystery of the sea, and the Land-under-Waves, and the Seal Country—and the strangeness of the people who dwelt therein, mortal and yet not mortal, equally at home in the sea or on the land.

It was on such a night that his seal-wife came to him.    Blue on the dreaming water the islands lay.    The salt sea-odour mingled with the sweet smell of the turf.    In his ears was the music that holds the beauty and the sorrow of the sea, and the joy of drifting with the brown wrack over fathoms of swinging water.

The seals lay on the rocks at the southern point of the bay, basking in the evening sun.    To the north were other rocks at the end of a low reef, and there the young fisherman thought he saw the brown head of a solitary seal.    Or was it the head of a woman?    The sun on the water dazzled his eyes ;  he could not be sure.    But if it were a woman he must warn her. The tide was rising soundlessly.    Soon the low reef would be covered, and she cut off from the shore.

ROBINSON CRUSOE

When he espied me, he came running to me, laying
himself down again on the ground, with all the possible signs
of a humble, thankful disposition. (Page 146)

THE WALRUS AND THE CARPENTER

"I weep for you", the Walrus said,
"I deeply sympathise." (Page 188)

Over the bay the strange song went, liquid and sweet. It brought him a sense of elation as he scrambled over the slippery tangle and the little rock-pools; as he hunted for the woman among the rocks.

He found her at last, looking out towards the sunset, the glistening seal-skin lying by her side.

She was lovelier than the land women are, this daughter of the seals, rosy and white and dreamy-eyed. The young fisherman fell in love with her at sight. He knew that if he could capture her seal-skin she would not be able to return to her own country, so, stealthily, he managed to get hold of it.

The maiden saw him then, and prayed him wildly to give it up to her, but he would not. He held on to it stubbornly and begged her to come with him and be his wife. At last she consented and he took her home and married her.

Kind and gentle he was to her, never forgetting that she was far from her kinsfolk of the seals. She for her part made an excellent wife, as good and industrious as she was beautiful, and for the love she bore to her husband she hid the sorrow she still felt for her home under the waves.

But sometimes, in the long hazy afternoons, the blue luminous evenings, she would hear the seal-folk calling to her from the reef, and answer their plaintive melody with a song as poignant as their own. Once she went down to the rocks to talk with them.

"It is pleasant to lie in the sun," said an old seal lazily, "but pleasanter far to swim in the cool green depths of the sea; and pleasantest of all to dwell in the clear brightness of the country that lies beneath."

The seal woman sighed.

"Alas, what can I do? My husband has hidden my seal-skin—I cannot return."

"Your little sister has married a prince in the Seal Country, and theirs was a great feast and merrymaking."

"Would I were there to join in it!"

"Your father and mother, your brothers and sisters, they all were there, and they grieved because you were not with them. They think that you are lost to them for ever."

The seal woman went home and wept. Yet when the time came for her husband to return she could not help thinking how sad it would be if she were not there to welcome him. So she dried her tears and met him with a smile.

A year or two passed by, and

*Once she went down to the rocks to talk with them.*

one day he bade her farewell with a strange heart-sinking which he could not account for. It seemed to him that some danger threatened his wife, and he would gladly have stayed at home to protect her. But he did not want to look foolish, and besides he had their living to earn, so off he went.

When he was gone his wife went blithely about her household tasks, and then, for want of something better to do, she turned out an old chest that lay in the kitchen. What should she come upon but her own smooth seal-skin! The sight of it, the feel of it, filled her with a great longing for her own land. Then the thought of her husband held her back; he was so kind, so firm, so faithful. But again the temptation came. She took the glistening skin to the water's edge, played with it awhile, slipped it on. . . . In a moment she was a seal, diving into the cool water, rising again to bask in the sun on the rocks.

Other seal-folk were about. She heard their deep melodious tune, and presently she dived in again and swam off to join them.

When the fisherman returned he found the hut empty and his wife gone. The open chest, the vanished seal-skin, told their own story, and in bitterness of heart he ran to the shore and called her name. There was no response : the seals were gone.

Day after day he sought her, scanning the waves from his boat, searching the rocky coast, but though he sometimes heard the seal-music far out at sea never a sign had he that his wife could hear him.

## II

ONCE on a wild and stormy day, when the white horses raced over the water, he stood on the beach and called his wife's name piteously. A voice reached him through the noise of the wind.

"Why weep you there, young fisherman?"

He turned in surprise and there was an old gray man with a bundle strapped on his back. So kind, so gentle was the stranger's aspect that he was moved to tell his story, and "Oh, that some one would take me to the Country of the Seals!" said he.

"I too am of the seal-folk," said the stranger. "Perhaps I may be able to help you."

He undid his pack, and lo! there were two shining gray seal-skins.

"One is mine," said he; "if you really wish to visit the Country of the Seals you may wear the other."

Together they donned the strange garb, and felt themselves growing into seals.

Together they slipped into the churning water, and down, down, down they went, until it seemed as though they never would stop. But at last they emerged in the Country of the Seals.

Before them was a lovely landscape. Woods and hills and valleys were brighter and more colourful than in the world above the waves. The streets were cobbled with shells, and the houses built of coral and pearl. Here they discarded their seal-skins and became men again.

" You must stay with me in the meantime," said the old gray man, " and I will bring you news of your wife."

The young fisher was full of impatience, but it seemed that his wife was a princess in her own country, and there were certain forms to be observed. However, the old man, who also appeared to be a person of importance, promised him tidings on the morrow, if he would be his guest for the night.

Alas, on the morrow the stranger returned with the woeful tidings that the fisherman's wife was about to be married to a seal.

" Can I have but one word with her ? " asked the young man piteously.

" I think I can do that for you."

A little while longer he waited, and there stood his wife before him. He kissed her with joy and tears. She told him then that it was the wish of the seal-folk that she should marry one of their number. In vain he pleaded with her to return.

" They would not let me go," she said mournfully ; " or they would call me back again, and I must come."

" They could not bring you back if you would stay," he urged.

" There are spells in the Seal Country that you know nothing of ; we could not fight against these."

It seemed that nothing he could say would move her. Sorrowfully at last she took her leave, and he was obliged to let her go.

Day after day he stayed on in the house of the seal-man, and every day brought the wedding of the princess nearer. At last in despair he sought the advice of his host.

" It is a hard thing," the old man said, " to mix the earth world with the countries under the sea. Yet since she is your wife I will tell you what to do. On the day of the wedding you must go to the palace, taking your seal-skin with you. I will give you a spell to put upon her so that she will follow you through the sea and over the sea, yes, to the earth-world itself."

The young fisherman thanked him warmly.

" When you bring her to your home," the old man went on, " see that you guard her well, for if you lose her this time you shall never see her again."

Nearer came the wedding. Now all the seal-people talked of it—the beauty of the bride, the dignity of the bridegroom, the great feast which the old king would make in honour of the event. Nobody thought of the poor fisherman whose wife the princess was ; but he too was busy with his preparations.

At last the great day dawned. Guests came from far and near to the wedding of the king's daughter. Among them the young man mingled, carrying his seal-skin carefully hidden under his cloak. His host had fitted him out richly, so that he was brave as any of them, and a great deal handsomer than the bridegroom.

When the bride appeared he laid the spells which the old man had taught him. Then he went out and donned the magic seal-skin. In a moment his wife had joined him. She also became a seal, and together they floated up through leagues of dark water.

Glad was the young fisherman to behold once more the land above the waves. He threw his seal-skin back into the sea, and would have thrown his wife's also, but she cried out in alarm :

" If you destroy it I shall die," she said. " I am of the sea, and I cannot live without it."

So again he hid it away, but this time she secretly watched where he was putting it.

They went back to the little hut between the wood and the shingle, and there for a time they lived happily, though always with a sense of foreboding which they could not quite throw off.

Then one day they heard again the call of the seal-folk, and this time there was something strangely menacing in the sound. Mournful and sad was the fisherman, unwilling to leave his young wife while the seals were about, but at length off he went. When he returned they were gone, but alas, his wife was with them.

All day he paced the beach, listening eagerly for the voices of the Strange People, but no sound could he hear. Day after day he wandered disconsolately along the shore, but this time there was no wise stranger to help him. So at last he went to the rock where he had first met his wife, and calling aloud on her name, jumped into the sea.

But that did not help him either. He drifted with the brown wrack on the fathoms of green water, and the Country of the Seals was far away.

## II

## THE HEATHER ALE

HEATHER is something more than heather in the Scottish mind. It is a symbol of the vigour and hardihood, the richness, the wild yet delicate flavour of the landscape and the race. It is the bloom on our history as well as on our hills.

And the old lost brew of the Heather Ale—honey-sweet and potent—seems not so much a drink as a distillation of enchantments. Yet a drink it was in the olden time, a drink to warm the hearts of heroes and fire the muse of the bards ; wisdom of age to the young, and to the old the glory of youth. . . . Among the hills they brewed it, the vanished people—Picts or an older race—who play so large a part in our tradition. Garb them in green mantles and pointed rush hats, and they become fairies ; clothe them with heroic stature and lo ! they are the hunters of the Fein. They have even passed into our idiom under the quaint name of Hottentots ! . . . They lived in green mounds and subterranean dwellings, and there they drank the liquor of the heather-bell. How well they kept the secret of their brewing is told in the following legend of Galloway.

The little swarthy folk had had their day. Ruthlessly the tall, fair strangers drove them back into crevice and cranny, into caves and holes in the rock ; relentlessly they crushed the old rude civilisation with its strange outlandish ways and—here and there—its jewels of barbaric achievement.

At last there was a great conflict between them. Back and forth went

*The Scottish king sat proudly on his horse.*

the tide of battle until the little people were completely wiped out. So at least thought the King of the Scots, as he rode proudly over the battlefield. He was glad that the barbarians would trouble him no more with their teasing, cunning warfare. One thing only he regretted—that before he had stamped them out utterly he had not learnt the secret of the Heather Ale.

Rich old wines they drank at the Scottish court; good strong ale; but none had the charm, the potency of the Pictish beverage. Strange ecstasies, they said, fell upon those who drank it; cold and hunger were forgotten; on a raging winter night they could see the heather-blush on far blue island hills, and listen to the drone of bees over miles of knee-high, honey-scented heather.

"Fool that I was!" the king muttered impatiently.

At that moment two dwarfish figures started up from under his horse's feet and leapt into the flaming gorse bushes.

"After them!" cried the king; and presently they were brought back, bound, resentful, darting quick, sullen glances from under their bushy brows.

Father and son they were, last of all the hill folk; broad and muscular despite their little stature; dark, primitive and rude.

The Scottish king sat proudly on his horse, a fine upstanding figure, fair of face and nobly featured, stern and imperious, every inch a king. He looked on the captives as he might look on some repulsive animals. There was but one thing he wanted of them.

"Dogs!" he said, "I will spare your lives on one condition—that you reveal to me the secret of the Heather Ale! To the cliff!"

They rode a little distance to the brink of a cliff. Far below the waves fretted among the cruel rocks. The little men shrank back appalled.

"Now," said the king, "I give you but a short time to choose which you will do—surrender the secret and spare your lives, or—suffer torture and perish over yonder!"

The younger of the two tossed back his matted hair, clenched his teeth and strained at his bonds, but the elder crept to the king's side, crafty cunning in his eyes.

"Sire," he said, and his speech was rough and uncouth as his appearance; "give me but a chance to speak with you apart!"

The king looked down on him with loathing, but he rode a few paces away from the cliff edge. The little man drew closer to his side.

"Sire," he said again, "I am old and my life has grown dear to me! Yet I fear my son would kill me if I should tell you the secret we have sworn to keep. But if you will throw my son over the cliff first, then, sire, then——"

The king looked at him with greater loathing than ever, but he ordered his men to throw the lad over the cliff into the sea.

This was quickly done. Struggling, scratching, biting, the youth was seized and flung into the sea where the bitter waves foamed and fretted among the sharp rocks.

The king frowned and bit his lip.

"Now," he said impatiently, "the secret!"

The little, swarthy, old man was laughing! His crafty eyes glittered through his wildly tangled hair.

"Ah-a!" said he, a note of triumph in his animal speech; "you thought I sent my son to his death because I was afraid. Nay, I did but fear that he would betray our secret, for he was only a boy. Now you can do to me what you will—torture or slay, I care not; the secret of the Heather Ale will perish with me!"

The Scots king looked down on him with a queer new interest. He saw something there—be it ever so rudely expressed—something dauntless, indomitable, to which he himself was no stranger.

"I see, indeed," he said drily, "that torture would avail little with such as thou!" He bade his followers release the barbarian, who henceforth lived quietly among the Scots until his death.

The secret of the Heather Ale he never revealed, and a secret it remains to this day.

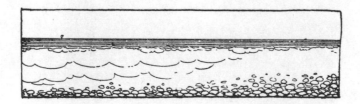

## LAZY MOLLY

*A Devonshire Legend by Cecily M. Rutley*

HERE once lived in Tavistock two serving girls. Their names were Molly and Kate, and they were both very fond of the pixies.

They knew how these little people love water, and every night, before they went to bed, they filled a bucket with fresh, clear water, and placed it in the kitchen. In the morning when they came downstairs they often found some silver pennies lying at the bottom of the bucket, which the grateful little pixies had dropped into the water for them.

One night Molly and Kate forgot all about filling the bucket, and went to bed leaving it standing empty in the chimney-nook. Perhaps they had been out, or had had some friends to visit them, or perhaps they were very tired. We are not told the reason of their forgetfulness, but there it was.

Presently the pixies came flying into the house through crannies and keyholes to look for their bucket of water. When they found it empty they were very disappointed. "Those tiresome girls have forgotten to fill it!" one little pixy cried. "Let us go up and ask them why!"

So upstairs whisked the pixies in the twinkling of an eye. Through the keyhole into the girls' bedroom they popped, and skipped and hopped excitedly about.

"The girls have forgotten our water!" cried one of them.

"It is very tiresome of them!" cried another.

"We are *very* much annoyed!" said a third.

Now Kate was still awake, and she heard what the pixies said. She nudged Molly who was fast asleep. "Wake up, Molly!" she cried. "Wake up at once!"

*When the pixies found the bucket empty they were very disappointed.*

"What is the matter?" asked Molly in a very sleepy voice. "Why are you waking me? I was having *such* a beautiful dream."

"We forgot to fill the pixies' bucket with water," said Kate. "They are very annoyed at our neglect. Listen! You can hear them grumbling and complaining in this room."

But Molly just pulled the bedclothes over her head, and turned over on her side. "Let them complain," she said. "I'm going to sleep again."

"Oh, you *mustn't*, Molly," cried Kate. "Jump up, and let us go down and fill the bucket now."

"Not I," said foolish Molly in a very drowsy voice. "I wouldn't get out of my bed now to please all the pixies in Devonshire!" And next moment she was fast asleep.

Alas! The pixies had heard her, and Molly was to be punished for her laziness as you soon shall hear.

"I'll go anyway," said Kate. "Poor little pixies. They shall have their water. They are always very kind to us."

So she jumped out of bed and ran downstairs. She filled the empty bucket, then crept upstairs again. When she went back into the bedroom the pixies were still there. She could not see them, for it was too dark. But she could hear their shrill little voices quite clearly.

"How shall we punish that lazy girl?" asked one.

"Let's pinch her all over!" suggested another.

"Let's nip her hard!" cried a third.

"Let us tear to bits her new cherry-coloured bonnet and ribbons!" suggested a fourth.

"Let's give her the toothache!" said a fifth pixy.

"Let's give her a red nose!" cried a sixth.

"Oh, she is too pretty for us to do that!" cried a seventh little pixy who was rather kinder than the rest.

"I know!" cried an eighth pixy. "We'll give her a lame leg!"

"Not to last for always!" said the kind one.

"No!" replied the other. "It shall last for seven years. But then it shall only be cured if Molly finds this plant that grows on Dartmoor. Its name is . . ." and the pixy pronounced, very slowly and clearly, the name of a plant that had seven syllables.

"Oh, how shall I remember it!" cried Kate who had been listening to the pixies' debate. "It *is* a long word. Let me see, this is it," and she repeated the name over and over again to herself until she fell asleep.

The next morning, when she woke, the first thing she thought of was the long name. "Oh!" she cried, sitting up in bed. "I have quite forgotten it," and although she tried her hardest to recall it to her mind not one syllable could she remember.

Then Molly woke, and jumped out of bed. "Oh, whatever *has* happened to me?" she cried. "Oh, Kate, one of my legs is quite lame!"

"That is the punishment the pixies have sent you for being lazy last night, and not getting up and going downstairs with me to fill their bucket with water," said Kate sadly.

"Oh, the horrid, nasty, unkind little creatures," cried Molly, stamping her good leg on the floor.

"Hush!" cried Kate. "Do be careful what you are saying. If the pixies hear you they may send you a worse punishment." Then she told Molly all that she had heard them saying, and how in seven years' time she would be cured of her lameness if she could find a certain plant that grew on Dartmoor.

"What is its name?" asked Molly.

"I have forgotten it," said Kate. "All I know is that it is a very long name, but I cannot remember a single syllable."

"Oh, how *stupid* of you!" cried Molly, and she stamped her foot again. But it was not the slightest use her being cross and angry. Lame she was, and lame she continued to be in her right leg for nearly seven years.

Then one day, when the seven years were drawing to an end, Molly said, "I am going on to the Moor to gather mushrooms. Come with me, Kate. Perhaps we may find the plant the pixies spoke of." Molly was not cross about her lameness any longer, and had grown quite cheerful and patient. But each time she went on to Dartmoor she hoped she might find the plant the name of which had seven syllables.

"I am tired of looking for it!" said Kate. "We have been looking for nearly seven years now, and all we can find are plants with short and simple names that we know quite well."

"Perhaps the pixies have not allowed us to find it yet," said Molly. "They said I was to be lame for seven years. But now that time is nearly over, perhaps we shall be able to discover it."

"I cannot come to-day, anyway," said Kate. "I have some work to finish."

So Molly took her basket, and climbed up on to Dartmoor by herself. She knew where the best mushrooms were always to be found, and sure enough, there were more than ever about, and such beauties they were this bright sunny morning.

Molly was stooping down to pluck a mushroom, when a short distance away she saw a strange little boy, with a very merry face, suddenly start up from the ground and come tumbling head over heels towards her. In his hand he was holding a plant.

"Who are you?" asked Molly, standing up.

The boy did not answer, but he tumbled right up to Molly, and struck her lame leg with the plant. And the next moment her lameness had gone!

The boy had gone too, so Molly could not thank him. She filled her basket with mushrooms, then hastened home. Kate was standing at the door of the house watching for her. "Why, Molly," she cried as Molly came skipping gaily up the path, "whatever *has* happened? Why, you are not lame any longer!"

"No!" cried Molly in a very joyful voice. "I am *not*." Then she told Kate about the strange boy and his plant.

"That must have been the plant the pixies mentioned," said Kate. "I don't expect, as you said, that they ever meant us to find it for ourselves in case you should have been cured too soon. But, oh, Molly," she added, "now you are cured *do* be careful never to annoy the pixies again."

"You need have no fear of that," cried Molly. "It is much too nasty and tiresome being lame for me to forget. Dear little pixies ! I *do* thank you for sending that plant to make me well again."

" I expect the pixies have heard you," said Kate.

" I hope they have," said Molly. " For I *am* grateful."

After that Molly found that her dancing had very much improved. She could now dance much more gracefully than before she became lame. And on May Day, when the festivities and frolics were held on the village green, the best dancer of all who were there dancing round the Maypole was lazy Molly.

# THE TALE OF ST. PIRAN

### *A Cornish Legend by Cecily M. Rutley*

MANY saints or holy men and women lived and worked in Cornwall long ago, and there are numbers of interesting and beautiful legends about them.

The chief of them, and the one who may be called the patron saint of Cornwall, is St. Piran. He is first heard of in Ireland, where he taught the people and performed many marvellous acts. He is said to have brought to life soldiers who had been killed in battle, and dogs which had been killed while hunting the wild boar ! But, in spite of all that he did for them, the kings of Ireland grew tired of St. Piran, and one day commanded that he should be thrown into the sea.

So the unfortunate saint was put into chains, and taken to the top of a steep precipice overlooking the sea. A crowd of wild Irish followed him, and some of them pushed a huge millstone to the top of the hill, where poor St. Piran was fastened to it.

Then one of the kings gave a signal, and St. Piran and the millstone were rolled over the edge of the cliff. Far below the angry waves were dashing over the rocks, and the sky was dull and overcast. But as soon as the saint had been pushed over the cliff the sun shone forth brilliantly, the wind, which a moment before had been blowing tempestuously, died down, and the sea became smooth and calm. Sitting quietly and happily upon the large stone, St. Piran landed upon the water, and went floating away.

When the crowd of wild Irish folk, who were watching from the cliff top, beheld the wonder that had happened, it is said that many of them became Christians from that moment. But St. Piran did not return to them. He floated on over the water, until he reached the north coast of Cornwall.

On March 5th, the millstone floated up on to that glorious stretch of golden sands which lies between Newquay and Perranporth, and which is now known as Perran Beach after St. Piran. The saint then left the great stone which had borne him safely over the water. He went ashore, and built himself a little chapel upon the sands, and began to work amongst and teach the Cornish people, who loved and honoured him far more than the Irish had done. They came to services in the lovely little church with its altar decorated with the most beautiful flowers that St. Piran could find, or which he had given to him, and when any of them were in trouble or difficulty they went to see him in his little cell which he made bright and gay with crystals that he collected from the rocks around. The vast sands of Perranporth are edged with wonderful arched rocks which are very large and tall, and there is one great mass of rock known as Chapel Rock that can only be reached on foot at low tide. At high tide it stands up out of the sea. No doubt at some time or another a little chapel stood upon it. It *might* have been the one St. Piran built. All these you will see if you visit Perranporth to-day, and wander over the sands where St. Piran wandered long ago.

In his wanderings St. Piran often looked up at the slate rocks of which the cliffs at this part of Cornwall are formed, and noticed the lines or veins of different minerals running through them. He made a collection of as many different kinds as he could find.

One day he took a heavy black stone to form part of the fireplace he was building on the sands. When his fire was lighted to cook his meal it burned with greater strength and intensity than usual, and presently St. Piran saw a stream of beautiful white metal flowing out from it upon the sand.

" Oh ! " cried St. Piran in great joy. " Praise be to God, Who, indeed, is Great and Good. He has allowed me to discover something which will surely be of great use to man."

St. Piran wished to tell some one about his great discovery. So he sought out another saint, St. Chiwidden, who lived nearby. " Come and see what is flowing out of my fire ! " he cried.

" 'Tis surely a great discovery ! " St. Chiwidden exclaimed, when he had been shown the wondrous sight. " That black rock is being melted by the fire, and changed into the beautiful white metal."

Now St. Chiwidden was a learned man. He soon found out a way of

obtaining the metal in large quantities. Perhaps he built the first smelting house, and gave his name to it. That, for certain, we do not know. But *chi-wadden* is the Cornish word for a " white house," and in a smelting or blowing-house the black ore of tin is changed into the white metal !

Then, as there were large quantities of the black ore in the rocks and cliffs, St. Piran and St. Chiwidden called on all the Cornishmen who lived thereabouts, and told them of their great discoveries. They taught them how to dig the ore out of the earth, and then how to obtain the metal. The Cornish folk were greatly rejoiced, and celebrated the discovery of tin by many days of feasting and merrymaking. And for years afterwards two days were always kept apart by them for such rejoicings. One was the 5th of March, the day on which St. Piran arrived on their shores, and the other was the second Thursday before Christmas. White Thursday, they called it, in memory of the day when St. Chiwidden first showed their forefathers how to change the black tin ore into the white tin metal.

After the first days of rejoicing were over the men of Perranporth, and of St. Agnes too, set to work with a will. They dug up large quantities of the tin ore, and smelted it into the white metal which they then took down to the southern coasts of their county, where it was bought by merchants from Gaul as in those days France was called.

The news of the discovery of tin soon spread far and wide, and when it reached the ears of the rich merchants of Tyre, that great city of the East, Phœnician sailors set sail for Cornwall to seek the precious metal.

" Whatever happens," the Cornish folk then said amongst themselves, " none of these foreigners must ever find out whence we obtain the ore. We are willing to sell them the tin, and as much of it as they want. But they must never come ashore, and get it for themselves."

So, in order to safeguard themselves against such an event, the Cornishmen built earthworks and entrenchments all around the ground where the tin ore was found, and many of these old defences and " hill castles " are still to be seen in the neighbourhood of St. Agnes to-day. They forbade, also, any foreigner to land upon their shores, and they set up markets where tin could be bought on the islands along their coast. These Tin Islands were known by the old Cornish standard which was hoisted upon each of them, the banner of St. Piran and St. Chiwidden, a white cross upon a black ground as symbols of the black tin ore and the white tin metal.

Small wonder that St. Piran was beloved by the Cornish folk, not only on account of his good life and noble deeds, but also because that it was to him they owed the discovery of tin. When at last he grew old and died he was buried by his people in the Penhale Sands, a number of large sand-hills a short distance inland from the sands of Perranporth where St. Piran had floated ashore on the millstone. Over his grave they built St. Piran's Chapel, which has long since been almost completely buried beneath the sands, but of which some of the ruins may still be seen.

Many places also were named after Cornwall's and the tinners' patron saint, whose name was sometimes spelt Perran as well as Piran. Besides Perranporth, there is Perranzabuloe, which means " Perran in the Sands," Perranwell, which is near Falmouth, Perranuthroe on Mount's Bay, and others which you can find for yourselves.

# TWO WELSH LEGENDS

*by* HILDA A. E. ROBERTS

## THE LEGEND OF BEDDGELERT

EDDGELERT lies near the mighty Snowdon in Carnarvonshire, about eight miles inland from the sea. "Bedd" is the Welsh word for "grave," so Beddgelert means the "Grave of Gelert." This is the story of how it came to be so called.

Many years ago there lived a brave chieftain, called Llewellyn, in Snowdonia. Now Llewellyn had a faithful hound which had been presented to him by King John of England, and this hound was the leader of all Llewellyn's pack. At home he was as gentle as a lamb but in the hunt there was not another to compare with him.

One day when Llewellyn and his men had assembled on the mountainside ready for hunting the hare, the huntsman blew a loud blast on his horn to rally the pack of hounds. To the huntsman's surprise, Gelert, the leader of the pack, was not there. So he blew again upon his horn. Still Gelert did not come. " It seems very strange that Gelert does not come in answer to my call," said the hunstman.

But they could not wait for him any longer and the huntsmen and the rest of the pack went on without him.

But somehow or other things went wrong that day. The chase was poor, the hounds failed to run their quarry to earth.

At twilight Llewellyn rode sadly towards his castle. He was wondering greatly where Gelert had been all day. Just then he heard the familiar sound of his barking.

" Ah ! Bad dog ! Why did you fail me to-day ? Where have you been ? " Llewellyn began. But as he rode nearer he could see that something was amiss.

The dog did not bound forward to greet him as he usually did. He crouched low and licked his lips. Then, looking more closely at him, Llewellyn perceived that Gelert's coat was tangled and matted with clots of blood.

" What is the matter ? Whence came all this blood ? " cried his master.

Here, there and everywhere the ground was smeared with it. Llewellyn dismounted hastily and ran into the castle. Here there were signs everywhere of a struggle. Blood, freshly-spilled, lay all over the floor. No servants were there to answer to his call. Gelert followed at his master's heels, dragging his hind legs somewhat.

Quickly Llewellyn's gaze travelled to the cradle in which he had left his baby son. He rushed up to it. The baby was not there ! The coverlet was torn and smeared with blood. All was in disorder. Llewellyn had only one thought at the time. " Cruel monster ! " he cried to the dog. " Thou hast betrayed thy trust and devoured my son ! "

The poor dumb creature's eyes searched his master's face.

173

"If only I could speak!" he seemed to say. He crouched low and tried to lick his master's feet. But Llewellyn was furious.

"Thou, too, shalt die, treacherous hound!" And so saying he plunged his sword into Gelert's side.

His dying yelp was heard from afar. It woke Llewellyn's sleeping child who murmured and cried out.

The chieftain searched in the direction from whence the sound came. There, in another room, quite safe and sound, beneath a heap of blood-stained clothes, lay the child.

At his side, torn and mangled, but quite dead, lay an enormous wolf!

Now the truth was made clear to Llewellyn. The gallant hound had fought with the wolf and had killed him, in order to save the life of the child he so jealously guarded.

Llewellyn's grief was pitiful to behold. "The frantic deed which laid thee low, this heart shall ever rue," said he.

So Gelert was buried with ceremony and there beneath a mound of stones, his grave can still be seen to this day.

> "The grey old man in the chimney corner
> Of his father heard this story,
> Which from his father he had heard
> And after them have I remembered."
> So now I tell it unto you!

## THE LADY OF LLYN Y FAN FACH

MANY years ago, some folks say during the twelfth century, there lived a poor widow, near Llanddeusant, in Carmarthenshire.

She had an only son, well-favoured and good to look upon, and each day this son drove his mother's cows up the side of the Black Mountain, to graze.

One day they came in their wanderings to the edge of a deep lake called Llyn y Fan Fach. Imagine the youth's surprise when he saw, standing on the calm surface of the water, a beautiful maiden. She was singing softly to herself and arranging her golden, curling locks.

Shyly the young man held out to her a piece of his barley bread, hoping that she would take it from him. She came to the edge of the lake but no farther, saying as she came:

> "Cras dy fara
> Nid hawdd fy nala!"

which meant,

> "Hard baked is thy bread,
> Hard it is to catch me."

*" This is the second time you have given me a blow without cause, husband,"*
*she sighed. " The third time, remember, I shall leave you."*

With these words she dived away out of sight. The young man was
overcome with love for her. That night when he had brought his cattle
safely home and he was sitting by the fireside with his mother, he told her
all about the beautiful maiden.

" She must be one of the ' Tylwyth-Teg ' (the fairies), my boy," said
his mother. " Take with you some unbaked dough to-morrow and see if
that will tempt her."

The youth set out early on the following morning and again he drove
his cows up to the lake.

All day long he waited but the maiden did not appear. Just as he was
giving up all hope, however, one of the cows strayed rather too close to
the edge, slipped into some soft mud and fell.

The youth rushed to help the cow, and as he did so, he saw the lady
appear again in the lake.

With shining eyes he held out his bread, unbaked this time. Again the
maiden refused it, saying :

" Llaith dy fara
Ti ni fynna ! "

which means,

" Too moist is thy bread,
I will not come to thee."

Again she plunged into the lake. Early next morning the boy visited
the lake once more, taking with him, this time, bread that was neither too
moist nor too hard.

The maiden again appeared and the moderately baked bread seemed to please her very much for she took it and consented to be the young man's wife.

"But one thing I must tell you," she said, "before we are wed. You must never on any account whatsoever strike me three blows without cause. If you do, then I shall go, never to come back."

When she had said this she plunged again beneath the waters. In a few minutes, a gray-bearded old man arose from the lake. With him were his three daughters and, wonder of wonders, they were all three exactly alike !

"These are my daughters," said the old man. "If thou canst pick out the one that thou didst ask to be thy wife, then thou shalt have her."

Now this was a puzzle to the young man. He really could not tell one from the other. Suddenly he remembered that his lover had worn sandals on her feet, which had attracted his attention. He looked down at their feet. One had sandals on and the others had nothing ! Moreover, the one with the sandals thrust out one foot as if to make him notice the fact.

"That is the maiden," said he.

"Thou art right," said the old man. "Take her, and with her I will give thee cattle in plenty, so that thou shalt never want. But remember this. Never strike her without cause. If thou dost strike her three times, on the third time she will leave thee."

As the young couple went down the slope of the hill, so did the herds of cattle come from out the waters of the lake, walking five by five.

For a long time all went well. One day the young couple were invited to attend a christening, some distance away. So the husband fetched a horse that they might ride, and as he helped her on to the horse's back, he tapped her playfully with his glove upon her shoulder, saying, "Dos ! Dos !" which meant "Hurry !"

She gazed at him with sadness in her eyes. That was the first of the three blows !

As time passed three sons were born to them. They were very handsome and very clever too.

One day the man and his wife were present at a wedding. In the midst of all the rejoicings, the wife began to cry loudly.

Her husband, greatly wondering, tapped her gently on the shoulder, saying :

"Wife ! Wife ! Why do you cry ?"

"That is the second time you have given me a blow without cause, husband," she sighed. "The third time, remember, I shall leave you."

Her husband felt very cross with himself for having been so thoughtless, but as time wore on, he almost forgot about it.

Then one day, years afterwards, the man and his wife were present at a funeral in the house of another neighbour.

Without a word of warning, the wife indulged in a fit of hearty laughter.

"Wife ! Wife ! Why do you laugh when every one else is crying ?" asked her husband.

As she did not stop laughing, her husband went to her and again patted her on the shoulder, asking her what was the matter.

Now this was the third blow !

### THE BUTTERFLY'S BALL

See the children of earth and the tenants of air
For an evening's amusement together repair. (Page 222)

DON QUIXOTE BECOMES A KNIGHT

The inn-keeper repeated some pious oration,
then gave Don Quixote a gentle slap on the back
with the flat of his sword. (Page 266)

" People when they die go out of their troubles," said the wife, " and so do I go."

That was how she left him. As suddenly as she had entered his life so did she go out of it, crying upon her cows to follow her :

> " Brindled cow, white speckled,
> Spotted cow, bold freckled,
> With the White Bull
> From the court of the King,
> And the little black calf
> That is hanging on the hook,
> Come thou also, quite well home ! "

And the little black calf that had just been killed, and was hanging from a hook, became alive and well and with the rest of the herd followed the woman. Back into the waters of Llyn y Fan Fach they returned, and were never seen again.

The husband, they say, died soon afterwards of a broken heart.

As for the three sons, they used to walk, by night, at the edge of the lake in the hope of seeing their mother again.

One night she appeared to them near what is now called " Llidiad-y-Meddygion," the " Doctors' Gate," and bade her sons take up the study of healing the sick.

Later on, she appeared again, this time at " Pant-y-Meddygion," the " Doctors' Dingle," and there she pointed out to them certain plants and herbs well known for their powers of healing.

Be all this as it may, the fame of those three sons, as physicians, spread through the length and breadth of the land. The graves of the Physicians of Myddfai can still be seen in the little churchyard.

> [1] " The grey old man in the chimney-corner
> Of his father heard this story
> Which from his father he had heard
> And after them have I remembered."
> So now I tell it unto you.
>     [1] Trans. Old Welsh Pennill.

# Two Irish Fairy Tales

*Adapted from Thomas Crofton Croker*

## THE GIANT'S STAIRS

ON the road between Cork and Kinsale, stands a great house, where a noble lord and his lady lived many years ago.

They had a little son about seven years old, who was called Philip, after no less a person than the King of Spain.

Philip was a bright little fellow, with big blue eyes and curly brown hair. He was very clever at his books too. No wonder his father and mother were proud of him.

He must have felt very lonely with no brothers to play with; for often he would go away for hours, to chase butterflies in the beautiful gardens. The butterflies and the flowers, you see, were his only playmates.

One afternoon, however, Philip was missing, and no one could think what had become of him. Servants were sent, on horseback and on foot, along all the roads; but they came home without hearing anything of the little boy. His father offered a large sum of money to any one who would bring back his son, but the years passed and Philip was never heard of again.

Now, at this time, there lived in the village a blacksmith called Robin Kelly—a merry fellow who could shoe a horse better than any man in Ireland. One night Robin had a strange dream. He dreamed that Philip came to him in the middle of the night and spoke to him. The lost boy was mounted on a beautiful white horse, but his voice was very sad, and his eyes were full of tears. He told Robin how he had been carried off many years ago by the giant Mahon, and had been forced to work in his forge.

"All the little boys who are stolen are kept for seven years in his palace, among the rocks near the village," said Philip. "After that they are sent far away to another of the giant's castles. "My seven years of service end to-night, and, if you can rescue me before morning, I will see that you get plenty of money." "But how am I to know," said Robin—cunning enough, even in his sleep, "that this is not a silly dream?"

"Take that as a sign," said the boy, and at these words the white horse struck out with one of his hind legs. Robin got a kick on the forehead, and he roared so loudly that he woke up!

He was glad to find himself in bed; but, on putting a hand to his brow, he felt a great lump where the horse had kicked him.

Robin at once made up his mind to try to rescue Philip. He had often heard strange stories about the giant Mahon. The villagers often talked about the Giant's Stairs. This was the name they gave to a number of great rocks which rose from the sea like a flight of stairs, and led to the top of the cliffs. Robin had heard too that sometimes the giants had really been seen climbing up these stairs; but no one knew where they went.

*The lost boy was mounted on a beautiful white horse, but his voice was very sad, and his eyes were full of tears.*

The blacksmith was not long in getting ready for his visit. At the last moment, he thought he would take his big hammer with him.

"The giants may give up Philip more readily if they see this," he said to himself.

A few minutes later he was rowing towards the great rocks. It was a beautiful, calm night; the little boat glided swiftly along, and was soon under the dark shadows of the steps.

Robin looked for the door of the Giant's Castle. This, it was said, may be found by any one seeking it at midnight; but nothing could be seen in the darkness.

"I wonder if I am too late," he said. At the moment he spoke, he saw a little light on the rock. It grew larger and larger, and a door slowly opened in the cliff, just on the edge of the water.

Robin rowed towards the light, and, jumping ashore, tied his boat to the rock. Then, holding his hammer tightly in his hand, he entered boldly. He found himself in a long passage cut out of the solid rock. All of a sudden he heard a rumbling noise, and felt as if the rocks were going to swallow him up for ever. But nothing happened.

"Robin, Robin," said he, "why didn't you stay at home, and forget all about giants and lost children?" Just then he saw a small light twinkling in the darkness like a star. On he went towards it, until he came at last to a great hall, lit by the lamp whose light he had seen. Robin, peeping through the door, could see several giants seated in silence round a great stone table. At the head of the table sat the great Mahon himself. The giant had sat there so long that his beard had taken root and grown into the table; while the table itself was thickly covered with dust. Indeed, there was dust everywhere, and some of it must have got into Robin's nose, for he suddenly sneezed loudly, "Atchoo! Atchoo!"

Robin had no time to slip out of sight. The giant sat up with such a jerk that half his beard was torn away. For he had slept so long that he did not know his beard had taken root in the table. Of course, this made him very angry. "What are you doing here?" he roared in a voice of thunder.

"I have come," replied Robin, "to claim young Philip, whose time of service ends to-night. You are not going to be so unfair as to keep him longer."

"Ho-ho! you speak very boldly," said the giant, with a laugh that made the whole room shake. "If that is what you have come for, then you must pick him out from among my pages; but, if you fix on the wrong one, you shall die. Follow me."

He led Robin into another great hall. Along each side were rows of children, all about seven years old. Every one was dressed in green, and they all looked so much alike that Robin saw it would not be easy to pick out Philip.

"Here," said Mahon, "you are free to take Philip if you will; but remember, I give you only one chance."

Robin was puzzled, for there were hundreds of children to choose from; and he was afraid he might miss Philip. He walked slowly down the hall by the side of Mahon. They had nearly reached the end without speaking, when Robin thought he would try to make friends with the giant.

"If I speak to him nicely," he thought, "he might help me to pick out the right boy."

"Well, the children all look nice and healthy," he said to the giant, "although they have had no fresh air for such a long time. You must have taken good care of them."

"Ay, you speak truth," said the giant, showing his yellow teeth in a horrible smile. "Give me your hand, for you are a very honest fellow for a blacksmith."

At the first glance, Robin did not care to trust his hand in the giant's great paw; so he handed him his hammer instead. The giant took it, and broke it as if it had been a potato stalk. On seeing this, all the children burst into laughter. In the midst of their mirth, Robin thought he heard his name called softly.

He put his hand on the boy whom he thought had spoken, and cried out, "Let me live or die for it, but this is young Philip."

"It is Philip—happy Philip," cried the other children; and in a moment the hall became dark.

Loud crashes were heard on all sides, as tables and chairs were upset in the darkness; but Robin held fast to his prize, and rushed out of the hall and down the passage with the young boy in his arms.

When he got outside, dawn was breaking. He soon stepped safely into the boat and started on his way back to the village. The joyful news spread, and a crowd quickly gathered to hear Robin's wonderful story.

*Along each side were rows of children, all about seven years old.*

"Are you quite sure it is young Philip you have brought back with you?" cried an old woman.

"Am I sure? why, that's a queer question," replied Robin. "Look at the boy! He has the blue eyes of his mother and the brown hair of his father; and look, there is a mark on the side of his little nose."

"Take me to my father and mother and they will know their son," smiled Philip.

So off they went, as quickly as horses could take them, to the big house. You may be sure there was great joy, when the long-lost child was safely brought home again. Philip's father, of course, gave Robin a large sum of money, so there was no need for him to toil in the smithy. He bought a little cottage near the big house, and Philip would often visit his brave friend for a talk about the Giant's Stairs.

# THE STORY OF BOTTLE HILL

IN olden days, when the fairies were seen more often than they are now, a farmer lived in a cabin near Mallow. From sunrise to sunset he toiled on his farm. His wife did what she could to help him, as their children were too young to work in the fields.

The poor woman looked after the house, milked the cow, boiled the potatoes, and carried the eggs to market. At the end of the summer, they always had saved enough money to pay the rent.

At last came a bad year. Day after day the rain poured down. Their small crop of oats was spoiled, the chickens died, and the pigs fell ill! When the rent was due there was no money to pay the landlord.

"What can we do, Molly?" said the farmer sadly to his wife.

"You must take the cow to the fair of Cork, Mick, and sell her," said Molly. "Monday is fair day, so you must go to-morrow."

"And what shall we do when she is gone?" he asked, not very willing to part with the cow.

"Och! now you are looking for trouble before it meets you."

"I believe you are right, Molly. I will go to-morrow; and now you must put a needle and thread through my coat, for it is torn under the arm."

Early next morning he took his stick in his hand, and drove his cow slowly along the road. It was a fine day and the sun shone brightly on the fields. After six long miles the farmer came to the top of a hill— Bottle Hill it is called now, but that was not the name of it then. Just then a man overtook him.

"Good-morning," said he.

"Good-morning," said the farmer, looking at the stranger, who was a very little man. His face was yellow, his nose sharp as a bird's beak, and his eyes were bright and piercing.

Mick did not like the look of the little man. He drove his cow faster along the road, but the dwarf kept up with him, gliding along like a shadow, without noise. The farmer was wishing he had not come out that day, but had stayed in his cottage, when the dwarf asked:

"Where are you going with the cow, my honest man?"

"To the fair of Cork," said Mick, trembling at the shrill tone of his voice.

"Are you going to sell her?" asked the stranger.

"Why, what would I be going to market for? Of course I am going to sell her."

"Will you sell her to me?"

Mick started. He was afraid to have anything to do with the little man, and yet more afraid to say no.

"What will you give for her?" he asked.

"I'll give you this bottle," said the dwarf, pulling a bottle from under his coat.

The farmer looked first at him and then at the bottle. In spite of his fear he burst into a loud peal of laughter.

" Laugh if you will," cried the little man angrily. " I tell you this bottle is better for you than all the money you will get in Cork."

Mick laughed again. " Do you think I am so silly as to give my good cow for an empty bottle ? What would Molly say ? How could we pay the rent without a penny of money ? "

" Take the bottle, Mick, and give me the cow."

" How do you know my name ? " asked the farmer.

" Never mind ! " said the dwarf ; then he added, more gently, " I like you, Mick. Come, do as I tell you, or you may be sorry for it. Who knows what ill luck may befall you ! Your cow may die before you get to the fair. There may be many cattle at the fair, and you will get a bad price. Perhaps you will be robbed on your road home. But why should I talk to you when you will not listen ? "

" If I thought the bottle was as good as you say, I would give you the cow."

" I would not tell you a lie," said the stranger. " Here, take the bottle, and when you go home do just as I tell you."

But the farmer could not make up his mind to part with the cow.

" Well, then, good-bye ! I can stay no longer. Once more, take it and be rich. If not, you will beg for your living, see your children in rags, and your wife die for want," said the dwarf with a grin, which made him look ten time more ugly.

At length Mick took the bottle. " Take the cow," said he ; " but if you are telling a lie——"

" You will find I have spoken the truth, if you do what I tell you. When you go home, ask your wife to sweep the floor clean, and spread a clean cloth on the table. Then put the bottle on the ground, saying these words, ' Bottle, do your duty,' and see what happens."

" Is that all ? " asked Mick.

" No more," said the stranger. " Good-bye ; you are a rich man ! "

As the dwarf led away the cow, Mick turned back towards the cabin, fearing what his wife would say to him for his foolishness.

Towards night, he reached home again. As he entered the cabin, Molly rose from her seat by the turf fire.

" You have come back very quickly," she said ; " what has happened ? Did you sell the cow ? How much money did you get for her ? "

" Why, Molly, if you will give me time I will tell you all about it," he cried, placing the bottle on the table. " I did sell the cow, and—and that's all I got for her."

His poor wife looked at him in surprise. " All you got ! What good is that ? I never thought you were so silly. How can we pay the rent with that ? " and she sat down, and began to weep bitterly.

" Now listen, Molly, and I will tell you the whole story." Then and there he told of his meeting with the strange dwarf, and how he had sold the cow for an empty bottle.

Now, his wife had faith in the good works of the fairies.

When he had finished, she rose without saying a word, and began to sweep the earthen floor with her broom. Then she spread a clean cloth on the table, and Mick, placing the bottle on the ground, cried, " Bottle, do your duty ! "

" Look there ! Look there, mammy ! " cried his chubby little son, who was barely five years old. He ran to his mother's side, as two tiny fairies rose from the bottle and climbed upon the table.

In a few moments they had covered the table with dishes, and plates of gold and silver, full of the richest food. When all was ready the fairies went back into the bottle again.

The farmer and his wife looked at each other. Never had they seen such splendid dishes.

" Well, Molly, the little man spoke the truth after all."

" Oh, what beautiful plates ! " cried Molly, with a happy laugh. " Come and sit down. You must be hungry after such a good day's work."

They all sat down at the table and made a hearty meal, though they could not eat half the food that the good fairies had brought.

" Now," said Molly, when they had finished, " I wonder if the fairies will carry away these fine things again."

They waited, but no one came ; so Molly put away the dishes and plates very carefully. After the children had been put to bed, the farmer and his wife sat by the fire, planning how they would sell the gold dishes and buy more land.

Next day Mick went to Cork, sold a gold dish, and bought a horse and cart. Molly and he kept their secret closely. Often they called forth the fairies, had a splendid meal, and in this way added to their store of dishes.

One day, however, the landlord asked Mick how he had become so rich, and the farmer told him about the fairies and the magic bottle. The landlord offered him a large sum of money for the bottle, but Mick would not give it up. At last, he offered to give him his farm for ever, in exchange for the bottle. Mick, being a kind-hearted man, and thinking he would never want any more money, agreed.

But, alas ! he spent his money very quickly. He became poorer and poorer, till at last he had nothing left but one poor cow.

One morning before daybreak, he set out again with his cow for the fair at Cork. He hoped that he would meet the dwarf and get another bottle.

He walked at a good pace till he reached the big hill. The mist was lying in the valley, and curling like smoke upon the brown heath around him. As he reached the top of the hill, he stopped to watch the sunrise, and listen to the sweet song of the lark.

" Well, Mick," said a voice behind him. " I told you, you would be a rich man."

The farmer looked round and, sure enough, there was the dwarf.

" Indeed, I was rich, but now I am poor again," he said. " If you have another bottle, sir, here is the cow."

" And here is the bottle," said the old man, smiling ; " you know what to do with it. And now good-bye. I said that you would be a rich man."

" Good-bye to you, sir," said the farmer joyfully, as he turned back. " Good luck to you ! Good luck to the big hill. It lacks a name, so we will call it Bottle Hill ! "

He went home, not daring to look back at the little man and the cow, so eager was he to make the bottle work.

He reached his cabin safely, and as soon as he saw Molly, cried, "Hurrah! I have another bottle!"

In a moment she put a clean cloth on the table. Mick, looking at the bottle, cried, "Bottle, do you duty!"

At once two big men, armed with stout sticks, came out. (Only the fairies knew how they found room in the bottle.) They beat poor Mick and his wife, and even the children, till they fell on their knees and begged for mercy. Then they hid in the bottle again.

Slowly the farmer rose to his feet and looked about him. He gave poor Molly and the children what comfort he could. Then, taking up the bottle, he ran off to his landlord.

Now that night the old gentleman had a number of people at supper. When he heard that the farmer wanted to see him, he came to the door in none too good a temper.

"Well, what do you want now?"

"Nothing, sir," said Mick; "only I have another bottle."

"Oh, ho! is it as good as the first?"

"Better, sir, better! If you like, I will show it to you before all the ladies and gentlemen."

"Come along, then," and he led Mick into the hall. At once the farmer caught sight of his old bottle standing high on a shelf. "Ah, ha!" he thought to himself, "I will have you before long!"

"Now," said the landlord, "show us your bottle."

Mick set it on the floor and spoke the proper words.

The next moment out jumped the men with the sticks. The landlord was thrown to the floor; ladies and gentlemen, servants, and every one were running and roaring and sprawling! Wine glasses and plates and dishes were thrown about the room, until the landlord cried out, "Stop these two men, Mick, or I'll have you hanged."

"Not until I get my own bottle back," he cried.

"Give it to him—quickly—before we are all killed," gasped the landlord.

Mick took his precious bottle, while the two men jumped into their bottle again. Quickly he ran home with his burden.

Little more remains to be told. The farmer became richer than ever. Having learned his lesson, he did not spend his money foolishly. When he died he left the biggest farm in County Cork to his eldest son. At his wake the bottle at last was broken, and was of no further use to any one; but the hill, where the farmer first met the strange little man, is called Bottle Hill even to this day.

# THE WALRUS AND THE CARPENTER

## by LEWIS CARROLL

THE sun was shining on the sea,
  Shining with all his might:
He did his very best to make
  The billows smooth and bright—
And this was odd, because it was
  The middle of the night.

The moon was shining sulkily,
  Because she thought the sun
Had got no business to be there
  After the day was done—
" It's very rude of him," she said,
  " To come and spoil the fun ! "

The sea was wet as wet could be,
  The sands were dry as dry.
You could not see a cloud, because
  No cloud was in the sky:
No birds were flying overhead—
  There were no birds to fly.

The Walrus and the Carpenter
  Were walking close at hand:
They wept like anything to see
  Such quantities of sand:
" If this were only cleared away,"
  They said, " it *would* be grand ! "

" If seven maids with seven mops
  Swept it for half a year,
Do you suppose," the Walrus said,
  " That they could get it clear ? "
" I doubt it," said the Carpenter,
  And shed a bitter tear.

" O Oysters, come and walk with us ! "
  The Walrus did beseech.
" A pleasant walk, a pleasant talk,
  Along the briny beach :
We cannot do with more than four,
  To give a hand to each."

The eldest Oyster looked at him,
　But never a word he said :
The eldest Oyster winked his eye,
　And shook his heavy head—
Meaning to say he did not choose
　To leave the oyster-bed.

But four young Oysters hurried up,
　All eager for the treat :
Their coats were brushed, their faces washed,
　Their shoes were clean and neat—
And this was odd, because you know,
　They hadn't any feet.

Four other Oysters followed them,
　And yet another four ;
And thick and fast they came at last,
　And more, and more, and more—
All hopping through the frothy waves,
　And scrambling to the shore.

The Walrus and the Carpenter
　Walked on a mile or so,
And then they rested on a rock
　Conveniently low :
And all the little Oysters stood
　And waited in a row.

" The time has come," the Walrus said,
　" To talk of many things :
Of shoes—and ships—and sealing-wax—
　Of cabbages—and kings—
And why the sea is boiling hot—
　And whether pigs have wings."

" But wait a bit," the Oysters cried,
　" Before we have our chat ;
For some of us are out of breath,
　And all of us are fat ! "
" No hurry ! " said the Carpenter.
　They thanked him much for that.

" A loaf of bread," the Walrus said,
　" Is what we chiefly need :
Pepper and vinegar besides
　Are very good indeed—
Now, if you're ready, Oysters dear,
　We can begin to feed."

" But not on us ! " the Oysters cried,
  Turning a little blue.
" After such kindness, that would be
  A dismal thing to do ! "
" The night is fine," the Walrus said,
  " Do you admire the view ?

" It was so kind of you to come !
  And you are very nice ! "
The Carpenter said nothing but
  " Cut us another slice.
I wish you were not quite so deaf—
  I've had to ask you twice ! "

" It seems a shame," the Walrus said,
  " To play them such a trick.
After we've brought them out so far,
  And made them trot so quick ! "
The Carpenter said nothing but
  " The butter's spread too thick !

" I weep for you," the Walrus said :
  " I deeply sympathise."
With sobs and tears he sorted out
  Those of the largest size,
Holding his pocket-handkerchief
  Before his streaming eyes.

" O Oysters," said the Carpenter,
  " You've had a pleasant run !
Shall we be trotting home again ! "
  But answer came there none—
And this was scarcely odd, because
  They'd eaten every one.

# A CHRISTMAS CAROL

*Old Scrooge sat busy in his counting-house.*

*by*

## CHARLES DICKENS

(*Abridged*)

### STAVE ONE

MARLEY'S GHOST

MARLEY was dead, to begin with. Old Marley was as dead as a door-nail. Scrooge knew he was dead? Of course he did. How could it be otherwise? Scrooge and he were partners for I don't know how many years. Scrooge was his sole executor, his sole administrator, his sole assign, his sole residuary legatee, his sole friend, and sole mourner. And even Scrooge was not so dreadfully cut up by the sad event, but that he was an excellent man of business on the very day of the funeral, and solemnised it with an undoubted bargain.

Scrooge never painted out Old Marley's name. There it stood, years afterwards, above the warehouse door : Scrooge and Marley. The firm was known as Scrooge and Marley. Sometimes people new to the business called Scrooge Scrooge, and sometimes Marley, but he answered to both names. It was all the same to him.

Oh ! But he was a tight-fisted hand at the grindstone, Scrooge ! a squeezing, wrenching, grasping, scraping, clutching, covetous old sinner ! Hard and sharp as flint, from which no steel had ever struck out generous fire ; secret, and self-contained, and solitary as an oyster. The cold within him froze his old features, nipped his pointed nose, shrivelled his cheek, stiffened his gait ; made his eyes red, his thin lips blue ; and spoke out shrewdly in his grating voice. A frosty rime was on his head, and on his eyebrows, and his wiry chin. He carried his own low temperature always about with him ; he iced his office in the dog-days ; and didn't thaw it one degree at Christmas.

Nobody ever stopped him in the street to say, with gladsome looks, " My dear Scrooge, how are you ? When will you come to see me ? " No beggars implored him to bestow a trifle, no children asked him what it was o'clock, no man or woman ever once in all his life inquired the way to such and such a place, of Scrooge. Even the blind men's dogs appeared to know him ; and when they saw him coming on, would tug their owners into doorways and up courts; and then would wag their tails as though they said, "No eye at all is better than an evil eye, dark master!"

But what did Scrooge care! It was the very thing he liked. To edge his way along the crowded paths of life, warning all human sympathy to keep its distance, was what the knowing ones call "nuts" to Scrooge.

Once upon a time—of all the good days in the year, on Christmas Eve—old Scrooge sat busy in his counting-house. It was cold, bleak, biting weather: foggy withal: and he could hear the people in the court outside go wheezing up and down, beating their hands upon their breasts, and stamping their feet upon the pavement stones to warm them.

The door of Scrooge's counting-house was open that he might keep his eye upon his clerk, who, in a dismal little cell beyond, a sort of tank, was copying letters. Scrooge had a very small fire, but the clerk's fire was so very much smaller that it looked like one coal. But he couldn't replenish it, for Scrooge kept the coal-box in his own room; and so surely as the clerk came in with the shovel, the master predicted that it would be necessary for them to part. Wherefore the clerk put on his white comforter, and tried to warm himself at the candle; in which effort, not being a man of strong imagination, he failed.

"A Merry Christmas, uncle! God save you!" cried a cheerful voice. It was the voice of Scrooge's nephew, who came upon him so quickly that this was the first intimation he had of his approach.

"Bah!" said Scrooge. "Humbug!"

He had so heated himself with rapid walking in the fog and frost, this nephew of Scrooge's, that he was all in a glow; his face was ruddy and handsome; his eyes sparkled, and his breath smoked again.

"Christmas a humbug, uncle!" said Scrooge's nephew. "You don't mean that, I am sure?"

"I do," said Scrooge. "Merry Christmas! What right have you to be merry? What reason have you to be merry? You're poor enough."

"Come, then," returned the nephew gaily. "What right have you to be dismal? What reason have you to be morose? You're rich enough."

Scrooge, having no better answer ready on the spur of the moment, said, "Bah!" again; and followed it up with "Humbug."

"Don't be cross, uncle!" said the nephew.

"What else can I be," returned the uncle, "when I live in such a world of fools as this? Merry Christmas! Out upon merry Christmas! What's Christmas time to you but a time for paying bills without money; a time for finding yourself a year older, and not an hour richer; a time for balancing your books and having every item in 'em through a round dozen of months presented dead against you? If I could work my will," said Scrooge indignantly, "every idiot who goes about with 'Merry Christmas' on his lips, should be boiled with his own pudding, and buried with a stake of holly through his heart. He should!"

"Uncle!" pleaded the nephew.

"Nephew!" returned the uncle sternly, "keep Christmas in your own way, and let me keep it in mine."

"Keep it!" repeated Scrooge's nephew. "But you don't keep it."

"Let me leave it alone, then," said Scrooge. "Much good may it do you! Much good it has ever done you!"

"There are many things from which I might have derived good, by which I have not profited, I dare say," returned the nephew— "Christmas among the rest. But I am sure I have always thought of Christmas time, when it has come round— apart from the veneration due to its sacred name and origin, if anything belonging to it can be apart from that—as a good time; a kind, forgiving, charitable, pleasant time; the only time I know of, in the long calendar of the year, when men and women seem by one consent to open their shut-up hearts freely, and to think of people below them as if they really were fellow-passengers to the grave, and not another

*"Let me leave it alone, then," said Scrooge.*

race of creatures bound on other journeys. And therefore, uncle, though it has never put a scrap of gold or silver in my pocket, I believe that it *has* done me good, and *will* do me good; and I say, God bless it!"

The clerk in the tank involuntarily applauded. Becoming immediately sensible of the impropriety, he poked the fire, and extinguished the last frail spark for ever.

"Let me hear another sound from *you*," said Scrooge, "and you'll keep your Christmas by losing your situation! You're quite a powerful speaker, sir," he added, turning to his nephew. "I wonder you don't go into Parliament."

"Don't be angry, uncle. Come! Dine with us to-morrow."

Scrooge said that he would see him—— Yes, indeed he did. He went the whole length of the expression, and said that he would see him in that extremity first.

"But why?" cried Scrooge's nephew. "Why?"

"Why did you get married?" said Scrooge.

"Because I fell in love."

"Because you fell in love!" growled Scrooge, as if that were the only one thing in the world more ridiculous than a merry Christmas. "Good-afternoon!"

"Nay, uncle, but you never came to see me before that happened. Why give it as a reason for not coming now?"

" Good-afternoon," said Scrooge.

" I want nothing from you ; I ask nothing of you ; why cannot we be friends ? "

" Good-afternoon," said Scrooge.

" I am sorry, with all my heart, to find you so resolute. We have never had any quarrel, to which I have been a party. But I have made the trial in homage to Christmas, and I'll keep my Christmas humour to the last. So A Merry Christmas, uncle ! "

" Good-afternoon ! " said Scrooge.

" And A Happy New Year ! "

" Good-afternoon ! " said Scrooge.

His nephew left the room without an angry word, notwithstanding. He stopped at the outer door to bestow the greetings of the season on the clerk, who, cold as he was, was warmer than Scrooge ; for he returned them cordially.

" There's another fellow," muttered Scrooge, who overheard him ; " my clerk, with fifteen shillings a week, and a wife and family, talking about a merry Christmas. I'll retire to Bedlam."

This lunatic, in letting Scrooge's nephew out, had let two other people in. They were portly gentlemen, pleasant to behold, and now stood, with their hats off, in Scrooge's office. They had books and papers in their hands, and bowed to him.

" Scrooge and Marley's, I believe," said one of the gentlemen, referring to his list. " Have I the pleasure of addressing Mr. Scrooge, or Mr. Marley ? "

" Mr. Marley has been dead these seven years," Scrooge replied. " He died seven years ago, this very night."

" We have no doubt his liberality is well represented by his surviving partner," said the gentleman, presenting his credentials.

It certainly was ; for they had been two kindred spirits. At the ominous word " liberality," Scrooge frowned, and shook his head, and handed the credentials back.

" At this festive season of the year, Mr. Scrooge," said the gentleman, taking up a pen, " it is more than usually desirable that we should make some slight provision for the poor and destitute, who suffer greatly at the present time. Many thousands are in want of common necessaries ; hundreds of thousands are in want of common comforts, sir."

" Are there no prisons ? " asked Scrooge.

" Plenty of prisons," said the gentleman, laying down the pen again.

" And the union workhouses ? " demanded Scrooge. " Are they still in operation ? "

" They are. Still," returned the gentleman, " I wish I could say they were not."

" The treadmill and the Poor Law are in full vigour, then ? " said Scrooge.

" Both very busy, sir."

" Oh ! I was afraid, from what you said at first, that something had occurred to stop them in their useful course," said Scrooge. " I'm very glad to hear it."

" Under the impression that they scarcely furnish Christian cheer of mind or body to the multitiude," returned the gentleman, " a few of us are endeavouring to raise a fund to buy the poor some meat and drink, and means of warmth. We choose this time, because it is a time, of all others, when want is keenly felt, and abundance rejoices. What shall I put you down for?"

"Nothing!" Scrooge replied.

"You wish to be anonymous?"

"I wish to be left alone," said Scrooge. "Since you ask me what I wish, gentlemen, that is my answer. I don't make merry myself at Christmas, and I can't afford to make idle people merry. I help to support the establishments I have mentioned—they cost enough; and those who are badly off must go there."

"Many can't go there; and many would rather die."

"If they would rather die," said Scrooge, "they had better do it, and decrease the surplus population. Besides—excuse me—I don't know that."

"But you might know it," observed the gentleman.

"It's not my business," Scrooge returned. "It's enough for a man to understand his own business, and not to interfere with other people's. Mine occupies me constantly. Good-afternoon, gentlemen!"

Seeing clearly that it would be useless to pursue their point, the gentlemen withdrew. Scrooge resumed his labours with an improved opinion of himself, and in a more facetious temper than was usual with him.

Foggier yet, and colder! Piercing, searching, biting cold. If the good St. Dunstan had but nipped the evil spirit's nose with a touch of such weather as that, instead of using his familiar weapons, then indeed he would have roared to lusty purpose. The owner of one scant young nose, gnawed and mumbled by the hungry cold as bones are gnawed by dogs, stooped down at Scrooge's keyhole to regale him with a Christmas carol; but at the first sound of—

"God bless you, merry gentleman!
May nothing you dismay!"

Scrooge seized the ruler with such energy of action, that the singer fled in terror, leaving the keyhole to the fog and even more congenial frost.

At length the hour of shutting up the counting-house arrived. With an ill-will Scrooge dismounted from his stool, and tacitly admitted the fact to the expectant clerk in the tank, who instantly snuffed his candle out, and put on his hat.

"You'll want all day to-morrow, I suppose?" said Scrooge.

"If quite convenient, sir."

"It's not convenient," said Scrooge, "and it's not fair. If I was to stop half a crown for it, you'd think yourself ill-used, I'll be bound?"

The clerk smiled faintly.

"And yet," said Scrooge, "you don't think *me* ill-used, when I pay a day's wages for no work."

The clerk observed that it was only once a year.

"A poor excuse for picking a man's pocket every twenty-fifth of December!" said Scrooge, buttoning his greatcoat to the chin. "But I suppose you must have the whole day. Be here all the earlier next morning."

The clerk promised that he would ; and Scrooge walked out with a growl. The office was closed in a twinkling, and the clerk, with the long ends of his white comforter dangling below his waist (for he boasted no great-coat), went down a slide on Cornhill, at the end of a lane of boys, twenty times, in honour of its being Christmas Eve, and then ran home to Camden Town as hard as he could pelt, to play at blindman's-buff.

Scrooge took his melancholy dinner in his usual melancholy tavern ; and having read all the newspapers, and beguiled the rest of the evening with his banker's book, went home to bed. He lived in chambers which had once belonged to his deceased partner. They were a gloomy suite of rooms, in a lowering pile of building up a yard, where it had so little business to be, that one could scarcely help fancying it must have run there when it was a young house, playing at hide-and-seek with other houses, and have forgotten the way out again. It was old enough now, and dreary enough, for nobody lived in it but Scrooge, the other rooms being all let out as offices. The yard was so dark that even Scrooge, who knew its every stone, was fain to grope with his hands.

Now, it is a fact that there was nothing at all particular about the knocker on the door, except that it was very large. It is also a fact that Scrooge had seen it, night and morning, during his whole residence in that place ; also that Scrooge had as little of what is called fancy about him as any man in the city of London. And then let any man explain to me, if he can, how it happened that Scrooge, having his key in the lock of the door, saw in the knocker, without its undergoing any intermediate process of change—not a knocker, but Marley's face.

Marley's face. It was not in impenetrable shadow as the other objects in the yard were, but had a dismal light about it, like a bad lobster in a dark cellar. It was not angry or ferocious, but looked at Scrooge as Marley used to look, with ghostly spectacles turned up on its ghostly forehead. The hair was curiously stirred, as if by breath or hot air ; and, though the eyes were wide open, they were perfectly motionless. That, and its livid colour, made it horrible ; but its horror seemed to be in spite of the face and beyond its control, rather than a part of its own expression.

As Scrooge looked fixedly at this phenomenon, it was a knocker again.

To say that he was not startled, or that his blood was not conscious of a terrible sensation to which it had been a stranger from infancy, would be untrue. But he put his hand upon the key he had relinquished, turned it sturdily, walked in, and lighted his candle.

He *did* pause, with a moment's irresolution, before he shut the door ; and he *did* look cautiously behind it first, as if he half expected to be terrified with the sight of Marley's pigtail sticking out into the hall. But there was nothing on the back of the door, except the screws and nuts that held the knocker on, so he said, " Pooh, pooh ! " and closed it with a bang.

The sound resounded through the house like thunder. Every room above, and every cask in the wine-merchant's cellars below, appeared to have a separate peal of echoes of its own. Scrooge was not a man to be frightened by echoes. He fastened the door, and walked across the hall, and up the stairs ; slowly, too ; trimming his candle as he went.

He closed his door, and locked himself in—double-locked himself in, which was not his custom. Thus secured against surprise, he took off his cravat; put on his dressing-gown and slippers, and his nightcap; and sat down before the fire to take his gruel.

As he threw his head back in the chair, his glance happened to rest upon a bell, a disused bell, that hung in the room, and communicated, for some purpose now forgotten, with a chamber in the highest story of the building. It was with great astonishment, and with a strange, inexplicable dread, that as he looked he saw this bell begin to swing. It swung so softly at the outset that it scarcely made a sound; but soon it rang out loudly, and so did every bell in the house.

This might have lasted half a minute, or a minute, but it seemed an hour. The bells ceased as they had begun, together. They were succeeded by a clanking noise,

*Scrooge saw . . . Marley's face.*

deep down below; as if some person were dragging a heavy chain over the casks in the wine-merchant's cellar. Scrooge then remembered to have heard that ghosts in haunted houses were described as dragging chains.

The cellar door flew open with a booming sound, and then he heard the noise much louder, on the floors below; then coming up the stairs; then coming straight towards his door.

" It's humbug still ! " said Scrooge. " I won't believe it."

His colour changed, though, when, without a pause, it came on through the heavy door, and passed into the room before his eyes. Upon its coming in, the dying flame leaped up, as though it cried, " I know him ! Marley's ghost ! " and fell again.

The same face : the very same. Marley in his pigtail, usual waistcoat, tights, and boots ; the tassels on the latter bristling, like his pigtail, and his coat-skirts, and the hair upon his head. The chain he drew was clasped about his middle. It was long, and wound about him like a tail ; and it was made (for Scrooge observed it closely) of cash-boxes, keys, padlocks, ledgers, deeds, and heavy purses wrought in steel. His body was transparent ; so that Scrooge, observing him, and looking through his waistcoat, could see the two buttons on his coat behind.

" How now ! " said Scrooge, caustic and cold as ever. " What do you want with me ? "

" Much ! "—Marley's voice, no doubt about it.

" Who are you? "

" Ask me who I *was*."

" Who *were* you then ? " said Scrooge, raising his voice.

" In life I was your partner, Jacob Marley."

" Can you—can you sit down ? " asked Scrooge, looking doubtfully at him.

" I can."

" Do it, then."

Scrooge asked the question, because he didn't know whether a ghost so transparent might find himself in a condition to take a chair ; and felt that in the event of its being impossible, it might involve the necessity of an embarrassing explanation.    But the ghost sat down on the opposite side of the fireplace, as if he were quite used to it.

" You don't believe in me," observed the ghost.

" I don't," said Scrooge.

" What evidence would you have of my reality beyond that of your senses ? "

" I don't know," said Scrooge.

" Why do you doubt your senses ? "

" Because," said Scrooge, " a little thing affects them.  A slight disorder of the stomach makes them cheats.  You may be an undigested bit of beef, a blot of mustard, a crumb of cheese, a fragment of an underdone potato.  There's more of gravy than of grave about you, whatever you are ! "

The ghost sat perfectly motionless, its hair, and skirts, and tassels were still agitated as by the hot vapour from an oven.

" You see this toothpick ? " said Scrooge, returning quickly to the charge, and wishing, though it were only for a second, to divert the vision's stony gaze from himself.

" I do," replied the ghost.

" You are not looking at it," said Scrooge.

" But I see it," said the ghost, " notwithstanding."

" Well ! " returned Scrooge.  " I have but to swallow this, and be for the rest of my days persecuted by a legion of goblins, all of my own creation. Humbug, I tell you—humbug ! "

At this the spirit raised a frightful cry, and shook its chain with such a dismal and appalling noise, that Scrooge held on tight to his chair, to save himself from falling in a swoon.  But how much greater was his horror, when the phantom taking off the bandage round its head, as if it were too warm to wear indoors, its lower jaw dropped down upon its breast !

Scrooge fell upon his knees, and clasped his hands before his face.

" Mercy ! " he said.  " Dreadful apparition, why do you trouble me ? "

" Man of the worldly mind," replied the ghost, " do you believe in me or not ? "

" I do," said Scrooge.  " I must.  But why do spirits walk the earth, and why do they come to me ? "

" It is required of every man," the ghost returned, " that the spirit within him should walk abroad among his fellow-men, and travel far and wide ; and if that spirit goes not forth in life, it is condemned to do so after death. It is doomed to wander through the world—oh, woe is me !—and witness what it cannot share, but might have shared on earth, and turned to happiness ! "

Again the spectre raised a cry, and shook its chain and wrung its shadowy hands.

" You are fettered," said Scrooge, trembling. " Tell me why ! "

" I wear the chain I forged in life," replied the ghost. " I made it link by link, and yard by yard ; I girded it on of my own free will, and of my own free will I wore it. Is its pattern strange to *you* ? "

Scrooge trembled more and more.

" Or would you know," pursued the ghost, " the weight and length of the strong coil you bear yourself ? It was full as heavy and long as this, seven Christmas Eves ago. You have laboured on it, since. It is a ponderous chain ! "

Scrooge glanced about him on the floor, in the expectation of finding himself surrounded by some fifty or sixty fathoms of iron cable : but he could see nothing.

" Jacob," he said imploringly. " Old Jacob Marley, tell me more. Speak comfort to me, Jacob ! "

" I have none to give," the ghost replied. " It comes from other regions, Ebenezer Scrooge, and is conveyed by other ministers, to other kinds of men. Nor can I tell you what I would. A very little more, is all permitted to me. I cannot rest, I cannot stay, I cannot linger anywhere. My spirit never walked beyond our counting-house—mark me !—in life my spirit never roved beyond the narrow limits of our money-changing hole; and weary journeys lie before me!"

*" You will be haunted," resumed the ghost, " by three spirits."*

" You must have been very slow about it, Jacob," Scrooge observed, in a business-like manner, though with humility and deference.

" Slow ! " the ghost repeated.

" Seven years dead," mused Scrooge. " And travelling all the time ? "

" The whole time," said the ghost. " No rest, no peace. Incessant torture of remorse."

It held up its chain at arm's length, as if that were the cause of all its unavailing grief, and flung it heavily upon the ground again.

"At this time of the rolling year," the spectre said, "I suffer most. Why did I walk through crowds of fellow-beings with my eyes turned down, and never raise them to that blessed Star which led the Wise Men to a poor abode? Were there no poor homes to which its light would have conducted *me*?"

Scrooge was very much dismayed to hear the spectre going on at this rate, and began to quake exceedingly.

"Hear me!" cried the ghost. "My time is nearly gone."

"I will," said Scrooge. "But don't be hard upon me! Don't be flowery, Jacob! Pray!"

"How it is that I appear before you in a shape that you can see I may not tell. I have sat invisible beside you many and many a day."

It was not an agreeable idea. Scrooge shivered, and wiped the perspiration from his brow.

"That is no light part of my penance," pursued the ghost. "I am here to-night to warn you, that you have yet a chance and hope of escaping my fate. A chance and hope of my procuring, Ebenezer."

"You were always a good friend to me," said Scrooge. "Thank'ee."

"You will be haunted," resumed the ghost, "by three spirits."

Scrooge's countenance fell almost as low as the ghost's had done.

"Is that the chance and hope you mentioned, Jacob?" he demanded, in a faltering voice.

"It is."

"I—I think I'd rather not," said Scrooge.

"Without their visits," said the ghost, "you cannot hope to shun the path I tread. Expect the first to-morrow, when the bell tolls one."

"Couldn't I take 'em all at once, and have it over, Jacob?" hinted Scrooge.

"Expect the second on the next night at the same hour. The third upon the next night when the last stroke of twelve has ceased to vibrate. Look to see me no more; and look that, for your own sake, you remember what has passed between us!"

## STAVE TWO

### THE FIRST OF THE THREE SPIRITS

WHEN Scrooge awoke, it was so dark, that, looking out of bed, he could scarcely distinguish the transparent window from the opaque walls of his chamber. He was endeavouring to pierce the darkness with his ferret eyes, when the chimes of a neighbouring church struck the four quarters. So he listened for the hour.

To his great astonishment the heavy bell went on from six to seven, and from seven to eight, and regularly up to twelve; then stopped. Twelve! It was past two when he went to bed. The clock was wrong. An icicle must have got into the works. Twelve!

He touched the spring of his repeater, to correct this most preposterous clock. Its rapid little pulse beat twelve; and stopped.

"Why, it isn't possible," said Scrooge, "that I can have slept through a whole day and far into another night. It isn't possible that anything has happened to the sun, and this is twelve at noon!"

Scrooge lay until the chime had gone three quarters more, when he remembered, on a sudden, that the ghost had warned him of a visitation when the bell tolled one. He resolved to lie awake until the hour was passed; and, considering that he could no more go to sleep than go to heaven, this was perhaps the wisest resolution in his power.

The quarter was so long that he was more than once convinced he must have sunk into a doze unconsciously, and missed the clock. At length it broke upon his listening ear.

"*I am the Ghost of Christmas Past.*"

"Ding, dong!"

"A quarter past," said Scrooge, counting.

"Ding, dong!"

"Half-past!" said Scrooge.

"Ding, dong!"

"A quarter to it," said Scrooge.

"Ding, dong!"

"The hour itself," said Scrooge triumphantly, "and nothing else!"

He spoke before the hour bell sounded, which it now did with a deep, dull, hollow, melancholy ONE. Light flashed up in the room upon the instant, and the curtains of his bed were drawn.

The curtains of his bed were drawn aside, I tell you, by a hand. Not the curtains at his feet, nor the curtains at his back, but those to which his face was addressed. The curtains of his bed were drawn aside; and Scrooge, starting up into a half-recumbent attitude, found himself face to face with the unearthly visitor, who drew them: as close to it as I am now to you, and I am standing in the spirit at your elbow.

It was a strange figure—like a child; yet not so like a child as like an old man, viewed through some supernatural medium which gave him the appearance of having receded from the view, and being diminished to a child's proportions. Its hair, which hung about its neck and down its back, was white as if with age; and yet the face had not a wrinkle in it, and the tenderest bloom was on the skin. The arms were very long and muscular ; the hands the same, as if its hold were of uncommon strength. Its legs and feet, most delicately formed, were, like those upper members, bare. It wore a tunic of the purest white ; and round its waist was bound a lustrous belt, the sheen of which was beautiful. It held a branch of fresh green holly in its hand ; and, in singular contradiction of that wintry emblem, had its dress trimmed with summer flowers. But the strangest thing about it was, that from the crown of its head there sprang a bright, clear jet of light, by which all this was visible ; and which was doubtless the occasion of its using, in its duller moments, a great extinguisher for a cap, which it now held under its arm.

" Are you the spirit, sir, whose coming was foretold to me ? " asked Scrooge.

" I am ! "

The voice was soft and gentle. Singularly low, as if, instead of being so close beside him, it were at a distance.

" Who, and what are you ? " Scrooge demanded.

" I am the Ghost of Christmas Past."

" Long past ? " inquired Scrooge, observant of its dwarfish stature.

" No. Your past."

Perhaps Scrooge could not have told anybody why, if anybody could have asked him, but he had a special desire to see the spirit in his cap ; and begged him to be covered.

" What ! " exclaimed the ghost, " would you so soon put out, with worldly hands, the light I give ? Is it not enough that you are one of those whose passions made this cap, and force me through whole trains of years to wear it low upon my brow ? "

Scrooge reverently disclaimed all intention to offend, or any knowledge of having wilfully " bonneted " the spirit at any period of his life. He then made bold to inquire what business brought him there.

" Your welfare ! " said the ghost.

Scrooge expressed himself much obliged, but could not help thinking that a night of unbroken rest would have been more conducive to that end. The spirit must have heard him thinking, for it said immediately—

" Your reclamation, then. Take heed ! "

It put out its strong hand as it spoke, and clasped him gently by the arm.

" Rise ! and walk with me ! "

The grasp, though gentle as a woman's hand, was not to be resisted. He rose ; but finding that the spirit made towards the window, clasped its robe in supplication.

" I am a mortal," Scrooge remonstrated, " and liable to fall."

" Bear but a touch of my hand *there*," said the spirit, laying it upon his heart, " and you shall be upheld in more than this ! "

As the words were spoken, they passed through the wall, and stood upon an open country road, with fields on either hand. The city had entirely vanished. Not a vestige of it was to be seen. The darkness and the mist had vanished with it, for it was a clear, cold, winter day, with snow upon the ground.

" Good Heaven ! " said Scrooge, clasping his hands together, as he looked about him. " I was bred in this place. I was a boy here ! "

The spirit gazed upon him mildly. Its gentle touch, though it had been light and instantaneous, appeared still present to the old man's sense of feeling. He was conscious of a thousand odours floating in the air, each one connected with a thousand thoughts, and hopes, and joys, and cares long, long forgotten !

" Your lip is trembling," said the ghost. " And what is that upon your cheek ? "

Scrooge muttered, with an unusual catching in his voice, that it was a pimple ; and begged the ghost to lead him where he would.

" You recollect the way ? " inquired the spirit.

" Remember it ! " cried Scrooge, with fervour ; " I could walk it blindfold."

" Strange to have forgotten it for so many years ! " observed the ghost. " Let us go on."

They walked along the road—Scrooge recognising every gate, and post, and tree—until a little market-town appeared in the distance, with its bridge, its church, and winding river.

" The school is not quite deserted," said the ghost. " A solitary child, neglected by his friends, is left there still."

Scrooge said he knew it. And he sobbed.

They left the high-road, by a well-remembered lane, and soon approached a mansion of dull red brick, with a little weather-cock-surmounted cupola on the roof, and a bell hanging in it. It was a large house, but one of broken fortunes ; for the spacious offices were little used, their walls were damp and mossy, their windows broken, and their gates decayed. Fowls clucked and strutted in the stables ; and the coach-houses and sheds were overrun with grass.

They went, the ghost and Scrooge, across the hall, to a door at the back of the house. It opened before them, and disclosed a long, bare, melancholy room, made barer still by lines of plain deal forms and desks. At one of these a lonely boy was reading near a feeble fire ; and Scrooge sat down upon a form, and wept to see his poor forgotten self as he had used to be.

The spirit touched him on the arm, and pointed to his younger self, intent upon his reading. Suddenly a man, in foreign garments—wonderfully real and distinct to look at—stood outside the window, with an axe stuck in his belt, and leading by the bridle an ass laden with wood.

" Why, it's Ali Baba ! " Scrooge exclaimed in ecstasy. " It's dear old honest Ali Baba ! Yes, yes, I know ! One Christmas time, when yonder solitary child was left here all alone, he *did* come, for the first time, just like that. Poor boy ! And Valentine," said Scrooge, " and his wild brother, Orson ; there they go ! And what's his name, who was put down in his drawers, asleep, at the gate of Damascus, don't you see him ? And the Sultan's Groom turned upside-down by the Genii ; there he is upon his head ! Serve him right ! I'm glad of it. What business had *he* to be married to the Princess ? "

To hear Scrooge expending all the earnestness of his nature on such subjects, in a most extraordinary voice between laughing and crying, and

*A lonely boy was reading by a feeble fire.*

to see his heightened and excited face, would have been a surprise to his business friends in the city, indeed.

" There's the parrot," cried Scrooge. " Green body and yellow tail, with a thing like a lettuce growing out of the top of his head ; there he is ! Poor Robin Crusoe, he called him, when he came home again after sailing round the island. ' Poor Robin Crusoe, where have you been, Robin Crusoe ? ' The man thought he was dreaming, but he wasn't. It was the parrot, you know. There goes Friday, running for his life to the little creek ! Hollo ! Hoop! Hollo ! "

Then, with a rapidity of transition very foreign to his usual character, he said, in pity for his former self, " Poor boy ! " and cried again.

" I wish," Scrooge muttered, putting his hand in his pocket, and looking about him, after drying his eyes with his cuff— " but it's too late now."

" What is the matter ? " asked the spirit.

" Nothing," said Scrooge. " Nothing. There was a boy singing a Christmas carol at my door last night. I should like to have given him something ; that's all."

The ghost smiled thoughtfully, and waved its hand, saying as it did so, " Let us see another Christmas ! "

The ghost stopped at a certain warehouse door, and asked Scrooge if he knew it.

" Know it ! " said Scrooge. " Was I apprenticed here ! "

They went in. At sight of an old gentleman in a Welsh wig, sitting behind such a high desk, that if he had been two inches taller he must have knocked his head against the ceiling, Scrooge cried in great excitement—

" Why, it's old Fezziwig ! Bless his heart ; it's Fezziwig alive again ! "

Old Fezziwig laid down his pen, and looked up at the clock, which pointed to the hour of seven. He rubbed his hands ; adjusted his capacious waistcoat ; laughed all over himself, from his shoes to his organ of benevolence ; and called out in a comfortable, oily, rich, fat, jovial voice—

" Yo, ho, there ! Ebenezer ! Dick ! "

Scrooge's former self, now grown a young man, came briskly in, accompanied by his fellow-'prentice.

" Dick Wilkins, to be sure ! " said Scrooge to the ghost. " Bless me, yes. There he is. He was very much attached to me, was Dick. Poor Dick ! Dear, dear ! "

" Yo ho, my boys ! " said Fezziwig. " No more work to-night. Christmas Eve, Dick. Christmas, Ebenezer ! Let's have the shutters up," cried old Fezziwig, with a sharp clap of his hands, " before a man can say Jack Robinson ! "

You wouldn't believe how those two fellows went at it ! They charged into the street with the shutters—one, two, three—had 'em up in their places—four, five, six—barred 'em and pinned 'em—seven, eight, nine—and came back before you could have got to twelve, panting like racehorses.

" Hilli-ho ! " cried old Fezziwig, skipping down from the high desk with wonderful agility. " Clear away, my lads, and let's have lots of room here ! Hilli-ho, Dick ! Chirrup, Ebenezer ! "

Clear away ! There was nothing they wouldn't have cleared away, or couldn't have cleared away, with old Fezziwig looking on. It was done in a minute. Every movable was packed off, as if it were dismissed from public life for evermore ; the floor was swept and watered, the lamps were trimmed, fuel was heaped upon the fire ; and the warehouse was as snug, and warm, and dry, and bright a ballroom, as you would desire to see upon a winter's night.

In came a fiddler with a music-book, and went up to the lofty desk, and made an orchestra of it, and tuned like fifty stomach-aches. In came Mrs. Fezziwig, one vast substantial smile. In came the three Misses Fezziwig, beaming and lovable. In came the six young followers whose hearts they broke. In came all the young men and women employed in the business. In came the housemaid, with her cousin, the baker. In came the cook, with her brother's particular friend, the milkman. In came the boy from over the way. In they all came, one after another ; some shyly, some boldly, some gracefully, some awkwardly, some pushing, some pulling ; in they all came, anyhow and everyhow. Away they all went, twenty couple at once ; hands half round and back

" *Yo ho, my boys !* " *said Fezziwig.* " *No more work to-night. It's Christmas Eve.*"

again the other way; down the middle and up again; round and round in various stages of affectionate grouping; old top couple always turning up in the wrong place; new top couple starting off again, as soon as they got there; all top couples at last and not a bottom one to help them! When this result was brought about, old Fezziwig, clapping his hands to stop the dance, cried out, "Well done!" and the fiddler plunged his hot face into a pot of porter, especially provided for that purpose.

There were more dances, and there were forfeits, and more dances, and there was cake, and there was negus, and there was a great piece of cold roast, and there was a great piece of cold boiled, and there were mince-pies, and plenty of beer. But the great effect of the evening came after the roast and boiled, when the fiddler struck up " Sir Roger de Coverley." Then old Fezziwig stood out to dance with Mrs. Fezziwig. Top couple, too; with a good stiff piece of work cut out for them; three or four-and-twenty pair of partners; people who were not to be trifled with; people who *would* dance, and had no notion of walking.

When the clock struck eleven, this domestic ball broke up. Mr. and Mrs. Fezziwig took their stations, one on either side the door, and shaking hands with every person individually as he or she went out, wished him or her A Merry Christmas. When everybody had retired but the two 'prentices, they did the same to them; and thus the cheerful voices died away, and the lads were left to their beds; which were under a counter in the back shop.

During the whole of this time, Scrooge had acted like a man out of his wits. His heart and soul were in the scene, and with his former self. He corroborated everything, remembered everything, enjoyed everything, and underwent the strangest agitation. It was not until now, when the bright faces of his former self and Dick were turned from them, that he remembered the ghost, and became conscious that it was looking full upon him, while the light upon its head burned very clear.

" A small matter," said the ghost, " to make these silly folks so full of gratitude."

" Small!" echoed Scrooge.

The spirit signed to him to listen to the two apprentices, who were pouring out their hearts in praise of Fezziwig; and when he had done so, said—

" Why! Is it not? He has spent but a few pounds of your mortal money; three or four, perhaps. Is that so much that he deserves this praise? "

" It isn't that," said Scrooge, heated by the remark, and speaking unconsciously like his former, not his latter, self. " It isn't that, spirit. He has the power to render us happy or unhappy; to make our service light or burdensome; a pleasure or a toil. Say that his power lies in words and looks; in things so slight and insignificant that it is impossible to add and count 'em up—what then? The happiness he gives us is quite as great as if it cost a fortune."

He felt the spirit's glance, and stopped.

" What is the matter? " asked the ghost.

" Nothing particular," said Scrooge.

" Something, I think? " the ghost insisted.

" No," said Scrooge. " No. I should like to be able to say a word or two to my clerk just now. That's all."

He was conscious of being exhausted, and overcome by an irresistible drowsiness ; and, further, of being in his own bedroom. He gave the cap a parting squeeze, in which his hand relaxed ; and had barely time to reel to bed, before he sank into a heavy sleep.

## STAVE THREE

### THE SECOND OF THE THREE SPIRITS

Awaking in the middle of a prodigiously tough snore, and sitting up in bed to get his thoughts together, Scrooge had no occasion to be told that the bell was again upon the stroke of one.

Now, being prepared for almost anything, he was not by any means prepared for nothing ; and, consequently, when the bell struck one, and no shape appeared, he was taken with a violent fit of trembling. Five minutes, ten minutes, a quarter of an hour went by, yet nothing came. All this time, he lay upon his bed, the very core and centre of a blaze of ruddy light, which streamed upon it when the clock proclaimed the hour ; and which, being only light, was more alarming than a dozen ghosts, as he was powerless to make out what it meant, or would be at ; and was sometimes apprehensive that he might be at that very moment an interesting case of spontaneous combustion, without having the consolation of knowing it.

At last, however, he began to think that the source and secret of this ghostly light might be in the adjoining room, from whence, on further tracing it, it seemed to shine. He got up softly and shuffled in his slippers to the door.

The moment Scrooge's hand was on the lock, a strange voice called him by his name, and bade him enter. He obeyed.

It was his own room. There was no doubt about that. But it had undergone a surprising transformation. The walls and ceiling were so hung with living green, that it looked a perfect grove ; from every part of which, bright gleaming berries glistened. The crisp leaves of holly, mistletoe, and ivy reflected back the light, as if so many little mirrors had been scattered there ; and such a mighty blaze went roaring up the chimney, as that dull petrifaction of a hearth had never known in Scrooge's time, or Marley's, or for many and many a winter season gone. Heaped up on the floor, to form a kind of throne, were turkeys, geese, game, poultry, brawn, great joints of meat, sucking-pigs, long wreaths of sausages, mince-pies, plum-puddings, barrels of oysters, red-hot chestnuts, cherry-cheeked apples, juicy oranges, luscious pears, immense twelfth-cakes, and seething bowls of punch, that made the chamber dim with their delicious steam. In easy state upon this couch, there sat a jolly giant, glorious to see ; who bore a glowing torch, in shape not unlike Plenty's horn, and held it up, high up, to shed its light on Scrooge, as he came peeping round the door.

" Come in ! " exclaimed the ghost. " Come in ! and know me better, man ! "

Scrooge entered timidly, and hung his head before this spirit. He was not the dogged Scrooge he had been; and though the spirit's eyes were clear and kind, he did not like to meet them.

"I am the Ghost of Christmas Present," said the spirit. "Look upon me!"

Scrooge reverently did so. It was clothed in one simple, deep-green robe, or mantle, bordered with white fur. This garment hung so loosely on the figure, that its capacious breast was bare, as if disdaining to be warded or concealed by any artifice. Its feet, observable beneath the ample folds of the garment, were also bare; and on its head it wore no other covering than a holly wreath, set here and there with shining icicles. Its dark-brown curls were long and free; free as its genial face, its sparkling eye, its open hand, its cheery voice, its unconstrained demeanour, and its joyful air. Girded round its middle was an antique scabbard; but no sword was in it, and the ancient sheath was eaten up with rust.

*" I am the Ghost of Christmas Present," said the spirit. " Look upon me ! "*

"You have never seen the like of me before!" exclaimed the spirit.

"Never," Scrooge made answer to it.

"Have never walked forth with the younger members of my family; meaning (for I am very young) my elder brothers born in these later years?" pursued the phantom.

"I don't think I have," said Scrooge. "I am afraid I have not. Have you had many brothers, spirit?"

"More than eighteen hundred," said the ghost.

"A tremendous family to provide for!" muttered Scrooge.

The ghost of Christmas Present rose.

"Spirit," said Scrooge submissively. "conduct me where you will. I went forth last night on compulsion, and I learned a lesson which is working now. To-night, if you have aught to teach me, let me profit by it."

"Touch my robe!"

Scrooge did as he was told, and held it fast.

Holly, mistletoe, red berries, ivy, turkeys, geese, game, poultry, brawn, meat, pigs, sausages, oysters, pies, puddings, fruit, and punch, all vanished instantly. So did the room, the fire, the ruddy glow, the hour of night, and they stood in the city streets on Christmas morning, where (for the weather was severe) the people made a rough, but brisk and not unpleasant, kind of music, in scraping the snow from the pavement in front of their dwellings, and from the tops of their houses, whence it was mad delight to the boys to see it come plumping down into the road below, and splitting into artificial little snow-storms.

There was nothing very cheerful in the climate or the town, and yet there was an air of cheerfulness abroad that the clearest summer air and brightest summer sun might have endeavoured to diffuse in vain.

For the people who were shovelling away on the housetops were jovial and full of glee; calling out to one another from the parapets, and now and then exchanging a facetious snowball, laughing heartily if it went right, and not less heartily if it went wrong. The poulterers' shops were still half open, and the fruiterers' were radiant in their glory. There were great, round, pot-bellied baskets of chestnuts, shaped like the waistcoats of jolly old gentlemen, lolling at the doors, and tumbling out into the street in their apoplectic opulence.

There were ruddy, brown-faced, broad-girthed Spanish onions, shining in the fatness of their growth like Spanish friars, and winking from their shelves in wanton slyness at the girls as they went by, and glanced demurely at the hung-up mistletoe. There were pears and apples, clustered high in blooming pyramids; there were bunches of grapes, made, in the shopkeepers' benevolence, to dangle from conspicuous hooks, that people's mouths might water gratis as they passed; there were piles of filberts, mossy and brown; there were Norfolk biffins, squab and swarthy, setting off the yellow of the oranges and lemons, and, in the great compactness of their juicy persons, urgently entreating and beseeching to be carried home in paper-bags and eaten after dinner.

The grocers'! oh, the grocers'! nearly closed, with perhaps two shutters down, or one; but through those gaps such glimpses! It was not alone that the scales descending on the counter made a merry sound, or that the twine and roller parted company so briskly, or that the canisters were rattled up and down like juggling tricks, or even that the blended scents of tea and coffee were so grateful to the nose, or even that the raisins were so plentiful and rare, the almonds so extremely white, the sticks of cinnamon so long and straight, the other spices so delicious, the candied fruits so caked and spotted with molten sugar as to make the coldest lookers-on feel faint and subsequently bilious.

Nor was it that the figs were moist and pulpy, or that the French plums blushed in modest tartness from their highly-decorated boxes, or that everything was good to eat and in its Christmas dress. But the customers were all so hurried and so eager in the hopeful promise of the day, that they tumbled up against each other at the door, crashing their wicker baskets wildly, and left their purchases upon the counter, and came running back to fetch them, and committed hundreds of the like mistakes, in the best humour possible; while the grocer and his people were so frank and fresh that the polished hearts with which they fastened their aprons behind might have been their own, worn outside for general inspection, and for Christmas daws to peck at if they chose.

Perhaps it was the pleasure the good spirit had in showing off this power of his, or else it was his own kind, generous, hearty nature, and his sympathy with all poor men, that led him straight to Scrooge's clerk's; for there he went, and took Scrooge with him, holding to his robe; and on the threshold of the door the spirit smiled, and stopped to bless Bob Cratchit's dwelling with the sprinklings of his torch. Think of that! Bob had but fifteen "Bob" a week himself; he pocketed on Saturdays but fifteen copies of his Christian name; and yet the Ghost of Christmas Present blessed his four-roomed house!

Then up rose Mrs. Cratchit, Cratchit's wife, dressed out but poorly in a twice-turned gown, but brave in ribbons, which are cheap and make a goodly show for sixpence; and she laid the cloth, assisted by Belinda Cratchit, second of her daughters, also brave in ribbons; while Master Peter Crachit plunged a fork into the saucepan of potatoes, and getting the corners of his monstrous shirt-collar (Bob's private property conferred upon his son and heir in honour of the day) into his mouth, rejoiced to find himself so gallantly attired, and yearned to show his linen in the fashionable parks.

And now two smaller Cratchits, boy and girl, came tearing in, screaming that outside the baker's, they had smelled the goose, and known it for their own; and basking in luxurious thoughts of sage and onion, these young Cratchits danced about the table, and exalted Master Peter Cratchit to the skies, while he (not proud, although his collars nearly choked him) blew the fire, until the slow potatoes bubbling up, knocked loudly at the saucepan-lid to be let out and peeled.

"What has ever got your precious father then?" said Mrs. Cratchit. "And your brother, Tiny Tim! And Martha warn't as late last Christmas Day by half an hour."

"Here's Martha, mother!" said a girl, appearing as she spoke.

"Here's Martha, mother!" cried the two young Cratchits. "Hurrah! There's *such* a goose, Martha!"

"Why, bless your heart alive, my dear, how late you are!" said Mrs. Cratchit, kissing her a dozen times, and taking off her shawl and bonnet for her with officious zeal.

"We'd a deal of work to finish up last night," replied the girl, "and had to clear away this morning, mother!"

"Well! Never mind so long as you are come," said Mrs. Cratchit. "Sit ye down before the fire, my dear, and have a warm, Lord bless ye!"

"No, no! There's father coming," cried the two young Cratchits, who were everywhere at once. "Hide, Martha, hide!"

So Martha hid herself, and in came little Bob, the father, with at least three feet of comforter exclusive of the fringe, hanging down before him; and his threadbare clothes darned up and brushed, to look seasonable; and Tiny Tim upon his shoulder. Alas for Tiny Tim, he bore a little crutch, and had his limbs supported by an iron frame!

"Why, where's our Martha?" cried Bob Cratchit, looking round.

"Not coming," said Mrs. Cratchit.

"Not coming!" said Bob, with a sudden declension in his high spirits:

for he had been Tim's blood-horse all the way from church, and had come home rampant. " Not coming upon Christmas Day ! "

Martha didn't like to see him disappointed, if it were only in joke ; so she came out prematurely from behind the closet door, and ran into his arms, while the two young Cratchits hustled Tiny Tim, and bore him off into the wash-house, that he might hear the pudding singing in the copper.

" And how did little Tim behave ? " asked Mrs. Cratchit, when she had rallied Bob on his credulity, and Bob had hugged his daughter to his heart's content.

" As good as gold," said Bob, " and better. Somehow he gets thoughtful, sitting by himself so much, and thinks the strangest things you ever heard. He told me, coming home, that he hoped the people saw him in the church, because he was a cripple, and it might be pleasant to them to remember upon Christmas Day who made lame beggars walk and blind men see."

Bob's voice was tremulous when he told them this, and trembled more when he said that Tiny Tim was growing strong and hearty.

His active little crutch was heard upon the floor, and back came Tiny Tim before another word was spoken, escorted by his brother and sister to his stool beside the fire ; and while Bob, turning up his cuffs—as if, poor fellow, they were capable of being made more shabby—compounded some hot mixture in a jug with gin and lemons, and stirred it round and round, and put it on the hob to simmer ;

*In came little Bob . . . and Tiny Tim upon his shoulder.*

Master Peter and the two ubiquitous young Cratchits went to fetch the goose, with which they soon returned in high procession.

Such a bustle ensued that you might have thought a goose the rarest of all birds ; a feathered phenomenon, to which a black swan was a matter of course—and in truth it was something very like it in that house. Mrs. Cratchit made the gravy (ready beforehand in a little saucepan) hissing hot ; Master Peter mashed the potatoes with incredible vigour ; Miss Belinda sweetened up the apple-sauce ; Martha dusted the hot plates ; Bob took Tiny Tim beside him in a tiny corner at the table ; the two young Cratchits set chairs for everybody, not forgetting themselves, and mounting guard upon their posts, crammed spoons into their mouths, lest they should shriek for goose before their turn came to be helped.

At last the dishes were set on, and grace was said. It was succeeded by a breathless pause, as Mrs. Cratchit, looking slowly all along the carving-knife, prepared to plunge it in the breast; but when she did, and when the long expected gush of stuffing issued forth, one murmur of delight arose all round the board, and even Tiny Tim, excited by the two young Cratchits, beat on the table with the handle of his knife, and feebly cried Hurrah!

There never was such a goose. Bob said he didn't believe there ever was such a goose cooked. Its tenderness and flavour, size and cheapness, were the themes of universal admiration. Eked out by apple-sauce and mashed potatoes, it was a sufficient dinner for the whole family; indeed, as Mrs. Cratchit said with great delight (surveying one small atom of a bone upon the dish), they hadn't ate it all at last! Yet every one had had enough, and the youngest Cratchits in particular, were steeped in sage and onion to the eyebrows! But now, the plates being changed by Miss Belinda, Mrs. Cratchit left the room alone—too nervous to bear witnesses—to take the pudding up, and bring it in.

Suppose it should not be done enough! Suppose it should break in turning out! Suppose somebody should have got over the wall of the back-yard, and stolen it, while they were merry with the goose—a supposition at which the two young Cratchits became livid! All sorts of horrors were supposed.

Hallo! A great deal of steam! The pudding was out of the copper. A smell like a washing-day! That was the cloth. A smell like an eating-house and a pastrycook's next door to each other, with a laundress's next door to that! That was the pudding! In half a minute Mrs. Cratchit entered—flushed, but smiling proudly—with the pudding, like a speckled cannon-ball, so hard and firm, blazing in half of half a quartern of ignited brandy, and bedight with Christmas holly stuck into the top.

Oh, a wonderful pudding! Bob Cratchit said, and calmly too, that he regarded it as the greatest success achieved by Mrs. Cratchit since their marriage. Mrs. Cratchit said that now the weight was off her mind, she would confess she had had her doubts about the quantity of flour. Everybody had something to say about it, but nobody said or thought it was at all a small pudding for a large family. It would have been flat heresy to do so. Any Cratchit would have blushed to hint at such a thing.

At last the dinner was all done, the cloth was cleared, the hearth swept, and the fire made up. The compound in the jug being tasted, and considered perfect, apples and oranges were put upon the table, and a shovelful of chestnuts on the fire. Then all the Cratchit family drew round the hearth, in what Bob Cratchit called a circle, meaning half a one; and at Bob Cratchit's elbow stood the family display of glass. Two tumblers, and a custard-cup without a handle.

These held the hot stuff from the jug, however, as well as golden goblets would have done; and Bob served it out with beaming looks, while the chestnuts on the fire sputtered and cracked noisily. Then Bob proposed:

" A Merry Christmas to us all, my dears. God bless us!"

Which all the family re-echoed.

" God bless us every one ! " said Tiny Tim, the last of all.

He sat very close to his father's side, upon his little stool. Bob held his withered little hand in his, as if he loved the child, and wished to keep him by his side, and dreaded that he might be taken from him.

" Spirit," said Scrooge, with an interest he had never felt before, " tell me if Tiny Tim will live."

" I see a vacant seat," replied the ghost, " in the poor chimney-corner, and a crutch without an owner, carefully preserved. If these shadows remain unaltered by the future, the child will die."

" No, no," said Scrooge. " Oh, no, kind spirit ! say he will be spared."

" If these shadows remain unaltered by the future, none other of my race," returned the ghost, " will find him here. What then ? If he be like to die, he had better do it, and decrease the surplus population."

Scrooge hung his head to hear his own words quoted by the spirit, and was overcome with penitence and grief.

" Man," said the ghost ; " if man you be in heart, not adamant—forbear that wicked cant until you have discovered what the surplus is, and where it is. Will you decide what men shall live, what men shall die ? It may be, that in the sight of Heaven, you are more worthless and less fit to live than millions like this poor man's child. O God ! to hear the insect on the leaf pronouncing on the too much life among his hungry brothers in the dust ! "

Scrooge bent before the ghost's rebuke, and, trembling, cast his eyes upon the ground. But he raised them speedily, on hearing his own name.

" Mr. Scrooge ! " said Bob ; " I'll give you Mr. Scrooge, the founder of the feast ! "

" The founder of the feast indeed ! " cried Mrs. Cratchit, reddening. " I wish I had him here. I'd give him a piece of my mind to feast upon, and I hope he'd have a good appetite for it."

" My dear," said Bob, " the children ! Christmas Day."

" It should be Christmas Day, I am sure," said she, " on which one drinks the health of such an odious, stingy, hard, unfeeling man as Mr. Scrooge. You know he is, Robert ! Nobody knows it better than you do, poor fellow ! "

" My dear," was Bob's mild answer, " Christmas Day."

" I'll drink his health for your sake and the day's," said Mrs. Cratchit, " not for his. Long life to him ! A Merry Christmas and A Happy New Year ! He'll be very merry and very happy, I have no doubt ! "

The children drank the toast after her. It was the first of their proceedings which had no heartiness in it. Tiny Tim drank it last of all, but he didn't care twopence for it. Scrooge was the ogre of the family. The mention of his name cast a dark shadow on the party, which was not dispelled for full five minutes.

They were not a handsome family ; they were not well dressed ; their shoes were far from being waterproof ; their clothes were scanty ; and Peter might have known, and very likely did, the inside of a pawnbroker's. But they were happy, grateful, pleased with one another, and contented with the time ; and when they faded, and looked happier yet in the bright sprinklings of the spirit's torch at parting, Scrooge had his eye upon them, and especially on Tiny Tim, until the last.

*The spirit then led Scrooge to see how Christmas was being spent deep in the coal mines, up in the lighthouses and away on the high seas. Every one was making merry as best he could.*

*At last they reached the home of Scrooge's nephew.*

It was a great surprise to Scrooge to find himself in a bright, dry, gleaming room, with the spirit standing smiling by his side, and looking at that same nephew with approving affability !

"Ha, ha !" laughed Scrooge's nephew. "Ha, ha, ha !"

If you should happen, by any unlikely chance, to know a man more blessed in a laugh than Scrooge's nephew, all I can say is, I should like to know him too. Introduce him to me, and I'll cultivate his acquaintance.

It is a fair, even-handed, noble adjustment of things, that while there is infection in disease and sorrow, there is nothing in the world so irresistibly contagious as laughter and good humour. When Scrooge's nephew laughed in this way—holding his sides, rolling his head, and twisting his face into the most extravagant contortions—Scrooge's niece, by marriage, laughed as heartily as he. And their assembled friends being not a bit behindhand, roared out lustily.

"Ha, ha ! Ha, ha, ha, ha !"

"He said that Christmas was a humbug, as I live !" cried Scrooge's nephew. "He believed it, too !"

"More shame for him, Fred !" said Scrooge's niece indignantly. Bless those women ; they never do anything by halves. They are always in earnest.

"He's a comical old fellow," said Scrooge's nephew, " that's the truth ; and not so pleasant as he might be. However, his offences carry their own punishment, and I have nothing to say against him."

"I'm sure he is very rich, Fred," hinted Scrooge's niece. "At least, you always tell *me* so."

"What of that, my dear ?" said Scrooge's nephew. "His wealth is of no use to him. He don't do any good with it. He don't make himself comfortable with it. He hasn't the satisfaction of thinking—ha, ha, ha !— that he is ever going to benefit us with it."

"I have no patience with him," observed Scrooge's niece. Scrooge's niece's sisters, and all the other ladies, expressed the same opinion.

"Oh, I have !" said Scrooge's nephew. "I am sorry for him ; I couldn't be angry with him if I tried. Who suffers by his ill whims ? Himself, always. Here, he takes it into his head to dislike us, and he won't come and dine with us. What's the consequence ? He don't lose much of a dinner."

"Indeed, I think he loses a very good dinner," interrupted Scrooge's niece. Everybody else said the same, and they must be allowed to have been competent judges, because they had just had dinner ; and, with the dessert upon the table, were clustered round the fire, by lamplight.

"Well ! I am very glad to hear it," said Scrooge's nephew ; "because I haven't any great faith in these young housekeepers. What do *you* say, Topper ?"

Topper had clearly got his eye upon one of Scrooge's niece's sisters, for he answered that a bachelor was a wretched outcast, who had no right to express an opinion on the subject. Whereat Scrooge's niece's sister—the plump one with the lace tucker; not the one with the roses—blushed.

"Do go on, Fred," said Scrooge's niece, clapping her hands. "He never finishes what he begins to say! He is such a ridiculous fellow!"

Scrooge's nephew revelled in another laugh, and as it was impossible to keep the infection off—though the plump sister tried hard to do it with aromatic vinegar—his example was unanimously followed.

"I was only going to say," said Scrooge's nephew, "that the consequence of his taking a dislike to us, and not making merry with us, is, as I think, that he loses some pleasant moments, which could do him no harm. I am sure he loses pleasanter companions than he can find in his own thoughts, either in his mouldy old office, or his dusty chambers. I mean to give him the same chance every year, whether he likes it or not, for I pity him. He may rail at Christmas till he dies, but he can't help thinking better of it— I defy him—if he finds me going there, in good temper, year after year, and saying, Uncle Scrooge, how are you? If it only puts him in the vein to leave his poor clerk fifty pounds, *that's* something; and I think I shook him, yesterday."

After tea, they had some music, and after a while played at forfeits; for it is good to be children sometimes, and never better than at Christmas, when its mighty Founder was a child Himself.

"Here is a new game," said Scrooge. "One half-hour, spirit, only one!"

It was a game called Yes and No, where Scrooge's nephew had to think of something, and the rest must find out what; he only answering to their questions yes or no, as the case was. The brisk fire of questioning to which he was exposed, elicited from him that he was thinking of an animal, a live animal, rather a disagreeable animal, a savage animal, an animal that growled and grunted sometimes, and talked sometimes, and lived in London, and walked about the streets, and wasn't made a show of, and wasn't led by anybody, and didn't live in a menagerie, and was never killed in a market, and was not a horse, or an ass, or a cow, or a bull, or a tiger, or a dog, or a pig, or a cat, or a bear. At every fresh question that was put to him, this nephew burst into a fresh roar of laughter; and was so inexpressibly tickled, that he was obliged to get up off the sofa and stamp. At last the plump sister, falling into a similar state, cried out:

"I have found it out! I know what it is, Fred! I know what it is!"

"What is it?" cried Fred.

"It's your uncle Scro-o-o-o-oge!"

Which it certainly was. Admiration was the universal sentiment, though some objected that the reply to "Is it a bear?" ought to have been "Yes"; inasmuch as an answer in the negative was sufficient to have diverted their thoughts from Mr. Scrooge, supposing they had ever had any tendency that way.

"He has given us plenty of merriment, I am sure," said Fred, "and it would be ungrateful not to drink his health. Here is a glass of mulled wine ready to our hand at the moment; and I say, 'Uncle Scrooge!'"

"Well! Uncle Scrooge!" they cried.

*At every fresh question Scrooge's nephew burst into a fresh roar of laughter.*

" A Merry Christmas and A Happy New Year to the old man, whatever he is ! " said Scrooge's nephew. " He wouldn't take it from me, but may he have it, nevertheless. Uncle Scrooge ! "

Uncle Scrooge had imperceptibly become so gay and light of heart, that he would have pledged the unconscious company in return, and thanked them in an inaudible speech, if the ghost had given him time. But the whole scene passed off in the breath of the last word spoken by his nephew ; and he and the spirit were again upon their travels.

Much they saw, and far they went, and many homes they visited, but always with a happy end. The spirit stood beside sick-beds, and they were cheerful ; on foreign lands, and they were close at home ; by struggling men, and they were patient in their greater hope ; by poverty, and it was rich. In alms-house, hospital, and jail, in misery's every refuge, where vain man in his little brief authority had not made fast the door, and barred the spirit out, he left his blessing, and taught Scrooge his precepts.

It was a long night, if it were only a night ; but Scrooge had his doubts of this, because the Christmas holidays appeared to be condensed into the space of time they passed together. It was strange, too, that while Scrooge remained unaltered in his outward form, the ghost grew older, clearly older. Scrooge had observed this change, but never spoke of it, until they left a children's Twelfth Night party, when, looking at the spirit as they stood together in an open space he noticed that its hair was grey.

" Are spirits' lives so short ? " asked Scrooge.

" My life upon this globe is very brief," replied the ghost. " It ends to-night."

" To-night ! " cried Scrooge.

" To-night at midnight. Hark ! The time is drawing near."

The bell struck twelve.

Scrooge looked about for the ghost, and saw it not. As the last stroke ceased to vibrate, he remembered the prediction of old Jacob Marley, and lifting up his eyes, beheld a solemn phantom, draped and hooded, coming, like a mist along the ground, towards him.

## STAVE FOUR

### THE LAST OF THE SPIRITS

THE phantom slowly, gravely, silently approached. When it came near him, Scrooge bent down upon his knee; for in the very air through which this spirit moved it seemed to scatter gloom and mystery.

It was shrouded in a deep-black garment, which concealed its head, its face, its form, and left nothing of it visible save one outstretched hand. But for this it would have been difficult to detach its figure from the night, and separate it from the darkness by which it was surrounded.

He felt that it was tall and stately when it came beside him, and that its mysterious presence filled him with a solemn dread. He knew no more, for the spirit neither spoke nor moved.

" I am in the presence of the Ghost of Christmas Yet to Come ? " said Scrooge.

The spirit answered not, but pointed onward with its hand.

" Lead on ! " said Scrooge. " Lead on ! The night is waning fast, and it is precious time to me, I know. Lead on, spirit ! "

The phantom moved away as it had come towards him. Scrooge followed in the shadow of its dress, which bore him up, he thought, and carried him along.

*The phantom showed the future, and Scrooge heard what people were saying of a much disliked man who had recently died. He even saw how the man's home, his furnishings and belongings were stolen even while his body lay cold in the house. No one cared a rap about this friendless, unfortunate man.*

" Spectre," said Scrooge, " something informs me that our parting moment is at hand. I know it, but I know not how. Tell me what man that was whom we saw lying dead ? "

The Ghost of Christmas Yet to Come conveyed him, as before

*The spirit answered not, but pointed onward with its hand.*

—though at a different time, he thought : indeed, there seemed no order in these latter visions, save that they were in the future—into the resorts of business men, but showed him not himself.

Scrooge hastened to the window of his office, and looked in. It was an office still, but not his. The furniture was not the same, and the figure in the chair was not himself. The phantom pointed as before.

He joined it once again, and wondering why and whither he had gone, accompanied it until they reached an iron gate. He paused to look round before entering.

A churchyard. Here, then, the wretched man whose name he had now to learn lay underneath the ground. It was a worthy place. Walled in by houses ; overrun by grass and weeds, the growth of vegetation's death, not life ; choked up with too much burying ; fat with repleted appetite. A worthy place !

The spirit stood among the graves, and pointed down to one. He advanced towards it, trembling. The phantom was exactly as it had been, but he dreaded that he saw new meaning in its solemn shape.

" Before I draw nearer to that stone to which you point," said Scrooge, " answer me one question. Are these the shadows of the things that will be, or are they the shadows of the things that may be, only ? "

Still the ghost pointed downward to the grave by which it stood.

Scrooge crept towards it, trembling as he went ; and following the finger, read upon the stone of the neglected grave his own name, EBENEZER SCROOGE.

" Am *I* that man who lay upon the bed ? " he cried, upon his knees.

The finger pointed from the grave to him, and back again.

" No, spirit ! Oh, no no ! "

The finger still was there.

" Spirit ! " he cried, tight clutching at its robe, " hear me. I am not the man I was. I will not be the man I must have been but for this intercourse. Why show me this, if I am past all hope ? "

For the first time the hand appeared to shake.

" Good spirit," he pursued, as down upon the ground he fell before it, " your nature intercedes for me, and pities me. Assure me that I yet may change these shadows you have shown me, by an altered life ! "

The kind hand trembled.

" I will honour Christmas in my heart, and try to keep it all the year. I will live in the past, the present, and the future. The spirits of all three shall strive within me. I will not shut out the lessons that they teach. Oh, tell me I may sponge away the writing on this stone ! "

In his agony, he caught the spectral hand. It sought to free itself, but he was strong in his entreaty, and detained it. The spirit, stronger yet, repulsed him.

Holding up his hands in a last prayer to have his fate reversed, he saw an alteration in the phantom's hood and dress. It shrank, collapsed, and dwindled down into a bedpost.

## STAVE FIVE

### THE END OF IT

YES! and the bedpost was his own. The bed was his own, the room was his own. Best and happiest of all, the time before him was his own, to make amends in!

"I will live in the past, the present, and the future!" Scrooge repeated, as he scrambled out of bed. "The spirits of all three shall strive within me. O Jacob Marley! Heaven, and the Christmas time be praised for this! I say it on my knees, old Jacob; on my knees!"

He was so fluttered and so glowing with his good intentions, that his broken voice would scarcely answer to his call. He had been sobbing violently in his conflict with the spirit, and his face was wet with tears.

*"No, spirit! Oh, no, no!"*

His hands were busy with his garments; turning them inside out, putting them on upside down, tearing them, mislaying them, making them parties to every kind of extravagance.

"I don't know what to do!" cried Scrooge, laughing and crying in the same breath, and making a perfect Laocoon of himself with his stockings. "I am as light as a feather, as happy as an angel, as merry as a schoolboy. I am as giddy as a drunken man. A Merry Christmas to everybody! A Happy New Year to all the world. Hallo, here! Whoop! Hallo!"

He had frisked into the sitting-room, and was now standing there, perfectly winded.

"There's the saucepan that the gruel was in!" cried Scrooge, starting off again, and going round the fireplace. "There's the door, by which the Ghost of Jacob Marley entered! There's the corner where the ghost of Christmas Present sat! There's the window where I saw the wandering spirits! It's all right, it's all true, it all happened. Ha, ha, ha!"

Really, for a man who had been out of practice for so many years, it was a splendid laugh, a most illustrious laugh. The father of a long, long line of brilliant laughs!

" I don't know what day of the month it is ! " said Scrooge. " I don't know how long I've been among the spirits. I don't know anything. I'm quite a baby. Never mind. I don't care. I'd rather be a baby. Hallo ! Whoop ! Hallo, here ! "

He was checked in his transports by the churches ringing out the lustiest peals he had ever heard. Clash, clang, hammer ; ding, dong, bell. Bell, dong, ding ; hammer, clang, clash ! Oh, glorious, glorious !

Running to the window, he opened it, and put out his head. No fog, no mist ; clear, bright, jovial, stirring, cold ; cold, piping for the blood to dance to ; golden sunlight ; heavenly sky ; sweet fresh air ; merry bells. Oh, glorious. Glorious !

" What's to-day ? " cried Scrooge, calling downward to a boy in Sunday clothes, who perhaps had loitered in to look about him.

" Eh ? " returned the boy, with all his might of wonder.

" What's to-day, my fine fellow ? " said Scrooge.

" To-day ! " replied the boy. " Why, CHRISTMAS DAY."

" It's Christmas Day ! " said Scrooge to himself. " I haven't missed it. The spirits have done it all in one night. They can do anything they like. Of course they can. Of course they can. Hallo, my fine fellow ! "

" Hallo ! " returned the boy.

" Do you know the poulterer's in the next street but one, at the corner ? "

" I should hope I did," replied the lad.

" An intelligent boy ! " said Scrooge. " A remarkable boy ! Do you know whether they've sold the prize turkey that was hanging up there ? —Not the little prize turkey : the big one ? "

" What, the one as big as me ? " returned the boy.

" What a delightful boy ! " said Scrooge. " It's a pleasure to talk to him. Yes, my buck ! "

" It's hanging there now," replied the boy.

" Is it ? " said Scrooge. " Go and buy it."

" Walk-ER ! " exclaimed the boy.

" No, no," said Scrooge, " I am in earnest. Go and buy it, and tell 'em to bring it here, that I may give them the direction where to take it. Come back with the man, and I'll give you a shilling. Come back with him in less than five minutes, and I'll give you half a crown ! "

The boy was off like a shot. He must have had a steady hand at a trigger who could have got a shot off half so fast.

" I'll send it to Bob Cratchit's ! " whispered Scrooge, splitting with a laugh. " He shan't know who sends it. It's twice the size of Tiny Tim. Joe Miller never made such a joke as sending it to Bob's will be ! "

The hand in which he wrote the address was not a steady one, but write it he did, somehow, and went downstairs to open the street door, ready for the coming of the poulterer's man. As he stood there, waiting his arrival, the knocker caught his eye.

" I shall love it, as long as I live ! " cried Scrooge, patting it with his hand. " I scarcely ever looked at it before. What an honest expression it has in its face. It's a wonderful knocker. Here's the turkey. Hallo ! Whoop ! How are you ? Merry Christmas ! "

It *was* a turkey ! He never could have stood upon his legs, that bird.

He would have snapped 'em short off in a minute, like sticks of sealing-wax.

"Why, it's impossible to carry that to Camden Town," said Scrooge. "You must have a cab."

The chuckle with which he said this, and the chuckle with which he paid for the turkey, and the chuckle with which he paid for the cab, and the chuckle with which he recompensed the boy, were only to be exceeded by the chuckle with which he sat down breathless, and chuckled till he cried.

He dressed himself " all in his best," and at last got out into the streets. The people were by this time pouring forth, as he had seen them with the Ghost of Christmas Present ; Scrooge regarded every one with a delighted smile. He looked so irresistibly pleasant, in a word, that three or four good-humoured fellows said, " Good-morning, sir. A Merry Christmas to you ! " And Scrooge said often afterwards, that of all the blithe sounds he had ever heard, those were the blithest in his ears.

He had not gone far, when coming on towards him he beheld the portly gentleman who had walked into his counting-house the day before, and said, " Scrooge and Marley's, I believe ? " It sent a pang across his heart to think how this old gentleman would look upon him when they met ; but he knew what path lay straight before him, and he took it.

"My dear sir," said Scrooge, quickening his pace, and taking the old gentleman by both his hands. " How do you do ? I hope you succeeded yesterday. It was very kind of you. A Merry Christmas to you, sir ! "

" Mr. Scrooge ? "

" Yes," said Scrooge. " That is my name, and I fear it may not be pleasant to you. Allow me to ask your pardon. And will you have the goodness——" here Scrooge whispered in his ear.

" Lord bless me ! " cried the gentleman, as if his breath were taken away. " My dear Mr. Scrooge, are you serious ? "

" If you please," said Scrooge. " Not a farthing less. A great many back-payments are included in it. Will you do me that favour ? "

" My dear sir," said the other, shaking hands with him. " I don't know what to say to such munifi——"

"*Why, it's impossible to carry that to Camden Town,*" *said Scrooge.*

" Don't say anything, please," retorted Scrooge. " Come and see me. Will you come and see me ? "

" I will ! " cried the old gentleman. And it was clear he meant to do it.

" Thank'ee," said Scrooge. " I am much obliged to you. I thank you fifty times. Bless you ! "

He went to church, and walked about the streets, and watched the people hurrying to and fro, and patted children on the head, and questioned beggars, and looked down into the kitchens of houses, and up to the windows ; and found that everything could yield him pleasure. He had never dreamed that any walk—that anything—could give him so much happiness. In the afternoon, he turned his steps towards his nephew's house.

He passed the door a dozen times, before he had the courage to go up and knock. But he made a dash and did it.

" Is your master at home, my dear ? " said Scrooge to the girl. Nice girl ! Very.

" Yes, sir."

" Where is he, my love ? " said Scrooge.

" He's in the dining-room, sir, along with mistress. I'll show you upstairs."

" Thank'ee. He knows me," said Scrooge, with his hand already on the dining-room lock. " I'll go in here, my dear."

He turned it gently, and sidled his face in, round the door. They were looking at the table (which was spread out in great array) ; for these young housekeepers are always nervous on such points, and like to see that everything is right.

" Fred ! " said Scrooge.

Dear heart alive, how his niece by marriage started !

" Why, bless my soul ! " cried Fred, " who's that ? "

" It's I. Your uncle Scrooge. I have come to dinner. Will you let me in, Fred ? "

Let him in ! It is a mercy he didn't shake his arm off. He was at home in five minutes. Nothing could be heartier. His niece looked just the same. So did Topper when *he* came. So did the plump sister when *she* came. So did every one when *they* came. Wonderful party, wonderful games, wonderful unanimity, won-der-ful happiness !

But he was early at the office next morning. Oh, he was early there. If he could only be there first, and catch Bob Cratchit coming late ! That was the thing he had set his heart upon.

And he did it ; yes, he did ! The clock struck nine. No Bob. A quarter past. No Bob. He was full eighteen minutes and a half behind his time. Scrooge sat with his door open, that he might see him come into the tank.

His hat was off before he opened the door ; his comforter too. He was on his stool in a jiffy ; driving away with his pen, as if he were trying to overtake nine o'clock.

" Hallo ! " growled Scrooge, in his accustomed voice, as near as he could feign it. " What do you mean by coming here at this time of day ? "

" I am very sorry, sir," said Bob. " I *am* behind my time."

" You are ? " repeated Scrooge. " Yes. I think you are. Step this way."

" It's only once a year, sir," pleaded Bob, appearing from the tank. " It shall not be repeated. I was making rather merry yesterday, sir."

"Now, I'll tell you what, my friend," said Scrooge; "I am not going to stand this sort of thing any longer. And therefore," he continued, leaping from his stool, and giving Bob such a dig in the waistcoat that he staggered back into the tank again; "and therefore I am about to raise your salary!"

Bob trembled, and got a little nearer to the ruler. He had a momentary idea of knocking Scrooge down with it, holding him, and calling to the people in the court for help and a strait waistcoat.

"A Merry Christmas, Bob!" said Scrooge, with an earnestness that could not be mistaken, as he clapped him on the back. "A merrier Christmas Bob, my good fellow, than I have given you for many a year. I'll raise your salary, and endeavour to assist your struggling family, and we will discuss your affairs this very afternoon, over a Christmas bowl of smoking bishop, Bob! Make up the fires, and buy another coal-scuttle before you dot another i, Bob Cratchit!"

"*I am about to raise your salary.*"

Scrooge was better than his word. He did it all, and infinitely more; and to Tiny Tim, who did NOT die, he was a second father. He became as good a friend, as good a master, and as good a man, as the good old city knew, or any other good old city, town, or borough, in the good old world. Some people laughed to see the alteration in him, but he let them laugh, and little heeded them; for he was wise enough to know that nothing ever happened on this globe, for good, at which some people did not have their fill of laughter in the outset; and knowing that such as these would be blind anyway, he thought it quite as well that they should wrinkle up their eyes in grins, as have the malady in less attractive forms. His own heart laughed; and that was quite enough for him.

He had no further intercourse with spirits, but lived upon the total abstinence principle, ever afterwards; and it was always said of him, that he knew how to keep Christmas well, if any man alive possessed the knowledge. May that be truly said of us, and all of us! And so, as Tiny Tim observed, God bless us every one!

# THE BUTTERFLY'S BALL
## By WILLIAM ROSCOE

Come, take up your hats, and away let us haste,
To the butterfly's ball and the grasshopper's feast;
The trumpeter gadfly has summoned the crew,
And the revels are now only waiting for you.

On the smooth-shaven grass by the side of the wood,
Beneath a broad oak that for ages has stood,
See the children of earth and the tenants of air
For an evening's amusement together repair.

And there came the beetle, so blind and so black,
Who carried the emmet, his friend, on his back;
And there was the gnat, and the dragonfly too,
With all their relations, green, orange and blue.

And there came the moth in his plumage of down,
And the hornet in jacket of yellow and brown,
Who with him the wasp, his companion, did bring,
But they promised that evening to lay by their sting.

And the shy little dormouse crept out of his hole,
And led to the feast his blind brother the mole;
And the snail, with his horns peeping out from his shell,
Came from a great distance—the length of an ell.

A mushroom their table, and on it was laid,
A water dock leaf which a table-cloth made;
The viands were various, to each of their taste,
And the bee brought his honey to crown the repast.

There close on his haunches, so solemn and wise,
The frog from a corner looked up to the skies;
And the squirrel, well pleased such diversion to see,
Sat cracking his nuts overhead in a tree.

Then out came the spider, with fingers so fine,
To show his dexterity on the tight line;
From one branch to another his cobwebs he slung,
Then quick as an arrow he darted along.

But just in the middle, oh! shocking to tell!
From his rope in an instant poor Harlequin fell;
Yet he touched not the ground, but with talons outspread
Hung suspended in air at the end of a thread.

Then the grasshopper came with a jerk and a spring
Very long was his leg, though but short was his wing;
He took but three leaps, and was soon out of sight,
Then chirped his own praises for the rest of the night.

With step so majestic the snail did advance,
And promised the gazers a minuet to dance;
But they all laughed so loud that he pulled in his head,
And went in his own little chamber to bed.

Then as evening gave way to the shadows of night,
The watchman, the glow-worm, came out with his light;
Then home let us hasten while yet we can see,
For no watchman is waiting for you and for me.

# THE JACKDAW OF RHEIMS
## BY THOMAS INGOLDSBY (RICHARD BARHAM)

THE Jackdaw sat on the Cardinal's chair!
Bishop and abbot, and prior were there;
Many a monk, and many a friar,
Many a knight, and many a squire,
With a great many more of lesser degree,—
In sooth a goodly company;
And they served the Lord Primate on bended knee.
Never, I ween, Was a prouder seen,
Read of in books, or dreamt of in dreams,
Than the Cardinal Lord Archbishop of Rheims!

In and out through the motley rout,
That little Jackdaw kept hopping about;
Here and there, Like a dog in a fair,
Over comfits and cakes, And dishes and plates,
Cowl and cope, and rochet and hall,
Mitre and crosier! he hopp'd upon all!
With saucy air, He perch'd on the chair
Where, in state, the great Lord Cardinal sat
In the great Lord Cardinal's great red hat;
And he peer'd in the face Of his Lordship's Grace,
With a satisfied look, as if he would say,
"We two are the greatest folks here to-day!"
And the priests, with awe, As such freaks they saw,
Said, "The Devil must be in that little Jackdaw!"

The feast was over, the board was clear'd,
The flawns and the custards had all disappear'd
And six little Singing-boys,—dear little souls!

In nice clean faces, and nice white stoles,
   Came, in order due, Two by two,
Marching that grand refectory through!
A nice little boy held a golden ewer,
Emboss'd and fill'd with water, as pure
As any that flows between Rheims and Namur,
Which a nice little boy stood ready to catch
In a fine golden hand-basin made to match.
Two nice little boys, rather more grown,
Carried lavender-water, and eau de Cologne;
And a nice little boy had a nice cake of soap,
Worthy of washing the hands of the Pope.
   One little boy more  A napkin bore,
Of the best white diaper, fringed with pink,
And a Cardinal's Hat mark'd in " permanent ink."

The great Lord Cardinal turns at the sight
Of these nice little boys dress'd all in white:
   From his finger he draws  His costly turquoise;
And, not thinking at all about little Jackdaws,
   Deposits it straight  By the side of his plate,
While the nice little boys on his Eminence wait;
Till, when nobody's dreaming of any such thing,
That little Jackdaw hops off with the ring!

   There's a cry and a shout, And a deuce of a rout,
And nobody seems to know what they're about,
But the monks have their pockets all turn'd inside out;
   The friars are kneeling, And hunting, and feeling
The carpet, the floor, and the walls, and the ceiling.

   The Cardinal drew  Off each plum-colour'd shoe,
And left his red stockings exposed to the view:
   He peeps, and he feels  In the toes and the heels;
They turn up the dishes,—they turn up the plates,—
They take up the poker and poke out the grates,
—They turn up the rugs, They examine the mugs—
   But, no!—no such thing;—They can't find THE RING!
And the Abbot declared that, " when nobody twigg'd it,
Some rascal or other had popp'd in, and prigg'd it! "

The Cardinal rose with a dignified look,
He call'd for his candle, his bell, and his book!
   In holy anger, and pious grief,
   He solemnly cursed that rascally thief!
   He cursed him at board, he cursed him in bed;
   From the sole of his foot to the crown of his head;
   He cursed him in sleeping, that every night
   He should dream of the devil, and wake in a fright;

He cursed him in eating, he cursed him in drinking,
  He cursed him in coughing, in sneezing, in winking;
He cursed him in sitting, in standing, in lying;
  He cursed him in walking, in riding, in flying,
  He cursed him in living, he cursed him dying!—
Never was heard such a terrible curse!
  But what gave rise  To no little surprise,
Nobody seem'd one penny the worse!

  The day was gone, The night came on,
The Monks and the Friars they search'd till dawn;
  When the Sacristan saw, On crumpled claw,
Come limping a poor little lame Jackdaw!
  No longer gay, As on yesterday;
His feathers all seem'd to be turn'd the wrong way;—
His pinions droop'd—he could hardly stand,—
His head was as bald as the palm of your hand;
  His eye so dim, So wasted each limb,
That, heedless of grammar, they all cried, " THAT'S HIM!—

That's the scamp that has done this scandalous thing!
That's the thief that has got my Lord Cardinal's Ring!"
  The poor little Jackdaw, When the monks he saw,
Feebly gave vent to the ghost of a caw;
And turn'd his bald head, as much as to say;
" Pray, be so good as to walk this way!"
  Slower and slower  He limp'd on before,
Till they came to the back of the belfry door,
  Where the first thing they saw, Midst the sticks and the straw
Was the RING in the nest of that little Jackdaw!

Then the great Lord Cardinal call'd for his book,
And off that terrible curse he took;
  The mute expression  Served in lieu of confession,
And, being thus coupled with full restitution,
The Jackdaw got plenary absolution!
  —When those words were heard, That poor little bird
Was so changed in a moment, 'twas really absurd,
  He grew sleek, and fat; In addition to that,
A fresh crop of feathers came thick as a mat!

  His tail waggled more  Even than before;
But no longer it wagged with an impudent air,
No longer he perch'd on the Cardinal's chair
  He hopp'd now about  With a gait devout;
At Matins, at Vespers, he never was out;
And, so far from any more pilfering deeds,
He always seem'd telling the Confessor's beads.

If any one lied,—or if any one swore,—
Or slumber'd in prayer-time and happen'd to snore,
   That good Jackdaw Would give a great " Caw ! "
As much as to say, " Don't do so any more ! "
While many remark'd, as his manners they saw,
That they " never had known such a pious Jackdaw ! "
   He long lived the pride Of that country-side,
And at last in the odour of sanctity died ;
   When, as words were too faint His merits to paint,
The Conclave determined to make him a Saint ;
And on newly-made Saints and Popes, as you know,
It's the custom, at Rome, new names to bestow,
So they canonised him by the name of Jim Crow !

# The Lake Isle of Innisfree

### *by* W. B. YEATS

I WILL arise and go now, and go to Innisfree,
   And a small cabin build there, of clay and wattles made ;
Nine bean rows will I have there, a hive for the honey bee,
   And live alone in the bee-loud glade.

And I shall have some peace there, for peace comes dropping slow,
   Dropping from the veils of the morning to where the cricket sings;
There midnight's all a glimmer, and noon a purple glow,
   And evening full of the linnet's wings.

I will arise and go now, for always night and day
   I hear lake water lapping with low sounds by the shore ;
While I stand on the roadway, or on the pavements gray,
   I hear it in the deep heart's core.

# THE HELPFUL WAITER

*from "David Copperfield"*

## *by* CHARLES DICKENS

THE coach was in the yard, shining very much all over, but without any horses to it as yet; and it looked in that state as if nothing was more unlikely than its ever going to London. I was thinking this, and wondering what would ultimately become of my box, which Mr. Barkis had put down on the yard-pavement by the pole (he having driven up the yard to turn his cart), and also what would ultimately become of me, when a lady looked out of a bow-window where some fowls and joints of meat were hanging up, and said:

" Is that the little gentleman from Blunderstone? "

" Yes, ma'am," I said.

" What name? " inquired the lady.

" Copperfield, ma'am," I said.

" That won't do," returned the lady. " Nobody's dinner is paid for here, in that name."

" Is it Murdstone, ma'am? " I said.

" If you're Master Murdstone," said the lady, " why do you go and give another name, first? "

I explained to the lady how it was, who then rang a bell, and called out, " William! show the coffee-room! " upon which a waiter came running out of a kitchen on the opposite side of the yard to show it, and seemed a good deal surprised when he found he was only to show it to me.

It was a large, long room with some large maps in it. I doubt if I could have felt much stranger if the maps had been real foreign countries, and I cast away in the middle of them. I felt it was taking a liberty to sit down, with my cap in my hand, on the corner of the chair nearest the door; and when the waiter laid a cloth on purpose for me, and put a set of castors on it, I think I must have turned red all over with modesty.

He brought me some chops, and vegetables, and took the covers off in such a bouncing manner that I was afraid I must have given him some offence. But he greatly relieved my mind by putting a chair for me at the table, and saying, very affably, " Now, six-foot! come on! "

I thanked him and took my seat at the board; but found it extremely difficult to handle my knife and fork with anything like dexterity, or to avoid splashing myself with the gravy, while he was standing opposite, staring so hard, and making me blush in the most dreadful manner every time I caught his eye. After watching me into the second chop, he said:

" There's half a pint of ale for you. Will you have it now? "

I thanked him, and said " Yes." Upon which he poured it out of a jug into a large tumbler, and held it up against the light, and made it look beautiful.

" My eye! " he said. " It seems a good deal, don't it? "

" It does seem a good deal," I answered, with a smile. For it was quite delightful to me, to find him so pleasant. He was a twinkling-eyed, pimple-

228

*" What have we got here ? " he said. " Hot chops ? "*

faced man, with his hair standing upright all over his head ; and as he stood with one arm akimbo, holding up the glass to the light with the other hand, he looked quite friendly.

" There was a gentleman here, yesterday," he said, " a stout gentleman, by the name of Topsawyer—perhaps you know him ! "

" No," I said, " I don't think——"

" In breeches and gaiters, broad-brimmed hat, gray coat, speckled choker," said the waiter.

" No," I said, bashfully, " I haven't the pleasure——"

" He came in here," said the waiter, looking at the light through the tumbler, " ordered a glass of this ale—*would* order it—I told him not—drank it, and fell dead. It was too old for him. It oughtn't to be drawn ; that's the fact."

I was very much shocked to hear of this melancholy accident, and said I thought I had better have some water.

" Why, you see," said the waiter, still looking at the light through the tumbler, with one of his eyes shut up, " our people don't like things being ordered and left. It offends 'em. But *I*'ll drink it, if you like. I'm used to it, and use is everything. I don't think it'll hurt me, if I throw my head back, and take it off quick. Shall I ? "

I replied that he would much oblige me by drinking it, if he thought he could do it safely, but by no means otherwise. When he did throw his head back, and take it off quick, I had a horrible fear, I confess, of seeing him meet the fate of the lamented Mr. Topsawyer, and fall lifeless on the carpet. But it didn't hurt him. On the contrary, I thought he seemed the fresher for it.

" What have we got here ? " he said, putting a fork into my dish.  " Not chops ? "

" Chops," I said.

" Lord bless my soul ! " he exclaimed, " I didn't know they were chops. Why, a chop's the very thing to take off the bad effects of that beer ! Ain't it lucky ? "

So he took a chop by the bone in one hand, and a potato in the other and ate away with a very good appetite, to my extreme satisfaction. He afterwards took another chop, and another potato ; and after that, another chop and another potato. When we had done, he brought me a pudding, and having set it before me, seemed to ruminate, and to become absent in his mind for some moments.

" How's the pie ? " he said, rousing himself.

" It's a pudding," I made answer.

" Pudding ! " he exclaimed.  " Why, bless me, so it is ! What ! " looking at it nearer.  " You don't mean to say it's a batter-pudding ! "

" Yes, it is indeed."

" Why, a batter-pudding," he said, taking up a tablespoon, " is my favourite pudding ! Ain't that lucky ? Come on, little 'un, and let's see who'll get most."

The waiter certainly got most. He entreated me more than once to come in and win, but what with his tablespoon to my teaspoon, his despatch to my despatch, and his appetite to my appetite, I was left far behind at the first mouthful, and had no chance with him. I never saw any one enjoy a pudding so much, I think ; and he laughed, when it was all gone, as if his enjoyment of it lasted still.

Finding him so very friendly and companionable, it was then that I asked for the pen and ink and paper, to write to Peggotty. He not only brought it immediately, but was good enough to look over me while I wrote the letter. When I had finished it, he asked me where I was going to school.

I said, " Near London," which was all I knew.

" Oh, my eye ! " he said, " I am sorry for that."

" Why ? " I asked him.

" Oh, Lord ! " he said, shaking his head, " that's the school where they broke the boy's ribs—two ribs—a little boy he was. I should say he was —let me see—how old are you, about ? "

I told him between eight and nine.

" That's just his age," he said.  " He was eight years and six months old when they broke his first rib ; eight years and eight months old when they broke his second, and did for him."

I could not disguise from myself, or from the waiter, that this was an uncomfortable coincidence, and inquired how it was done. His answer was not cheering, for it consisted of two dismal words, " With whopping."

The blowing of the coach-horn in the yard was a seasonable diversion, which made me get up and hesitatingly inquire, in the mingled pride and diffidence of having a purse (which I took out of my pocket), if there were anything to pay.

" There's a sheet of letter-paper," he returned.  " Did you ever buy a sheet of letter-paper ? "

I could not remember that I ever had.

" It's dear," he said, " on account of the duty. Threepence. That's the way we're taxed in this country. There's nothing else, except the waiter. Never mind the ink. *I* lose by that."

" Why should you—what should I—how much ought I to—what would it be right to pay the waiter, if you please ? " I stammered, blushing.

" If I hadn't a family, and that family hadn't the cow-pock," said the waiter, " I wouldn't take a sixpence. If I didn't support a aged pairint, and a lovely sister "—here the waiter was greatly agitated—" I wouldn't take a farthing. If I had a good place, and was treated well here, I should beg acceptance of a trifle, instead of taking it. But I live on broken wittles—and I sleep on the coals "—here the waiter burst into tears.

I was very much concerned for his misfortunes, and felt that any recognition short of ninepence would be mere brutality and hardness of heart. Therefore I gave him one of my three bright shillings, which he received with much humility and veneration, and spun up with his thumb, directly afterwards, to try the goodness of.

It was a little disconcerting to me, to find, when I was being helped up behind the coach, that I was supposed to have eaten all the dinner without any assistance. I discovered this, from overhearing the lady in the bow-window, say to the guard, " Take care of that child, George, or he'll burst ! " and from observing that the women-servants who were about the place came out to look and giggle at me as a young phenomenon. My unfortunate friend the waiter, who had quite recovered his spirits, did not appear to be disturbed by this, but joined in the general admiration without being at all confused. It I had any doubt of him, I suppose this half-awakened it ; but I am inclined to believe that with the simple confidence of a child, and the natural reliance of a child upon superior years, I had no serious mistrust of him on the whole, even then.

I felt it rather hard, I must own, to be made, without deserving it, the subject of jokes between the coachman and guard as to the coach drawing heavy behind, on account of my sitting there, and as to the greater expediency of my travelling by wagon. The story of my supposed appetite getting wind among the outside passengers, they were merry upon it likewise ; and asked me whether I was going to be paid for, at school, as two brothers or three, and whether I was contracted for, or went upon the regular terms ; with other pleasant questions. But the worst of it was, that I knew I should be ashamed to eat anything, when an opportunity offered, and that, after a rather light dinner, I should remain hungry all night—for I had left my cakes behind, at the hotel, in my hurry. My apprehensions were realised. When we stopped for supper I couldn't muster courage to take any, though I should have liked it very much, but sat by the fire and said I didn't want anything. This did not save me from more jokes, either ; for a husky-voiced gentleman with a rough face, who had been eating out of a sandwich-box all the way, except when he had been drinking out of a bottle, said I was like a boa constrictor who took enough at one meal to last him a long time ; after which, he actually brought a rash out upon himself with boiled beef

# FOLLOW MY LEADER

### *by* STEPHEN SOUTHWOLD

### (With fullest acknowledgment to Henri Fabre).

DAY after day a long line of Caterpillars would come creeping over the beds of the great garden to the cabbage-patch. Whence they came no one knew, but every morning just after daybreak, when the young sun scattered his first joyous beams, the line would appear.

It was always a line of Caterpillars, one behind the other, following their leader, noses touching tails in one wriggling stretch of unbroken green.

A Frog had watched their daily journey for a long while; and at last one morning he sat upon a garden-bed, and as the leader of the long thin line approached him, the Frog said affably, " Good-morning, Captain, where are you going ? "

" Don't talk to me," said the leading Caterpillar; " my work is too important : I have no time to stay talking with idlers. I lead my fellows onward, onward, onward, to the rich pastures."

The Frog smiled, but said nothing; and hopping along the line, he stopped beside the tenth Caterpillar, and said, " Good-morning, Wriggler; where are *you* off to ? "

" Away with you ! " cried the tenth Caterpillar, " I have work to do."

" What work ? " giggled the Frog.

" I have to follow the fellow in front, and have no time for chatter."

Away hopped the Frog, and coming to the twentieth Caterpillar, he said with a chuckle, " Good-morning, old Half-Way; and do you follow the fellow in front ? "

" Do I *what* ? " snapped the twentieth Caterpillar.

"I beg your pardon," grinned the Frog, "but may I ask what you are doing?"

"My work in the world," replied the twentieth Caterpillar.

"And what might that be?" inquired the Frog amiably, "following?"

"*And* leading," said the twentieth Caterpillar, with an impatient wriggle; "I follow the one in front and lead the one behind. Be off with you, and do not hinder the work of the world."

Chuckling to himself the Frog hopped away, and coming to the last Caterpillar in the line, he said, "Good-morning, old Whip-Behind, and what might *you* be doing?"

"Don't be rude!" snapped the end Caterpillar, "I am following; cannot you see for yourself?"

"I can see very well," giggled the Frog, "but where are you going?"

"That is not *my* business, nor yours either," replied the last Caterpillar; "I follow the one in front, and that is enough for me. Now you go away, and don't interfere in matters which you cannot understand."

"Bless your legs, old Greenback!" cried the Frog agreeably, "don't get cross. I think you are perfectly wonderful, all of you. Mind you don't get lost." And away hopped the Frog to think over the curious and quaint spectacle.

He thought and thought and thought about it all through the day. And then, toward evening, he hurried off to find a wise old Toad who lived in a hole under the sundial in the middle of the garden.

When the Toad had heard the story he laughed and croaked and chuckled so much that he nearly choked. And then he whispered for a long while to the Frog. And then both the Toad and the Frog laughed and croaked and chuckled together so much that they both nearly choked, and had to pat each other upon the back.

The next morning the Frog awaited the line of Caterpillars; and when the leader drew near, the Frog hopped up to him, made a low bow, and said, "Most noble Captain, I have news for you."

"Out with it then," said the leader of the Caterpillars; "for I have no time to waste."

"I wonder," went on the Frog, "that you should go to that old cabbage-patch——"

"Who told *you* where we went?" interrupted the leader of the Caterpillars, continuing on his way.

"My dear old friend, the kind-hearted Toad," replied the Frog, taking little hops to keep pace with the leader's slow progress.

"I see nothing to wonder at," said the Caterpillar; "I go where the food is best."

"Oh, most noble Captain," said the Frog gravely, "I assure you there are finer cabbages than in that old patch."

"Where?" asked the leader, half pausing and moving his head from side to side.

"Follow me!" cried the Frog eagerly; "and you shall have the feast of your lives."

The Frog set off with little slow hops, the Caterpillar leader followed him, and all the long line came wriggling after.

The Frog led the leader to the sundial, and then saying, " Now follow me closely," led him gradually round the sundial until he caught up with the Caterpillar at the end of the line. The leader of the Caterpillars was puzzled for a moment, but finding a Caterpillar in front of him, began to follow it nose to tail, forgetting all about his leadership.

And so now there was a ring of Caterpillars about the sundial, going round and round and round.

Round and round and round they went, never getting anywhere, but all going on hopefully and trustfully, in perfect faith that as long as there was some one in front he would lead them somewhere.

And upon the sundial sat the Toad and the Frog, hugging one another, and shaking with laughter.

All through the hot morning, and through the hotter afternoon, the thin green circle went round and round the sundial.

All the creatures of the garden came hurrying up to watch the amazing spectacle. And ever and again a Snail or Bee or Frog or Lizard or Ant would say to one of the members of that thin, green and giddy circle, " Where are you going, old Roundabouts ? " And always the Caterpillar spoken to would reply, " That's none of *your* business—I follow my leader."

At last the creatures of the garden grew weary of watching, and even the Frog and the Toad tired of the joke. And so, as twilight fell, the Caterpillars remained there alone, ever going round and round and round.

Whether they are still going round in that endless line, or whether (as the Frog said afterward) they went on and on till they died from starvation, I do not know. But certainly if they follow their leader, and do not die, they will go on for ever and ever and ever.

# THE BLUE BIRD

### *by* COUNTESS D'AULNOY

NCE upon a time there was a king who was very rich both in lands and money. His wife died, and he was in great grief.

All his subjects agreed amongst themselves that they would try to calm his grief. Some made speeches, while others tried pleasant talk, but he was so sad he scarcely heard a word they said to him.

At last a woman came before him, weeping and sobbing so much and so loudly that he was quite surprised. She said that she had lost the best of husbands, and had made up her mind to weep as long as she had eyes in her head.

The king listened to this visitor more than to the others. He talked to her of his dear, dead wife, and she told him all about her late husband. They talked so much of their sorrow that at last they were puzzled to know what more to say about it.

Soon he spoke less and less of his wife : at last he ceased to speak of her altogether. In fact, to the surprise of everybody, it was not long until the king was married to the cunning widow.

The king had an only daughter who was thought the eighth wonder of the world. She was named Florine, and was only fifteen when the king re-married.

The new queen sent for her own daughter, who had been brought up by her godmother, the Fairy Souci. Souci had tried to make her pretty, but all in vain. Yet she loved her dearly. Her name was Truton.

The queen, her mother, doted on her ; she talked of nothing but the charming Truton. As Florine looked so beautiful beside her daughter, it annoyed her, and she sought by every means to hurt the poor princess in the eyes of her father.

The king came one day to the queen and said, " Florine and Truton are of an age to be married.  The first prince who visits the court shall have the hand of one of them in marriage."

" I wish," said the queen, " my daughter to be married first ; she is older than yours, and a thousand times more amiable."

The king, who did not like arguing, answered that he was quite willing it should be so, and that he left her to do as she pleased.

A short time after this, news came that a visit from Prince Charming might be expected.  Never was any prince more noted for bravery and wealth.

When the queen heard this news, she had all the work-people making dresses for Truton, and told the king to give nothing new to Florine.

She then bribed the waiting-women to steal all the princess's clothes and jewels the very day Prince Charming came, so that when Florine went to dress she could not find even a ribbon.  She was left with only the gown she had on her back, and it was very much soiled.  She was so ashamed of her clothes that, when Prince Charming arrived, she hid herself in a corner of the hall.

The queen welcomed the prince with great pomp, and presented her daughter to him.  Prince Charming turned his eyes from her as soon as possible.

He asked if there was not another princess named Florine.  " Yes," said Truton, pointing to her with her finger ; " there she is, hiding herself, because she is not finely dressed."

Florine blushed and looked so lovely that Prince Charming was quite dazzled.  He rose at once and made a deep bow to the princess.

" Madam," said he, " your beauty does not need the help of fine clothes." Then he went and talked with her for three whole hours.

The queen was in despair, and Truton could not believe that the princess could be thus preferred to her.

They went to the king and made him agree that, during the visit of Prince Charming, Florine should be shut up in a tower.  No sooner had Florine retired to her rooms than four men in masks seized and carried her to a room at the top of the tower.

The prince awaited impatiently the hour when he hoped to meet her again.  He talked of her to the gentlemen whom the king had placed about his person to do him honour, but, as they had been ordered by the queen, they said all the ill of her they could think of.

The queen, anxious to learn if Prince Charming was much annoyed at not seeing the princess, sent for the courtiers she had placed with him. Everything they told showed that the prince was in love with Florine.

But how shall I describe to you the wretched state of that poor princess ? She lay stretched on the floor in the keep of that terrible tower.

" I should have borne it easier," said she, " if I had been put in prison before I had seen that amiable prince."

She then began to weep so bitterly that her worst enemy would have pitied her.  Thus passed the night.

Prince Charming visited the king and queen as often as he could in hopes of meeting Florine in the royal apartments.  His eyes were everywhere in search of her. The queen easily guessed what was passing in his mind ; but she pretended to take no notice of it. At last he asked her plainly where the Princess Florine was.

" Sir," replied the queen haughtily, " the king, her father, has forbidden her to quit her own rooms until my daughter is married."

" And what reason," inquired Prince Charming, " can there be for making a prisoner of that beautiful princess ? "

" I know not," said the queen, " and if I did, I should not think I had need to answer any of your questions ! "

The prince felt his anger rising fearfully. He cast an angry glance upon Truton. Then he abruptly left the queen's presence.

On his return to his own apartments in the palace he asked a young prince, who had come with him as a friend, to win over, at any cost, one of the princess's attendants, to allow him to speak to Florine for one moment.

The prince soon found one of the ladies, who promised him that Florine should that very evening be at a little lower window, which looked upon the garden. From there she could talk with the prince if he was very careful that no one should be aware of it.

The prince ran to tell his royal friend.

But the false attendant in the meantime went and told the queen all about the secret meeting.

The queen decided to place her daughter at the little window instead of Florine.

The night was so dark that it was impossible for Prince Charming to know that a trick was being played on him, and when he drew near to the window he poured forth to Truton all the tender things he would have said to Florine.

The prince vowed to her, that if she would accept him for her husband, he would be delighted to share with her his heart and crown. He thereupon drew his ring from his finger, and placing it on one of Truton's, begged her to take it as a sign of his faith, and added that she had only to fix the hour for their flight.

The queen felt happy that her plans were going so well.

So Prince Charming prepared to carry off his beloved in a flying chariot, drawn by winged frogs, a present which had been made to him by a friend who was a magician. The night fixed for the flight was very dark. Truton stole out by a little door, and the prince, who was waiting for her, led her into the chariot.

As he was anxious to marry his beloved princess at once, he asked her where she would like their wedding to be held. She answered that she had a godmother, named Souci, who was a very famous fairy, and she thought they should go at once to her castle.

Truton asked to see her godmother alone. Then she told her how she had entrapped the prince, and pleaded on the fairy to win him for her.

" Ah ! my child," said the fairy ; " the task will not be an easy one : he is too fond of Florine. I feel certain he will give us a great deal of trouble."

In the meantime the prince was awaiting them in a saloon, the walls of which were of diamonds so clear that through them he could see Souci and

Truton talking together. At first he thought he must be dreaming. But soon he saw he had been tricked.

Souci then entered the saloon and said, " Prince Charming, here is the Princess Truton, whom you have promised to marry ; she is my god daughter, and I wish you to marry her at once."

" I ! " exclaimed he, " I have made no promise to her."

" Am not I your princess, faithless one ? " said Truton, showing him his ring. " To whom didst thou give this ring as a pledge of thy truth ? "

" How then ! " he cried ; " have I been cheated ? I would away instantly ! "

" Oho, it is not in your power to go away," exclaimed Souci.

She touched him, and his feet were fixed to the floor as if they had been nailed to it.

" You may stone me to death," cried the prince, " but I will marry no one but Florine. You may use your power upon me as you please ! "

Souci and Truton tried in turn every means but in vain. The prince did not say another word, looking on them both with an air of great scorn.

Twenty days and twenty nights passed without their ceasing to talk. They did not sleep or sit down. At length Souci, quite tired out, said to the prince, " Well, since you will not listen to reason, choose at once whether you will marry my god daughter, or do penance for seven years as a punishment for breaking your word."

The prince, who up to this time had been silent, suddenly said, " Do what you will with me, but I will not marry this wretch."

" You are a wretch yourself," said Truton, in a passion.

" No, no, she shall not be your wife," said Souci angrily ; " you may fly out of that window if you like, for you shall be a Blue Bird for the next seven years ! "

At the same moment the prince's person became quite changed. He saw his body had shrunk, and indeed he had the form of a bird with blue plumage. When he beheld himself in this state, he gave a cry and flew from the fatal palace of Souci as fast as his wings could carry him.

The Fairy Souci sent Truton back to the queen. When she saw her daughter, and heard from her lips all that had happened, she got into a terrible passion, and blamed the poor Florine.

She went up to the tower with Truton, whom she had dressed in her richest clothes.

" My daughter has come to show you the wedding presents," said the queen. " Prince Charming and she are married. He loves her to distraction." Thereupon they showed the princess heaps of costly dresses, jewels, lace, and ribbons. Truton took care to show Florine Prince Charming's brilliant ring.

The pretty little princess fainted with grief, and the cruel queen, pleased to see this, would not let any one help her. The queen also asked the king that great care should be taken to keep her from leaving the tower, and the king told her to do as she pleased.

The princess sat at an open window and wept the whole night long. When day began to break she shut the window, but kept on weeping. The next night she again opened the window. At dawn she hid herself in the corner of her chamber.

In the meanwhile Prince Charming, or, to speak more correctly, the beautiful Blue Bird, never ceased flying round the palace. He believed his dear princess was in prison there. He came as near the windows as he could to look into the rooms, but he was afraid of being seen by Truton.

The Blue Bird perched upon a high cypress, and had scarcely done so when he heard some one moaning. " How much longer shall I suffer ? " said the mourner. " Will not death kindly come to my aid ? "

The Blue Bird had not lost one word of this. He longed for daylight to see the lady, but before the morning dawned she had closed her window.

The Bird came again the next night. It was moonlight, and he saw a girl at an open window of the tower. She was weeping bitterly. The Blue Bird flew to the top of a tree near the window.

" *You shall be a Blue Bird for the next seven years !* "

" Adorable Florine," he cried, " I can help you in your misfortunes."

" Ah ! who speaks to me," she cried, " in such kind words ? "

" An unhappy prince," replied the Bird, " who loves you, and will never love any other than you."

" A prince who loves me ! " rejoined Florine ; " is this a snare set for me by my enemy ? "

" No, my princess," replied the Bird ; " the lover who addresses you could not betray you," and, as he said these words, he flew to the window.

Florine was at first much alarmed at the sight of so strange a bird, who spoke with so much sense, and yet in the sweet voice of a nightingale. The beauty of his plumage, however, and his kind words soon drove away her fear.

" Can I once more look upon you, my Princess ! " he exclaimed. " Can I have such happiness ! But alas ! how troubled I am because you are a captive and because I am changed into a bird by the wicked Souci for seven years ! "

" And who are you, charming Bird ? " asked the princess, caressing him.

" You have said my name," said the prince.

" How ! the greatest prince in the world, Prince Charming ! " cried the princess ; " can the little bird I hold in my hand be he ? "

Then the Blue Bird told Florine what had really happened.

Florine felt so happy in listening to the explanation of her lover that she quite forgot how unhappy she had been. Day dawned, and it cost them a thousand pangs to part, after agreeing that they would meet every night in the same way.

As he was anxious to pay Florine a favour, the Bird flew to his palace and brought back a pair of diamond ear-rings so perfect that none in the world has ever been equal to them. That evening he took them to Florine, and begged her to wear them.

" I would do so," she said, " if you visited me by daylight ; but as I only see you at night, you must excuse me."

The Bird promised he would come to the tower whenever she wished ; upon which she put the ear-rings in her ears, and the night passed as happily as the one before.

As soon as morning came, the Bird flew back to his hollow tree, where he lived upon wild fruits. Sometimes he sang the finest airs, to the great delight of all who passed that way. They could see no one, so they fancied it must be the voice of a spirit.

This made people afraid, and at last nobody dared enter the wood.

Not a day passed without his making Florine some present, till at last she had a heap of valuables. She wore her jewels only by night to please the prince, and in the day-time she hid them carefully in the straw of her mattress.

Two years thus passed away without Florine once complaining.

In the meantime the queen, who kept her so cruelly in prison, vainly tried to get some one to marry Truton. She sent messengers with proposals to all the princes she knew the names of ; but they were bowed out almost as soon as they arrived.

" If your message had to do with the Princess Florine, you would be received with joy," was the answer.

These tidings made both mother and daughter furious against the innocent princess. They said Florine must be secretly plotting with foreign lands. They sat very late talking over these things, and it was past midnight when they made up their minds to go up to the tower to question Florine.

She was at the window with the Blue Bird, with all her jewels on. The queen listened at the door. She fancied she heard an air sung by two persons.

" Ah, my Truton ! we are betrayed," exclaimed the queen, suddenly opening the door and rushing into the room. Fancy the alarm of Florine at this ! She quickly pushed open the casement to give the Royal Bird a chance to fly off without being seen. But he felt he had not the power to fly. He had noticed the danger the princess was in.

" Your plots against the state are found out," cried the queen.

" Plots with whom, madam ? " inquired the princess. " Have you not been my jailer these two years ? " Whilst she spoke, the queen and her daughter looked about in surprise.

" And where did you get, madam," said the queen, " these jewels that outshine the sun ? "

" I have found them," said Florine, " that is all I know about it."

Ths queen fixed her eyes upon Florine. " You think you can deceive us ! " she cried, " but, princess, we are aware of what you do from morning till night. These jewels have been given to you with the sole object of getting you to sell your father's kingdom." She began to hunt everywhere, and coming to the mattress she emptied it, and found such a great quantity of jewels that she could not think where they all came from.

She had hoped to hide in some place papers which would prove the princess guilty. So when she thought nobody saw her, she was about to thrust them into the chimney. By good luck the Blue Bird, who had eyes as sharp as a lynx, saw everything.

" Beware, Florine ! " he cried, " of thy enemy." This voice, so unexpected, made the queen so afraid that she dared not hide the papers.

" I believe," exclaimed the queen, in a rage, " that you are in league with demons."

The queen left her, greatly worried by all she had seen and heard. She thought she would try to find out the mystery. So she sent a young girl to sleep in Florine's apartment, saying that she was placed there to wait upon her.

The princess looked on her, of course, as a spy.

" What, then ! shall I never be able to talk again with the Bird that

*Then the Blue Bird told Florine what had really happened.*

is so dear to me ! " thought she. " Our affection was everything to us ! What will become of him ? What will become of me ? " Thinking of all these things, she shed rivers of tears.

She no longer dared go to the little window, though she heard the Bird fluttering around it. She was dying to open it ; but she feared what might happen to her dear lover. She passed a whole month without seeing the prince.

The spy, who had watched day and night, felt quite overcome with drowsiness, and at last sank into a sound slumber. Florine saw it. She opened her little window and called on the Blue Bird.

The Bird was at the window in an instant. What delight once more to see and talk to each other ! At last the hour of parting arrived, without the spy awaking, and they bade each other farewell in the most touching manner.

They thought the spy found so much pleasure in sleeping that she would do so every night. But on the third night, the sleeper, being awakened by some noise, listened, without seeming to be awake and, peeping as well as she could, saw by the light of the moon the most beautiful bird in the world talking to the princess. She overheard part of their talk and was much surprised.

The spy ran to the queen, and told her all she had seen and heard. The queen sent for Truton and her maids. They talked the matter over and became sure that the Blue Bird was Prince Charming.

The queen sent the spy back to the tower, ordering her to appear more sleepy than ever. She went to bed early, and snored as loudly as she could.

The poor princess, opening the little window, called once more on her lover, but in vain she called him the whole night long. He came not ; for the wicked queen had caused swords, knives and daggers to be put in the cypress-tree, so that when he flew rapidly into it, these weapons cut off his feet. He reached his own tree, leaving behind him a long track of blood.

He took no care to save his life, because he thought it was Florine who had been guilty of this cruel treachery. As he began more and more to believe this, he made up his mind to die.

But the prince had a friend, the Enchanter, who had seen his car return without him. He was so troubled to think what had become of him that he went eight times round the world to find him. He was on a ninth journey, when, in passing through the wood in which the poor prince was lying, he blew a long blast on his horn, and then cried five times, in a loud voice, " Prince Charming ! Prince Charming ! where art thou ? "

The prince knew the voice of his best friend. " Come near this tree," he cried, " and see the wretched prince you love."

The Enchanter looked about him everywhere, without seeing any one.

" I am a Blue Bird," exclaimed the prince in a feeble voice.

At these words the Enchanter found him, without more trouble, in his little nest. It took him a few moments to heal the wound from which the blood was flowing. Then with some herbs he found in the wood he cured the prince as perfectly as if he had never been hurt.

Prince Charming told his friend the whole story of his troubles and asked to be taken back to his palace. The Enchanter took him home and put him in a cage out of danger.

Florine, in despair at no longer seeing her prince, passed her days and nights at the window in great grief. Although the girl was always with her in the room she did not care now and called aloud for her lover.

" What has become of you, Prince Charming ? " she would say. " Have our enemies made you suffer from their cruel rage ? " She felt sure that the prince had been killed.

The queen and Truton were glad. It gave them great pleasure that they had had their revenge on Florine.

But soon a change came over the affairs of the country. Florine's father, who had grown old, fell ill, and died. The wicked queen and her daughter were not liked by the people. They rose and ran in a body to the palace, demanding the Princess Florine, whom alone they wished to have as their ruler.

The angry queen tried to carry matters with a high hand ; she stepped out on a balcony and ordered them to go to their homes. But they would not listen to her. They broke into her rooms, and stoned her to death ! Truton fled for safety to her godmother, the Fairy Souci.

The leaders of the people went up to the tower, where the princess was lying very ill. She knew neither of the death of her father nor of the punishment of her enemy.

Her subjects, flinging themselves at her feet, told her of the happy change in her fortunes. They carried her to the palace and crowned her.

Florine soon got back her health, and she was able to choose a council to govern the kingdom during her absence. Then she set out on her journey one night quite alone, without any one knowing where she had gone.

The Enchanter, who looked after the affairs of Prince Charming, not being able to undo what the Fairy Souci had done, went to seek her and ask her to give the Prince his natural form.

Enchanters and fairies are on an equal footing. These two had known each other for five or six hundred years. She received him very politely.

" Is there anything in my power that I can do for you ? "

" Yes," answered the magician. " It has to do with one of my best friends, a prince whom you have made very unhappy."

" Aha ! I understand you ! " cried Souci. " I'm very sorry, but he has no mercy to hope for, unless he promises to marry my god daughter, Truton. There she is in all her beauty, as you may see." Truton was visiting Souci at the time.

The Enchanter was almost struck dumb at the sight of her, so hideous did she seem to him ; yet he could not leave without coming to something like a bargain with Souci, for the prince now ran the risk of losing his kingdom. His heirs were daily trying to prove he was dead.

So at last the Enchanter came to an understanding with the Fairy, that she should bring Truton to Prince Charming's palace, where she should live for some months. During this time the king should be left to make up his mind to marry her, and would have his true form. If he still refused to marry the Fairy's god daughter, he would again be turned into a bird.

In the meantime Queen Florine, disguised as a peasant, with a sack upon her shoulder, went on her long journey to find the prince. Sometimes she walked, sometimes rode, now by sea, now by land, going as quickly as she could.

One day she stopped to take a rest beside a fountain. A little woman, who, bent almost double and leaning on a stout stick, was passing that way, stopped and said to her :

" What are you doing there, my pretty girl, all alone ? "

" My good mother," answered the queen, " I have plenty of company, for I have my sorrows and troubles." At these words her eyes filled with tears.

" Ah, my child," said the good woman, " do not give way to sorrow ; tell me truly what is the matter, and I may be able to help you."

The queen willingly told her all her troubles, and how she was at present seeking the Blue Bird.

The little old woman changed suddenly into a lovely young lady, and smiling on the queen, said, " Good Florine, the prince you seek is no longer a bird ; my sister Souci has given him his former shape. He is in his own kingdom. Do not worry, you will reach it and get your reward. Here are four eggs ; break one of them whenever you are most in need of help, and you will find in it what will be useful."

As she ended these words, she disappeared.

Florine put the eggs in her sack, and hurried on towards the kingdom of Prince Charming.

After walking eight days and nights without stopping, she came to the foot of a very high mountain, all of ivory, and so steep that one could not keep one's footing upon it.

The queen tried a thousand times, stepping down every time. Suddenly she remembered the eggs the Fairy had given her.

She took one out of her sack and broke it. Joy ! She found inside some little golden cramps, which she fastened on her hands and feet.

By the aid of these she climbed up the ivory mountain without the least trouble, for the points of the cramps kept her from slipping.

When she got to the top, Florine found herself in as great trouble to get down the other side. She broke another egg, out of which came two pigeons yoked to a car, which at the same time became large enough for her to sit in with comfort. The pigeons then went slowly down the mountain with the queen, and got to the bottom without the least accident.

" My little friends," said she to them, " if you will just drive me to the spot where Prince Charming holds his court, you will oblige me."

The pigeons rested neither day nor night till they stopped at the gates of the city. Florine alighted, and gave each of them a sweet kiss.

Oh, how her heart beat as she walked into the city !

She stained her face that she might not be known. She asked some people where she could see the prince. Some of them began to laugh at her.

The queen said nothing, but passed on quietly. The next person she met she also asked about the prince.

" He is to go to the temple to-morrow with the Princess Truton, for he has at last agreed to be her husband," was the answer.

What tidings! Florine felt like dying! she had no longer power to speak or move. She sank down on a heap of stones under a gateway.

"Unhappy creature that I am!" cried she. "It was for her, then, the Blue Bird left me!"

When people are very sad they rarely have much appetite, so the poor queen found a lodging for the night, and went to bed without any supper.

She rose with the sun, and hurried to the temple. But the soldiers and attendants at the door would not let her in. She tried again and again, but in vain.

So she broke her third egg and out of it came a coach of polished steel, inlaid with gold, drawn by six green mice, and driven by a rose-coloured rat. In a moment the coach carried her through a hole below a window

*A little woman, bent almost double, was passing that way.*

at the back of the temple, and she found herself inside the temple at last.

There she saw the king's throne and that of Truton, whom the people already looked upon as queen.

How downcast Florine was! She leant against a marble pillar near the throne, wondering how she could make the prince believe she was Florine. Then the prince came in, looking more handsome than ever. He did not look towards her.

How could she get his attention? She broke her fourth and last egg, and there in her hands lay a pair of costly bracelets exactly like those Prince Charming had given her.

Florine had not thought of bringing her bracelets with her, and, as there was only one pair of the kind in the world, she knew that by some kind of magic they had been brought to her.

Just then Truton came to her throne richly dressed and ugly enough to frighten everybody. She frowned on seeing Florine.

"Who art thou," said she, "to dare come near our golden throne?"

"I am a poor woman," replied Florine; "I come from a great distance to sell you some curios," and so saying she took out of her sack the emerald bracelets.

"Aha!" said Truton, "these are pretty ornaments. Will you take a threepenny piece for them?"

"Show them, madame, to some one who knows the value of jewels," said the queen, "and then we will make our bargain."

Truton, who was as fond of the prince as such a creature could be, and liked to have a reason for talking to him, went to his throne and showed him the bracelets, asking what he thought of their value.

The sight of them at once brought to his mind those he had given to Florine. He turned pale, sighed, and stood for some time without speaking.

Then suddenly he turned to go towards the poor woman.

Every one in the temple looked towards her, but what was their surprise to see, not the poor woman, but a beautiful lady, dressed in a robe of light taffeta. Florine's coarse disguise had gone.

For a second the prince and Florine looked at each other, then he threw himself at her feet, bathing her hands with his tears, and felt ready to die with joy.

Florine was not less moved. Her heart seemed to stop beating; she could scarcely breathe. She looked earnestly at the prince without saying a word, and when she found strength to speak to him, she could not be angry with him.

At length they explained everything. Their love became stronger than ever, and all they feared was the Fairy Souci. But at this moment the Enchanter, who was so fond of the prince, appeared with a famous Fairy, no other than she who gave the four eggs to Florine. After the first compliments had passed between them, the Enchanter and the Fairy said their power was so great that Souci could do nothing against them, and that their marriage would take place without delay.

Truton was so astonished that she stood saying nothing. But when she heard the word "marriage," she got into a great rage and began to abuse Florine.

Florine shrank from her in fear, but at once the Enchanter and the Fairy stepped forward and changed Truton into a sow.

The sow danced about madly, and then rushed out of the temple and through the streets of the city.

Prince Charming and Queen Florine, now that they had got rid of so odious a person, thought only of their wedding, which was soon held in great splendour.

For many years they reigned together over Prince Charming's kingdom and were so happy that in time they forgot about the troubles they had suffered.

# THE KING OF THE PEACOCKS

*by*

COUNTESS D'AULNOY

KING and queen had two handsome boys of whom they were very fond. Then a baby girl was born, and the queen named her Rosette. She was a beautiful child, but the fairies, who had come to see her, were unwilling to talk about her future.

"Ah," said the queen, "that bodes me no good; you do not wish to hurt my feelings by foretelling some misfortune; but I entreat you to let me know all—hide nothing from me."

They made every sort of excuse, but that only further increased the queen's desire for information.

At last the principal fairy said: "We fear, madam, that Rosette will be the cause of some great misfortune to her brothers, and that through her they will lose their lives. That is all we can foresee respecting this beautiful little girl, and we are sorry we cannot tell you anything more agreeable."

After their departure, the queen remained so melancholy that the king, who could not help noticing her sadness, asked what was the matter. She replied that she had been sitting too near the fire and had burnt all the wool off her spindle.

"Is that all?" said the king, who instantly went up into the loft and brought down more wool than she could possibly spin in a thousand years.

The queen continued in low spirits, and the king again asked what the matter was. This time she replied that, while walking by the riverside, she had lost one of her green satin slippers.

"Is that all?" said the king, and immediately sent an order to all the shoemakers in the kingdom to furnish her Majesty with ten thousand green satin slippers.

The queen wished to keep her husband from becoming as miserable as herself, but at last she felt obliged to tell him the truth, and to ask what could be done. After much thought, the king replied that the only safe plan was to put Rosette to death; but to this, of course, the queen would not consent.

Later, a serving woman informed her that in a great forest near the city there lived an old hermit in a hollow tree, who was consulted by people from all parts of the world.

" I must seek him out," the queen declared ; " the fairies have told me the danger, perhaps this hermit will be able to show me the remedy."

She rose very early, and mounted a beautiful little white mule, shod with gold ; and two of her maids of honour, each on a handsome horse, rode with her. When they were near the wood, the queen and her ladies dismounted, out of respect for the hermit, and went on foot to the tree where he lived.

The hermit objected to the sight of women, but, when he saw the queen, he said, " You are welcome ; what is your will with me ? " Whereupon the queen repeated what the fairies had foretold about Rosette, and asked his advice.

To this he replied that the princess should be placed in a tower, out of which she should never be permitted to step. The queen thanked the old man for his advice, made him a handsome present, and returned with her information to the palace.

When the king heard this account, he ordered a great tower to be built as quickly as possible ; he put his daughter into it, and, in order that she might not feel dull, all the royal family went every day to visit her. The elder brother was called the Great Prince, the younger the Little Prince, and both were very fond of their sister, for she was the most beautiful and amiable creature ever seen.

When Rosette was about sixteen years old, her parents were taken very ill, and died almost on the same day as each other. Everybody was very sorry, there was general mourning, and the bells tolled throughout the city. Rosette grieved sadly for the loss of her loved mother and father.

After the funeral, the dukes and lords of the kingdom seated the Great Prince on a throne of gold and diamonds, with a crown on his head, and wearing robes of violet velvet covered all over with stars and moons. The whole court then shouted three times, " Long live the King ! " and nothing was thought of but rejoicing.

The very first thing that the new king and his brother said to each other was, " Now that we have the power we will remove our sister from the prison in which she has passed so many weary years." They had only to cross the garden to reach the tower, which had been built in a corner of it, as high as possible, for her parents had intended the princess to remain in it all her life.

Rosette was making a beautiful robe on a frame before her, but when she saw her brothers she rose, and took the king's hands, saying, " Good-morning, sire, you are now king and I am your little servant. I beseech you to take me out of this tower, where I am very dull," and with that she began to weep.

The king embraced her, and told her not to cry ; that he had come to set her free, and conduct her to a fine house. The prince had his pockets full of sweetmeats, which he gave to his sister, saying, " Come, let us quit this gloomy prison ; you shall not suffer any longer."

When Rosette saw the beautiful garden, all full of flowers, fruits, and fountains, she was so astonished that she could not utter a word, for she had never seen anything of the sort before. She gazed eagerly about her, now walking, now stopping, now gathering fruit from the trees, or flowers from their beds. Her little dog, named Fretillon, who was as green as a parrot, had but one ear, and danced to perfection, ran barking before her, with a thousand jumps and capers.

Suddenly Fretillon ran into a little wood, and the princess followed quickly. Never was any one so astonished as she at seeing in the wood a great peacock, with his tail spread, and looking so beautiful, that she could not take her eyes off him. In answer to her questions, her brothers, who had now come up, replied that the peacock was a bird which was sometimes cooked in a pie.

" What," she exclaimed, " do they dare to kill and eat such a beautiful bird ? I declare to you that I will never marry any one but the king of the peacocks, and when I am queen I will take good care that none shall be eaten."

" But, sister," cried the astonished king, " where would you that we should find the king of the peacocks ? "

" Wherever you please, sire," was the answer, " but I certainly will marry no one else."

After she had made this resolve, the brothers conducted her to the palace, whither they were obliged to bring the peacock also, since it was her wish. All the ladies, who had never seen Rosette, hastened to salute her and pay their court to her. Some brought preserves, others sugar, others dresses of gold stuff, beautiful ribbons, dainty shoes, pearls and diamonds. She was entertained everywhere, and was so well-bred and polite, that not a lady or gentleman left her without being charmed.

Meanwhile, the two brothers resolved to find the king of the peacocks, if there was one in the world. They decided that a portrait of the princess should be taken, and had one painted so finely that it did all but speak. Then they said to her, " Since you will not marry any one but the king of the peacocks, we are about to set out together in search of him. If we find him, we shall be very happy. Take charge of the kingdom until we return."

Rosette thanked them prettily for all the trouble they were taking. She said she would govern the kingdom carefully, and that, while they were away, all her pleasure would consist in looking at the peacock, and making the dog dance. They could not keep from tears in bidding each other farewell.

Behold these two princes, then, on their journey, inquiring of every one, " Do you know the king of the peacocks ? " Every one answered " No." They travelled on farther, and at last went so far that nobody has ever been such a distance.

They arrived at the Kingdom of Mayflies. Never before were seen so many ; they made such a buzzing that the king was afraid he would never hear distinctly again. He asked one, who seemed the most sensible of them, if he knew where the king of the peacocks could be found.

" Sire," replied the mayfly, " his kingdom is very, very far from this place ; you have come the longest road to it."

" How do you know that ? " the king asked.

" Because," replied the mayfly, " we know you very well, and go every year to pass two or three months in your gardens."

The brothers became great friends with the mayfly, and dined with him.

They saw and admired all the sights of the kingdom, afterwards setting out again to finish their journey, and, as they had learned the way, they were not long about it.  They saw all the trees laden with peacocks, and every part of the kingdom so full of them, that you could hear them scream a long distance off.

Both brothers now felt a little anxious.  " It is a most unfortunate whim that our sister has got into her head," said the prince.  " What could have made her believe there was a king of the peacocks in the world ? "

When they arrived at the principal city, they perceived it was full of men and women ; but that they were dressed in clothes made of peacocks' feathers, and wore a number of them as very fine ornaments.  They met the king, who was driving out in a coach of gold and diamonds, drawn by twelve handsome peacocks.

This king of the peacocks was so handsome, that his visitors were charmed with him.  He had long, curly, light hair and very fair skin, and he wore a crown of feathers from the tail of a peacock.  On seeing the two brothers, he judged that, as their clothes were of a different fashion from those worn by the people of the country, they must be foreigners, so he stopped his coach and ordered them to be brought  before him.

The travellers approached, and, making a deep bow, said, " Sire, we have come from a far distance to show you a beautiful portrait," at the same time handing him the portrait of their sister.

When the king of the peacocks had regarded it for some time, " I cannot believe," he said, with a sigh, " that there is such a beautiful maid in the world."

" She is a hundred times more beautiful," declared her elder brother.

" Oh, you are jesting," replied the king of the peacocks.

" Sire," said the prince, " there is my brother, who is a king as well as you.  He is styled the king, and I am called the prince.  Our sister, of whom this is the portrait, is the Princess Rosette.  We came to ask if you will marry her.  She is beautiful and very virtuous, and we will give her a bushel of golden crowns."

" Yes, truly," replied the king, " I will marry her with all my heart. She shall lack for nothing at my court ;  I will devote myself to her ;  but I declare to you that I expect her to be as handsome as her picture, and that if the picture flatter her in the slightest degree I will put you to death."

" We consent," said the brothers.

" You consent," replied the king ;  " then to prison with you, and there you shall remain until the princess arrives."

He treated them well, and often went up to see them, keeping the picture in his own castle.  They were quite happy, being perfectly certain that their sister was handsomer than her portrait.  They wrote immediately to Rosette, asking her to come with all speed, as the king of the peacocks was awaiting her.  They did not say that they were prisoners, for fear of alarming her.

When the letter arrived, the princess was overjoyed, and told every one that the king of the peacocks was found and desired to marry her.  The people kindled bonfires, fired guns, and made feasts of sweetmeats and sugar throughout the country.  The princess then left the charge of the kingdom in the hands of the wisest old men in the city, ordering them to take great care of everything, to spend very little, and to save up money against their royal master's return. She begged them to preserve her peacock, and would have no one go with her but her nurse, her foster-sister, and her little green dog.

They put to sea in a boat, carrying with them the bushel of gold crowns, and clothes enough to change their dress twice a day for ten years. When they were nearing the end

"*I will marry her with all my heart.*"

of their journey, the nurse seated herself beside the boatman and whispered, " If thou choosest, thou shalt be rich for ever."

He answered, " I should like it much."

" Thou must help me to-night," the nurse continued ; " when the princess is asleep, let us throw her into the sea. I will then dress my daughter in the fine clothes, and we will conduct her to the king of the peacocks, who will be happy to marry her ; and for the reward we will load thee with diamonds."

Ths boatman was very much surprised by this speech. He said it was a pity to drown so beautiful a princess—that she aroused his pity. But the nurse produced a bottle of wine, and made him drink so much, that he could no longer refuse her anything.

As soon as it was dark, the princess lay down as she was wont ; the little dog was snugly established at the bottom of the bed, moving neither foot nor paw. Rosette slept soundly, and the wicked nurse, who was wide-awake, fetched the boatman. She led him into the cabin, where without waking the sleeper, they took her up, with the feather-bed, mattress, sheets, and counterpane, and flung the whole into the sea, the princess being now so fast asleep that she never woke.

By good fortune the bed was stuffed with Phœnix feathers, which are very rare, and possess the property of never sinking in the water, so that Rosette floated on her bed just as if she had been in the boat. The water, however, soaked through and disturbed her, and she roused Fretillon.

The dog had an excellent nose, and smelt the soles and the codfish so close, that he began barking loudly, and so woke all the rest of the fish. They swam about, the great fish running their heads against the bed, which, having nothing to steady it, spun round and round like a whirligig.

The princess was very much surprised. " Has our boat taken to dancing on the water ? " she said, " I have never been so uncomfortable as to-night," and still the dog kept on barking and making a loud pother.

The wicked nurse and the boatman heard the noise a long distance off, and said, " There is that little rogue of a dog drinking with his mistress to our good health. Let us make haste to land," for they had now come in sight of the city.

His majesty had sent down to the beach a hundred coaches, drawn by all sorts of rare animals. There were lions, bears, stags, wolves, horses, oxen, asses, eagles, peacocks; and the coach intended to convey Rosette was drawn by six blue monkeys, who could jump and dance the tight-rope, and play all manner of amusing tricks. They had beautiful harness of crimson velvet plated with gold. There were also sixty young ladies, whom the king had chosen to entertain the princess. They were dressed in all sorts of colours: gold and silver were the meanest ornaments about them.

Ths nurse had taken great pains to deck out her daughter. She had covered her with diamonds from head to foot, and dressed her in the richest robes; but the girl, despite her finery, looked very ugly. When the servants saw her step from the boat, they were so surprised that they could not speak.

" What does this mean?" she said, " are you asleep? Come, bring me something to eat; you are a nice set of rascals; I will have you all hanged." All this while she played the mistress, giving slaps on the face and blows with her fist, for next to nothing, to everybody near her.

" What a vile creature!" said the servants, " she is as wicked as she is ugly! Here's a fine wife for our king! It surely was not worth while to send for her from the other end of the world!"

As her train was very numerous, the false princess proceeded slowly. She sat in her coach like a queen: but all the peacocks that had perched in the trees to salute her, and had resolved to cry, " Long live the beautiful Queen Rosette!" when they perceived her to be such a horrible fright, cried, " Fie! fie! how ugly she is!"

Very angry and mortified, she turned to her guards, saying, " Kill those rogues of peacocks who are insulting me!" but the birds flew off quickly and continued to make fun of her.

The boatman, who saw this, whispered to the nurse, " Gossip, all is not well with us. Your daughter should have been handsomer."

" Hold your tongue, stupid," she replied, " thou wilt bring some misfortune upon us."

When the king heard that the princess was coming, he said, " Well, have her brothers spoken the truth? Is she really more beautiful than her picture?"

" Sire," replied his courtiers, " it is quite enough for her to be as beautiful."

" Surely," the king agreed, " I shall be perfectly satisfied with that. Let us go to meet her," for he knew by the noise in the court that she had arrived, and he could not distinguish anything except, " Fie! fie! how ugly she is!" He thought the words were meant for some dwarf or animal she had brought, for it never could have entered his head that they were spoken about herself.

The wonderful portrait was carried at the end of a long staff, uncovered, and the king walked slowly after it, with all his barons and all his peacocks, followed by the great men from other kingdoms. He was impatient to see his bride. Mercy! when he did see her he was ready to die on the spot.

He flew into the greatest passion in the world. He rent his clothes, he would not go near her; she frightened him.

"How!" he cried, "the two scoundrels I hold in prison are bold, indeed, to have made sport of me, and to have proposed that I should marry such a woman. They shall die. Go! Lock up instantly that girl, her nurse, and the fellow who brought them hither. Fling them into the lowest cell of my great tower."

Meanwhile, the two brothers, who knew the day on which their sister ought to arrive, put on their best clothes to receive her. However, instead of opening their prison and setting them at liberty the jailer came with several soldiers and forced them to descend into a cell, perfectly dark and filled with horrid reptiles, where they stood up to their necks in water.

"Alas," they cried to each other, "this is a sad wedding for us. What can have brought so great a misfortune?"

They knew not what to think, except that they were doomed to die; and they were completely overcome with sorrow. Three days passed without their hearing a word, and then their captor came to mock at them.

"You have taken the titles of king and prince," said he, "in order to cheat me and engage me to marry your sister, but you are nothing better than vagabonds. I will find judges who will quickly sentence you to death. The rope is already twisting which shall hang you both."

"King of the peacocks," replied the elder brother, in great wrath, "be less hasty in this matter, for you may have cause to repent. I am a king as surely as you are. I have a kingdom, robes, crowns, and jewels. It is a fine joke truly for you to talk of hanging us. Have we stolen anything from you, pray?"

The king, hearing this bold speech, knew not what to think, and he was tempted at times to let them go with their sister; but his chief adviser talked to him, saying that, unless he punished them sharply, every one would laugh at him, and think him a mean, petty sovereign, not worth a groat. He declared that he would not forgive them, and ordered their trial to take place. This did not last long, as it was enough only to show the portrait of the real princess by the side of the person who had come to the city under that title.

The brothers were sentenced to die as false traitors, who had promised to give the king a beautiful princess in marriage, and had offered him only an ordinary and ill-looking girl. The court went in full state to the prison to read the sentence to the prisoners, who declared they had not been guilty of falsehood, and that their sister was fairer than the day. They insisted there was something going on which they could not understand, and demanded seven days' delay before they were put to death, as in that time their innocence would probably be proved. The king, who was very angry, granted them this favour very unwillingly.

While all this is passing at Court, we must say a word about the real princess. When day broke, she was greatly astonished to find herself in the middle of the sea, without boat or assistance. She began to cry so bitterly, that all the fishes pitied her. She knew not what to do, or what would become of her.

"Surely," she said, "I have been thrown into the sea by order of the

*She began to cry so bitterly that all the fishes cried out.*

king of the peacocks. He has repented his promise to marry me, and, to get rid of me, has ordered me to be drowned. What a strange man," she continued; "I should have been so proud of him, and we should have lived happily together," whereupon she wept still more bitterly.

She remained there for two days, floating on her little bed on the ocean, turning first on one side and then on the other, soaked to her bones, with a cold enough to kill her, and all but frozen. Had it not been for the dog, who imparted a little warmth to her heart, she would have died a hundred times over. She was also very hungry. She saw the oysters in their shells, and, taking as many as she chose, ate them. The dog had little liking for them, but he was obliged to eat something. When it grew dark, she became very frightened, and said to her dog, "Fretillon, keep on barking, for fear the soles should eat us."

The bed was now not far off the shore, where a good old man lived all alone, in a hut which no one ever came near. Early in the morning, he was surprised to hear a dog bark, for dogs rarely passed that way. He thought some travellers had lost their road, and came out to direct them. Suddenly he saw the bed floating on the water, and the princess, seeing him, stretched out her arms, crying, "Good old man, save me, for I am perishing here."

Hearing her speak so sorrowfully, he was filled with pity, and, returning to his dwelling, fetched a long boat-hook. He waded into the water up to his neck, and thought twice or thrice that he would be drowned. At length, however, he managed to pull the bed to the shore, and Rosette felt vastly glad to be upon dry land. She thanked the good man warmly, and, wrapping herself up in her counterpane, walked barefooted into the hut, where the old man made a small fire with dry leaves, and drew out of a box his dead wife's best gown, with stockings and shoes, which the princess put on. Though dressed as a peasant, she looked lovely as the day, and Fretillon danced around to amuse her.

The old man saw plainly that Rosette was a lady of rank, for the coverlet of her bed was of gold and silver, and the mattress of satin. He begged her to tell him her history, assuring her that he would keep it a secret if she wished. She recounted the whole of it, weeping very much, for she still believed that the king of the peacocks had ordered her to be drowned.

"What shall we do, my daughter?" asked the old man; "you are a great princess, used to all kinds of dainties, and I have nothing to offer but black bread and radishes. You will fare badly with me, and, if you take my advice, you will permit me to inform the king that you are here. I am sure that had he seen you he would have married you."

"Ah," exclaimed Rosette, "he is a wicked creature and will put me to death, but, if you have a little basket, let me tie it round my dog's neck, and it will be very unlucky if he does not bring back something to eat."

The old man handed the princess a basket, and she tied it round the dog's neck, saying, "Go to the best saucepan in the city and bring me what may be in it."

*He was much surprised to see a little green dog.*

Fretillon ran to the city, and there being no better saucepans than the king's, he entered the royal kitchen, took the lid off the largest, pulled out the contents, and returned with all speed to the hut.

"Now, go back to the buttery," said Rosette, "and bring me the best of everything."

Fretillon at once returned to the buttery and filled his basket with white bread, muscatel wine, and all sorts of fruits and preserves. He was so heavily laden that he could hardly make his way back.

When the king called for his dinner, there was nothing in the saucepan or in the buttery. The servants all stared at each other, and their royal master was in a fearful rage. "Very well," said he, "there is no dinner for me, but be careful that the spit is put down early this evening and that I have something extra nice roasted."

When evening arrived, the princess said to the dog, "Go to the city, enter the best kitchen, and bring back some nice roast meat."

Fretillon did as his mistress ordered, and, knowing no better kitchen than the king's, stole into it softly while the cooks' backs were turned, and took all the roast meat off the spit, so nicely done that the mere sight of it gave one an appetite. He brought his basket home quite full, and the princess at once sent him back to the buttery, where he filled his basket with all the royal preserves and sweetmeats.

The king, who had not dined, being very hungry, desired to sup early; there was, however, nothing to set before him. He put himself into an awful passion and went to bed supperless. Next day, at dinner and supper time, it was just the same, for, when his majesty was ready to sit down to table, it was discovered that everything had been carried off.

Now the king's chief adviser, being greatly disturbed, hid himself in a corner of the kitchen, and kept his eyes constantly on the pot that was boiling. Presently he was much surprised to see a little green dog, with one ear, enter softly, take off the cover, and put all the meat into his basket. He watched the animal go out of the city, and followed it to the hut on the shore. Then he returned to inform the king that all his boiled and roast meat was carried day and night to the hovel of a poor peasant.

The king, very much astonished, ordered the man to be brought before him, and his adviser resolved to go himself with the archers of the guard. They found the old man dining with his companion upon the king's boiled meat. The archers seized and bound them with strong cords, and secured the dog also.

As soon as they arrived at the palace, the king was informed. " Ah," he exclaimed, " to-morrow will be the seventh and last day granted to those impudent impostors. They shall die with these thieves who have stolen my dinner," and so saying he entered the hall.

The peasant fell on his knees and offered to confess everything. While he related his story, the king gazed on the beautiful girl and pitied her, but, when the speaker declared that she was the Princess Rosette, who had been thrown into the sea, the king, notwithstanding he was so weak and faint for want of food, jumped three times for joy, and hastily untied the cords with which she was bound.

At the same time the princes were sent for, and they, thinking it was for their execution, came sadly, hanging down their heads ; the nurse and her daughter were also brought out. With a cry of joy Rosette ran to embrace her brothers. The nurse, her daughter, and the boatman, flung themselves on their knees and prayed for mercy, and the general joy was so great that the king and the brothers forgave them. The good old man was richly rewarded, and lived all the rest of his days in the palace.

The king of the peacocks, in short, made every sort of amends to Rosette's brothers, proving his regret at having ill-treated them. The nurse gave back the rich robes and the bushel of gold crowns, and the wedding feast lasted fifteen days. Everybody was satisfied, down to Fretillon, who from that day never ate anything but the wings of partridges.

---

# The Grasshopper and the Cricket

### by John Keats

THE poetry of earth is never dead :
  When all the birds are faint with the hot sun,
  And hide in cooling trees, a voice will run
From hedge to hedge about the new-mown mead ;
That is the grasshopper's—he takes the lead
  In summer luxury—he has never done
  With his delights ; for when tired out with fun
He rests at ease beneath some pleasant weed.
The poetry of earth is ceasing never :
  On a lone winter evening when the frost
  Has wrought a silence, from the stove there shrills
The cricket's song, in warmth increasing ever,
  And seems to one in drowsiness half lost,
The Grasshopper's among some grassy hills.

# HOW DON QUIXOTE WAS DUBBED A KNIGHT

## by MIGUEL DE CERVANTES

AT a certain village in La Mancha, in Aragon, the name of which I have no wish to recall, there lived not long ago one of those old-fashioned gentlemen, who are never without a lance upon a rack, an old target, a lean horse, and a greyhound. His diet consisted more of beef than mutton; and with minced meat on most nights, lentils on Fridays, eggs and collops on Saturdays, and a pigeon on Sundays, he consumed three-quarters of his revenue; the rest was laid out in a plush coat, velvet breeches, with slippers of the same, for holidays; and a suit of the very best homespun cloth, which he bestowed on himself for working days.

His whole family was a housekeeper something turned of forty, a niece not twenty, and a man that served him either a-field or for marketing, and could saddle a horse, and handle the pruning-hook. The master himself was nigh fifty years of age, of a hale and strong complexion, lean-bodied and thin-faced, an early riser, and a lover of hunting.

You must know then, that when our gentleman had nothing to do (which was almost all the year round), he passed his time in reading books of knight-errantry, which he did with so much delight that at last he wholly left off his country sports, and even the care of his estate. Nay, he grew so strangely besotted with these amusements that he sold many acres of arable land to purchase books of that kind, by which means he collected as many of them as were to be had. But, among them all, none pleased him like the works of the famous Feliciano de Sylva; especially when he came to read the challenges, and the amorous addresses, many of them in this extraordinary style: "The reason of your unreasonable usage of my reason does so enfeeble my reason that I have reason to expostulate with your beauty." And this: "The sublime heavens, which with your divinity divinely fortify you with the stars, and fix you the deserver of the desert that is deserved by your grandeur." These, and such-like expressions, strangely puzzled the poor gentleman's understanding, while he was breaking his brain to unravel their meaning, which Aristotle himself could never have found, though he should have been raised from the dead for that very purpose.

He did not so well like those dreadful wounds which Don Belianis gave and received; for he considered that all the art of surgery could never keep his face and body from being strangely disfigured with scars. However, he highly commended the author for concluding his book with a promise to finish that unfinishable adventure; and many times he had a desire to put pen to paper, and finish it himself.

In short, he gave himself up so wholly to the reading of romances, that at nights he would pore on until it was day, and by day he would read on until it was night. Thus by sleeping little and reading much, the moisture

257

of his brain was so exhausted that at last he lost the use of his reason. A world of disorderly notions, picked out of his books, crowded into his imagination. Now his head was full of nothing but enchantments, quarrels, battles, challenges, wounds, complaints, amours, torments, and abundance of stuff and impossibilities ; while all the fables and fantastic tales which he read seemed to him now as true as the truest histories.

He would say, that the Cid Ruy Diaz was a very brave knight, but not worthy to compare with the Knight of the Burning-sword, who, with a single back-stroke, had cut in sunder two fierce and mighty giants. He liked better Bernardo del Carpio, who, at Roncesvalles, killed the enchanted Orlando, having lifted him from the ground, and choked him in the air, as Hercules did Antæus, the son of the Earth.

As for the giant Morgante, he always spoke very civil things of him ; for though he was one of that monstrous brood, who ever were intolerably proud and brutish, he still behaved himself like a civil and well-bred person.

But of all men in the world he admired Rinaldo of Montalban, and particularly his sallying out of his castle to rob all he met ; and then again when abroad he carried away the idol of Mahomet, which was all massy gold, as the history says. But he so hated that traitor Galalon, that for the pleasure of kicking him handsomely, he would have given up his housekeeper ; nay, and his niece into the bargain.

Having thus lost his understanding, he unluckily stumbled upon the oddest fancy that ever entered into a madman's brain ; for now he thought it convenient and necessary to turn knight-errant, and roam through the whole world, armed cap-a-pie, and mounted on his steed, in quest of adventures. Thus by imitating those knights-errant of whom he had read, and following their course of life, redressing all manner of grievances, and exposing himself to danger on all occasions, he believed that at last, he might purchase everlasting honour and renown. Transported with these agreeable delusions, the poor gentleman prepared with all speed to take the field.

The first thing he did was to scour a suit of armour that had belonged to his great-grandfather, and had lain time out of mind carelessly rusting in a corner. But when he had cleaned and repaired it as well as he could, he perceived there was a material piece wanting ; for, instead of a complete helmet, there was only a single head-piece. However, his industry supplied that defect ; for with some pasteboard he made a kind of half-beaver, or visor, which, being fitted to the head-piece, made it look like an entire helmet.

Then, to know whether it were cutlass-proof, he drew his sword, and tried its edge upon the pasteboard visor ; but with the very first stroke he unluckily undid in a moment what he had been a whole week a-doing. He did not like its being broke with so much ease, and therefore he made it anew, and strengthened it with thin plates of iron, which he fixed on the inside of it so cunningly, that at last he had reason to be satisfied with the solidity of the work. And so, without any further experiment, he resolved it should pass to all intents and purposes for a full and sufficient helmet.

It was time to look to his horse, who was a sorry jade ; however, his master thought that no other horse could be compared with him. He was four days considering what name to give him. He argued with himself there was no reason why a horse bestrid by so famous a knight, and withal so excellent in himself, should not have a particular name. It was but just, since the owner changed his profession, that the horse should also change his title, and be dignified with another; a good big word, such a one as should fill the mouth, and seem to fit the quality and profession of his master.

And thus after many names which he devised, rejected, changed, liked, disliked, and pitched upon again, he concluded to call him Rozinante; a name, in his opinion, lofty, sounding, and significant.

When he had thus given his horse a name so much to his satisfaction, he thought of choosing one for himself; and having seriously pondered on the matter eight whole days more, at last he determined to call himself Don Quixote. And observing that the valiant Amadis, not satisfied with the bare appellation of Amadis, added to it the name of his country, that it might grow more famous by his exploits, and so styled himself Amadis de Gaul; so he, like a true lover of his native soil, resolved to call himself Don Quixote de la Mancha. This addition, to his thinking, denoted very plainly his parentage and country, and consequently would fix a lasting honour on that part of the world.

And now, his armour being scoured, his head-piece improved to a helmet, his horse and himself new named, he perceived he wanted nothing but a lady, on whom he might bestow the empire of his heart; for he was sensible that a knight-errant without a mistress was a tree without either fruit or leaves, and a body without a soul. Should I, said he to himself, by good or ill fortune, chance to encounter some giant, as is common in knight-errantry, and happen to lay him prostrate on the ground, transfixed with my lance, or cleft in two, or, in short, overcome him, and have him at my mercy, would it not be proper to have some lady, to whom I may send him as a trophy of my valour? Then when he comes into her presence, throwing himself at her feet, he may thus make his humble submission: "Lady, I am the giant Caraculiambro, lord of the island of Malindrania, vanquished in single combat by that never-deservedly-enough-extolled knight-errant Don Quixote de la Mancha, who has commanded me to cast myself most humbly at your feet, that it may please your honour to dispose of me according to your will."

Oh! how elevated was the knight with the fancy of this imaginary submission of the giant; especially having withal bethought himself of a person, on whom he might confer the title of his mistress! Near the place where he lived dwelt a good likely country lass, for whom he had formerly had a sort of an inclination, though, it is believed, she never heard of it, nor regarded it in the least. Her name was Aldonza Lorenzo, and this was she whom he thought he might entitle to the sovereignity of his heart. He studied to find her out a new name, that might have some affinity with her old one, and yet at the same time sound somewhat like that of a princess or lady of quality. So at last he resolved to call her Dulcinea, with the addition of del Toboso, from the place where she was born; a name, in his opinion, sweet, harmonious, unusual, and no less meaningful than the others which he devised.

These preparations being made, he found his designs ripe for action, and thought it now a crime to deny himself any longer to the injured world, that wanted such a deliverer ; the more when he considered what grievances he was to redress, what wrongs and injuries to remove, what abuses to correct, and what duties to discharge. So one morning before day, in the greatest heat of July, he planned to set out. He did not acquaint any one with his design. With all the secrecy imaginable he armed himself cap-a-pie, laced on his ill-contrived helmet, braced on his target, grasped his lance, and mounted Rozinante. At the private door of his backyard he sallied out into the fields, wonderfully pleased to see with how much ease he had succeeded in the beginning of his enterprise.

He had not gone far ere a terrible thought alarmed him, a thought that almost made him renounce his great undertaking. It came into his mind that the honour of knighthood had not yet been conferred upon him, and therefore, according to the laws of chivalry, he neither could, nor ought to appear in arms against any professed knight. Nay, he also considered, that though he were already knighted, it would become him to wear white armour, and not to adorn his shield with any device, until he had deserved one by some special proof of his valour.

These thoughts shook his resolve ; but his folly prevailing over his reason, he resolved to be dubbed a knight by the first he should meet, after the example of several others, who, as his distracting romances informed him, had formally done the like. As for the other difficulty, about wearing white armour, he proposed to overcome it by scouring his own at leisure until it should look whiter than ermine. And having thus dismissed his scruples, he very calmly rode on, leaving it to his horse's discretion to go which way he pleased ; firmly believing, that in this consisted the very being of adventures.

He travelled almost all that day without meeting any adventure worth the trouble of relating, which put him into a kind of despair ; for he desired nothing more than to meet at once with some person on whom he might try the vigour of his arm.

Some authors say, that his first adventure was that of the pass called Puerto Lapice ; others, that of the Wind-mills ; but all that I could discover of certainty in this matter, and that I meet with in the annals of La Mancha, is, that he travelled all that day. Toward the evening, he and his horse being heartily tired and almost famished, Don Quixote looked about him, in hopes to discover some castle, or at least some shepherd's cottage, where he might repose and refresh himself. At last near the road which he kept he espied an inn, as welcome a sight to his longing eyes as if he had discovered a star directing him to the gate.

Thereupon hastening towards the inn with all the speed he could, he got thither just at the close of the evening. There stood by chance at the inn-door two young wenches, who were going to Seville, with some carriers that happened to take up their lodging there that very evening. As whatever our knight-errant saw, thought, or imagined, was all of a romantic cast, he no sooner saw the inn, but he fancied it to be a castle fenced with four towers, and lofty pinnacles glittering with silver, with a deep moat and a drawbridge.

Therefore when he came near it, he stopped a while at a distance from the gate, expecting that some dwarf would appear on the battlements, and sound his trumpet to give notice of the arrival of a knight. At that very moment, a swineherd getting together his hogs from the stubble-field, wound his horn. Don Quixote imagined this was the wished-for signal, which some dwarf gave to notify his approach. Therefore with the greatest joy in the world, he rode up to the inn. The wenches, affrighted at the approach of a man cased in iron, and armed with a lance and target, were for running into their lodging; but Don Quixote perceiving their fear by their flight, lifted up the pasteboard beaver of his helmet, and discovering his withered dusty face, with comely grace and grave delivery accosted them in this manner: " I beseech ye, ladies, do not fly, nor fear the least offence; the order of the knighthood, which I profess, does not permit me to countenance or offer injuries to any one in the universe, and, least of all, to virgins of such high rank as your presence denotes." The wenches looked earnestly upon him. They could not forbear laughing outright, which Don Quixote resented as a great affront. " Give me leave to tell ye, ladies," cried he, " that modesty and civility are very becoming in the fair sex; whereas laughter without ground is the highest piece of indiscretion; however," added he, " I do not presume to say this to offend you, or incur your displeasure; no, ladies, I assure you, I have no other design but to do you service."

This uncommon way of expression, joined to the knight's scurvy figure, increased their mirth, which made him very angry. Luckily the innkeeper appeared at that juncture. He was a man whose burden of fat inclined him to peace and quietness, yet when he had observed such a strange disguise of human shape in his old armour and equipage, he could hardly forbear keeping the wenches company in their laughter. But having the fear of such a warlike appearance before his eyes, he accosted him civilly: " Sir Knight," said he, " if your worship be disposed to alight you will fail of nothing here but a bed; as for all else you may be supplied to your mind."

Don Quixote observing the humility of the governor of the castle (for such the innkeeper and the inn seemed to him), " Señor Castellano," said he, " the least thing in the world suffices me: for arms are the only things I value, and combat is my bed of repose."

" At this rate, Sir Knight, your bed might be a pavement, and your rest to be still awake. You may then safely alight, and I dare assure you, you can hardly miss being kept awake all the year long in this house, much less one single night."

With that he went and held Don Quixote's stirrup, who, not having broke fast that day, dismounted with no small trouble or difficulty. He immediately desired the governor (that is, the innkeeper) to have special care of his steed, assuring him that there was not a better in the universe; upon which the innkeeper viewed him narrowly, but could not think him to be half so good as Don Quixote said.

However, having set him up in the stable, he came back to the knight to see what he wanted, and found him pulling off his armour with the help of the good-natured wenches. But though they had eased him of his corslet and back-plate, they could by no means undo his gorget, nor take off his ill-contrived beaver, which he had tied so fast with green ribbons, that it was impossible to get it off without cutting them. Now he would by no means permit that, and so was forced to keep on his helmet all night, which was one of the most pleasant sights in the world. While his armour was being taken off by the two kind lasses, imagining them to be persons of quality, and ladies of that castle, he very gratefully made them the following compliment (an imitation of an old romance),—

> " There never was on earth a knight
>     So waited on by ladies fair,
> As once was he, Don Quixote hight,
>     When first he left his village dear ;
> Damsels to undress him ran with speed,
> And princesses to dress his steed.

O Rozinante ! for that is my horse's name, ladies, and mine Don Quixote de la Mancha. I never thought to have disclosed, until some feats of arms, achieved by me in your service, had made me better known to your ladyships. Necessity has extorted the secret from me before its time ; yet a day will come, when you shall command, and I obey, and then the valour of my arm shall show the reality of my zeal to serve your ladyships."

The two females, who were not used to such high-flown speeches, could make no answer to this ; they only asked him whether he would eat anything ? " That I will with all my heart," cried Don Quixote, " whatever it be, for I am of opinion nothing can come to me more seasonably." Now, as ill-luck would have it, it happened to be Friday, and there was nothing to be had at the inn but some pieces of fish, which was nothing.

Thereupon they laid the cloth at the inn-door, for the benefit of the fresh air, and the landlord brought him a piece of that salt fish, but ill-watered, and as ill-dressed ; and as for the bread, it was as mouldy and brown as the knight's armour. But it would have made one laugh to have seen him eat. For having his helmet on, with his beaver lifted up, it was impossible to feed himself without help. As for drink, he must have gone without it, had not the innkeeper bored a cane, and setting one end of it in his mouth, poured the wine in at the other ; all which the knight suffered patiently because he would not cut the ribbons that fastened his helmet.

While he was at supper, a swine-herd happened to sound his cane-trumpet, or whistle of reeds, four or five times as he came near the inn, which made Don Quixote the more positive of his being in a famous castle, where he was entertained with music at supper. He imagined that the poor jack was young trout, the bread of the finest flour, the wenches great ladies, and the innkeeper the governor of the castle, which made him applaud himself for his resolution, and his setting out on such an account. The only thing that vexed him was, that he was not yet dubbed a knight ; for he fancied he could not lawfully undertake any adventure till he had received the order of knighthood.

Don Quixote's mind being disturbed with that thought, he abridged even this short supper. As soon as he had done, he called his host, then shut him and himself up in the stable, and falling at his feet, " I will never rise from this place," cried he, " most valorous knight, till you have graciously vouchsafed to grant me a boon, which will redound to your honour and the good of mankind." The innkeeper, strangely at a loss to find his guest at his feet, and talking at this rate, endeavoured to make him rise; but all in vain, till he had promised to grant him what he asked. "I expected no less from your great magnificence, noble sir," replied Don Quixote: "and therefore I make bold to tell you that the boon which I beg, and you generously condescend to grant me, is, that to-morrow you will be pleased to bestow the honour of knighthood upon me. This night I will watch my armour in the chapel of your castle, and then in the morning you shall gratify me, as I passionately desire that I may be duly qualified to seek out adventures in every corner of the universe, to relieve the distressed, according to the laws of chivalry, and the inclinations of knights-errant like myself."

*The innkeeper poured the wine, through a cane, into Don Quixote's mouth.*

The innkeeper, who was a sharp fellow, and had already a shrewd suspicion of the disorder in his guest's understanding, was fully convinced of it when he heard him talk after this manner. To make sport that night he resolved to humour him in his desires, telling him he was highly to be commended for his choice of such an employment, which was altogether worthy a knight of the first order, such as his gallant deportment discovered him to be: that he himself had in his youth followed that honourable profession, ranging through many parts of the world in search of adventures, doing wrongs in abundance, and making himself famous in most of the courts of judicature in Spain, till at length he retired to this castle, where he lived on his own estate and those of others, entertaining all knights-errant of what quality or condition soever, purely for the great affection he bore them, and to partake of what they had in recompense of his good-will.

He added, that his castle at present had no chapel where the knight might keep the vigil of his arms, it being pulled down in order to be new built;

but that he knew they might lawfully be watched in any other place in a
case of necessity, and therefore he might do it that night in the courtyard
of the castle. In the morning (God willing) all the necessary ceremonies
should be performed so that he might assure himself he should be dubbed a
knight, nay, as much a knight as any one in the world could be.

He then asked Don Quixote whether he had any money. " Not a cross,"
replied the knight, " for I never read in any history of chivalry that any
knight-errant ever carried money about him."—" You are mistaken," cried
the innkeeper; " for admit that histories are silent in this matter, the
authors thinking it needless to mention things so evidently necessary as
money and clean shirts, yet there is no reason to believe the knights went
without either; and you may rest assured, that all the knights-errant, of
whom so many histories are full, had their purses well lined to supply themselves with necessaries, and carried also with them some shirts, and a small
box of salves to heal their wounds; I must therefore advise you," continued
he, " nay, I might even charge and command you, as you are shortly to be
my son in chivalry, never from this time forwards to ride without money, nor
without the other necessaries of which I spoke to you, which you will find
very beneficial when you least expect it."

Don Quixote promised to perform very punctually all his injunctions;
and so they disposed everything in order to his watching his arms in a great
yard that adjoined to the inn. To which purpose the knight, having got
them all together, laid them in a horse-trough close by a well in that yard.
Then bracing his target, and grasping his lance, just as it grew dark, he
began to walk about by the horse-trough with a graceful deportment. In
the meanwhile the innkeeper acquainted all those that were in the house
with the oddities of his guest, his watching his arms, and his hopes of being
made a knight. They all marvelled very much at so strange a kind of folly,
and went on to observe him at a distance; where they saw him sometimes
walk about with a great deal of gravity, and sometimes lean on his lance,
with his eyes all the while fixed upon his arms. It was now undoubted
night, but yet did the moon shine so that the knight was wholly exposed to
the spectators' view.

While he was thus employed, one of the carriers who lodged in the inn
came out to water his mules, which he could not do without removing the
arms out of the trough. With that, Don Quixote, who saw him make towards
him cried out to him aloud, " O thou, whoever thou art, rash knight that
prepared to lay thy hands on the arms of the most valorous knight-errant
that ever wore a sword, take heed. Do not attempt to profane them with
a touch lest instant death be the reward of thy temerity."

But the carrier never regarded these dreadful threats. Laying hold on
the armour by the straps, without more ado he threw it a good way from
him. Don Quixote no sooner saw this than he lifted up his eyes to heaven,
and addressed his thoughts, as it seemed, to his lady Dulcinea; " Assist
me, lady," cried he, " in the first opportunity that offers itself to your faithful
slave; nor let your favour and protection be denied me in this first trial
of my valour!"

With this he let slip his target, and lifting up his lance with both his
hands, he gave the carrier such a terrible knock on his inconsiderate head

with his lance, that he laid him at his feet in a woeful condition. This done, Don Quixote took up his armour, laid it again in the horse-trough, and then walked on backwards and forwards with as great unconcern as he did at first.

Soon after another carrier, not knowing what had happened, came also to water his mules, while the first yet lay on the ground in a trance; but as he offered to clear the trough of the armour, Don Quixote, without speaking a word, lifted up his lance, and then let it fall so heavily on the fellow's pate, that he broke the carrier's head in three or four places. His outcry soon alarmed and brought thither all the people in the inn, and the landlord among the rest. Don Quixote called upon his Dulcinea, " Thou Queen of Beauty," cried he, bracing on his shield, and drawing his sword, " thou courage and vigour of my weakened heart, now is the time when thou must enliven thy adventurous slave with the beams of thy greatness, while this moment he is engaging in so terrible an adventure!" With this, in his opinion, he found himself supplied with such an additional courage, that had all the carriers in the world at once attacked him, he would undoubtedly have faced them all.

On the other side, the carriers, enraged to see their comrades thus used, gave the knight such a volley of stones, that he was forced to shelter under the cover of his target, without daring to go far from the horse-trough, lest he should seem to abandon his arms.

The innkeeper called to the carriers as loud as he could to let him alone; that he had told them already he was mad, and consequently the law would acquit him, though he should kill them. Don Quixote also made yet more noise, calling them false and treacherous villains and the lord of the castle base and unhospitable, and a discourteous knight, for suffering a knight-errant to be so abused. " I would make thee know," cried he, " what a perfidious wretch thou art, had I but received the order of knighthood; but for you, base rabble! fling on, do your worst; and receive the reward of your insolence."

This he spoke with so much spirit that he struck terror into all his assailants. Partly through fear, and partly through the innkeeper's persuasions, they gave over flinging stones at him; and he, on his side, permitted the enemy to carry off their wounded, and then returned to the guard of his arms as calm and composed as before.

The innkeeper, who began somewhat to disrelish these mad tricks of his guest, resolved to despatch him forthwith, and bestow on him that unlucky knighthood, to prevent further mischief. So coming to him, he excused himself for the insolence of those base scoundrels, as being done without his knowledge or consent; but their boldness, he said, was sufficiently punished. . . . He added, that he had already told him there was no chapel in his castle; and that indeed there was no need of one to finish the rest of the ceremony of knighthood, which consisted only in the application of the sword to the neck and shoulders. This might be performed as well in a field as anywhere else. Also, he had already fulfilled the obligation of watching his arms, which required no more than two hours' watch, whereas he had been four hours upon the guard.

Don Quixote, who easily believed him, desired him to make an end of the business as soon as possible, for if he were but knighted, and should see himself once attacked, he believed he should not leave a man alive in the castle, except those whom he should desire him to spare for his sake.

Upon this the innkeeper, lest the knight should proceed to such lengths, fetched the book in which he used to set down the carriers' accounts for straw and barley, and having brought with him the two wenches and a boy that held a piece of lighted candle in his hand, he ordered Don Quixote to kneel. Then reading in his manual, as if he had been repeating some pious oration, in the midst of his devotion he lifted up his hand and gave him a good blow on the neck, and then a gentle slap on the back with the flat of his sword, still mumbling some words between his teeth in the tone of a prayer.

After this he ordered one of the wenches to gird the sword about the knight's waist; which she did with much solemnity, and I may add, discretion, considering how hard a thing it was to forbear laughing at every circumstance of the ceremony: it is true, the thoughts of the knight's late prowess did not a little contribute to the suppression of her mirth. Don Quixote desired to know her name, that he might understand to whom he was indebted for the favour she had bestowed upon him, and also make her partaker of the honour he was to acquire by the strength of his arm. The lady answered with all humility, that her name was Tolosa, a cobbler's daughter.

Don Quixote begged of her to do him the favour to add hereafter the title of lady to her name, and for his sake to be called from that time Donna Tolosa; which she promised to do. Her companion having buckled on his spurs, occasioned a like conference between them; and when he had asked her name, she told him she went by the name of Molinera, being the daughter of an honest miller of Antequera. Our new knight entreated her also to style herself the Donna Molinera, making her new offers of service.

These extraordinary ceremonies (the like never seen before) being thus hurried over in a kind of post-haste, Don Quixote could not rest till he had taken the field in quest of adventures. Therefore having immediately saddled his Rozinante, and being mounted, he embraced the innkeeper, and returned him so many thanks for the obligation he had laid upon him in dubbing him a knight, that it is impossible to give a true relation of them all: to which the innkeeper, in haste to get rid of him, answered him shortly but in the same stream; and without stopping his horse for the reckoning, was glad with all his heart to see him go.

# NONSENSE RHYMES

*by* EDWARD LEAR

There was an Old Man with a beard,
Who said, " It is just as I feared !—
  Two Owls and a Hen,
  Four Larks and a Wren,
Have all built their nests in my beard ! "

There was an Old Man with a nose,
Who said, " If you choose to suppose,
  That my nose is too long,
  You are certainly wrong ! "
That remarkable Man with a nose.

There was a Young Lady whose bonnet
Came untied when the birds sat
      upon it;
  But she said, " I don't care !
  All the birds in the air
Are welcome to sit on my
          bonnet ! "

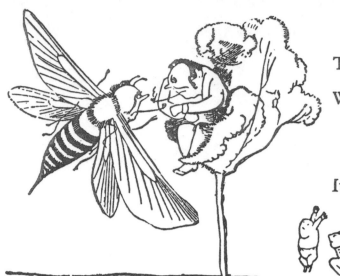

There was an Old Man in a
    tree,
Who was horribly bored by a
    Bee;
    When they said, "Does it
      buzz?"
    He replied, "Yes, it does!
It's a regular brute of a Bee!"

There was an Old Man in a boat,
Who said, "I'm afloat! I'm afloat!"
    When they said, "No! you ain't!"
    He was ready to faint,
That unhappy Old Man in a boat.

There was a Young Lady
    whose chin
Resembled the point of a pin:
So she had it made sharp,
And purchased a harp,
And played several tunes with her
    chin.

There was an Old Man who supposed,
That the street door was partially closed;
   But some very large rats
   Ate his coats and his hats,
While that futile old gentleman dozed.

There was an Old Person whose habits
Induced him to feed upon Rabbits;
   When he'd eaten eighteen,
   He turned perfectly green,
Upon which he relinquished those habits.

There was a Young Lady whose nose
Was so long that it reached to her toes:
   So she hired an Old Lady,
   Whose conduct was steady,
To carry that wonderful nose.

There was an Old Man of Apulia,
Whose conduct was very peculiar;
   He fed twenty sons
   Upon nothing but buns,
That whimsical Man of Apulia.

There was an Old Man with a poker,
Who painted his face with red oker;
   When they said, " You're a Guy ! "
   He made no reply,
But knocked them all down with his poker.

There was an Old Man of the
    Nile,
Who sharpened his nails with
   a file;
   Till he cut off his thumbs,
   And said calmly, " This
    comes—
Of sharpening one's nails
   with a file ! "

There was an Old Man
    of Dundee,
Who frequented the top
    of a tree;
    When disturbed by the crows,
    He abruptly arose,
And exclaimed, " I'll return to Dundee."

There was an Old Man of Coblenz,
The length of whose legs was immense;
He went with one prance
    From Turkey to France,
    That surprising Old Man of
        Coblenz.

There was an Old Person of
    Dutton
Whose head was as small as a
    button;
    So to make it look big,
    He purchased a wig,
And rapidly rushed about
    Dutton.

There was an Old Man who said, " Hush !
I perceive a young bird in this bush ! "
    When they said, " Is it small ? "
    He replied, " Not at all !
It is four times as big as the bush ! "

There was an Old Person of Anerley,
Whose conduct was strange and unmannerly :
    He rushed down the Strand,
    With a Pig in each hand,
But returned in the evening to Anerley.

There was a Young Lady of Troy,
Whom several large flies did annoy ;
    Some she killed with a thump,
    Some she drowned at the pump,
And some she took with her to Troy.

There was an Old Person of Cheadle,
Was put in the stocks by the beadle
   For stealing some pigs,
    Some coats, and some wigs,
That horrible Person of Cheadle.

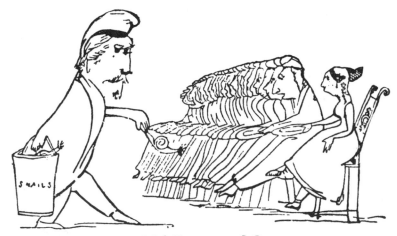

There was an Old Person of Sparta,
Who had twenty-five sons and one daughter;
   He fed them on snails,
    And weighed them in scales,
That wonderful Person of Sparta.

There was a Young Lady of Clare,
Who was sadly pursued by a bear;
   When she found she was tired,
    She abruptly expired,
That unfortunate Lady of Clare.

# THE SNORING GHOST

*from " Mrs. Overtheway's Remembrances "*

## *by* JULIANA H. EWING

"I REMEMBER," began Mrs. Overtheway, "I remember my first visit. That is, I remember the occasion on which I and my sister Fatima did, for the first time in our lives, go out visiting without our mother, or any grown-up person to take care of us.

"The invitation came on my thirteenth birthday.

"'In four more years,' I said to Fatima, as we sat on the eve of my birthday, discussing its many advantages, 'in four more years, I shall be grown-up.'

"'Do people always grow much on their birthdays?' asked one of the little ones. I had boasted in the nursery that, when I was thirteen, I should be 'nearly grown up,' and I myself had hardly outlived the idea that on one's birthday one was a year older than on the previous day, and might naturally expect to have made a year's growth during the night.

"This birthday, however, produced no such striking change. As usual, the presents were charming; the wreath as lovely as Fatima's deft fingers could make it, the general holiday and pleasure-making almost too much of a good thing. Otherwise there was little to mark it from other days in the year.

"Towards evening we were all sitting on the grass, and there had been an outcry for a story to which no one had responded. We had remained some time without speaking, and the idea was becoming general that the boys were napping, when the summer silence was broken by the distant footfalls of a horse upon the high road.

"'Trotting,' observed one of the supposed sleepers. We were not, as a family, given to explanations, and we drew a few more breaths of the evening air in silence.

"Then some one said, 'We might make a story out of *that*, and fancy

274

all sorts of things. Who is it? Where does he come from? and where is he going?'

"'It is a messenger from the seat of war,' drawled one boy, without moving, 'To horse, gentlemen, to horse! The enemy will be at Barter's Mill by midnight.'

"There was a pause; the solitary footfalls came nearer through the evening mists, and a small brother, of a quaint turn of mind, sat up and said slowly, 'It is one of Job's messengers. The Chaldeans made out three bands, and fell upon the camels, and have carried them away. Yea, and slain the servants with the edge of the sword; and I only am escaped alive to tell thee.'

"The other boys laughed, but he lay down again, as solemnly as he had risen.

"'That was a foot messenger,' said one.

"'It doesn't say so,' retorted the small brother.

"'Well, anyway, the camels had been carried off—so what did he ride upon?'

"'Listen,' I said; 'it's the post. The mail from the north was stopped on the highway, but he has saved the bags and is riding hard for London.'

"But the new suggestion was drowned in a general shout of, 'It's coming up the lane.'

"The footfalls had diverged from the main road, and were coming up the sandy lane that skirted our wall. The boys lifted their heads, and we sat expectant. There was a pause, and a familiar gate click, and then the footfalls broke upon the carriage-road, close by us. A man in livery upon a well-groomed horse—nothing more, but rather an uncommon sight with us. Moreover, the man and his livery looked strange, and the horse looked tired.

"This event broke up the sitting, and we were strolling up to the house, when a maid met us, saying that my mother wished to see me and Fatima.

"We found my mother sewing, with an open letter beside her. It was written on one of the large sheets then in use, and it was covered and crossed at every corner in a vague, scratchy hand.

"'I have heard from an old friend of mine, Mary,' said my mother. 'She has come to live about twelve miles from here. There is something in the letter about you and Fatima, and you may read that part aloud if you can. The top of the last page.'

"I found the place with some difficulty and began. 'The dear Major was——'

"'No, no,' said my mother, 'the next sentence.'

"'Dear Cecilia was all sweetness. The dress was——'

"My mother took the letter and found the right place herself, and then I read: 'If you cannot come yourself, at least let us renew acquaintance in our children. I think you have two girls about thirteen. My Lucy, a dear child just fifteen, feels keenly the loss of her only sister, and some young companions would be a boon, as all our company will be elders. Pray send them. They can come by the coach, and shall be met at Durnfurd, at the Elephant and Castle.'

"'Is the other sister dead?' asked Fatima, pityingly.

" ' Oh, no, only married,' said my mother.

" It was decided that we should go.  This decision was not arrived at at once, or without some ups and downs.  My mother could not go herself, and had some doubts as to our being old enough, as yet, to go out visiting alone.  It may be believed that I made much of being able to say, ' But, you know, I am thirteen, now.'

" Next day, in the evening, my father was busy in his study, and my mother sat at the open window, with Fatima and me at her feet.  The letter of acceptance had been duly sent by the messenger, but she had yet a good deal of advice to give, and some doubts to express.

" ' We can't take all our good habits with us if you don't come,' I said, ' what is to become of the Sunday readings ? '

" My mother used to read to us every Sunday evening, and we were just in the middle of that wonderful book—*The Pilgrim's Progress*.

" ' If it were not for the others, and if you would trust us with it,' said Fatima thoughtfully, ' we might take the book with us, and Mary might read to me if she would—I like her reading.'

" My mother consented.  There was another copy in the house, and though this volume was a favourite, she said it was time we learned to take care of valuable books.  We talked no more that evening ; and the clouds drifted out of sight.

" ' They have gone to bed in a big dark cloud on the other side,' said Fatima, yawning ; and we went to bed also.

" I will not describe the big box which my father lent us, nor the joys of packing.  How Fatima's work-box dovetailed with my desk.  How the books did not make comfortable paving for the bottom of the trunk ; whilst folded stockings may be called the packer's delight, from their usefulness to fill up corners.  How, having packed the whole week long, we were barely ready, and a good deal flurried at the last moment ; and how we took all our pro-perty with us, and left the key of the trunk behind.

" Fancy for yourself how the green coach picked us up at the toll bar, and how, as it jingled on, we felt the first qualm of home sickness, and, stretching our heads and hands out of the window, waved good-bye and kisses to home, regardless of our fellow-traveller in the corner, an old gentle-man, with a yellow silk handkerchief on his head, who proved in the end a very pleasant companion.

" I remember that we told him all our family history, and that he gave us the most clear, the most sweet, the most amber-coloured sticks of barley-sugar I have ever had the good fortune to meet with.

" Shall I tell you how we were met at the Elephant and Castle, by a footman of most gentlemanly appearance (his livery excepted), who, with a wisdom which somewhat startled us, discovered that we were ' the young ladies that were expected,' and led us to the carriage, firmly opposing my efforts to fulfil the last home orders I had received, to ' look after the box ! '

" In the carriage we found a lady dressed in handsome black, who came out to meet us, and seemed so anxious for our comfort, and so much inter-ested in our arrival that we naturally supposed her to be the lady who had invited us, till we discovered that she was the lady's maid.  On arriving we found our hostess quite another sort of person, with no appearance at all of being interested in our arrival.

" It was a large house, reminding me of the Manor, within, but prettier outside ; old and irregular, built with odd wings and corners. A glowing well-kept garden contrasted prettily with the gray stones, and the grounds seemed magnificent in our eyes.

" We were shown into the drawing-room, where the real lady of the house sat at a dainty writing-table, scratching away at a letter that was no doubt as affectionate as the one which my mother had received. She was short-sighted, which seemed to be the case also with most of the other ladies in the room. This perhaps was why they stared so hard at us, and then went on with the pieces of needlework on which all of them were engaged.

" It seemed to take our hostess a second or two to see us, and another second or two to recall who we were. Then she came forward very kindly, showed us where to sit, and asked after my mother. Whilst I was replying, she crossed to the fireplace and rang the bell ; and I felt slightly surprised by her seeming wish for no further news of her old friend.

" She asked if we had had a pleasant journey, and Fatima had hardly pronounced a modest ' Yes,' before she begged we would allow her to finish her letter, and went back to the spindle-legged table. Whilst she scratched, we looked around us. Three or four ladies were in the room, more or less young, more or less pretty, more or less nicely dressed, and all with pieces of needlework.

" There was one gentleman, young and dark, with large brown eyes, who seemed to be employed in making paper pellets of an old letter, chatting the while in a low voice to a young lady with a good deal of red hair. We afterwards found out that he was an Irishman, familiarly called ' Pat ' by some of the young ladies, who seemed to be related to him. We had seen all this when the manservant appeared at the door.

" ' Where is Miss Lucy, Thompson ? ' our hostess asked sharply.

" ' I will inquire, ma'am,' Thompson replied with the utmost softness, and vanished.

" The scratching began again, the Irishman went on gently chatting, and it all felt very like a horrid dream. Then Thompson reappeared.

" ' Miss Lucy is out, ma'am.'

" ' Did she know what time these young ladies were to arrive ? '

" ' Miss Lucy knew that the carriage had gone to meet them, ma'am.'

" ' Very thoughtless ! Very thoughtless, indeed ! ' said the lady. Thompson paused respectfully, as if to receive the full weight of the remark, and then vanished noiselessly as before.

" There was an awkward pause. Our hostess left off scratching and looked very cross ; the Irishman fired one of his pellets across the room and left off chatting ; the red-haired young lady got up and rustled across to us. I remember her so well, Ida, for we fell deeply in love with her and her kindness. I remember her green and white dress. She had a fair, round face, more pleasant than really pretty, a white star-like forehead, almost too firm a mouth, but a very gentle voice, at least so we thought when she said, ' As Lucy is out, may I take these young ladies to their room ? '

" Our hostess hesitated, and murmured something about Bedford, who

was the lady's maid.  The red-haired young lady said rather strongly:
'As Lucy is not in to receive her friends, I thought, perhaps, I might supply
her place.'

"'Well, my dear, if you will be so kind,' said our hostess, 'I must
finish these letters.'

"'The yellow room?' said the young lady, and swept us off without
further parley.  The Irish gentleman opened the door for us, staring with a
half-puzzled, half-amused look at the lofty air with which the young lady
passed out.  He followed us into the hall, where we left him discharging
his remaining pellets at the furniture, and whistling, "Kathleen Mavourneen," as clearly as a bird.

*" It's years and years ago," Lucy began.*

"The yellow room was a large, airy one, with white-painted wainscoting,
a huge four-post bed with yellow curtains, and a pretty view from the
windows.  In the middle of the floor we saw our box standing in all its
dignity, uncorded and ready.  Then it was that the terrible fact broke
upon our minds, that the key was left behind.  My sufferings during the few
seconds before I found courage to confide this misfortune to our new friend
were considerable.  When I did tell her, the calmness and good nature
with which she received the confession were both surprising and delightful.

"'The lock doesn't look a very uncommon one,' she said, as she opened
the door, 'I dare say I may find a key to fit it.'

"'What's the matter?' said a voice outside.  It was the Irish gentleman.
She explained.

"'Keys?' said the Irish gentleman; 'got lots in my pocket, besides
their not being wanted, as I'm a capital hand at lockpicking.  Let me see.'

" With which he slipped in, seeming quite as much at his ease as in the drawing-room, and in another second had squatted upon the floor before our box, where he seemed to be quite as comfortable as in the arm-chair he had left. Here he poked, and fitted, and whistled, and chatted without a pause.

" ' I've locks and keys to everything I possess,' he cheerfully remarked, ' and as I never lock up anything, there's no damage done if the keys are left behind, which is a good thing, you see, as I always leave everything everywhere.'

" He had opened the box, and was leaning against the bedpost with a twinkle in his brown eyes, which faded, however, under the silent severity of the red-haired young lady, and gave place to a look of melancholy that might have melted granite.

" ' I'm all alone, you see,' he added, ' that's what does it. I believe I'm the neatest creature breathing, if I'd only somebody to keep me up to it.'

" Neither his untidiness nor his lonely lot, however, seemed to weigh heavily on his mind ; for he withdrew whistling, and his notes were heard about the passages for some little time. When they had died away in a distant part of the house, the red-haired young lady left us also.

" Bedford came in while we were in the midst of our unpacking, and warmly begged us to leave everything to her, as she would put our things away for us. The red-haired young lady had sent her, and she became a great comfort to us during our visit. From her we got odd meals when we were hungry, spirits of wine when Fatima's tooth ached, warnings when we were near to being late for breakfast, and stories of this household and others in which she had lived. I remember her with gratitude.

" Miss Lucy came home before our putting away was finished, and we had tea with her in the schoolroom. She was a slight, sharp, lively young lady, looking older than fifteen to us, rather pretty, and very self-possessed. She scanned us from head to foot when we first met, and I felt as if her eyes had found many defects, which seemed the less likely, as she was short-sighted also.

" As her governess was away visiting a sick relative, Miss Lucy did the honours of the schoolroom. She was cold at first, but ended by being gracious. In her gracious mood she was even affectionate. She called us, ' my dear girls,' put her arms round us as we sat in the dark, and chatted without a pause about herself, her governess, her sister, and her sister's husband.

" ' A wedding in the house is very good fun,' she observed, ' particularly if you take a principal part in it. I was chief bridesmaid, you know, my dear girls. But I'll tell you the whole affair from the first. I had never been bridesmaid before, and I couldn't make up my mind how I should like the dresses.' And we had got no further in the story than Miss Lucy's own costume, when we were called to dress and go downstairs.

" ' What are you going to put on ? ' she asked, balancing herself at our door and peering in.

" ' White muslin ! ' we said with some pride, for they were new frocks and splendid in our eyes.

" ' I have had so many muslins I am tired of them,' she said ; ' I shall wear a pink silk to-night. The trimming came from London. Perhaps I may wear a muslin to-morrow ; I have an Indian one. But you shall see my dresses to-morrow, my dear girls.'

" With which she left us, and we put on our new frocks (which were to be *the* evening dresses of our visit), in depressed spirits.

" Affectionate as Miss Lucy had been when we were alone together, she was no sooner among the grown-ups downstairs, than she kept with them as much as she was permitted, and seemed to forget us altogether. The red-haired young lady had made her fetch us a large scrap-book, and we sat with this before our eyes, and the soft chit-chat of our hostess in our ears, as she talked and worked with some elder ladies on the sofa.

" The next day's post brought news from Bath of more general interest to the household. Cecilia and the Major were coming to her mother's on the following Monday.

" ' My dear girls, I *am* glad,' said Miss Lucy ; ' you'll see them. But you will have to be moved out of your room, I'm sorry to say.'

" Sunday was a day of mixed experiences to us ; some pleasant and some the reverse. After breakfast we dawdled about till it was time to dress for church, and, as most of the ladies took five minutes more than they had allowed for, it seemed likely that we should be late. At the last moment Miss Lucy lost her prayer-book, and it was not until another five minutes had gone in the search that she remembered having left it in the church the Sunday before.

" This being settled, we all stowed away in the carriage and drove off. It was only a short drive ; but when we came in sight of the quaint church there was no sound of bells, and it became evident that we were late. In the porch we shook out our dresses, the Irishman divided the prayer-books he had been gallantly bearing, and we swept up the church into a huge square pew.

" We returned as we came.

" The evening slipped by, and our Sunday reading had not been accomplished. We had found good habits less easy to maintain in a strange household than we had thought, and this one seemed likely to follow some others that had been allowed to slip.

" The red-haired young lady had been absent for about half an hour, and the Irishman had been prowling restlessly round the room, when she returned with a book in her hand, which she settled herself resolutely to read. The Irishman gave a comical glance at the volume, and then, seating himself on a chair just behind her, found apparent peace in the effort to sharpen a flat ruler on his knee.

" I began to feel uncomfortable. Fatima was crouched down near Lucy. listening to the history of a piece of lace. I waited some time to catch her eye, and then beckoned her to me.

" ' We haven't read,' I whispered.

" ' Dare you go ? ' asked Fatima.

" ' We ought,' I said.

" It required more daring than may appear. To such little people as ourselves it was rather an undertaking to cross the drawing-room, stealing over the soft carpet ; to attack the large smooth handle, open the heavy door, and leave the room in the face of the company.

" We did it, however, our confusion being much increased by the Irish gentleman, who jumped up to open the door for us. We were utterly unable to thank him, and, stumbling over each other in the passage, flew up to our own room like caged birds set free.

" Fatima drew out the pillows, and made herself easy on the floor. I found the book and climbed into the window-seat.

" I lifted up my voice and read till I could see no longer ; then we went downstairs slowly, hand in hand.

" ' I wonder what mother is doing,' said Fatima.

" The next day, Lucy very good-naturedly helped us to move our belongings into the smaller room we were now to occupy. It was in another part of the house, and we rather enjoyed the running to and fro.

" ' This is the oldest part of the house,' Lucy said, as we sat on the bed resting from our labours, for the day was sultry, 'and it breaks off here in an odd way. There are no rooms beyond this. There were some that matched the other side of the house, but they were pulled down.'

" ' Why ? ' we asked.

" ' Well, there's a story about it in the family,' she said. ' But it's a ghost story. I'll tell you, if you like. Some people are afraid of ghost stories. I'm not, but if you are, I won't tell it.'

" Of course, we declared we were not afraid. Sitting down together, on a sunny summer's afternoon, perhaps we were not.

" ' It's years and years ago,' Lucy began ; ' you know the place has been in our family for generations. At last it came down to an old Mr. Bartlett, who had one daughter, who, of course, was to be the heiress. But she fell in love with a man whose name I forget, but her father would not hear of it, and declared that if she married him he would disinherit her. She would have married the man in spite of this, but what he wanted was her money ; so, when he found that the old man was quite resolute, and that there was little chance of his dying soon, he murdered him.'

" We both cried out, for this fairly took our breath away. Lucy's nerves were stronger, however, and she rattled on.

" ' He smothered him in bed, and, as he was a very old man, and might have died in the night some other way, and as nothing could be proved, the man got off. Well, he married the daughter and got the property, but the very first evening as he was passing the old man's room, he heard some one breathing heavily inside, and, when he looked in, there was the old father asleep in his bed.'

" ' Not really ? ' we cried.

" ' Of course not really, but so it was said. That's the ghost part of it. Do what he would, he never could get rid of the old man, who was always there asleep, so he pulled the rooms down. At last he went abroad, and there both he and his wife died, and the property went to a cousin, who took the name of Bartlett.'

" ' How awful ! ' we murmured ; but Lucy laughed and told us other family anecdotes. The ghost story somewhat passed from our minds, especially as a little later we heard wheels, and, peeping down from the landing-windows, beheld a post-chaise drive up.

"'It's Cecilia!' screamed Lucy, and left us at once.

" I may as well say here, my dear Ida, that Cecilia and her husband proved altogether different from our expectations. Cecilia was really pretty, soft, and gentle, while the Major was kind and sensible. They seemed a happy couple, more like the rest of the world than we had been led to suppose.

" The newcomers took up most of our attention during the evening, and it was not until we were fairly entering the older part of the house on our way to bed, that the story of the old man's ghost came back to my mind. It was a relief to meet Bedford at this point, to hear her cheerful good-night, and to see her turn into a room only two doors from us.

" Once, while we were undressing, I said, 'What a horrid story that was Lucy told us.'

" To which sensible Fatima made answer, 'Don't talk about it.'

" We dismissed the subject by consent, got into bed, and I fell asleep. I do not quite know how far on it was into the night, when I was roused by Fatima's voice repeating my name over and over again in tones of subdued terror. I know nothing more alarming, when one is young and nervous, than to be roused thus, by a voice in which the terror is evident and the cause unknown.

" 'What is the matter?' I asked.

" 'Don't you hear?' gasped Fatima in a whisper. If she had said at once there was a robber under the bed, a burglar at the window, or a ghost in the wardrobe, I should have been prepared for the worst, and it would have been less alarming than this unknown evil.

" 'I hear nothing,' I said crossly. 'I wish you'd go to sleep, Fatima.'

" 'There! Now!' said Fatima.

" I held my breath, and in the silence heard distinctly the sound of some one snoring in another room.

" 'It's only some one snoring,' I said.

" 'Where?' asked Fatima, with all the terror still in her voice.

" 'In the room behind us, of course,' I replied impatiently. 'Can't you hear?'

" Fatima's voice might have been the voice of a shadow as she answered, 'There is no room there!'

" A cold chill crept over me, for I remembered that the wall from beyond which the snoring proceeded was an outer wall. There had been the room of old Mr. Bartlett which his son-in-law and murderer had pulled down. There he had been heard 'breathing heavily' and had been seen asleep upon his bed, long after he was smothered with his own pillows, and his body shut up in the family vault.

" At least so it was said, and at that particular moment we felt no comfort from the fact that Lucy had said that 'of course it wasn't true.' I said something, to which Fatima made no reply, and I could feel her trembling, and hear a half-choked sob. Fear for her overpowered my other alarm, and gave me a sort of strength.

" 'Don't dear,' I begged. 'Let's be brave. It must be something else.

And there's nothing in the room.  Let's go to Bedford.  She's next door
but one.'

"Fatima could speak no more.  By the moonlight through the blind I
jumped up, and half dragged, half helped her out of bed across the room.
Opening the door was the worst.  To touch anything at such a moment is
a trial.  We groped down the passage, I felt the handle of the first door, and
turned that of the second, and in we went.  The window-blind of this room
was drawn up, and the moonlight streamed over everything.

"A nest of white drapery covered one chair, a muslin dress lay like a
sick ghost over a second, black satin shoes and weblike stockings were on
the floor, a gold watch and one or two feminine ornaments lay on the table ;
and in the bed reposed—not Bedford, but our friend Kate, fast asleep, with
one arm over the bed clothes, and her long red hair in a pigtail streaming
over the pillow.

"I climbed up and treated her as Fatima had treated me, calling her in
low, frightened tones, over and over again.  She woke at last and sat up.

"'You sprites !  What *is* the matter ? ' she exclaimed.

"I stumbled through an account of our misfortunes, in the middle of
which the young lady lay down, and before it was ended I believe she was
asleep again.  Poor Fatima, who saw nothing before us but to return to our
room with all its terrors, here began to sob violently, which roused our
friend once more, and she became full of pity.

"'You poor children,' she said, ' I am so sleepy.  I cannot get up and
go after the ghost now ;  besides, one might meet somebody.  But you may
get into bed if you like ; there's plenty of room and nothing to frighten
you.'

"In we both crept, most willingly.  She gave us the long tail of her
hair and said, ' If you want me, pull.  But go to sleep if you can '—and,
before she had well finished the sentence, her eyes closed once more.  In
such good company, a snoring ghost seemed hardly possible.  We held the
long plait between us, and, clinging to it as drowning men do to a rope,
we soon slept also.

"When we returned to our room next day, there was no snoring to be
heard, and in the full sunshine of a summer morning our fright seemed to
be completely a thing of the past.  I persuaded myself that it might have
been fancy, but Fatima said, ' What's the use of trying to believe what's
not true ?  I heard it, and shall know that I heard it, if I live to a hundred.'

"In all proper ghost stories, when the hero comes down in the morning,
valiant, but exhausted from the terrors of the night, to breakfast, his host
always asks him how he slept.  When we came down, we found Kate and the
Irishman alone together in the breakfast-room.

"Now, it certainly was in keeping with our adventure when he stepped
forward, and bowing, asked how we had passed the night.  Still, in spite of
his grave face, there was a twinkle in the big brown eyes that showed we
were being made fun of, and I felt slightly angry with our friend, who had
faithfully promised not to betray us to Lucy, and might, I thought, have
saved us from the Irishman's jokes.

"The rest of the company, however, began to assemble, and to our relief
the subject was dropped.  But, though he kept our secret, we had every

reason to suspect that he did not forget it ; he looked terribly roguish through breakfast, and was kept in order only by Kate's severe glances.

" ' Always breathe through the nose,' he suddenly began, ' it prevents snoring.'

" ' Very true,' said the Major.

" ' It may be laid down,' continued the Irishman gravely, ' that the man who snores is sure to disturb somebody ; and also that the man who doesn't snore till he dies is not likely to live to be a snoring ghost when he is dead.'

" Kate looked daggers. The Major laughed, and said, ' Let me give you some beef.' When he didn't understand a remark he always laughed and generally turned the conversation to eatables.

" A little later the Irishman asked, ' What's the origin of the saying, " to stir up with a long pole ? " ' which turned the conversation to wild beasts.

" Presently he inquired, ' What's the meaning of putting a thing up the spout ? '

" ' Pawning it,' replied the Major quickly.

" ' People pawn their family jewels sometimes,' said Pat. ' Did you ever hear of anybody pawning the family ghosts ? ' he asked suddenly, turning to me.

" I gave a distressed ' No,' and he continued in a whisper, ' You never saw a ghost up the spout ? '

" Before I could answer he caught Kate's eye, and making a penitent face became silent.

" We were in the drawing-room after breakfast, when the Irishman passed the window outside, whistling ' Kathleen Mavourneen.' We were sitting at Kate's feet, and she got up, and whispering, ' He's got something to show you, but he wouldn't let me tell,' went out into the garden, we following her.

" There we found the Irishman with a long pole, which he was waving in the air. He bowed as we approached.

" ' This, young ladies,' he said, ' is the original long pole spoken of at the breakfast-table. With this I am about to stir up and bring forth for your inspection the living ghost whose snoring disturbed your repose last night.'

" The little Irishman's jokes reassured me. I guessed that he had found some clue to our mysterious noise ; but with Fatima it was different. She had been too deeply frightened to recover easily. She clung trembling to me, as I was following him, and whispered, ' I'd rather not.'

" On her behalf I summoned courage to say, ' If you please, sir, Fatima would rather not ; and, if you please, don't tease us any more.'

" The young lady added her entreaties, but they were not needed. The good-natured gentleman no sooner saw Fatima's real distress than he lowered his pole, and sank upon his knees on the grass, looking really penitent.

" ' I *am* so sorry I have been tormenting you so,' he exclaimed. ' I forgot you were really frightened, and, you see, I knew it wasn't a ghost.'

" ' I heard it,' murmured Fatima resolutely, with her eyes half shut.

" ' So did I,' said the Irishman gaily ; ' I've heard it dozens of times. It's the owls.'

" We both cried out.

" ' Ah,' he said comically, ' I see you don't believe me ! That's what comes of telling so many fibs. But it's true, I assure you. (And the brown eyes did look particularly truthful.) Barn owls do make a noise that is very like the snoring of an old man. And there are some with young ones who live in the spout at the corner of the wall in your room. They're snoring and scrambling in and out of the spout all night.'

" It was quite true, Ida, as we found when Fatima was at last persuaded to visit the corner where the rooms had been pulled down, and where, decorated with ivy, the old spout formed a home for the snoring owls.

" By the aid of the long pole he brought out a young one to our view—a shy, soft, lovely, shadow-tinted creature, ghostly enough to behold, who felt like a mass of fluff, refused to be kissed, and went blinking back into his spout at the first opportunity. His snoring alarmed us no more."

" And the noise was really that ? " said Ida.

" It really was, my dear."

" It's a splendid story," said Ida, " you see I didn't go to sleep this time. And what became of everybody, please ? Did the red-haired young lady marry the Irishman ? "

" Very soon afterwards, my dear," said Mrs. Overtheway. " We kept up our friendship, too, in after life ; and I have many times amused their children with the story of the Snoring Ghost."

---

# Welcome to the New Year

*by* ELEANOR FARJEON

HEY, my lad ! ho, my lad !
Here's a New Broom.
Heaven's your housetop
And Earth is your room.

Tuck up your shirt-sleeves,
There's plenty to do—
Look at the muddle
That's waiting for you !

Dust in the corners
And dirt on the floor,
Cobwebs still clinging
To window and door.

Hey, my lad ! ho, my lad !
Nimble and keen—
Here's your New Broom, my lad !
See you sweep clean.

# THE FAIRIES' PASSAGE.
## JAMES CLARENCE MANGAN.

TAP, tap, rap, rap! "Get up, gaffer Ferryman."
"Eh! Who is there?" The clock strikes three.
"Get up, do, gaffer! You are the very man
We have been long, long, longing to see."
The ferryman rises, growling and grumbling,
And goes fum-fumbling, and stumbling, and tumbling
Over the wares on his way to the door.
But he sees no more
Than he saw before,
Till a voice is heard: "O Ferryman, dear!
Here we are waiting, all of us, here.
We are a wee, wee colony, we;
Some two hundred in all, or three.
Ferry us over the River Lee
Ere dawn of day,
And we will pay
The most we may
In our own wee way!"

"Who are you? Whence came you?
What place are you going to?"
"Oh, we have dwelt over-long in this land:
The people get cross, and are growing so knowing, too!
Nothing at all but they now understand.

We are daily vanishing under the thunder
Of some huge engine or iron wonder;
That iron—ah! it has entered our souls."
"Your souls?   O gholes!
You queer little drolls,
Do you mean—"   "Good gaffer, do aid us with speed,
For our time, like out stature, is short indeed!
And a very long way we have to go:
Eight or ten thousand miles or so,
Hither and thither, and to and fro,
With our pots and pans
And little gold cans;
But our light caravans
Run swifter than man's."

"Well, well, you may come," said the ferryman affably;
"Patrick, turn out, and get ready the barge."
Then again to the little folk: "Tho' you seem laughably
Small, I don't mind, if your coppers be large."
Oh, dear! what a rushing, what pushing, what crushing
(The waterman making vain efforts at hushing
The hubbub the while), there followed these words!
What clapping of boards,
What strapping of cords,
What stowing away of children and wives,
And platters, and mugs, and spoons, and knives!
Till all had safely got into the boat,
And the ferryman, clad in his tip-top coat,
And his wee little fairies were safely afloat;
Then ding, ding, ding,
And kling, kling, kling,
How the coppers did ring
In the tin pitcherling!

Off, then, went the boat, at first very pleasantly,
Smoothly, and so forth; but after a while
It swayed and it swagged this and that way, and presently
Chest after chest, and pile after pile
Of the little folk's goods began tossing and rolling,
And pitching like fun, beyond fairy controlling.
O Mab! if the hubbub were great before,
It was now some two or three million times more.
Crash! went the wee crocks and the clocks; and the locks
Of each little wee box were stove in by hard knocks;
And then there were oaths, and prayers, and cries:
"Take care!"—"See there!"—"Oh, dear, my eyes!"—
"I am killed!"—"I am drowned!"—with groans and sighs,

Till to land they drew,
"Yeo-ho!   Pull to!
Tiller-rope, thro' and thro'!"
And all's right anew,
"Now jump upon shore, ye queer little oddities.

(Eh, what is this? . . . Where are they, at all?
Where are they, and where are their tiny commodities?
Well, as I live! . . .)" He looks blank as a wall,
Poor ferryman!   Round him and round him he gazes,
But only gets deeplier lost in the mazes
Of utter bewilderment.   All, all are gone,
And he stands alone,
Like a statue of stone,
In a doldrum of wonder.   He turns to steer,
And a tinkling laugh salutes his ear,
With other odd sounds: "Ha, ha, ha, ha!
Fol lol! zidzizzle! quee, quee! bah, bah!
Fizzigigiggidy! pshee! sha, sha!"
"O ye thieves, ye thieves, ye rascally thieves!"
The good man cries.   He turns to his pitcher,
And there, alas, to his horror perceives
That the little folk's mode of making him richer
Has been to pay him with withered leaves!

**THE FAIRIES' PASSAGE**

Oh, dear! What a rushing, what pushing, what crushing. (Page 287)

THE BABY AND THE BEAR

He rowed rapidly away, just as the old bear dragged
herself up on the raft. (Page 325)

# The LOST CITY of ATLANTIS

## from Twenty Thousand Leagues Under the Sea

### by JULES VERNE

ONE evening, about 11 p.m., I received the very unexpected visit of Captain Nemo. He asked me very graciously if I felt fatigued from sitting up so late the night before. I answered in the negative.

"Then, M. Aronnax, I have a curious excursion to propose to you."

"What is it, captain?"

"You have as yet only been on the sea-bottom by daylight. Should you like to see it on a dark night?"

"I should like it much."

"It will be a fatiguing walk, I warn you. You will have to go far, and climb a mountain. The roads are not very well kept in repair."

"What you tell me makes me doubly curious. I am ready to follow you."

"Come, then, professor. We will go and put on our diving dresses."

When we reached the ward-room I saw that neither my companions nor any of the crew were to follow us in our excursion. Captain Nemo had not even asked me to take Ned or Conseil.

In a few minutes we had put on our apparatus. They placed on our backs the reservoirs full of air, but the electric lamps were not prepared. I said as much to the captain.

"They would be of no use to us," he answered.

I thought I had not heard aright, but I could not repeat my observation, for the captain's head had already disappeared under its metallic covering. I finished harnessing myself, felt that some one placed an iron spiked stick in my hand, and a few minutes later, after the usual manœuvre, we set foot on the bottom of the Atlantic, at a depth of 150 fathoms.

Midnight was approaching. The waters were in profound darkness, but Captain Nemo showed me a reddish point in the distance, a sort of large light shining about two miles from the *Nautilus*. What this fire was, with what fed, why and how it burnt in the liquid mass, I could not tell. Anyway it lighted us, dimly it is true, but I soon became accustomed to the peculiar darkness, and I understood, under the circumstances, the uselessness of the Ruhmkorff apparatus.

Captain Nemo and I walked side by side directly towards the light. The flat soil ascended gradually. We took long strides, helping ourselves with our sticks, but our progress was slow, for our feet often sank in a sort of mud covered with seaweed and flat stones.

As we went along I heard a sort of pattering above my head. The noise sometimes redoubled, and produced something like a continuous shower. I soon understood the cause. It was rain falling violently and crisping the surface of the waves. Instinctively I was seized with the idea that I should be wet through. By water, in water ! I could not help laughing at the odd idea. But the truth is that under a thick diving dress the liquid element is no longer felt, and it only seems like an atmosphere rather denser than the terrestrial atmosphere, that is all.

After half an hour's walking the soil became rocky. The medusæ, the microscopic crustaceans, the pennatules slightly lighted us with their phosphorescent gleams. I caught a glimpse of heaps of stones covered by some millions of zoophytes and thickets of seaweed. My foot often slipped upon this viscous carpet of seaweed and without my stick I should have fallen several times. Turning, I still saw the white light of the *Nautilus* beginning to gleam in the distance.

The heaps of stones of which I have just spoken were heaped on the bottom of the ocean with a sort of regularity I could not explain to myself. I perceived gigantic furrows which lost themselves in the distant darkness, the length of which escaped all valuation. Other peculiarities presented themselves that I did not know how to account for. It seemed to me that my heavy leaden shoes were crushing a litter of bones that cracked with a dry noise. What then was this vast plain I was thus moving across ! I should have liked to question the captain, but his language by signs, that allowed him to talk to his companions when they followed him in his submarine excursions, was still incomprehensible to me.

In the meantime the reddish light that guided us increased and inflamed the horizon. The presence of this fire under the seas excited my curiosity to the highest pitch. Was it some electric effluence ? Was I going towards a natural phenomenon still unknown to the *savants* of the earth ? Or—for this thought crossed my mind—had the hand of man any part in the conflagration ? Had it lighted this fire ? Was I going to meet in this deep sea companions and friends of Captain Nemo living the same strange life, and whom he was going to see ? All these foolish and inadmissible ideas pursued me, and in that state of mind, ceaselessly excited by the series of marvels that passed before my eyes, I should not have been surprised to see at the bottom of the sea, one of the submarine towns Captain Nemo dreamed of.

Our road grew lighter and lighter. The white light shone from the top of a mountain about eight hundred feet high. But what I perceived was only a reflection made by the crystal of the water. The fire, the source of the inexplicable light, was on the opposite side of the mountain.

Amidst the stony paths that furrowed the bottom of the Atlantic Captain Nemo went on without hesitating. He knew the dark route, had doubtless often been along it, and could not lose himself in it. I followed him with unshaken confidence. He appeared, whilst walking before me, like one of the sea genii, and I admired his tall stature like a black shadow on the luminous background of the horizon.

It was one o'clock in the morning. We had reached the first slopes of the mountain. But the way up led through the difficult paths of a vast thicket.

Yes, a thicket of dead trees, leafless, sapless, mineralised under the action of the water, overtopped here and there by gigantic pines. It was like a coal-series, still standing, holding by its roots to the soil that had given way, and whose branches, like fine black paper-cuttings, stood out against the watery ceiling. My readers may imagine a forest on the side of the Hartz Mountains, but forest and mountain sunk to the bottom of the sea. The paths were encumbered with seaweed and fucus, amongst which swarmed a world of crustaceans. I went on climbing over the rocks, leaping over the fallen trunks, breaking the sea-creepers that balanced from one tree to another, startling the fish that flew from branch to branch. Pressed onwards I no longer felt any fatigue. I followed my guide, who was never fatigued.

What a spectacle! How can I depict it? How describe the aspect of the woods and rocks in this liquid element, their lower parts sombre and wild, the upper coloured with red tints in the light which the reverberating power of the water doubled? We were climbing rocks which fell in enormous fragments directly afterwards with the noise of an avalanche. Right and left were deep dark galleries where sight was lost. Here opened vast clearings that seemed made by the hand of man, and I asked myself sometimes if some inhabitant of these submarine regions was not about to appear suddenly.

But Captain Nemo still went on climbing. I would not be left behind. My stick lent me useful aid. A false step would have been dangerous in these narrow paths, hollowed out of the sides of precipices; but I walked along with a firm step without suffering from vertigo. Sometimes I jumped over a crevice the depth of which would have made me recoil on the glaciers of the earth; sometimes I ventured on the vacillating trunks of trees thrown from one abyss to another without looking under my feet, having only eyes to admire the savage sites of that region. There, monumental rocks perched on these irregularly-cut bases seemed to defy the laws of equilibrium. Between their stony knees grew trees like a jet of water under strong pressure, sustaining and sustained by the rocks. Then, natural towers, large scarps cut perpendicularly like a fortress curtain, inclining at an angle which the laws of gravitation would not have authorised on the surface of the terrestrial regions.

And did I not myself feel the difference due to the powerful density of the water, when, notwithstanding my heavy garments, my brass headpiece, my metal soles, I climbed slopes impracticably steep, clearing them, so to speak, with the lightness of an isard or a chamois?

I feel that this recital of an excursion under the sea cannot sound probable.

I am the historian of things that seem impossible, and that yet are real and incontestable. I did not dream. I saw and felt.

Two hours after having quitted the *Nautilus* we had passed the trees, and a hundred feet above our heads rose the summit of the mountain, the projection of which made a shadow on the brilliant irradiation of the opposite slope. A few petrified bushes were scattered hither and thither in grimacing zigzags. The fish rose in shoals under our footsteps like birds surprised in the tall grass. The rocky mass was hollowed out into impenetrable confractuosities, deep grottoes, bottomless holes, in which I heard formidable noises. My blood froze in my veins when I perceived some enormous antennæ barricading my path, or some frightful claw shutting up with a noise in the dark cavities. Thousands of luminous points shone amidst the darkness. They were the eyes of gigantic crustaceans, giant lobsters setting themselves up like halberdiers, and moving their claws with the clanking sound of metal ; titanic crabs pointed like cannon on their carriages, and frightful poulps, intertwining their tentacles like a living nest of serpents.

What was this exorbitant world that I did not know yet ? To what order belonged these articulates to which the rock formed a second carapace ? Where had Nature found the secret of their vegetating existence, and for how many centuries had they lived thus in the lowest depths of the ocean ?

But I could not stop. Captain Nemo, familiar with these terrible animals, paid no attention to them. We had arrived at the first plateau, where other surprises awaited me. There rose picturesque ruins which betrayed the hand of man, and not that of the Creator. They were vast heaps of stones in the vague outlines of castles and temples, clothed with a world of zoophytes in flower, and, instead of ivy, seaweed and fucus clothed them with a vegetable mantle.

But what, then, was this portion of the globe swallowed up by cataclysms ? Who had placed these rocks and stones like dolmens of ante-historical times ? Where was I ? Where had Captian Nemo's whim brought me to ?

I should have liked to question him. As I could not do that, I stopped him. I seized his arm. But he, shaking his head, and pointing to the last summit, seemed to say to me,—

" Higher ! Still higher ! "

I followed him with a last effort, and in a few minutes I had climbed the peak that overtopped for about thirty feet all the rocky mass.

I looked at the side we had just climbed. The mountain only rose seven or eight hundred feet above the plain ; but on the opposite side it commanded from twice that height the depths of this portion of the Atlantic. My eyes wandered over a large space lighted up by a violent fulguration. In fact, this mountain was a volcano. At fifty feet below the peak, amidst a rain of stones and scoriæ, a wide crater was vomiting forth torrents of lava which fell in a cascade of fire into the bosom of the liquid mass. Thus placed, the volcano, like an immense torch, lighted up the lower plain to the last limits of the horizon.

I have said that the submarine crater threw out lava, but not flames. The oxygen of the air is necessary to make a flame, and it cannot exist in water ; but the streams of red-hot lava struggled victoriously against the liquid element, and turned it to vapour by its contact. Rapid currents carried away all this gas in diffusion, and the lava torrent glided to the foot of the mountain like the eruption of Vesuvius on another Torre del Greco.

There, before my eyes, ruined, destroyed, overturned, appeared a town, its roofs crushed in, its temples thrown down, its arches dislocated, its columns lying on the ground, with the solid proportions of Tuscan architecture still discernible upon them ; farther on were the remains of a gigantic aqueduct ; here, the encrusted base of an Acropolis, and the outlines of a Parthenon ; there, some vestiges of a quay, as if some ancient port had formerly sheltered, on the shores of an extinct ocean, merchant vessels and war triremes ; farther on still, long lines of ruined walls, wide deserted streets, a second Pompeii buried under the waters, raised up again for me by Captain Nemo.

*I followed him and in a few minutes I had climbed the peak.*

Where was I ? Where was I ? I wished to know at any price. I felt I must speak, and tried to take off the globe of brass that imprisoned my head.

But Captain Nemo came to me and stopped me with a gesture. Then picking up a piece of clayey stone he went up to a black basaltic rock and traced on it the single word—

" ATLANTIS."

What a flash of lightning shot through my mind ! Atlantis, the ancient Meropis of Theopompus, the Atlantis of Plato, the continent disbelieved in by Origen, Iamblichus, D'Anville, Malte-Brun, and Humboldt, who placed its disappearance amongst legendary tales ; believed in by Possidonius, Pliny, Ammianus, Marcellinus, Tertullian, Engel, Sherer, Tournefort, Buffon, and

D'Avezac, was there before my eyes bearing upon it the unexceptionable testimony of its catastrophe! This, then, was the engulfed region that existed beyond Europe, Asia, and Lybia, beyond the columns of Hercules, where the powerful Atlantides lived, against whom the first wars of Ancient Greece were waged!

The historian who put into writing the grand doings of the heroic times was Plato himself. His dialogue of Timotheus and Critias was, thus to speak, written under the inspiration of Solon, poet and legislator.

One day Solon was talking with some wise old men of Sais, a town already eight hundred years old, as the annals engraved on the sacred walls of its temples testified. One of these old men related the history of another town, a thousand years older. This first Athenian city, nine hundred centuries old, had been invaded and in part destroyed by the Atlantides. These Atlantides, said he, occupied an immense continent, larger than Africa and Asia joined together, which covered a surface between the twelfth and fortieth degree of north latitude. Their dominion extended even as far as Egypt. They wished to impose it upon Greece, but were obliged to retire before the indomitable resistance of the Hellenes. Centuries went by. A cataclysm occurred with inundations and earthquakes. One night and one day sufficed for the extinction of this Atlantis, of which the highest summits, the Madeiras, Azores, Canaries, and Cape Verde Islands still emerge.

Such were the historical souvenirs that Captain Nemo's inscription awoke in my mind. Thus, then, led by the strangest fate, I was treading on one of the mountains of this continent! I was touching with my hand these ruins a thousand times secular and contemporaneous with the geological epochs. I was walking where the contemporaries of the first man had walked. I was crushing under my heavy soles the skeletons of animals of fabulous times, which these trees, now mineralised, formerly covered with their shade.

Ah! why did time fail me? I should have liked to descend the abrupt sides of this mountain, and go over the whole of the immense continent that doubtless joined Africa to America, and to visit the great antediluvian cities. There, perhaps, before my gaze, stretched Makhinios the warlike, Eusebius the pious, whose gigantic inhabitants lived entire centuries, and who were strong enough to pile up these blocks which still resisted the action of the water. One day, perhaps, some eruptive phenomenon would bring these engulfed regions back to the surface of the waves. Sounds that announced a profound struggle of the elements have been heard, and volcanic cinders projected out of the water have been found. All this ground, as far as the Equator, is still worked by underground forces. And who knows if in some distant epoch, increased by the volcanic dejections and by successive strata of lava, the summits of ignivome mountains will not appear on the surface of the Atlantic?

Whilst I was thus dreaming, trying to fix every detail of the grand scene in my memory, Captain Nemo, leaning against a moss-covered fragment of ruin, remained motionless as if petrified in mute ecstasy. Was he dreaming about the long-gone generations and asking them the secret of human destiny? Was it here that this strange man came to refresh his historical memories and live again that ancient existence?—he who would have no modern one. What would I not have given to know his thoughts, to share and understand them!

We remained in the same place for a whole hour, contemplating the vast plain in the light of the lava that sometimes was surprisingly intense. The interior bubblings made rapid tremblings pass over the outside of the mountain. Deep noises, clearly transmitted by the liquid medium, were echoed with majestic amplitude.

At that moment the moon appeared for an instant through the mass of waters and threw her pale rays over the engulfed continent. It was only a gleam, but its effect was indescribable. The captain rose, gave a last look at the immense plain, and then, with his hand, signed to me to follow him.

We rapidly descended the mountain. When we had once passed the mineral forest I perceived the lantern of the *Nautilus* shining like a star. The captain walked straight towards it, and we were back on board as the first tints of dawn whitened the surface of the ocean.

# I'm a Rover

*by* GEORGE DARLEY

I'M a rover! I'm a rover
  Of the greenwood and the glade!
And I'll teach you to discover
  Every Beauty of the shade!

I'm a rover! I'm a rover
  Of the woodland and the dell!
And I know the leafy cover
  Where the maiden-roses dwell!

I'm a rover! I'm a rover!
  Where her couch the lily keeps;
And I'll bring you slily over—
  You may kiss her as she sleeps!

I'm a rover! I'm a rover!
  Where the cowslip quaffs the dew,
Where the bee delights to hover,
  Come! I'll choose a cup for you!

# THE PYGMIES

*from " Tanglewood Tales "*

### *by* NATHANIEL HAWTHORNE

A GREAT while ago, when the world was full of wonders, there lived an earth-born Giant, named Antæus, and a million or more of curious little earth-born people, who were called Pygmies. This Giant and these Pygmies, being children of the same mother (that is to say, our good old Grandmother Earth), were all brethren, and dwelt together in a very friendly and affectionate manner, far, far off, in the middle of hot Africa. The Pygmies were so small, and there were so many sandy deserts and such high mountains between them and the rest of mankind, that nobody could get a peep at them oftener than once in a hundred years. As for the Giant, being of a very lofty nature, it was easy enough to see him, but safest to keep out of his sight.

Among the Pygmies, I suppose, if one of them grew to the height of six or eight inches, he was reckoned a prodigiously tall man. It must have been very pretty to behold their little cities, with streets two or three feet wide, paved with the smallest pebbles, and bordered by habitations about as big as a squirrel's cage. The king's palace attained to the stupendous magnitude of Periwinkle's baby house, and stood in the centre of a spacious square, which could hardly have been covered by our hearthrug. Their principal temple, or cathedral, was as lofty as yonder bureau, and was looked upon as a wonderfully sublime and magnificent edifice. All these structures were built neither of stone nor wood. They were neatly plastered together by the Pygmy workmen, pretty much like birds' nests, out of straw, feathers, egg shells, and other small bits of stuff, with stiff clay instead of mortar;

and, when the hot sun had dried them, they were just as snug and comfortable as a Pygmy could desire.

The country round about was conveniently laid out in fields, the largest of which was nearly of the same extent as one of Sweet Fern's flower beds. Here the Pygmies used to plant wheat and other kinds of grain, which, when it grew up and ripened, overshadowed these tiny people as the pines, and the oaks, and the walnut and chestnut trees overshadow you and me, when we walk in our own tracts of woodland. At harvest time they were forced to go with their little axes and cut down the grain, exactly as a woodcutter makes a clearing in the forest ; and when a stalk of wheat, with its over-burdened top, chanced to come crashing down upon an unfortunate Pygmy, it was apt to be a very sad affair. If it did not smash him all to pieces, at least, I am sure, it must have made the poor little fellow's head ache. And oh, my stars ! if the fathers and mothers were so small, what must the children and babies have been ? A whole family of them might have been put to bed in a shoe, or have crept into an old glove, and played at hide-and-seek in its thumb and fingers. You might have hidden a year-old baby under a thimble.

Now these funny Pygmies, as I told you before, had a Giant for their neighbour and brother, who was bigger, if possible, than they were little. He was so very tall that he carried a pine tree, which was eight feet through the butt, for a walking-stick. It took a far-sighted Pygmy, I can assure you, to discern his summit without the help of a telescope ; and sometimes, in misty weather, they could not see his upper half, but only his long legs, which seemed to be striding about by themselves. But at noonday, in a clear atmosphere, when the sun shone brightly over him, the Giant Antæus presented a very grand spectacle. There he used to stand, a perfect mountain of a man, with his great countenance smiling down upon his little brothers, and his one vast eye (which was as big as a cart wheel, and placed right in the centre of his forehead) giving a friendly wink to the whole nation at once.

The Pygmies loved to talk with Antæus ; and fifty times a day, one or another of them would turn up his head, and shout through the hollow of his fists, " Halloo, brother Antæus ! How are you, my good fellow ? " and when the small, distant squeak of their voices reached his ear, the Giant would make answer, " Pretty well, brother Pygmy, I thank you," in a thunderous roar that would have shaken down the walls of their strongest temple, only that it came from so far aloft.

It was a happy circumstance that Antæus was the Pygmy people's friend ; for there was more strength in his little finger than in ten million of such bodies as theirs. If he had been as ill-natured to them as he was to everybody else, he might have beaten down their biggest city at one kick, and hardly have known that he did it. With the tornado of his breath, he could have stripped the roofs from a hundred dwellings and sent thousands of the inhabitants whirling through the air. He might have set his immense foot upon a multitude ; and when he took it up again there would have been a pitiful sight, to be sure. But, being the son of Mother Earth, as they like-wise were, the Giant gave them his brotherly kindness, and loved them with as big a love as it was possible to feel for creatures so very small. And, on their parts, the Pygmies loved Antæus with as much affection as their tiny hearts could hold.  He was always ready to do them any good offices that lay in his power ;  as for example, when they wanted a breeze to turn their windmills, the Giant would set all the sails agoing with the mere natural respiration of his lungs.  When the sun was too hot, he often sat himself down, and let his shadow fall over the kingdom, from one frontier to the other ;  and as for matters in general, he was wise enough to let them alone, and leave the Pygmies to manage their own affairs—which, after all, is about the best thing that great people can do for little ones.

In short, as I said before, Antæus loved the Pygmies, and the Pygmies loved Antæus.  The Giant's life being as long as his body was large, while the lifetime of a Pygmy was but a span, this friendly intercourse had been going on for innumerable generations and ages.  It was written about in the Pygmy histories, and talked about in their ancient traditions.  The most venerable and white-bearded Pygmy had never heard of a time, even in his greatest of grandfather's days, when the Giant was not their enormous friend.  Once, to be sure (as was recorded on an obelisk, three feet high, erected on the place of the catastrophe), Antæus sat down upon about five thousand Pygmies, who were assembled at a military review.  But this was one of those unlucky accidents for which nobody is to blame ;  so that the small folks never took it to heart, and only requested the Giant to be careful for ever afterwards to examine the acre of ground where he intended to squat himself.

It is a very pleasant picture to imagine Antæus standing among the Pygmies, like the spire of the tallest cathedral that ever was built, while they ran about like ants at his feet ;  and to think that, in spite of their difference in size, there were affection and sympathy between them and him !  Indeed, it has always seemed to me that the Giant needed the little people more than the Pygmies needed the Giant.  For, unless they had been his neighbours and well wishers, and, as we may say, his playfellows, Antæus would not have had a single friend in the world.  No other being like himself had ever been created.  No creature of his own size had ever talked with him, in thunder-like accents, face to face.  When he stood with his head among the clouds he was quite alone, and had been so for hundreds of years, and would be so for ever.  Even if he had met another Giant, Antæus would have fancied the world not big enough for two such vast personages, and, instead of being friends with him, would have fought him till one of the two was killed.  But with the Pygmies he was the most sportive and humorous, and merry-hearted, and sweet-tempered old Giant that ever washed his face in a wet cloud.

His little friends, like all other small people, had a great opinion of their own importance, and used to assume quite a patronising air towards the Giant.

" Poor creature ! " they said one to another.  " He has a very dull time of it, all by himself ;  and we ought not to grudge wasting a little of our precious time to amuse him.  He is not half so bright as we are, to be sure ;  and, for that reason, he needs us to look after his comfort and happiness.  Let us be kind to the old fellow.  Why, if Mother Earth had not been very kind to ourselves, we might all have been Giants too."

On all their holidays the Pygmies had excellent sport with Antæus. He often stretched himself out at full length on the ground, where he looked like the long ridge of a hill ; and it was a good hour's walk, no doubt, for a short-legged Pygmy to journey from head to foot of the Giant. He would lay down his great hand flat on the grass, and challenge the tallest of them to clamber upon it, and straddle from finger to finger. So fearless were they, that they made nothing of creeping in among the folds of his garments. When his head lay sidewise on the earth, they would march boldly up, and peep into the great cavern of his mouth, and take it all as a joke (as indeed it was meant) when Antæus gave a sudden snap with his jaws, as if he were going to swallow fifty of them at once. You would have laughed to see the children dodging in and out among his hair, or swinging from his beard. It is impossible to tell half of the funny tricks that they played with their huge comrade ; but I do not know that anything was more curious than when a party of boys were seen running races on his forehead, to try which of them could get first round the circle of his one great eye. It was another favourite feat with them to march along the bridge of his nose, and jump down upon his upper lip.

If the truth must be told, they were sometimes as troublesome to the Giant as a swarm of ants or mosquitoes, especially as they had a fondness for mischief, and liked to prick his skin with their little swords and lances, to see how thick and tough it was. But Antæus took it all kindly enough ; although, once in a while, when he happened to be sleepy, he would grumble out a peevish word or two, like the muttering of a tempest, and ask them to have done with their nonsense. A great deal oftener, however, he watched their merriment and gambols until his huge, heavy, clumsy wits were completely stirred up by them ; and then would he roar out such a tremendous volume of immeasurable laughter, that the whole nation of Pygmies had to put their hands to their ears, else it would certainly have deafened them.

"Ho, ho, ho!" quoth the Giant, shaking his mountainous sides. "What a funny thing it is to be little! If I were not Antæus, I should like to be a Pygmy, just for the joke's sake."

The Pygmies had but one thing to trouble them in the world. They were constantly at war with the cranes, and had always been so ever since the long-lived Giant could remember. From time to time, very terrible battles had been fought, in which sometimes the little men won the victory, and sometimes the cranes. According to some historians, the Pygmies used to go to the battle mounted on the backs of goats and rams ; but such animals as these must have been far too big for Pygmies to ride upon ; so that, I rather suppose, they rode on squirrel-back, or rabbit-back, or rat-back, or perhaps got upon hedgehogs, whose prickly quills would be very terrible to the enemy. However this might be, and whatever creatures the Pygmies rode upon, I do not doubt that they made a formidable appearance, armed with sword and spear, and bow and arrow, blowing their tiny trumpets, and shouting their little war-cry. They never failed to exhort one another to fight bravely, and recollect that the world had its eyes upon them ; although, in simple truth, the only spectator was the Giant Antæus, with his one, great, stupid eye in the middle of his forehead.

When the two armies joined battle, the cranes would rush forward,

flapping their wings and stretching out their necks, and would perhaps
snatch up some of the Pygmies crosswise in their beaks. Whenever this
happened, it was truly an awful spectacle to see those little men of might
kicking and sprawling in the air, and at last disappearing down the crane's
long, crooked throat, swallowed up alive. A hero, you know, must hold
himself in readiness for any kind of fate; and doubtless the glory of the
thing was a consolation to him, even in the crane's gizzard. If Antæus
observed that the battle was going hard against his little allies, he generally
stopped laughing, and ran with mile-long strides to their assistance, flourishing
his club aloft and shouting at the cranes, who quacked and croaked, and
retreated as fast as they could. Then the Pygmy army would march homeward
in triumph. attributing the victory entirely to their own valour, and to the
warlike skill and strategy of whomseover happened to be captain-general;
and for a tedious while afterwards nothing would be heard of but grand
processions, and public banquets, and brilliant illuminations, and
shows of wax-work, with likenesses of the distinguished officers as small
as life.

In the above-described warfare, if a Pygmy chanced to pluck out a
crane's tail feather, it proved a very great feather in his cap. Once or twice,
if you will believe me, a little man was made chief ruler of the nation for no
other merit in the world than bringing home such a feather.

But I have now said enough to let you see what a gallant little people
these were, and how happily they and their forefathers, for nobody knows
how many generations, had lived with the immeasurable Giant Antæus.
In the remaining part of the story, I shall tell you of a far more astonishing
battle than any that was fought between the Pygmies and the cranes.

One day the mighty Antæus was lolling at full length among his little
friends. His pine-tree walking-stick lay on the ground, close by his side.
His head was in one part of the kingdom, and his feet extended across the
boundaries of another part; and he was taking whatever comfort he could
get, while the Pygmies scrambled over him, and peeped into his cavernous
mouth, and played among his hair. Sometimes, for a minute or two, the
Giant dropped asleep, and snored like the rush of a whirlwind. During
one of these little bits of slumber, a Pygmy chanced to climb upon his
shoulder, and took a view around the horizon, as from the summit of a
hill; and he beheld something, a long way off, which made him rub the
bright specks of his eyes, and look sharper than before. At first he mistook
it for a mountain, and wondered how it had grown up so suddenly out of
the earth. But soon he saw the mountain move. As it came nearer and
nearer, what should it turn out to be but a human shape, not so big as
Antæus, it is true, although a very enormous figure, in comparison with
Pygmies, and a vast deal bigger than the men we see nowadays.

When the Pygmy was quite satisfied that his eyes had not deceived him,
he scampered, as fast as his legs would carry him, to the Giant's ear, and
stooping over its cavity shouted lustily into it:

"Halloo, brother Antæus! Get up this minute, and take your pine-
tree walking-stick in your hand. Here comes another Giant to have a
tussle with you."

"Poh, poh!" grumbled Antæus, only half awake. "None of your

nonsense, my little fellow! Don't you see I'm sleepy? There is not a Giant on earth for whom I would take the trouble to get up."

But the Pygmy looked again, and now perceived that the stranger was coming directly towards the prostrate form of Antæus. With every step he looked less like a blue mountain and more like an immensely large man. He was soon so nigh that there could be no possible mistake about the matter. There he was, with the sun flaming on his golden helmet, and flashing from his polished breastplate; he had a sword by his side, and a lion's skin over his back, and on his right shoulder he carried a club, which looked bulkier and heavier than the pine-tree walking-stick of Antæus.

By this time, the whole nation of the Pygmies had seen the new wonder, and a million of them set up a shout all together; so that it really made quite an audible squeak.

"Get up, Antæus! Bestir yourself, you lazy old Giant! Here comes another Giant, as strong as you are, to fight with you."

"Nonsense, nonsense!" growled the sleepy Giant. "I'll have my nap out, come who may."

Still the stranger drew nearer; and now the Pygmies could plainly discern that, if his stature were less lofty than the Giant's, yet his shoulders were even broader. And, in truth, what a pair of shoulders they must have been! As I told you, a long while ago, they once upheld the sky. The Pygmies, being ten times as vivacious as their great numskull of a brother, could not abide the Giant's slow movements, and were determined to have him on his feet. So they kept shouting to him, and even went so far as to prick him with their swords.

"Get up, get up, get up!" they cried. "Up with you, lazy bones! The strange Giant's club is bigger than your own, his shoulders are the broadest, and we think him the stronger of the two."

Antæus could not endure to have it said that any mortal was half so mighty as himself. This latter remark of the Pygmies pricked him deeper than their swords; and, sitting up, in rather a sulky humour, he gave a gape of several yards wide, rubbed his eyes, and finally turned his stupid head in the direction whither his little friends were eagerly pointing.

No sooner did he set eyes on the stranger, than, leaping on his feet, and seizing his walking-stick, he strode a mile or two to meet him; all the while brandishing the sturdy pine-tree, so that it whistled through the air.

"Who are you?" thundered the Giant. "And what do you want in my dominions?"

There was one strange thing about Antæus, of which I have not yet told you, lest, hearing of so many wonders all in a lump, you might not believe much more than half of them. You are to know, then, that, whenever this redoubtable Giant touched the ground, either with his hand, his foot, or any other part of his body, he grew stronger than ever he had been before. The Earth, you remember, was his mother, and was very fond of him, as being almost the biggest of her children; and so she took this method of keeping him always in full vigour. Some persons affirm that he grew ten times stronger at every touch; others say that it was only twice as strong. But only think of it! Whenever Antæus took a walk, supposing it were but ten miles, and that he stepped a hundred yards at a stride, you may try to

*Hercules caught him round the middle and lifted him in the air.*

cipher out how much mightier he was, on sitting down again, than when he first started. And whenever he flung himself on the earth to take a little repose, even if he got up the very next instant, he would be as strong as exactly ten just such giants as his former self. It was well for the world that Antæus happened to be of a sluggish disposition, and liked ease better than exercise ; for, if he had frisked about like the Pygmies, and touched the earth as often as they did, he would long ago have been strong enough to pull down the sky about people's ears. But these great lubberly fellows resemble mountains, not only in bulk, but in their disinclination to move.

Any other mortal man, except the very one whom Antæus had now encountered, would have been half frightened to death by the Giant's ferocious aspect and terrible voice. But the stranger did not seem at all disturbed. He carelessly lifted his club, and balanced it in his hand, measuring Antæus with his eye, from head to foot, not as if wonder-smitten at his stature, but as if he had seen a great many Giants before, and this was by no means the biggest of them. In fact, if the Giant had been no bigger than the Pygmies (who stood pricking up their ears, and looking and listening to what was going forward), the stranger could not have been less afraid of him.

"Who are you, I say ? " roared Antæus again. " What's your name ? Why do you come hither ? Speak, you vagabond, or I'll try the thickness of your skull with my walking-stick."

" You are a very discourteous Giant," answered the stranger quietly, " and I shall probably have to teach you a little civility, before we part. As for my name, it is Hercules. I have come hither because this is my most convenient road to the garden of the Hesperides, whither I am going to get three of the golden apples for King Eurystheus."

" Caitiff, you shall go no farther ! " bellowed Antæus, putting on a grimmer look than before ; for he had heard of the mighty Hercules, and hated him because he was said to be so strong. " Neither shall you go back whence you came ! "

" How will you prevent me," asked Hercules, " from going whither I please ? "

" By hitting you a rap with this pine tree here," shouted Antæus, scowling so that he made himself the ugliest monster in Africa. " I am fifty times stronger than you ; and, now that I stamp my foot upon the ground, I am five hundred times stronger ! I am ashamed to kill such a puny little dwarf as you seem to be. I will make a slave of you, and you shall likewise be the slave of my brethren here, the Pygmies. So throw down your club and your other weapons ; and as for that lion's skin, I intend to have a pair of gloves made of it."

" Come and take it off my shoulders, then," answered Hercules, lifting his club.

Then the Giant, grinning with rage, strode tower-like towards the stranger (ten times strengthened at every step), and fetched a monstrous blow at him with his pine tree, which Hercules caught upon his club ; and being more skilful than Antæus he paid him back such a rap upon the sconce that down tumbled the great lumbering man-mountain, flat upon the ground. The poor little Pygmies (who really never dreamed that anybody in the world was half so strong as their brother Antæus) were a good deal dismayed at this. But no sooner was the Giant down than up he bounced again, with tenfold might, and such a furious visage as was horrible to behold. He aimed another blow at Hercules, but struck away, being blinded with wrath, and only hit his poor innocent Mother Earth, who groaned and trembled at the stroke. His pine tree went so deep into the ground, and stuck there so fast, that, before Antæus could get it out, Hercules brought down his club across his shoulders with a mighty thwack, which made the Giant roar as if all sorts of intolerable noises had come screeching and rumbling out of his immeasurable lungs in that one cry. Away it went, over mountains and valleys, and, for aught I know, was heard on the other side of the African deserts.

As for the Pygmies, their capital city was laid in ruins by the concussion and vibration of the air ; and, though there was uproar enough without their help, they all set up a shriek out of three millions of little throats, fancying, no doubt, that they swelled the Giant's bellow by at least ten times as much. Meanwhile, Antæus had scrambled upon his feet again, and pulled his pine tree out of the earth ; and, all aflame with fury, and more outrageously strong than ever, he ran at Hercules, and brought down another blow.

"This time, rascal," shouted he, "you shall not escape me."

But once more Hercules warded off the stroke with his club, and the Giant's pine tree was shattered into a thousand splinters, most of which flew among the Pygmies, and did them more mischief than I like to think about. Before Antæus could get out of the way, Hercules let drive again, and gave him another knock-down blow, which sent him heels over head, but served only to increase his already enormous and insufferable strength. As for his rage, there is no telling what a fiery furnace it had now got to be. His one eye was nothing but a circle of red flame. Having now no weapons but his fists, he doubled them up (each bigger than a hogshead), smote one against the other, and danced up and down with absolute frenzy, flourishing his immense arms about, as if he meant not merely to kill Hercules, but to smash the whole world to pieces.

"Come on !" roared this thundering Giant. "Let me hit you but one box on the ear, and you'll never have the headache again."

Now Hercules (though strong enough, as you already know, to hold the sky up) began to be sensible that he should never win the victory, if he kept on knocking Antæus down ; for, by and by, if he hit him such hard blows, the Giant would inevitably, by the help of his Mother Earth, become stronger than the mighty Hercules himself. So, throwing down his club, with which he had fought so many dreadful battles, the hero stood ready to receive his antagonist with naked arms.

"Step forward," cried he. "Since I've broken your pine tree, we'll try which is the better man at a wrestling match."

"Aha ! then I'll soon satisfy you," shouted the Giant ; for, if there was one thing on which he prided himself more than another, it was his skill in wrestling. "Villain, I'll fling you where you can never pick yourself up again."

On came Antæus, hopping and capering with the scorching heat of his rage, and getting new vigour wherewith to wreak his passion, every time

LITTLE SNOW WHITE

As soon as morning dawned, Snow White awoke, and was quite
frightened when she saw the seven little men. (Page 341)

GUY OF WARWICK

Guy, however, had so much the advantage that,
coming with his spear directly on the other's breast, he forced
a passage through it to his heart. (Page 349)

he hopped. But Hercules, you must understand, was wiser than this numb-skull of a Giant, and had thought of a way to fight him—huge, earth-born monster that he was—and to conquer him too, in spite of all that his Mother Earth could do for him. Watching his opportunity, as the mad Giant made a rush at him, Hercules caught him round the middle with both hands, lifted him high into the air, and held him aloft overhead.

Just imagine it, my dear little friends. What a spectacle it must have been, to see this monstrous fellow sprawling in the air, face downward, kicking out his long legs and wriggling his whole vast body, like a baby when its father holds it at arm's length towards the ceiling.

But the most wonderful thing was, that, as soon as Antæus was fairly off the earth, he began to lose the vigour which he had gained by touching it. Hercules very soon perceived that his troublesome enemy was growing weaker, both because he struggled and kicked with less violence, and because the thunder of his big voice subsided into a grumble. The truth was that unless the giant touched Mother Earth as often as once in ten minutes, not only his overgrown strength, but the very breath of his life would depart from him. Hercules had guessed this secret; and it may be well for us all to remember it, in case we should ever have to fight a battle with a fellow like Antæus. For these earth-born creatures are only difficult to conquer on their own ground, but may easily be managed if we can contrive to lift them into a loftier and purer region. So it proved with the poor Giant, whom I am really a little sorry for, notwithstanding his uncivil way of treating strangers who came to visit him.

When his strength and breath were quite gone, Hercules gave his huge body a toss, and flung it about a mile off, where it fell heavily, and lay with no more motion than a sand hill. It was too late for the Giant's Mother Earth to help him now; and I should not wonder if his ponderous bones were lying on the same spot to this very day, and were mistaken for those of an uncommonly large elephant.

But, alas me! What a wailing did the poor little Pygmies set up when they saw their enormous brother treated in this terrible manner! If Hercules heard their shrieks, however, he took no notice, and perhaps fancied them only the shrill, plaintive twittering of small birds that had been frightened from their nests by the uproar of the battle between himself and Antæus. Indeed, his thoughts had been so much taken up with the Giant that he had never once looked at the Pygmies, nor even knew that there was such a funny little nation in the world. And now, as he had travelled a good way, and was also rather weary with his exertions in the fight, he spread out his lion's skin on the ground, and, reclining himself upon it, fell fast asleep.

As soon as the Pygmies saw Hercules preparing for a nap, they nodded their little heads at one another, and winked with their little eyes. And when his deep, regular breathing gave them notice that he was asleep, they assembled together in an immense crowd, spreading over a space of about twenty-seven feet square. One of their most eloquent orators (and a valiant warrior enough, besides, though hardly so good at any other weapon as he was with his tongue) climbed upon a toadstool, and, from that elevated position, addressed the multitude. His sentiments were pretty much as

follows ; or, at all events, something like this was probably the upshot of
his speech :

"Tall Pygmies and mighty little men! You and all of us have seen
what a public calamity has been brought to pass, and what an insult has
here been offered to the majesty of our nation. Yonder lies Antæus, our
great friend and brother, slain, within our territory, by a miscreant who took
him at disadvantage, and fought him (if fighting it can be called) in a way
that neither man, nor Giant, nor Pygmy ever dreamed of fighting, until
this hour. And, adding a grievous contumely to the wrong already done us,
the miscreant has now fallen asleep as quietly as if nothing were to be dreaded
from our wrath! It behoves you, fellow-countrymen, to consider in what
aspect we shall stand before the world, and what will be the verdict of im-
partial history, should we suffer these accumulated outrages to go unavenged.

"Antæus was our brother, born of that same beloved parent to whom
we owe the thews and sinews, as well as the courageous hearts, which made
him proud of our relationship. He was our faithful ally, and fell fighting
as much for our national rights and immunities as for his own personal ones.
We and our forefathers have dwelt in friendship with him, and held affectionate intercourse as man to man, through immemorial generations. You
remember how often our entire people have reposed in his great shadow,
and how our little ones have played at hide-and-seek in the tangles of his
hair, and how his mighty footsteps have familiarly gone to and fro among
us, and never trodden upon any of our toes. And there lies this dear brother
—this sweet and amiable friend—this brave and faithful ally—this virtuous
Giant—this blameless and excellent Antæus—dead! Dead! Silent!
Powerless! A mere mountain of clay! Forgive my tears! Nay, I behold
your own. Were we to drown the world with them, could the world
blame us?

"But to resume : Shall we, my countrymen, suffer this wicked stranger
to depart unharmed, and triumph in his treacherous victory among distant
communities of the earth? Shall we not rather compel him to leave his
bones here on our soil, by the side of our slain brother's bones ? so that,
while one skeleton shall remain as the everlasting monument of our sorrow,
the other shall endure as long, exhibiting to the whole human race a terrible
example of Pygmy vengeance! Such is the question. I put it to you in
full confidence of a response that shall be worthy of our national character,
and calculated to increase, rather than diminish, the glory which our
ancestors have transmitted to us, and which we ourselves have proudly
vindicated in our warfare with the cranes."

The orator was here interrupted by a burst of irrepressible enthusiasm ;
every individual Pygmy crying out that the national honour must be preserved at all hazards. He bowed, and, making a gesture for silence, wound
up his harangue in the following admirable manner :

"It only remains for us, then, to decide whether we shall carry on the
war in our national capacity—one united people against a common enemy—
or whether some champion, famous in former fights, shall be selected to
defy the slayer of our brother Antæus to single combat. In the latter case,
though not unconscious that there may be taller men among you, I hereby
offer myself for that enviable duty. And, believe me, dear countrymen,

whether I live or die, the honour of this great country, and the fame bequeathed us by our heroic progenitors, shall suffer no diminution in my hands. Never, while I can wield this sword, of which I now fling away the scabbard—never, never, never, even if the crimson hand that slew the great Antæus shall lay me prostrate, like him, on the soil which I give my life to defend."

So saying, this valiant Pygmy drew out his weapon (which was terrible to behold, being as long as the blade of a penknife), and sent the scabbard whirling over the heads of the multitude. His speech was followed by an uproar of applause, as its patriotism and self-devotion unquestionably deserved; and the shouts and clapping of hands would have been greatly prolonged, had they not been rendered quite inaudible by a deep respiration, vulgarly called a snore, from the sleeping Hercules.

It was finally decided that the whole nation of Pygmies should set to work to destroy Hercules; not, be it understood, from any doubt that a single champion would be capable of putting him to the sword, but because he was a public enemy, and all were desirous of sharing in the glory of his defeat. There was a debate whether the national honour did not demand that a herald should be sent with a trumpet, to stand over the ear of Hercules, and, after blowing a blast right into it, to defy him to the combat by formal proclamation. But two or three venerable and sagacious Pygmies, well versed in state affairs, gave it as their opinion that war already existed, and that it was their rightful privilege to take the enemy by surprise. Moreover, if awakened, and allowed to get upon his feet, Hercules might happen to do them a mischief before he could be beaten down again. For, as these sage counsellors remarked, the stranger's club was really very big, and had rattled like a thunderbolt against the skull of Antæus. So the Pygmies resolved to set aside all foolish punctilios, and assail their antagonist at once.

Accordingly, all the fighting men of the nation took their weapons, and went boldly up to Hercules, who still lay fast asleep. A body of twenty thousand archers marched in front, with their little bows all ready, and the arrows on the string. The same number clambered upon Hercules, some with spades to dig his eyes out, and others with bundles of hay, and all manner of rubbish with which they intended to plug up his mouth and nostrils, so that he might perish for lack of breath. These last, however, could by no means perform their appointed duty; inasmuch as the enemy's breath rushed out of his nose in an obstreperous hurricane and whirlwind, which blew the Pygmies away as fast as they came nigh.

After holding a council, the captains ordered their troops to collect sticks, straws, dry weeds, and whatever combustible stuff they could find, and make a pile of it, heaping it high around the head of Hercules. The archers, meanwhile, were stationed within bow shot, with orders to let fly at Hercules the instant that he stirred. Everything being in readiness, a torch was applied to the pile, which immediately burst into flames, and soon waxed hot enough to roast the enemy, had he but chosen to lie still. But no sooner did Hercules begin to be scorched, than up he started, with his hair in a red blaze.

"What's all this?" he cried, bewildered with sleep, and staring about him as if he expected to see another Giant.

At that moment the twenty thousand archers twanged their bowstrings, and the arrows came whizzing, like so many winged mosquitoes, right into the face of Hercules. But I doubt whether more than half a dozen of them punctured the skin, which was remarkably tough, as you know the skin of a hero has good need to be.

"Villain!" shouted all the Pygmies at once. "You have killed the Giant Antæus, our great brother, and the ally of our nation. We declare war to the death against you, and will slay you on the spot."

Surprised at the shrill piping of so many little voices, Hercules, after putting out the conflagration of his hair, gazed all round about, but could see nothing. At last, however, looking narrowly on the ground, he espied the innumerable assemblage of Pygmies at his feet. He stooped down, and taking up the nearest one, set him on the palm of his left hand, and held him at a proper distance for examination. It chanced to be the very identical Pygmy who had spoken from the top of the toadstool.

"What in the world, my little fellow," ejaculated Hercules, "may you be?"

"I am your enemy," answered the valiant Pygmy, in his mightiest squeak. "You have slain the enormous Antæus, our brother by the mother's side, and for ages the faithful ally of our illustrious nation. We are determined to put you to death; and for my own part, I challenge you to instant battle, on equal ground."

Hercules was so tickled with the Pygmy's big words and warlike gestures that he burst into a great explosion of laughter, and almost dropped the poor little mite of a creature off the palm of his hand, through the ecstasy and convulsion of his merriment.

"Upon my word," cried he, "I thought I had seen wonders before to-day—hydras with nine heads, stags with golden horns, six-legged men, three-headed dogs, giants with furnaces in their stomachs, and nobody knows what besides. But here, on the palm of my hand, stands a wonder that outdoes them all! Your body, my little friend, is about the size of an ordinary man's finger. Pray, how big may your soul be?"

"As big as your own!" said the Pygmy.

Hercules was touched with the little man's dauntless courage, and could not help acknowledging such a brotherhood with him as one hero feels for another.

"My good little people," said he, making a low obeisance to the grand nation, "not for all the world would I do an intentional injury to such brave fellows as you! Your hearts seem to be so exceedingly great, that, upon my honour, I marvel how your small bodies can contain them. I sue for peace, and, as a condition of it, will take five strides, and be out of your kingdom at the sixth. Good-bye. I shall pick my steps carefully, for fear of treading upon some fifty of you, without knowing it. Ha, ha, ha! Ho, ho, ho! For once Hercules acknowledges himself vanquished."

Some writers say that Hercules gathered up the whole race of Pygmies in his lion's skin, and carried them home to Greece, for the children of King Eurystheus to play with. But this is a mistake. He left them, one and all, within their own territory, where, for aught I can tell, their descendants are alive to the present day.

# TOM SAWYER
# WHITEWASHES A FENCE

## *by* MARK TWAIN

SATURDAY morning was come, and all the summer world was bright and fresh, and brimming with life. There was a song in every heart; and if the heart was young the music issued at the lips. There was cheer in every face and a spring in every step. The locust trees were in bloom and the fragrance of the blossoms filled the air. Cardiff Hill, beyond the village and above it, was green with vegetation, and it lay just far enough away to seem a Delectable Land, dreamy, reposeful, and inviting.

Tom appeared on the side-walk with a bucket of whitewash and a long-handled brush. He surveyed the fence, and all gladness left him and a deep melancholy settled down upon his spirit. Thirty yards of board-fence nine feet high. Life to him seemed hollow and existence but a burden. Sighing, he dipped his brush and passed it along the topmost plank; repeated the operation; did it again; compared the insignificant white-washed streak with the far-reaching continent of unwhitewashed fence, and sat down on a tree-box discouraged. Jim came skipping out at the gate with a tin pail, and singing " Buffalo Gals." Bringing water from the town pump had always been hateful work in Tom's eyes, before, but now it did not strike him so. He remembered that there was company at the pump. White, mulatto, and negro boys and girls were always there waiting their turns, resting, trading playthings, quarrelling, fighting, skylarking. And he remembered that although the pump was only a hundred and fifty yards off, Jim never got back with a bucket of water under an hour—and even then, somebody generally had to go after him. Tom said: " Say, Jim, I'll fetch the water if you'll whitewash some."

Jim shook his head, and said:

" Can't, Mars Tom. Ole missis, she tole me I got to go an' git dis water an' not stop foolin' roun' wid anybody. She say she spec' Mars Tom gwine to ax me to whitewash, an' so she tole me go 'long an' 'tend to my own business—she 'lowed *she'd* 'tend to de whitewashin'."

" Oh, never you mind what she said, Jim. That's the way she always talks. Gimme the bucket—I won't be gone only a minute. *She* won't ever know."

" Oh, I dasn't, Mars Tom. Ole missis she'd take an' tar de head off'n me. 'Deed she would."

" *She !* She never licks anybody—whacks 'em over the head with her thimble—and who cares for that, I'd like to know. She talks awful, but talk don't hurt—anyway, it don't if she don't cry. Jim, I'll give you a marvel. I'll give you a white alley ! "

Jim began to waver.

" White alley, Jim ! And it's a bully taw."

" My ! Dat's a mighty gay marvel, I tell you ! But, Mars Tom, I's powerful 'fraid ole missis——"

" And besides, if you will, I'll show you my sore toe."

Jim was only human—this attraction was too much for him. He put down his pail, took the white alley, and bent over the toe with absorbing interest while the bandage was being unwound. In another moment he was flying down the street with his pail and a tingling rear, Tom was white-washing with vigour, and Aunt Polly was retiring from the field with a slipper in her hand and triumph in her eye.

But Tom's energy did not last. He began to think of the fun he had planned for this day. and his sorrows multiplied. Soon the free boys would come tripping along on all sorts of delicious expeditions, and they would make a world of fun of him for having to work—the very thought of it burnt him like fire. He got out his worldly wealth and examined it—bits of toys, marbles, and trash ; enough to buy an exchange of *work*, maybe, but not half enough to buy so much as half an hour of pure freedom. So he returned his straitened means to his pocket, and gave up the idea of trying to buy the boys. At this dark and hopeless moment an inspiration burst upon him ! Nothing less than a great, magnificent inspiration.

He took up his brush and went tranquilly to work. Ben Rogers hove in sight presently—the very boy, of all boys, whose ridicule he had been dreading. Ben's gait was the hop-skip-and-jump—proof enough that his heart was light and his anticipations high. He was eating an apple, and giving a long, melodious whoop at intervals, followed by a deep-toned ding-dong-dong, ding-dong-dong, for he was personating a steamboat. As he drew near, he slackened speed, took the middle of the street, leaned far over to starboard and rounded to ponderously, and with laborious pomp and circumstance—for he was personating the *Big Missouri*, and considered himself to be drawing nine feet of water. He was a boat, and captain, and engine-bells combined, so he had to imagine himself standing on his own hurricane-deck giving the orders and executing them.

" Stop her, sir ! Ting-a-ling-ling ! " The headway ran almost out and he drew up slowly toward the side-walk.

" Ship up to back ! Ting-a-ling-ling ! " His arms straightened and stiffened down his sides.

" Set her back on the stabboard ! Ting-a-ling-ling ! Chow ! ch-chow-wow ! Chow ! " His right hand, meantime, describing stately circles—for it was representing a forty-foot wheel.

" Let her go back on the labboard ! Ting-a-ling-ling ! Chow-ch-chow-chow ! " The left hand began to describe circles.

" Stop the stabboard ! Ting-a-ling-ling ! Stop the labboard ! Come ahead on the stabboard ! Stop her ! Let your outside turn over slow ! Ting-a-ling-ling ! Chow-ow-ow ! Get out that head-line ! *Lively* now ! Come—out with your spring-line—what're you about there ? Take a turn round that stump with the bight of it ! Stand by that stage, now—let her go ! Done with the engines, sir ! Ting-a-ling-ling ! *Sh't ! sh't ! sh't !* " (trying the gauge-cocks).

Tom went on whitewashing—paid no attention to the steamboat. Ben stared a moment, and then said :

"Hi-*yi*! *You're* up a stump, ain't you!"

No answer. Tom surveyed his last touch with the eye of an artist, then he gave his brush another gentle sweep and surveyed the result, as before. Ben ranged up alongside of him. Tom's mouth watered for the apple, but he stuck to his work. Ben said:

"Hallo, old chap, you got to work, hey?"

*Tom went on whitewashing.*

Tom wheeled suddenly, and said:

"Why, it's you, Ben! I warn't noticing."

"Say—I'm going in a-swimming, I am. Don't you wish you could? But of course you'd rather *work*—wouldn't you? Course you would!"

Tom contemplated the boy a bit, and said:

"What do you call work?"

"Why, ain't *that* work?"

Tom resumed his whitewashing, and answered carelessly: "Well, maybe it is, and maybe it ain't. All I know is, it suits Tom Sawyer."

"Oh, come, now, you don't mean to let on that you *like* it?"

The brush continued to move.

"Like it? Well, I don't see why I oughn't to like it. Does a boy get a chance to whitewash a fence every day?"

That put the thing in a new light. Ben stopped nibbling his apple. Tom swept his brush daintily back and forth—stepped back to note the effect—added a touch here and there—criticised the effect again—Ben watching every move and getting more and more interested, more and more absorbed. Presently he said:

"Say, Tom, let *me* whitewash a little."

Tom considered, was about to consent; but he altered his mind.

"No—no—I reckon it wouldn't hardly do, Ben. You see, Aunt Polly's awful particular about this fence—right here on the street, you know—but if it was the back fence I wouldn't mind and *she* wouldn't. Yes, she's awful particular about this fence; it's got to be done very careful; I reckon there ain't one boy in a thousand, maybe two thousand, that can do it the way it's got to be done."

"No—is that so? Oh, come, now—lemme just try. Only just a little —I'd let *you*, if you was me, Tom."

"Ben, I'd like to, honest injun; but Aunt Polly—well, Jim wanted to do it, but she wouldn't let him; Sid wanted to do it, and she wouldn't let

Sid. Now don't you see how I'm fixed? If you was to tackle this fence and anything was to happen to it——"

"Oh, shucks, I'll be just as careful. Now lemme try. Say—I'll give you the core of my apple."

"Well, here. . . . No, Ben, now don't. I'm afeard——"

"I'll give you *all* of it!"

Tom gave up the brush with reluctance in his face, but alacrity in his heart. And while the late steamer, *Big Missouri*, worked and sweated in the sun, the retired artist sat on a barrel in the shade close by, dangled his legs, munched his apple, and planned the slaughter of more innocents. There was no lack of material; boys happened along every little while; they came to jeer, but remained to whitewash. By the time Ben was fagged out, Tom had traded the next chance to Billy Fisher for a kite, in good repair; and when *he* played out, Johnny Miller bought in for a dead rat and a string to swing it with—and so on, and so on, hour after hour.

And when the middle of the afternoon came, from being a poor poverty-stricken boy in the morning, Tom was literally rolling in wealth. He had beside the things before mentioned, twelve marbles, part of a jews'-harp, a piece of blue bottle-glass to look through, a spool cannon, a key that wouldn't unlock anything, a fragment of chalk, a glass stopper of a decanter, a tin soldier, a couple of tadpoles, six fire-crackers, a kitten with only one eye, a brass door-knob, a dog-collar—but no dog—the handle of a knife, four pieces of orange peel, and a dilapidated old window-sash.

He had a nice, good, idle time all the while—plenty of company—and the fence had three coats of whitewash on it! If he hadn't run out of white-wash, he would have bankrupted every boy in the village.

Tom said to himself that it was not such a hollow world, after all. He had discovered a great law of human action—without knowing it—namely, that in order to make a man or boy covet a thing, it is only necessary to make the thing difficult to attain. If he had been a great and wise philosopher, like the writer of this book, he would now have comprehended that Work consists of whatever a body is *obliged* to do, and that Play consists of whatever a body is not obliged to do. And this would help him to understand why constructing artificial flowers or performing on a treadmill is work, while rolling ten-pins or climbing Mont Blanc is only amusement.

There are wealthy gentlemen in England who drive four-horse passenger-coaches twenty or thirty miles on a daily line, in the summer because the privilege costs them considerable money; but if they were offered wages for the service, that would turn it into work and then they would resign.

The boy mused a while over the substantial change which had taken place in his worldly circumstances, and then wended toward headquarters to report.

# BURIED TREASURE

*From* " Tom Sawyer " *by* MARK TWAIN

ABOUT noon the next day the boys arrived at the dead tree;
they had come for their tools. Tom was impatient to go to
the haunted house; Huck was measurably so, also, but suddenly
said :

"Looky here, Tom, do you know what day it is?"

Tom mentally ran over the days of the week and then quickly
lifted his eyes with a startled look in them :

"My! I never once thought of it, Huck!"

"Well, I didn't, neither, but all at once it popped on to me that it was
Friday."

"Blame it; a body can't be too careful, Huck. We might a got into
an awful scrape, tackling such a thing on a Friday."

"Might! Better say we would! There's some lucky days, maybe, but
Friday ain't."

"Any fool knows that. I don't reckon you was the first that found it
out, Huck."

"Well, I never said I was, did I? And Friday ain't all, neither. I had
a rotten bad dream last night—dreamt about rats."

"No! Sure sign of trouble. Did they fight?"

"No."

"Well, that's good, Huck. When they don't fight, it's only a sign that
there's trouble around, you know. All we got to do is to look mighty sharp
and keep out of it. We'll drop this thing for to-day, and play. Do you
know Robin Hood, Huck?"

" No.  Who's Robin Hood ? "

" Why, he was one of the greatest men that was ever in England—and
the best.  He was a robber."

" Cracky, I wisht I was.  Who did he rob ? "

" Only sheriffs and bishops and rich people and kings, and such like.
But he never bothered the poor.  He loved 'em.  He always divided up
with 'em perfectly square."

" Well, he must a been a brick."

" I bet you he was, Huck.  Oh, he was the noblest man that ever was.
They ain't any such men now, I can tell you.  He could lick any man in
England with one hand tied behind him ;  and he could take his yew bow
and plug a ten-cent piece every time, a mile and a half."

" What's a *yew* bow ? "

" I don't know.  It's some kind of a bow, of course.  And if he hit that
dime only on the edge he would set down and cry—and curse.  But we'll
play Robin Hood—it's noble fun.  I'll learn you."

" I'm agreed."

So they played Robin Hood all the afternoon, now and then casting a
yearning eye down upon the haunted house and passing a remark about the
morrow's prospects and possibilities there.  As the sun began to sink into
the west, they took their way homeward athwart the long shadows of the
trees and soon were buried from sight in the forests of Cardiff Hill.

On Saturday, shortly after noon, the boys were at the dead tree again.
They had a smoke and a chat in the shade, and then dug a little in their last
hole, not with great hope, but merely because Tom said there were so many
cases where people had given up a treasure after getting down within six
inches of it, and then somebody else had come along and turned it up with
a single thrust of a shovel.  The thing failed this time, however, so the boys
shouldered their tools and went away, feeling that they had not trifled with
fortune, but had fulfilled all the requirements that belong to the business
of treasure-hunting.

When they reached the haunted house, there was something so weird
and grisly about the dead silence that reigned there under the baking sun,
and something so depressing about the loneliness and desolation of the
place, that they were afraid, for a moment, to venture in.  Then they crept
to the door and took a trembling peep.  They saw a weed-grown, floorless
room, unplastered, an ancient fireplace, vacant windows, a ruinous staircase ;
and here, there, and everywhere, hung ragged and abandoned cobwebs.  They
presently entered softly, with quickened pulses, talking in whispers, ears alert
to catch the slightest sound, and muscles tense and ready for instant retreat.

In a little while familiarity modified their fears and they gave the place
a critical and interested examination, rather admiring their own boldness,
and wondering at it, too.  Next they wanted to look upstairs.  This was something like cutting off retreat, but they got to daring each other, and of course
there could be but one result—they threw their tools into a corner and made
the ascent.  Up there were the same signs of decay.  In one corner they
found a closet that promised mystery, but the promise was a fraud—there
was nothing in it.  Their courage was up now, and well in hand.  They
were about to go down and begin work when—

" *Sh !* " said Tom.

" What is it ? " whispered Huck, blanching with fright.

" *Sh !* There ! Hear it ? "

" Yes ! O my ! Let's run ! "

" Keep still ! Don't you budge ! They're coming right towards the door."

The boys stretched themselves upon the floor with their eyes to knot-holes in the planking, and lay waiting in a misery of fear.

" They've stopped—— No—coming—— Here they are. Don't whisper another word, Huck. My goodness, I wish I was out of this ! "

Two men entered. Each boy said to himself :

" There's the old deaf and dumb Spaniard that's been about town once or twice lately—never saw t'other man before."

" T'other " was a ragged, unkempt creature, with nothing very pleasant in his face. The Spaniard was wrapped in a *serape* ; he had bushy white whiskers, long white hair flowed from under his sombrero, and he wore green goggles. When they came in, " t'other " was talking in a low voice ; they sat down on the ground, facing the door, with their backs to the wall, and the speaker continued his remarks. His manner became less guarded and his words more distinct as he proceeded.

" No," said he, " I've thought it all over, and I don't like it. It's dangerous."

" Dangerous ! " grunted the " deaf and dumb " Spaniard, to the vast surprise of the boys. " Milk-sop ! "

This voice made the boys gasp and quake. It was Injun Joe's ! There was silence for some time. Then Joe said :

" What's any more dangerous than that job up yonder—but nothing's come of it."

" That's different. Away up the river so, and not another house about. 'Twon't ever be known that we tried, anyway, long as we didn't succeed."

" Well, what's more dangerous than coming here in the daytime ?—anybody would suspicion us that saw us."

" I know that. But there wasn't any other place as handy after that fool of a job. I want to quit this shanty. I wanted to yesterday, only it wasn't any use trying to stir out of here with those infernal boys playing over there on the hill right in full view."

" Those infernal boys " quaked again under the inspiration of this remark, and thought how lucky it was that they had remembered it was Friday and concluded to wait a day. They wished in their hearts they had waited a year. The two men got out some food and made a luncheon. After a long and thoughtful silence, Injun Joe said :

" Look here, lad, you go back up the river where you belong. Wait there till you hear from me. I'll take the chances on dropping into this town just once more, for a look. We'll do that ' dangerous ' job after I've spied around a little and think things look well for it. Then for Texas ! We'll leg it together ! "

This was satisfactory. Both men presently fell to yawning, and Injun Joe said : ·

" I'm dead for sleep ! It's your turn to watch."

He curled down in the weeds and soon began to snore. His comrade stirred him once or twice, and he became quiet. Presently the watcher began to nod; his head drooped lower and lower; both men began to snore now.

The boys drew a long grateful breath. Tom whispered:

" Now's our chance—come ! "

Huck said: " I can't—I'd die if they was to wake."

Tom urged—Huck held back. At last Tom rose slowly and softly, and started alone. But the first step he made wrung such a hideous creak from the crazy floor that he sank down almost dead with fright. He never made a second attempt. The boys lay there counting the dragging moments till it seemed to them that time must be done and eternity growing grey; and then they were grateful to note that at last the sun was setting.

Now one snore ceased. Injun Joe sat up, stared around—smiled grimly upon his comrade, whose head was drooping upon his knees—stirred him up with his foot, and said:

" Here ! You're a watchman, ain't you ? "

" All right, though—nothing's happened."

" My ! Have I been asleep ? "

" Oh, partly, partly. Nearly time for us to be moving, pard. What'll we do with what little swag we've got left ? "

" I don't know—leave it here as we've always done, I reckon. No use to take it away till we start south. Six hundred and fifty in silver's something to carry."

" Well—all right—it won't matter to come here again."

" No—but I'd say come in the night as we used to do—it's better."

" Yes, but look here; it may be a good while before I get the right chance at that job; accidents might happen, 'taint in such a very good place; we'll just regularly bury it—and bury it deep."

" Good idea," said the comrade, who walked across the room, knelt down, raised one of the rearward hearthstones, and took out a bag that jingled pleasantly. He subtracted from it twenty or thirty dollars for himself and as much for Injun Joe, and passed the bag to the latter, who was on his knees in the corner, now, digging with his bowie-knife.

The boys forgot all their fears, all their miseries in an instant. With gloating eyes they watched every movement. Luck ! the splendour of it was beyond all imagination ! Six hundred dollars was money enough to make half a dozen boys rich ! Here was treasure-hunting under the happiest auspices—there would not be any bothersome uncertainty as to where to dig. They nudged each other every moment—eloquent nudges and easily understood, for they simply meant, " Oh, but ain't you glad now we're here ! "

Joe's knife struck upon something.

" Hallo ! " said he.

" What is it ? " said his comrade.

" Half-rotten plank—no, it's a box, I believe. Here, bear a hand, and we'll see what it's here for. Never mind, I've broke a hole."

He reached his hand in and drew it out.

" Man, it's money ! "

Ths two men examined the handful of coins. They were gold. The boys above were as excited as themselves, and as delighted.

Joe's comrade said:

"We'll make quick work of this. There's an old rusty pick over amongst the weeds in the corner, the other side of the fireplace—I saw it a minute ago."

He ran and brought the boys' pick and shovel. Injun Joe took the pick, looked it over critically, shook his head, muttered something to himself, and then began to use it.

Ths box was soon unearthed. It was not very large; it was iron-bound and had been very strong before the slow years had injured it. The men contemplated the treasure a while in blissful silence.

"Pard, there's thousands of dollars here," said Injun Joe.

"'Twas always said that Murrel's gang used around here one summer," the stranger observed.

*He reached in his hand and drew it out, "Man, it's money!"*

"I know it," said Injun Joe; "and this looks like it, I should say."

"Now you won't need to do that job."

The half-breed frowned. Said he:

"You don't know me. Least you don't know all about that thing. 'Tain't robbery altogether—it's revenge!" and a wicked light flamed in his eyes. "I'll need your help in it. When it's finished—then Texas. Go home to your Nance and your kids, and stand by till you hear from me."

"Well, if you say so. What'll we do with this—bury it again?"

"Yes" (ravishing delight overhead). "No! by the great Sachem, no!" (profound distress overhead). "I'd nearly forgot. That pick had fresh earth on it!" (The boys were sick with terror in a moment.) "What business has a pick and a shovel here? What business with fresh earth on them? Who brought them here—and where are they gone? Have you heard anybody?—

seen anybody? What! bury it again and leave them to come and see the ground disturbed? Not exactly—not exactly. We'll take it to my den."

" Why, of course! Might have thought of that before. You mean number one?"

" No—number two—under the cross. The other place is bad—too common."

" All right. It's nearly dark enough to start."

Injun Joe got up and went about from window to window, cautiously peeping out. Presently he said :

" Who could have brought those tools here? Do you reckon they can be upstairs?"

The boys' breath forsook them. Injun Joe put his hand on his knife, halted a moment undecided, and then turned towards the stairway. The boys thought of the closet, but their strength was gone. The steps came creaking up the stairs—the intolerable distress of the situation woke the stricken resolution of the lads—they were about to spring for the closet, when there was a crash of rotten timbers, and Injun Joe landed on the ground amid the debris of the ruined stairway. He gathered himself up cursing, and his comrade said :

" Now what's the use of all that? If it's anybody, and they're up there, let them stay there—who cares? If they want to jump down, now, and get into trouble, who objects? It will be dark in fifteen minutes—and then let them follow us if they want to ; I'm willing. In my opinion, whoever hove those things in here caught a sight of us, and took us for ghosts or devils or something. I'll bet they're running yet."

Joe grumbled awhile ; then he agreed with his friend that what daylight was left ought to be economised in getting things ready for leaving. Shortly afterwards they slipped out of the house in the deepening twilight, and moved towards the river with their precious box.

Tom and Huck rose up, weak but vastly relieved, and stared after them through the chinks between the logs of the house. Follow? Not they—they were content to reach the ground again without broken necks, and take the townward track over the hill. They did not talk much, they were too much absorbed in hating themselves—hating the ill-luck that made them take the spade and the pick there. But for that, Injun Joe never would have suspected. He would have hidden the silver with the gold to wait there till his " revenge " was satisfied, and then he would have had the misfortune to find that money turn up missing. Bitter, bitter luck that the tools were ever brought there! They resolved to keep a look-out for that Spaniard when he should come to town spying out for chances to do his revengeful job, and follow him to " number two," wherever that might be. Then a ghastly thought occurred to Tom :

" Revenge? What if he means *us*, Huck!"

" Oh, don't," said Huck, nearly fainting.

They talked it all over, and as they entered town they agreed to believe that he might possibly mean somebody else—at least that he might at least mean nobody but Tom, since only Tom had testified.

Very, very small comfort it was to Tom to be alone in danger! Company would be a palpable improvement, he thought.

*"Bill's raft's carrying me away!"*

# THE BABY AND THE BEAR

## By C. G. D. ROBERTS

A STIFFISH breeze was blowing over Silverwater. Close inshore where the Babe was fishing, the water was fairly calm—just sufficiently ruffled to keep the trout from distinguishing too clearly that small, intent figure at the edge of the raft. But out in the middle of the lake the little whitecaps were chasing each other boisterously.

The raft was a tiny one, of small logs pinned together with two lengths of spruce pole. It was made for just the use to which the Babe was now putting it. A raft was so much more convenient than a boat or a canoe when the water was still and one had to make long, delicate casts in order to drop one's fly along the edges of the lily-pads. But the Babe was not making long, delicate casts. On such a day as this the somewhat unsophisticated trout of Silverwater demanded no subtleties. They were hungry, and they were feeding close inshore, and the Babe was having great sport. The fish were not large, but they were clean, trim-jawed, bright fellows, some of them not far short of the half-pound; and the only bluebottle in the ointment of the Babe's exultation was that Uncle Andy was not on hand to see his triumph. To be sure, the proof would be in the pan that night, browned in savoury corn-meal after the fashion of the New Brunswick backwoods. But the Babe had in him the makings of a true sportsman, and for him a trout had just one brief moment of unmatchable perfection—the moment when it was taken off the hook and held up to be gloated over or coveted.

The raft had been anchored, carelessly enough, by running an inner corner lightly aground. The Babe's weight, slight as it was, on the outer end, together with his occasional ecstatic, though silent, hoppings up and down, had little by little sufficed to slip the haphazard mooring. This the Babe was far too absorbed to notice.

All at once, having just slipped a nice half-pounder which he had just caught into his fishing-basket, he noticed that the wooded point which had been shutting off his view on the right seemed to have politely drawn back. His heart jumped into his throat. He turned—and there were twenty yards or so of clear water between the raft and the shore. The raft was gently but none too slowly gliding out towards the tumbling whitecaps.

Always methodical, the Babe laid his rod and his basket of fish carefully down on the logs, and then stood for a second or two quite rigid. This was one of those dreadful things which, as he knew, did happen, sometimes, to other people, so that he might read about it. But that it should actually happen to him! Why, it was as if he had been reading some terrible adventure and suddenly found himself thrust trembling into the midst of it. All at once those whitecaps out in the lake seemed to be turning dreadful eyes his way, and clamouring for him. He opened his mouth and gave two piercing shrieks, which cut the air like saws.

"What's the matter?" shouted a very anxious voice from among the trees.

It was the voice of Uncle Andy. He had returned sooner than he was expected. And instantly the Babe's terror vanished. He knew that everything would be all right in just no time.

"I'm afloat. Bill's raft's carrying me away!" he replied in an injured voice.

"Oh!" said Uncle Andy, emerging from the trees and taking in the situation. "You are afloat, are you! I was afraid from the noise you made that you were sinking. Keep your hair on, and I'll be with you in five seconds. And we'll see what Bill's raft has to say for itself after such extraordinary behaviour."

Putting the canoe into the water, he thrust out, overtook the raft in a dozen strokes of his paddle, and proceeded to tow it back to the shore in disgrace.

"What on earth did you make those dreadful noises for," demanded Uncle Andy, "instead of simply calling for me, or Bill, to come and get you?"

"You see, Uncle Andy," answered the Babe, after some consideration, "I was in a hurry, rather, and I thought you or Bill might be in a hurry too, if I made a noise like that, instead of just calling."

"Well, I believe," said Uncle Andy, seating himself on the bank and getting out his pipe, "that at last the unexpected has happened. I believe, in other words, that you are right. I once knew of a couple of youngsters who might have saved themselves and their parents a lot of trouble if they could have made some such sound as you did, at the right time. But they couldn't, or, at least, they didn't; and, therefore, things happened, which I'll tell you about if you would like me to."

The Babe carefully laid his basket of fish in a cool place under some leaves, and then came and sat on the grass at his uncle's feet.

They were an odd pair of youngsters (began Uncle Andy —and paused to get his pipe going).

*Flung her arms about the bear*

They were a curious pair, and they eyed each other curiously. One was about five years old, and the other about five months. One was all pink and white, and ruddy tan, and fluffy gold, and the other all glossy black. One, in fact, was a baby, and the other was a bear.

Neither had come voluntarily into this strange fellowship; and it would have been hard to say which of the pair regarded the other with most suspicion. The bear, to be sure, at five months old was more grown up, more self-sufficing and efficient than the baby at five years; but he had the disadvantage of feeling himself an interloper. He had come to the raft quite uninvited, and found the baby in possession! On that account, of course, he rather expected the baby to show her white little teeth, and snarl at him, and try to drive him off into the water. In that case, he would have resisted desperately, because he was in mortal fear of the boiling, seething flood. But he was very uneasy, and kept up a whimpering that was intended to be conciliatory; for though the baby was small, and by no means ferocious, he regarded her as the possessor of the raft, and it was an axiom of the wilds that very small and harmless-looking creatures might become dangerous when resisting an invasion of their rights.

The baby, on the other hand, was momentarily expecting that the bear would come over and bite her. Why else, if not from some such sinister motive, had he come aboard her raft, when he had been travelling on a perfectly good tree? The tree looked so much more interesting than her bare raft, on which she had been voyaging for over an hour, and of which she was now heartily tired. To be sure, the bear was not much bigger than her own Teddy Bear at home, which she was wont to carry around by one leg, or to spank without ceremony whenever she thought it needed discipline. But the glossy black of the stranger was quite unlike the wild and grubby whiteness of her Teddy, and his shrewd little twinkling eyes were quite unlike the shoe buttons which adorned the face of her uncomplaining pet. She wondered when her mother would come and relieve the strain of the situation.

All at once the raft, which had hitherto voyaged with a discreet delibera-
tion, seemed to become agitated. Boiling upthrusts of the current, caused by
some hidden unevenness on the bottom, shouldered it horridly from beneath,
threatening to tear it apart, and unbridled eddies twisted it this way and that
with sickening lurches. The tree was torn from it and snatched off reluctantly
all by itself, rolling over and over in a fashion that must have made the cub
rejoice to think that he had quitted a refuge so eccentric in its behaviour.
As a matter of fact, the flood was now sweeping the raft over what was, at
ordinary times, a series of low falls, a succession of saw-toothed ledges which
would have ripped the raft to bits. Now the ledges were buried deep under
the immense volume of the freshet. But they were not to be ignored, for all
that. And they made their submerged presence felt in a turmoil that became
more and more terrifying to the two little passengers on the raft.

There was just one point in the raft, one only, that was farther away than
any other part from those dreadful, seething-crested black surges—and that
was the very centre. The little bear backed toward it, whimpering and
shivering, from his corner.

From her corner, directly opposite, the baby too backed towards it,
hitching herself along and eyeing the waves in the silence of terror. They
arrived at the same instant. Each was conscious of something alive and
warm, and soft, and comfortable—with motherly suggestion in the contact.
The baby turned with a sob, and flung her arms about the bear. The bear,
snuggling his narrow black snout under her arm as if to shut out the fearful
sight of the waves, made futile efforts to crawl into a lap that was many sizes
too small to accommodate him.

In some ten minutes more the wild ledges were past. The surges sank to
foaming swirls, and the raft once more journeyed smoothly. The two little
voyagers, recovering from their ecstasy of fear, looked at each other in surprise
—and the bear, slipping off the baby's lap, squatted on his furry haunches,
and eyed her with a sort of guilty apprehension.

Here it was that the baby showed herself of the dominant breed. The bear
was still uneasy and afraid of her. But she, for her part, had no more dread
of him whatever. Through all her panic she had been dimly conscious that
he had been in the attitude of seeking her protection. Now she was quite
ready to give it—quite ready to take possession of him, in fact, as really a sort
of glorified Teddy Bear come to life; and she felt her authority
complete.

Half coaxingly, but quite firmly, and with a note of command in her little
voice which the animal instinctively understood, she said: "Tum here,
Teddy!" and pulled him back unceremoniously to her lap. The bear, with
the influence of her comforting warmth still strong upon him, yielded. It
was nice, when one was frightened and had lost one's mother, to be cuddled
so softly by a creature that was evidently friendly, in spite of the dreaded
man-smell that hung about her. His mother had tried to teach him that that
smell was the most dangerous of all the warning smells his nostrils could
encounter. But the lesson had been most imperfectly learned, and now was
easily forgotten. He was tired, moreover, and wanted to go to sleep. So he
snuggled his glossy, roguish face down into the baby's lap and shut his eyes.
And the baby, filled with delight over such a novel and interesting plaything,

*He bent to the oars*

shook her yellow hair down over his black fur and crooned to him a soft, half-articulate babble of endearment.

The swollen flood was comparatively quiet now, rolling full and turbid over the drowned lands, and gleaming sullenly under a blaze of sun. The bear having gone to sleep, the baby presently followed his example, her rosy face falling forward into his woodsy-smelling black fur. At last, the raft catching in the trees of a submerged islet, came softly to a stop, so softly as not to awaken the little pair of sleepers.

In the meantime two distraught mothers, quite beside themselves with fear and grief, were hurrying downstream in search of the runaway raft and its burden.

The mother of the baby, when she saw the flood sweeping the raft away, was for some moments perilously near to flinging herself in after it. Then her backwoods common sense came to the rescue. She reflected, in time, that she could not swim—while the raft, on the other hand, could and did, and would carry her treasure safely enough for a while. Wading waist-deep through the drowned fields behind the house, she gained the uplands, and rushed dripping along the ridge to the next farm, where, as she knew, a boat was kept. This farmhouse, perched on a bluff, was safe from all floods; and the farmer was at home, congratulating himself. Before he quite knew what was happening, he found himself being dragged to the boat—for his neighbour was a strenuous woman, whom few men in the settlement presumed to argue with, and it was plain to him now that she was labouring under an unwonted excitement. It was not until he was in the boat, with the oars in his hands, that he gathered clearly what had happened. Then, however, he bent to the oars with a will which convinced even that frantic and vehement mother that nothing better could be demanded of him. Dodging logs and wrecks and uprooted trees, the boat went surging down the flood, while the woman sat stiffly erect in the stern, her face white as death, while from time to time she muttered angry phrases which sounded as if the baby had gone off on a pleasure trip without leave and was going to be called to sharp account for it.

The other mother had the deeper and more immediate cause for anguish. Coming to the bank where she had left her cub in the tree, she found the bank caved in, and tree and cub together vanished. Unlike the baby's mother, she could swim; but she knew that she could run faster and farther. In stoic silence she started on a gallop down the half-drowned shores, clambering the heaps of debris, and swimming the deep, still estuaries where the flood had backed up into the valleys of the tributary brooks.

At last, with labouring lungs and pounding heart, she came upon a low, bare bluff overlooking the flood, and saw, not a hundred yards out, the raft with its two little passengers asleep. She saw her cub, lying curled up with his head in the baby's arms, his black fur mixed with the baby's yellow locks. Her first thought was that he was dead—that the baby had killed him and was carrying him off. With a roar of pain and vengeful fury, she rushed down the bluff and hurled herself into the water.

Not till then did she notice that a boat was approaching the raft—a boat

*Clutched the baby hysterically to her breast*

with two human beings in it. It was very much nearer the raft than she was —and travelling very much faster than she could swim. Her savage heart went near to bursting with rage and fear. She knew those beings in the boat could have but one object—the slaughter, or at least the theft, of her little one. She swam frantically, her great muscles heaving as she shouldered the waves apart. But in that race she was hopelessly beaten from the first.

The boat reached the raft, bumped hard upon it—and the baby's mother leaped out while the man, with his boathook, held the two craft close together. The woman, thrusting the cub angrily aside, clutched the baby hysterically to her breast, sobbing over her, and muttering strange threats of what she would do to her when she got her home to punish her for giving so much trouble. The baby did not seem in the least disturbed by these threats—to which the man in the boat was listening with a grin—but when her mother started to carry her to the boat she reached out rebelliously for the cub.

"Won't go wivout my Teddy Bear," she announced tearfully.

"Ye'd better git a move on, Mrs. Murdoch," admonished the man in the boat. "Here's the old b'ar comin' after her young-un."

The woman hesitated. She was willing enough to indulge the baby's whim, the more so as she felt in her heart that it was in some respects her fault that the raft had got away. She measured the distance to that formidable black head, cleaving the waters some thirty yards away.

"Well," said she, "we may's well take the little varmint along, if baby wants him." And she stepped over to pick up the now shrinking cub.

"You quit that an' git into the boat, quick!" ordered the man, in a voice of curt authority. The woman whipped round and stared at him in amazement. She was accustomed to having people defer to her; and Jim Simmons, in particular, she had always considered such a mild-mannered man.

"Get in!" reiterated the man, in a voice that she found herself obeying.

"D'ye want to see baby et up afore yer eyes?" he continued sternly, hiding a grin beneath the sandy droop of his big moustache. And with the baby kicking and wailing, and stretching out her arms to the cub, he rowed rapidly away, just as the old bear dragged herself up on the raft.

"Then Mrs. Murdoch's wrath found words, and she let it flow forth while the man listened as indifferently as if it had been the whistling of the wind. At last she stopped.

"Anything more to say, ma'am?" he asked politely.

Mrs. Murdoch snorted a negative.

"Then all I hev to say," he went on, "is, that to my mind mothers has rights. That there b'ar's a mother, an' she's got feelin's, like you, an' she's come after her young-un, like you—an' I wasn't agoin' to see her robbed of him."

G.G.B.—M

# FEATHERTOP

## by NATHANIEL HAWTHORNE

"DICKON," cried Mother Rigby, " a coal for my pipe ! "

The pipe was in the old dame's mouth when she said these words. She had thrust it there after filling it with tobacco, but without stopping to light it at the hearth—where, indeed, there was no appearance of a fire having been kindled that morning. Forthwith, however, as soon as the order was given, there was an intense red glow out of the bowl of the pipe and a whiff of smoke from Mother Rigby's lips. Whence the coal came and how brought hither by an invisible hand I have never been able to discover.

"Good ! " quoth Mother Rigby, with a nod of her head. " Thank ye, Dickon ! And now for making this scarecrow. Be within call, Dickon, in case I need you again."

The good woman had risen thus early (for as yet it was scarcely sunrise) in order to set about making a scarecrow, which she intended to put in the middle of her corn patch. It was now the latter week in May, and the crows and blackbirds had already discovered the little green, rolled-up leaf of the Indian corn just peeping out of the soil. She was determined, therefore, to contrive as lifelike a scarecrow as ever was seen, and to finish it immediately, from top to toe, so that it should begin its sentinel's duty that very morning.

Now, Mother Rigby (as everybody must have heard) was one of the most cunning and potent witches in New England, and might with very little trouble have made a scarecrow ugly enough to frighten the minister himself. But on this occasion, as she had awakened in an uncommonly pleasant humour, and was further dulcified by her pipe of tobacco, she resolved to produce something fine, beautiful, and splendid rather than hideous and horrible.

" I don't want to set up a hobgoblin in my own corn patch, and almost at my own doorstep," said Mother Rigby to herself, puffing out a whiff of smoke. "I could do it if I pleased, but I'm tired of doing marvellous things, and so I'll keep within the bounds of everyday business, just for variety's sake. Besides, there is no use in scaring the little children for a mile round about, though 'tis true I'm a witch." It was settled, therefore, in her own mind, that the scarecrow should represent a fine gentleman of the period, so far as the materials at hand would allow.

Perhaps it may be as well to enumerate the chief of the articles that went to the composition of this figure. The most important item of all, probably, although it made so little show, was a certain broomstick on which Mother Rigby had taken many an airy gallop at midnight, and which now served the scarecrow by way of a spinal column—or, as the unlearned phrase it, a backbone. One of its arms was a disabled flail which used to be wielded by Goodman Rigby before his spouse worried him out of this troublesome world; the other, if I mistake not, was composed of the pudding stick and a broken rung of a chair, tied loosely together at the elbow. As for its legs, the right was a hoe handle, and the left an undistinguished and miscellaneous stick from the wood pile. Its lungs, stomach, and other affairs of that kind were nothing better than a meal bag stuffed with straw. Thus we have made out the skeleton and entire corporosity of the scarecrow, with the exception of its head, and this was admirably supplied by a somewhat withered and shrivelled pumpkin, in which Mother Rigby cut two holes for the eyes and a slit for the mouth, leaving a bluish-coloured knob in the middle to pass for a nose. It was really quite a respectable face.

"I've seen worse on human shoulders, at any rate," said Mother Rigby. "And many a fine gentleman has a pumpkin head, as well as my scarecrow."

But the clothes in this case were to be the making of the man; so the good old woman took down from a peg an ancient plum-coloured coat of London make and with relics of embroidery on its seams, cuffs, pocket flaps, and button holes, but lamentably worn and faded, patched at the elbows, tattered at the skirts, and threadbare all over. On the left breast was a round hole whence either a star of nobility had been rent away or else the hot heart of some former wearer had scorched it through and through. The neighbours said that this rich garment belonged to the Black Man's wardrobe, and that he kept it at Mother Rigby's cottage for the convenience of slipping it on whenever he wished to make a grand appearance at the governor's table.

To match the coat there was a velvet waistcoat of very ample size, and formerly embroidered with foliage that had been as brightly golden as the maple leaves in October, but which had now quite vanished out of the substance of the velvet. Next came a pair of scarlet breeches once worn by the French governor of Louisbourg, and the knees of which had touched the lower step of the throne of Louis le Grand. The Frenchman had given these small clothes to an Indian pow-wow, who parted with them to the old witch for a gill of strong waters at one of their dances in the forest. Furthermore, Mother Rigby produced a pair of silk stockings and put them on the figure's legs, where they showed as unsubstantial as a dream, with the wooden reality of the two sticks making itself miserably apparent through the holes. Lastly, she put her dead husband's wig on the bare scalp of the pumpkin, and surmounted the whole with a dusty three-cornered hat, in which was stuck the longest tail feather of a rooster.

Then the old dame stood the figure up in a corner of her cottage and chuckled to behold its yellow semblance of a visage, with its nobby little nose thrust into the air. It had a strangely self-satisfied aspect, and seemed to say, " Come, look at me ! "

" And you are well worth looking at, that's a fact ! " quoth Mother Rigby, in admiration at her own handiwork. " I've made many a puppet since I've been a witch, but methinks this is the finest of them all. 'Tis almost too good for a scarecrow. And, by the by, I'll just fill a fresh pipe of tobacco, and then take him out to the corn patch."

While filling her pipe the old woman continued to gaze with almost motherly affection at the figure in the corner. To say the truth, whether it were chance or skill, or downright witchcraft, there was something wonderfully human in this ridiculous shape bedizened with its tattered finery, and, as for the countenance, it appeared to shrivel its yellow surface into a grin— a funny kind of expression betwixt scorn and merriment, as if it understood itself to be a jest at mankind. The more Mother Rigby looked, the better she was pleased.

" Dickon," cried she sharply, " another coal for my pipe ! "

Hardly had she spoken than, just as before, there was a red-glowing coal on the top of the tobacco. She drew in a long whiff, and puffed it forth again into the bar of morning sunshine which struggled through the one dusty pane of her cottage window. Mother Rigby always liked to flavour her pipe with a coal of fire from the particular chimney whence this had been brought. But where that chimney corner might be or who brought the coal from it—further than that the invisible messenger seemed to respond to the name of Dickon—I cannot tell.

" That puppet yonder," thought Mother Rigby, still with her eyes fixed on the scarecrow, " is too good a piece of work to stand all summer in a corn patch frightening away the crows and blackbirds. He's capable of better things. Why, I've danced with a worse one when partners happened to be scarce at our witch meetings in the forest ! What if I should let him take his chance among other men of straw and empty fellows who go bustling about the world ? "

The old witch took three or four more whiffs of her pipe and smiled.

" He'll meet plenty of his brethren at every street corner," continued she. " Well, I didn't mean to dabble in witchcraft to-day further than the lighting of my pipe, but a witch I am, and a witch I'm likely to be, and there's no use trying to shirk it. I'll make a man of my scarecrow, were it only for the joke's sake."

While muttering these words, Mother Rigby took the pipe from her mouth, and thrust it into the crevice which represented the same feature in the pumpkin visage of the scarecrow.

" Puff, darling, puff ! " she said. " Puff away, my fine fellow ! Your life depends upon it ! "

This was a strange exhortation, undoubtedly, to be addressed to a mere thing of sticks, straw, and old clothes, with nothing better than a shrivelled pumpkin for a head, as we know to have been the scarecrow's case. Nevertheless, as we must carefully hold in remembrance, Mother Rigby was a witch of singular power and dexterity; and, keeping this fact duly before our minds, we shall see nothing beyond credibility in the remarkable incidents of our story. Indeed, the great difficulty will be at once got over if we can only bring ourselves to believe that as soon as the old dame bade him puff there came a whiff of smoke from the scarecrow's mouth. It was the very feeblest of whiffs, to be sure, but it was followed by another and another, each more decided than the preceding one.

"Puff away, my pet! Puff away, my pretty one!" Mother Rigby kept repeating, with her pleasantest smile. "It is the breath of life to ye, and you may take my word for it."

Beyond all question, the pipe was bewitched. There must have been a spell either in the tobacco or in the fiercely glowing coal that so mysteriously burned on top of it, or in the pungently aromatic smoke which exhaled from the kindled weed. The figure, after a few doubtful attempts, at length blew forth a volley of smoke extending all the way from the obscure corner into the bar of sunshine. There it eddied and melted away among the motes of dust. It seemed a convulsive effort, for the two or three next whiffs were fainter, although the coal still glowed and threw a gleam over the scarecrow's visage.

The old witch clapped her skinny hands together, and smiled encouragingly upon her handiwork. She saw that the charm had worked well. The shrivelled yellow face, which heretofore had been no face at all, had already a thin fantastic haze, as it were, of human likeness, shifting to and fro across it, sometimes vanishing entirely, but growing more perceptible than ever with the next whiff from the pipe. The whole figure, in like manner, assumed a show of life such as we impart to ill-defined shapes among the clouds, and half deceive ourselves with the pastime of our own fancy.

If we must needs pry closely into the matter, it may be doubted whether there was any real change, after all, in the sordid, worn-out, worthless, and ill-jointed substance of the scarecrow, but merely a spectral illusion and a cunning effect of light and shade, so coloured and contrived as to delude the eyes of most men. The miracles of witchcraft seem always to have had a very shallow subtlety, and at least, if the above explanations do not hit the truth of the process, I can suggest no better.

"Well puffed, my pretty lad!" still cried old Mother Rigby. "Come! another good stout whiff, and let it be with might and main. Puff for thy life, I tell thee! Puff out of the very bottom of thy heart, if any heart thou hast, or any bottom to it. Well done, again! Thou didst suck in that mouthful as if for the pure love of it."

And then the witch beckoned to the scarecrow, throwing so much magnetic potency into her gesture that it seemed as if it must inevitably be obeyed like the mystic call of the loadstone when it summons the iron.

"Why lurkest thou in the corner, lazy one?" said she. "Step forth! Thou hast the world before thee."

In obedience to Mother Rigby's word and extending its arm as if to reach her outstretched hand, the figure made a step forward—a kind of hitch and jerk, however, rather than a step—then tottered, and almost lost its balance. What could the witch expect? It was nothing, after all, but a scarecrow stuck upon two sticks. But the strong-willed old beldam scowled and beckoned, and flung the energy of her purpose so forcibly at this poor combination of rotten wood and musty straw and ragged garments that it was compelled to show itself a man, in spite of the reality of things ; so it stepped into the bar of sunshine. There it stood, with only the thinnest vesture of human similitude about it, through which was evident the stiff, rickety, incongruous, faded, tattered, good-for-nothing patchwork of its substance, ready to sink in a heap upon the floor, as conscious of its own unworthiness to be erect.

But the fierce old hag began to get angry and show a glimpse of her diabolic nature (like a snake's head peeping with a hiss out of her bosom) at this pusillanimous behaviour of the thing which she had taken the trouble to put together.

" Puff away, wretch ! " cried she wrathfully. " Puff, puff, puff, thou thing of straw and emptiness ! thou rag or two ! thou meal bag ! thou pumpkin head ! thou nothing ! Where shall I find a name vile enough to call thee by ? Puff, I say, and suck in thy fantastic life along with the smoke, else I snatch the pipe from thy mouth and hurl thee where that red coal came from."

Thus threatened, the unhappy scarecrow had nothing for it but to puff away for dear life. As need was, therefore, it applied itself lustily to the pipe, and sent forth such abundant volleys of tobacco smoke that the small cottage kitchen became all-vaporous. The one sunbeam struggled mistily through, and could but imperfectly define the image of the cracked and dusty window pane on the opposite wall.

*" Puff away, wretch ! " cried she wrathfully. " Puff, puff, puff, thou thing of straw and emptiness ! "*

Mother Rigby, meanwhile, with one brown arm akimbo and the other stretched toward the figure, loomed grimly amid the obscurity with such port and expression as when she was wont to heave a ponderous nightmare on her victims and stand at the bedside to enjoy their agony. In fear and trembling did this poor scarecrow puff. But its efforts, it must be acknowledged, served an excellent purpose, for with each successive whiff the figure lost more and more of its dizzy and perplexing tenuity and seemed to take denser substance. Its very garments, moreover, partook of the magical change and shone with the gloss of novelty, and glistened with the skilfully embroidered gold that had long ago been rent away ; and, half-revealed among the smoke, a yellow visage bent its lustreless eyes on Mother Rigby.

At last the old witch clenched her fist and shook it at the figure.

" Thou hast a man's aspect," said she sternly ; " have also the echo and mockery of a voice. I bid thee speak ! "

The scarecrow gasped, struggled, and at length emitted a murmur which was so incorporated with its smoky breath that you could scarcely tell whether it were indeed a voice or only a whiff of tobacco.

" Mother," mumbled the poor stifled voice, " be not so awful with me ! I would fain speak, but, being without wits, what can I say ? "

" Thou canst speak, darling, canst thou ? " cried Mother Rigby, relaxing her grim countenance into a smile. " And what shalt thou say, quotha ? Say, indeed ! Art thou of the brotherhood of the empty skull and demandest of me what thou shalt say ? Thou shalt say a thousand things, and, saying them a thousand times over, thou shalt still have said nothing. Be not afraid, I tell thee ! When thou comest into the world—whither I purpose sending thee forthwith—thou shalt not lack the wherewithal to talk. Talk ! Why, thou shalt babble like a mill stream, if thou wilt. Thou hast brains enough for that, I trow."

" At your service, mother," responded the figure.

" And that was well said, my pretty one ! " answered Mother Rigby. " Then thou spakest like thyself, and meant nothing. Thou shalt have a hundred such set phrases, and five hundred to the boot of them. And now, darling, I have taken so much pains with thee, and thou art so beautiful that, by my troth, I love thee better than any witch's puppet in the world ; and I've made them of all sorts—clay, wax, straw, sticks, night fog, morning mist, sea foam, and chimney smoke. But thou art the very best ; so give heed to what I say."

" Yes, kind mother," said the figure, " with all my heart."

" With all thy heart ! " cried the old witch, setting her hands to her sides, and laughing loudly. " Thou hast such a pretty way of speaking ! With all thy heart ! And thou didst put thy hand to the left side of thy waistcoat, as if thou really hadst one ! "

So now, in high good humour with this fantastic contrivance of hers, Mother Rigby told the scarecrow that it must go and play its part in the great world, where not one man in a hundred, she affirmed, was gifted with more real substance than itself. And that he might hold up his head with the best of them, she endowed him on the spot with an unreckonable amount of wealth. It consisted partly of a gold mine in Eldorado, and of ten thousand shares in a broken bubble, and of half a million acres of vineyard at the

North Pole, and of a castle in the air and a chateau in Spain, together with all the rents and income therefrom accruing. She further made over to him the cargo of a certain ship laden with salt of Cadiz which she herself by her necromantic arts had caused to founder ten years before in the deepest part of mid-ocean. If the salt were not dissolved and could be brought to market it would fetch a pretty penny among the fishermen. That he might not lack ready money, she gave him a copper farthing of Birmingham manufacture, being all the coin she had about her, and likewise a great deal of brass, which she applied to his forehead, thus making it yellower than ever.

"With that brass alone," quoth Mother Rigby, "thou canst pay thy way all over the earth. Kiss me, pretty darling! I have done my best for thee."

Furthermore, that the adventurer might lack no possible advantage toward a fair start in life, this excellent old dame gave him a token by which he was to introduce himself to a certain magistrate, member of the council, merchant, and elder of the church (the four capacities constituting but one man), who stood at the head of society in the neighbouring metropolis. The token was neither more nor less than a single word, which Mother Rigby whispered to the scarecrow, and which the scarecrow was to whisper to the merchant.

"Gouty as the old fellow is, he'll run thy errands for thee when once thou hast given him that word in his ear," said the old witch. "Mother Rigby knows the worshipful Justice Gookin, and the worshipful justice knows Mother Rigby!"

Here the witch thrust her wrinkled face close to the puppet's, chuckling irrepressibly, and fidgeting all through her system with delight at the idea which she meant to communicate.

"The worshipful Master Gookin," whispered she, "hath a comely maiden to his daughter. And hark ye, my pet. Thou hast a fair outside, and a pretty wit enough of thine own. Yea, a pretty wit enough! Thou wilt think better of it when thou hast seen more of other people's wits. Now, with thy outside and thy inside, thou art the very man to win a young girl's heart. Never doubt it; I tell thee it shall be so. Put but a bold face on the matter, sigh, smile, flourish thy hat, thrust forth thy leg like a dancing master, put thy right hand to the left side of thy waistcoat, and pretty Polly Gookin is thine own."

All this while the new creature had been sucking in and exhaling the vapoury fragrance of his pipe, and seemed now to continue this occupation as much for the enjoyment it afforded as because it was an essential condition of his existence. It was wonderful to see how exceedingly like a human being it behaved. Its eyes (for it appeared to possess a pair) were bent on Mother Rigby, and at suitable juncture it nodded or shook its head. Neither did it lack words proper for the occasion: "Really!"—"Indeed!"— "Pray tell me!"—"Is it possible!"—"Upon my word!"—"By no means!"—"Oh!"—"Ah!"—"Hem!" and other such weighty utterances as imply attention, inquiry, acquiescence, or dissent on the part of the auditor. Even had you stood by and seen the scarecrow made you could scarcely have resisted the conviction that it perfectly understood the cunning counsels which the old witch poured into its counterfeit of an ear. The more earnestly it applied its lips to the pipe, the more distinctly was its human likeness stamped among visible realities; the more sagacious grew its expression, the more lifelike its gestures and movements, and the more intelligibly audible its voice. Its garments, too, glistened so much the brighter with an illusory magnificence. The very pipe in which burned the spell of all this wonder work ceased to appear as a smoke-blackened earthen stump, and became a meerschaum with painted bowl and amber mouthpiece.

It might be apprehended, however, that, as the life of the illusion seemed identical with the vapour of the pipe, it would terminate simultaneously with the reduction of the tobacco to ashes. But the beldam foresaw the difficulty.

"Hold thou the pipe, my precious one," said she, "while I fill it for thee again."

It was sorrowful to behold how the fine gentleman began to fade back into a scarecrow while Mother Rigby shook the ashes out of the pipe and proceeded to replenish it from her tobacco-box.

"Dickon," cried she, in her high, sharp tone, "another coal for this pipe."

No sooner said than the intensely red speck of fire was glowing within the pipe bowl, and the scarecrow, without waiting for the witch's bidding, applied the tube to his lips and drew in a few short, convulsive whiffs, which soon, however, became regular and equable.

"Now, mine own heart's darling," quoth Mother Rigby, "whatever may happen to thee, thou must stick to thy pipe. Thy life is in it; and that, at least, thou knowest well, if you knowest naught besides. Stick to thy pipe, I say! Smoke, puff, blow thy cloud, and tell people, if any questions be made, that it is for thy health, and that so the physician orders thee to do. And, sweet one, when thou shalt find thy pipe getting low, go apart into some corner, and—first filling thyself with smoke—cry sharply, ' Dickon, a fresh pipe of tobacco!' and ' Dickon, another coal for my pipe!' and have it into thy pretty mouth as speedily as may be, else, instead of a gallant gentleman in a gold-laced coat, thou wilt be but a jumble of sticks and tattered clothes, and a bag of straw and a withered pumpkin. Now depart, my treasure, and good luck go with thee!"

"Never fear, mother," said the figure, in a stout voice, and sending forth a courageous whiff of smoke. "I will thrive if an honest man and a gentleman may."

"Oh, thou will be the death of me!" cried the old witch, convulsed with laughter. "That was well said! If an honest man and a gentleman may! Thou playest thy part to perfection. Get along with thee for a smart fellow, and I will wager on thy head, as a man of pith and substance, with a brain and what they call a heart, and all else that a man should have, against any other thing on two legs. I hold myself a better witch than yesterday, for thy sake. Did I not make thee? And I defy any witch in New England to make such another! Here! take my staff along with thee."

The staff, though it was but a plain oaken stick, immediately took the aspect of a gold-headed cane.

"That gold head has as much sense in it as thine own," said Mother Rigby, "and it will guide thee straight to worshipful Master Gookin's door. Get thee gone, my pretty pet, my darling, my precious one, my treasure;

and if any ask thy name, it is 'Feathertop,' for thou hast a feather in thy hat, and I have thrust a handful of feathers into the hollow of thy head. And thy wig, too, is of the fashion they call 'feather-top,' so be 'Feathertop' thy name."

And, issuing from the cottage, Feathertop strode manfully towards town. Mother Rigby stood at the threshold, well pleased to see how the sunbeams glistened on him, as if all his magnificence were real, and how diligently and lovingly he smoked his pipe, and how handsomely he walked, in spite of a little stiffness of his legs. She watched him until out of sight, and threw a witch benediction after her darling when a turn of the road snatched him from her view.

Betimes in the forenoon, when the principal street of the neighbouring town was just at its acme of life and bustle, a stranger of very distinguished

*A stranger of very distinguished figure was seen on the sidewalk.*

figure was seen on the sidewalk. His port as well as his garments betokened nothing short of nobility. He wore a richly embroidered plum-coloured coat, a waistcoat of costly velvet magnificently adorned with golden foliage, a pair of splendid scarlet breeches, and the finest and glossiest of white silk stockings. His head was covered with a peruke so daintily powdered and adjusted that it would have been sacrilege to disorder it with a hat, which, therefore (and it was a gold-laced hat set off with a snowy feather), he carried beneath his arm. On the breast of his coat glistened a star. He managed his gold-headed cane with an airy grace peculiar to the fine gentleman of the period, and, to give the highest possible finish to his equipment, he had long lace ruffles at his wrist of a most ethereal delicacy, sufficiently avouching how idle and aristocratic must be the hands which they half-concealed.

It was a remarkable point in the accoutrement of this brilliant personage that he held in his left hand a fantastic kind of a pipe with an exquisitely painted bowl and an amber mouthpiece. This he applied to his lips as often as every five or six paces, and inhaled a deep whiff of smoke, which after being retained a moment in his lungs might be seen to eddy gracefully from his mouth and nostrils.

As may well be supposed, the street was astir to find out the stranger's name.

" It is some great nobleman, beyond question," said one of the towns-people. " Do you see the star at his breast ? "

" Nay, it is too bright to be seen," said another. " Yes, he must needs be a nobleman, as you say. But by what conveyance, think you, can his lordship have voyaged or travelled hither ? There has been no vessel from the old country for a month past ; and if he have arrived overland from the southward, pray where are his attendants and equipage ? "

" He needs no equipage to set off his rank," remarked a third. " If he came among us in rags, nobility would shine through a hole in his elbow. I never saw such dignity of aspect. He has the old Norman blood in his veins, I warrant him."

" I rather take him to be a Dutchman or one of your High Germans," said another citizen. " The men of those countries have always the pipe at their mouths."

" And so has a Turk," answered his companion. " But in my judgment, this stranger hath been bred at the French court, and hath there learned politeness and grace of manner, which none understand so well as the nobility of France. That gait, now ! A vulgar spectator might deem it stiff —he might call it a hitch and a jerk—but, to my eye, it hath an unspeakable majesty, and must have been acquired by constant observation of the deportment of the Grand Monarque. The stranger's character and office are evident enough. He is a French ambassador come to treat with our rulers about the cession of Canada."

" More probably a Spaniard," said another, " and hence his yellow complexion. Or, most likely, he is from Havana or from some port on the Spanish main, and comes to make investigation about the piracies which our governor is thought to connive at. Those settlers in Peru and Mexico have skins as yellow as the gold which they dig out of their mines."

" Yellow or not," cried a lady, " he is a beautiful man ! So tall, so slender ! Such a fine, noble face, with so well-shaped a nose and all that delicacy of expression about the mouth ! And, bless me ! How bright his star is ! It positively shoots out flames."

" So do your eyes, fair lady," said the stranger, with a bow and a flourish of his pipe, for he was just passing at the instant. " Upon my honour, they have quite dazzled me ! "

" Was ever so original and exquisite a compliment ? " murmured the lady, in an ecstasy of delight.

Amid the general admiration excited by the stranger's appearance there were only two dissenting voices. One was that of an impertinent cur which, after sniffing at the heels of the glistening figure, put its tail between its legs and skulked into its master's back yard, vociferating an execrable howl.

The other dissentient was a young child who squalled at the fullest stretch of his lungs and babbled some unintelligible nonsense about a pumpkin.

Feathertop, meanwhile, pursued his way along the street. Except for the few complimentary words to the lady, and now and then a slight inclination of the head in requital of the profound reverences of the bystanders, he seemed wholly absorbed in his pipe. With a crowd gathering behind his footsteps, he finally reached the mansion house of the worshipful Justice Gookin, entered the gate, ascended the steps of the front door and knocked. In the interim before his summons was answered the stranger was observed to shake the ashes out of his pipe.

" What did he say in that sharp voice ? " inquired one of the spectators.

" Nay, I know not," answered his friend. " But the sun dazzles my eyes strangely. How dim and faded his lordship looks all of a sudden ! Bless my wits, what is the matter with me ? "

" The wonder is," said the other, " that his pipe, which was out only an instant ago, should be all alight again, and with the reddest coal I ever saw. There is something mysterious about this stranger. What a whiff of smoke was that ! ' Dim and faded,' did you call him ? Why, as he turns about the star on his breast is all ablaze."

" 'Tis, indeed," said his companion, " and it will go near to dazzle pretty Polly Gookin, whom I see peeping at it out of the chamber window."

The door being now opened, Feathertop turned to the crowd, made a stately bend of his body, like a great man acknowledging the reverence of the meaner sort, and vanished into the house. There was a mysterious kind of smile—if it might not better be called a grin or grimace—upon his visage, but, of all the throng that beheld him, not an individual appears to have possessed insight enough to detect the illusive character of the stranger, except a little child and a cur dog.

Polly Gookin was a damsel of a soft, round figure, with light hair and blue eyes, and a fair rosy face which seemed neither very shrewd nor very simple. This young lady had caught a glimpse of the glistening stranger while standing at the threshold, and had forthwith put on a laced cap, a string of beads, her finest kerchief, and her stiffest damask petticoat, in preparation for the interview. Hurrying from her chamber to the parlour, she had ever since been viewing herself in the large looking-glass and practising pretty airs—now a smile, now a ceremonious dignity of aspect, and now a softer smile than the former, kissing her hand, likewise, tossing her head, and managing her fan, while within the mirror an unsubstantial little maid repeated every gesture and did all the foolish things that Polly did, but without making her ashamed of them.

No sooner did Polly hear her father's gouty footsteps approaching the parlour door, accompanied with the stiff clatter of Feathertop's high-heeled shoes, than she seated herself bolt upright and began warbling a song.

" Polly ! Daughter Polly ! " cried the merchant. " Come hither, child."

Master Gookin's aspect, as he opened the door, was doubtful.

" This gentleman," continued he, presenting the stranger, " is the Chevalier Feathertop—nay, I beg his pardon, my Lord Feathertop—who hath brought me a token of remembrance from an ancient friend of mine. Pay your duty to his lordship, child, and honour him as his quality deserves."

After these few words of introduction the worshipful magistrate immediately quitted the room.

Feathertop paused, and, throwing himself into an imposing attitude, seemed to summon the fair girl to survey his figure and resist him longer if she could. His star, his embroidery, his buckles, glowed at that instant with unutterable splendour ; the picturesque hues of his attire took a richer depth of colouring ; there was a gleam and polish over his whole presence betokening the perfect witchery of well-ordered manners. The maiden raised her eyes and suffered them to linger upon her companion with a bashful and admiring gaze. Then, as if desirous of judging what value her own simple comeliness might have side by side with so much brilliancy, she cast a glance toward the full-length looking-glass, in front of which they happened to be standing. It was one of the truest plates in the world, and incapable of flattery. No sooner did the images therein reflected meet Polly's eye than she shrieked, shrank from the stranger's side, gazed at him for a moment in the wildest dismay, and sank insensible upon the floor. Feathertop, likewise, had looked toward the mirror and there beheld, not the glittering mockery of his outside show, but a picture of the sordid patchwork of his real composition stripped of all witchcraft.

Mother Rigby was seated by her kitchen hearth in the twilight of this eventful day, and had just shaken the ashes out of a new pipe, when she heard a hurried tramp along the road. Yet it did not seem so much the tramp of human footsteps as the clatter of sticks or the rattling of dry bones.

" Ha ! " thought the old witch ; " what step is that ? Whose skeleton is out of its grave now, I wonder ? "

A figure burst headlong into the cottage door. It was Feathertop. His pipe was still alight, the star still flamed upon his breast, the embroidery still glowed upon his garments, nor had he lost in any degree or manner that could be estimated the aspect that assimilated him with our mortal brotherhood. But yet, in some indescribable way (as is the case with all that has deluded us when once found out), the poor reality was felt beneath the cunning artifice.

" What has gone wrong ? " demanded the witch. " Did yonder sniffing hypocrite thrust my darling from his door ? The villain ! I'll set twenty fiends to torture him till he offer thee his daughter on his bended knees ! "

" No, mother," said Feathertop despondingly, " it was not that. But," he added, after a brief pause, and then a howl of self-contempt, " I've seen myself, mother ! I've seen myself for the wretched, ragged, empty thing I am. I'll exist no longer."

Snatching the pipe from his mouth, he flung it with all his might against the chimney, and at the same instant sank upon the floor, a medley of straw and tattered garments, with some sticks protruding from the heap and a shrivelled pumpkin in the midst. The eyeholes were now lustreless, but the rudely carved gap that just before had been a mouth still seemed to twist itself into a despairing grin, and was so far human.

" Poor fellow ! " quoth Mother Rigby, with a rueful glance at the relics of her ill-fated contrivance. " My poor dear pretty Feathertop ! There are thousands upon thousands of coxcombs and charlatans in the world made up of just such a jumble of worn-out, forgotten, and good-for-nothing trash as he was, yet they live in fair repute, and never see themselves for what they are. And why should my poor puppet be the only one to know himself and perish for it?"

While thus muttering the witch had filled a fresh pipe of tobacco, and held the stem between her fingers, as doubtful whether to thrust it into her own mouth or Feathertop's.

"Poor Feathertop!" she continued. "I could easily give him another chance, and send him forth again to-morrow. But no! His feelings are too tender—his sensibilities too deep. He seems to have too much heart to bustle for his own advantage in such an empty and heartless world. Well, well! I'll make a scarecrow of him, after all. 'Tis an innocent and useful vocation, and will suit my darling well; and if each of his human brethren has as fit a one, 'twould be the better for mankind. And, as for this pipe of tobacco, I need it more than he."

So saying, Mother Rigby put the stem between her lips.

"Dickon," cried she, in her sharp tone, "another coal for my pipe!"

---

# Daybreak

*by* H. W. LONGFELLOW

A WIND came up out of the sea,
And said, "O mists, make room for me."

It hailed the ships, and cried, "Sail on,
Ye mariners, the night is gone."

And hurried landward far away,
Crying, "Awake! it is the day."

It said unto the forest, "Shout!
Hang all your leafy banners out!"

It touched the wood-bird's folded wing,
And said, "O bird, awake and sing."

And o'er the farms, "O chanticleer,
Your clarion blow; the day is near."

It whispered to the fields of corn,
"Bow down, and hail the coming morn."

It shouted through the belfry-tower,
"Awake, O bell! proclaim the hour."

It crossed the churchyard with a sigh,
And said, "Not yet! in quiet lie."

# LITTLE Snow-White

## *by* THE BROTHERS GRIMM

ONCE upon a time in the depth of winter, when the flakes of snow were falling like feathers from the clouds, a Queen sat at her palace window, which had an ebony black frame, stitching her husband's shirts. While she was thus engaged, and looking out at the flakes, she pricked her finger, and three drops of blood fell upon the snow. And because the red looked so well upon the white, she thought to herself, " Had I now but a child as white as this snow, as red as this blood, and as black as the wood of this frame ! "

Soon afterwards a little daughter was born to her, who was as white as snow, and red as blood, and with hair as black as ebony, and thence she was named " Snow-White "; but when the child was born the mother died.

About a year afterwards the King married another wife, who was very beautiful, but so proud and haughty that she could not bear any one to be prettier than herself. She possessed a wonderful mirror, and when she stepped before it, and said :

> " Oh, mirror, mirror on the wall,
> Who is the fairest of us all ? "

it replied :

> " Thou art the fairest, lady Queen."

Then she was pleased, for she knew that the mirror spoke truly.

Little Snow-White, however, grew up, and became pretty and prettier, and when she was seven years old she was as beautiful as the noon-day, and fairer far than the Queen herself. When the Queen now asked her mirror :

> " Oh mirror, mirror on the wall,
> Who is the fairest of us all ? "

it replied :

> " Thou wert the fairest, lady Queen ;
> Snow-White is fairest now, I ween."

This answer so vexed the Queen that she became quite yellow with envy.

From that hour, whenever she perceived Snow-White, her heart was hardened against her, and she hated the maiden.

Her envy and jealousy increased, so that she had no rest day nor night, till at length she said to a Huntsman, "Take the child away into the forest; I will never look upon her again. You must kill her, and bring me her heart and tongue for a token."

The Huntsman listened, and took the maiden away; but, when he drew out his knife to kill her, she began to cry, saying, "Ah, dear Huntsman, give me my life! I will run into the wild forest, and never come home again."

This speech softened his heart, and her beauty so touched him that he had pity on her, and said, "Well, run away, then, poor child;" but he thought to himself, "The wild beasts will soon devour you." Still, he felt as if a stone had been taken from his heart, because her death was not by his hand. Just at that moment a young boar came roaring along to the spot, and as soon as he caught sight of it the Huntsman pursued it, and, killing it, took out the tongue and heart, and carried them to the Queen for a token of his deed.

Now poor little Snow-White was left motherless and alone, and overcome with grief; she was bewildered at the sight of so many trees, and knew not which way to turn. Presently she set off running, and ran over stones and through thorns; and wild beasts bellowed as she passed them, but they did her no harm. She ran on till her feet refused to go farther, and, as it was getting dark, she saw a little house near, and entered in to rest.

In this cottage everything was very small, but more neat and elegant than I can tell you. In the middle stood a little table with a white cloth over it, and seven little plates upon the cloth, each plate having a spoon and a knife and fork, and there were also seven little mugs. Against the wall were seven little beds ranged in a row, each covered with a white counterpane. Snow-White, being both hungry and thirsty, ate a morsel of bread and meat from each plate, and drank a little out of each mug, for she did not wish to take away the whole share of any one.

After that, because she was so tired, she laid herself down on one bed, but it did not suit; she tried another, but that was too long; a fourth was too short, a fifth too hard, but the seventh was just the thing, and, tucking herself up in it, she went to sleep, first commending herself to God.

When it became quite dark the lords of the cottage came home, seven Dwarfs, who dug and delved for ore in the mountains. They first lighted seven little lamps, and perceived at once—for they illuminated the whole apartment—that somebody had been in, for everything was not in the order in which they had left it.

The first Dwarf asked, "Who has been sitting on my chair?" The second, "Who has been eating off my plate?" The third, "Who has been nibbling at my bread?" The fourth, "Who has been at my meat?" The fifth, "Who has been meddling with my fork?" The sixth grumbled out, "Who has been cutting with my knife?" The seventh said, "Who has been drinking out of my mug?" Then the first, looking round, began again. "Who has been lying in my bed?" he asked, for he saw that the sheets were tumbled. At these words the others came, and, looking at their beds, cried out too, "Some one has been lying in our beds!"

But the seventh little man, running up to his, saw Snow-White asleep; so he called his companions, who shouted with wonder, and held up their seven lamps, so that the light fell upon the maiden.

"Oh! oh!" exclaimed they, "what a beauty she is!" and they were so much delighted that they would not awaken her, but left her to her repose, and the seventh dwarf, in whose bed she was, slept with each of his fellows one hour, and so passed the night.

As soon as morning dawned, Snow-White awoke, and was quite frightened when she saw the seven little men; but they were very friendly, and asked her what she was called. "My name is Snow-White," was her reply.

"Why have you entered our cottage?" they asked.

Then she told them how her stepmother would have had her killed, but the Huntsman had spared her life; and how she had wandered about the whole day until at last she had found their house. When her tale was finished, the Dwarfs said, "Will you see after our household—be our cook, make the beds, wash, sew, and knit for us, and keep everything in neat order? If so, we will keep you here, and you shall want for nothing."

And Snow-White answered, "Yes, with all my heart and will;" and so she remained with them, and kept their house in order. In the mornings the Dwarfs went into the mountains and searched for ore and gold, and in the evenings they came home and found their meals nicely cooked ready for them.

During the day the maiden was left alone, and therefore the good Dwarfs warned her, and said, "Be careful of your stepmother, who will soon know of your being here; therefore, let nobody enter the cottage."

The Queen, meanwhile, supposing she had eaten the heart and tongue of her stepdaughter, did not think but that she was above all comparison the most beautiful of every one around. One day she stepped before her mirror, and said:

> "Oh, mirror, mirror on the wall,
> Who is the fairest of us all?"

and it replied:

> "Thou wert the fairest, lady Queen;
> Snow-White is fairest now, I ween.
> Amid the forest, darkly green,
> She lives with Dwarfs—the hills between."

This reply annoyed her, for she knew that the mirror spoke the truth, and she perceived that the Hunstman had deceived her, and that Snow-White was still alive. Now the Queen thought and thought how she should accomplish her purpose, for so long as she was not the fairest in the whole country, jealousy left her no rest.

At last a thought struck her, and she dyed her face and clothed herself as a pedlar woman, so that no one could recognise her. In this disguise she went over the seven hills to the seven Dwarfs, knocked at the door of the hut, and called out, "Fine goods for sale! beautiful goods for sale!"

Snow-White peeped out of the window, and said, "Good-day, my good woman. What have you to sell?" "Fine goods, beautiful goods!" the Queen replied, "stays of all colours;" and she held up a pair that was made of variegated silks.  " I may let in this honest woman," thought Snow-White ;  and she unbolted the door and bargained for one pair of stays.  " You can't think, my dear, how it becomes you ! " exclaimed the old woman.  " Come, let me lace it up for you."

Snow-White expected no evil, and let her do as she wished, but the old woman laced her up so quickly and so tightly that all her breath went, and she fell down like one dead.  " Now," thought the Queen, hastening away ; " now am I once more the most beautiful of all ! "

Not long after her departure, at eventide, the seven Dwarfs came home, and were much frightened at seeing their dear little maid lying on the ground, neither moving nor breathing, as if she were dead.  They raised her up, and when they saw she was laced too tightly they cut the stays in pieces, and presently she began to breathe, and little by little revived.

When the Dwarfs heard what had taken place, they said, " The old pedlar woman was no other than your wicked stepmother : take care of yourself, and let no one enter when we are not with you."

Meanwhile, the Queen had reached home, and, going before her mirror, she repeated her usual words :

> " Oh, mirror, mirror on the wall,
> Who is the fairest of us all ? "

and it replied as before :

> " Thou wert the fairest, lady Queen ;
> Snow-White is fairest now, I ween.
> Amid the forest darkly green,
> She lives with Dwarfs—the hills between."

As soon as it had finished all the blood rushed to her heart, for she was angry to hear that Snow-White was yet living.  " But now," thought she to herself, " will I contrive something which shall destroy her completely."

## Mirror, Mirror on the Wall

Thus saying, she made a poisoned comb, by arts which she understood, and then, disguising herself, she took the form of an old widow. She went over the seven hills to the house of the seven Dwarfs, and, knocking at the door, called out, " Good wares to sell to-day ! "

Snow-White peeped out, and said, " You must go farther, for I dare not let you in."

" Still, you may look," said the old woman, drawing out her poisoned comb and holding it up. The sight pleased the maiden so much that she allowed herself to be persuaded, and opened the door. As soon as she had made a purchase, the old woman said, " Now, let me for once comb you properly," and Snow-White consented ; but scarcely was the comb drawn through the hair when the poison began to work, and the maiden fell down senseless. " You pattern of beauty," cried the wicked Queen, " it is now all over with you ; " and so saying, she departed.

Fortunately, evening came on, and the seven Dwarfs returned, and as soon as they saw Snow-White lying like dead upon the ground, they suspected the Queen, and discovering the poisoned comb, immediately drew it out, and the maiden reviving related all that had happened. Then they warned her again against the wicked stepmother, and bade her to open the door to nobody.

Meanwhile, the Queen, on her arrival home, had consulted her mirror, and received the same answer as twice before. This made her tremble and foam with rage and jealousy, and she swore Snow-White should die, if it cost her her own life. Thereupon she went into an inner secret chamber where no one could enter, and made an apple of the most deep and subtle poison. Outwardly it looked nice enough, and had rosy cheeks which would make the mouth of every one who looked at it water ; but whoever ate the smallest piece would surely die.

As soon as the apple was ready, the Queen dyed her face and clothed herself like a peasant's wife, and then over the seven mountains to the seven Dwarfs she made her way. She knocked at the door, and Snow-White,

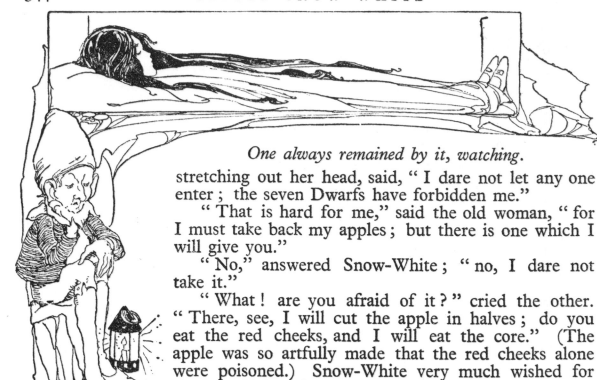

*One always remained by it, watching.*

stretching out her head, said, " I dare not let any one enter ; the seven Dwarfs have forbidden me."

" That is hard for me," said the old woman, " for I must take back my apples ; but there is one which I will give you."

" No," answered Snow-White ; " no, I dare not take it."

" What ! are you afraid of it ? " cried the other. " There, see, I will cut the apple in halves ; do you eat the red cheeks, and I will eat the core." (The apple was so artfully made that the red cheeks alone were poisoned.) Snow-White very much wished for the beautiful apple, and when she saw the woman eating the core could no longer resist, but, putting out her hand, took the poisoned part. Scarcely had she placed a piece in her mouth when she fell dead upon the ground.

Then the Queen, looking at her with glittering eyes, and laughing bitterly, exclaimed, " White as snow, red as blood, black as ebony ! This time the Dwarfs cannot reawaken you."

When she reached home and consulted her mirror :

" Oh, mirror, mirror on the wall,
Who is the fairest of us all ? "

it answered :

" Thou art the fairest, lady Queen."

Then her envious heart was at rest, as peacefully as an envious heart can rest.

When the Dwarfs returned home in the evening, they found Snow-White lying on the ground, and there appeared to be no life in her body ; she seemed quite dead. They raised her up, and searched if they could find anything poisonous, unlaced her, and even uncombed her hair, and washed her with water and with wine ; but nothing availed—the dear child was really and truly dead. Then they laid her upon a bier, and all seven placed themselves around it, and wept and wept for three days without ceasing.

Afterwards they would bury her ; but she looked still fresh and life-like, and even her cheeks were still red, so they said to one another, " We cannot bury her in the black ground," and they ordered a case to be made of transparent glass. In this one could view the body on all sides, and the Dwarfs wrote her name with golden letters upon the glass, saying that she was a King's daughter. Then they placed the glass case upon the ledge of a rock, and one always remained by it watching. Even the beasts bewailed the loss

"*See, I will cut the apple in halves; do you eat the red cheeks, and I will eat the core*," said the old woman.

B.F.                                                                 T

of Snow-White; first came an owl, then a raven, and last of all a dove.

For a long time Snow-White lay peacefully in her case, and changed not, but looked as if she were only asleep, for she was still white as snow, red as blood, and black-haired as ebony. By and by it happened that a King's son was travelling in the forest, and came to the Dwarfs' house to pass the night. He perceived the glass case upon the rock, and the beautiful maiden lying within, and he read also the golden inscription.

When he had examined it, he said to the Dwarfs, " Let me have this case, and I will pay what you like for it."

But the Dwarfs replied, " We will not sell it for all the gold in the world."

" Then give it to me," said the Prince, " for I cannot live without Snow-White. I will honour and protect her so long as I live."

When the Dwarfs saw he was so much in earnest, they pitied him, and at last gave him the case, and the Prince ordered it to be carried away on the shoulders of his attendants. Presently it happened that they stumbled over a rut, and with the shock the piece of poisoned apple which lay in Snow-White's mouth fell out. Almost immediately she opened her eyes, and, raising the lid of the glass case, rose up, and asked, " Where am I ? "

Full of joy, the Prince answered, " You are safe with me ; " and he related what she had suffered, and how he would rather have her than any other for his wife ; and he asked her to accompany him to the castle of the King his father. Snow-White consented, and when they arrived there the wedding between them was celebrated as speedily as possible, with all the splendour and magnificence proportionate to the happy event.

By chance the stepmother of Snow-White was also invited to the wedding, and, when she was dressed in all her finery to go, she first stepped in front of her mirror, and asked :

> " Oh, mirror, mirror on the wall,
> Who is the fairest of us all ? "

and it replied :

> " Thou wert the fairest, O lady Queen ;
> The Prince's bride is more fair, I ween."

At these words she was in a fury, and so terribly mortified that she knew not what to do with herself. At first she resolved not to go to the wedding, but she could not resist the wish for a sight of the young Queen, and as soon as she entered she recognised Snow-White, and was so terrified with rage and astonishment that she remained rooted to the ground. Then a pair of red-hot iron shoes were brought in with a pair of tongs and set before her, and these she was forced to put on and to dance in till she died.

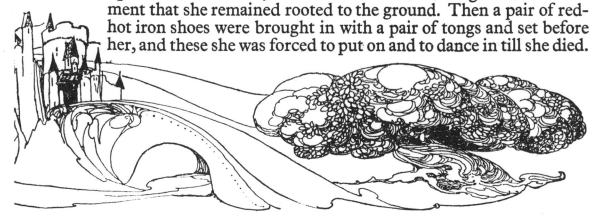

# Guy of Warwick

## by
## W. J. Thoms

HE story of Guy of Warwick, one of the most popular of the early English romances, was first printed before the middle of the sixteenth century.

In the sixth year of the reign of King Edgar the Great, Guy was born in the city of Warwick. His father, Segard, was a gentleman of Northumberland, in which county, during the time of the Mercian kings, he had been the possessor of a fair estate ; but, when the arms of Edgar prevailed over the King of Mercia, as well as the rest of the Saxon kings, Segard lost all his property.

Afterwards, seeking to mend his fortunes in our more southern climates, he came to Warwick, and was well received by the people of every class, especially by Earl Rohand, who was then the king's governor, both of the town and of the castle.

At that time Rohand was one of the most powerful nobles in England, brave, wise, and liberal, and uniting, in his own person, the Earldoms of Warwick, of Oxford, and of Rockingham. The proudest barons of the land respected the laws of this great noble, who made Segard his steward and counsellor, and raised him to high power.

Segard, whose wife was the daughter of an eminent knight in the town, had a son, Guy, who, even as a small boy, gave evidence of enormous strength and courage. In running, wrestling, and similar games he exceeded boys that were both older and bigger than himself, and, as he grew to manhood, he delighted in hardships, and such exercises as needed both strength and labour. When he was only sixteen years old, there were few durst encounter with him ; for then he would use to enter the lists and always came off victorious.

First among all the pages of the Earl of Warwick the youthful Guy stood, in manly beauty, in learning, and in warlike ardour, which, added to grace and addresse at " bordes " (tables), at tournaments, and at chess, made him worthy of knighthood.

Such was the state of Rohand's court, when he was called upon to celebrate, according to annual custom, the feast of Pentecost. This splendid ceremony, which drew together all the nobility of the country, began by the celebration of high mass, which was followed by a grand banquet, to which, again, succeeded the amusement of the chase, or of dancing. The following days, for the great festivals of the year generally occupied a whole fortnight, were marked by jousts, and tournaments, and other warlike diversions, as well as by hawking and hunting.

Guy, who had been raised to the honour of being the earl's principal cup-bearer, had taken his station near his lord, and he now received instruction to go to the rooms of Felice, the earl's daughter, and to superintend the service of the ladies during dinner.

In the old chronicle one reads the most marvellous accounts of Felice's beauty and learning, while she was also one of the richest heiresses in England. It is easy, therefore, to understand that many famous knights of noble birth sought her hand in marriage. Felice, however, promised her hand to Guy, when he should have been made a knight, and proved his valour in a suitable number of tournaments.

The knighting of Guy at the hand of Earl Rohand was a very splendid affair :

After the ceremony, Sir Guy, as he now was, begged his father to let him pass without delay into foreign countries, for the purpose of proving his valour. Segard, unable to refuse his consent to this proposal, gave him two knights, Sir Thorold and Sir Urry, a number of attendants suitable to his rank, and a large sum of money. The faithful Heraud, too, formed one of the party, which, embarking in a stout ship, arrived safely off the coast of Normandy.

Now Guy's main object was to seek warlike adventures, so that he might prove worthy of Felice, and, taking the captain of the ship with him, he went ashore and put up at an inn.

They had not been there long, before the loud shouts of a number of people, with the louder noise of drums and trumpets, arose outside, upon which Guy, sending for the landlord, demanded to know the reason for this tumult.

His host replied that a beautiful young lady, named Dorinda, had been accused by three knights of treason against the Duke, and that, unless she could find a champion able and willing to overcome her accusers in open fight, she was to be put to death.

Having learned that the lady was really innocent of any crime, Guy ordered his horse and his arms to be got ready, took leave of his host, directed the captain, who would willingly have gone with him, to await his return, and rode off alone to the place of combat. Here he saw Dorinda fastened to the stake, her friends weeping around her, and the three false knights, well armed and well mounted, awaiting proudly in the lists.

One of them, wheeling his horse, demanded loudly whether any knight would break a lance in defence of the lady. " Let him come forth," he said, " and I shall soon make him repent his rash undertaking."

Hereupon, Guy, all on fire, entered the lists, and riding up cried, " Here is a man, false knight, that dares do battle for a lady's honour, and know, that I so little fear you, that I will revenge her quarrel, not singly, with one only, but with you altogether, so that the matter may be sooner ended."

After this bold speech the trumpets sounded, both knights couched their spears, and so encountered each other, and with so much fury that the earth trembled under them.  Guy, however, had so much the advantage that, coming with his spear directly on the other's breast, he forced a passage through it to his heart, so that he straight fell down, and with one groan expired.

*" Here is a man, false knight, that dares do battle for a lady's honour."*

His two companions, vowing revenge, charged with desperate fury on Guy, who, drawing out his trusty blade, soon made them feel that it was like the sword of fate, which there was no withstanding ; so that one fell dead by the side of his leader, and the other, being wounded, begged for his life, and confessed that he had received a heavy bribe to bear false witness against Dorinda.

Guy now unbound the lady, who joyfully embraced his knees, and calling down thousands of blessings on his head, offered him her whole fortune as a reward, but he answered that he desired no payment, and that what he did was " out of love to virtue and to honour."

Gently bidding her farewell, he rode back to the coast, and there related to the captain what had befallen him.  Then, judging it prudent not to stay longer in that harbour, they weighed their anchors and sailed out to sea.

# A SEA-FIGHT

ALTHOUGH Guy and the captain made great haste to get out of the harbour, yet were they not altogether out of danger. The duke's son was so angered at the overthrow of his knights, and the death of two of them, that he resolved to wreak his malice on the head of Guy, for doing him so grave an injury.

Secretly arming sixty of his servants and attendants, he made all the haste possible to the port, where he had information Guy's ship lay, thinking to surprise him there. Finding that Guy had set sail three hours before his coming, his disappointment made his rage boil higher, especially believing Guy fled for fear of him, and that he was also conveying the lady away with him.

Whereupon, going on board a stout vessel that lay in the harbour, he commanded the sailors to weigh anchor, and make all the sail they could after the English ship, which, by a small boat just come into port, was sailed to the eastward. The mariners immediately got ready, and, having a fair wind, and the ship being a very good sailer, in the running of a glass and a half they came within sight of the ship wherein Guy was.

No sooner was the French ship come in sight, but the mariners gave notice of it to their captain, who, viewing of the ship with his prospect glass, told Guy that he was sure they were pursued, and that the enemy, being treble their number, their best way was to hoist up all their sails, and to make the best of their way; and that then, by the help of the evening, he did not doubt but to get clear of them.

" Why, how many ships," said Guy, " are they that chase us ? "

" Why," said the captain, " I see no more than one at present, but it is a good stout ship, and carries thrice the men on board that we do."

" Well, well," said Guy, " if that be all, be of good courage; and the first thing we do, let us tack about, and meet them like brave Englishmen. I will bear the brunt of war myself alone. I would not for the crown of France, I swear it, have it reported that Guy ever fled."

This speech had such effect upon the seamen that one and all cried, " Let us engage them straight."

Nor did the captain now appear less willing. And so they cried, " All hands aloft," to put them in a posture of defence; which they had no sooner done, but up the French ship comes and grapples them. This Guy was glad to see, hoping he should be with them presently, and, therefore, he gave orders to let the French board them without much difficulty; who, by that means supposing they had been victorious, gave such a shout as victors do on land.

This insolence made Guy to lay about him; each blow he struck had more than human force, and in a few moments all the deck was nothing but a scene of slaughter. No armour was of proof against his sword, which caused a fresh wound at every blow.

The French knight was amazed at the dismal sight, and wished himself in his own ship again. He ordered those few that were left alive, if possible, to get to his own ship, and then immediately ungrapple; which, Guy perceiving, having cleared his deck, he soon leaped on board of the French ship, and, singly, there maintained the fight with so much fury that many of them, to escape his sword, leaped into the sea.

The French leader seeing this, gave all the encouragement to his men that was possible; and, as one now grown desperate, charged on Guy's helmet with such force as made it sparkle fire; at which Guy returned him such a blow, as made him fall down at his feet for dead, which made the soldiers all throw down their arms and cry aloud for quarter.

*Guy began to lay about him; each blow he struck had more than human force.*

Thereupon Guy, who was always merciful to conquered foes, ended the battle, commanding all his men to fight no more. Having removed the Frenchmen into his own ship, he set fire to the French ship, and sailed on his intended voyage, coasting along the shore, until they touched upon that part of Normandy that borders on Germany. Here Guy landed, and was welcomed with the pleasing news that a tournament was to be held on the following day in honour of Blanche-fleur, the emperor's daughter, and a most beautiful and accomplished lady.

Many famous knights were already arrived, for the purpose of contending for the prize, which consisted of a milk-white falcon, a white horse, and two white greyhounds. In addition, the victor was entitled to claim the hand of the princess, unless he had already chosen in his own country the lady of his affections.

Upon hearing this welcome news, Guy discharged the captain of the ship, leaving the prisoners with him to dispose of at his pleasure, who, putting them to ransom, they obtained their liberty.

Sir Guy, according to the knightly custom, now gave a beautiful palfrey to his host, as a reward for the joyous news, and rode off with his companions to the royal tilting.

## GUY GAINS GREAT FAME

OUR English knight then prepared for the field, where kings and princes, dukes and earls, had gathered to joust for such a rare and beauteous prize. Though one only could win and hundreds fail, yet each man imagined the prize his own. The spacious field, wherein they were assembled, hardly afforded room for the armed knights. The golden, glittering armour that was there, darted the sunbeams back into the clouds. The pampered horses pranced about proudly at the sound of the trumpets.

Sir Guy's first victory was over a German prince, and then he was challenged by Duke Otho, who coming on, cried, " Prepare to breathe thy last." The two joined together valiantly, the clattering armour sounded, the splinters flew, they were covered by the rising dust. Both their swords broke, they jumped from their horses, and with main force Sir Guy at length threw his rival to the ground.

Then Otho's cousin entered the lists in the stead of his kinsman. " I see," quoth Sir Guy, " that you are less than men, that with a blow or fall are vexed so soon. But come and welcome, I am ready for you. We say in England that the weakest must go to the wall."

They rushed together, shaking the ground, whilst the trumpets sounded the alarm. But the combat was soon over, and Sir Guy remained the victor.

For a while all stood amazed, none being forward to encounter him, till the Duke of Lowayne resolved to try his fortune, having good hope that he might better speed. Sitting fair on a proud steed that ill endured the bit, well mounted and well armed, he cried, " I think thou art some enchanter, that hast in thine arm the force of magic."

" I will teach thee to believe ere I have done," Sir Guy replied, " for thou shalt feel that I can charm. I will, however, conjure with no other spell but iron." With that he gave him such a shrewd stroke that the duke could make but a weak return ; then, with a second, and a third, he broke his helmet.

With that, " Hold, hold," cried the beaten man, " I have enough, I will rather yield than die."

Then not a man would encounter the victor, but all were terrified and stood in fear, though all were filled with anger.

" What," cried they, " shall a stranger bear the honour of this great day ? What ill-fortune is this, that he should have the glory of the field ? " So they talked amongst themselves, and would gladly have killed him, but no man durst put his life in danger to come against him.

Thus it was plain that he must be named the victor, and the emperor sent a knight to bring him to the royal seat, and asked his name, and of his birth and country, to all of which questions the hero frankly replied.

Then said his majesty, " I must commend thy skill and courage ; brave Englishman, thou art thy country's pride ; in Europe lives not such another man. I do admire thy worth ; great is thy valour ; my tongue cannot speak all thy praise. This day thy hand has shown me more than I ever saw in my life before. Take this jewel, wear it for my sake, which shall be as a witness of my regard."

Sir Guy thanked his highness for his gracious favour, and vowed him service whilst his life did last. Then to the princess, with a mild behaviour, he cast a humble look and said :

" Madam, accept your loyal English knight, to do you service when you shall command it ; who, while he hath a drop of blood to spend, will spend it all on your behalf, against any who shall dare to contradict you."

Then the emperor gave a grand feast, after which Sir Guy sent two of his attendants into England, with orders to commend him to Rohand and his fair daughter, and to lay at their feet the spoils of his victory.

Without staying any longer in Normandy, he now proceeded into " far lands," travelling through Spain, Lombardy, and the more distant parts of Europe. Wherever a tournament was being held, there went Sir Guy, gaining the prize in every one, and making his name known as that of the most valiant knight in the world.

At the end of a year, his friend Heraud advised that they should return to England, and Sir Guy, being of the same opinion, it was agreed that they should, on the next morning, set off for home. After a short stay in London, where they were received with great kindness by Athelstane, the Saxon king, they journeyed to Warwick, to the joy of Segard and his wife, who were impatient to welcome their famous son.

Felice, however, was not yet satisfied with the hero's fame, so he resolved to go abroad once more and win fresh honour.

" At home, my honourable lord," he said to her father, " I find that valour has no stage for action, I will therefore search what is to be done abroad ; from kingdom to kingdom will I go and find out work, for no good comes of idleness ; it only bringeth men up to sloth."

" Dear Guy," Rohand returned, " thou makest me grieve at this sad news, and more because thou hast disappointed me. I hoped I should enjoy thy company, and thou wouldst go no more abroad, and now thou speakest of new adventures. Fortune, though she hath dealt so kindly with thee, may yet leave thee to an unlucky hour, and turn her many favours into frowns. Do not over rashly hazard thy glory ; lost honour is not easily got again."

To this, Sir Guy answered, " My noble lord, I will never fear I shall be overcome, while I have hands to fight or legs to stand. Therefore, I will leave your honour, wishing all health into your happy state."

The earl, seeing him resolved to go, told him that he would be no hindrance to his proceedings, and only would ask one question of him before he went. Guy told him, whatsoever he asked that was in his power to perform, he should not be denied.

" Then," said the earl, " it is this, that when you are once again come safe to England, you will go abroad no more, but live at home with me," and Sir Guy gave his promise.

His parents were even more sorrowful, and begged him, his mother with tears, to remain at home.

But though their tender pleadings sank deep into the heart of Sir Guy he felt that his promise to Felice must be kept.

## GUY IS NEAR TO DEATH

HAVING taken leave of his sorrowful parents, Sir Guy, with his faithful attendants, Heraud, Thorold, and Urry, proceeded to the seaside, there to embark for France, but the wind proved contrary, and so they continued for six days together.

During this time, rumour, through each corner of the land, had made a mighty noise of an exceeding great and monstrous cow, lurking within the woods not many miles from Warwick. The animal was making most dreadful havoc, destroying man and beast, and putting all the keepers to flight, being so mighty strong that it was not possible to kill her. She was of a dun colour, and thence named the dun cow; and the place where she lay, being on the borders of a wide heath, was thence called Dunsmore Heath, which name it retains to this day.

Upon notice being given to the king (who was then at York), of the havoc made by this creature, he offered knighthood and other gifts to any one who would undertake to destroy her. But, such was the terror she had spread throughout the country, that none was found so hardy as to venture upon such a dangerous enterprise; and the absence of Sir Guy (who by this time was supposed to be in France), was generally lamented, all believing he would undertake it.

Sir Guy (who was all this time waiting for a fair wind), hearing the discourse, and hating to be idle, resolved privately to go and engage with this destroyer of his country. Taking his sword, a strong battle-axe, and his bow and quiver with him, he rode to the place where this monster used to lodge, which was in a thicket of trees, which grew on the side of a heath, near a pool of standing water.

Finding, as he rode along, the cottages and houses everywhere deserted, and the bodies of men and beasts lying scattered round about, he was filled with pity and compassion, and his anger at the destroyer grew hotter and hotter.

When, at last, he was come within bow-shot of the place, the monster spied him, and thrust her head through the thicket. Her dreadful eyes were enough to fill any heart but that of the brave Guy with terror. Being one of the expertest archers England then could boast of, he, notwithstanding her horrid roaring, drawing his arrow to the head, let fly at the oncoming monster.

To his amazement the arrow, striking the animal's hide, rebounded as from an iron wall, without the least impression being made, and the dreadful beast, swift as the wind, came running towards him, with her sharp pointed horns aiming directly at him. Observing this, he lifted his battle-axe on

*Notwithstanding the animal's horrid roaring, he let fly his arrow.*

high, and struck her such a blow on the forehead as made her to recoil, and
roar most hideously.

Nevertheless, she came on again in a great rage, and, clapping her horns
upon his breast, dinted his armour, though of highest proof, before he could
avoid her. Wheeling his warlike steed about, he met her again, and gave her
a desperate wound under the ear, the only place in which she could be
wounded sensibly. Again she roared, snorting, and stamped on the ground,
and by this, Sir Guy, seeing she was mortal, followed that stroke with others
no less forcible, by which at last she fell upon the ground. Sir Guy, alighting
from his horse, dealt her another blow, so that she lay there breathing
her last.

Leaving her lying there, he rode off to the next town that was inhabited,
and there made known the monster's death, to the joy of the inhabitants.
The people loaded him with presents, and honoured him with thanks, and
all the country came in to see that monster dead, of which when alive they
were so much afraid.

The hero thought to get away before the king had notice of it, yet fame
was swifter far than he, and he was sent for by the king before he could get
on shipboard, and so was forced to go to York. There he was no sooner
arrived but the monarch embraced him, and after a splendid entertainment
loaded him with many rich gifts, and caused one of the monster's ribs to be
hanged up in Warwick Castle.

The wind now being favourable, Sir Guy embarked with his friends, and
again travelled in quest of adventure, bearing away the prize in every tournament. But Duke Otho, whom Sir Guy had formerly overthrown, made a

plot to get him into his power. Sending for Earl Lombard and fifteen other knights, he placed them in a wood through which Sir Guy was obliged to pass, and directed them to fall on the travellers by surprise; to kill the attendants without mercy, but, if possible, to capture the leader alive.

Never before was Sir Guy in such distress, but seeing how it was, " Now, friends," said he, " show yourselves right bred English gentlemen. Here is indeed some odds, sixteen to three, but I, the fourth, will stand you in some stead."

Our hero, lately, had been dangerously wounded in a tournament, and was riding, without his coat of mail, on a mule. Springing down, he put on his armour and prepared to face the enemy, while his three faithful knights begged in vain that he would save his life by a timely retreat, leaving them to stem the onslaught.

The encounter was long and hotly contested, and, although Sir Guy finally remained the victor, both Sir Urry and Sir Thorold were slain, while Sir Heraud was so sorely wounded that his leader believed him to be dead. A holy man who lived in a nearby forest buried the first two, but the body of Heraud Sir Guy placed on his own steed and proceeded slowly to the nearest abbey. Here he left the body in charge of the abbot for honourable burial, and retired to the cave of a hermit, for the purpose of lying in hiding until his wounds were healed.

As soon as his cure was complete, he went on his way, travelling now in this country and now in that, gaining honour and glory, and spreading abroad the fame of his name.

Now it chanced that, while he journeyed towards Louvain, he met a pilgrim, faint with travel, from whom he sought news.

" Sir," replied the pilgrim, sighing, " with news I have little business; there is but one thing in the world I care for; and only that and nothing else I mind. In despair I do seek a man, because I have long sought and cannot find him; a man more to me than all the men in the world beside."

" Thou speakest," said Sir Guy, " like one that hast some gratitude. But tell me, pray, what man art thou? And what is he for whom thou hast expressed so great a kindness? "

" I am an Englishman of knight's degree," quoth the pilgrim, " and the subject of my grief is the loss of one Sir Guy, my countryman."

With tears of joy in his eyes, Sir Guy embraced him. " And art thou living, Heraud, my dear friend? " he cried, and kindly took him in his arms. " Then here I bid my sorrows all adieu; how comes it that thou art still living? "

Heraud, no less surprised with joy and wonder to find his countryman again, cried out, " And have I found thee thus, my friend? My pains and travels have been well rewarded. It was a monk in the abbey, who knew the virtue of many a grass, that cured my wounds."

Then each embraced, and both renewed their joy at this so good and happy meeting.

The faithful Heraud, indeed, was weak and poor; but Sir Guy, taking him up behind him on his horse, and conveying him to the next town, soon supplied all his wants.

## GUY CHALLENGES THE SOUDAN

OUR hero's next exploit was to assist the Duke of Louvain, whose chief city was besieged by the forces of the emperor. With fifty knights he entered the city without the knowledge of the enemy, and to the satisfaction of the duke.

" Now," quoth the latter, " we have an honourable, valiant man ; advise me, martial knight, what is to be done to free us from our present danger."

" My lord," returned Guy, " great as the danger seems, we will find a way to set you free. Let us presently issue forth upon them ; our courage will make the cowards flee."

The duke thought the plan good, and early in the morning they sallied forth with such fury that the enemy were put to instant flight. A second army was now sent to invest the city, and to starve the defenders into surrender.

But Sir Guy, appearing upon the walls, laughed at them and said, " You shall never win the town, and as for starving us, we can spare you all the provisions you need." With that he ordered abundance of food to be flung down from the city walls.

Not content with this taunt, he made a second surprise attack, and gained a second victory, so that the emperor was forced to withdraw his soldiers, and to change the siege into a blockade.

Now it chanced that one day the emperor, in order to amuse himself, went a-hunting in the forest, and there was surprised by Sir Guy, who, holding an olive-branch in his hand, requested him to go with him to the city, where he would be treated with great consideration and respect.

All resistance being hopeless, the emperor, by the advice of his barons, went quietly with his conqueror into the city, where, though really a prisoner, he was treated as a master, and served with the greatest humility by Sir Guy, through whose good offices the two enemies were made friends, and a treaty of peace was signed between them.

Both entreated Sir Guy to rest, but just then ill news arrived from Constantinople, where Ernis, the Greek emperor, was besieged by the infidels. These tidings roused our hero to instant action. Choosing two thousand of the bravest knights that could be found, he embarked them on ten ships of war, and, after an exciting adventure with some Sallee rovers, cast anchor in a harbour near the town.

He arrived only just in time, for Coldran, the Saracen leader, was beginning an attack upon the walls. During the battle the two leaders met in single combat, and the Saracens, to their intense astonishment, saw their invincible champion slain by this English knight from overseas. The second in command also being killed, the pagans withdrew in disorder.

The danger, however, was not yet past. Angry at such a crushing defeat, the Soudan resolved to assault the town with all the force he could muster. This intention coming by means of spies to the ears of Sir Guy, he determined to meet the enemy in the field, instead of waiting their attack, and took post in a spot already strong by nature, and made stronger by his efforts. As a result of his skill and valour, the Saracens were completely defeated, and retired swiftly to their camp.

In order to stop all this bloodshed, Guy now proposed to visit the Soudan and challenge him to mortal combat. In vain Ernis implored him not to run into such danger. But Guy put on his armour and mounted his steed.

Coming to the Soudan's tent he delivered his challenge to the astonished monarch, who at length inquired his name, and learning that it was Guy of Warwick, gave orders that he should be seized instantly and put to death. But it was more easy to command than to obey! Sir Guy drew his terrible sword, and, in the fight that followed, cut off the Soudan's head, and, setting spurs to his horse, made his way through the camp, though attacked on all sides by the enemy.

The good emperor, Ernis, more and more astonished at Sir Guy's valour, wished the hero to marry his daughter Loret, and to rule the country after him. Nor would Sir Guy have been unwilling, but for the memory of Felice, from whom he had now been so long absent, and to whom he resolved to return.


## GUY SLAYS THE DRAGON

AFTER many gallant adventures, in which Sir Guy always bore himself nobly, he arrived in England with Sir Heraud, and the pair immediately set out for York, where King Athelstane was holding his court. The king received them with much kindness, and praised them heartily for their martial doings.

He had scarcely finished speaking, when there came a messenger bringing tidings of a terrible dragon who was then laying waste the country of Northumberland. This monster was black as coal, had paws like those of a lion, and was winged. No man could stand before it.

" Dear lord," exclaimed Guy, on hearing these tidings, " as I am an English knight, faithful to God and loyal to my king, I am resolved to see this dragon, and try whether my sword cannot work upon him."

Then, taking his humble leave, he rode into Northumberland, having a dozen knights to be his guide, who brought him where the dragon kept his den, feasting himself with naught but human flesh.

" Now it is enough," said Guy, " so you stand off and leave me. He that has fed so much on human flesh shall never devour a man again."

As he approached the cave, the dragon espied him, and forth he started, of form most dreadful, and with lofty speckled breast. The battle was long and obstinate; but at length the knight, watching his opportunity, drove his sword down the throat of his enemy, after which he cut off his head, and carried it in triumph to Athelstane.

Looking on the fearful head, " Heaven shield," said the king, " and save me from all harm. I will have the monster's picture drawn on cloth of Arras, curiously wrought, and place it in Warwick Castle, there to remain and tell the ages of Guy's matchless strength and courage."

Having by this feat noised his name abroad through all the country, Sir Guy suddenly withdrew from the Court in order to seek his parents.

But alas ! they were no more, so he now hurried to Warwick, to offer at the feet of Felice the laurels which he had won in every part of the continent.

Amidst great rejoicings, and in the presence of King Athelstane and his queen, the two were married, but their happiness did not endure long. Sir Guy's mind was troubled as he thought of all the enemies he had slain throughout his adventurous life.

His sole desire now was to do penance for his former life, and so he told Felice. She, unable to change this fixed resolve, placed on his finger a gold ring, begging him to bestow at least a thought on her, whenever he looked upon it.

So they parted, and Guy, in homespun gray, with staff and script, and in his hat a scollop shell, wended his way towards the Holy Land, leaving his wife to mourn his absence.

Now it chanced that while Guy was away the Danes came in force to England. King Athelstane was in deep distress, shut up with a few troops in Winchester, and altogether unable to oppose his numerous foes.

At last Anlaf, the Danish king, proposed to decide the quarrel by single combat between a Dane and an Englishman, and he brought forth his champion, a mighty giant named Colbrand, who, throwing down his glove, cried, " If there be one dare meet me here, let him stand forth, or else the English are the worst of cowards."

Athelstane was well aware that such a champion could not be found in Winchester, nor perhaps in all the land ; but in a vision he was instructed to entrust his defence to the first pilgrim whom he should meet at the entrance to his palace. This, though unknown to Athelstane, was Sir Guy, who, after hearing the king's story, agreed to fight for England.

Stoutly armed and bestriding a noble war-horse, Sir Guy rode against the Danish giant. The combat was a long and terrible one, but in the end Sir Guy conquered. Colbrand was slain, and the Danish warriors, downcast and astonished, returned to their own country.

Sir Guy, to the sounds of drums, trumpets, and other martial music, was carried in triumph to Winchester, but he seemed to take no share in the general joy. In vain the king offered him costly jewels and rich rewards, and only with difficulty could he be persuaded to tell Athelstane, and him only, his name. Then he took his departure, and in pilgrim's dress proceeded to Warwick, where he lived in a cave.

During all this long interval, Felice had passed her whole time in acts of devotion and charity. Of all palmers who came to the castle for alms, she would ask if they were ever in the Holy Land ; or if in their travels they had seen an Englishman, lord of that noble castle, who many years from hence had been away ? Her husband himself, coming to her gate in his pilgrim's weeds, was invited into the hall, and treated with much kindness, though his wife wist not who he was.

So time passed, until Sir Guy felt that he was dying. Then, calling to a passing herdsman, he sent to Felice the gold ring she had given him at parting, whereupon she knew that the sender was her husband, and immediately accompanied the messenger to the cave. There she arrived in time to hear his last words and to receive his last breath, and she herself dying soon afterwards, they were both buried in the one grave.

# THE OPEN ROAD
## by
## KENNETH GRAHAME

"RATTY," said the Mole suddenly, one bright summer morning, "if you please, I want to ask you a favour."

The Rat was sitting on the river bank, singing a little song. He had just composed it himself, so he was very taken up with it, and would not pay proper attention to Mole or anything else. Since early morning he had been swimming in the river, in company with his friends the ducks. And when the ducks stood on their heads suddenly, as ducks will, he would dive down and tickle their necks, just under where their chins would be if ducks had chins, till they were forced to come to the surface again in a hurry, spluttering and angry and shaking their feathers at him, for it is impossible to say quite *all* you feel when your head is under water. At last they implored him to go away and attend to his own affairs and leave them to mind theirs. So the Rat went away, and sat on the river bank in the sun and made up a song about them, which he called

### "DUCKS' DITTY"

All along the backwater,
Through the rushes tall,
Ducks are a-dabbling,
Up tails all!

Ducks' tails, drakes' tails,
Yellow feet a-quiver,
Yellow bills all out of sight
Busy in the river!

360

Slushy green undergrowth
Where the roach swim—
Here we keep our larder,
Cool and full and dim.

Every one for what he likes !
*We* like to be
Heads down, tails up,
Dabbling free !

High in the blue above
Swifts whirl and call—
*We* are down a-dabbling
Up tails all !

" I don't know that I think so *very* much of that little song, Rat,"
observed the Mole cautiously. He was no poet himself and didn't care
who knew it ; and he had a candid nature.

" Nor don't the ducks neither," replied the Rat cheerfully. " They say,
' *Why* can't fellows be allowed to do what they like *when* they like and *as*
they like, instead of other fellows sitting on banks and watching them all
the time and making remarks and poetry and things about them ? What
*nonsense* it all is ! ' That's what the ducks say."

" So it is, so it is," said the Mole, with great heartiness.

" No, it isn't ! " cried the Rat indignantly.

" Well then, it isn't, it isn't," replied the Mole soothingly. " But what
I wanted to ask you was, won't you take me to call on Mr. Toad ? I've
heard so much about him, and I do so want to make his acquaintance."

" Why, certainly," said the good-natured Rat, jumping to his feet and
dismissing poetry from his mind for the day. " Get the boat out, and we'll
paddle up there at once. It's never the wrong time to call on Toad. Early
or late he's always the same fellow. Always good-tempered, always glad
to see you, always sorry when you go ! "

" He must be a very nice animal," observed the Mole, as he got into
the boat and took the sculls, while the Rat settled himself comfortably
in the stern.

" He is indeed the best of animals," replied Rat. " So simple, so good-
natured, and so affectionate. Perhaps he's not very clever—we can't all
be geniuses ; and it may be that he is both boastful and conceited. But he
has got some great qualities, has Toady."

Rounding a bend in the river, they came in sight of a handsome, dignified
old house of mellowed red brick, with well-kept lawns reaching down to
the water's edge.

" There's Toad Hall," said the Rat ; " and that creek on the left, where
the notice-board says, ' Private. No landing allowed,' leads to his boat-
house, where we'll leave the boat. The stables are over there to the right.
That's the banqueting-hall you're looking at now—very old, that is. Toad
is rather rich, you know, and this is really one of the nicest houses in these
parts, though we never admit as much to Toad."

They glided up the creek, and the Mole shipped his sculls as they passed into the shadow of a large boat-house. Here they saw many handsome boats, slung from the cross-beams or hauled up on a slip, but none in the water ; and the place had an unused and a deserted air.

The Rat looked around him. " I understand," said he. " Boating is played out. He's tired of it, and done, with it. I wonder what new fad he has taken up now ? Come along and let's look him up. We shall hear all about it quite soon enough."

They disembarked, and strolled across the gay flower-decked lawns in search of Toad, whom they presently happened upon resting in a wicker garden-chair, with a preoccupied expression of face, and a large map spread out on his knees.

" Hooray ! " he cried, jumping up on seeing them, " this is splendid ! " He shook the paws of both of them warmly, never waiting for an introduction to the Mole. " How *kind* of you ! " he went on, dancing round them. " I was just going to send a boat down the river for you, Ratty, with strict orders that you were to be fetched up here at once, whatever you were doing. I want you badly—both of you. Now what will you take ? Come inside and have something ! You don't know how lucky it is, your turning up just now ! "

" Let's sit quiet a bit, Toady ! " said the Rat, throwing himself into an easy-chair, while the Mole took another by the side of him and made some civil remark about Toad's " delightful residence."

" Finest house on the whole river," cried Toad boisterously. " Or anywhere else, for that matter," he could not help adding.

Here the Rat nudged the Mole. Unfortunately the Toad saw him do it, and turned very red. There was a moment's painful silence. Then Toad burst out laughing. " All right, Ratty," he said. " It's only my way, you know. And it's not such a very bad house, is it ? You know you rather like it yourself. Now, look here. Let's be sensible. You are the very animals I wanted. You've got to help me. It's most important ! "

" It's about your rowing, I suppose," said the Rat, with an innocent air. " You're getting on fairly well, though you splash a good bit still. With a great deal of patience, and any quantity of coaching, you may——"

" O, pooh ! boating ! " interrupted the Toad, in great disgust. " Silly boyish amusement. I've given that up *long* ago. Sheer waste of time, that's what it is. It makes me downright sorry to see you fellows, who ought to know better, spending all your energies in that aimless manner. No, I've discovered the real thing, the only genuine occupation for a lifetime. I propose to devote the remainder of mine to it, and can only regret the wasted years that lie behind me, squandered in trivialities. Come with me, dear Ratty, and your amiable friend also, if he will be so very good, just as far as the stable-yard, and you shall see what you shall see ! "

He led the way to the stable-yard accordingly, the Rat following with a most mistrustful expression ; and there, drawn out of the coach-house into the open, they saw a gipsy caravan, shining with newness, painted a canary-yellow picked out with green, and red wheels.

" There you are ! " cried the Toad, straddling and expanding himself. " There's real life for you, embodied in that little cart. The open road, the dusty highway, the heath, the common, the hedgerows, the rolling downs ! Camps, villages, towns, cities ! Here to-day, up and off to somewhere else to-morrow ! Travel, change, interest, excitement ! The whole world before you, and a horizon that's always changing ! And mind, this is the very finest cart of its sort that was ever built, without any exception. Come inside and look at the arrangements. Planned 'em all myself, I did ! ''

The Mole was tremendously interested and excited, and followed him eagerly up the steps and into the interior of the caravan. The Rat only snorted and thrust his hands deep into his pockets, remaining where he was.

It was indeed very compact and comfortable. Little sleeping-bunks— a little table that folded up against the wall—a cooking-stove, lockers, book-shelves, a bird-cage with a bird in it ; and pots, pans, jugs and kettles of every size and variety.

"All complete ! '' said the Toad triumphantly, pulling open a locker. "You see—biscuits, potted lobster, sardines—everything you can possibly want. Soda-water here—baccy there—letter-paper, bacon, jam, cards and dominoes—you'll find," he continued, as they descended the steps again, " you'll find that nothing whatever has been forgotten, when we make our start this afternoon."

"I beg your pardon," said the Rat slowly, as he chewed a straw, " but did I overhear you say something about ' we,' and ' start,' and ' this afternoon ? ' ''

"Now, you dear good old Ratty," said Toad imploringly, " don't begin talking in that stiff and sniffy sort of way, because you know you've got to come. I can't possibly manage without you, so please consider it settled, and don't argue—it's the one thing I can't stand. You surely don't mean to stick to your dull fusty old river all your life, and just live in a hole in a bank, and boat ? I want to show you the world ! I'm going to make an animal of you, my boy ! ''

"I don't care," said the Rat doggedly. " I'm not coming, and that's flat. And I am going to stick to my old river, and live in a hole, and boat, as I've always done. And what's more, Mole's going to stick to me and do as I do, aren't you, Mole ? ''

"Of course I am," said the Mole loyally. " I'll always stick to you, Rat, and what you say is to be—has got to be. All the same, it sounds as if it might have been—well, rather fun, you know ! '' he added wistfully. Poor Mole ! The Life Adventurous was so new a thing to him, and so thrilling ; and this fresh aspect of it was so tempting ; and he had fallen in love at first sight with the canary-coloured cart and all its little fitments.

The rat saw what was passing in his mind, and wavered. He hated disappointing people, and he was fond of the Mole, and would do almost anything to oblige him. Toad was watching both of them closely.

"Come along in and have some lunch," he said diplomatically, " and we'll talk it over. We needn't decide anything in a hurry. Of course, I don't really care. I only want to give pleasure to you fellows. ' Live for others ! ' That's my motto in life."

During luncheon—which was excellent, of course, as everything at Toad Hall always was—the Toad simply let himself go. Disregarding the

Rat, he proceeded to play upon the inexperienced Mole as on a harp. Naturally a voluble animal, and always mastered by his imagination, he painted the prospects of the trip and the joys of the open life and the roadside in such glowing colours, that the Mole could hardly sit in his chair for excitement. Somehow, it soon seemed taken for granted by all three of them that the trip was a settled thing; and the Rat, though still unconvinced in his mind, allowed his good-nature to override his personal objections. He could not bear to disappoint his two friends, who were already deep in schemes and anticipations, planning out each day's separate occupation for several weeks ahead.

When they were quite ready, the now triumphant Toad led his companions to the paddock and set them to capture the old gray horse, who, without having been consulted, and to his own extreme annoyance, had been told off by Toad for the dustiest job in this dusty expedition. He frankly preferred the paddock, and took a deal of catching. Meantime,

*The Rat knotted the horse's reins over his back and took him by the head.*

Toad packed the lockers still tighter with necessaries, and hung nose-bags, nets of onions, bundles of hay, and baskets from the bottom of the cart. At last the horse was caught and harnessed and they set off, all talking at once, each animal either trudging by the side of the cart or sitting on the shaft, as the humour took him. It was a golden afternoon. The smell of the dust they kicked up was rich and satisfying; out of thick orchards on either side the road, birds called and whistled to them cheerily; good-natured wayfarers, passing them, gave them 'Good-day,' or stopped to say nice things about their beautiful cart; and rabbits, sitting at their front doors in the hedgerows, held up their fore-paws, and said, "O my! O my! O my!"

Late in the evening, tired and happy and miles from home, they drew up on a remote common far from habitations, turned the horse loose to graze, and ate their simple supper sitting on the grass by the side of the cart. Toad talked big about all he was going to do in the days to come, while stars grew fuller and larger all around them, and a yellow moon, appearing suddenly and silently from nowhere in particular, came to keep them company and listen to their talk. At last they turned into their little bunks in the cart; and Toad, kicking out his legs, sleepily said, " Well, good-night, you fellows ! This is the real life for a gentleman ! Talk about your old river ! "

" I *don't* talk about my river," replied the patient Rat. " You *know* I don't, Toad. But I *think* about it," he added pathetically, in a lower tone : " I think about it—all the time ! "

The Mole reached out from under his blanket, felt for the Rat's paw in the darkness, and gave it a squeeze. " I'll do whatever you like, Ratty," he whispered. " Shall we run away to-morrow morning, quite early— *very* early—and go back to our dear old hole on the river ? "

" No, no, we'll see it out," whispered back the Rat. " Thanks awfully, but I ought to stick by Toad till this trip is ended. It wouldn't be safe for him to be left to himself. It won't take very long. His fads never do. Good-night ! "

The end was indeed nearer than even the Rat suspected.

After so much open air and excitement the Toad slept very soundly, and no amount of shaking could rouse him out of bed next morning. So the Mole and Rat turned to, quietly and manfully, and while the Rat saw to the horse, and lit a fire, and cleaned last night's cups and platters, and got things ready for breakfast, the Mole trudged off to the nearest village, a long way off, for milk and eggs and various necessaries the Toad had, of course, forgotten to provide. The hard work had all been done, and the animals were resting, thoroughly exhausted, by the time Toad appeared on the scene, fresh and gay, remarking what a pleasant easy life it was they were all leading now, after the cares and worries and fatigues of house-keeping at home.

They had a pleasant ramble that day over grassy downs and along narrow by-lanes, and camped, as before, on a common, only this time the two guests took care that Toad should do his fair share of work. In consequence, when the time came for starting next morning, Toad was by no means so rapturous about the simplicity of the primitive life, and indeed attempted to resume his place in his bunk, whence he was hauled by force. Their way lay, as before, across country by narrow lanes, and it was not till the afternoon that they came out on the high road, their first high road ; and there disaster, fleet and unforeseen, sprang out on them—disaster momentous indeed to their expedition, but simply overwhelming in its effect on the after-career of Toad.

They were strolling along the high road easily, the Mole by the horse's head, talking to him, since the horse had complained that he was being frightfully left out of it, and nobody considered him in the least ; the Toad and the Water Rat walking behind the cart talking together—at least Toad was talking, and Rat was saying at intervals, " Yes, precisely ; and what did *you* say to *him* ? "—and thinking all the time of something very different, when far behind them they heard a faint warning hum, like a drone of a distant bee. Glancing back, they saw a small cloud of dust, with a dark centre of energy, advancing on them at incredible speed, while from out the dust a faint " Poop-poop ! " wailed like an uneasy animal in pain. Hardly regarding it, they turned to resume their conversation, when in an instant (as it seemed), the peaceful scene was changed, and with a blast of wind and a whirl of sound that made them jump for the nearest ditch, It was on them! The "poop-poop" rang with a brazen shout in their ears, they had a moment's glimpse of an interior of glittering plate-glass and rich morocco, and the magnificent motor-car, immense, breath-snatching, passionate, with its pilot tense and hugging his wheel, possessed all earth and air for the fraction of a second, flung an enveloping cloud of dust that blinded and enwrapped them utterly, and then dwindled to a speck in the far distance, changed back into a droning bee once more.

The old gray horse, dreaming, as he plodded along, of his quiet paddock, in a new raw situation such as this simply abandoned himself to his natural emotions. Rearing, plunging, backing steadily, in spite of all the Mole's efforts at his head, and all the Mole's lively language directed at his better feelings, he drove the cart backwards towards the deep ditch at the side of the road. It wavered an instant—then there was a heartrending crash— and the canary-coloured cart, their pride and their joy, lay on its side in the ditch, an irredeemable wreck.

The Rat danced up and down in the road, simply transported with passion. "You villains!" he shouted, shaking both fists, "you scoundrels, you highwaymen, you—you—road-hogs!—I'll have the law of you! I'll report you! I'll take you through all the Courts!" His home-sickness had quite slipped away from him, and for the moment he was the skipper of the canary-coloured vessel driven on a shoal by the reckless jockeying of rival mariners, and he was trying to recollect all the fine and biting things he used to say to masters of steam-launches when their wash, as they drove too near the bank, used to flood his parlour carpet at home.

Toad sat straight down in the middle of the dusty road, his legs stretched out before him, and stared fixedly in the direction of the disappearing motor-car. He breathed short, his face wore a placid, satisfied expression, and at intervals he faintly murmured "Poop-poop!"

The Mole was busy trying to quiet the horse, which he succeeded in doing after a time. Then he went to look at the cart, on its side in the ditch. It was indeed a sorry sight. Panels and windows smashed, axles hopelessly bent, one wheel off, sardine-tins scattered over the wide world, and the bird in the bird-cage sobbing pitifully and calling to be let out.

The Rat came to help him, but their united efforts were not sufficient to right the cart. "Hi! Toad!" they cried. "Come and bear a hand, can't you!"

The Toad never answered a word, or budged from his seat in the road; so they went to see what was the matter with him. They found him in a sort of trance, a happy smile on his face, his eyes still fixed on the dusty wake of their destroyer. At intervals he was still heard to murmur "Poop-poop!"

The Rat shook him by the shoulder. "Are you coming to help us, Toad?" he demanded sternly.

"Glorious, stirring sight!" murmured Toad, never offering to move. "The poetry of motion! The *real* way to travel! The *only* way to travel! Here to-day—in next week to-morrow! Villages skipped, towns and cities jumped—always somebody else's horizon! O bliss! O poop-poop! O my! O my!"

"O *stop* being an ass, Toad!" cried the Mole despairingly.

"And to think I never *knew*!" went on the Toad in a dreamy monotone. "All those wasted years that lie behind me, I never knew, never even *dreamt*! But *now*—but now that I know, now that I fully realise! O what a flowery track lies spread before me, henceforth! What dust-clouds shall spring up behind me as I speed on my reckless way! What carts I shall fling carelessly into the ditch in the wake of my magnificent onset! Horrid little carts—common carts—canary-coloured carts!"

"What are we to do with him?" asked the Mole of the Water Rat.

"Nothing at all," replied the Rat firmly. "Because there is really nothing to be done. You see, I know him from of old. He is now possessed. He has got a new craze, and it always takes him that way, in its first stage. He'll continue like that for days now, like an animal walking in a happy dream, quite useless for all practical purposes. Never mind him. Let's go and see what there is to be done about the cart."

A careful inspection showed them that, even if they succeeded in righting it by themselves, the cart would travel no longer. The axles were in a hopeless state, and the missing wheel was shattered into pieces.

The Rat knotted the horse's reins over his back and took him by the head, carrying the bird-cage and its hysterical occupant in the other hand. "Come on!" he said grimly to the Mole. "It's five or six miles to the nearest town, and we shall just have to walk it. The sooner we make a start the better."

"But what about Toad?" asked the Mole anxiously, as they set off together. "We can't leave him here, sitting in the middle of the road by himself, in the distracted state he's in! It's not safe. Supposing another Thing were to come along?"

"O, *bother* Toad," said the Rat savagely; "I've done with him!"

They had not proceeded very far on their way, however, when there was a pattering of feet behind them, and Toad caught them up and thrust a paw inside the elbow of each of them; still breathing short and staring into vacancy.

"Now, look here, Toad!" said the Rat sharply: "as soon as we get to the town, you'll have to go straight to the police-station, and see if they know anything about that motor-car and who it belongs to, and lodge a complaint against it. And then you'll have to go to a blacksmith's or a wheelwright's and arrange for the cart to be fetched and mended and put to rights. It'll take time, but it's not quite a hopeless smash. Meanwhile, the Mole and I will go to an inn and find comfortable rooms where we can stay till the cart's ready, and till your nerves have recovered their shock."

"Police-station! Complaint!" murmured Toad dreamily. "Me *complain* of that beautiful, that heavenly vision that has been vouchsafed me! *Mend the cart*! I've done with carts for ever. I never want to see the cart, or to hear of it, again. O, Ratty! You can't think how obliged I am to you for consenting to come on this trip! I wouldn't have gone without you, and then I might never have seen that—that swan, that sunbeam, that thunderbolt ! I might never have heard that entrancing sound, or smelt that be-witching smell ! I owe it all to you, my best of friends ! "

The Rat turned from him in despair. " You see what it is ? " he said to the Mole, addressing him across Toad's head : " He's quite hopeless. I give it up—when. we get to the town we'll go to the railway-station, and with luck we may pick up a train there that'll get us back to River Bank to-night. And if ever you catch me going a-pleasuring with this provoking animal again ! "—He snorted, and during the rest of that weary trudge addressed his remarks exclusively to Mole.

On reaching the town they went straight to the station and deposited Toad in the second-class waiting-room, giving a porter twopence to keep a strict eye on him. They then left the horse at an inn stable, and gave what directions they could about the cart and its contents.

Eventually, a slow train having landed them at a station not very far from Toad Hall, they escorted the spellbound, sleep-walking Toad to his door, put him inside it, and instructed his housekeeper to feed him, undress him, and put him to bed. Then they got out their boat from the boat-house, sculled down the river home, and at a very late hour sat down to supper in their own cosy riverside parlour, to the Rat's great joy and contentment.

The following evening the Mole, who had risen late and taken things very easy all day, was sitting on the bank fishing, when the Rat, who had been looking up his friends and gossiping, came strolling along to find him. " Heard the news ? " he said. " There's nothing else being talked about, all along the river bank. Toad went up to Town by an early train this morning. And he has ordered a large and very expensive motor-car."

# DICK TURPIN'S RIDE TO YORK

ADAPTED FROM THE STORY
BY
W. HARRISON AINSWORTH

IT was a delicious evening. The sun was slowly declining, and glowed like a ball of fire amid the thick foliage of a neighbouring elm. Whether, like the robber Moor, Tom King was touched by this glorious sunset, we pretend not to determine. Certain it was that a shade of inexpressible melancholy passed across his handsome countenance, as he gazed in the direction of Harrow-on-the-Hill, which, lying to the west of the green upon which they walked, stood out with its pointed spire and lofty college against the ruddy sky. He spoke not. But Dick noticed the passing emotion.

"What ails you, Tom?" said he, with much kindness of manner; "are you not well, lad?"

"Yes, I am well enough," said King; "I know not what came over me, but looking at Harrow, I thought of my schooldays, and what I was *then*, and that bright prospect reminded me of my boyish hopes."

"Tut—tut!" said Dick, "this is idle—you are a man now."

"I know I am," replied Tom, "but I *have* been a boy. Had I any faith in presentiments, I should say this is the last sunset I shall ever see."

"Here comes our host," said Dick, smiling. "I've no presentiment that this is the last bill I shall ever pay."

The bill was brought and settled. As Turpin paid it, the man's conduct was singular, and awakened his suspicions.

"Are our horses ready?" asked Dick quickly.

"They are, sir," said the landlord.

"Let us be gone," whispered Dick to King; "I don't like this fellow's manner. I thought I heard a carriage draw up at the inn door just now—there may be danger. Be fly!" added he to Jerry and the Magus. "Now, sir," said he to the landlord, "lead the way. Keep on the alert, Tom."

Dick's hint was not lost upon the two bowlers. They watched their comrades; and listened intently for any manifestation of alarm.

· · · · · · · · · · ·

While Turpin and King are walking across the bowling-green, we will see what has taken place outside the inn. Tom's presentiments of danger were not, it appeared, without foundation. Scarcely had the ostler brought forth our two highwaymen's steeds, when a post-chaise, escorted by two or three horsemen, drove furiously up to the door. The sole occupant of the carriage was a lady, whose slight and pretty figure was all that could be distinguished, her face being closely veiled. The landlord, who was busied in casting up Turpin's account, rushed forth at the summons. A word or two passed between him and the horsemen, upon which the former's countenance fell. He posted in the direction of the garden; and the horsemen instantly dismounted.

"We have him now, sure enough," said one of them, a very small man.

"By the powers! I begin to think so," replied the other horseman. "But don't spoil all, Mr. Coates, by being too precipitate."

"Never fear that, Mr. Tyrconnel," said Coates, the gallant attorney; "he's sure to come for his mare. That's a *trap* certain to catch him, eh, Mr. Paterson? With the Chief Constable of Westminster to back us, the devil's in it if we are not a match for him."

"And for Tom King too," replied the chief constable; "the game's up with him, too. We've long had an eye upon him, and now we'll have a finger. He's one of your dashing trouts to whom we always give a long line, but we'll *land* him this time, anyhow. If you'll look after Dick Turpin, gemmen, I'll make sure of Tom."

"I'd rather you would help *us*, Mr. Paterson," said Coates; "never mind Tom King; another time will do for him."

"No such thing," said Paterson; "one *weighs* just as much for that matter as t' other. I'll take Tom to myself, and surely you two, with the landlord and ostler, can manage Turpin amongst you."

"I don't know that," said Coates doubtfully; "he's a devil of a fellow to deal with."

"Take him quietly," said Paterson. "Draw the chaise out of the way, lad. Take our horses to one side, and place their nags near the door, ostler. Shall you be able to see him, ma'am, where you are?" asked the chief constable, walking to the carriage, and touching his hat to the lady within. Having received a satisfactory nod from the bonnet and veil, he returned to his companions. "And now, gemmen," added he, "let's step aside a little. Don't use your fire-arms too soon."

As if conscious what was passing around her, and of the danger that awaited her master, Black Bess exhibited so much impatience, and plunged so violently, that it was with difficulty the ostler could hold her. "The devil's in the mare," said he; "what's the matter with her? She was quiet enough a few minutes since. Soho! lass, stand."

Turpin and King, meanwhile, walked quickly through the house, preceded by the host, who conducted them, not without some inward trepidation, towards the door. Arrived there, each man rushed swiftly to his horse. Dick was in the saddle in an instant, and stamping her foot upon the ostler's leg, Black Bess compelled the man, yelling with pain, to quit his hold of the bridle. Tom King was not equally fortunate. Before he could mount his horse, a loud shout was raised, which startled the animal, and caused him to swerve, so that Tom lost his footing in the stirrup, and fell to the ground. He was instantly seized by Paterson, and a struggle commenced, King endeavouring, but in vain, to draw a pistol.

"Shoot him, Dick; fire, or I'm taken," cried King. "Fire! Why don't you fire?" shouted he, in desperation, still struggling vehemently with Paterson, who was a strong man, and more than a match for a light-weight like King.

"I can't," cried Dick; "I shall hit you, if I fire."

"Take your chance," shouted King. "Is *this* your friendship?"

Thus urged, Turpin fired. The ball ripped up the sleeve of Paterson's coat, but did not wound him.

"Again!" cried King. "Shoot him, I say. Don't you hear me? Fire again!"

Pressed as he was by foes on every side, himself their mark, for both Coates and Tyrconnel had fired upon him, and were now mounting their steeds to give chase, it was impossible that Turpin could take sure aim; added to which, in the struggle, Paterson and King were each moment changing their relative positions. He, however, would no longer hesitate, but again, at his friend's request, fired. The ball lodged itself in King's breast! He fell at once. At this instant a shriek was heard from the chaise: the window was thrown open, and her thick veil being drawn aside, the features of a very pretty woman, now impressed with terror and contrition, were suddenly exhibited.

King fixed his glazing eyes upon her.

"Susan!" sighed he, "is it you that I behold?"

"Yes, yes, 'tis she, sure enough," said Paterson. "You see, ma'am, what you and such-like have brought him to. However, you'll lose your reward; he's going fast enough."

"Reward!" gasped King; "reward! Did she betray me?"

"Aye, aye, sir," said Paterson, "she blowed the gaff, if it's any consolation to you to know it."

"Consolation!" repeated the dying man; "perfidious!—oh!—the prophecy—my best friend—Turpin—I die by his hand."

And vainly striving to raise himself, he fell backwards and expired. Alas, poor Tom!

"Mr. Paterson! Mr. Paterson!" cried Coates; "leave the landlord to look after the body of that dying ruffian, and mount with us in pursuit of the living rascal. Come, sir; quick! mount! dispatch! You see he is yonder; he seems to hesitate; we shall have him now."

"Well, gemmen, I'm ready," said Paterson; "but how came you to let him escape?"

"Saint Patrick only knows!" said Titus; "he's as slippery as an eel —and, like a cat, turn him which way you will, he is always sure to alight upon his legs. I wouldn't wonder but we lose him now, after all, though he has such a small start. The mare flies like the wind."

"He shall have a tight run for it, at all events," said Paterson, putting spurs into his horse. " I've got a good nag under me, and you are neither of you badly mounted. He's only three hundred yards before us, and the devil's in it if we can't run him down. It's a three-hundred-pound job, Mr. Coates, and well worth a race."

" You shall have another hundred from me, sir, if you take him," said Coates, urging his steed forward.

" Thank you, sir, thank you. Follow my directions, and we'll make sure of him," said the constable. " Gently, gently, not so fast up the hill— you see he's breathing his horse. All in good time, Mr. Coates—all in good time, sir."

And maintaining an equal distance, both parties cantered leisurely up the ascent now called Windmill Hill. We shall now return to Turpin.

Aghast at the deed he had accidentally committed, Dick remained for a few moments irresolute ; he perceived that King was mortally wounded, and that all attempts at rescue would be fruitless ; he perceived, likewise, that Jerry and the Magus had effected their escape from the bowling-green, as he could detect their figures stealing along the hedgeside. He hesitated no longer. Turning his horse, he galloped slowly off, little heeding the pursuit with which he was threatened.

" Every bullet has its billet," said Dick ; " but little did I think that I really should turn poor Tom's executioner. To the devil with this rascally snapper," cried he, throwing the pistol over the hedge. " I could never have used it again. 'Tis strange, too, that he should have foretold his own fate—devilish strange ! And then that he should have been betrayed by the very woman he trusted ! "

.      .      .      .      .      .      .      .      .      .      .

Arrived at the brow of the hill, whence such a beautiful view of the country surrounding the metropolis is obtained, Turpin turned for an instant to reconnoitre his pursuers. Coates and Titus he utterly disregarded ; but Paterson was a more formidable foe, and he well knew that he had to deal with a man of experience and resolution. It was then, for the first time, that the thoughts of executing his extraordinary ride to York first flashed across him ; his bosom throbbed high with rapture, and he involuntarily exclaimed aloud, as he raised himself in the saddle, " By God ! I will do it ! "

He took one last look at the great Babel that lay buried in a world of trees beneath him ; and as his quick eye ranged over the magnificent prospect, lit up by that gorgeous sunset, he could not help thinking of Tom King's last words. " Poor fellow ! " thought Dick, " he said truly. He will never see another sunset." Aroused by the approaching clatter of his pursuers, Dick struck into a lane which lies on the right of the road, now called Shoot-up-hill Lane, and set off at a good pace in the direction of Hampstead.

" Now," cried Paterson, " put your horses to it, my boys. We must not lose sight of him for a second in these lanes."

Accordingly, as Turpin was by no means desirous of inconveniencing his mare in this early stage of the business, and as the ground was still upon an ascent, the parties preserved their relative distances.

At length, after various twistings and turnings in that deep and devious lane ; after scaring one or two farmers, and riding over a brood or two of ducks ; dipping into the verdant valley of West End, and ascending another hill, Turpin burst upon the gorsy, sandy, and beautiful heath of Hampstead. Shaping his course to the left, Dick then made for the lower part of the heath, and skirted a path that leads towards North End, passing the furze-crowned summit which is now crested by a clump of lofty pines.

It was here that the chase first assumed a character of interest. Being open ground, the pursued and pursuers were in full view of each other ; and as Dick rode swiftly across the heath, with the shouting trio hard at his heels, the scene had a very animated appearance. He crossed the hill —the Hendon Road—passed Crackskull Common—and dashed along the cross-road to Highgate.

Hitherto no advantage had been gained by the pursuers ; they had not lost ground, but still they had not gained an inch, and much spurring was required to maintain their position. As they approached Highgate, Dick slackened his pace, and the other party redoubled their efforts. To avoid the town, Dick struck into a narrow path at the right, and rode easily down the hill.

His pursuers were now within a hundred yards, and shouted to him to stand. Pointing to a gate which seemed to bar their further progress, Dick unhesitatingly charged it, clearing it in beautiful style. Not so with Coates's party ; and the time they lost in unfastening the gate, which none of them chose to leap, enabled Dick to put additional space betwixt them. It did not, however, appear to be his intention altogether to outstrip his pursuers : the chase seemed to give him excitement, which he was willing to prolong as much as was consistent with his safety. Scudding rapidly

*" Reward ! " gasped King ; " reward ! Did she betray me ? "*

past Highgate, like a swift-sailing schooner with three lumbering Indiamen in her wake, Dick now took the lead along a narrow lane that threads the fields in the direction of Hornsey. The shouts of his followers had brought others to join them, and as he neared Crouch End, traversing the lane which takes its name from Du-Val, and in which a house frequented by that gayest of robbers stands, or stood, " A highwayman ! a highwayman ! " rang in his ears, in a discordant chorus of many voices.

The whole neighbourhood was alarmed by the cries, and by the tramp of horses : the men of Hornsey rushed into the road to seize the fugitive, and women held up their babes to catch a glimpse of the flying cavalcade, which seemed to gain number and animation as it advanced. Suddenly three horsemen appear in the road—they hear the uproar and the din. " A highwayman ! a highwayman ! " cry the voices : " stop him, stop him ! " But it is no such easy matter. With a pistol in each hand, and his bridle in his teeth, Turpin passed boldly on. His fierce looks—his furious steed —the impetus with which he pressed forward, bore down all before him. The horsemen gave way, and only served to swell the list of his pursuers.

" We have him now—we have him now ! " cried Paterson, exultingly. " Shout for your lives. The Turnpike-man will hear us. Shout again— again ! The fellow has heard it. The gate is shut. We have him. Ha, ha ! "

The old Hornsey toll-bar was a high gate with a spiked top. The gate was swung into its lock, and, like a tiger in his lair, the prompt custodian of the turnpike held himself in readiness to spring upon the runaway. But Dick kept steadily on. He coolly calculated the height of the gate ; he looked to the right and to the left—nothing better offered ; he spoke a few words of encouragement to Bess, gently patted her neck, then stuck spurs into her sides, and cleared the spikes by an inch. Out rushed the amazed turnpike-man, thus unmercifully bilked, and was nearly trampled to death under the feet of Paterson's horse.

" Open the gate, fellow, and be expeditious," shouted the chief constable.

" Not I," said the man sturdily, " unless I gets my dues. I've been done once already. But strike me stupid if I'm done a second time."

" Don't you perceive that's a highwayman ? Don't you know that I'm Chief Constable of Westminster ? " said Paterson, showing his staff. " How dare you oppose me in the discharge of my duty ? "

" That may be, or it may not be," said the man doggedly. " But you don't pass, unless I gets the blunt, and that's the long and short on it."

Amidst a storm of oaths Coates flung down a crown piece, and the gate was thrown open.

Turpin took advantage of this delay to breathe his mare ; and, striking into a by-lane at Duckett's Green, cantered easily along in the direction of Tottenham. Little repose was allowed him. Yelling like a pack of hounds in full cry, his pursuers were again at his heels. He had now to run the gauntlet of the long straggling town of Tottenham, and various were the devices of the populace to entrap him. The whole place was up in arms, shouting, screaming, running, dancing, and hurling every possible description of missile at the horse and her rider. Dick merrily responded to their clamour as he flew past, and laughed at the brickbats that were showered thick as hail, and quite as harmlessly, around him.

A few more miles hard riding tired the volunteers, and before the chase reached Edmonton most of them were "*nowhere.*" Here fresh relays were gathered, and a strong field was again mustered. John Gilpin himself could not have excited more astonishment amongst the good folks of Edmonton, than did our highwayman as he galloped through their town. Unlike the men of Tottenham, the mob received him with acclamations, thinking, no doubt, that, like "the citizens of famous London town," he rode for a wager. Presently, however, borne on the wings of the blast, came the cries of "Turpin! Dick Turpin!" and the hurrahs were changed to hootings; but such was the rate at which our highwayman rode, that no serious opposition could be offered to him.

A man in a donkey-cart, unable to get out of the way, drew himself up in the middle of the road. Turpin cleared the driver and his little wain with ease. This was a capital stroke, and well adapted to please the multitude, who are ever taken with a brilliant action. "Hark away, Dick!" resounded on all hands, while hisses were as liberally bestowed upon his pursuers.

.   .   .   .   .   .   .   .   .   .

Away they fly past scattered cottages, swiftly and skimmingly, like eagles on the wing, along the Enfield highway. All were well mounted, and the horses, now thoroughly warmed, had got into their paces, and did their work beautifully. None of Coates's party lost ground, but they maintained it at the expense of their steeds, which were streaming like water-carts, while Black Bess had scarcely turned a hair.

Turpin was a crack rider; he was *the* crack rider of England of his time, and, perhaps, of any time. The craft and mystery of jockeyship was not so well understood in the eighteenth as it is in the nineteenth century; men treated their horses differently, and few rode them as well as many ride now, when every youngster takes to the field as naturally as if he had been bred a gaucho. Dick Turpin was a glorious exception to the rule, and anticipated a later age. He rode wonderfully lightly, yet sat his saddle to perfection, distributing the weight so exquisitely that his horse scarcely felt his pressure; he yielded to every movement made by the animal, and became, as it were, part and parcel of itself; he took care Bess should be neither strained nor wrung. Freely, and as lightly as a feather, was he borne along; beautiful was it to see her action—to watch her style and temper of covering the ground; and many a first-rate Meltonian might have got a wrinkle from Turpin's seat and conduct.

We have before stated that it was not Dick's object to *ride away* from his pursuers—he could have done that at any moment. He liked the fun of the chase, and would have been sorry to put a period to his own excitement. Confident in his mare, he just kept her at such speed as should put his pursuers completely to *it*, without in the slightest degree inconveniencing himself. Some judgment of the speed at which they went may be formed, when we state that little better than an hour had elapsed and nearly twenty miles had been ridden over.

"By the mother that bore me," said Titus, as they went along in this slapping style—Titus, by the by, rode a big, Roman-nosed, powerful horse, well adapted to his weight, but which required a plentiful exercise both of leg and arm to call forth all his action, and keep his rider alongside his companions—" by the mother that bore me," said he, almost thumping the wind out of his flea-bitten Bucephalus with his calves, after the Irish fashion, " if the fellow isn't lighting his pipe ! I saw the sparks fly on each side of him, and there he goes like a smoky chimney on a frosty morning ! See, he turns his impudent phiz, with the pipe in his mouth ! Are we to stand that, Mr. Coates ? "

" Wait awhile, sir—wait awhile," said Coates ; " we'll smoke *him* by and by."

It was now gray twilight. The mists of coming night were weaving a thin curtain over the rich surrounding landscape. All the sounds and hum of that delicious hour were heard, broken only by the regular clatter of the horses' hoofs. Tired of shouting, the chasers now kept on their way in deep silence ; each man held his breath, and plunged his spurs, rowel deep, into his horse ; but the animals were already at the top of their speed, and incapable of greater exertion. Paterson, who was a hard rider, and perhaps a thought better mounted, kept the lead. The rest followed as they might.

Had it been undisturbed by the rush of the cavalcade, the scene would have been still and soothing. Overhead a cloud of rooks were winging their garrulous flight to the ancestral avenue of an ancient mansion to the right ; the bat was on the wing ; the distant lowing of a herd of kine saluted the ear at intervals ; the blithe whistle of the rustic herdsman, and the merry chime of wagon bells, rang pleasantly from afar. But these cheerful sounds, which make the still twilight hour delightful, were lost in the tramp of the horsemen, now three abreast. The hind fled to the hedge for shelter, and the wagoner pricked up his ears, and fancied he heard the distant rumbling of an earthquake.

On rush the pack, whipping, spurring, tugging for very life. Again they gave voice, in hopes the wagoner might succeed in stopping the fugitive. But Dick was already by his side. " Hark 'ee, my tulip," cried he, taking the pipe from his mouth as he passed, " tell my friends behind they will hear of me at York."

" What did he say ? " asked Paterson, coming up the next moment.

" That you'll find him at York," replied the wagoner.

" At York ! " echoed Coates, in amaze.

Turpin was now out of sight, and although our trio flogged with might and main, they could never catch a glimpse of him until, within a short distance of Ware, they beheld him at the door of a little public-house, standing with his bridle in his hand, coolly quaffing a tankard of ale. No sooner were they in sight, than Dick vaulted into the saddle, and rode off.

" Devil seize you, sir ! why didn't you stop him ? " exclaimed Paterson, as he rode up. " My horse is dead lame. I cannot go any farther. Do you know what a prize you have missed ? Do you know who that was ? "

" No, sir, I don't," said the publican. " But I know he gave his mare more ale than he took himself, and he has given me a guinea instead of a shilling. He's a regular good 'un."

" A good 'un ! " said Paterson ; " it was Turpin, the notorious highwayman. We are in pursuit of him. Have you any horses ? our cattle are all blown."

" You'll find the post-house in the town, gentlemen. I'm sorry I can't accommodate you. But I keeps no stabling. I wish you a very good-evening, sir." Saying which, the publican retreated to his domicile.

" That's a flash crib, I'll be bound," said Paterson. " I'll chalk you down, my friend, you may rely upon it. Thus far we're done, Mr. Coates. But curse me if I give it in. I'll follow him to the world's end first."

" Right, sir—right," said the attorney. " A very proper spirit, Mr. Constable. You would be guilty of neglecting your duty were you to act otherwise. You must recollect my father, Mr. Paterson—Christopher, or Kit Coates ; a name as well known at the Old Bailey as Jonathan Wild's. You recollect him—eh ? "

" Perfectly well, sir," replied the chief constable.

" The greatest thief-taker, though I say it," continued Coates, " on record. I inherit all his zeal—all his ardour. Come along, sir. We shall have a fine moon in an hour—bright as day. To the post-house ! to the post-house ! "

Accordingly to the post-house they went ; and, with as little delay as circumstances admitted, fresh hacks being procured, accompanied by a postillion, the party again pursued their onward course, encouraged to believe they were still in the right scent.

Night had now spread her mantle over the earth : still it was not wholly dark. A few stars were twinkling in the deep, cloudless heavens, and a pearly radiance in the eastern horizon heralded the rising of the orb of night. A gentle breeze was stirring ; the dews of evening had already fallen ; and the air felt bland and dry. It was just the night one would have chosen for a ride, if one ever rode by choice at such an hour ; and to Turpin, whose chief excursions were conducted by night, it appeared little less than heavenly.

Full of ardour and excitement, determined to execute what he had mentally undertaken, Turpin held on his solitary course. Everything was favourable to his project ; the roads were in admirable condition, his mare was in like order ; she was inured to hard work, had rested sufficiently in town to recover from the fatigue of her recent journey, and had never been in more perfect training. " She has now got her wind in her," said Dick ; " I'll see what she can do—hark away, lass—hark away ! I wish they could see her now," added he, as he felt her almost fly away with him.

Encouraged by her master's voice and hand, Black Bess started forward at a pace which few horses could have equalled, and scarcely any have sustained so long. Even Dick, accustomed as he was to her magnificent action, felt electrified at the speed with which he was borne along. " Bravo ! bravo ! " shouted he, " hark away, Bess ! "

. . . . . . . . . .

Bess is now in her speed, and Dick happy. Happy ! he is enraptured —maddened—furious—intoxicated as with wine. Pshaw ! wine could never throw him into such a burning delirium. Its choicest juices have no inspiration like this. Its fumes are slow and heady. This is ethereal, transporting. His blood spins through his veins ; winds round his heart ; mounts to his brain. Away ! away ! He is wild with joy. Hall, cot, tree, tower, glade, mead, waste, or woodland, are seen, passed, left behind, and vanish as in a dream. Motion is scarcely perceptible—it is impetus ! volition ! The horse and her rider are driven forward, as it were, by self-accelerated speed. A hamlet is visible in the moonlight. It is scarcely discovered ere the flints sparkle beneath the mare's hoofs. A moment's clatter upon the stones, and it is left behind. Again, it is the silent, smiling country. Now they are buried in the darkness of woods ; now sweeping along on the wide plain ; now clearing the unopened toll-bar ; now trampling over the hollow-sounding bridge, their shadows momentarily reflected in the placid mirror of the stream ; now scaling the hill-side a thought more slowly ; now plunging, as the horses of Phœbus into the ocean, down its precipitous sides.

The limits of two shires are already past. They are within the confines of a third. They have entered the merry county of Huntingdon ; they have surmounted the gentle hill that slips into Godmanchester. They are by the banks of the rapid Ouse. The bridge is past ; and as Turpin rode through the deserted streets of Huntingdon, he heard the eleventh hour given from the iron tongue of St. Mary's spire. In four hours (it was about seven when he started) Dick had accomplished full sixty miles !

Huntingdon is left behind, and he is once more surrounded by dew-gemmed hedges and silent slumbering trees. Broad meadows, or pasture land, with drowsy cattle, or low bleating sheep, lie on either side. But what to Turpin, at that moment, is nature, animate or inanimate ? He thinks only of his mare—his future fame. None are by to see him ride ; no stimulating plaudits ring in his ears ; no thousand hands are clapping ; no thousand voices huzzaing ; no handkerchiefs are waved ; no necks strained ; no bright eyes rain influence upon him ; no eagle orbs watch his motions ; no bells are rung ; no cup awaits his achievement ; no sweepstakes—no plate. But his will be renown—everlasting renown ; his will be fame which will not die with him—which will keep his reputation, albeit a tarnished one, still in the mouths of men.

He trembled with excitement, and Bess trembled under him. But the emotion was transient. On, on they fly ! The torrent leaping from the crag—the bolt from the bow—the air-cleaving eagle—thoughts themselves are scarce more winged in their flight !

. . . . . . . . . .

The night had hitherto been balmy and beautiful, with a bright array of stars, and a golden harvest moon, which seemed to diffuse even warmth with its radiance ; but now Turpin was approaching the region of fog and fen, and he began to feel the influence of that dank atmosphere. The inter-secting dykes, yawners, gullies, or whatever they are called, began to send forth their steaming vapours, and chilled the soft and wholesome air, obscuring the void, and in some instances, as it were, choking up the road itself with vapour. But fog or fen was the same to Bess ; her hoofs rattled merrily along the road, and she burst from a cloud, like Eous at the break of dawn.

It chanced, as he issued from a fog of this kind, that Turpin burst upon the York stage coach. It was no uncommon thing for the coach to be stopped ; and so furious was the career of our highwayman, that the man involuntarily drew up his horses. Turpin had also to draw in the rein, a task of no little difficulty, as charging a huge lumbering coach, with its full complement of passengers, was more than even Bess could accomplish. The moon shone brightly on Turpin and his mare. He was unmasked, and his features were distinctly visible. An exclamation was uttered by a gentleman on the box, who, it appeared, instantly recognised him.

"Pull up—draw your horses across the road!" cried the gentleman; "that's Dick Turpin, the highwayman. His capture would be worth three hundred pounds to you," added he, addressing the coachman, "and is of equal importance to me. Stand!" shouted he, presenting a cocked pistol.

This resolution of the gentleman was not apparently agreeable, either to the coachman or the majority of the passengers—the name of Turpin acting like magic upon them. One man jumped off behind, and was with difficulty afterwards recovered, having tumbled into a deep ditch at the road-side. An old gentleman with a cotton nightcap, who had popped out his head to swear at the coachman, drew it suddenly back. A faint scream in a

*Dick rode up, pistol in hand, to the gentleman who had fired.*

female key issued from within, and there was a considerable hubbub on the roof. Amongst other ominous sounds, the guard was heard to click his long horse-pistols. "Stop the York four-day stage!" said he, forcing his smoky voice through a world of throat-embracing shawl; "the fastest coach in the kingdom: vos ever sich atrocity heard of? I say, Joe, keep them 'ere leaders steady; we shall all be in the ditch. Don't you see where the hind wheels are? Who—whoop, I say."

The gentleman on the box now discharged his pistol, and the confusion within was redoubled. The white nightcap was popped out like a rabbit's head, and as quickly popped back on hearing the highwayman's voice. Owing to the plunging of the horses, the gentleman had missed his aim.

Prepared for such emergencies as the present, and seldom at any time taken aback, Dick received the fire without flinching. He then lashed the horses out of his course, and rode up, pistol in hand, to the gentleman who had fired.

"Major Mowbray," said he, in a stern tone, "I know you. I meant not either to assault you or these gentlemen. Yet you have attempted my life, sir, a second time. But you are now in my power, and if you do not answer the questions I put to you, nothing earthly shall save you."

"If you ask aught I may not answer, fire!" said the major; "I will never ask life from such as you."

"Have you seen aught of Sir Luke Rookwood?" asked Dick.

"The villain you mean is not yet secured," replied the major, "but we have traces of him. 'Tis with the view of procuring more efficient assistance that I ride to town."

"They have not met, then, since?" said Dick carelessly.

"Met! Whom do you mean?"

"Your sister and Sir Luke," said Dick.

"My sister meet him!" cried the major angrily—"think you he dares show himself at Rookwood?"

"Ho, ho!" laughed Dick; "she *is* at Rookwood, then? A thousand thanks, major. Good-night to you, gentlemen."

"Take that with you, and remember the guard," cried the fellow, who, unable to take aim from where he sat, had crept along the coach roof, and discharged thence one of his large horse-pistols at what he took to be the highwayman's head, but which, luckily for Dick, was his hat, which he had raised to salute the passengers.

"Remember you," said Dick, coolly replacing his perforated beaver on his brow; "you may rely upon it, my fine fellow, I'll not forget you the next time we meet."

And off he went like the breath of the whirlwind.

.     .     .     .     .     .     .     .     .     .     .

Eighty and odd miles had now been traversed—the boundary of another county, Northampton, passed; yet no rest nor respite had Dick Turpin or his unflinching mare enjoyed. But here he deemed it fitting to make a brief halt.

Bordering the beautiful domains of Burleigh House stood a little retired hostelry of some antiquity, which bore the great Lord Treasurer's arms. With this house Dick was not altogether unacquainted. The lad who acted as ostler was known to him. It was now midnight, but a bright and beaming night. To the door of the stable then did he ride, and knocked in a peculiar manner. Reconnoitring Dick through a broken pane of glass in the lintel, and apparently satisfied with his scrutiny, the lad thrust forth a head of hair as full of straw as Mad Tom's is represented to be upon the stage. A chuckle of welcome followed his sleepy salutation. "Glad to see you, Captain Turpin," said he; "can I do anything for you?"

"Get me a couple of bottles of brandy and a beefsteak," said Dick.

"As to the brandy, you can have that in a jiffy—but the steak, Lord love ye, the old ooman won't stand it at this time; but there's a cold round, mayhap a slice of that might do—or a knuckle of ham?"

" A pest on your knuckles, Ralph," cried Dick; " have you any raw meat in the house ? "

" Raw meat ! " echoed Ralph, in surprise. " Oh, yes, there's a rare rump of beef. You can have a cut off that, if you like."

" That's the thing I want," said Dick, ungirthing his mare. " Give me the scraper. There, I can get a wisp of straw from your head. Now run and get the brandy. Better bring three bottles. Uncork 'em, and let me have half a pail of water to mix with the spirit."

" A pailful of brandy and water to wash down a raw steak ! My eyes ! " exclaimed Ralph, opening wide his sleepy peepers; adding, as he went about the execution of his task, " I always thought them rum-padders, as they call themselves, rum fellows, but now I'm sartin sure on it."

The most sedulous groom could not have bestowed more attention upon the horse of his heart than Dick Turpin now paid to his mare. He scraped, chafed, and dried her, sounded each muscle, traced each sinew, pulled her ears, examined the state of her feet, and, ascertaining that her " withers were unwrung," finally washed her from head to foot in the diluted spirit, not, however, before he had conveyed a thimbleful of the liquid to his own parched throat, and replenished what Falstaff calls a " pocket pistol," which he had about him. While Ralph was engaged in rubbing her down after her bath, Dick occupied himself, not in dressing the raw steak in the manner the stable-boy had anticipated, but in rolling it round the bit of his bridle.

" She will now go as long as there's breath in her body," said he, putting the flesh-covered iron within her mouth.

The saddle being once more replaced, after champing a moment or two at the bit, Bess began to snort and paw the earth, as if impatient of delay; and, acquainted as he was with her indomitable spirit and power, her condition was a surprise even to Dick himself. Her vigour seemed inexhaustible, her vivacity was not a whit diminished, but, as she was led into the open space, her step became as light and free as when she started on her ride, and her sense of sound as quick as ever. Suddenly she pricked her ears, and uttered a low neigh. A dull tramp was audible.

" Ha ! " exclaimed Dick, springing into his saddle; " they come."

" Who come, captain ? " asked Ralph.

" The road takes a turn here, don't it ? " asked Dick; " sweeps round to the right by the plantations in the hollow ? "

" Aye, aye, captain," answered Ralph; " it's plain you knows the ground."

" What lies behind yon shed ? "

" A stiff fence, captain—a reg'lar rasper. Beyond that a hill-side steep as a house; no 'oss as was ever shod can go down it."

" Indeed ! " laughed Dick.

A loud halloo from Major Mowbray, who seemed advancing upon the wings of the wind, told Dick that he was discovered. The major was a superb horseman, and took the lead of his party. Striking his spurs deeply into his horse, and giving him bridle enough, the major seemed to shoot forward like a shell through the air.

The Burleigh Arms retired some hundred yards from the road, the space in front being occupied by a neat garden, with low, clipped edges. No tall timber intervened between Dick and his pursuers, so that the motions of both parties were visible to each other. Dick saw in an instant that if he now started he should come into collision with the major exactly at the angle of the road, and he was by no means desirous of hazarding such a rencontre. He looked wistfully back at the double fence.

"Come into the stable. Quick, captain, quick!" exclaimed Ralph.

"The stable?" echoed Dick, hesitating.

"Aye, the stable; it's your only chance. Don't you see he's turning the corner, and they are all coming? Quick, sir, quick!"

Dick, lowering his head, rode into the tenement, the door of which was unceremoniously slapped in the major's face, and bolted on the other side.

"Villain!" cried Major Mowbray, thundering at the door, "come forth. You are now fairly trapped at last—caught like the woodcock in your own spring. We have you. Open the door, I say, and save us the trouble of forcing it. You cannot escape us. We will burn the building down but we will have you."

"What dun you want, measter?" cried Ralph, from the lintel, whence he reconnoitred the major, and kept the door fast. "You're clean mista'en. There be no one here."

"We'll soon see that," said Paterson, who had now arrived; and, leaping from his horse, the chief constable took a short run, to give himself impetus, and with his foot burst open the door. This being accomplished, in dashed the major and Paterson, but the stable was vacant. A door was open at the back; they rushed to it. The sharply sloping sides of a hill slipped abruptly downwards, within a yard of the door. It was a perilous descent to the horseman, yet the print of a horse's heels was visible in the dislodged turf and scattered soil.

"Confusion!" cried the major, "he has escaped us."

"He is yonder," said Paterson, pointing out Turpin moving swiftly through the steaming meadow. "See, he makes again for the road—he clears the fence. A regular throw he has given us, by the Lord!"

"Nobly done, by Heaven!" cried the major. "With all his faults, I honour the fellow's courage, and admire his prowess. He's already ridden to-night as I believe never man rode before. I would not have ventured to slide down that wall, for it's nothing else, with the enemy at my heels. What say you, gentlemen, have you had enough? Shall we let him go, or—— ?"

"As far as the chase goes, I don't care if we bring the matter to a conclusion," said Titus. "I don't think, as it is, that I shall have a sate to sit on this week to come. I've lost leather most confoundedly."

"What says Mr. Coates?" asked Paterson. "I look to him."

"Then mount, and off," cried Coates. "Public duty requires that we should take him."

"And private pique," returned the major. "No matter! The end is the same. Justice shall be satisfied. To your steeds, my merry men all Hark, and away."

Once more upon the move, Titus forgot his distress, and addressed himself to the attorney, by whose side he rode.

" What place is that we're coming to ? " asked he, pointing to a cluster of moonlit spires belonging to a town they were rapidly approaching.

" Stamford," replied Coates.

" Stamford ! " exclaimed Titus ; " by the powers ! then, we've ridden a matter of ninety miles. Why, the great deeds of Redmond O'Hanlon were nothing to this ! I'll remember it to my dying day, and with reason," added he, uneasily shifting his position on the saddle.

.    .    .    .    .    .    .    .    .    .    .

Dick Turpin, meanwhile, held bravely on his course. Bess was neither strained by her gliding passage down the slippery hill-side, nor shaken by *larking* the fence in the meadow. As Dick said, " It took a devilish deal to take it out of her." On regaining the high road she resumed her old pace, and once more they were distancing Time's swift chariot in its whirling passage o'er the earth. Stamford, and the tongue of Lincoln's fenny shire, upon which it is situated, are passed almost in a breath. Rutland is won and passed, and Lincolnshire once more entered. The road now verged within a bowshot of Melton Mowbray. Bess here *let out* in a style with which it would have puzzled the best Leicestershire squire's best prad to have kept pace. The spirit she imbibed through the pores of her skin, and the juices of the meat she had champed, seemed to have communicated preternatural excitement to her. Her pace was absolutely terrific. Her eyeballs were dilated, and glowed like flaming carbuncles ; while her widely distended nostrils seemed, in the cold moonshine, to snort forth smoke, as from a

*Bess suddenly floundered and fell, throwing her master over her head.*

hidden fire. Fain would Turpin have controlled her; but without bringing into play all his tremendous nerve, no check could be given her headlong course, and for once, and the only time in her submissive career, Bess resolved to have her own way—and she had it. Like a sensible fellow, Dick conceded the point. There was something even of conjugal philosophy in his self-communion upon the occasion. " E'en let her take her own way and be hanged to her, for an obstinate, self-willed jade as she is," said he : " now her back is up there'll be no stopping her, I'm sure : she rattles away like a woman's tongue, and when that once begins, we all know what chance the curb has. Best to let her have it out, or rather to lend her a lift. 'Twill be over the sooner. Tantivy, lass ! tantivy ! I know which of us will tire first."

. . . . . . . . . . .

Time presses. We may not linger in our course. We must fly on before our flying highwayman. Full forty miles shall we pass over in a breath. Two more hours have elapsed, and he still urges his headlong career, with heart resolute as ever, and purpose yet unchanged. Fair Newark, and the dashing Trent, " most loved of England's streams," are gathered to his laurels. Broad Notts, and its heavy paths and sweeping glades ; its waste (forest no more) of Sherwood past ; bold Robin Hood and his merry men, his Marian and his moonlight rides, recalled, forgotten, left behind. Hurrah ! hurrah ! That wild halloo, that waving arm, that enlivening shout—what means it ? He is once more upon Yorkshire ground ; his horse's hoof beats once more the soil of that noble shire. So transported was Dick that he could almost have flung himself from the saddle to kiss the dust beneath his feet. Thrice fifty miles has he run, nor has the morn yet dawned upon his labours. Hurrah ! the end draws nigh ; the goal is in view. Halloo ! halloo ! on !

Bawtrey is past. He takes the lower road by Thorne and Selby. He is skirting the waters of the deep-channelled Don.

Bess now began to manifest some slight symptoms of distress. There was a strain in the carriage of her throat, a dullness in her eye, a laxity in her ear, and a slight stagger in her gait, which Turpin noticed with apprehension. Still she went on, though not at the same gallant pace as heretofore. But, as the tired bird still battles with the blast upon the ocean, as the swimmer still stems the stream, though spent, on went she : nor did Turpin dare to check her, fearing that, if she stopped, she might lose her force, or, if she fell, she would rise no more.

The moon had set. The stars had all—save one, the herald of the dawn —withdrawn their lustre. A dull mist lay on the stream, and the air became piercing cold. Turpin's chilled fingers could scarcely grasp the slackening rein, while his eyes, irritated by the keen atmosphere, hardly enabled him to distinguish surrounding objects, or even to guide his steed. It was owing, probably, to this latter circumstance, that Bess suddenly floundered and fell, throwing her master over her head.

Turpin instantly recovered himself. His first thought was for his horse. But Bess was instantly upon her legs—covered with dust and foam, sides and cheeks—and with her large eyes glaring wildly, almost piteously, upon her master.

*When Turpin and his horse were nearly across, Paterson fired, but did not do much mischief.*

"Art hurt, lass?" asked Dick, as she shook herself, and slightly shivered. And he proceeded to the horseman's scrutiny. "Nothing but a shake; though that dull eye—those quivering flanks——" added he, looking earnestly at her. "She won't go much farther, and I must give it up—what! give up the race just when it's won? No, that can't be. Ha! well thought on. I've a bottle of liquid, given me by an old fellow, who was a knowing cove and a famous jockey in his day, which he swore would make a horse go as long as he'd a leg to carry him, and bade me keep it for some great occasion. I've never used it; but I'll try it now. It should be in this pocket. Ah! Bess, wench, I fear I'm using thee, after all, as Sir Luke did his mistress, that I thought so like thee. No matter! It will be a glorious end."

Raising her head upon his shoulder, Dick poured the contents of the bottle down the throat of his mare. Nor had he to wait long, for its invigorating effects were instantaneous. The fire was kindled in the glassy orb; her crest was once more erected; her flank ceased to quiver; and she neighed loud and joyously.

"Egad, the old fellow was right," cried Dick. "The drink has worked wonders. What the devil could it have been? It smells like spirit," added he, examining the bottle. "I wish I'd left a taste for myself. But here's that which will do as well." And he drained his flask of the last drop of brandy.

Once more, at a gallant pace, he traversed the banks of the Don, skirting the fields of flax that bound its sides, and hurried far more swiftly than its current to its confluence with the Aire.

Snaith was past. He was on the road to Selby when dawn first began to break. Here and there a twitter was heard in the hedge; a hare ran across his path, gray-looking as the morning self; and the mists began to rise from the earth. A bar of gold was drawn against the east, like the roof of a gorgeous palace. But the mists were heavy in this world of rivers and their tributary streams. The Ouse was before him, the Trent and Aire behind; the Don and Derwent on either hand, all on their way to commingle their currents ere they formed the giant Humber. Amid a region so prodigal of water, no wonder the dews fell thick as rain. Here and there the ground was clear; but then again came a volley of vapour, dim and palpable as smoke.

. . . . . . . . . . .

The sun had just o'ertopped the "high eastern hill," as Turpin reached the Ferry of Cawood, and its beams were reflected upon the deep and sluggish waters of the Ouse. Wearily had he dragged his course thither— wearily and slow. The powers of his gallant steed were spent, and he could scarcely keep her from sinking. It was now midway 'twixt the hours of five and six. Nine miles only lay before him, and that thought again revived him. He reached the water's edge, and hailed the ferry-boat, which was then on the other side of the river. At that instant a loud shout smote his ear; it was the halloo of his pursuers. Despair was in his look. He shouted to the boatman, and bade him pull fast. The man obeyed; but he had to breast a strong stream, and had a lazy bark and heavy sculls to contend with. He had scarcely left the shore, when another shout was raised from the pursuers. The tramp of their steeds grew louder and louder.

The boat had scarcely reached the middle of the stream. His captors were at hand. Quietly did he walk down the bank, and as cautiously enter the water. There was a plunge, and steed and rider were swimming down the river.

Major Mowbray was at the brink of the stream. He hesitated an instant, and stemmed the tide. Seized, as it were, by a mania for equestrian distinction, Mr. Coates braved the torrent. Not so Paterson. He very coolly took out his bull-dogs, and, watching Turpin, cast up in his own mind the pros and cons of shooting him as he was crossing. " I could certainly hit him," thought, or said, the constable; " but what of that? A dead highwayman is worth nothing—alive, he *weighs* £300. I won't shoot him, but I'll make a pretence." And he fired accordingly.

The shot skimmed over the water, but did not, as it was intended, do much mischief. It, however, occasioned a mishap, which nearly proved fatal to our aquatic attorney. Alarmed at the report of the pistol, in the nervous agitation of the moment Coates drew in his rein so tightly that his steed instantly sank. A moment or two afterwards he rose, shaking his ears, and floundering heavily towards the shore, and such was the chilling effect of this sudden immersion, that Mr. Coates now thought much more of saving himself than of capturing Turpin. Dick, meanwhile, had reached the opposite bank, and, refreshed by her bath, Bess scrambled up the sides of the stream, and speedily regained the road. " I shall do it yet," shouted Dick; " that stream has saved her. Hark away, lass! Hark away!"

Bess heard the cheering cry, and she answered to the call. She roused all her energies; strained every sinew; and put forth all her remaining strength. Once more, on wings of swiftness, she bore him away from his pursuers, and Major Mowbray, who had now gained the shore, and made certain of securing him, beheld him spring, like a wounded hare, from beneath his very hand.

"It cannot hold out," said the major; "it is but an expiring flash; that gallant steed must soon drop."

"She be regularly booked, that's certain," said the postboy. "We shall find her on the road."

Contrary to all expectation, however, Bess held on, and set pursuit at defiance. Her pace was swift as when she started. But it was unconscious and mechanical action. It wanted the ease, the lightness, the life of her former riding. She seemed screwed up to a task which she must execute. There was no flogging, no gory heel; but the heart was throbbing, tugging at the sides within. Her spirit spurred her onwards. Her eye was glazing; her chest heaving; her flank quivering; her crest again fallen. Yet she held on. "She is dying!" said Dick. "I feel it——" No, she held on.

Fulford is past. The towers and pinnacles of York burst upon him in all the freshness, the beauty, and the glory of a bright, clear, autumnal morn. The ancient city seemed to smile a welcome—a greeting. The noble minster and its serene and massive pinnacles, crocketed, lantern-like, and beautiful; Saint Mary's lofty spire, All-Hallows tower, the massive mouldering walls of the adjacent postern, the grim castle, and Clifford's neighbouring keep—all beamed upon him, "like a bright-eyed face, that laughs out openly."

"It is done—it is won," cried Dick. "Hurrah, hurrah!" And the sunny air was cleft with his shouts.

Bess was not insensible to her master's exultation. She neighed feebly in answer to his call, and reeled forwards. It was a piteous sight to see her —to mark her staring, protruding eyeball—her shaking flanks; but, while life and limb held together, she held on.

Another mile is past. York is near.

"Hurrah!" shouted Dick; but his voice was hushed. Bess tottered —fell. There was a dreadful gasp—a parting moan—a snort; her eye gazed, for an instant, upon her master, with a dying glare; then grew glassy, rayless, fixed. A shiver ran through her frame. Her heart had burst.

Dick's eyes were blinded, as with rain. His triumph, though achieved, was forgotten—his own safety was disregarded. He stood weeping and swearing, like one beside himself.

"And art thou gone, Bess?" cried he, in a voice of agony, lifting up his courser's head, and kissing her lips, covered with blood-flecked foam. "Gone, gone! and I have killed the best steed that was ever crossed! And for what?" added Dick, beating his brow with his clenched hand; "for what? for what?"

At this moment the deep bell of the minster clock tolled out the hour of six.

"I am answered," gasped Dick; "*it was to hear those strokes!*"

# THE LEGEND OF SLEEPY HOLLOW

## by WASHINGTON IRVING

IN the bosom of one of those spacious coves which indent the eastern shore of the Hudson, at that broad expansion of the river denominated by the ancient Dutch navigators the Tappaan Zee, and where they always prudently shortened sail, and implored the protection of St. Nicholas when they crossed, there lies a small market-town or rural port, which by some is called Greensburgh, but which is more generally and properly known by the name of Tarry Town. Not far from this village, perhaps about two miles, there is a little valley, or rather lap of land, among high hills, which is one of the quietest places in the whole world. A small brook glides through it, with just murmur enough to lull one to repose; and the occasional whistle of a quail or tapping of a woodpecker is almost the only sound that ever breaks in upon the uniform tranquillity.

From the listless repose of the place, and the peculiar character of its inhabitants, who are descendants from the original Dutch settlers, this sequestered glen has long been known by the name of SLEEPY HOLLOW, and its rustic lads are called the Sleepy Hollow Boys throughout all the neighbouring country. A drowsy dreamy influence seems to hang over the land, and to pervade the very atmosphere. The whole neighbourhood abounds with local tales, haunted spots, and twilight superstitions; stars shoot and meteors glare oftener across the valley than in any other part of the country, and the nightmare, with her whole nine fold, seems to make it the favourite scene of her gambols.

The dominant spirit, however, that haunts this enchanted region, and seems to be commander-in-chief of all the powers of the air, is the apparition of a figure on horseback without a head. It is said by some to be the ghost of a Hessian trooper, whose head had been carried away by a cannon-ball, in some nameless battle during the revolutionary war; and who is ever and anon seen by the country folk, hurrying along in the gloom of night, as if on the wings of the wind. His haunts are not confined to the valley, but extend at times to the adjacent roads, and especially to the vicinity of a church at no great distance. Indeed, certain of the most authentic historians of those parts, who have been careful in collecting and collating the floating facts concerning this spectre, allege that the body of the trooper having been buried in the churchyard, the ghost rides forth to the scene of battle in nightly quest of his head; and that the rushing speed with which he sometimes passes along the Hollow, like a midnight blast, is owing to his being belated, and in a hurry to get back to the churchyard before daybreak.

Such is the general purport of this legendary superstition, which has furnished materials for many a wild story in that region of shadows; and the spectre is known at all the country firesides by the name of the Headless Horseman of Sleepy Hollow.

It is remarkable that the visionary propensity I have mentioned is not confined to the native inhabitants of the valley, but is unconsciously imbibed by every one who resides there for a time. However wide awake they may have been before they entered that sleepy region, they are sure, in a little time, to inhale the witching influence of the air, and begin to grow imaginative —to dream dreams, and see apparitions.

In this by-place of nature there abode, in a remote period of American history, that is to say, some thirty years since, a worthy wight of the name of Ichabod Crane; who sojourned, or, as he expressed it, "tarried," in Sleepy Hollow, for the purpose of instructing the children of the vicinity. He was a native of Connecticut; a state which supplies the Union with pioneers for the mind as well as for the forest, and sends forth yearly its legions of frontier woodmen and country schoolmasters. The cognomen of Crane was not inapplicable to his person. He was tall, but exceedingly lank, with narrow shoulders, long arms and legs, hands that dangled a mile out of his sleeves, feet that might have served for shovels, and his whole frame most loosely hung together. His head was small, and flat at top, with huge ears, large green glassy eyes, and a long snipe nose, so that it looked like a weather cock, perched upon his spindle neck, to tell which way the wind blew. To see him striding along the profile of a hill on a windy day, with his clothes bagging and fluttering about him, one might have mistaken him for the genius of famine descending upon the earth, or some scarecrow eloped from a cornfield.

His school-house was a low building of one large room, rudely constructed of logs; the windows partly glazed, and partly patched with leaves of old copybooks. It was ingeniously secured at vacant hours, by a withe twisted in the handle of the door, and stakes set against the window-shutters; so that, though a thief might get in with perfect ease, he would find some embarrassment in getting out; an idea most probably borrowed by the architect, Yost Van Houten, from the mystery of an eel-pot. The school-house stood in a rather lonely but pleasant situation, just at the foot of a woody hill, with a brook running close by, and a formidable birch-tree growing at one end of it. From hence the low murmur of his pupils' voices, conning over their lessons, might be heard in a drowsy summer's day, like the hum of a beehive; interrupted now and then by the authoritative voice of the master, in the tone of menace or command ; or, peradventure, by the appalling sound of the birch, as he urged some tardy loiterer along the flowery path of knowledge. Truth to say, he was a conscientious man, and ever bore in mind the golden maxim, " Spare the rod and spoil the child." Ichabod Crane's scholars certainly were not spoiled.

When school-hours were over, he was even the companion and playmate of the larger boys ; and on holiday afternoons would convoy some of the smaller ones home, who happened to have pretty sisters, or good housewives for mothers, noted for the comforts of the cupboard. Indeed, it behoved him to keep on good terms with his pupils. The revenue arising from his school was small, and would have been scarcely sufficient to furnish him

*Ichabod's appearance was apt to occasion some little stir at the tea-table.*

with daily bread, for he was a huge feeder, and though lank, had the dilating powers of an anaconda ; but to help out his maintenance, he was, according to country custom in those parts, boarded and lodged at the houses of the farmers whose children he instructed. With these he lived successively a week at a time ; thus going the rounds of the neighbourhood, with all his worldly effects tied up in a cotton handkerchief.

That all this might not be too onerous on the purses of his rustic patrons, who are apt to consider the costs of schooling a grievous burden, and school-masters as mere drones, he had various ways of rendering himself both useful and agreeable. He assisted the farmers occasionally in the lighter labours of their farms ; helped to make hay ; mended the fences ; took the horses to water ; drove the cows from pasture ; and cut wood for the winter fire. He found favour in the eyes of the mothers by petting the children, particularly the youngest ; and would sit with a child on one knee, and rock a cradle with his foot for whole hours together.

In addition to his other vocations, he was the singing-master of the neighbourhood, and picked up many bright shillings by instructing the young folks in psalmody. It was a matter of no little vanity to him, on Sundays, to take his station in front of the church gallery, with a band of chosen singers, where, in his own mind, he completely carried away the palm from the parson.

The schoolmaster is generally a man of some importance in the female circle of a rural neighbourhood ; being considered a kind of idle gentleman-like personage, of vastly superior taste and accomplishments to the rough country swains, and, indeed, inferior in learning only to the parson. His appearance, therefore, is apt to occasion some little stir at the tea-table of a farm-house, and the addition of a supernumerary dish of cakes or sweetmeats, or peradventure the parade of a silver teapot. Our man of letters, therefore, was peculiarly happy in the smiles of all the country damsels. How he would figure among them in the churchyard between services on Sundays ! gathering grapes for them from the wild vines that overran the surrounding trees ; reciting for their amusement all the epitaphs on the tombstones ; or sauntering with a whole bevy of them along the banks of the adjacent mill-pond ; while the more bashful country bumpkins hung sheepishly back, envying his superior elegance and address.

From his half-itinerant life, also, he was a kind of travelling gazette, carrying the whole budget of local gossip from house to house ; so that his appearance was always greeted with satisfaction. He was, moreover, esteemed by the women as a man of great erudition, for he had read several books quite through, and was a perfect master of Cotton Mather's *History of New England Witchcraft*, in which, by the way, he most firmly and potently believed.

It was often his delight, after his school was dismissed in the afternoon, to stretch himself on the rich bed of clover, bordering the little brook that whimpered by his school-house, and there con over old Mather's direful tales, until the gathering dusk of the evening made the printed page a mere mist before his eyes. Then, as he wended his way by swamp and stream and awful woodland, to the farm-house where he happened to be quartered, every sound of nature, at that witching hour, fluttered his excited imagination. His only resource on such occasions, either to drown thought or drive away evil spirits, was to sing psalm tunes ;—and the good people of Sleepy Hollow, as they sat by their doors of an evening, were often filled with awe at hearing his nasal melody, " in linked sweetness long drawn out," floating from the distant hill, or along the dusky road.

These, however, were mere terrors of the night, phantoms of the mind that walk in darkness ; and though he had seen many spectres in his time, and been more than once beset by Satan in divers shapes, in his lonely perambulations, yet daylight put an end to all these evils ; and he would have passed a pleasant life of it, in despite of the devil and all his works, if his path had not been crossed by a being that causes more perplexity to mortal man than ghosts, goblins, and the whole race of witches put together, and that was—a woman.

Among the musical disciples who assembled one evening in each week to receive his instructions in psalmody, was Katrina Van Tassel, the daughter and only child of a substantial Dutch farmer. She was a blooming lass of fresh eighteen; plump as a partridge; ripe and melting and rosy-cheeked as one of her father's peaches, and universally famed, not merely for her beauty, but her vast expectations. She was, withal, a little of a coquette, as might be perceived even in her dress, which was a mixture of ancient and modern fashions, as most suited to set off her charms. She wore the ornaments of pure yellow gold, which her great-great-grandmother had brought over from Saardam; the tempting stomacher of the olden time; and withal a provokingly short petticoat, to display the prettiest foot and ankle in the country round.

Ichabod Crane had a soft and foolish heart towards the sex; and it is not to be wondered at that so tempting a morsel soon found favour in his eyes, more especially after he had visited her in her paternal mansion. Old Baltus Van Tassel was a perfect picture of a thriving, contented, liberal-hearted farmer. He seldom, it is true, sent either his eyes or his thoughts beyond the boundaries of his own farm; but within those, everything was snug, happy, and well-conditioned. He was satisfied with his wealth, but not proud of it; and piqued himself upon the hearty abundance, rather than the style in which he lived. His stronghold was situated on the banks of the Hudson, in one of those green, sheltered, fertile nooks, in which the Dutch farmers are so fond of nestling. A great elm-tree spread its broad branches over it, at the foot of which bubbled up a spring of the softest and sweetest water, in a little well formed of a barrel, and then stole sparkling away through the grass to a neighbouring brook that bubbled along among alders and dwarf willows. Hard by the farm-house was a vast barn that might have served for a church, every window and crevice of which seemed bursting forth with the treasures of the farm; the flail was busily resounding within it from morning to night; swallows and martins skimmed twittering about the eaves; and rows of pigeons, some with one eye turned up, as if watching the weather, some with their heads under their wings, or buried in their bosoms, and others swelling, and cooing, and bowing about their dames, were enjoying the sunshine on the roof. Sleek unwieldy porkers were grunting in the repose and abundance of their pens, whence sallied forth now and then troops of sucking pigs, as if to snuff the air. A stately squadron of snowy geese were riding in an adjoining pond, convoying whole fleets of ducks; regiments of turkeys were gobbling through the farm-yard, and guinea-fowls fretting about it, like ill-tempered housewives, with their peevish, discontented cry. Before the barn door strutted the gallant cock, that pattern of a husband, a warrior, and a fine gentleman, clapping his burnished wings, and crowing in the pride and gladness of his heart—sometimes tearing up the earth with his feet, and then generously calling his ever-hungry family of wives and children to enjoy the rich morsel which he had discovered.

The pedagogue's mouth watered as he looked upon his sumptuous promise of luxurious winter fare. In his devouring mind's eye he pictured to himself every roasting-pig running about with a pudding in its belly, and an apple in its mouth; the pigeons were snugly put to bed in a comfortable pie, and tucked in with a coverlet of crust; the geese were swimming in their own gravy; and the ducks pairing cosily in dishes, like snug married couples, with a decent competency of onion sauce. In the porkers he saw carved out the future sleek side of bacon and juicy relishing ham ; not a turkey but he beheld daintily trussed-up, with its gizzard under its wing, and, peradventure, a necklace of savoury sausages ; and even bright chanticleer himself lay sprawling on his back in a side dish, with uplifted claws, as if craving that quarter which his chivalrous spirit disdained to ask while living.

When he entered the house, the conquest of his heart was complete. It was one of those spacious farm-houses, with high-ridged, but lowly-sloping roofs, built in the style handed down from the first Dutch settlers : the low projecting eaves forming a piazza along the front, capable of being closed up in bad weather. Under this were hung flails, harness, various utensils of husbandry, and nets for fishing in the neighbouring river. Benches were built along the sides for summer use ; and a great spinning-wheel at one end, and a churn at the other, showed the various uses to which this important porch might be devoted. From this piazza the wondering Ichabod entered the hall, which formed the centre of the mansion and the place of usual residence. Here rows of resplendent pewter, ranged on a long dresser, dazzled his eyes. In one corner stood a huge bag of wool ready to be spun ; in another, a quantity of linsey-woolsey just from the loom ; ears of Indian corn, and strings of dried apples and peaches, hung in gay festoons along the wall, mingled with the gaud of red peppers ; and a door left ajar gave him a peep into the best parlour, where the claw-footed chairs and dark mahogany tables shone like mirrors ; and irons, with their accompanying shovel and tongs, glistened from their covert of asparagus tops ; mock oranges and conch-shells decorated the mantel-piece ; strings of various coloured birds' eggs were suspended above it ; a great ostrich egg was hung from the centre of the room, and a corner cupboard, knowingly left open, displayed immense treasures of old silver and well-mended china.

From the moment Ichabod laid his eyes upon these regions of delight, the peace of his mind was at an end, and his only study was how to gain the affections of the peerless daughter of Van Tassel. In this enterprise, however, he had more real difficulties than generally fell to the lot of a knight-errant of yore, who seldom had anything but giants, enchanters, fiery dragons, and such like easily conquered adversaries, to contend with ; he had to encounter a host of fearful adversaries of real flesh and blood, the numerous rustic admirers who beset every portal to her heart, keeping a watchful and angry eye upon each other, but ready to fly out in the common cause against any new competitor.

Among these the most formidable was a burly, roaring, roistering blade, of the name of Abraham, or, according to the Dutch abbreviation, Brom Van Brunt, the hero of the country round, which rang with his feats of strength and hardihood. He was broad-shouldered and double-jointed, with short curly black hair, and a bluff but not unpleasant countenance, having a mingled air of fun and arrogance. From his Herculean frame and great powers of limb, he had received the nickname of BROM BONES, by which he was universally known. He was famed for great knowledge and skill in horsemanship, being as dexterous on horseback as a Tartar. He was foremost at all races and cock-fights, and, with the ascendancy which bodily strength acquires in rustic life, was the umpire in all disputes, sitting his hat on one side, and giving his decisions with an air and tone admitting of no gainsay or appeal. He was always ready for either a fight or frolic, but had more mischief than ill-will in his composition ; and, with all his overbearing roughness, there was a strong dash of waggish good humour at bottom. He had three or four boon companions, who regarded him as their model, and at the head of whom he scoured the country, attending every scene of feud or merriment for miles round.

This rantipole hero had for some time singled out the blooming Katrina for the object of his uncouth gallantries, and it was whispered that she did not altogether discourage his hopes.

Such was the formidable rival with whom Ichabod Crane had to contend.

To have taken the field openly against his rival would have been madness ; for he was not a man to be thwarted in his amours, any more than that stormy lover, Achilles. Ichabod, therefore, made his advances in a quiet and gently-insinuating manner. Under cover of his character of singing-master, he made frequent visits at the farm-house ; not that he had anything to apprehend from the meddlesome interference of parents, which is so often a stumbling-block in the path of lovers. Balt Van Tassel was an easy, in-dulgent soul ; he loved his daughter better even than his pipe, and, like a reasonable man and an excellent father, let her have her way in everything. His notable little wife, too, had enough to do to attend to her housekeeping, and manage her poultry ; for, as she sagely observed, ducks and geese are foolish things, and must be looked after, but girls can take care of themselves. Thus, while the busy dame bustled about the house, or plied her spinning-

*A scoundrel dog whined in the most ludicrous manner.*

wheel at one end of the piazza, honest Balt would sit smoking his evening pipe at the other, watching the achievements of a little wooden warrior, who, armed with a sword in each hand, was most valiantly fighting the wind on the pinnacle of the barn. In the meantime, Ichabod would carry on his suit with the daughter by the side of the spring under the great elm, or sauntering along in the twilight.

From the moment Ichabod Crane made his advances, the interests of Brom Bones evidently declined; his horse was no longer seen tied at the palings on Sunday nights, and a deadly feud gradually arose between him and the preceptor of Sleepy Hollow.

Brom, who had a degree of rough chivalry in his nature, would fain have carried matters to open warfare, and have settled their pretensions to the lady, according to the mode of those most concise and simple reasoners, the knights-errants of yore—by single combat; but Ichabod was too conscious of the superior might of his adversary to enter the lists against him; he had overheard a boast of Bones, that he " would double the schoolmaster up, and lay him on a shelf of his own school-house "; and he was too wary to give him an opportunity. There was something extremely provoking in this obstinately pacific system; it left Brom no alternative but to draw upon the funds of rustic waggery in his disposition, and to play off boorish practical jokes upon his rival. Ichabod became the object of whimsical persecution to Bones and his gang of rough riders. They harried his hitherto peaceful domains; smoked out his singing-school, by stopping up the chimney; broke into the school-house at night, in spite of his formidable fastenings of withe and window stakes, and turned everything topsy-turvy; so that the poor schoolmaster began to think all the witches in the country held their meetings there. But what was still more annoying, Brom took all opportunities of turning him into ridicule in presence of his mistress, and had a scoundrel dog whom he taught to whine in the most ludicrous manner, and introduced as a rival of Ichabod's to instruct her in psalmody.

In this way matters went on for some time, without producing any material effect on the relative situation of the contending powers. On a fine autumnal afternoon, Ichabod, in pensive mood, sat enthroned on the lofty stool whence he usually watched all the concerns of his little literary realm. In his hand he swayed a ferule, that sceptre of despotic power; the birch of justice reposed on three nails behind the throne, a constant terror to evil-doers; while on the desk before him might be seen sundry contraband articles and prohibited weapons, detected upon the persons of idle urchins; such as half-munched apples, pop-guns, whirligigs, fly-cages, and whole legions of rampant little paper game-cocks. Apparently there had been some appalling act of justice recently inflicted, for his scholars were all busily intent upon their books, or slyly whispering behind them with one eye kept upon the master; and a kind of buzzing stillness reigned throughout the schoolroom. It was suddenly interrupted by the appearance of a negro, in tow-cloth jacket and trousers, a round-crowned fragment of a hat, like the cap of Mercury, and mounted on the back of a ragged, wild, half-broken colt, which he managed with a rope by way of halter. He came clattering up to the school door with an invitation to Ichabod to attend a merry-making, or " quilting frolic," to be held that evening at Mynheer Van Tassel's; and having delivered

*Old and broken-down as he looked, there was more of the lurking devil in him than in any young filly in the country.*

his message with that air of importance and effort at fine language which a negro is apt to display on petty embassies of the kind, he dashed over the brook, and was seen scampering away up the hollow, full of the importance and hurry of his mission.

All was now bustle and hubbub in the late quiet schoolroom. The scholars were hurried through their lessons without stopping at trifles ; those who were nimble skipped over half with impunity, and those who were tardy had a smart application now and then in the rear, to quicken their speed, or help them over a tall word. Books were flung aside without being put away on the shelves ; inkstands were overturned, benches thrown down, and the whole school was turned loose an hour before the usual time, bursting forth like a legion of young imps, yelping and racketing about the green in joy at their early emancipation.

The gallant Ichabod now spent at least an extra half-hour at his toilet, brushing and furbishing up his best, and indeed only suit of rusty black, and arranging his locks by a bit of broken looking-glass that hung up in the school-house. That he might make his appearance before his mistress in the true style of a cavalier, he borrowed a horse from the farmer with whom he was domiciliated, a choleric old Dutchman, of the name of Hans Van Ripper, and, thus gallantly mounted, issued forth like a knight-errant in quest of adventures.

The animal he bestrode was a broken-down plough-horse that had outlived almost everything but his viciousness. He was gaunt and shagged, with a ewe neck and a head like a hammer ; his rusty mane and tail were tangled and knotted with burrs; one eye had lost its pupil, and was glaring and spectral; but the other had the gleam of a gonuine devil in it. Still he must have had fire and mettle in his day, if we may judge from the name he bore of Gunpowder. He had, in fact, been a favourite steed of his master's, the choleric Van Ripper, who was a furious rider, and had infused, very probably, some of his own spirit into the animal; for, old and broken-down as he looked, there was more of the lurking devil in him than in any young filly in the country.

Ichabod was a suitable figure for such a steed. He rode with short stirrups, which brought his knees nearly up to the pommel of the saddle; his sharp elbows stuck out like grasshoppers'; he carried his whip perpendicularly in his hand, like a sceptre, and, as his horse jogged on, the motion of his arms was not unlike the flapping of a pair of wings. A small wool hat rested on the top of his nose, for so his scanty strip of forehead might be called; and the skirts of his black coat fluttered out almost to the horse's tail. Such was the appearance of Ichabod and his steed, as they shambled out of the gate of Hans Van Ripper, and it was altogether such an apparition as is seldom to be met with in broad daylight.

As Ichabod jogged slowly on his way, his eye, ever open to every symptom of culinary abundance, ranged with delight over the treasures of jolly autumn. On all sides he beheld vast stores of apples; some hanging in oppressive opulence on the trees; some gathered into baskets and barrels for the market; others heaped up in rich piles for the cider-press. Farther on he beheld great fields of Indian corn, with its golden ears peeping from their leafy coverts, and holding out the promise of cakes and hasty-pudding; and the yellow pumpkins lying beneath them, turning up their fair round bellies to the sun, and giving ample prospects of the most luxurious of pies; and anon he passed the fragrant buckwheat fields breathing the odour of the beehive, and as he beheld them, soft anticipations stole over his mind of dainty slapjacks, well buttered, and garnished with honey or treacle, by the delicate little dimpled hand of Katrina Van Tassel.

Thus feeding his mind with many sweet thoughts and " sugared suppositions," he journeyed along the sides of a range of hills which look out upon some of the goodliest scenes of the mighty Hudson.

It was toward evening that Ichabod arrived at the castle of the Heer Van Tassel, which he found thronged with the pride and flower of the adjacent country. Old farmers, a spare leathern-faced race, in homespun coats and breeches, blue stockings, huge shoes, and magnificent pewter buckles. Their brisk, withered little dames, in close crimped caps, long-waisted short gowns, homespun petticoats, with scissors and pincushions, and gay calico pockets hanging on the outside. Buxom lasses, almost as antiquated as their mothers, excepting where a straw hat, a fine riband, or perhaps a white frock, gave symptoms of city innovation. The sons, in short square-skirted coats with rows of stupendous brass buttons, and their hair generally queued in the fashion of the times, especially if they could procure an eel-skin for the purpose, it being esteemed throughout the country as a potent nourisher and strengthener of the hair.

Brom Bones, however, was the hero of the scene, having come to the gathering on his favourite steed Daredevil, a creature like himself, full of mettle and mischief, and which no one but himself could manage. He was, in fact, noted for preferring vicious animals, given to all kinds of tricks, which kept the rider in constant risk of his neck, for he held a tractable, well-broken horse as unworthy of a lad of spirit.

Fain would I pause to dwell upon the world of charms that burst upon the enraptured gaze of my hero, as he entered the state parlour of Van Tassel's mansion. Not those of the bevy of buxom lasses, with their luxurious display of red and white; but the ample charms of a genuine Dutch country tea-table in the sumptuous time of autumn. Such heaped-up platters of cakes of various and almost indescribable kinds, known only to experienced Dutch housewives! There was the doughty doughnut, the tenderer oly koek, and the crisp and crumbling cruller; sweet-cakes and short-cakes, ginger-cakes and honey-cakes, and the whole family of cakes. And then there were apple-pies and peach-pies and pumpkin-pies; besides slices of ham and smoked beef; and, moreover, delectable dishes of preserved plums, and peaches, and pears, and quinces; not to mention broiled shad and roasted chickens; together with bowls of milk and cream, all mingled higgledy-piggledy with the motherly teapot sending up its clouds of vapour from the midst!

Ichabod was a kind and thankful creature, whose heart dilated in proportion as his skin was filled with good cheer; and whose spirits rose with eating as some men's do with drink. He could not help, too, rolling his large eyes round him as he ate, and chuckling with the possibility that he might one day be lord of all this scene of almost unimaginable luxury and splendour. Then, he thought, how soon he'd turn his back upon the old school-house, snap his fingers in the face of Hans Van Ripper and every other niggardly patron, and kick any itinerant pedagogue out of doors that should dare to call him comrade!

Old Baltus Van Tassel moved about among his guests with a face dilated with content and good humour, round and jolly as the harvest moon. His hospitable attentions were brief, but expressive, being confined to a shake of the hand, a slap on the shoulder, a loud laugh, and a pressing invitation to "fall to, and help themselves."

And now the sound of the music from the common room or hall summoned to the dance. The musician was an old gray-headed negro, who had been the itinerant orchestra of the neighbourhood for more than half a century. His instrument was as old and battered as himself. The greater part of the time he scraped on two or three strings, accompanying every movement of the bow with a motion of the head; bowing almost to the ground, and stamping with his foot whenever a fresh couple were to start.

Ichabod prided himself upon his dancing as much as upon his vocal powers. Not a limb, not a fibre about him was idle; and to have seen his loosely-hung frame in full motion, and clattering about the room, you would have thought Saint Vitus himself, that blessed patron of the dance, was figuring before you in person. He was the admiration of all the negroes; who, having gathered, of all ages and sizes, from the farm and the neighbourhood, stood forming a pyramid of shining black faces, at every door and window, gazing with delight at the scene, rolling their white eyeballs, and showing grinning rows of ivory from ear to ear. How could the flogger of urchins be otherwise than animated and joyous? The lady of his heart was his partner in the dance, and smiling graciously in reply to all his amorous oglings; while Brom Bones, sorely smitten with love and jealousy, sat brooding by himself in one corner.

When the dance was at an end, Ichabod was attracted to a knot of the sager folks, who, with old Van Tassel, sat smoking at one end of the piazza, gossiping over former times, and drawing out long stories about the war.

But all these were nothing to the tales of ghosts and apparitions that succeeded. Many dismal tales were told about funeral trains, and mourning cries and wailings heard and seen about the great tree where the unfortunate Major André was taken, and which stood in the neighbourhood. Some mention was made also of the woman in white that haunted the dark glen at Raven Rock, and was often heard to shriek on winter nights before a storm, having perished there in the snow. The chief part of the stories, however, turned upon the favourite spectre of Sleepy Hollow, the headless horseman who had been heard several times of late, patrolling the country; and, it was said, tethered his horse nightly among the graves in the churchyard.

The sequestered situation of this church seems always to have made it a favourite haunt of troubled spirits. It stands on a knoll surrounded by locust-trees and lofty elms, from among which its decent whitewashed walls shine modestly forth, like Christian purity, beaming through the shades of retirement. A gentle slope descends from it to a silver sheet of water, bordered by high trees, between which peeps may be caught at the blue hills of the Hudson. To look upon its grass-grown yard, where the sunbeams seem to sleep so quietly, one would think that there at least the dead might rest in peace. On one side of the church extends a wide woody dell, along which raves a large brook among broken rocks and trunks of fallen trees. Over a deep black part of the stream, not far from the church, was formerly thrown a wooden bridge; the road that led to it, and the bridge itself, were thickly shaded by overhanging trees, which cast a gloom about it, even in the day-time; but occasioned a fearful darkness at night. Such was one of the favourite haunts of the headless horseman, and the place where he was most frequently encountered. The tale was told of old Brouwer, a most heretical disbeliever in ghosts, how he met the horseman returning from his foray into Sleepy Hollow, and was obliged to get up behind him; how they galloped over bush and brake, over hill and swamp, until they reached the bridge; when the horseman suddenly turned into a skeleton, threw old Brouwer into the brook, and sprang away over the tree-tops with a clap of thunder.

This story was immediately matched by a thrice marvellous adventure of Brom Bones, who made light of the galloping Hessian as an arrant jockey. He affirmed that, on returning one night from the neighbouring village of Sing-Sing, he had been overtaken by this midnight trooper; that he had offered to race with him for a bowl of punch, and should have won it too, for Daredevil beat the goblin horse all hollow, but, just as they came to the church bridge, the Hessian bolted, and vanished in a flash of fire.

All these tales, told in that drowsy undertone with which men talk in the dark, the countenances of the listeners only now and then receiving a casual gleam from the glare of a pipe, sank deep in the mind of Ichabod.

He repaid them in kind, with large extracts from his invaluable author Cotton Mather, and added many marvellous events that had taken place in his native state of Connecticut, and fearful sights which he had seen in his nightly walks about Sleepy Hollow.

The revel now gradually broke up. The old farmers gathered together their families in their wagons, and were heard for some time rattling along the hollow roads, and over the distant hills. Some of the damsels mounted on pillions behind their favourite swains, and their light-hearted laughter, mingling with the clatter of hoofs, echoed along the silent woodlands, sounding fainter and fainter until they gradually died away—and the late scene of

*The lady of his heart was his partner in the dance, while Brom Bones sat brooding in a corner.*

noise and frolic was all silent and deserted. Ichabod only lingered behind, according to the custom of country lovers, to have a *tête-à-tête* with the heiress, fully convinced that he was now on the high road to success. What passed at this interview I will not pretend to say, for in fact I do not know. Something, however, I fear me, must have gone wrong, for he certainly sallied forth, after no very great interval, with an air quite desolate and chop-fallen. Oh, these women! these women! Could that girl have been playing off any of her coquettish tricks?—Was her encouragement of the poor pedagogue all a mere sham to secure her conquest of his rival?—Heaven only knows, not I!—Let it suffice to say, Ichabod stole forth with the air of one who had been sacking a hen-roost, rather than a fair lady's heart. Without looking to the right or left to notice the scene of rural wealth on which he had so often gloated, he went straight to the stable, and with several hearty cuffs and kicks, roused his steed most uncourteously from the comfortable quarters in which he was soundly sleeping, dreaming of mountains of corn and oats, and whole valleys of timothy and clover.

It was the very witching time of night that Ichabod, heavy-hearted and crestfallen, pursued his travel homewards, along the sides of the lofty hills which rise above Tarry Town, and which he had traversed so cheerily in the afternoon. The hour was as dismal as himself. All the stories of ghosts and goblins that he had heard in the afternoon now came crowding upon his recollection. The night grew darker and darker; the stars seemed to sink deeper in the sky, and driving clouds occasionally hid them from his sight.

He had never felt so lonely and dismal. He was, moreover, approaching the very place where many of the scenes of the ghost-stories had been laid. In the centre of the road stood an enormous tulip-tree, which towered like a giant above all the other trees of the neighbourhood, and formed a kind of landmark. Its limbs were gnarled and fantastic, large enough to form trunks for ordinary trees, twisting down almost to the earth, and rising again into the air. It was connected with the tragical story of the unfortunate André, who had been taken prisoner hard by; and was universally known by the name of Major André's tree. The common people regarded it with a mixture of respect and superstition, partly out of sympathy for the fate of its ill-starred namesake, and partly from the tales of strange sights and doleful lamentations told concerning it.

As Ichabod approached this fearful tree, he began to whistle; he thought his whistle was answered; it was but a blast sweeping sharply through the dry branches. As he approached a little nearer, he thought he saw something white hanging in the midst of the tree—he paused and ceased whistling; but on looking more narrowly, perceived that it was a place where the tree had been scathed by lightning, and the white wood laid bare. Suddenly he heard a groan—his teeth chattered, and his knees smote against the saddle; it was but the rubbing of one huge bough upon another, as they were swayed about by the breeze. He passed the tree in safety, but new perils lay before him.

About two hundred yards from the tree a small brook crossed the road, and ran into a marshy and thickly-wooded glen, known by the name of Wiley's Swamp. A few rough logs, laid side by side, served for a bridge over this stream. On that side of the road where the brook entered the wood a group of oaks and chestnuts, matted thick with wild grapevines, threw a cavernous gloom over it. To pass this bridge was the severest trial. It was at this identical spot that the unfortunate André was captured and under the covert of those chestnuts and vines were the sturdy yeomen concealed who suprised him. This has ever since been considered a haunted stream, and fearful are the feelings of the schoolboy who has to pass it alone after dark.

As he approached the stream, his heart began to thump; he summoned up, however, all his resolution, gave his horse half a score of kicks in the ribs, and attempted to dash briskly across the bridge; but instead of starting forward, the perverse old animal made a lateral movement, and ran broadside against the fence. Ichabod, whose fears increased with the delay, jerked the reins on the other side, and kicked lustily with the contrary foot: it was all in vain; his steed started, it is true, but it was only to plunge to the

opposite side of the road into a thicket of brambles and alderbushes. The
schoolmaster now bestowed both whip and heel upon the starveling ribs of
old Gunpowder, who dashed forward, snuffling and snorting, but came to
a stand just by the bridge, with a suddenness that had nearly sent his rider
sprawling over his head. Just at this moment a plashy tramp by the side
of the bridge caught the sensitive ear of Ichabod. In the dark shadow of
the grove, on the margin of the brook, he beheld something huge, mis-
shapen, black and towering. It stirred not, but seemed gathered up in the
gloom, like some gigantic monster ready to spring upon the traveller.

The hair of the affrighted pedagogue rose upon his head with terror.
What was to be done? To turn and fly was now too late; and besides, what
chance was there of escaping ghost or goblin, if such it was, which could

*Ichabod was horror-struck on perceiving that his fellow-traveller was headless.*

ride upon the wings of the wind? Summoning up, therefore, a show of
courage, he demanded in stammering accents, "Who are you?" He
received no reply. He repeated his demand in a still more agitated voice.
Still there was no answer. Once more he cudgelled the sides of the in-
flexible Gunpowder, and, shutting his eyes, broke forth with involuntary
fervour into a psalm tune. Just then the shadowy object of alarm put itself
in motion, and with a scramble and a bound, stood at once in the middle
of the road. Though the night was dark and dismal, yet the form of the
unknown might now in some degree be ascertained. He appeared to be a
horseman of large dimensions, and mounted on a black horse of powerful
frame. He made no offer of molestation or sociability, but kept aloof on
one side of the road, jogging along on the blind side of old Gunpowder,
who had now got over his fright and waywardness.

Ichabod, who had no relish for this strange midnight companion, and bethought himself of the adventure of Brom Bones with the Galloping Hessian, now quickened his steed, in hopes of leaving him behind. The stranger, however, quickened his horse to an equal pace. Ichabod pulled up, and fell into a walk, thinking to lag behind—the other did the same. His heart began to sink within him ; he endeavoured to resume his psalm tune, but his parched tongue clove to the roof of his mouth, and he could not utter a stave. There was something in the moody and dogged silence of this pertinacious companion that was mysterious and appalling. It was soon fearfully accounted for. On mounting a rising ground, which brought the figure of his fellow-traveller in relief against the sky, gigantic in height, and muffled in a cloak, Ichabod was horror-struck on perceiving that he was headless !—but his horror was still more increased on observing that the head, which should have rested on his shoulders, was carried before him on the pommel of the saddle ; his terror rose to desperation ; he rained a shower of kicks and blows upon Gunpowder, hoping, by a sudden movement, to give his companion the slip—but the spectre started full jump with him. Away then they dashed, through thick and thin ; stones flying and sparks flashing at every bound. Ichabod's flimsy garments fluttered in the air, as he stretched his long lank body away over his horse's head, in the eagerness of his flight.

They had now reached the road which turns off to Sleepy Hollow ; but Gunpowder, who seemed possessed with a demon, instead of keeping up it, made an opposite turn, and plunged headlong down the hill to the left. This road leads through a sandy hollow, shaded by trees for about a quarter of a mile, where it crosses the bridge famous in goblin story, and just beyond swells the green knoll on which stands the whitewashed church.

As yet the panic of the steed had given his unskilful rider an apparent advantage in the chase ; but just as he had got half-way through the hollow, the girths of the saddle gave way, and he felt it slipping from under him. He seized it by the pommel, and endeavoured to hold it firm, but in vain ; and had just time to save himself by clasping old Gunpowder round the neck, when the saddle fell to the earth, and he heard it trampled underfoot by his pursuer. For a moment the terror of Hans Van Ripper's wrath passed across his mind—for it was his Sunday saddle ; but this was no time for petty fears ; the goblin was hard on his haunches ; and (unskilful rider that he was !) he had much ado to maintain his seat ; sometimes slipping on one side, sometimes on the other, and sometimes jolted on the high ridge of his horse's back-bone, with a violence that he verily feared would cleave him asunder.

An opening in the trees now cheered him with the hopes that the church bridge was at hand. The wavering reflection of a silver star in the bosom of the brook told him that he was not mistaken. He saw the walls of the church dimly glaring under the trees beyond. He recollected the place where Brom Bones's ghostly competitor had disappeared. " If I can but reach that bridge," thought Ichabod, " I am safe." Just then he heard the black steed panting and blowing close behind him ; he even fancied that he felt his hot breath. Another convulsive kick in the ribs, and old Gunpowder sprang upon the bridge ; he thundered over the resounding planks ; he gained the opposite side; and now Ichabod cast a look behind to see if his pursuer should vanish, according to rule, in a flash of fire and brimstone. Just then he saw the goblin rising in his stirrups, and in the very act of hurling his head at him. Ichabod endeavoured to dodge the horrible missile, but too late. It encountered his cranium with a tremendous crash—he was tumbled headlong into the dust, and Gunpowder, the black steed, and the goblin rider passed by like a whirlwind.

The next morning the old horse was found without his saddle, and with the bridle under his feet, soberly cropping the grass at his master's gate. Ichabod did not make his appearance at breakfast—dinner-hour came, but no Ichabod. The boys assembled at the school-house, and strolled idly about the banks of the brook; but no schoolmaster. Hans Van Ripper now began to feel some uneasiness about the fate of poor Ichabod and his saddle. An inquiry was set on foot, and after diligent investigation they came upon his traces. In one part of the road leading to the church was found the saddle trampled in the dirt; the track of horses' hoofs deeply dented in the road, and evidently at furious speed, were traced to the bridge, beyond which, on the bank of a broad part of the brook, where the water ran deep and black, was found the hat of the unfortunate Ichabod, and close beside it a shattered pumpkin.

The brook was searched, but the body of the schoolmaster was not to be discovered. Hans Van Ripper, as executor of his estate, examined the bundle, which contained all his worldly effects. They consisted of two shirts and a half; two stocks for the neck; a pair or two of worsted stockings; an old pair of corduroy small-clothes; a rusty razor; a book of psalm tunes, full of dog's-ears; and a broken pitch-pipe. As to the books and furniture of the school-house, they belonged to the community, excepting Cotton Mather's *History of Witchcraft*, a New England Almanac, and a book of dreams and fortune-telling; in which last was a sheet of foolscap much scribbled and blotted in several fruitless attempts to make a copy of verses in honour of the heiress of Van Tassel. These magic books and the poetic scrawl were forthwith consigned to the flames by Hans Van Ripper; who from that time forward determined to send his children no more to school, observing that he never knew any good come of this same reading and writing. Whatever money the schoolmaster possessed, and he had received his quarter's pay but a day or two before, he must have had about his person at the time of his disappearance.

The mysterious event caused much speculation at the church on the following Sunday. Knots of gazers and gossips were collected in the church-yard, at the bridge, and at the spot where the hat and pumpkin had been found. The stories of Brouwer, of Bones, and a whole budget of others, were called to mind; and when they had diligently considered them all, and compared them with the symptoms of the present case, they shook their heads, and came to the conclusion that Ichabod had been carried off by the Galloping Hessian. As he was a bachelor, and in nobody's debt, nobody troubled his head any more about him: the school was removed to a different quarter of the Hollow, and another pedagogue reigned in his stead.

Brom Bones, who shortly after his rival's disappearance conducted the blooming Katrina in triumph to the altar, was observed to look exceedingly knowing whenever the story of Ichabod was related, and always burst into a hearty laugh at the mention of the pumpkin ; which led some to suspect that he knew more about the matter than he chose to tell.

The old country wives, however, who are the best judges of these matters, maintain to this day that Ichabod was spirited away by supernatural means ; and it is a favourite story often told about the neighbourhood round the winter evening fire. The bridge became more than ever an object of super-stitious awe, and that may be the reason why the road has been altered of late years, so as to approach the church by the border of the mill-pond. The school-house being deserted, soon fell to decay, and was reported to be haunted by the ghost of the unfortunate pedagogue ; and the plough-boy, loitering homeward of a still summer evening, has often fancied his voice at a distance, chanting a melancholy psalm tune among the tranquil solitudes of Sleepy Hollow.

# The Piper

*by* WILLIAM BLAKE

PIPING down the valleys wild,
 Piping songs of pleasant glee,
On a cloud I saw a child,
 And he laughing said to me :

" Pipe a song about a Lamb ! "
 So I piped with merry cheer.
" Piper, pipe that song again ; "
 So I piped : he wept to hear.

" Drop thy pipe, thy happy pipe ;
 Sing thy songs of happy cheer : "
So I sang the same again,
 While he wept with joy to hear.

" Piper, sit thee down and write
 In a book, that all may read."
So he vanished from my sight,
 And I pluck'd a hollow reed,

And I made a rural pen,
 And I stain'd the water clear,
And I wrote my happy songs
 Every child may joy to hear.

# HO-TI DISCOVERS ROAST PIG

## by CHARLES LAMB

ANKIND, says a Chinese manuscript, which my friend M. was obliging enough to read and explain to me, for the first seventy thousand ages ate their meat raw, clawing or biting it from the living animal, just as they do in Abyssinia to this day. This period is not obscurely hinted at by their great Confucius in the second chapter of his Mundane Mutations, where he designates a kind of golden age by the term Cho-fang, literally the Cooks' Holiday. The manuscript goes on to say, that the art of roasting, or rather broiling (which I take to be the elder-brother) was accidentally discovered in the manner following. The swineherd, Ho-ti, having gone out into the woods one morning, as his manner was, to collect mast for his hogs, left his cottage in the care of his eldest son, Bo-bo, a great lubberly boy, who, being fond of playing with fire, as younkers of his age commonly are, let some sparks escape into a bundle of straw, which, kindling quickly, spread the conflagration over every part of their poor mansion, till it was reduced to ashes. Together with the cottage (a sorry antediluvian make-shift of a building, you may think it), what was of much more importance, a fine litter of new-farrowed pigs, no less than nine in number, perished. China pigs have been esteemed a luxury all over the East, from the remotest periods that we read of. Bo-bo was in the utmost consternation, as you may think, not so much for the sake of the tenement, which his father and he could easily build up again with a few dry branches, and the labour of an hour or two, at any time, as for the loss of the pigs. While he was thinking what he should say to his father, and wringing his hands over the smoking remnants of one of those untimely sufferers, an odour assailed his nostrils, unlike any scent which he had before experienced. What could it proceed from? not from the burned cottage—he had smelt that smell before—indeed this was by no means the first accident of the kind which had occurred through the negligence of this unlucky young firebrand. Much less did it resemble that of any known herb, weed, or flower. He knew not what to think. He next stooped down to feel the pig, if there were any signs of life in it. He burned his fingers, and to cool them he applied them in his booby fashion to his mouth. Some of the crumbs of the scorched skin had come away with his fingers, and for the first time in his life (in the world's life indeed, for before him no man had known it) he tasted—*crackling*! Again he felt and fumbled at the pig. It did not burn him so much now, still he licked his fingers from a sort of habit. The truth at length broke into his slow understanding that it was the pig that smelt so, and the pig that tasted so delicious; and surrendering himself up to the new-born pleasure, he fell to tearing up whole handfuls of the scorched skin with the flesh next it, and was cramming it down his throat in his beastly fashion, when his sire entered amid the smoking rafters, armed with retributory cudgel, and finding how affairs stood, began to rain blows upon the young rogue's shoulders, as thick as hail-stones, which Bo-bo heeded not any more than if they had been flies. The tickling pleasure, which he experienced in his lower regions, had rendered him quite callous to any inconveniences he might feel in those remote quarters. His father might lay on, but he could not beat him from his pig, till he had fairly made an end of it, when, something like the following dialogue ensued.

"You graceless whelp, what have you got there devouring? Is it not enough that you have burned me down three houses with your dog's tricks, and be hanged to you! but you must be eating fire, and I know not what— what have you got there, I say?"

"O father, the pig, the pig! do taste how nice the burned pig eats."

The ears of Ho-ti tingled with horror. He cursed his son, and he cursed himself that ever he should beget a son that should eat burned pig.

Bo-bo, whose scent was wonderfully sharpened since morning, soon raked out another pig, and fairly rending it asunder, thrust the lesser half by main force into the fists of Ho-ti, still shouting out, "Eat, eat, eat the burned pig, father, only taste—O Lord!"—with such-like barbarous ejaculations, cramming all the while as if he would choke.

Ho-ti trembled every joint while he grasped the abominable thing, wavering whether he should not put his son to death for an unnatural young monster, when, the crackling scorching his fingers, as it had done his son's, and applying the same remedy to them, he in his turn tasted some of its flavour, which, make what sour mouths he would for pretence, proved not altogether displeasing to him. In conclusion (for the manuscript here is a little tedious), both father and son fairly set down to the mess, and never left off till they had despatched all that remained of the litter.

Bo-bo was strictly enjoined not to let the secret escape, for the neighbours would certainly have stoned them for a couple of abominable wretches, who could think of improving upon the good meat which God had sent them. Nevertheless, strange stories got about. It was observed that Ho-ti's cottage was burned down now more frequently than ever. Nothing but fires from this time forward. Some would break out in broad day, others in the night-time. As often as the sow farrowed, so sure was the house of Ho-ti to be in a blaze; and Ho-ti himself, which was the more remarkable, instead of chastising his son, seemed to grow more indulgent to him than ever. At length they were watched, the terrible mystery discovered, and father and son summoned to take their trial at Pekin, then an inconsiderable assize town. Evidence was given, the obnoxious food itself produced in court, and verdict about to be produced, when the foreman of the jury begged that some of the burned pig, of which the culprits stood accused, might be handed into the box. He handled it, and they all handled it; and burning their fingers, as Bo-bo and his father had done before them, and nature prompting to each of them the same remedy, against the face of all the facts, and the clearest charge which judge had ever given—to the surprise of the whole court, townsfolk, strangers, reporters, and all present—without leaving the box, or any manner of consultation whatever, they brought in a verdict of Not Guilty.

The judge, who was a shrewd fellow, winked at the manifest iniquity of the decision; and, when the court was dismissed, went privily, and bought up all the pigs that could be had for love or money. In a few days his Lordship's town house was observed to be on fire. The thing took wing, and now there was nothing to be seen but fires in every direction. Fuel and pigs grew enormously dear all over the district. The insurance offices, one and all, shut up shop. People built slighter and slighter every day, until it was feared that the very science of architecture would in no long time be lost to the world. Thus this custom of firing houses continued, till in process of time, says my manuscript, a sage arose, like our Locke, who made a discovery, that the flesh of swine, or indeed of any other animal, might be cooked (*burned*, as they called it) without the necessity of consuming a whole house to dress it. Then first began the rude form of a gridiron. Roasting by the string, or spit, came in a century or two later, I forget in whose dynasty. By such slow degrees, concludes the manuscript, do the most useful, and seemingly the most obvious arts, make their way among mankind.

---

# Outward Bound

## *by* CHARLES HARPUR

AWAY, away she plunged,
   With her white sails o'er her spread,
Like the sheety clouds that gather
   On some great hill's piny head.
Still away she plungéd rampant,
   Like a lion roused to wrath,
And the late proud wave lies humbled
   In the foam-track of her path.

Yet ho! my gallant sailors,
   Wear her head from off the land!
As his steed obeys the Arab,
   How she feels the steering hand!
And the deep is her wide dwelling,
   Her wild spouse the gipsy wind;
Like a soul from earth departing
   So she leaves the coast behind.

# RIP VAN WINKLE.

FROM WASHINGTON IRVING

AT the foot of the Kaatskill mountains, the voyager may have descried the light smoke curling up from a village, whose shingle roofs gleam among the trees, just where the blue tints of the upland melt away into the fresh green of the nearer landscape.

In that same village and in one of these very houses there lived many years since, while the country was yet a province of Great Britain, a simple good-natured fellow, of the name of Rip Van Winkle. He was a kind neighbour, and an obedient henpecked husband.

He was a great favourite among all the good wives of the village, who, as usual with the amiable sex, took his part in all family squabbles; and never failed, whenever they talked those matters over in their evening gossipings, to lay all the blame on Dame Van Winkle. The children of the village, too, would shout with joy whenever he approached. He assisted at their sports, made their playthings, taught them to fly kites and shoot marbles, and told them long stories of ghosts, witches, and Indians. Whenever he went dodging about the village, he was surrounded by a troop of them, hanging on his skirts, clambering on his back, and playing a thousand tricks on him with impunity; and not a dog would bark at him throughout the neighbourhood.

The great error in Rip's composition was an insuperable aversion to all kinds of profitable labour. It could not be from the want of assiduity or perseverance; for he would sit on a wet rock, with a rod as long and heavy as a Tartar's lance, and fish all day without a murmur, even though he should not be encouraged by a single nibble. He would carry a fowling-piece on his shoulder for hours together, trudging through woods and swamps, and up hill and down dale, to shoot a few squirrels or wild pigeons. He would never refuse to assist a neighbour even in the roughest toil, and was a foremost man at all country frolics for husking Indian corn, or building stone fences; the women of the village, too, used to employ him to run their errands, and to do such little odd jobs as their less obliging husbands would not do for them. In a word, Rip was ready to attend to anybody's business but his own; but as to doing family duty, and keeping his farm in order, he found it impossible.

His children, too, were as ragged and wild as if they belonged to nobody. His son Rip, an urchin begotten in his own likeness, promised to inherit the habits, with the old clothes of his father. He was generally seen trooping like a colt at his mother's heels, equipped in a pair of his father's cast-off galligaskins, which he had much ado to hold up with one hand, as a fine lady does her train in bad weather.

Rip Van Winkle, however, was one of those happy mortals, of foolish, well-oiled dispositions, who take the world easy, eat white bread or brown, whichever can be got with least thought or trouble, and would rather starve on a penny than work for a pound. If left to himself, he would have whistled life away in perfect contentment; but his wife kept continually dinning in his ears about his idleness, his carelessness, and the ruin he was bringing on his family. Morning, noon, and night, her tongue was incessantly going, and everything he said or did was sure to produce a torrent of household eloquence. Rip had but one way of replying to all lectures of the kind, and that, by frequent use, had grown into a habit. He shrugged his shoulders, shook his head, cast up his eyes, but said nothing.

Rip's sole domestic adherent was his dog Wolf, who was as much henpecked as his master; for Dame Van Winkle regarded them as companions in idleness, and even looked upon Wolf with an evil eye, as the cause of his master's going so often astray. True it is, in all points of spirit befitting an honourable dog, he was as courageous an animal as ever scoured the woods— but what courage can withstand the ever-during and all-besetting terrors of a woman's tongue? The moment Wolf entered the house, his crest fell, his tail drooped to the ground, or curled between his legs, he sneaked about with a gallows air, casting many a sidelong glance at Dame Van Winkle, and at the least flourish of a broomstick or ladle, he would fly to the door with yelping precipitation.

Times grew worse and worse with Rip Van Winkle. For a long while he used to console himself, when driven from home, by frequenting a kind of perpetual club of the sages, philosophers, and other idle personages of the village; which held its sessions on a bench before a small inn, designated by a rubicund portrait of his Majesty George the Third. Here they used to sit in the shade, of a long lazy summer's day, talk listlessly over village gossip, or tell endless sleepy stories about nothing. But it would have been worth any statesman's money to have heard the profound discussions that sometimes took place, when by chance an old newspaper fell into their hands from some passing traveller. How solemnly they would listen to the contents as drawled out by Derrick Van Bummel, the schoolmaster, a dapper, learned little man, who was not to be daunted by the most gigantic word in the dictionary.

The opinions of this junto were completely controlled by Nicholas Vedder, a patriarch of the village, and landlord of the inn, at the door of which he took his seat from morning till night, just moving sufficiently to avoid the sun and keep in the shade of a large tree; so that the neighbours could tell the hour by his movements as accurately as by a sundial. It is true, he was rarely heard to speak, but smoked his pipe incessantly. His adherents, however, perfectly understood him, and knew how to gather his opinions. When anything that was read or related displeased him, he was observed to smoke his pipe vehemently, and to send forth short, frequent, and angry puffs, but when pleased he would inhale the smoke slowly and tranquilly, and emit it in light and placid clouds; and sometimes, taking the pipe from his mouth, and letting the fragrant vapour curl about his nose, would gravely nod his head in token of perfect approbation.

From even this stronghold the unlucky Rip was at length routed by his termagant wife, who would suddenly break in upon the tranquillity of the assemblage and call the members all to naught; nor was that august personage, Nicholas Vedder himself, sacred from her daring tongue who charged him outright with encouraging her husband in habits of idleness.

Poor Rip was at last reduced almost to despair; and his only alternative to escape from the labour of the farm and clamour of his wife, was to take gun in hand, and stroll away into the woods. Here he would sometimes seat himself at the foot of a tree, and share the contents of his wallet with Wolf, with whom he sympathised as a fellow-sufferer in persecution. "Poor Wolf," he would say, "thy mistress leads thee a dog's life of it; but never mind, my lad, whilst I live thou shalt never want a friend to stand by thee!" Wolf would wag his tail, look wistfully in his master's face, and if dogs can feel pity, I verily believe he reciprocated the sentiment with all his heart.

In a long ramble of the kind on a fine autumnal day, Rip had unconsciously scrambled to one of the highest parts of the Kaatskill mountains. He was after his favourite sport of squirrel-shooting, and the still solitudes had echoed and re-echoed with the reports of his gun. Panting and fatigued, he

*He was a short, square fellow . . . and bore on his shoulder a stout keg.*

threw himself, late in the afternoon, on a green knoll, covered with mountain herbage, that crowned the brow of a precipice. From an opening between the trees he could overlook all the lower country for many a mile of rich woodland. He saw at a distance the lordly Hudson, far, far below him.

On the other side he looked down into a deep mountain glen, wild, lonely, and shagged, the bottom filled with fragments from the impending cliffs, and scarcely lighted by the reflected rays of the setting sun. For some time Rip lay musing on this scene; evening was advancing; the mountains began to throw their long blue shadows over the valleys; he saw that it would be dark long before he could reach the village, and he heaved a heavy sigh when he thought of encountering the terrors of Dame Van Winkle.

As he was about to descend, he heard a voice from a distance, hallooing, "Rip Van Winkle! Rip Van Winkle!" He looked round, but could see nothing but a crow winging its solitary flight across the mountain. He thought his fancy must have deceived him, and turned again to descend, when he heard the same cry ring through the still evening air: "Rip Van Winkle! Rip Van Winkle!"—at the same time Wolf bristled up his back, and, giving a loud growl, skulked to his master's side, looking fearfully down into the glen. Rip now felt a vague apprehension stealing over him; he looked anxiously in the same direction, and perceived a strange figure slowly toiling up the rocks, and bending under the weight of something he carried on his back.

On nearer approach he was still more surprised at the singularity of the stranger's appearance. He was a short, square-built old fellow, with thick bushy hair and a grizzled beard. His dress was of the antique Dutch fashion —a cloth jerkin, strapped round the waist—several pair of breeches, the outer one of ample volume, decorated with rows of buttons down the sides, and bunches at the knees. He bore on his shoulder a stout keg, that seemed full of liquor, and made signs for Rip to approach and assist him with the load.

Though rather shy and distrustful of this new acquaintance, Rip complied with his usual alacrity, and, mutually relieving each other, they clambered up a narrow gully, apparently the dry bed of a mountain torrent. As they ascended, Rip every now and then heard long rolling peals, like distant thunder, that seemed to issue out of a deep ravine, or rather cleft, between lofty rocks, toward which their rugged path conducted. He paused for an instant, but supposing it to be the muttering of one of those transient thunder-showers which often take place in mountain heights, he proceeded.

Passing through the ravine, they came to a hollow, like a small amphi-theatre, surrounded by perpendicular precipices, over the brinks of which impending trees shot their branches, so that you only caught glimpses of the azure sky and the bright evening cloud. During the whole time Rip and his companion had laboured on in silence, for though the former mar-velled greatly what could be the object of carrying a keg of liquor up this wild mountain, yet there was something strange and incomprehensible about the unknown that inspired awe and checked familiarity.

On entering the amphitheatre, new objects of wonder presented them-selves. On a level spot in the centre was a company of odd-looking personages playing at ninepins. They were dressed in a quaint outlandish fashion; some wore short doublets, others jerkins, with long knives in their belts, and most of them had enormous breeches, of similar style with that of the guide's. Their visages, too, were peculiar: one had a large head, broad face, and small piggish eyes; the face of another seemed to consist entirely of nose, and was surmounted by a white sugar-loaf hat, set off with a little red cock's tail. They all had beards, of various shapes and colours.

There was one who seemed to be the commander. He was a stout old gentleman, with a weather-beaten countenance; he wore a laced doublet, broad belt and hanger, high-crowned hat and feather, red stockings, and high-heeled shoes, with roses in them.

What seemed particularly odd to Rip was, that though these folks were evidently amusing themselves, yet they maintained the gravest faces, the most mysterious silence, and were, withal, the most melancholy party of pleasure he had ever witnessed. Nothing interrupted the stillness of the scene but the noise of the balls, which, whenever they were rolled, echoed along the mountains like rumbling peals of thunder.

As Rip and his companion approached them, they suddenly desisted from their play, and stared at him with such fixed, statue-like gaze, and such strange, uncouth, lack-lustre countenances, that his heart turned within him, and his knees smote together. His companion now emptied the contents of the keg into large flagons, and made signs to him to wait upon the company. He obeyed with fear and trembling; they quaffed the liquor in profound silence, and then returned to their game.

By degrees Rip's awe and apprehension subsided. He even ventured, when no eye was fixed upon him, to taste the beverage, which he found had much of the flavour of excellent Hollands. He was naturally a thirsty soul, and was soon tempted to repeat the draught. One taste provoked another; and he reiterated his visits to the flagon so often, that at length his senses were overpowered, his eyes swam in his head, his head gradually declined, and he fell into a deep sleep.

On waking, he found himself on the green knoll whence he had first seen the old man of the glen. He rubbed his eyes—it was a bright sunny morning. The birds were hopping and twittering among the bushes, and the eagle was wheeling aloft, and breasting the pure mountain breeze. "Surely," thought Rip, "I have not slept here all night." He recalled the occurrences before he fell asleep. The strange man with a keg of liquor— the mountain ravine—the wild retreat among the rocks—the woebegone party at ninepins—the flagon—"Oh! that flagon! that wicked flagon!" thought Rip; "what excuse shall I make to Dame Van Winkle?"

He looked round for his gun, but in place of the clean, well-oiled fowling-piece, he found an old firelock, lying by him, the barrel incrusted with rust, the lock falling off, and the stock worm-eaten. He now suspected that the grave roysters of the mountain had put a trick upon him, and, having dosed him with liquor, had robbed him of his gun. Wolf, too, had disappeared. but he might have strayed away after a squirrel or partridge. He whistled after him, and shouted his name, but all in vain; the echoes repeated his whistle and shout, but no dog was to be seen.

He determined to revisit the scene of the last evening's gambol, and, if he met with any of the party, to demand his dog and gun. As he rose to walk he found himself stiff in the joints, and wanting in his usual activity. " These mountain beds do not agree with me," thought Rip ; " and if this frolic should lay me up with a fit of the rheumatism, I shall have a blessed time with Dame Van Winkle."

At length he reached to where the ravine had opened through the cliffs to the amphitheatre ; but no traces of such opening remained. The rocks presented a high impenetrable wall, over which the torrent came tumbling in a sheet of feathery foam, and fell into a broad, deep basin, black from the shadows of the surrounding forest. Here, then, poor Rip was brought to a stand. He again called and whistled after his dog ; he was only answered by the cawing of a flock of idle crows, sporting high in air about a dry tree that overhung a sunny precipice ; and who, secure in their elevation, seemed to look down and scoff at the poor man's perplexities.

What was to be done ?—the morning was passing away, and Rip felt famished for want of his breakfast. He grieved to give up his dog and his gun ; he dreaded to meet his wife ; but it would not do to starve among the mountains. He shook his head, shouldered the rusty firelock, and, with a heart full of trouble and anxiety, turned his steps homeward.

As he approached the village he met a number of people, but none whom he knew, which somewhat surprised him, for he had thought himself acquainted with every one in the country round. Their dress, too, was of a different fashion from that to which he was accustomed. They all stared at him with equal marks of surprise, and, whenever they cast their eyes upon him, invariably stroked their chins. The constant recurrence of this gesture induced Rip, involuntarily, to do the same, when, to his astonishment, he found his beard had grown a foot long !

He had now entered the skirts of the village. A troop of strange children ran at his heels, hooting after him, and pointing at his gray beard. The dogs, too, not one of which he recognised for an old acquaintance, barked at him as he passed. The very village was altered ; it was larger and more populous. There were rows of houses which he had never seen before, and those which had been his familiar haunts had disappeared. Strange names were over the doors—strange faces at the windows—everything was strange.

His mind now misgave him ; he began to doubt whether both he and the world around him were not bewitched. Surely this was his native village, which he had left but the day before. There stood the Kaatskill mountains—there ran the silver Hudson at a distance—there was every hill and dale precisely as it had always been. Rip was sorely perplexed. " That flagon last night," thought he, " has addled my poor head sadly ! "

It was with some difficulty that he found the way to his own house, which he approached with silent awe, expecting every moment to hear the shrill voice of Dame Van Winkle. He found the house gone to decay—the roof fallen in, the windows shattered, and the doors off the hinges. A half-starved dog that looked like Wolf was skulking about it. Rip called him by name, but the cur snarled, showed his teeth, and passed on. This was an unkind cut indeed—" My very dog," sighed poor Rip, " has forgotten me ! "

He entered the house, which, to tell the truth, Dame Van Winkle had always kept in neat order. It was empty, forlorn, and apparently abandoned. The desolateness overcame all his connubial fears—he called loudly for his wife and children—the lonely chambers rang for a moment with his voice, and then all again was silence.

He now hurried forth, and hastened to his old resort, the village inn—but it too was gone. A large, rickety, wooden building stood in its place, with great gaping windows, some of them broken and mended with old hats and petticoats, and over the door was painted, " The Union Hotel, by Jonathan Doolittle." Instead of the great tree that used to shelter the quiet little Dutch inn of yore, there was now reared a tall naked pole, with something on the top that looked like a red nightcap, and from it was fluttering a flag, on which was a singular assemblage of stars and stripes—all this was strange and incomprehensible.

He recognised on the sign, however, the ruby face of King George, under which he had smoked so many a peaceful pipe; but even this was singularly metamorphosed. The red coat was changed for one of blue and buff, a sword was held in the hand instead of a sceptre, the head was decorated with a cocked hat, and underneath was painted in large characters, GENERAL WASHINGTON.

There was, as usual, a crowd of folks about the door, but none that Rip recollected. The very character of the people seemed changed. There was a busy, bustling, disputatious tone about it, instead of the accustomed phlegm and drowsy tranquillity. He looked in vain for the sage Nicholas Vedder, with his broad face, double chin, and fair long pipe, uttering clouds of tobacco-smoke instead of idle speeches; or Van Bummel, the school-master, doling forth the contents of an ancient newspaper. In place of these, a lean, bilious-looking fellow, with his pockets full of hand-bills, was haranguing vehemently about rights of citizens—elections—members of Congress—liberty—Bunker's Hill—heroes of seventy-six—and other words, which were a perfect Babylonish jargon to the bewildered Van Winkle.

The appearance of Rip, with his long grizzled beard, his rusty fowling-piece, his uncouth dress, and an army of women and children at his heels, soon attracted the attention of the tavern politicians. They crowded round him, eyeing him from head to foot with great curiosity. The orator bustled up to him, and, drawing him partly aside, inquired " on which side he voted ? "

Rip stared in vacant stupidity. Another short but busy little fellow pulled him by the arm, and, rising on tiptoe, inquired in his ear, " Whether he was Federal or Democrat ? " Rip was equally at a loss to comprehend the question; when a knowing, self-important old gentleman, in a sharp cocked hat, made his way through the crowd, putting them to the right and left with his elbows as he passed, and planting himself before Van Winkle, with one arm akimbo, the other resting on his cane, his keen eyes and sharp hat penetrating, as it were, into his very soul, demanded in an austere tone, " What brought him to the election with a gun on his shoulder, and a mob at his heels, and whether he meant to breed a riot in the village ? "—" Alas ! gentlemen," cried Rip, somewhat dismayed, " I am a poor quiet man, a native of the place, and a loyal subject of the king, God bless him ! "

Here a general shout burst from the bystanders—" A Tory ! a Tory !

a spy ! a refugee ! hustle him ! away with him ! " It was with great difficulty that the self-important man in the cocked hat restored order ; and, having assumed a tenfold austerity of brow, demanded again of the unknown culprit, what he came there for, and whom he was seeking ? The poor man humbly assured him that he meant no harm, but merely came there in search of some of his neighbours, who used to keep about the tavern.

" Well—who are they !—name them."

Rip bethought himself a moment, and inquired, " Where's Nicholas Vedder ? "

There was a silence for a little while, when an old man replied in a thin piping voice, " Nicholas Vedder ! why, he is dead and gone these eighteen years ! There was a wooden tombstone in the churchyard that used to tell all about him, but that's rotten and gone too."

" Where's Brom Dutcher ? "

" Oh, he went off to the army in the beginning of the war ; some say he was killed at the storming of Stony Point—others say he was drowned in a squall at the foot of Antony's Nose. I don't know—he never came back again."

" Where's Van Bummel, the schoolmaster ? "

" He went off to the wars too, was a great militia general, and is now in Congress."

Rip's heart died away at hearing of these sad changes in his home and friends, and finding himself thus alone in the world. Every answer puzzled him too, by treating of such enormous lapses of time, and of matters which he could not understand ; war—Congress—Stony Point ;—he had no courage to ask after any more friends, but cried out in despair, " Does nobody here know Rip Van Winkle ? "

" Oh, Rip Van Winkle ! " exclaimed two or three. " Oh, to be sure ! that's Rip Van Winkle yonder, leaning against the tree."

Rip looked, and beheld a precise counterpart of himself, as he went up the mountain : apparently as lazy, and certainly as ragged. The poor fellow was now completely confounded. He doubted his own identity, and whether he was himself or another man. In the midst of his bewilderment, the man in the cocked hat demanded who he was, and what was his name ?

" God knows," exclaimed he, at his wits' end ; " I'm not myself—I'm somebody else—that's me yonder—no—that's somebody else got into my shoes—I was myself last night, but I fell asleep on the mountain, and they've changed my gun, and everything's changed, and I'm changed, and I can't tell what's my name, or who I am ! "

The bystanders began now to look at each other, nod, wink significantly, and tap their fingers against their foreheads. There was a whisper, also, about securing the gun, and keeping the old fellow from doing mischief, at the very suggestion of which the self-important man in the cocked hat retired with some precipitation. At this critical moment a fresh, comely woman pressed through the throng to get a peep at the gray-bearded man. She had a chubby child in her arms, which, frightened at his looks, began to cry. " Hush, Rip," cried she, " hush, you little fool ; the old man won't hurt you." The name of the child, the air of the mother, the tone of her voice, all awakened a train of recollections in his mind.

" What is your name, my good woman ? " asked he.

" Judith Gardenier."

" And your father's name ? "

" Ah, poor man, Rip Van Winkle was his name ; it's twenty years since he went away from home with his gun, and never has been heard of since—his dog came home without him ; but whether he shot himself, or was carried away by the Indians, nobody can tell. I was then but a little girl."

Rip had but one question more to ask ; but he put it with a faltering voice :

" Where's your mother ? "

" Oh, she too had died but a short time since ; she broke a blood-vessel in a fit of passion at a New-England pedlar."

*" I am your father ! . . . Does nobody know poor Rip Van Winkle ? "*

There was a drop of comfort, at least, in this intelligence. The honest man could contain himself no longer. He caught his daughter and her child in his arms. " I am your father ! " cried he—" Young Rip Van Winkle once—old Rip Van Winkle now !—Does nobody know poor Rip Van Winkle ? "

All stood amazed, until an old woman, tottering out from among the crowd, put her hand to her brow, and peering under it in his face for a moment, exclaimed, " Sure enough ! it is Rip Van Winkle—it is himself ! Welcome home again, old neighbour—Why, where have you been these twenty long years ? "

Rip's story was soon told, for the whole twenty years had been to him but as one night. The neighbours stared when they heard it ; some were seen to wink at each other, and put their tongues in their cheeks : and the self-important man in the cocked hat, who, when the alarm was over, had returned to the field, screwed down the corners of his mouth, and shook his head—upon which there was a general shaking of the head throughout the assemblage.

It was determined, however, to take the opinion of old Peter Vanderdonk, who was seen slowly advancing up the road. He was a descendant of the historian of that name, who wrote one of the earliest accounts of the province. Peter was the most ancient inhabitant of the village, and well versed in all the wonderful events and traditions of the neighbourhood. He recollected Rip at once, and corroborated his story in the most satisfactory manner. He assured the company that it was a fact, handed down from his ancestor the historian, that the Kaatskill mountains had always been haunted by strange beings. That it was affirmed that the great Hendrick Hudson, the first discoverer of the river and country, kept a kind of vigil there every twenty years, with his crew of the *Half-moon*, being permitted in this way to revisit the scenes of his enterprise, and keep a guardian eye upon the river, and the great city called by his name. That his father had once seen them in their old Dutch dresses playing at ninepins in a hollow of the mountain; and that he himself had heard, one summer afternoon, the sound of their balls, like distant peals of thunder.

To make a long story short, the company broke up, and returned to the more important concerns of the election. Rip's daughter took him home to live with her : she had a snug, well-furnished house, and a stout cheery farmer for her husband, whom Rip recollected for one of the urchins that used to climb upon his back. As to Rip's son and heir, who was the ditto of himself, seen leaning against the tree, he was employed to work on the farm ; but evinced an hereditary disposition to attend to anything else but his business.

Rip now resumed his old walks and habits ; he soon found many of his former cronies, though all rather the worse for the wear and tear of time ; and preferred making friends among the rising generation, with whom he soon grew into great favour.

Having nothing to do at home, and being arrived at that happy age when a man can be idle with impunity, he took his place once more on the bench at the inn door, and was reverenced as one of the patriarchs of the village, and a chronicle of the old times " before the war." It was some time before he could get into the regular track of gossip, or could be made to comprehend the strange events that had taken place during his torpor. How that there had been a revolutionary war—that the country had thrown off the yoke of Old England—and that, instead of being a subject of his Majesty George the Third, he was now a free citizen of the United States. Rip, in fact, was no politician ; the changes of states and empires made but little impression on him ; but there was one species of despotism under which he had long groaned, and that was—petticoat government. Happily that was at an end ; he had got his neck out of the yoke of matrimony, and could go in and out whenever he pleased without dreading the tyranny of Dame Van Winkle. Whenever her name was mentioned, however, he shook his head, shrugged his shoulders, and cast up his eyes ; which might pass either for an expression of resignation to his fate, or joy at his deliverance.

# THE GOLDEN FLEECE

## *by* NATHANIEL HAWTHORNE

HE son of the dethroned King of Iolchos was named Jason. When he was a little boy, he was sent away from his parents, and placed under a very queer schoolmaster. This learned person was one of the people, or quadrupeds, called Centaurs. He lived in a cavern, and had the body and legs of a white horse, with the head and shoulders of a man. His name was Chiron; and, in spite of his odd appearance, he was a very excellent teacher, and had several scholars who afterwards did him credit by making a great figure in the world. The famous Hercules was one, and so was Achilles, and Philoctetes likewise, and Æsculapius, who acquired immense repute as a doctor. The good Chiron taught his pupils how to play upon the harp, and how to cure diseases, and how to use the sword and shield, together with various other branches of education in which the lads of those days used to be instructed, instead of writing and arithmetic.

I have sometimes suspected that Master Chiron was not really very different from other people, but that, being a kind-hearted and merry old fellow, he was in the habit of making believe that he was a horse, and scrambling about the schoolroom on all fours, and letting the little boys ride upon his back. And so, when his scholars had grown up, and grown old, and were trotting their grandchildren on their knees, they told them about the sports of their school days; and these young folks took the idea that their grandfathers had been taught their letters by a Centaur, half-man and half-horse. Little children not quite understanding what is said to them, often get such absurd notions into their heads, you know.

Be that as it may, it has always been told for a fact (and always will be told, as long as the world lasts), that Chiron, with the head of a school-master, had the body and legs of a horse. Just imagine the grave old gentleman clattering and stamping into the schoolroom on his four hoofs, perhaps treading on some little fellow's toes, flourishing his switch tail instead of a rod, and, now and then, trotting out of doors to eat a mouthful of grass ! I wonder what the blacksmith charged him for a set of iron shoes !

So Jason dwelt in the cave with this four-footed Chiron, from the time that he was an infant, only a few months old, until he had grown to the full height of a man. He became a very good harper, I suppose, and skilful in the use of weapons, and tolerably acquainted with herbs and other doctor's stuff, and, above all, an admirable horseman ; for, in teaching young people to ride, the good Chiron must have been without a rival among schoolmasters. At length, being now a tall and athletic youth, Jason resolved to seek his fortune in the world, without asking Chiron's advice, or telling him anything about the matter. This was very unwise, to be sure ; and I hope none of you, my little hearers, will ever follow Jason's example.

But, you are to understand, he had heard how that he himself was a prince royal, and how his father, King Æson, had been deprived of the kingdom of Iolchos, by a certain Pelias, who would also have killed Jason, had he not been hidden in the Centaur's cave. And, being come to the strength of a man, Jason determined to set all this business to rights, and to punish the wicked Pelias for wronging his dear father, and to cast him down from the throne, and seat himself there instead.

With this intention, he took a spear in each hand, and threw a leopard's skin over his shoulders, to keep off the rain, and set forth on his travels, with his long yellow ringlets waving in the wind. The part of his dress on which he most prided himself was a pair of sandals that had been his father's. They were handsomely embroidered, and were tied upon his feet with strings of gold. But his whole attire was such as people did not very often see ; and as he passed along, the women and children ran to the doors and windows, wondering whither this beautiful youth was journeying, with his leopard's skin and his golden-tied sandals, and what heroic deeds he meant to perform, with a spear in his right hand and another in his left.

I know not how far Jason had travelled, when he came to a turbulent river, which rushed right across his pathway, with specks of white foam among its black eddies, hurrying tumultuously onward, and roaring angrily as it went. Though not a very broad river in the dry seasons of the year, it was now swollen by heavy rains and by the melting of the snow on the sides of Mount Olympus ; and it thundered so loudly, and looked so wild and dangerous that Jason, bold as he was, thought it prudent to pause upon the brink. The bed of the stream seemed to be strewn with sharp and rugged rocks, some of which thrust themselves above the water. By and by, an uprooted tree, with shattered branches, came drifting along the current, and got entangled among the rocks. Now and then, a drowned sheep, and once the carcass of a cow, floated past.

In short, the swollen river had already done a great deal of mischief. It was evidently too deep for Jason to wade, and too boisterous for him to swim ; he could see no bridge ; and as for a boat, had there been any, the rocks would have broken it to pieces in an instant.

"See the poor lad," said a cracked voice close to his side. "He must have had but a poor education, since he does not know how to cross a little stream like this. Or is he afraid of wetting his fine golden-stringed sandals? It is a pity his four-footed schoolmaster is not here to carry him safely across on his back!"

Jason looked round greatly surprised, for he did not know that anybody was near. But beside him stood an old woman, with a ragged mantle over her head, leaning on a staff, the top of which was carved into the shape of a cuckoo. She looked very aged, and wrinkled, and infirm; and yet her eyes, which were as brown as those of an ox, were so extremely large and beautiful that, when they were fixed on Jason's eyes, he could see nothing else but them. The old woman had a pomegranate in her hand, although the fruit was then quite out of season.

"Whither are you going, Jason?" she now asked.

She seemed to know his name, you will observe; and, indeed, those great brown eyes looked as if they had a knowledge of everything, whether past or to come. While Jason was gazing at her a peacock strutted forward, and took his stand at the old woman's side.

"I am going to Iolchos," answered the young man, "to bid the wicked King Pelias come down from my father's throne, and let me reign in his stead."

"Ah, well, then," said the old woman, still with the same cracked voice, "if that is all your business you need not be in a very great hurry. Just take me on your back, there's a good youth, and carry me across the river. I and my peacock have something to do on the other side as well as yourself."

"Good mother," replied Jason, "your business can hardly be so important as the pulling down a king from his throne. Besides, as you may see for yourself, the river is very boisterous; and if I should chance to stumble, it would sweep both of us away more easily than it has carried off yonder uprooted tree. I would gladly help you if I could; but I doubt whether I am strong enough to carry you across."

"Then," said she, very scornfully, "neither are you strong enough to pull King Pelias off his throne. And, Jason, unless you will help an old woman at her need you ought not to be a king. What are kings made for, save to succour the feeble and distressed? But do as you please. Either take me on your back, or with my poor old limbs I shall try my best to struggle across the stream."

Saying this, the old woman poked with her staff in the river, as if to find the safest place in its rocky bed where she might make the first step. But Jason, by this time, had grown ashamed of his reluctance to help her. He felt that he could never forgive himself, if this poor feeble creature should come to any harm in attempting to wrestle against the headlong current. The good Chiron, whether half-horse or no, had taught him that the noblest use of his strength was to assist the weak; and also that he must treat every young woman as if she were his sister, and every old one like a mother. Remembering these maxims, the vigorous and beautiful young man knelt down, and requested the good dame to mount upon his back.

"The passage seems to me not very safe," he remarked. "But, as your business is so urgent, I will try to carry you across. If the river sweeps you away, it shall take me too."

" That, no doubt, will be a great comfort to both of us," quoth the old woman. " But never fear. We shall get safely across."

So she threw her arms around Jason's neck; and lifting her from the ground he stepped boldly into the raging and foaming current, and began to stagger away from the shore. As for the peacock, it alighted on the old dame's shoulder. Jason's two spears, one in each hand, kept him from stumbling, and enabled him to feel his way among the hidden rocks; although, every instant, he expected that his companion and himself would go down the stream, together with the driftwood of shattered trees, and the carcasses of the sheep and cow. Down came the cold, snowy torrent from the steep side of Olympus, raging and thundering as if it had a real spite against Jason, or, at all events, were determined to snatch off his living burden from his shoulders. When he was half-way across, the uprooted tree (which I have already told you about) broke loose from among the rocks, and bore down upon him, with all its splintered branches sticking out like the hundred arms of the giant Briareus. It rushed past, however, without touching him. But the next moment his foot was caught in a crevice between two rocks, and stuck there so fast, that, in the effort to get free, he lost one of his golden-stringed sandals.

At this accident Jason could not help uttering a cry of vexation.

" What is the matter, Jason ? " asked the old woman.

" Matter enough," said the young man. " I have lost a sandal here among the rocks. And what sort of a figure shall I cut at the court of King Pelias, with a golden-stringed sandal on one foot, and the other foot bare ! "

" Do not take it to heart," answered his companion cheerily. " You never met with better fortune than in losing that sandal. It satisfies me that you are the very person whom the Speaking Oak has been talking about."

There was no time, just then, to inquire what the Speaking Oak had said. But the briskness of her tongue encouraged the young man; and besides, he had never in his life felt so vigorous and mighty as since taking this old woman on his back. Instead of being exhausted he gathered strength as he went on; and, struggling up against the torrent, he at last gained the opposite shore, clambered up the bank, and set down the old dame and her peacock safely on the grass. As soon as this was done, however, he could not help looking rather despondently at his bare foot, with only a remnant of the golden string of the sandal clinging round his ankle.

" You will get a handsomer pair of sandals by and by," said the old woman, with a kindly look out of her beautiful brown eyes. " Only let King Pelias get a glimpse of that bare foot, and you shall see him turn as pale as ashes, I promise you. There is your path. Go along, my good Jason, and my blessing go with you. And when you sit on your throne remember the old woman whom you helped over the river."

With these words she hobbled away, giving him a smile over her shoulder as she departed. Whether the light of her beautiful brown eyes threw a glory round about her, or whatever the cause might be, Jason fancied that there was something very noble and majestic in her figure after all, and that, though her gait seemed to be a rheumatic hobble, yet she moved with as

much grace and dignity as any queen on earth. Her peacock, which had now
fluttered down from her shoulder, strutted behind her in prodigious pomp,
and spread out its magnificent tail on purpose for Jason to admire it.

When the old dame and her peacock were out of sight, Jason set forward
on his journey. After travelling a pretty long distance, he came to a town
situated at the foot of a mountain, and not a great way from the shore of
the sea. On the outside of the town there was an immense crowd of people,
not only men and women, but children too, all in their best clothes, and
evidently enjoying a holiday. The crowd was thickest towards the sea-shore ;
and in that direction, over the people's heads, Jason saw a wreath of smoke
curling upward to the blue sky. He inquired of one of the multitude what
town it was near by, and why so many persons were here assembled
together.

"This is the kingdom of Iolchos," answered the man, "and we are
the subjects of King Pelias. Our monarch has summoned us together that
we may see him sacrifice a black bull to Neptune, who, they say, is his
majesty's father. Yonder is the king, where you see the smoke going up from
the altar."

While the man spoke he eyed Jason with great curiosity ; for his garb was
quite unlike that of the Iolchians, and it looked very odd to see a youth
with a leopard's skin over his shoulders, and each hand grasping a spear.
Jason perceived, too, that the man stared particularly at his feet, one of
which, you remember, was bare, while the other was decorated with his
father's golden-stringed sandal.

"Look at him ! only look at him !" said the man to his next neighbour.
"Do you see ? He wears but one sandal !"

*Jason stood near the smoking altar, front to front with the angry King Pelias.*

Upon this, first one person, and then another, began to stare at Jason, and everybody seemed to be greatly struck with something in his aspect; though they turned their eyes much oftener towards his feet than to any other part of his figure. Besides, he could hear them whispering to one another.

"One sandal! One sandal!" they kept saying. "The man with one sandal! Here he is at last! Whence has he come? What does he mean to do? What will the king say to the one-sandalled man?"

Poor Jason was greatly abashed, and made up his mind that the people of Iolchos were exceedingly ill-bred, to take such public notice of an accidental deficiency in his dress. Meanwhile, whether it were that they hustled him forward, or that Jason of his own accord thrust a passage through the crowd, it so happened that he soon found himself close to the smoking altar, where King Pelias was sacrificing the black bull. The murmur and hum of the multitude, in their surprise at the spectacle of Jason with his one bare foot, grew so loud that it disturbed the ceremonies; and the king, holding the great knife with which he was just going to cut the bull's throat, turned angrily about and fixed his eyes on Jason. The people had now withdrawn from around him, so that the youth stood in an open space, near the smoking altar, front to front with the angry King Pelias.

"Who are you?" cried the king, with a terrible frown. "And how dare you make this disturbance, while I am sacrificing a black bull to my father Neptune?"

"It is no fault of mine," answered Jason. "Your majesty must blame the rudeness of your subjects, who have raised all this tumult because one of my feet happens to be bare."

When Jason said this the king gave a quick startled glance down at his feet.

"Ha!" muttered he, "here is the one-sandalled fellow, sure enough! What can I do with him!"

And he clutched more closely the great knife in his hand, as if he were in half a mind to slay Jason, instead of the black bull. The people round about caught up the king's words, indistinctly as they were uttered; and first there was a murmur amongst them, and then a loud shout.

"The one-sandalled man has come! The prophecy must be fulfilled!"

For you are to know, that, many years before, King Pelias had been told by the Speaking Oak of Dodona, that a man with one sandal should cast him down from his throne. On this account he had given strict orders that nobody should ever come into his presence, unless both sandals were securely tied upon his feet; and he kept an officer in his palace, whole sole business it was to examine people's sandals, and to supply them with a new pair, at the expense of the royal treasury, as soon as the old ones began to wear out. In the whole course of the king's reign, he had never been thrown into such a fright and agitation as by the spectacle of poor Jason's bare foot. But, as he was naturally a bold and hard-hearted man, he soon took courage, and began to consider in what way he might rid himself of this terrible one-sandalled stranger.

"My good young man," said King Pelias, taking the softest tone imaginable, in order to throw Jason off his guard, "you are excessively welcome to my kingdom. Judging by your dress, you must have travelled a long distance ; for it is not the fashion to wear leopard skins in this part of the world. Pray what may I call your name ? and where did you receive your education ? "

" My name is Jason," answered the young stranger. " Ever since my infancy, I have dwelt in the cave of Chiron the Centaur. He was my instructor, and taught me music, and horsemanship, and how to cure wounds, and likewise how to inflict wounds with my weapons ! "

" I have heard of Chiron the schoolmaster," replied King Pelias, " and how that there is an immense deal of learning and wisdom in his head, although it happens to be set on a horse's body. It gives me great delight to see one of his scholars at my court. But to test how much you have profited under so excellent a teacher, will you allow me to ask you a single question ? "

" I do not pretend to be very wise," said Jason. " But ask me what you please, and I will answer to the best of my ability."

Now King Pelias meant cunningly to entrap the young man, and to make him say something that should be the cause of mischief and destruction to himself. So, with a crafty and evil smile upon his face, he spoke as follows :

" What would you do, brave Jason, if there were a man in the world by whom, as you had reason to believe, you were doomed to be ruined and slain—what would you do, I say, if that man stood before you, and in your power ? "

When Jason saw the malice and wickedness which King Pelias could not prevent from gleaming out of his eyes, he probably guessed that the king had discovered what he came for, and that he intended to turn his own words against himself. Still he scorned to tell a falsehood. Like an upright and honourable prince as he was, he determined to speak out the real truth. Since the king had chosen to ask him the question, and since Jason had promised him an answer, there was no right way save to tell him precisely what would be the most prudent thing to do, if he had his worst enemy in his power.

Therefore, after a moment's consideration, he spoke up, with a firm and manly voice.

" I would send such a man," said he, " in quest of the Golden Fleece ! "

This enterprise, you will understand, was, of all others, the most difficult and dangerous in the world. In the first place it would be necessary to make a long voyage through unknown seas. There was hardly a hope or a possibility that any young man who should undertake this voyage would either succeed in obtaining the Golden Fleece, or would survive to return home, and tell of the perils he had run. The eyes of King Pelias sparkled with joy, therefore, when he heard Jason's reply.

" Well said, wise man with the one sandal ! " cried he. " Go, then, and at the peril of your life bring me back the Golden Fleece."

" I go," answered Jason composedly. " If I fail, you need not fear that I will ever come back to trouble you again. But if I return to Iolchos with the prize, then, King Pelias, you must hasten down from your lofty throne, and give me your crown and sceptre."

" That I will," said the king, with a sneer. " Meantime, I will keep them very safely for you."

The first thing that Jason thought of doing, after he left the king's presence, was to go to Dodona, and inquire of the Talking Oak what course it was best to pursue. This wonderful tree stood in the centre of an ancient wood. Its stately trunk rose up a hundred feet into the air, and threw a broad and dense shadow over more than an acre of ground. Standing beneath it, Jason looked up among the knotted branches and green leaves, and into the mysterious heart of the old tree, and spoke aloud, as if he were addressing some person who was hidden in the depths of the foliage.

"What shall I do," said he, "in order to win the Golden Fleece?"

At first there was a deep silence, not only within the shadow of the Talking Oak, but all through the solitary wood. In a moment or two, however, the leaves of the oak began to stir and rustle, as if a breeze were wandering amongst them, although the other trees of the wood were perfectly still. The sound grew louder, and became like the roar of a high wind. By and by, Jason imagined that he could distinguish words, but very confusedly, because each separate leaf of the tree seemed to be a tongue, and the whole myriad of tongues were babbling at once. But the noise waxed broader and deeper, until it resembled a tornado sweeping through the oak, and making one great utterance, out of the thousand and thousand of little murmurs which each leafy tongue had caused by its rustling. And now, though it still had the tone of a mighty wind roaring among the branches, it was also like a deep bass voice, speaking, as distinctly as a tree could be expected to speak, the following words:

"Go to Argus, the shipbuilder, and bid him build a galley with fifty oars."

Then the voice melted again into the indistinct murmur of the rustling leaves, and died gradually away. When it was quite gone, Jason felt inclined to doubt whether he had actually heard the words, or whether his fancy had not shaped them out of the ordinary sound made by a breeze while passing through the thick foliage of the tree.

But on inquiry among the people of Iolchos, he found that there was really a man in the city by the name of Argus who was a very skilful builder of vessels. This showed some intelligence in the oak; else how should it have known that any such person existed? At Jason's request, Argus readily consented to build him a galley so big that it should require fifty strong men to row it; although no vessel of such a size and burden had heretofore been seen in the world. So the head carpenter and all his journeymen and apprentices began their work; and for a good while afterwards there they were busily employed, hewing out the timbers, and making a great clatter with their hammers; until the new ship, which was called the *Argo*, seemed to be quite ready for sea. And, as the Talking Oak had already given him such good advice, Jason thought that it would not be amiss to ask for a little more. He visited it again, therefore, and standing beside its huge, rough trunk, inquired what he should do next.

This time, there was no such universal quivering of the leaves throughout the whole tree, as there had been before. But after a while, Jason observed that the foliage of a great branch which stretched above his head had begun to rustle, as if the wind were stirring that one bough while all the other boughs of the oak were at rest.

" Cut me off ! " said the branch, as soon as it could speak distinctly ; " cut me off ! cut me off ! and carve me into a figure-head for your galley."

Accordingly, Jason took the branch at its word and lopped it off the tree. A carver in the neighbourhood engaged to make the figure-head. He was a tolerably good workman, and had already carved several figure-heads, in what he intended for feminine shapes, and looking pretty much like those which we see nowadays stuck up under a vessel's bowsprit, with great staring eyes that never wink at the dash of the spray. But (what was very strange) the carver found that his hand was guided by some unseen power, and by a skill beyond his own, and that his tools shaped out an image which he had never dreamed of. When the work was finished, it turned out to

*Jason was delighted with the oaken image.*

be the figure of a beautiful woman, with a helmet on her head, from beneath which the long ringlets fell down upon her shoulders. On the left arm was a shield, and in its centre appeared a life-like representation of the head of Medusa with the snaky locks. The right arm was extended, as if pointing onward. The face of this wonderful statue, though not angry or forbidding, was so grave and majestic that perhaps you might call it severe ; and as for the mouth, it seemed just ready to unclose its lips and utter words of the deepest wisdom.

Jason was delighted with the oaken image, and gave the carver no rest until it was completed, and set up where a figure-head has always stood, from that time to this, in the vessel's prow.

" And now," cried he, as he stood gazing at the calm, majestic face of the statue, " I must go to the Talking Oak, and inquire what next to do."

" There is no need of that, Jason," said a voice which, though it was far lower, reminded him of the mighty tones of the great oak. " When you desire good advice you can seek it of me."

Jason had been looking straight into the face of the image when these words were spoken. But he could hardly believe either his ears or his eyes. The truth was, however, that the oaken lips had moved, and, to all appearance, the voice had proceeded from the statue's mouth. Recovering a little from his surprise, Jason bethought himself that the image had been carved out of the wood of the Talking Oak, and that, therefore, it was really no great wonder, but, on the contrary, the most natural thing in the world that it should possess the faculty of speech. It would have been very odd, indeed, if it had not. But certainly it was a great piece of good fortune that he should be able to carry so wise a block of wood along with him on his perilous voyage.

" Tell me, wondrous image," exclaimed Jason,—" since you inherit the wisdom of the Speaking Oak of Dodona, whose daughter you are— tell me, where shall I find fifty bold youths who will take each of them an oar of my galley ? They must have sturdy arms to row, and brave hearts to encounter perils, or we shall never win the Golden Fleece."

" Go," replied the oaken image, " go, summon all the heroes of Greece."

And, in fact, considering what a great deed was to be done, could any advice be wiser than this which Jason received from the figure-head of his vessel ? He lost no time in sending messengers to all the cities, and making known to the whole people of Greece that Prince Jason, the son of King Æson, was going in quest of the Fleece of Gold, and that he desired the help of forty-nine of the bravest and strongest young men alive, to row his vessel and share his dangers. And Jason himself would be the fiftieth.

At this news, the adventurous youths all over the country began to bestir themselves. Some of them had already fought with giants, and slain dragons ; and the younger ones, who had not yet met with such good fortune, thought it a shame to have lived so long without getting astride of a flying serpent, or sticking their spears into a Chimæra, or, at least, thrusting their right arms down a monstrous lion's throat. There was a fair prospect that they would meet with plenty of such adventures before finding the Golden Fleece. As soon as they could furbish up their helmets and shields, therefore, and gird on their trusty swords, they came thronging to Iolchos, and clambered on board the new galley. Shaking hands with Jason, they assured him that they did not care a pin for their lives, but would help row the vessel to the remotest edge of the world, and as much farther as he might think it best to go.

Many of these brave fellows had been educated by Chiron, the four-footed pedagogue, and were, therefore, old schoolmates of Jason, and knew him to be a lad of spirit. The mighty Hercules, whose shoulders afterwards upheld the sky, was one of them. And there were Castor and Pollux, the twin brothers, who were never accused of being chicken-hearted although they had been hatched out of an egg ; and Theseus, who was so renowned for killing the Minotaur, and Lynceus, with his wonderfully sharp eyes which could see through a millstone, or look right down into the depths of the earth, and discover the treasures that were there ; and Orpheus, the very best of harpers, who sang and played upon his lyre so sweetly that the brute beasts stood upon their hind legs and capered merrily to the music. Yes, and at some of his more moving tunes the rocks bestired their moss-grown bulk out of the ground, and a grove of forest trees uprooted themselves, and, nodding their tops to one another, performed a country dance.

One of the rowers was a beautiful young woman named Atalanta, who had been nursed among the mountains by a bear. So light of foot was this fair damsel that she could step from one foamy crest of a wave to the foamy crest of another, without wetting more than the sole of her sandal. She had grown up in a very wild way, and talked much about the rights of women, and loved hunting and war far better than her needle. But in my opinion, the most remarkable of this famous company were two sons of the North Wind (airy youngsters and of rather a blustering disposition) who had wings on their shoulders, and, in case of a calm, could puff out their cheeks and blow almost as fresh a breeze as their father. I ought not to forget the prophets and conjurers, of whom there were several in the crew, and who could foretell what would happen to-morrow or the next day, or a hundred years hence, but were generally quite unconscious of what was passing at the moment.

Jason appointed Tiphys to be helmsman, because he was a star-gazer, and knew the points of the compass. Lynceus, on account of his sharp sight, was stationed as a look-out in the prow, where he saw a whole day's sail ahead, but was rather apt to overlook things that lay directly under his nose. If the sea only happened to be deep enough, however, Lynceus could tell you exactly what kind of rocks or sands were at the bottom of it ; and he often cried out to his companions that they were sailing over heaps of sunken treasure, which yet he was none the richer for beholding. To confess the truth, few people believed him when he said it.

Well ! But when the Argonauts, as these fifty brave adventurers were called, had prepared everything for the voyage, an unforeseen difficulty threatened to end it before it was begun. The vessel, you must understand, was so long, and broad, and ponderous that the united force of all the fifty was insufficient to shove her into the water. Hercules, I suppose, had not grown to his full strength, else he might have set her afloat as easily as a little boy launches his boat upon a puddle. But here were these fifty heroes, pushing, and straining, and growing red in the face, without making the *Argo* start an inch. At last, quite wearied out, they sat themselves down on the shore exceedingly disconsolate, and thinking that the vessel must be left to rot and fall in pieces, and that they must either swim across the sea or lose the Golden Fleece.

All at once Jason bethought himself of the galley's miraculous figure-head.

" O daughter of the Talking Oak," cried he, " how shall we set to work to get our vessel into the water ? "

" Seat yourselves," answered the image (for it had known what ought to be done from the very first, and was only waiting for the question to be put)—" seat yourselves and handle your oars, and let Orpheus play upon his harp."

Immediately the fifty heroes got on board, and, seizing their oars, held them perpendicularly in the air, while Orpheus (who liked such a task far better than rowing) swept his fingers across the harp. At the first ringing note of the music they felt the vessel stir. Orpheus thrummed away briskly and the galley slid at once into the sea, dipping her prow so deeply that the figure-head drank the wave with its marvellous lips, and rising again as buoyant as a swan. The rowers plied their fifty oars; the white foam boiled up before the prow; the water gurgled and bubbled in their wake; while Orpheus continued to play so lively a strain of music that the vessel seemed to dance over the billows by way of keeping time to it. Thus triumphantly did the *Argo* sail out of the harbour, amidst the huzzas and good wishes of everybody except the wicked old Pelias, who stood on a promontory scowling at her, and wishing that he could blow out of his lungs the tempest of wrath that was in his heart, and so sink the galley with all on board. When they had sailed above fifty miles over the sea, Lynceus happened to cast his sharp eyes behind, and said that there was this bad-hearted king, still perched upon the promontory, and scowling so gloomily that it looked like a black thunder-cloud in that quarter of the horizon.

In order to make the time pass away more pleasantly during the voyage, the heroes talked about the Golden Fleece. It originally belonged, it appears, to a Bœotian ram, who had taken on his back two children, when in danger of their lives, and fled with them over land and sea as far as Colchis. One of the children, whose name was Helle, fell into the sea and was drowned. But the other (a little boy, named Phrixus) was brought safe ashore by the faithful ram, who, however, was so exhausted that he immediately lay down and died. In memory of this good deed, and as a token of his true heart, the fleece of the poor dead ram was miraculously changed to gold and became one of the most beautiful objects ever seen on earth. It was hung upon a tree in a sacred grove, where it had now been kept I know not how many years, and was the envy of mighty kings, who had nothing so magnificent in any of their palaces.

If I were to tell you all the adventures of the Argonauts, it would take me till nightfall, and perhaps a great deal longer. There was no lack of wonderful events, as you may judge from what you have already heard. At a certain island they were hospitably received by King Cyzicus, its sovereign, who made a feast for them, and treated them like brothers. But the Argonauts saw that this good king looked downcast and very much troubled, and they therefore inquired of him what was the matter. King Cyzicus hereupon informed them that he and his subjects were greatly abused and incommoded by the inhabitants of a neighbouring mountain, who made war upon them, and killed many people, and ravaged the country. And while they were talking about it, Cyzicus pointed to the mountain and asked Jason and his companions what they saw there.

" I see some very tall objects," answered Jason; " but they are at such a distance that I cannot distinctly make out what they are. To tell your majesty the truth, they look so very strangely that I am inclined to think them clouds, which have chanced to take something like human shapes."

" I see them very plainly," remarked Lynceus, whose eyes, you know, were as far-sighted as a telescope. " They are a band of enormous giants,

*The rowers plied their fifty oars, while Orpheus played upon his harp.*

all of whom have six arms apiece, and a club, a sword, or some other weapon in each of their hands."

" You have excellent eyes," said King Cyzicus. " Yes ; they are six-armed giants as you say, and these are the enemies whom I and my subjects have to contend with."

The next day, when the Argonauts were about setting sail, down came these terrible giants, stepping a hundred yards at a stride, brandishing their six arms apiece, and looking very formidable, so far aloft in the air. Each of these monsters was able to carry on a whole war by himself, for with one arm he could fling immense stones, and wield a club with another, and a sword with a third, while the fourth was poking a long spear at the enemy, and the fifth and sixth were shooting him with a bow and arrow. But, luckily, though the giants were so huge and had so many arms, they had each but one heart, and that no bigger nor braver than the heart of an ordinary man. Besides, if they had been like the hundred-armed Briareus, the brave Argonauts would have given them their hands full of fight. Jason and his friends went boldly to meet them, slew a great many, and made the rest take to their heels, so that if the giants had had six legs apiece instead of six arms it would have served them better to run away with.

Another strange adventure happened when the voyagers came to Thrace, where they found a poor blind king named Phineus, deserted by his subjects, and living in a very sorrowful way all by himself. On Jason's inquiring whether they could do him any service, the king answered that he was terribly tormented by three great winged creatures, called Harpies, which had the faces of women, and the wings, bodies, and claws of vultures. These ugly wretches were in the habit of snatching away his dinner, and allowed him no peace of his life. Upon hearing this the Argonauts spread a plentiful feast on the sea-shore, well knowing from what the blind king said of their greediness that the Harpies would snuff up the scent of the victuals, and quickly come to steal them away. And so it turned out; for, hardly was the table set, before the three hideous vulture women came flapping their wings, seized the food in their talons, and flew off as fast as they could. But the two sons of the North Wind drew their swords, spread out their pinions, and set off through the air in pursuit of the thieves, whom they at last overtook among some islands after a chase of hundreds of miles. The two winged youths blustered terribly at the Harpies (for they had the rough temper of their father), and so frightened them with their drawn swords that they solemnly promised never to trouble King Phineus again.

Then the Argonauts sailed onward, and met with many other marvellous incidents, any one of which would make a story by itself. At one time they landed on an island, and were reposing on the grass, when they suddenly found themselves assailed by what seemed a shower of steel-headed arrows. Some of them stuck in the ground, while others hit against their shields, and several penetrated their flesh. The fifty heroes started up and looked about them for the hidden enemy, but could find none, nor see any spot, on the whole island, where even a single archer could lie concealed. Still, however, the steel-headed arrows came whizzing among them; and, at last, happening to look upward, they beheld a large flock of birds hovering and wheeling aloft, and shooting their feathers down upon the Argonauts. These feathers were the steel-headed arrows that had so tormented them. There was no possibility of making any resistance; and the fifty heroic Argonauts might all have been killed or wounded by a flock of troublesome birds, without ever setting eyes on the Golden Fleece, if Jason had not thought of asking the advice of the oaken image.

So he ran to the galley as fast as his legs would carry him.

"O daughter of the Speaking Oak," cried he, all out of breath, "we need your wisdom more than ever before! We are in great peril from a flock of birds, who are shooting us with their steel-pointed feathers. What can we do to drive them away?"

"Make a clatter on your shields," said the image.

On receiving this excellent counsel, Jason hurried back to his companions (who were far more dismayed than when they fought with the six-armed giants), and bade them strike with their swords upon their brazen shields. Forthwith, the fifty heroes set heartily to work, banging with might and main, and raised such a terrible clatter that the birds made what haste they could to get away; and though they had shot half the feathers out of their wings they were soon seen skimming among the clouds, a long distance off, and looking like a flock of wild geese. Orpheus celebrated this victory by playing a triumphant anthem on his harp, and sang so melodiously that Jason begged him to desist, lest, as the steel-feathered birds had been driven away by an ugly sound, they might be enticed back again by a sweet one.

While the Argonauts remained on this island, they saw a small vessel approaching the shore in which were two young men of princely demeanour, and exceedingly handsome, as young princes generally were in those days. Now, who do you imagine these two voyagers turned out to be? Why, if you will believe me, they were the sons of that very Phrixus, who in his childhood had been carried to Colchis on the back of the golden-fleeced ram. Since that time, Phrixus had married the king's daughter; and the two young princes had been born and brought up at Colchis, and had spent their play-days in the outskirts of the grove, in the centre of which the Golden Fleece was hanging upon a tree. They were now on their way to Greece, in hopes of getting back a kingdom that had been wrongfully taken from their father.

When the princes understood whither the Argonauts were going, they offered to turn back and guide them to Colchis. At the same time, however, they spoke as if it were very doubtful whether Jason would succeed in getting the Golden Fleece. According to their account, the tree on which it hung was guarded by a terrible dragon, who never failed to devour at one mouthful every person who might venture within his reach.

"There are other difficulties in the way," continued the young princes. "But is not this enough? Ah, brave Jason, turn back before it is too late. It would grieve us to the heart, if you and your nine-and-forty brave companions should be eaten up, at fifty mouthfuls, by this execrable dragon."

"My young friends," quietly replied Jason, "I do not wonder that you think the dragon very terrible. You have grown up from infancy in the fear of this monster, and therefore still regard him with the awe that children feel for the bugbears and hobgoblins which their nurses have talked to them about. But, in my view of the matter, the dragon is merely a pretty large serpent, who is not half so likely to snap me up at one mouthful as I am to cut off his ugly head, and strip the skin from his body. At all events, turn back who may, I will never see Greece again unless I carry with me the Golden Fleece."

"We will none of us turn back!" cried his nine-and-forty brave comrades. "Let us get on board the galley this instant; and if the dragon is to make a breakfast of us, much good may it do him."

And Orpheus (whose custom it was to set everything to music) began to harp and sing most gloriously, and made every mother's son of them feel as if nothing in this world were so delectable as to fight dragons, and nothing so truly honourable as to be eaten up at one mouthful in case of the worst.

After this (being now under the guidance of the two princes, who were well acquainted with the way), they quickly sailed to Colchis. When the king of the country, whose name was Æetes, heard of their arrival, he instantly summoned Jason to court. The king was a stern and cruel looking potentate; and, though he put on as polite and hospitable an expression as he could Jason did not like his face a whit better than that of the wicked King Pelias, who dethroned his father.

"You are welcome, brave Jason," said King Æetes. "Pray, are you on a pleasure voyage?—or do you meditate the discovery of unknown islands?—or what other cause has procured me the happiness of seeing you at my court?"

"Great sir," replied Jason, with an obeisance—for Chiron had taught him how to behave with propriety, whether to kings or beggars—"I have come hither with a purpose which I now beg your majesty's permission to execute.  King Pelias, who sits on my father's throne (to which he has no more right than to the one on which your excellent majesty is now seated), has engaged to come down from it, and to give me his crown and sceptre provided I bring him the Golden Fleece.  This, as your majesty is aware, is now hanging on a tree here at Colchis ; and I humbly solicit your gracious leave to take it away."

In spite of himself the king's face twisted itself into an angry frown ; for, above all things else in the world, he prized the Golden Fleece, and was even suspected of having done a very wicked act in order to get it into his own possession.  It put him into the worst possible humour, therefore, to hear that the gallant Prince Jason and forty-nine of the bravest young warriors of Greece had come to Colchis with the sole purpose of taking away his chief treasure.

" Do you know," asked King Æetes, eyeing Jason very sternly, " what are the conditions which you must fulfil before getting possession of the Golden Fleece ? "

" I have heard," rejoined the youth, " that a dragon lies beneath the tree on which the prize hangs, and that whoever approaches him runs the risk of being devoured at a mouthful."

" True," said the king, with a smile that did not look particularly good-natured.  " Very true, young man.  But there are other things as hard, or perhaps a little harder, to be done before you can even have the privilege of being devoured by the dragon.  For example, you must first tame my two brazen-footed and brazen-lunged bulls, which Vulcan, the wonderful black-smith, made for me.  There is a furnace in each of their stomachs ; and they breathe such hot fire out of their mouths and nostrils that nobody has hitherto gone nigh them without being instantly burned to a small, black cinder.  What do you think of this, my brave Jason ? "

" I must encounter the peril," answered Jason composedly, " since it stands in the way of my purpose."

" After taming the fiery bulls," continued King Æetes, who was deter-mined to scare Jason if possible, " you must yoke them to a plough, and must plough the sacred earth in the Grove of Mars, and sow some of the same dragon's teeth from which Cadmus raised a crop of armed men.  They are an unruly set of reprobates, those sons of the dragon's teeth ; and unless you treat them suitably they will fall upon you sword in hand.  You and your nine-and-forty Argonauts, my bold Jason, are hardly numerous or strong enough to fight with such a host as will spring up."

" My master Chiron," replied Jason, " taught me, long ago, the story of Cadmus.  Perhaps I can manage the quarrelsome sons of the dragon's teeth as well as Cadmus did."

" I wish the dragon had him," muttered King Æetes to himself, " and the four-footed pedant, his schoolmaster, into the bargain.  Why, what a foolhardy, self-conceited coxcomb he is !  We'll see what my fire-breathing bulls will do for him.  Well, Prince Jason," he continued aloud and as complacently as he could, " make yourself comfortable for to-day, and to-morrow morning, since you insist upon it, you shall try your skill at the plough."

While the king talked with Jason, a beautiful young woman was standing behind the throne. She fixed her eyes earnestly upon the youthful stranger, and listened attentively to every word that was spoken; and, when Jason withdrew from the king's presence, this young woman followed him out of the room.

"I am the king's daughter," she said to him, "and my name is Medea. I know a great deal of which other young princesses are ignorant, and can do many things which they would be afraid so much as to dream of. If you will trust to me I can instruct you how to tame the fiery bulls, and sow the dragon's teeth, and get the Golden Fleece."

*"I am the king's daughter," she said. "My name is Medea."*

"Indeed, beautiful princess," answered Jason, "if you will do me this service, I promise to be grateful to you my whole life long."

Gazing at Medea, he beheld a wonderful intelligence in her face. She was one of those persons whose eyes are full of mystery; so that, while looking into them, you seem to see a very great way, as into a deep well, yet can never be certain whether you see into the farthest depths, or whether there be not something else hidden at the bottom. If Jason had been capable of fearing anything, he would have been afraid of making this young princess his enemy; for, beautiful as she now looked, she might the very next instant become as terrible as the dragon that kept watch over the Golden Fleece.

"Princess," he exclaimed, "you seem indeed very wise and very powerful. But how can you help me to do the things of which you speak? Are you an enchantress?"

"Yes, Prince Jason," answered Medea, with a smile, "you have hit upon the truth. I am an enchantress. Circe, my father's sister, taught me to be one, and I could tell you, if I pleased, who was the old woman with the peacock, the pomegranate, and the cuckoo staff, whom you carried over the river ; and, likewise, who it is that speaks through the lips of the oaken image that stands in the prow of your galley.  I am acquainted with some of your secrets, you perceive.  It is well for you that I am favourably inclined ; for otherwise you would hardly escape being snapped up by the dragon."

" I should not so much care for the dragon," replied Jason, " if I only knew how to manage the brazen-footed and fiery-lunged bulls."

" If you are as brave as I think you, and as you have need to be," said Medea, " your own bold heart will teach you that there is but one way of dealing with a mad bull.  What it is I leave you to find out in the moment of peril.  As for the fiery breath of these animals, I have a charmed ointment here, which will prevent you from being burned up, and cure you if you chance to be a little scorched."

So she put a golden box into his hand, and directed him how to apply the perfumed unguent which it contained, and where to meet her at midnight.

" Only be brave," added she, " and before daybreak the brazen bulls shall be tamed."

Ths young man assured her that his heart would not fail him.  He then rejoined his comrades and told them what had passed between the princess and himself, and warned them to be in readiness in case there might be need of their help.

At the appointed hour he met the beautiful Medea on the marble steps of the king's palace.  She gave him a basket, in which were the dragon's teeth just as they had been pulled out of the monster's jaws by Cadmus, long ago.  Medea then led Jason down the palace steps, and through the silent streets of the city, and into the royal pasture ground where the two brazen-footed bulls were kept.  It was a starry night, with a bright gleam along the eastern edge of the sky, where the moon was soon going to show herself.  After entering the pasture the princess paused and looked around.

" There they are," said she, " reposing themselves and chewing their fiery cuds in that farthest corner of the field.  It will be excellent sport, I assure you, when they catch a glimpse of your figure.  My father and all his court delight in nothing so much as to see a stranger trying to yoke them in order to come at the Golden Fleece.  It makes a holiday in Colchis whenever such a thing happens.  For my part, I enjoy it immensely.  You cannot imagine in what a mere twinkling of an eye their hot breath shrivels a young man into a black cinder."

" Are you sure, beautiful Medea," asked Jason, " quite sure that the unguent in the gold box will prove a remedy against those terrible burns ? "

" If you doubt, if you are in the least afraid," said the princess, looking him in the face by the dim starlight, " you had better never have been born than to go a step nigher to the bulls."

But Jason had set his heart steadfastly on getting the Golden Fleece ; and I positively doubt whether he would have gone back without it, even had he been certain of finding himself turned into a red-hot cinder, or a handful of white ashes, the instant he made a step farther.  He therefore let go Medea's hand and walked boldly forward in the direction whither she had pointed. At some distance before him he perceived four streams of fiery vapour, regularly appearing, and again vanishing, after dimly lighting up the surrounding obscurity. These, you will understand, were caused by the breath of the brazen bulls, which was quietly stealing out of their four nostrils, as they lay chewing their cuds.

At the first two or three steps which Jason made, the four fiery streams appeared to gush out somewhat more plentifully ; for the two brazen bulls had heard his foot tramp, and were lifting up their hot noses to snuff the air. He went a little farther, and by the way in which the red vapour now spouted forth, he judged that the creatures had got upon their feet. Now he could see glowing sparks and vivid jets of flame. At the next step, each of the bulls made the pasture echo with a terrible roar, while the burning breath, which they thus belched forth, lit up the whole field with a momentary flash. One other stride did bold Jason make ; and, suddenly as a streak of lightning, on came these fiery animals, roaring like thunder, and sending out sheets of white flame, which so kindled up the scene that the young man could discern every object more distinctly than by daylight. Most distinctly of all he saw the two horrible creatures galloping right down upon him, their brazen hoofs rattling and ringing over the ground, and their tails sticking up stiffly into the air, as has always been the fashion with angry bulls. Their breath scorched the herbage before them. So intensely hot it was, indeed, that it caught a dry tree, under which Jason was now standing, and set it all in a blaze. But as for Jason himself (thanks to Medea's enchanted ointment), the white flame curled around his body without injuring him a jot more than if he had been made of asbestos.

*He caught one of them by the horn and the other by his screwed-up tail.*

Greatly encouraged at finding himself not yet turned into a cinder, the young man awaited the attack of the bulls. Just as the brazen brutes fancied themselves sure of tossing him into the air, he caught one of them by the horn, and the other by his screwed-up tail, and held them in a grip like that of an iron vice, one with his right hand, the other with his left. Well, he must have been wonderfully strong in his arms, to be sure. But the secret of the matter was that the brazen bulls were enchanted creatures, and that Jason had broken the spell of their fiery fierceness by his bold way of handling them. And, ever since that time, it has been the favourite method of brave men, when danger assails them, to do what they call "taking the bull by the horns"; and to grip him by the tail is pretty much the same thing—that is, to throw aside fear, and overcome the peril by despising it.

It was now easy to yoke the bulls, and to harness them to the plough, which had lain rusting on the ground for a great many years gone by; so long was it before anybody could be found capable of ploughing that piece of land. Jason, I suppose, had been taught how to draw a furrow by the good old Chiron, who, perhaps, used to allow himself to be harnessed to the plough. At any rate, our hero succeeded perfectly well in breaking up the greensward; and, by the time that the moon was a quarter of her journey up the sky, the ploughed field lay before him a large tract of black earth, ready to be sown with the dragon's teeth. So Jason scattered them broadcast, and harrowed them into the soil with a brush-harrow, and took his stand on the edge of the field, anxious to see what would happen next.

"Must we wait long for harvest time?" he inquired of Medea, who was now standing by his side.

"Whether sooner or later, it will be sure to come," answered the princess. "A crop of armed men never fails to spring up, when the dragon's teeth have been sown."

The moon was now high aloft in the heavens, and threw its bright beams over the ploughed field, where as yet there was nothing to be seen. Any farmer, on viewing it, would have said that Jason must wait weeks before the green blades would peep from among the clods, and whole months before the yellow grain would be ripened for the sickle. But by and by, all over the field, there was something that glistened in the moonbeams like sparkling drops of dew. These bright objects sprouted higher, and proved to be the steel heads of spears. Then there was a dazzling gleam from a vast number of polished brass helmets, beneath which, as they grew farther out of the soil, appeared the dark and bearded visages of warriors, struggling to free themselves from the imprisoning earth. The first look that they gave at the upper world was a glare of wrath and defiance. Next were seen their bright breastplates; in every right hand there was a sword or a spear, and on each left arm a shield; and when this strange crop of warriors had but half grown out of the earth, they struggled—such was their impatience of restraint—and, as it were, tore themselves up by the roots. Wherever a dragon's tooth had fallen, there stood a man armed for battle. They made a clangour with their swords against their shields, and eyed one another fiercely; for they had come into this beautiful world, and into the peaceful moonlight, full of rage and stormy passions, and ready to take the life of every human brother, in recompense of the boon of their own existence.

There have been many other armies in the world that seemed to possess the same fierce nature with the one which had now sprouted from the dragon's teeth ; but these, in the moonlit field, were the more excusable, because they never had women for their mothers. And how it would have rejoiced any great captain, who was bent on conquering the world, like Alexander or Napoleon, to raise a crop of armed soldiers as easily as Jason did !

For a while, the warriors stood flourishing their weapons, clashing their swords against their shields, and boiling over with the red-hot thirst for battle. Then they began to shout—" Show us the enemy ! Lead us to the charge ! Death or victory ! Come on, brave comrades ! Conquer or die ! " and a hundred other outcries, such as men always bellow forth on a battle-field, and which these dragon people seemed to have at their tongues' ends. At last, the front rank caught sight of Jason, who, beholding the flash of so many weapons in the moonlight, had thought it best to draw his sword. In a moment all the sons of the dragon's teeth appeared to take Jason for an enemy ; and crying with one voice, " Guard the Golden Fleece ! " they ran at him with uplifted swords and protruded spears. Jason knew that it would be impossible to withstand this bloodthirsty battalion with his single arm, but determined, since there was nothing better to be done, to die as valiantly as if he himself had sprung from a dragon's tooth.

Medea, however, bade him snatch up a stone from the ground.

" Throw it among them quickly ! " cried she. " It is the only way to save yourself."

The armed men were now so nigh that Jason could discern the fire flashing out of their enraged eyes, when he let fly the stone, and saw it strike the helmet of a tall warrior, who was rushing upon him with his blade aloft. The stone glanced from this man's helmet to the shield of his nearest comrade, and thence flew right into the angry face of another, hitting him smartly between the eyes. Each of the three who had been struck by the stone took it for granted that his next neighbour had given him a blow ; and instead of running any farther towards Jason, they began to fight among themselves. The confusion spread through the host, so that it seemed scarcely a moment before they were all hacking, hewing, and stabbing at one another, lopping off arms, heads, and legs, and doing such memorable deeds that Jason was filled with immense admiration ; although, at the same time, he could not help laughing to behold these mighty men punishing each other for an offence which he himself had committed. In an incredibly short space of time (almost as short, indeed, as it had taken them to grow up), all but one of the heroes of the dragon's teeth were stretched lifeless on the field. The last survivor, the bravest and strongest of the whole, had just force enough to wave his crimson sword over his head and give a shout of exultation, crying, " Victory ! Victory ! Immortal fame ! " when he himself fell down, and lay quietly among his slain brethren.

And there was the end of the army that had sprouted from the dragon's teeth. That fierce and feverish fight was the only enjoyment which they had tasted on this beautiful earth.

" Let them sleep in the bed of honour," said the Princess Medea, with a sly smile at Jason. " The world will always have simpletons enough, just like them, fighting and dying for they know not what, and fancying that posterity will take the trouble to put laurel wreaths on their rusty and battered helmets. Could you help smiling, Prince Jason, to see the self-conceit of that last fellow, just as he tumbled down ? "

" It made me very sad," answered Jason gravely. " And, to tell you the truth, princess, the Golden Fleece does not appear so well worth the winning after what I have here beheld ! "

" You will think differently in the morning," said Medea. " True, the Golden Fleece may not be so valuable as you have thought it ; but then there is nothing better in the world ; and one must needs have an object, you know. Come ! Your night's work has been well performed ; and to-morrow you can inform King Æetes that the first part of your allotted task is fulfilled."

Agreeably to Medea's advice, Jason went betimes in the morning to the palace of King Æetes. Entering the presence chamber, he stood at the foot of the throne, and made a low obeisance.

" Your eyes look heavy, Prince Jason," observed the king ; " you appear to have spent a sleepless night. I hope you have been considering the matter a little more wisely, and have concluded not to get yourself scorched to a cinder, in attempting to tame my brazen-lunged bulls."

" That is already accomplished, may it please your majesty," replied Jason. " The bulls have been tamed and yoked ; the field has been ploughed ; the dragon's teeth have been sown broadcast and harrowed into the soil ; the crop of armed warriors have sprung up, and they have slain one another, to the last man. And now I solicit your majesty's permission to encounter the dragon, that I may take down the Golden Fleece from the tree, and depart with my nine-and-forty comrades."

King Æetes scowled, and looked very angry and excessively disturbed ; for he knew that, in accordance with his kingly promise, he ought now to permit Jason to win the Fleece, if his courage and skill should enable him to do so. But, since the young man had met with such good luck in the matter of the brazen bulls and the dragon's teeth, the king feared that he would be equally successful in slaying the dragon. And therefore, though he would gladly have seen Jason snapped up at a mouthful, he was resolved (and it was a very wrong thing of this wicked potentate) not to run any further risk of losing his beloved Fleece.

" You would never have succeeded in this business, young man," said he, " if my undutiful daughter Medea had not helped you with her enchantments. Had you acted fairly, you would have been, at this instant, a black cinder, or a handful of white ashes. I forbid you, on pain of death, to make any more attempts to get the Golden Fleece. To speak my mind plainly, you shall never set eyes on so much as one of its glistening locks."

Jason left the king's presence in great sorrow and anger. He could think of nothing better to be done than to summon together his forty-nine brave Argonauts, march at once to the Grove of Mars, slay the dragon, take possession of the Golden Fleece, get on board the *Argo*, and spread all sail for Iolchos. The success of this scheme depended, it is true, on the doubtful point whether all the fifty heroes might not be snapped up, at so many mouthfuls, by the dragon. But, as Jason was hastening down the palace steps, the Princess Medea called after him, and beckoned him to return.

*The king scowled, for he feared that Jason would be equally successful in slaying the dragon.*

Her black eyes shone upon him with such a keen intelligence that he felt as if there were a serpent peeping out of them ; and, although she had done him so much service only the night before, he was by no means very certain that she would not do him an equally great mischief before sunset. These enchantresses, you must know, are never to be depended upon.

"What says King Æetes, my royal and upright father ? " inquired Medea, slightly smiling. "Will he give you the Golden Fleece without any further risk or trouble ? "

"On the contrary," answered Jason, "he is very angry with me for taming the brazen bulls and sowing the dragon's teeth. And he forbids me to make any more attempts, and positively refuses to give up the Golden Fleece, whether I slay the dragon or no."

"Yes, Jason," said the princess, "and I can tell you more. Unless you set sail from Colchis before to-morrow's sunrise, the king means to burn your fifty-oared galley, and put yourself and your forty-nine brave comrades to the sword. But be of good courage. The Golden Fleece you shall have, if it lies within the power of my enchantments to get it for you. Wait for me here an hour before midnight."

At the appointed hour you might again have seen Prince Jason and the Princess Medea, side by side, stealing through the streets of Colchis, on their way to the sacred grove, in the centre of which the Golden Fleece was suspended to a tree. While they were crossing the pasture ground, the brazen bulls came towards Jason, lowing, nodding their heads, and thrusting forth their snouts, which, as other cattle do, they loved to have rubbed and

THE GOLDEN FLEECE

caressed by a friendly hand. Their fierce nature was thoroughly tamed ; and, with their fierceness, the two furnaces in their stomachs had likewise been extinguished, insomuch that they probably enjoyed far more comfort in grazing and chewing their cuds than ever before. Indeed, it had heretofore been a great inconvenience to these poor animals that, whenever they wished to eat a mouthful of grass, the fire out of their nostrils had shrivelled it up before they could manage to crop it. How they contrived to keep themselves alive is more than I can imagine. But now, instead of emitting jets of flame and streams of sulphurous vapour, they breathed the very sweetest of cow breath.

After kindly patting the bulls, Jason followed Medea's guidance into the Grove of Mars, where the great oak trees, that had been growing for centuries, threw so thick a shade that the moonbeams struggled vainly to find their way through it. Only here and there a glimmer fell upon the leaf-strewn earth, or now and then a breeze stirred the boughs aside, and gave Jason a glimpse of the sky, lest, in that deep obscurity, he might forget that there was one, overhead. At length, when they had gone farther and farther into the heart of the duskiness, Medea squeezed Jason's hand.

" Look yonder," she whispered. " Do you see it ? "

Gleaming among the venerable oaks there was a radiance, not like the moonbeams, but rather resembling the golden glory of the setting sun. It proceeded from an object which appeared to be suspended at about a man's height from the ground, a little farther within the wood.

" What is it ? " asked Jason.

" Have you come so far to seek it," exclaimed Medea, " and do you not recognise the meed of all your toils and perils, when it glitters before your eyes ? It is the Golden Fleece."

Jason went onward a few steps farther, and then stopped to gaze. Oh, how beautiful it looked, shining with a marvellous light of its own, that inestimable prize which so many heroes had longed to behold, but had perished in the quest of it, either by the perils of their voyage, or by the fiery breath of the brazen-lunged bulls.

" How gloriously it shines ! " cried Jason, in a rapture. " It has surely been dipped in the riches of gold sunset. Let me hasten onward and take it to my bosom."

" Stay," said Medea, holding him back. " Have you forgotten what guards it ? "

To say the truth, in the joy of beholding the object of his desires, the terrible dragon had quite slipped out of Jason's memory. Soon, however, something came to pass that reminded him what perils were still to be encountered. An antelope that probably mistook the yellow radiance for sunrise, came bounding fleetly through the grove. He was rushing straight towards the Golden Fleece, when suddenly there was a frightful hiss, and the immense head and half the scaly body of the dragon was thrust forth (for he was twisted round the trunk of the tree on which the Fleece hung), and seizing the poor antelope, swallowed him with one snap of his jaws.

After this feat the dragon seemed sensible that some other living creature was within reach, on which he felt inclined to finish his meal. In various directions he kept poking his ugly snout among the trees, stretching out his neck a terrible long way, now here, now there, and now close to the spot where Jason and the princess were hiding behind an oak. Upon my word, as the head came waving and undulating through the air, and reaching almost within arm's length of Prince Jason, it was a very hideous and uncomfortable sight. The gape of his enormous jaws was nearly as wide as the gateway of the king's palace.

"Well, Jason," whispered Medea (for she was ill-natured, as all enchantresses are, and wanted to make the bold youth tremble)," what do you think now of your prospect of winning the Golden Fleece?"

Jason answered only by drawing his sword, and making a step forward.

"Stay, foolish youth," said Medea, grasping his arm. "Do not you see you are lost without me as your good angel? In this gold box I have a magic potion, which will do the dragon's business far more effectually than your sword."

The dragon had probably heard the voices; for, swift as lightning, his black head and forked tongue came hissing among the trees again, darting full forty feet at a stretch. As it approached, Medea tossed the contents of the gold box right down the monster's wide-open throat. Immediately, with an outrageous hiss and a tremendous wriggle—flinging his tail up to the tip-top of the tallest tree, and shattering all its branches as it crashed heavily down again—the dragon fell at full length upon the ground, and lay quite motionless.

"It is only a sleeping potion," said the enchantress to Prince Jason. "One always finds a use for these mischievous creatures sooner or later;

*Medea tossed the contents of the gold box right down the dragon's throat.*

so I did not wish to kill him outright. Quick! Snatch the prize, and let us be gone. You have won the Golden Fleece."

Jason caught the Fleece from the tree and hurried through the grove. A little way before him, he beheld the old woman whom he had helped over the stream, with her peacock beside her. She clapped her hands for joy, and beckoning him to make haste, disappeared among the duskiness of the trees. Espying the two winged sons of the North Wind (who were disporting themselves in the moonlight, a few hundred feet aloft), Jason bade them tell the rest of the Argonauts to embark as speedily as possible. But Lynceus, with his sharp eyes, had already caught a glimpse of him, bringing the Golden Fleece, although several stone walls, a hill, and the black shadows of the Grove of Mars, intervened between them. By his advice, the heroes had seated themselves on the benches of the galley, with their oars held perpendicularly, ready to let fall into the water.

As Jason drew near, he heard the Talking Image calling to him:
" Make haste, Prince Jason! For your life make haste!"

With one bound he leaped aboard. At sight of the glorious radiance of the Golden Fleece the nine-and-forty heroes gave a mighty shout, and Orpheus, striking his harp, sang a song of triumph, to the cadence of which the galley flew over the water homeward bound, as if on wings!

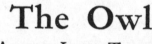

# The Owl

### by ALFRED LORD TENNYSON

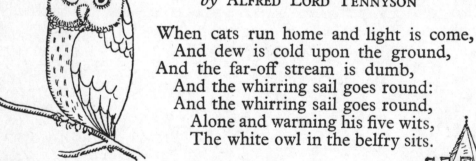

When cats run home and light is come,
And dew is cold upon the ground,
And the far-off stream is dumb,
And the whirring sail goes round:
And the whirring sail goes round,
Alone and warming his five wits,
The white owl in the belfry sits.

When merry milkmaids click the latch,
And rarely smells the new-mown hay,
And the cock hath sung beneath the thatch,
Twice or thrice his roundelay,
Twice or thrice his roundelay:
Alone and warming
his five wits,
The white owl in the
belfry sits.

# THE SELFISH GIANT

## *by* OSCAR WILDE

EVERY afternoon, as they were coming from school, the children used to go and play in the Giant's garden.

It. was a large lovely garden, with soft green grass. Here and there over the grass stood beautiful flowers like stars, and there were twelve peach-trees that in the spring-time broke out into delicate blossoms of pink and pearl, and in the autumn bore rich fruit. The birds sat on the trees and sang so sweetly that the children used to stop their games in order to listen to them. "How happy we are here !" they cried to each other.

One day the Giant came back. He had been to visit his friend the Cornish ogre, and had stayed with him for seven years. After the seven years were over he had said all that he had to say, for his conversation was limited, and he determined to return to his own castle. When he arrived he saw the children playing in the garden.

"What are you doing here ?" he cried in a very gruff voice, and the children ran away.

"My own garden is my own garden," said the Giant ; "any one can understand that, and I will allow nobody to play in it but myself." So he built a high wall all round it, and put up a notice-board

> TRESPASSERS
> WILL BE
> PROSECUTED.

He was a very selfish Giant.

The poor children had now nowhere to play. They tried to play on the road, but the road was very dusty and full of hard stones, and they did not like it. They used to wander round the high walls when their lessons were over, and talk about the beautiful garden inside. "How happy we were there !" they said to each other.

Then the Spring came, and all over the country there were little blossoms and little birds. Only in the garden of the Selfish Giant it was still winter. The birds did not care to sing in it as there were no children, and the trees forgot to blossom. Once a beautiful flower put its head out from the grass, but when it saw the notice-board it was so sorry for the children that it slipped back into the ground again, and went off to sleep. The only people who were pleased were the Snow and the Frost. "Spring has forgotten this garden," they cried, "so we will live here all the year round." The Snow covered up the grass with her great white cloak, and the Frost painted all the trees silver. Then they invited the North Wind to stay with them, and he came. He was wrapped in furs, and he roared all day about the garden, and blew the chimney-pots down. "This is a delightful spot," he said, " we must ask the Hail on a visit." So the Hail came. Every day for three hours he rattled on the roof of the castle till he broke most of the slates, and then he ran round and round the garden as fast as he could go. He was dressed in gray, and his breath was like ice.

"I cannot understand why the Spring is so late in coming," said the Selfish Giant, as he sat at the window and looked out at his cold, white garden ; " I hope there will be a change in the weather."

*The giant's face grew red with rage.*

But the Spring never came, nor the Summer. The Autumn gave golden fruit to every garden, but to the Giant's garden she gave none. "He is too selfish," she said. So it was always Winter there, and the North Wind and the Hail, and the Frost, and the Snow danced about through the trees.

One morning the Giant was lying awake in bed when he heard some lovely music. It sounded so sweet to his ears that he thought it must be the King's musicians passing by. It was really only a little linnet singing outside his window, but it was so long since he had heard a bird sing in his garden that it seemed to him to be the most beautiful music in the world. Then the Hail stopped dancing over his head, and the North Wind ceased roaring, and a delicious perfume came to him through the open casement. "I believe the Spring has come at last," said the Giant ; and he jumped out of bed and looked out.

What did he see?

He saw a most wonderful sight. Through a little hole in the wall the children had crept in, and they were sitting in the branches of the trees. In every tree that he could see there was a little child. And the trees were so glad to have the children back again that they had covered themselves with blossoms, and were waving their arms gently above the children's heads. The birds were flying about and twittering with delight, and the flowers were looking up through the green grass and laughing. It was a lovely scene, only in one corner it was still winter. It was the farthest corner of the garden, and in it was standing a little boy. He was so small that he could not reach up to the branches of the tree, and he was wandering all round it, crying bitterly. The poor tree was still covered with frost and snow, and the North Wind was blowing and roaring above it. " Climb up ! little boy," said the Tree, and it bent its branches down as low as it could ; but the boy was too tiny.

And the Giant's heart melted as he looked out. " How selfish I have been ! " he said ; " now I know why the Spring would not come here. I will put that poor little boy on the top of the tree, and then I will knock down the wall, and my garden shall be the children's playground for ever and ever." He was really very sorry for what he had done.

So he crept downstairs and opened the front door quite softly, and went out into the garden. But when the children saw him they were so frightened that they all ran away, and the garden became winter again. Only the little boy did not run for his eyes were so full of tears that he did not see the Giant coming. And the Giant stole up behind him and took him gently in his hand, and put him up into the tree. And the tree broke at once into blossom, and the birds came and sang on it, and the little boy stretched out his two arms and flung them round the Giant's neck, and kissed him. And the other children, when they saw that the Giant was not wicked any longer, came running back, and with them came the Spring. " It is your garden now, little children," said the Giant, and he took a great axe and knocked down the wall. And when the people were going to market at twelve o'clock they found the Giant playing with the children in the most beautiful garden they had ever seen.

All day long they played, and in the evening they came to the Giant to bid him good-bye.

" But where is your little companion ? " he said : " the boy I put into the tree." The Giant loved him the best because he had kissed him.

" We don't know," answered the children ; " he has gone away."

" You must tell him to be sure and come to-morrow," said the Giant. But the children said that they did not know where he lived, and had never seen him before ; and the Giant felt very sad.

Every afternoon, when school was over, the children came and played with the Giant. But the little boy whom the Giant loved was never seen again. The Giant was very kind to all the children, yet he longed for his first little friend. " How I would like to see him ! " he used to say.

Years went over, and the Giant grew very old and feeble. He could not play about any more, so he sat in a huge arm-chair, and watched the children at their games, and admired his garden. " I have many beautiful flowers," he said, "but the children are the most beautiful flowers of all."

One winter morning he looked out of his window as he was dressing. He did not hate the Winter now, for he knew that it was merely the Spring asleep, and that the flowers were resting.

Suddenly he rubbed his eyes in wonder and looked and looked. In the farthest corner of the garden was a tree quite covered with lovely white blossoms. Its branches were golden, and silver fruit hung down from them, and underneath it stood the little boy he had loved.

Downstairs ran the Giant in great joy, and out into the garden. He hastened across the grass, and came near to the child. And when he came quite close his face grew red with anger, and he said, " Who hath dared to wound thee ? " For on the palms of the child's hands were the prints of two nails, and the prints of two nails were on the little feet.

" Who hath dared to wound thee ? " cried the Giant ; " tell me, that I may take my big sword and slay him."

" Nay," answered the child ; " but these are the wounds of Love."

" Who art thou ? " said the Giant, and a strange awe fell on him, and he knelt before the little child.

And the child smiled on the Giant, and said to him, " You let me play once in your garden, to-day you shall come with me to my garden, which is Paradise."

And when the children ran in that afternoon, they found the Giant lying dead under the tree, all covered with white blossoms.

# And Did Those Feet
*by* WILLIAM BLAKE

AND did those feet in ancient time
   Walk upon England's mountains green?
And was the holy Lamb of God
   On England's pleasant pastures seen?

And did the Countenance Divine
   Shine forth upon our clouded hills?
And was Jerusalem builded here
   Among those dark Satanic mills?

Bring me my bow of burning gold!
   Bring me my arrows of desire!
Bring me my spear! O clouds, unfold!
   Bring me my chariot of fire!

I will not cease from mental fight,
   Nor shall my sword sleep in my hand,
Till we have built Jerusalem
   In England's green and pleasant land.